FORGIVING SAM

a novel by

POWELL CLARK

NewSouth Books

Montgomery

NewSouth Books
P.O. Box 1588
Montgomery, AL 36102

Library of Congress Cataloging-in-Publication Data
ISBN 1-58838-067-X

Design by Randall Williams
Printed in the United States of America

AUTHOR'S NOTE

To Pamela Smith, the wonderful reader, critic, friend I happened upon
in the check-out line at Food World and to Darlene McDonald, the
cashier who was thoughtful enough to introduce us—sincere thanks. For
once, I was in the right place at the right time.

My gratitude must also go to my early readers: Allie Hanna, Debbie
Swann, Eunice Russell, Joyce Fowler, Sherry Whitworth, Cathy Skotzky,
and Joy Binkley. They provided the courage I'm still running on.

Many thank-yous go to Bobby, Blakely, Blaire, and Bailey who
missed hot meals and quality time because I wanted to write a novel, to
Granny Duck who made sure I had the means, and to Randall Williams
who didn't leave *Sam* or me behind.

Joy and Marcia and Garrett, what can I say? It all means so much!

—POWELL

To Bobby,

MY LOVE AS ALWAYS

D on't talk to me about lowly sparrows, Reverend White." Ruth Ann's anger came out tired and flat. She tried harder. "His eye may be on the sparrow, but it seems to me He turns His face from the blood and tears of human babies!"

"Now, now, Sister McKinsey. Let's not say things we don't mean."

The pumped-up indignation of the preacher was chimney smoke to her, but his blustering about the room and scripture-quoting were more than her ravaged nerves could abide. His booming voice made Jared's stiff little muscles twitch. "I'm not your sister. I spoke only for myself, and I meant every word." She hugged her wounded child to her breast, rocked him back and forth, felt his moist heat seeping into her skin. Once, he had bubbled over with words and laughter. Once, he had played all day and slept through the night. Now, nightmares stole his sleep. Now, he rarely let go of handfuls of her clothing.

Seemingly paralyzed by her blasphemy, the preacher stopped and stared. Perspiration streamed down his florid face in shining rivulets. Ruth Ann knew the smell of his horror would soak into the fibers of her upholstery and carpeting. Sour and acrid, it would linger long after she was rid of him. "Sister McKinsey—" he halted as if he had suddenly realized all the religious babble inside him would be wasted on as hopeless a sinner as she had become.

Over the head of her fear-muted son, she narrowed her eyes at this black-suited oracle, waited until his gaping mouth snapped shut, then finished what she had started. "I just wonder what *He* was looking at while those demons took turns with my little boy. What do you think His eye was on? Do you think God was *bird watching* then, *Brother White?*"

—FROM *Little Birds* BY BRENAN ARMSTRONG MACCAULEY

CONTENTS

PART ONE
Every Wrong Direction

"He sees the lowly sparrow fall—somebody say amen!"—
common sing-song of TV evangelists, finger-shaking
dispensers of the Word, Sunday School teachers,—and
lesser and greater pulpits than these.

I

B Y THE TIME HE WAS TEN, he had stopped trying to recall those days. He wouldn't try for his parents or Dr. Collins. When he was thirteen, the scars around his hands and ankles were his only proof those days, four in all, had truly happened. People no longer asked him to remember. When the nightmare gripped him, if he was ten or thirty, he had no choice but to relive the brutal assaults, only to shiver their details out of his waking memory as soon as his eyes opened and his breath evened out. He never wanted the memories, but they rattled around inside him—hard, opportunistic seeds ever seeking places to sprout, maliciously determined to strangle him. As hard as he tried, yanking and slinging the seedlings away, there were times he couldn't keep ahead of them. Sometimes, they grew lush, hardy, twining tightly and barbed with thorns.

June 1965

SAM SPRINTED A LONG WAY down the shoulder of the blacktop before turning around to judge the distance. The old store had shrunk to the size of a matchbox, and Robbie Armstrong was just coming out. No need to hurry. With this much head start, Sam would easily beat Robbie home, so for a moment, he stood watching his smart aleck friend plugging along under a heavy bag of groceries. "Not such a hot shot now, huh, Robbie?"

The cloudless sky was so blue and sunny Sam couldn't look up without getting stinging sun spots in his eyes. Standing outside the fringe of Dark Water Woods, he heard the skittering and snap-popping of small animals playing, foraging deep in the thickets of evergreen and deadfall. A few steps closer and he could have made the forest fall as still and silent as death. The animals knew danger came with the scent of humans.

Sam sniffed, breathed deeply, and separated the smells in the air, singling out pine trees, cut grass, hot tar, freshly-turned garden soil, and his own sweat. All the sights and smells and sounds fit together to make this day feel like yesterday and the day before—perfect boy days, all.

If anything was out of the ordinary, it was the heat. The sun blazed too hot, even for the middle of the day. It had melted sticky black tar into small puddles that bubbled up through the roadbed gravel. Sam had heard Tighe, one of the farm hands, say, "Too early for dawg days." "Hotter'n a three-balled bulldog," the other hand, Jonsey, had answered. "Hotter'n a fire in a pepper patch." "Hotter'n a blister on the devil's ass." Tighe and Jonsey always tried to outdo each other as they worked in the fields. Sometimes, they put on a show just to make Sam laugh, but they'd been right about the heat. No breeze rose to stir away a heaviness not unlike Mama's kitchen on baking days.

Nine-year-old Sam MacCauley had just put third grade behind him forever and was feeling good about his life. He believed the long days of summer belonged to him. He had friends, stacks of mystery books, a horse of his own, woods to explore, and an honest-to-goodness cave. Standing in the weeds and the wilted morning-glory vines by the side of Russett Bridge Road, he felt as free and independent as one of Daddy's brindled barn cats.

His sweat-soaked hair stuck to his forehead. His blue-and-orange striped tee-shirt clung to his skin. The jeans he'd put on for an early morning hike to the cave had grown heavy on his legs. The sensations caused by the heat were far from unpleasant. He could almost feel the rays of the sun lightening his hair and darkening his arms and face. The warmth was familiar and good. The dark cavern had been as cool as the outside was hot. Its coolness had been just as pleasing.

Sam's mood was not dulled by the temperature nor the undignified begging he'd been forced to do to gain Mama's permission to come with Robbie. In fact, he was happy. He was nearly always happy.

He clamped his lips together in what Mama called his up-to-no-good grin and waved smugly to Robbie. Robbie was mad. Sam could tell by the choppy way his friend walked. If Sam had stayed, Mr. Peterson would have divided the groceries into a sack for each of them. Robbie wouldn't have to struggle with soft bananas riding on top of jars of olives and cans of beans. But Sam didn't feel like being a good friend. He didn't feel like being nice or helpful or careful. Continuing to wave, he trotted backward a few steps, tripped over a rock, then turned around the right way.

He was smaller but faster than any boy in his class at school. Being little and skinny could be aggravating, a real pain. Two years older and a lot bigger, Robbie's long legs covered in one stride what Sam's took in two, and every activity between them turned into a race of one kind or another. Now that Robbie, with his speed and extra years of experience, had finally started playing with him instead of telling him to "get lost, Short Stuff," Sam had real competition for the first time. He hated running like crazy to catch up. He resented Robbie's size and the sneering way names like Shrimp and PeeWee came out of his mouth. Most of all, Sam hated hearing Robbie promise Mama to look after her *little* boy. Robbie always acted like a big shot.

While Mr. Peterson was weighing bananas, Robbie had ordered Sam not to leave the store. "Don't you go out without me, Runt. You know I'm supposed to be watching you."

"What?" Sam had been looking through the glass part of the door but had made no move to leave.

"You heard me, Half-pint. Come away from that door. Now!"

"I don't hafta mind you!" Sam had shouted after the door had banged shut behind him. Of course, he couldn't have hung around and let Robbie talk to him like that.

He was jogging at a steady pace when he heard the clanky rumbling of an old car slowly rolling up behind him. The motor was so loud it sounded like an airplane. When it pulled even with him, Sam jumped to the far side of the shallow drainage ditch. He knew not to stop any closer to the road. Mama had made it clear that some people snatched kids, plucked them as easy as apples off a tree. She'd snapped her fingers. "Just like that and we'd never see you again." Grown-ups always worried about what *could* happen. They treated big kids like babies. Only a little while ago, Mama had hollered out the door, "I know how long it takes to walk two miles. You boys go straight there and back, and watch for cars! People think that road's a racetrack!" Still, being a little careful couldn't hurt.

Just as he turned around, a junky old rattletrap screeched to a stop. A dusty yellow station wagon with fake wood down the sides. Rusty scratches and dents covered the fenders and doors. It idled in front of him, shivering like a puppy just taken from its mother. A man stared out of the back seat window.

Sam frowned. His legs turned rubbery as the first pang of fear hit.

The man's grinning, crooked teeth were slimy with tobacco ooze. His nostrils flared. His blue-striped work shirt had a darker blue oval spot on the pocket where a name patch had been stripped off, and it was splattered with dirty gray and brown grease spots. The broken brim of an old straw hat fell down over his face, covering it from the middle of his nose up.

When the man spoke, Sam started running back toward the store and Robbie. A terrible thought burst into his head—this big man with nasty, crooked teeth was a *stranger*. Maybe he was *The Stranger* Mama was always talking about!

"Boy! Come back here," the man crooned in a gurgling, mucousy voice, a voice as deep and mean as Bluto's in a Popeye cartoon. A splat of tobacco juice sizzled on the pavement. "I jist wanna ast ya a question. Ain't no need bein' skeered a me!"

Over the sound of gravel scattering under his running feet, Sam heard the man cursing at the driver and the sputter of the car backing up. Robbie wasn't as far away, now, but he wasn't close, either. He had seen the station wagon and was yelling as he ran toward Sam. The loud engine and crunching gravel kept him from hearing the words, but when Robbie threw down the sack and pointed excitedly toward the woods, Sam knew he was being told to run into the trees to find a hiding place.

A good idea—a great idea—and he'd just about made up his mind to do it when the station wagon backed past him. More scared than he'd ever been, he hesitated a second too long.

The dull black barrel of a pistol pointed over the edge of the open window and froze him to the ground. Guns killed people! *Bang! Your dead!* He'd seen hundreds of Old West gunfights, dozens of cop-and-robber shoot 'em-outs. His frozen mouth filled with screams that couldn't get out.

But the man with the crooked teeth and the gun was already out of the car, across the ditch. A hand that stank of motor oil and onions stretched toward him. As soon as it touched him, Sam thawed. He kicked and punched and bit, but the stinking arm swept all the way around him.

As he was thrown into the back seat of the station wagon, he heard Robbie call his name. The man climbed in and touched the gun to Sam's nose. "Lay still, little man, or yore gunna wisht ya'z dead."

The station wagon started rolling forward again. Sam had a feeling if he looked, he'd see every person he loved standing in the weeds near the blacktop and waving good-bye. *The Stranger* had him, and the ugly old station wagon was taking him to the never-seen-again place. The sick, crawly feeling in his stomach and the pounding of his heart in his ears told him so.

2

THE PART OF THE DRIVE Sam would remember was confusing and miserable. His wrists were tied behind him with the same twine Daddy used on bales of hay. His shoulders cramped, and his fingers went from tingly to numb. The nasty smells inside the car—mildewed upholstery, oil, fried meat, sweat—made him sick to his stomach, and when he threw up on the floorboard, the man backhanded him. Afraid to cry, Sam closed his eyes and tried to think. The station wagon would eventually stop, and he would run away from these people. Having his hands tied would slow him down, but he was the fastest kid on his baseball team. He could outrun any flabby old man. He could outrun the silly looking woman behind the steering wheel.

The woman's hair was light yellow, almost white, but close to her head it was brown. It was pulled back in a ponytail held by the kind of rubber band that came around newspapers. She wore big sunglasses and red lipstick. A loose scarf around her neck made a cup in front of her face that was pulled up over her mouth and nose like a cowboy's bandanna or a bank robber's mask—a stupid thing to wear in the hot summertime. She spoke only when the man spat a wad of chewing tobacco out the window and told her to hand him a cigarette. "They're in yore pocket." Her voice was softer than Mama's.

The cigarette smoke and the mess he'd made on the floorboard made Sam feel sick again. The hot air that came in the windows blew smoke in his eyes and made them sting. No one at his house smoked. He took deep breaths through his mouth like Mama always had him do when he felt sick at home. He sure didn't want to throw up again. He didn't know what the man and woman wanted with him, but he already believed the man *liked* to hit people. Sam had traded licks with other boys on the playground. Once in a while his sister, Jackie, got mad enough to smack him, but no one else had ever raised a hand to him.

He had to stop worrying about being sick or getting slapped. He had to use his thoughts to find a way to escape. All his experiences with kidnaping had come from movies, books, and make-believe games. Calling up every Saturday morning TV hero, every matinee cowboy, every mystery-book sleuth, he searched for ideas, for the fastest, surest way to save himself.

Out of the blue of the western sky comes . . . a bird, a plane, no it's . . . Ringo . . . Whoa, Nellie Bell . . . Johnny Ringo . . . Sky King . . . Marshal Dillon . . . hi ho Silver away! What would the Cartwright boys do? Wyatt Earp? Tarzan of the Jungle?

While he was making and tossing out one plan after another, the man dragged him across the car seat, pulling him close—almost like a hug. He gritted his teeth to keep from crying out over the strain to the muscles in his shoulders. Thick fingers combed through his hair. Facing away, all he could see of the man was the lumpy shape of a knee under grimy dark blue pants. Sam's head was tipped back against the man's chest, and his right elbow rested in the man's lap. At first, the man petted him, smoothed his hair, rubbed rough hands over Sam's belly and chest. Maybe, if he was still and quiet and minded, the man would let him go. *"I'll think about something else. I'll think about . . . "*

> *. . . when I die, take my saddle from the wall,*
> *put it on my pony, and lead him from his stall.*
> *Tie my bones . . .*

Marty Robbins, Gene Autry, Roy Rogers. All singing together. Slow and sad. Very sad.

Then one of the hands pulled up the striped shirt and began to rub Sam's bare skin. The wrongness of the touch caused his whole body to shiver. Though he tried hard not to let it happen, he began to cry. He didn't make any noise, at first, but if the man didn't stop, Sam wouldn't have any more control of the crying than he had over anything else in the old station wagon.

> *. . . to his back. Turn our faces to the West,*
> *and we'll ride the prairie that we love the best.*
> *Ride around little doggies, ride around . . .*

While that hand continued to stroke him, the other one dropped lightly onto the front of his jeans. The fingers slid between his legs and cupped around him.

> *. . . slow.*
> *The fiery and snuffy are . . .*

The singing stopped.

Sam wanted to fight, but he had no weapons. His feet hadn't been tied, but in his position, they were useless. Kicking the car seat didn't help. He felt his nuts draw up inside him like they did when he jumped off the pier into the icy water of Smith Lake or at the movies when Dracula was about to bite the girl. Here, there was no shocking cold, no tingle of excitement. All the feelings were terrifying. Nobody had a right to touch him there. Mama and Daddy had talked to Sam and Jackie about people who liked to touch children. They said Sam and Jackie should tell if anybody ever tried. But there was no one *here* to tell!

The man made a racket in his throat like he'd hurt himself. The hand slid back and grabbed the waistband of Sam's blue jeans. One hard pull. The snap popped open, and the zipper went down. The other hand left his belly, then Sam heard the sound of another zipper. *"Come back, Roy! Marty! Sing . . . "* His crying became hard and loud, but the man didn't seem to notice. Except for the bawling, Sam was as paralyzed as he'd been when the gun had been pointed at him. He couldn't fight to keep the hands from lifting him and sliding his jeans and underpants down below his knees, couldn't fight to keep the rough, dirty fingers from grabbing his private parts. He couldn't even turn his head to see what the man was rubbing under his arm, against his side.

Then he *knew*. The man was evil.

Sam screamed.

The man laughed.

He rocked Sam back and forth. The pain caused by the coarse fingers became so great Sam's eyes squeezed shut and his screams caught in his throat. The hurt sounds that came from the man grew louder and turned to crackling laughter. Sam felt the man's hands and body stiffen and strain. Drops of thick, warm liquid slid down his side. Some of it splashed on his legs and belly. It smelled like dirty swimming pool water.

As soon as the hands let go, he leaned over and vomited on the man's leg. The hot, green liquid burned his throat and mouth. The man cursed and flung him back across the car seat.

After he was empty, Sam continued to gag and cough. He was no longer willing to believe an escape was coming. Had he ever really believed? Nothing short of a miracle would save him. He was looking out the window to see if he could recognize the road they were on when something banged against the side of his head.

ELLIS PETERSON BENT over the back of his old Zenith, turning the stems of broken knobs with pliers, in a wasted attempt to get rid of the wavy lines that made Bob Hughes's gray and white face look as if it was under water. With religious devotion, he watched *As the World Turns* every afternoon. He ignored everyone, including customers, to involve himself in the lives of Lisa and Bob, Grandpa and Pennie, all the fascinating citizens of Oakdale. That was why he became so riled when the Armstrong boy came back into the store, slamming the screen door as if no one would have to pay for it or fix it if it was torn off its hinges. The boy had already interrupted Ellis once.

"You little varmint," he swore, but when he saw the kid's panic, Ellis's anger cooled. "What's a matter?"

"Gotta use the phone!" The boy was out of breath and his face was ashy with alarm. "They got Sam!"

"Whoa, there." Ellis grabbed Robbie's heaving shoulders. "You mean A. D.'s boy? Who got him?"

"Man in a station wagon! Pulled a gun on him and threw him in!" The boy got loose, ran around the counter, and snatched up the telephone.

As the World Turns forgotten, Ellis was insisting on more information about what could turn out to be a boyish prank when Toby Baker butted through the screen with the same frantic energy as the boy. Toby limped past Ellis as if he didn't see him.

"Gimme that, boy. Sheriff Harrison'll sooner believe me."

Robbie surrendered the phone to the old farmer without an argument and stood, quivering and pale, while the police and Sam's parents were summoned to the little store.

Ellis stood next to Toby and Robbie at the grimy plate-glass window and bided the few minutes it took for the MacCauleys and the county sheriff's deputy to get there. Two automobiles pulled passed the gas pumps, a new Ford sedan followed by a battered green squad car. A third car, the Armstrongs', was only seconds behind them.

The boy confronted all of them in tears. "It's my fault. I got smart with him, and he ran out ahead of me."

Ellis felt sorry for the youngster as the adults surrounded him, all of them at once demanding the whole story in a word. When the deputy settled them down a little, the boy gave them all he knew. A beat up, rusty old yellow or white station wagon with wood-grain panels. A blond woman wearing shades and something over her mouth driving. A man with a handgun, wearing a work uniform—dark blue pants, a lighter blue shirt—and a straw hat. A mud-smeared Mississippi license plate. No, Robbie hadn't gotten any numbers. Sam had jumped the ditch and started running, but the car had slammed into reverse and shot past him. The man had put the gun on him, grabbed him, and threw him like a wad of paper into the back seat. Although the station wagon had been loud and smoking from the tailpipe, it had flown out of sight like a race car.

Toby Baker backed Robbie's story. "To the letter, it's the gospel. I seen it from the garden I got over there by the road. Run fast as I could, but with a gimp knee, I can't do good as I used to. Time I got there, they'uz plumb gone."

Ellis glanced guiltily at the old Zenith. He'd had his soap opera turned up so loud he couldn't have heard the dynamite blasts at the coal mine, and because of his preoccupation, as sure as dirt, a little boy was on his way to a horrifying death. He knew very well people who snatched kids off the side of the road didn't bring them home for supper.

3

SAM AWOKE FACEDOWN on a bed in a small cluttered room. Each wrist and ankle had been tied to a separate bedpost. The rough baling twine stretched his arms and legs straight out, making him a big X on the musty bed. He was wearing nothing but the ropes and his underpants. The room was hot and stuffy. It smelled as if it had been closed up for a long time. A room where stuff was tossed and forgotten, maybe. When he turned his head to either side, all he saw was junky looking boxes, stacked-up old furniture, and piles of clothes. Only a path from the door to the bed was clear. Close by, the sounds of water running and a television playing let him know he wasn't alone.

Every part of his body felt sore. When he tried to move, the ropes cut deeply. Pain burned up through his arms and shoulders and the calves of his legs. He needed to go to the bathroom, but he wouldn't call out for help. He remembered the man and the gun and what had happened in the back seat of the station wagon. He squeezed his eyelids tight and saw Mama and Daddy and Jackie, his room and bed at home. Then he cried. How could this have happened? Why? All Sam had wanted was to show Robbie he didn't like being bossed around. It wouldn't have meant anything to anyone else. If he had made it, what was the worst that could have happened? Mama could have found out and stopped letting Sam go places with Robbie. She could have sent him to his room for an hour to think about what he'd done wrong. She could have made him go a Sunday night without Bonanza.

But Sam hadn't made it. He rubbed his runny nose on the sheet as far away as he could reach from the place where he put down his head. Then when he couldn't hold it any longer, he peed the bed.

If he was kept tied up like this, forced to lie in his own pee, he'd get sick and die. Death wasn't the scariest notion in the world anymore. As good as some people made heaven sound, he doubted such a place was real. Still, he believed in souls. Where a soul went after its body stopped working, he didn't know. It didn't matter. The one thing he was certain of was that he'd rather be dead than *here*. He hoped dying wouldn't take long.

LAW ENFORCEMENT TEAMS all over Alabama and Mississippi were doing all they could. Leaving no stone unturned. Going over the highways and byways with fine-toothed combs. That's what A. D. and Freida MacCauley were told. Everything that could be done.

Their little boy's third grade school picture had smiled at them from Channel Nine's evening news while the commentator unemotionally read their plea. Darkness had fallen, and the steady stream of friends, neighbors, and officers of the law—all full of questions and condolences—had stopped knocking on the door. The sudden silence of the phone taunted them. Hope had darkened with the setting of the sun. For the parents of a missing child, solace did not exist.

Freida sat dry-eyed, rigid, unmoving, paralyzed by grief and shock. Beside her, for long, jarring intervals, A. D. wept with a child's abandon into the crook of his arm. Earlier he'd been loud and hostile, rudely dismissing any question he considered useless to the search. As soon as the door had closed behind Ellen Armstrong, the last to leave and who had taken little Jackie with her, A. D.'s anger had turned to something more frightening. Whenever his sobs got through to her, Freida reached to pat his hand or his knee. A mother's reflex, but he wasn't her child. A man unknown to shed tears, A. D.'s weeping confirmed the reality of the horror. Sam had been stolen.

Into the night, they sat on the sofa, the phone between them. Neither bothered to turn on a light. Neither spoke. In the shadowy dimness, they heard only the ticking of the mantel clock, A. D.'s wounded breathing, Freida's hard silence.

At some point during the darkest hours of early morning, she heard A. D. blow his nose, put the phone on the floor and speak her name. He then pulled her to him. She curled her body against his, letting him hold her as he had done hundreds of times. Feeble with grief, she gave herself to the residual strength in his arms. His fingers moved in intimate slowness over the stiff, tortured set of her back and shoulders. She welcomed the warmth of his hands. Listlessly, her muscles began to loosen and sag. She felt as though her body was collapsing into itself, becoming smaller, more frail. Her fingers gathered and clamped onto swatches of her husband's shirt. Everything else she could let go of now, including a wellspring of tears.

THE COMING OF DARK NIGHT brought an end to the horrible day then morning brought light to the room again. No curtain hung over the open window, and the blinding sun poured over Sam's body. He turned his face away from it. He no longer smelled the pee from last night, but he needed to go again. During the long darkness, he'd fallen asleep only long enough to dream.

In his senseless nightmare, the nasty man had come naked onto the bed, taken the ropes off, and used Sam's body in a string of disgusting, painful games. When he woke up, Sam was almost too tired and sore to think, and the coppery taste of blood was strong.

Other than the dream, he'd heard only small night sounds. Now, there were all kinds of noises. The man and woman talking, arguing. Kitchen racket, pans rattling, water running. Doors opening and closing. A TV switching on, and a few minutes later, off again. Outside, somewhere near the window, the man cursing. The growl of the old station wagon coming to life, a sound that instantly brought tears to Sam's eyes.

Then the house was quiet.

He tried to focus his thoughts on his family and how they must have reacted to his capture. He was important to them, and even though it was his own fault, they would be more hurt and sad than mad at him. Mama and Daddy had never held bad behavior against him for long. He wondered how they were going to get along without him.

THE DOOR EASED OPEN, and the woman came in from what appeared to be a narrow hall. She was wearing a fuzzy bathrobe, and her yellow-white hair was loose and messy. Sam didn't think she was as old as Mama, but her face wasn't young, either. It wasn't a happy face.

The smoking butt of a cigarette dangled between two of her fingers. She paused to tighten the belt of her robe then sat on the edge of the bed. Though the strain hurt his neck, he watched her. She wrinkled her nose, blew a puff of smoke toward the ceiling, and stubbed the cigarette out on the lid of an old metal tackle box.

"Pissed the bed. Stinks, don't it? Ralph didn't like that atall. Said ta warn ya good he ain't put nuthin' over yore mouth, so ain't no reason ya can't holler when ya gotta go. Next time, call me, hear? Best git ya up an' do somethin' 'bout it."

She untied his left hand, brought it down to his side, wrapped the thin, stiff rope around it several times. Next, she pulled the rope around his waist, back to his wrist and tied big knots in it there. When she undid the other wrist, she left it free. She untied both feet and was trying to remove Sam's wet underpants when he saw a chance to free himself. He yanked a handful of pale hair and slammed a knee into the underside of her chin.

Yelling, she threw herself across him like a blanket. "Whoa there!" She was strong. Before he could get away, she had him stripped and his feet tied together with only a short slack between them—just the way Daddy hobbled Appalachia and the other horses to keep them from running wild when he let them out to graze in the pasture.

"Damned near got away. Wouldn't that a been somethin'?" She didn't sound mad. "Now, le's git ya cleaned up, an' then I'll fix ya somethin' ta eat." She helped him off the bed.

He couldn't feel the floor with his feet. If the woman hadn't steadied him, he would have fallen.

"Here, lemme rub 'em. Pore kid. Ralph don't keer if he cuts yore feet plumb off. Ain't yore feet he wants."

Using his free hand to cover himself, he sat back on the bed and allowed her to massage some feeling back into his feet. When he could walk, she led him down the hall to a bathroom. He wished she'd freed his left hand. His right hand didn't work as well. It wouldn't have a chance at untying the ropes.

He'd never been inside a house trailer, but this didn't look like a regular house. Everything was smaller than what he was used to. The bathroom was barely big enough for the two of them to stand in at the same time. The tub and sink wouldn't have looked out of place in a child's playhouse.

"Go on. I don't wanna be bringin' ya back five minutes after I get ya somewheres else."

Sam didn't think he could pee with the woman watching. He stared down at the rust stains under the water in the toilet. He felt her brush against him as she reached to turn the water on in the bathtub. Letting the water splash over her hand, she adjusted the temperature then stoppered the drain with a washcloth. When he realized she wasn't interested in looking, he was able to relieve himself.

"Step over in here. When Ralph gits home, he'll want ya clean. No, I guess ya can't with them hobbles. Wait an' I'll lift ya over. Yore a little'n, ain't ya? Don't hardly weigh nuthin'. Not much more'n a baby. Ya better git used ta doin' like Ralph sez in a hurry. That other'n—that Tennessee boy never did, an' Ralph'uz mighty hard on 'im. Ya pay me some mind, hear?"

THE CORDS WERE DAMP and tight from the bath water. The woman dressed him in a clean button-up shirt that came to his knees. She put his right arm through a sleeve she'd rolled up and buttoned the tied-up arm inside the shirt, leaving the other sleeve empty. Keeping him close beside her, she washed his underpants in the bathtub and hung them on a metal crank that probably rolled the bathroom window open and closed. "I'll give 'em back soon as they dry." He hoped she kept her promises.

"Call me Deb, if ya want, or Debra Jean," she told him. "Git on up ta the table an' eat."

Sam shuffled through the cramped kitchen. A table with two chairs took up most of the floor space. He sat on the edge of a chair, but he didn't eat. He wasn't hungry. The fried eggs and potatoes didn't smell like the food Mama cooked. If he ate or drank, he'd have to go to the bathroom. Besides, he'd never eat food offered by these people. Mama had taught him better than that. And, he supposed, he'd die sooner if he didn't eat.

She tried to coax him, but when he continued to silently refuse, she gave up. "Have it yore way, but goin' hungry ain't gunna make it any better. Ralph'll beat the hell outta ya if he finds out. If he tells ya ta eat, ya better not back out then. He's crazy fer real now, an' he's got ways a body'd never bleve if he wadn't so free ta use 'em."

Sam hadn't spoken. He wanted to ask the woman questions, but she lived with that nasty man. Didn't that make her just as bad? Still, she'd been sort of decent. During the bath, her hands had been quick and gentle. Her touch had felt nothing like the man's. If she liked him enough, she might help him. He decided to try to find out more about her—and about the other boy she'd mentioned and about himself.

He licked his dry lips and asked, "Why am I here?"

She had just thrown his eggs and potatoes out the door—"fer the dogs"—and was washing dishes at a single sink no bigger than Mama's smallest soup pot.

"Ralph likes little boys. Who can say why? Talked about 'em fer years 'fore he ever got the nerve ta take 'im one. He's had me drivin' the roads ever evenin' since Fridy 'fore last. Took off work yestiddy, an' we rode up ta Cullman an' 'round the lake. Then on the way back, he seen you. I'm real sorry fer ya, but he'd kill me if I let ya go. He's meaner'n the devil when he's crossed up." She blotted her sweaty face, dried her hands on the tail of her bathrobe, and dropped into the other chair. "If there'uz a place on the green earth we could hide, both of us'd run away. But ya can't hide from Ralph."

"You mean you don't like him, but you still stay here with him?" Sam found that hard to believe.

"That's 'bout it. Been with 'im since I'uz thirteen. Took me in after my daddy got hisself sent down ta Tuscaloosa fer bein' crazy. Ralph'uz nicer back then. Rough an' all, but nicer'n he is now. Used ta laugh an' tell jokes an' act sweet as ya please some a the time. Now, only time he laughs is when he's doin' somethin' mean, an' he's done fergot what sweet is."

"Why don't you ask the police to help you? You could take me with you." A reasonable thing. He hoped she would think so, too.

She snorted. "They wouldn't lock 'im up. Not that he ain't done the kinda things they lock people up fer. Jist you an' the other boy'd be aplenty, but he'd git out of it. See, this is a tiny town. Ever'body thinks Ralph ain't nuthin' more'n the best car mechanic ever wuz. They like 'im. He does 'em favors an' gives 'em good deals. Lies like a dead dog, an' nobody doubts a word. It's like he's two people. He'd jist say somebody else musta set 'im up. Ain't nobody gunna bleve he picks up little boys ta play with. Why, he even goes ta the Baptist church. Hollers amen ta ever'thing comes outta that preacher's mouth."

Sam wasn't ready to give up. "If you took me back to Russett, my daddy'd help you. He knows how to do things, and he knows the county sheriff. He'd keep that man from being mean to you. I know he would."

"Boy, we drove ya around some. Through the strip pits an' snake trails, down Main Street Warrior as purty as ya please. Ralph likes darin' the law ta ketch 'im, too. You ain't ten miles from Russett, now. This here's Chesterville. Don't hurt none, ya knowin'—long as ya don't tell, an' ya ain't gunna get no chance ta tell. Nobody 'cept the meter man comes here, an' that's at the end a the month. Ralph put a Miss'ippi tag on that old junker wagon he's had in the wreck yard behind his garage fer a year or two. Got it runnin' good enough to go out prowlin' 'round. Been keepin' it hid out there in the backwoods behind the trailer. Left outta here with it at seven a'clock this mornin', a hour 'fore he opens up. It's at the bottom a Injun Creek by now. We got the same county sheriff you got, an' Ralph knows 'im, too. Works on the county po-lice cars real cheap."

Sam's hopes fell. "But my daddy can take care of us." He started crying softly.

"I can't do nuthin', boy. Ain't even gunna try."

"If you'd just untie me and tell him I got loose by myself, he might believe you. Then my daddy would come here with the police and get him. They'll believe Daddy. *I know they will!*"

"No. Now if ya don't hush, I'm gunna put ya back on that stinkin' bed all by yoreself. I don't wanna hafta do it." She reached across the table and lightly touched his face. "Be nice, an' ya kin sit in the livin' room an' look at the TV. Let that ol' feather tick air out some."

SAM SPENT THE DAY in a woolly armchair watching a small black and white television set with a fuzzy picture. An old wire-framed fan near an open push-out window swept a hot breeze across the room and back. A few times the woman stopped her chores to talk to him. When he asked her about the *other* boy, the *Tennessee* boy, she sadly told him the boy was bigger than Sam and that he'd gotten hurt a lot because he wouldn't mind Ralph. She refused to say more.

Ralph would soon come back to the trailer. Sam tried not to think about it. Thinking about the man made his stomach hurt, but he couldn't control his thoughts. Every move reminded him he'd been mistreated. Every muscle twitch called attention to the fact that he was a prisoner, that he'd been touched and somehow damaged. Daddy was the only person who had touched him where the man had, and that had been only once. It had happened when Sam was about six and had had to be rescued from the biting teeth of his zipper. The *only* person, the *only* time, and *only* to help.

During the last year or two, he'd become bashful about his nakedness, but before this onset of modesty, he'd felt no shame in stripping to his bare skin for his bath in the middle of the kitchen or living room. Jackie had done the same thing. He'd been taught the correct names for his body parts and used them as well as playground words, depending on who was listening. A time had come when running naked through the house in search of his pajamas or just to get a laugh out of his mother had made him feel shy and embarrassed. That was when he'd simply stopped doing it. Until now, he hadn't felt guilty that he had done those things.

He'd outgrown them, like he'd outgrown sleeping with Uncle Henry, his teddy bear.

The difference between Daddy and the man called Ralph was as big as an ocean. Sam couldn't figure out why the man had touched and hurt him, but whatever the reason, it was very *wrong*. He was only nine, but he wasn't stupid. He knew something dark and creepy was living inside that man.

4

THE AFTERNOON PASSED with Sam still curled in the armchair in Ralph and Deb's living room. His body was still, but his restless, jumbled thoughts coasted home where the best summer of his life was supposed to be taking place.

This was Daddy's first summer as a farmer. His workday was now spent at home, usually within calling distance of the back door. Last winter, he had sold all the MacCauley's Lumber and Building Supply stores—two in Birmingham, two in Montgomery, one in Anniston, and the old one next to the feed store in Russett. He'd bought tractors, seeds, hundred-pound bags of fertilizer, and two hundred acres of woods, pasture, and stumpy fields from Mrs. Meyers, a neighbor who had gone to live in Birmingham in a house full of old people. "The old broom driver couldn't get outta Russett quick enough with my money." Daddy liked to say Mrs. Meyers had been dying to unload her scrub pine and poison oak empire on him for years. The new land was separated from the old fifteen-acre home place by a steep-banked, rock-bottomed creek. Two wooden bridges—one wide enough to drive a truck or tractor over—connected the two pieces of land.

Sometimes on Sundays, Daddy took the family to visit Mrs. Meyers. She would ask if that old rattlesnake ranch had broken his back, yet. Then she'd say she wished he'd hurry up and tear down her old tinderbox house so she wouldn't have to look at it when she took the senior citizen bus to the cemetery to put fresh flowers on Mr. Meyers's grave. She would say lots of things that weren't easy to understand. Daddy would go on to confuse Sam even more with explanations. "She's just tryin' to get my goat, son." Sam didn't think Mrs. Meyers wanted a goat. She couldn't have kept one in the city, but if she could have and really wanted it, Daddy would have given her one. People were always saying A. D. MacCauley would give away the shirt off his back.

Daddy had seven goats, six nannies and a billy, that ate everything in front of them and kept the woods from taking back the farm. He also had two John Deere tractors—and the two hired men, Tighe and Jonsey, who came every day except Sunday to work the fields with him.

He'd told Sam that farming was what he'd always wanted to do, that it was the best way for an old sod-buster-at-heart to make a living. Sam had agreed mainly because he could run out to the fields and ask Daddy a question any time he wanted. He hadn't been crazy about farm chores, but instead of whining like a baby, he'd done most of the ones Daddy had given him. "Boy does a man's share, Freida—long as you can keep his mind outta the clouds. Strong as a yearlin' bull. When he takes the notion, he can just about keep up with me." Daddy would tell Mama, making sure Sam heard.

Dropping seeds into shallow furrows had been boring work. The exciting part had come a few days later when he'd gone back and found endless rows of identical green shoots bursting out of the ground. Unlike the small kitchen gardens they had every summer, the rows tilled and planted in the new fields were long and curvy. They wound around wooded corners, vanished, and reappeared. Sitting alone in a strange room, Sam realized he'd never know how much yellow squash or Silver Queen corn rows like those would produce.

Mama had been right all along. Too late, he was beginning to put tremendous value on her could-happens. He would never be a farmer like his father. He would never be a detective or a scientist. Thinking about his family, about all the things he would never become, he cried until the front of the big shirt was soaked. Home and happiness had quickly become only remembered things. Dying was going to take a long time. It was going to take more than a peed-on bed.

When Deb came in, he commenced begging. "Please! I wanna go home! I don't belong here. I want my daddy! I want my mama! *Please!*"

Deb left without offering the tiniest hope, but his pleading had hurt her. She was sobbing into her apron when she went out.

THE CAR RALPH DROVE home was quieter than the station wagon, but Sam had stopped daydreaming and was giving outside noise his full attention. Above the whirring of the fan, he heard the car pull up close to the trailer. He strained to make himself smaller, to disappear into the cushions of the scratchy old chair. The opening and closing of the car and trailer doors made sharp little cracks like the firing of an air rifle.

Ralph leaned over the chair and raked his oily fingers through Sam's hair. "Hope ya got over yore pukin'. I can take boo-hooin' an' carryin' on but can't stand pukin'. Don't think you'll get yore supper till after we have us some fun—jist in case. I'm gunna have mine, now. Hard work makes a man hongry—fer a lotta things."

Sam had an idea what kind of fun the man was talking about. His stomach felt as if he'd eaten nails. He listened to Ralph and Deb talking behind him. The mixed smells of beer and fried pork in the hot room were heavy and sour. The kitchen and living room were separated only by a rack of open shelving. The shelves held stacks of glass bowls and other kitchen things, but Sam knew if he looked over the back of the chair and had the stomach for it, he would be able to look right through and watch Ralph eat.

A picture on the television caught Sam's eye. The news man was talking about *him*. His photograph covered half the screen. The volume was low, and mixed with the kitchen sounds, the words of the news man ran together. Sam couldn't have heard anything over the booming thuds of his own heart, anyway. People were looking for him. Not make believe heroes. Real people.

But they wouldn't look *here!* So close to home, he'd never been farther away!

Too soon, Ralph came back to the living room. He turned up the volume on the TV and pulled Sam onto his lap as he sat down. "Yore a purty'n. Purty as a girl. Anybody ever tell ya that?"

Sam looked at the man's mocking, whiskery face.

"Not talkin'? Well, that's okay. I wouldn't wanna talk much myself if I had to go 'round in that ol' shirt-dress. Here, les get ridda that."

Sam wanted that shirt. Deb hadn't given back his underpants. He wanted more than anything to stay covered. Though he knew it was hopeless, he grabbed the front of the shirt with his free hand and tried to wriggle out of the stout arms. He put everything he had into the struggle, but the shirt was ripped from his body as if it had been made of paper. He continued to struggle until Ralph brought out a pocketknife, opened it, and froze him with one touch of cold, thin-bladed steel and four hoarse words. "I'll cut it off."

After that, Sam sat tamed and allowed the man to handle him at will. Fighting wouldn't save him. Nothing would.

Holding Sam tightly, stroking his hair, Ralph watched the rest of the news and called Deb to turn off the television. "What's yore name, boy?"

"Sam." He thought the man probably already knew his name.

"That's what the radio said. Well, Sambo, I hear tell the law's a-lookin' all over fer ya—mostly in Miss'ippi. Yore daddy done put up a ree-ward. Ten bigguns. By tomorrow, it'll be twenty. Wanna bet, Sambo? Might jist turn ya in myself when we get thoo playin'." Ralph laughed at his own joke. "How'd ya like that, Sambo? Ya wanna go home?"

Sam nodded, knowing the man wouldn't take him home. Tears squeezed through his lowered eyelids. Daddy wanted to buy him back. A ransom. But Daddy wasn't a Barkley or a Cartwright or Sky King. There would be no nick-of-time rescue. The man didn't want money. He had what he wanted.

Ralph laughed again and lit a cigarette. Coughing, he exhaled a puff of smoke and called over his shoulder, "Debra Jean, get yore ass back in here. An' bring us all a beer. We're 'bout to have us a little party." He ran a callused finger down Sam's face. "Damned if ya ain't purty."

EVEN IN PITCH-DARK SILENCE, Sam recognized his location. He was fastened down the same as before, but this time there was no slack in the cords. The raw circles around his ankles burned. When he tried to stretch the cramps from his fingers, something bit viciously into the palms of his hands and the stretchy skin between his thumbs and forefingers. Maybe the twine had been pulled across his palms and tied too tight, or maybe the man had used the pocketknife to slice Sam's hands. He didn't know because he'd blacked out before the man was done with him. He hurt other places, too, and he remembered more than he wanted to about the awful games the man had made him and Deb play, the games the man had played with him. Painful, nasty, confusing—so much like the games in the nightmare. The truth hit hard.

He had not slept. He had not dreamed.

He ran his dry tongue over his lips. A split ran down the middle of them. Every time he had gagged or fought back, Ralph had slapped him. When the openhanded smacks had turned into fisted punches, Sam had thought the worst had come. Then Ralph had gone on to teach him about real pain. Not like a bicycle wreck on an asphalt drive or falling out of a tree and getting the wind knocked out of you. Not like getting hit on the leg by a baseball. Pain that could not be described.

"Boy, this is s'posed ta make yore prick git hard an' stand up like a man's! Must be a goddamn girl!" He'd turned Sam onto his stomach, picked him up by his hips. "Yore daddy ever do this to ya, Sambo?" The new pain, hot and ripping, had exploded inside Sam's body. He hadn't known anything in the world could hurt so much. Just before the merciful blackness came to shield him from the rest of the game, Sam had heard Ralph ask again, "Say? Yore ol' man ever do *this* to ya?"

5

THE ACTIVITIES OF THE PAST three days made Deb feel dirty. The more soap and water she used, the more the filth seemed to soak into her skin. Ralph was crazy mean. She couldn't make him be decent any more than she could keep his muck from fouling her own hands and heart. Over the last year, she'd watched him go from cruel and sick to brutal and insane. She'd watched him do murder. Watched him kill the boy he'd picked up in Pulaski. Watched him hoist up a ballpeen hammer and, without batting an eye, turn that child's head into bloody pulp. Watched him roll up the small body in an old window curtain and kick it down a hole he'd scratched out behind the tool shed. Not more than a foot of dirt lay over that little body now. A foot of dirt and two old rusty rain barrels. If she told the county sheriff and found a place to hide long enough for them to dig it up, they might get Ralph before he had a chance to get her. She'd think on it. Yes, this time she'd think on it.

Ralph had had two whole evenings of his sick doings, plus whatever he'd done in the back seat of the station wagon and in the back bedroom that first night. The new boy was about used up. The little thing hadn't touched a bite of food or more than tiny sips of water and Pepsi she'd forced on him. She couldn't blame him. How could a kid eat with all the other stuff going on? His hands and ankles looked like raw hamburger. He didn't have energy to talk or fight at all any more. He was covered with proof of Ralph's temper. Bruises, deep scratches, dried blood everywhere, and a busted-up mouth. There had been times when she'd thought Ralph was going to choke him to death and times the boy had begged to die. Mercifully, during the roughest assaults, the kid had fainted dead away.

When she got out of the shower, Deb dressed in shorts, halter, and sandals, then went in to get the boy up.

He lay on his belly. So small and flat, so still under the spread of an old housecoat Ralph had thrown over him, he might not have been there at all. To be sure he was alive, she bent close and listened for the croupy breathing sounds he'd started making. He stirred in her a tenderness and kinship. He'd done nothing to be treated like this—just like the little girl she had once been had done nothing to make her daddy do the dirt he'd done to her. The ceaseless work, the men he'd brought home, the shame, the emptiness inside her. Ralph was torturing this boy, and he was torturing her. There was no sense to be made of his cruelty. Anybody would get fed-up after a lifetime of being knocked around.

Pulling back the house coat, she began to look him over, starting with his little red-scabbed hands. Softly, she called his name then shuddered. A name made him real, turned him into a shameful, accusing finger pointed at her. She should have waited until Ralph was passed-out drunk and loosened the ropes, but if she'd been caught, she'd have to deal with injuries of her own.

Blood had dried to crust in the cleft of the child's butt and in dark stripes down his legs. The bruises on his back had been the cause of the few drops of rust-colored water he'd pissed into the toilet yesterday. She knew because of the time Ralph had gotten kidney-punched in a ruckus at the Last Chance a couple of years back—before he'd become a born-again Baptist, before he'd started doing his drinking in secret. The rust was blood.

She removed all the bindings and rolled him over. He made some phlegmy noises in his throat. She knew he wouldn't resist. He didn't have any fight left. His front didn't show the bruises as plain as his back, but Ralph had thrown some mighty hard gut-punches. Each one had doubled the boy over like a jack knife. His ribs stood out too far. As she checked him over, Deb waited for the bluish eyelids to open, but even after she called his name a second time, they stayed shut. He was dying;

she could feel it. One more night would finish him off. Ralph wouldn't need his ballpeen hammer.

Her heart beat like a fist inside her chest. It pounded as if it wanted out. She had gone to church with Ralph. She'd learned about wrong. Killing was wrong. Torturing an innocent little boy was wrong. This child's death would be her fault as much as Ralph's—just like the other boy's. This one was going to be Dead Boy Number Two. Then after a while, there would be a Number Three. The numbers would grow as long as Ralph Sommers was alive and loose. He had started something he couldn't stop. And every boy he roughed up and killed, *every last one,* would be her fault. She had to find a way to stop him. The fist behind her breastbone continued to bang in hot anger and fright.

Her eyes narrowed at the boy's privates. His balls had crawled into his belly to escape the kicks and punches, and his pecker was as marbled and gray as tree bark. That, above everything else, stung her. Ralph had told her to go down on him and watched her perform the sick act—watched in twisted delight as she followed his orders to a tee, saving herself a beating. By God, she'd not do it again. She'd kill herself first!

Kill herself! Yes, of course! God, yes! So simple. Why hadn't the idea come years ago? There was a pistol and a box of shells on the shelf over the refrigerator. The pistol Ralph had taken on his boy hunts. The pistol that had stopped the kid from running like a startled deer into the woods. What had she to live for? More of this? She couldn't think of a blessed thing. She'd be better off! Death would rescue her from this slave existence. Shooting herself in the head wouldn't even hurt. First, while Ralph was at the garage, she'd take the boy to a safe place where his family could claim him. She'd tell the police about the body of the Tennessee boy. Oh, yes, she'd tell them *all* about Ralph! Then she'd put an end to her own suffering. Ralph couldn't beat a dead woman. She might even shoot him first! The blood in her veins sang with energy and purpose. God wouldn't hold against her the saving of a little boy, perhaps many boys—even if by murder and suicide.

The banging of her heart became something new and wonderful. Its rhythm applauded her decision, the first important one of her life. Yes, oh, yes! She'd dress the boy and take him away from here. She'd do it right now. If she thought about it too long, she'd risk letting fear get the better of her.

"Up, Sam!" She pulled him to the edge of the bed and balanced him seated against her. "I gotta surprise for ya! Open up them eyes!"

His eyelids fluttered and cracked open to slits. Behind the slits, his eyes were a dull gray, the whites tinged pink. The thin lids were spidery with blue veins. As Deb pulled one of Ralph's clean, oil-stained tee-shirts over his head, his eyelids slid back down. Ralph had ripped the boy's shirt to rags. She eased him down on his back while she worked his underpants and jeans up his legs. As she tugged his clothes into place, she felt a muscle or two ripple under his skin and heard a few weak moans leak from his throat. He was a doll to be handled and posed. She tucked the excess of the shirt into his pants. Its bulk helped to fill in the space created by the weight he'd lost. He needed bathing, but that could wait.

"I'm gunna take ya ta the sheriff! Hear that, Sam? I'm gunna git ya outta here, away from Ralph—jist like ya wanted!"

Deb wrapped her arms around him and tilted his head back. His eyes slowly widened and appeared to focus on her face. His dry, cracked lips twitched. A drop of blood bubbled out of the crusty split in the top one. She blotted it with the housecoat and reached for a cup of water she'd brought from the bathroom. Half the water sloshed onto them and the floor before she got the cup to his lips. "Mind me, an' drink some a this so ya can talk ta me. That's it. Wet yore lips real good." When he'd swallowed two or three sips, she put down the glass, shook him gently, and said, "I'm takin' ya outta here, boy. The law'll git ya back ta yore mama an' daddy. Ya understand that, now?"

Sam blinked and stared at her for a few seconds. She nodded vigorously to let him know she meant what she had said. A tiny smile curved across his injured mouth.

Mindful of his injuries, she hugged him. His warmth, his breath on her neck felt silky. She would do this thing for him—get him out of the devil's reach. After that, she would pluck her own self right out of the devil's hands. She could almost feel God's hand on her shoulder. Debra

Jean Sommers was paying for her ticket to heaven!

As she set about carrying out her new plans, she wondered if what she was feeling for this little boy was anything close to love. It was unlike any feeling she had known before.

IN THE AGED CHEVY Ralph kept in running order for her to get to and from the grocery store and laundry, Deb drove with a surety that amazed her. She was used to doing things Ralph's way, and before Ralph, her whiskey-soaked daddy's. Today, she was doing things on her own, making decisions right and left, and feeling good about all of them. She kept changing, praying, reworking her ideas so they'd come out perfect. She glanced at Sam sitting huddled up against the other door. She hadn't told him about any of her other plans—only that she was setting him free. She hadn't let him see the gun. She remembered all too well the panic on his face when Ralph had aimed it at him. If he was curious about her change of heart, he didn't ask questions.

Gradually, he'd become more alert, but his eyes told Deb the pain had waked up, too. The spoonful of paregoric she'd given him had come back up as soon as he'd swallowed. She'd waited a few minutes, tried the paregoric again with a little sugar and a piece of cold biscuit. That stayed down. She hoped it would help a little until he could be seen by a doctor.

Deb steered into a curbside space in front of a sooty red brick building with a dozen wide concrete steps leading up to its glass doors. She got out and carefully opened Sam's door. She glanced around warily but saw no one closer than the corner sidewalk by the First National Bank building two blocks away.

Leading gingerly by an elbow, she walked him across a strip of grass to the steps. The bandages she'd torn from a bleached white sheet were stiff with splotches of drying blood. She'd done her best, but the gashes made by the embedded twine needed stitches. She helped him lean back on the nearest of the three iron handrails that ran down the sides and middle of the steps.

"Here," she showed him a folded piece of tablet paper before slipping it into his back pocket. "Don't try ta get it out. Jist tell the po-lice it's there an' they'll get it. Gunna hafta take keer a them hands a spell, I expect. If ya keep yore fingers real still, they might not bleed much more." She stood back, tipping her head to keep the sun from taking her last picture of him. "Wait till I get outta sight 'fore ya go in. Hear? Good. Now remember this is the most important part. I need time ta do something 'bout Ralph. We don't wanna be chased by 'im from now on, do we? An' we don't want nobody else to get hurt. We wanna be *free,* so wait a spell 'fore ya say mine or Ralph's name. Make like ya can't think of it, at first. Ya gotta gimme enough time ta drive ta the garage, an' that's 'bout as long as it took us ta get here from the trailer. So try ta gimme a bit longer'n that. Then let 'em git the note outta yore pocket. Can ya do it?"

He gave a slight nod.

"I didn't wanna hurt ya. Never wanted ta hurt nobody. I wuz skeered like you. Ralph liked ta knock me around, too."

Sam nodded again. She needed him to understand.

"You be careful." She kissed the top of his head and ran.

She didn't cry. All her years of woe had dried her up. At the corner, she turned her head and waved at the tiny figure on the steps, saw one bandaged hand lift and flutter in the air.

She felt under the seat. It was still there. She'd found only four shells in the box—plenty. She only needed one for herself, but that Ralph was tough. It might take two or three to put him down. As she had slid the shells into their chambers, she'd known. Three were for Ralph, the *first* three. They had cried his name as they'd become seated in the cylinder, as they'd become readied to rip into flesh and bone and human gristle. Three bullets for Ol' Ralph. Three to get ready, and four to go!

6

S AM HAD WALKED up these same steps with Daddy. Before school had been dismissed for the summer, they had gone inside the brick building to buy tickets for the rides and games at the May Day carnival. Every year, the Sheriff's Department sponsored the carnival to make money for welfare kids to go to summer camp. Daddy had bought big rolls of tickets for Jackie's scout troop as well as Sam, Robbie, and their friend, Bud. Plus, he'd paid for rolls to be given to kids who didn't have much money. Daddy had called the sheriff Pete.

Sam had waited while Daddy talked to the sheriff. They'd talked about the carnival, the price of new cars, and the problems this year's crops were likely to have. Daddy had offered free plywood seconds and stuff he'd brought home and stored in the smoke house before the stores had been sold. "Send a truck over an' take whatever you can use for the booths. Got a few spare tools, too, if you need 'em." He liked to do things for other people, even when they didn't ask.

When he was through talking, Daddy had taken Sam to the shoe shop across the street to have new soles put on his school shoes. While the shoes were being repaired, they'd gone around the corner to Parker's Drug Store and eaten cheeseburgers, fried potatoes, and root beer floats at the lunch counter. Sam'd had to promise he wouldn't mention the food to Mama unless she asked. They didn't want to get on her bad side. A month ago. A whole month. Sam's life had changed in only a few days. He'd disobeyed, and he'd been hurt. Would Daddy and Mama want him back after all that had happened during those days? He didn't know. They'd have every right not to want him.

Deb had gone, but Sam couldn't go inside the building. His legs shook too hard. Only his arms hooked behind him over the rail kept his knees from buckling. The rail was hot. The heat burned through the tee-shirt and stung his skin. The sun was strong in his eyes. It glared off the pebbly concrete, so he looked only at the part that was in his shadow.

Between his feet a web of cracks looked as if someone had dropped a heavy rock on the step. He stared at the cracks for a long time. They fit together to make a tree. One long, wide crack with a crown of smaller ones spreading out from one end like branches. There was a single tiny split off to the side of the crack-tree. A broken branch that had fallen to the ground? A limb that had snapped in the wind? A branch torn from its tree couldn't be put back. The parting was final. But a tree was not a family, and a broken limb was not a boy. Sam would go home, and his body would heal. He would go back to being A. D. and Freida MacCauley's only son. He would sleep in his room at the top of the stairs. He would sit in his own chair at breakfast. He would do everything as he once had—*if* they wanted him back.

If.

He would never be exactly the same boy. Parts of him had died like broken twigs, and those parts were gone forever. Still, his parents would come for him, and he'd go back—*if* they wanted him. They would see the rips and bruises and raw places and know what caused them. They'd decide *if* they still wanted him. He would not think about what he'd do *if* they didn't. Would not. Could not.

He didn't know he was crying until two of his tears fell onto the cracked, dusty step. The toe of his tennis shoe caught a third. He had to go in sometime. Not just yet, but soon. He'd be able to walk in a minute or two. If he could have, he would have crossed his bandaged fingers for good luck. Ralph and the station wagon could come cruising up the street at any time. In spite of the heat, Sam felt a cold shiver scamper through him.

"Hey, kid?"

Sam looked up. He recognized the man right off as Deputy White, the father of his friend, Michael. Michael was the catcher on Sam's baseball team. He and Sam practiced together a lot—sometimes at Sam's house, sometimes at Michael's, sometimes at the ball field with the rest of the team—because Sam was the pitcher. Michael was fun to be around because he made jokes and told funny stories. If the difference in their sizes hadn't been so great, they might have become closer friends aside from baseball. Sam felt like an ant next to the bigger boy. Deputy White was as big as Hoss Cartwright, and Michael, at ten, was nearly as big as Sam's daddy.

"Son, you can't play here on the—*godallmightyjesus!* Why, you're the MacCauley boy, ain'tja?" Deputy White took Sam's arms between his big hands.

Sam, turning his head and hunching one shoulder to wipe his wet face on the old tee-shirt, sniffed and nodded. The weight of the man's hands caused the rail to press sharply into his armpits. He accepted the stabbing, stinging pain without a making a sound.

"Thank God! We'd about give up on findin' you alive. Where you been?"

Sam squinted harder against the sun and shrugged. His legs wobbled. The throbbing in his hands had turned into fiery little lightning bolts that made his fingers curl by themselves.

"You're a-shakin' like a leaf, son. You need me to tote you in there?" The big man tilted his head toward the building.

Deputy White's voice was soft. When he leaned down, Sam could see kindness and pity and the desire to help in his eyes, but Sam shook his head. He needed to walk by himself. He wanted Deputy White to stop touching him altogether, but without the support of those big hands, he probably wouldn't be able to go up the remaining steps. Hands could be scary.

"Come on then. Your folks are in for a surprise, huh? Been about crazy thinkin' you've been killed. We'll get 'em on the phone quick as a wink. They—sweetjesus, buddy! What *happened* to your hands?" The big man stopped suddenly and let his eyes trace over the bloody bandages. "Where in this old world an' the next have you been? Some devil sure messedja over!"

Deputy White gently pried Sam's arms from the rail. The large, powerful hands swallowed Sam's upper arms and braced him. Together, they began to take baby steps toward the door of the sheriff's office. Every movement hurt. A generous trickle of shiny red began to seep from under the bandage on his left hand, and the overflow laid a trail of bloody dimes on the concrete.

Sam stopped to look at the bright spatters of blood. A startling thought made his trembling harder, more jarring. His breathing sounded like a tomcat was purring inside his throat. The spots of blood could lead the man right to him! Ralph was an animal, and animals could smell blood. It would be easier to follow than bread crumbs or pebbles dropped on the ground, easier than a blazed trail. Deb had promised Ralph wouldn't come, but she could be wrong. As Sam started walking again, he wished with all his might for rain, a storm so great all the blood would be washed away.

7

A. D. CROSSED the back yard and was reaching to turn on the outdoor spigot when he heard the phone ring. He looked at his hands and frowned. After spending three hours riffling damp clods of dirt through his fingers, they were caked with red garden mud. He'd meant to start pushing seed potatoes into the rows one of the hired men had laid off, but after getting to the field, there hadn't seemed to be any point. Instead, he'd dumped the seed potatoes on the ground, upended the bucket for a stool, and sat playing in the dirt like a kid making mudpies. Though he'd played for hours, he'd found no joy in the game.

The loud burring of the telephone tensed his muscles into corded knots. He thought Freida would get it. But the ringing didn't stop. He straightened to look at the driveway. Her car wasn't there.

"No!" He muttered again as he ran across the patio and into the kitchen. *Where the Hades did you go, Freida? What were you thinkin' about? Somebody has to stay by the phone!*

Stuffing the receiver between his shoulder and ear, A. D. skimmed over a chalked note on the kitchen board—something about the Birmingham city morgue. His heart rose and stuck in his throat. "Yeah?"

"That you MacCauley?" A man's cigarette-husky voice.

"Yeah." A. D.'s muddy hands jerked with impatience and fear. He was still scanning the message Freida had scratched on the chalkboard. She'd gone to see a boy the police had found. Ellen was driving. Jackie was at the Armstrong house with Robbie and the Armstrong's housekeeper.

48

Gone to see a boy at the morgue! A dead boy!

"Pete Harrison here. Thought I wadn't gonna get an answer. You okay, A. D.?" Sheriff Harrison. Pete. Old friend asking stupid questions while A. D.'s boy might be lying dead in some dark, refrigerated mortician's drawer. *Why couldn't you have found my boy, Harrison? Why couldn't you? You're the sheriff. I voted for you. I trusted you.*

"No, Pete. If there's anything I ain't, it's okay. Didn't expect I would be, did you?"

"Well, no, guess not. Freida close by?"

We gonna talk about the price of cotton next, Pete? "No. I went out to the back field—tryin' to pass a little time. Just got back. Freida's gone off with Ellen Armstrong. She left a note sayin' she couldn't find me. She's been called to look at a dead kid in Birmingham." The impact of what he was saying folded him against the counter. All the air gushed from his lungs. He struggled to pull it back in. "Did—did somebody call you? Is it—is it Sam?"

"Whoa, now. I don't know nuthin' about what Birmingham's come up with, but I can tell you what I one hundred an' ten percent know— it ain't your boy. I'll call 'em on the other line, so they can get Freida settled an' on her way back here. A. D., stop worryin' an' catch your breath a little. I got a fella here I want you to talk to."

A. D. pulled himself straight then leaned against the wall. "How do you know it's not *him?*"

Freida's gone to see a boy!

"I'm a fortune teller! Just hold on one dern minute!"

The Birmingham city morgue!

A. D. waited. His heart beat too fast, making him feel light-headed. He couldn't seem to form a complete thought. Harrison wasn't making sense. The misery and fear of the last four days had made a doddering old man of him. The receiver in his hand shook like a baby rattle. Nine years ago, some supreme force had given him a family. A wife. A daughter. A son. All at once, after years of being alone, he'd been given everything he'd wanted from life. Now, he wondered if, one after the other, all would be snatched away—as his parents, his brother Henry, Gramma

Addie, and the son who had lived less than a month had been stolen—leaving him alone again.

He tried to concentrate on a jumble of sounds that came from the sheriff's office through the phone lines. Nothing was clear enough to identify. Bad reception from a radio just off the station. *Then* total silence as if everyone had stopped dead still, refusing to draw breath. A. D. caught and held his own.

Breathing was the next sound he heard. The short, stuffy, loudly impatient puffs of a child. Then into his ear came a sweet, husky voice that penetrated every molecule of A. D.'s body, every fiber of his soul.

"Daddy? It's me—Sam."

THE WINDOWS WERE OPEN, and a pair of ceiling fans droned. The inside of the building felt cooler and safer. Ralph wouldn't come for him in here. Deputy White had led Sam in, presenting him to Sheriff Harrison as if he was some kind of award. Shouting for his secretary to bring clean bandages for the boy's bleeding hands, the elated sheriff had tried to hug Sam.

Sam had hunched his shoulders, twisted away, and stood staring at a man he was supposed to know. He'd thought of the sheriff as a short, round, gruff-sounding man who could be hard and tough when needed but who was jelly-soft with kids. He made regular speeches and demonstrations at Sam's school, and every year he put on an old-timey striped bathing suit that looked a lot like long-handles and manned the dunking booth at the May Day carnival. Sam had heard Daddy and other people say Sheriff Harrison was a good man, and he'd believed them. He didn't want to believe the sheriff was Ralph's friend, but Deb had said he was. He couldn't be Daddy's friend and Ralph's at the same time. Until Sam could decide whose friend the sheriff really was, he didn't want to be touched by him. The sheriff didn't try again. Instead, he overlooked Sam's rudeness and pushed a straight-backed, wood-slatted chair up to his desk. "Sit down, son."

A woman who introduced herself as Naomi brought a first aid kit, a paper straw, and a bottle of Orange Crush to where Sam sat, shaking his head, politely refusing to give answers. *"I don't remember." "I'm sorry." "I don't know." "When can I go home?"* She baby-talked him into drinking some of the cold soda. Frowning and clucking over his injuries, she called him "poor baby" as she stripped the bloody rags from his hands and replaced them with fresh white gauze. He ground his teeth together to keep from crying. After cleansing the gnawed, rope-burned circles around his ankles, she smeared his crusty mouth with Vaseline.

The new bandages covered his fingertips. When she asked the name of his family doctor, Sam told her Mark Armstrong, Robbie's daddy. He waited until Naomi was through to tell the sheriff he would talk to Deputy White. Alone. A funny look crossed the sheriff's face, but he nodded and motioned for Naomi to follow. They left, leaving Sam alone in the room with Aaron White, the less frightening of the two men.

The deputy didn't seem to mind being singled out. He sat down behind the sheriff's desk. A white form that the sheriff had printed Sam's name on lay on the desk blotter, but he didn't write on it. Instead, he crossed his arms over it and leaned forward as he talked.

Trying to ease the burning pain in his bottom, Sam sat with his weight on one hip and an elbow over the desktop. For the first time since yesterday, maybe even the day before, he needed to go to the bathroom. When the Orange Crush bottle was held out to him once more, he drank most of the cold soda. It washed some of the bad taste out of his mouth.

"Why don't you just tell me what happened? If I need to, I'll ask questions later." Deputy White's face was a father's, trustworthy and caring, with eyes that showed pity.

Sam nodded then wondered what he should say. He thought it had been long enough that he could give names and Deb's note, but he'd wait a little longer to be sure. He took a deep breath and blew it slowly out through his injured mouth. He looked at the gray file cabinet, the wooden coat rack, the paper-filled wire basket on the desk. When his words began to come out, he was staring at the crowded bulletin board where notices and clippings whispered and waved in the ceiling fan's breeze.

"I couldn't go home or call 'cause I was tied with ropes. The man wouldn't let me loose, but the woman brought me here. She said she was sorry, but that man woulda kept doing it."

"What did they do to you?"

"I don't know—bad things. He hit me a lot." He worked to push the words out. His lungs made scratchy sounds.

"Just take your time."

"He asked me if my daddy does that kinda stuff to me. My daddy's not like that. He wouldn't hurt anybody."

Deputy White's smile showed he knew what Sam meant. "Doggone straight. I've known your daddy a long time. He's sure been in bad shape since you've been gone. Your mama, too."

"They might not want me back—"

"They'll want you. Don't you worry."

"I hope so." He blinked hard and sniffed. He didn't want to cry in front of Deputy White.

"This is real hard to talk about, huh? Why don't we try somethin' else? I can see some of what's been done to you. You ain't gonna have to describe a whole lot. Just say yes or no. Okay? Good."

The ceiling fan whirred. The bulletin board papers waved.

The questioning started. Sam was shocked that the deputy knew to ask such a question. He wondered if the things that had been done to him had also happened to other boys. Although he didn't want to, he nodded to show his answer was *yes*.

Another question.

Another nod.

And another.

"Who did it, Sam?"

Sam looked back at the waving bulletin board then out the small grimy window. "Ralph Summers and Debra Jean."

The deputy whistled. "You mean Ralph Sommers, the mechanic?"

"Yessir. Over in Chesterville."

"Son, you gotta tell this to the sheriff. Will you try—"

Sheriff Harrison swung back through the door but instead of waiting for the names to be dropped on him, he reached for the phone on his desk, placed a finger over a glowing red button. "Sorry for buttin' in, but your daddy's on the line. He don't know you're here, so surprise him." He punched the button and placed the receiver to Sam's ear.

DEPUTY WHITE WAS FLOORED, simply *floored* by the names the boy had given as his kidnapers. Ralph Sommers was a member of the Chesterville Baptist Church and a tither, and his wife, Debra Jean, was one of the sweetest, quietest little ladies Aaron had ever met. Aaron had been raised in that church and still made preaching most Sundays. The Sommers were simple folk who didn't have a lot of money or education. They didn't get out much socially, but a lot of shy country families had funny ways and kept to themselves. Ever since Ralph had gotten saved and stopped drinking, White hadn't heard a hard word about him. How could he have molested a child? Surely, the boy was mixed up. Maybe, the kidnapers had lied, told him they were Ralph and Deb. Animals had gotten hold of him. There was no doubt in his mind that little Sam MacCauley had been tortured and terrified in ways most people could scarcely imagine.

Looking baffled, Harrison went back out to the front office to dispatch a car to Sommers Garage. Aaron took over holding the receiver to the boy's ear.

Sam was as small for his age as Aaron's son, Mikey, was big for his. Still, they shared the kinship of childhood innocence and inexperience. They needed protection, kindness, and a mountain of patient instruction to grow into strong men. He doubted this child would recover from the assault he had endured at the hands of some demented man and woman.

As he listened to the low, plaintive voice, Aaron thought his heart would break.

AFTER A STAMMERED REQUEST, Aaron took the boy to the toilet. Standing in the square, utilitarian room, he felt his lunch begin to pitch and boil in his stomach. The extent of the injuries was appallingly plain.

Lifting the oil-stained shirt, he winced. He knew by the boy's face the passing of the reddish brown urine caused pain.

"Can I do anything to make waitin' easier?" He asked as he led Sam back into the office.

"I'm okay."

The boy perched nervously on the edge of his chair, an innocent kid with sad blue eyes. Aaron knew kids blamed themselves for the pain others inflicted on them and that some adults also blamed children. He prayed to God the MacCauleys would know better.

"Don't tell Michael," Sam said softly.

"You got my word on that."

"There's a note in my pocket. Deb said give it to you."

Aaron unfolded the paper and read to himself:

> The other boy is behind the shed under the rain barrels. Ralph got him in Pulaski, Tennessee. I think his name was Donald Baker. He had a little billfold he was buried with. Ralph picked him up by the road same as this one. I could not stop that killing, but I'll see to it he don't do it again.
>
> Debra Jean Sommers

"Can I stand by the door?"

"Sure." With the note in his hand, Aaron backed away. The horrors of this one day were piling high.

AS SAM GAZED OUT over the concrete steps, a phone behind him rang. He heard Deputy White answer.

"Sheriff's Department, White speakin'. — Yeah, Dave? — sweetjesus — dyin'! You sure? — What about Debra Jean? Think she'll make it? — You done radioed an ambulance, I hope. — Good. I'll put you on with Harrison, but first the real kicker. I think there's a dead kid buried out behind Sommer's shed. — No, at his trailer, I think. — Shocked the bejesus outta me, too. Who'd a thought it? Listen, Dave, you keep quiet about the boy. You know how folks around here act about things they don't understand. You gotta a little girl an' wouldn't want talk goin' on about her. He was nabbed, then he was brought back. No matter what you hear, that's *all*. Period. Far as you know, he never saw Ralph Sommers. You got that?"

Hearing only half of a conversation was confusing. He understood only little pieces. *The Tennessee boy.* That's what must have been in the note. Ralph had killed the Tennessee boy. If Deb hadn't brought him here, Sam would have died, too. He didn't know why an ambulance instead of a hearse would be needed for a body that had been dead a long time, but he decided not to think about the Tennessee boy.

More deputies were in the room behind him. One of them said Ralph might be dead, too, but when Sam became interested, they quit talking about Ralph.

Deputy White stopped on his way out and knelt by Sam. He said, "You're a brave young man. Remember that, you hear?"

"No, I'm not," Sam whispered back.

The deputy brushed Sam's hair back from his face. "Yes, son, you really are. I hope those hands are in good shape soon. The team needs you on the mound, Lefty."

Sam looked at the bulky dressings on his hands. "Maybe next year. They were playing me too young, anyway. I'm just nine."

"Yeah, but you smoke a batter like you're at least fifteen."

Sam didn't feel like smiling, but because he knew what Deputy White was attempting to do, he tried. He watched the broad, brown-uniformed man go down the steps and drive off in an olive green cruiser.

He pressed close to the glass, keeping a lookout on those steps.

The first glimpse of Daddy was a blur because he was running. Doctor Mark was running, too. They didn't touch half of those old steps. Sam's heart beat so fast he felt dizzy. Daddy stopped short of the door, and Doctor Mark drew up beside him. They stared through the squares of glass.

Sam looked into eyes the color of creamed coffee. Those eyes didn't lie. Some things could still be counted on. Even before Daddy figured out how to move again, how to get through the doors, Sam felt some of the fear falling away. Daddy wanted him! For the time being, nothing else mattered.

He waited, and when the time was right, he took a step to meet the front of Daddy's overalls. Nothing had ever felt as good as the denim against his face and the muscular arms that locked around him.

8

EACH DAY THAT FALL was a trek through a minefield. Any step could bring a chance victory or a lesson too late for the learning. A hit or a miss. A. D. enviously watched Freida as she set about restoring their child. Relying on her intuitive wisdom, he made himself available, completed any task. All he could manage without her prompting was a tremendous amount of love. Next to her mystifying mother-love, even that seemed to fall short. As the magnitude of the horror Sam had endured began to settle and impact in his brain, A. D.'s feelings of inadequacy grew heavy.

During his first days home, when a plague of dreams followed by formidable asthma attacks began to rob him of sleep, Sam became afraid of his own bed, his own room. There seemed to be no peace for him. Slowly, the physical wounds began to close. Some were replaced by scars. Impaired nerve endings in his small fingers began to regain strength and agility. The stain of bruises faded, soreness ebbed, but the spiritual pain stayed fresh. Many months would pass, even with Freida's intuition and patient resolve, before their son would feel safe anywhere. A. D. knew what his wife wouldn't accept: despite all the love and tending, mental scars would be as lasting as the physical.

Sam's recovery depended on unity and open communication—no room for A. D.'s petty jealousy—so he cordially bowed to his wife's good sense. Neither could afford to become an island. They would find three people could divide and carry a load that would break the back of one person. Each took a share of the others' fear and pain, thus balancing the weight of his own.

They learned to appreciate and rejoice over every minuscule speck of progress. Setbacks would come and be overcome. And Sam would once again begin to grow.

ON AN OCTOBER SATURDAY, Freida propped the door open a little wider than a crack with an old flat iron that had belonged to A. D.'s grandmother. Keeping Sam's door from closing during the night was the first practical use the relic had seen in half a century, long before A. D.'s time. Even at the pinnacle of its usefulness, she doubted it had held a more serviceable position.

She returned to the bedside of her sleeping son. The nightmare beaten back for the time being, the asthma attack calmed, the wheezing subsiding to a kitten's soft purr, Sam was finally at peace. The flat iron doorstop, the lights in his closet and the hall bathroom, the cloth-shaded lamp on his night table—household concessions effected in hopes of offering a single grain of security to her child.

She gazed down, straightened the covers over his chest and shoulders, smiled and sighed. His dusky gold lashes were long with a deep curl, and his hair fell in wild, loose ringlets. His lips were slightly parted, the lower edges of his top teeth showing. Sweet and beautiful and innocent. And so wounded.

After A. D. had gotten Jackie back to bed and returned to his book and his recliner in the den, Freida had stayed behind. It was her turn in an unspoken agreement. They didn't leave Sam alone in his room after the monstrous dreams and asthma attacks. One of them always waited to be sure his sleep was sound and his breathing untroubled. Sometimes, the dreams and asthma skipped a night or two. On occasion, they came two or three in a night. There were times when Freida or A. D. passed the night beside him on his narrow bed, times when they took him into to their own bed, enveloping him in a secure trough between their bodies.

Studying the relaxed contour of his face, she thought she'd never known a child to look more like or be more fundamentally different from his natural father. For a moment, she allowed her mind to drift back to her first marriage and the insipid despondency it had created inside her.

Charles Smith had been handsome, unbendingly formal, and full of Old South notions about manly deportment and role-playing. His husband-father-provider part had had to be acted out to the letter each day, turning his family time into an unvarying routine. Neatly typed agendas had been posted weekly at his home as businesslike as the work schedules at the mine. Breakfast at five-thirty. Dinner at six. Laundry on Tuesdays and Fridays. Hardwood floors waxed every other Monday. The maid's duties and Freida's had been listed in separate columns on the same page. If he had survived the accident at the mine, the lives of his children would have been different and most likely quite difficult at times.

When his first child had been born female, Charles had insisted on making an immediate repeat attempt for a son. The girl he'd met and married less than two years before during a business trip to New York City wasn't asked her opinion. The fact that she was only nineteen, anxious over her new station, and unversed in motherhood swayed him not at all. He'd owned one of the most profitable coal companies in Alabama. Providing housekeepers and anything else Freida needed to free herself for child bearing and rearing would have been of no consequence. Charles Smith had pictured himself the father of a half-dozen sons and whatever number of daughters who came incidental to the begetting process.

Freida had been a trophy, a mysterious dark-eyed Yankee of Italian Jewish lineage who had further set him apart—and, to his thinking, higher up—from the two-thirds of the small town population who, by circumstance, found themselves dependent upon his payroll. She'd been behind the counter of a small cafe where she'd worked evenings after her papa had been given his dinner. Smith had wandered in for coffee. He'd taken a stool and leered across catsup bottles and metal napkin holders and gasped, "Heavens to hoss harness! as my old daddy used to say. Where'd this Yankee town get you? You belong on my sunporch with my beagle hounds in Russett, Alabama! Sit all day sipping minted iced tea and watching peafowl strut around on the greenest grass you ever saw. What is you're name, Sugar?"

Not once after the marriage had he referred to her in any way other than Missus Smith or Sugar.

By the time she had begun to suspect she was pregnant with a second child, Freida's brain had commenced working overtime, trying to find an out for herself and her children. During the mid-fifties, opportunities for an unskilled, pregnant woman with an infant daughter to make a sufferable living were next to nonexistent, but Freida's determination had already begun to emerge. She would not have returned to the father who had handed her, at barely seventeen, without a second thought to a silver-tongued stranger, never have asked him for a dime toward the support of her children. She would not have asked anything of anyone, but she would have managed. She certainly would not have lived much longer with a man who saw her as something less than a person, a man who expected her to be satisfied in the roll of brood mare. Nor would she have remained a servant in his house, a polite decoration for his arm, a receptacle for his semen.

Fate, however, had made other designs. Freida would not have to go alone into the world to save herself and her babies. Her rigid, unloving husband hadn't lived to see his son. His oldest, deepest mine had caved in on him during a rare, grudging trip underground to investigate a year's worth of complaints about the working conditions. Two white and seven colored miners had been buried with him under tons of coal-seamed rock. The story flew through Russett. Charles Smith had had to be dug out of the rubble of his own miserly failure to shore up the tunnels and shafts with adequate timber and brace. The just reward for his stinginess, many said. His comeuppance.

Freida had taken no pleasure in Charles's death, nor had she grieved. However, she had grasped the measure of relief it had provided. Not without some inherent knowledge of money and business, she had quickly sold the mining operation and put most of the money in trust for her children. She'd held onto the enormous house and grounds for only a short time. More to her taste was this old-fashioned, two-story farmhouse where, at once, she'd become the center of one wonderful man's universe.

She rolled her eyes reflectively toward the ceiling.

A local lumber store owner and part-time handyman, A. D. had been a dream come true. She'd met him in a long line at the Jitney Jungle when he'd accidentally stepped on her foot and plied her with apologies. He'd made a fuss over her baby daughter who was sitting in a wire grocery cart, contentedly sucking her fingers. During the resulting introductions and dialogue, Freida had admitted, yes, she was Charles Smith's widow, and without embarrassment, he'd described the store he'd inherited from an otherwise heirless man he'd worked for since his early teens. While inching up to the checkout counter, jokes about found money had passed between them. "Who says you can't be poor as Job's turkey one day an' eatin' high on the hog the next?" She'd hardly been surprised when he'd stuttered a request for her to wait for him in the parking lot. Something had clicked.

Strong but gentle, he'd believed a woman to be a man's equal, and treated her with a respect that was wholly foreign to her. She'd fallen hard for his easy smile and warm brown eyes. She'd yet to have the first regret.

New York had been a cold place for a motherless girl to be raised by a stern, unloving father with a quick disciplinary hand. Charles had been an even more abasing experience. Trust might have come harder to a woman with less confidence in her own judgement. The possibility that A. D. could have turned out to be just another man who required a woman to cater to his every whim had been briefly entertained then discarded. She'd believed in him, she'd fallen in love, and three weeks before Sam was born, she'd married this marvelous, slightly rough-edged man.

He had become the hero of the best romance novels, the dark, handsome man in her youthful daydreams, and beside him, she had grown, matured into a woman. He'd encouraged this growth, applauded and celebrated each accomplishment. In him, her children found a father who loved and nurtured them as his own. In him, she'd found the definition of joy.

The wind had shifted and her world had warmed. Until recently, she'd taken for granted the peace and wholeness of her family, but never again. Looking down at her son, she was well aware of where her true though vulnerable fortune lay.

She turned her attention to a stack of loose notebook paper on Sam's small desk, a written exercise his therapist had asked him to complete. Several times during the day, she'd seen him sitting at the desk, a Black Warrior pencil in his left hand and his school dictionary within easy reach, alternating writing with intense concentration and dreamily gazing out the window. Giving in to curiosity, she quietly gathered up the papers and took them out with her.

IN THE DEN, Freida frowned with mock irritation at A. D. who was stretched as flat as his recliner allowed and asleep with his mouth open. One shoe lay on its side on the floor, the other dangled off the toes of a stockinged foot. She sighed and sat down to see what her son had written.

The lined paper, dotted with gray erasure stains and occasional lapses into printing, was covered in Sam's careless, back-slanted script. There were more pages than she'd anticipated. She counted. Nine, front side only, single-spaced. He couldn't be accused of skimping on effort. With the slightest of guilty prickles over the invasion of Sam's personal territory, she flicked on the table lamp next to her and began to read.

> I am Sam. I am Somebody. I have to write down stuff that tells about the Somebody who I am. Dr. Collins is making me. He wants to know why I don't like him. My parents make me go to him every Tuesday. He has a pointy beard and nothing but glass unicorns on his desk. I think those things are weird, but they don't bother me much. I just don't want to answer questions. He keeps telling me I am Somebody who is as important as any other person. He thinks I don't believe it, so I have to write down stuff about the Somebody I think I am. I am a boy, and I am nine-and-a-half years old. I live in Russett, Alabama. That's close to Birmingham, but it's not a city. Russett has farms and houses that are far apart and little stores. I live on a farm. I go to Smith-Briley Elementary School. I am in fourth grade. The kids and people have stopped asking so many questions. They used to ask

all kinds of stuff when this term first started. I wouldn't tell them much. Just that I don't remember all of it and that I want to forget the stuff I do remember. That is what Mama told me to say. Anyway, they all know I got kidnapped. Daddy says they don't know about the other because Sheriff Harrison and Dr. Mark didn't let that part get in the newspaper. I'm glad they don't know, but I think my mother told my teacher. I could have gone to private school where nobody knows me, but I wanted to stay with my friends. I don't like to be around people I don't know. I am the littlest kid in my class. I make honor roll, and I like to read mysteries, books about cowboys, and newspapers. My teacher says I could be a writer. I like to write adventure stories. I don't like to write this, and I want Dr. Collins to know it's not fair to make me. My hand is tired. I'm going to take a break. I am going to be serious now so I can stop going to therapy. (Get the hint, Dr. Collins?) I am just a kid who gets scared sometimes. There is nothing weird about it. I am scared of the dark and people, especially car mechanics and most men and PSYCHOLOGISTS. I am scared of station wagons, being by myself, eating food my mother didn't make, and going out in my own yard. I get scared when I get asthma attacks because I can't get my breath. I'm afraid my friends will stop liking me because they think I'm not as good as them even though I am. The dreams scare me more than anything else because when I have them they feel real and they make me have asthma. I don't like my parents to go to the store or anywhere unless we all go because something might happen and they can't come back. I don't like them to close their door at night or my sister Jackie's door because I want to be able to get out of bed and see them if I get scared or hear something. I don't think this is a big deal, because my sister is scared of everything, too. It's time for another break. I HATE this, so I know it is not helping me. I do not hate Dr. Collins. I just don't like talking to him. (You SAID be honest) I was worried I would get back and nobody would want me, but I was wrong. They are nice to me and don't get mad if I have nightmares and wake them up. They try to make me feel safe. They tell me over and over it was not my fault. They promise it won't happen again because the man is dead and the woman is in Tutwiler Prison. That is a jail just for women. She shot and killed the man. She shot herself but didn't die. The gun messed up. I'm glad she didn't die. I'm not mad at her because she let me go. She might get out of prison soon. When I first got back, Mama and Daddy had to do everything for me like when I was a baby. My hands were bandaged and had all those stitches for a long time. They only touched me when they had to, so it was different from that man touching me. I know what I mean by that even if no one else does. They were gentle because they were so afraid it would hurt. They hug me and say they love me, so I guess you could say my parents think I'm Somebody, too. They cried a lot when I got back because they were happy I was not dead like they thought I was and because they were sad about me being hurt. I don't like writing this down. It makes me feel creepy. It's nobody's business but mine and my family's. They never ask me if I liked what the man did, but Dr. Collins does. (That's mostly why I don't like you.) They know how bad I hated it. I'm taking a long break this time. I rode my horse Appalachia. My friend Robbie rode double with me. His horse Sadie has a colt. We went almost all the way to our cave. Robbie wanted to get down, climb the hill, and go in, but he knows I'm scared because it is dark. We used to play in the cave all the time. He didn't fuss too much because he knows I am getting better and soon I won't be afraid any more. He is my best friend. It's not his fault I got hurt, but sometimes he thinks it is. He keeps my secrets. I'm going to take Karate. Daddy says I can start after Christmas. He says he might take lessons with me if the teacher will let him wear overalls. Tomorrow is Halloween. My sister and I are not going to trick-or-treat this year. We are having a party at our house for the kids in our neighborhood. Daddy is going to cook hamburgers and hotdogs on the grill. Trick-or-treating can be dangerous, and there are a lot of other ways to have fun. All the families who live close to my house are more worried about kids than last year. They watch us all the time. I think most of them will bring their kids to my party. I am tired of writing. My hand gets tired easy. You can see where they put all those stitches. They look like zippers or railroad tracks or something

Frankenstein's monster would have. They really don't bother me. I hope Dr. Collins tears it up when he is through. (That is a hint.) I hope he knows I believe I am Somebody who is good because I do, and I hope he tells my parents I don't have to come back any more. I don't ask anybody about their problems, and I don't like telling them about mine.

FREIDA WAS SHAKEN over the depth and sophistication of the composition. Sam had always been precocious and performed on an unusually high level. The creative style of Sam's writing bothered her less than the tone, the clearly expressed aversion to his therapy sessions with Dr. Collins. Why hadn't he complained? Why hadn't he made his feelings known to her or his father? What else had he kept to himself?

"A. D., wake up."

Sam had come a long way since June. She wouldn't try to fool herself. He still had a long, difficult road ahead, but he'd responded to her and to A. D. better than Dr. Collins all along. Whether the psychologist would agree or not, she didn't care. In her mind, his services had been terminated at the end of page one of the Somebody essay.

Lately, Sam had shown an interest in martial arts training. Freida knew how powerless he felt, that he was searching for something to give him more confidence in his ability to fend for himself. As a father-son venture, A. D. had signed himself and Sam up for karate and tae kwon do. At three-foot-ten, forty-six pounds, Sam looked like a six-year-old. How could he stand next to his towering friends and not feel at a disadvantage.

"A. D.," Freida spoke his name softly but poked his shoulder sharply with the tips of her fingers. When he grunted without rousing further, she knocked off the dangling shoe.

He jerked, opened his eyes and shaded them from the light. "What?"

"Wake up. We've got to talk."

9

April 1966

. . . choking, suffocating. His mouth and throat were slimed with rot and jammed by a living piston, growing bigger and wedging tighter. The pressure inside his head forced his nostrils to flatten shut and his eyes to bulge from their sockets. It squeezed into his brain. His lashings cut deep, bloody troughs in his hands and sawed the flesh of his ankles. His ears filled with rhythmic grunting. Let this be the last time! The dying time! The overhead light was at first as bright as the sun but rapidly began to dim. His skull was caving in, crushed by hands as big as catcher's mitts . . . "Did yore daddy ever . . . "

THEN, ABOVE THE GRUNTING, rode a chorus of garbled, worried voices. Gentle but strong hands slid over his body, plucking away the ropes, yanking the stinking piston from his mouth, prying the giant hands from his head.

In the returning light, the faces of his rescuers drifted toward him. "Shhh—s'okay, baby—settle down—all over now."

The nightmare began to slink away, but the asthma refused to give up its power, refused to let go of the air in his overfilled lungs. The sound of his struggle was the chugging of a freight train, the roar of a tornado. It competed with the voices to fill the room.

"—listen, honey—gotta relax—open your eyes so you can—"

Slowly, his muscles began to loosen, allowing tiny bursts of air to escape. The nightmare was gone and the asthma was leaving. But they were faithful. They would return.

When his eyes adjusted to the light, he quickly looked around. His family was faithful, too. Everyone was here. In Mama's hand was a syringe that she'd used to stop the asthma attack. The bite of the needle lingered on the top of his thigh. If he concentrated, he could pull in small gulps of fresh, cool oxygen. Daddy, kneeling on the floor by the head of the bed, was holding Sam tightly—like a baby. In her pajamas, Jackie yawned and leaned against the door frame. Like so many other nights.

"You're all right, son. Nobody's hurtin' you now. Daddy's here."

Sam hid his face behind his rope-scarred hands. His breathing was quiet enough now to hear Daddy's heart beating against his ear. "I'm sorry, Daddy," he whispered. His voice sounded like rusty screen door hinges. Just like so many other nights and, Sam was certain, so many nights yet to come.

HE WAS COUGHING AND WHEEZING when he climbed the fence. Balancing one foot on the top split-rail, the other on an upright post, he held the rawhide reins tightly and made an effortless leap. He landed with his legs forked across the saddle that he had, without help, strapped to Appalachia. He hoped the cinch was tight enough to hold. He'd waited until she'd breathed out to give one last tug before buckling it.

The cough was partly due to his struggle with the saddle, but fear played a part, too. Whenever he was afraid, he had asthma. He felt for his atomizer, found it in a pocket of his corduroy jacket, and fired a nasty-tasting squirt into his throat. He held it in for a few seconds. His next breath was easier.

Quietly, he looked around the pasture. He hated being sneaky, but there were things he hated more.

In the distance, at the edge of the new-plowed south field, he saw the fuzzy shapes of Jonsey, Tighe, and Daddy. Daddy was slinging his arms and pacing back and forth in the grass. He looked angry. Sam grinned because Daddy wasn't mad. That was just his way. He was only giving instructions to the farm hands.

Mama was always saying she didn't think either Daddy or Sam could talk without moving their hands and arms. Daddy probably couldn't. Sam could, if he concentrated, but somehow it didn't feel right. His hands helped his words, helped other people understand what he meant, and now that the scars weren't so dark and easy to notice, he used them a lot. Sometimes, it was hard for him to make people see things. And even more times, it was hard for him to understand what people tried to tell him.

He stretched his feet into the shortened stirrups and nudged Appalachia forward. If Daddy turned around, there would be trouble. Sam wasn't supposed to go out on her alone, but today he wanted to start proving to himself he could do something to make his own fears go away. He didn't want to feel like a sissy the rest of his life. Besides, summer was coming, and Robbie was already talking about the cave.

He let the reins droop loosely in his hands and gently rocked himself with the mare's canter. The flashlight jutting out of his waistband poked his belly, so he moved it a little to the side. He tried to ignore the way his nuts slid up inside him as soon as he felt the movement of the saddle. Whenever they did that, he was reminded of something he didn't want to think about.

Behind him a door slammed. He jumped and swung around in the saddle.

Jackie stood outside the stable door. She crossed her arms and began happily swinging her body side to side. Just like a witch's, her smile was evil. Her dark hair was skinned back into a tight ponytail. Her bangs rippled in the breeze. Her braces caught and reflected the sun, making her look like she had a mouthful of diamonds or crumpled up tinfoil. More tinfoil than diamonds.

Jackie didn't really need braces, but she thought she did. "They make her feel better. Let her alone about 'em, hear?" Daddy had warned. "Better learn now that girls are like that." Mama had frowned at both of them. Even though he thought the whole idea of wearing braces on straight teeth was crazy, he'd kept quiet. He had plenty other things to rag Jackie about. But he didn't have time today.

Her eyes were squinty and mean. "I'm gonna tell," she sang. Her voice was as gritty as boot heels on broken glass.

"Tell what? I'm not doing anything." He had to act braver than he felt around her. She could be plenty rough on him when she was of a mind. She was eleven, more than a year older than Sam, but she was three or four years *bigger.*

"Sneakin' off on that stupid horse. Mama'll have a fit."

"You're the one who's stupid. When you gonna start minding your own business?"

"You're my baby brother. That makes you my business." She flashed her nasty tinfoil grin again.

Sam knew he couldn't win an argument with her, so he kicked the horse and took off again. "Who cares what you tell? Dummy!" he snapped, knowing she'd also tell Mama he'd called her a name.

He took the path into the woods. For once in a long time, he was doing what he wanted. Jackie wasn't going to stop him. Neither was the fluttery thing in his stomach nor the asthma.

The trail was spongy from the winter's fallen leaves. Sawbriars flung prickly purple and green runners in front of him. Here and there deadfall littered the wide footpath. None of this hindered Appalachia. She high-stepped it all. In places, stands of wild dogwood whitened the leafy umbrella overhead. He felt as if he had wandered into another world where the only music was wind in the trees and the chittering of the birds, where time had no meaning, where a boy could find a hiding place when he needed one.

Nearing the cave, the path became steeper, and the trees began to grow bigger and farther apart. Sam stopped in a grassy clearing a short way below the hidden cavern entrance and pitched himself over the side of the mare. He tied the reins to a scrubby pine and continued on foot.

In the thick of the woods, he had felt surprisingly sheltered and protected, but now his skin began to crawl around. Imaginary bugs tiptoed up the back of his neck. What if some monster was hiding in the cave—waiting for him? Maybe Ralph's ghost—as spiteful a ghost as the man had been—sending signals out to him, tricking him. "No," he said out loud, "no ghosts, no tricks. It's *my* cave."

Every step took him closer to one of his favorite places. A safe place until it came into the nightmare. Sometimes in the dream, a junky little room turned into the cave. A smelly bed turned into a pile of limestone boulders. Baling twine to kite string. An old station wagon to . . .

Stupid things happened in dreams. He couldn't think of a real reason to be afraid of the cave. Only a few people knew it existed. No one but he and Robbie had ever gone deep inside. They hadn't even shown Bud. Bud didn't always remember his promises to keep secrets. Sam and Robbie had played there a hundred times, and nothing had bothered them. But fear was like the settling of the house in the quiet of night, like the blackness behind his own eyelids. It didn't need a *reason*.

He hoped the cave would turn out to be a cool, damp, dark answer place, a thinking place where he could sort out and take care of things that upset him, a place he could come back to again and again. After all, it was *his* cave. *His*. No, not exactly *his* anymore because his brain had lumped it in with the hidden monsters that called out to him from the endless fog of the nightmare. It would only be *his* again if he made himself take it back. He supposed that was what he was here to do.

Each time he picked up one of his feet, it was heavier than the last, but he leaned into the steep slope and kept climbing. Grasping the trunks of saplings and handfuls of grass, he pulled himself along the steepest spots. He looked back only once to see if his horse was still there, and when he reached the summit and the mouth of the cave, he looked once at the trees that hid his home in the valley below. Then he gave his full regard to the honeysuckle that grew in snarled ropes over one side of the dark opening. Waves of sweet perfume aggravated his breathing and made him feel a little giddy. Though the breeze was cool, beads of sweat popped up on his forehead and upper lip. He drew his pocketknife and began to hack and pull at the tangle of vines until the cave mouth was free. He wanted all the daylight possible to follow him inside the circular opening that was as high as a man's head and wider than a garage door.

The rumbling purr of the house cat in his chest was a warning. Sam patted his pocket to make sure the canister of medicine was still there, but he didn't use it. He might need it more later on. Taking as deep a breath as his tightening lungs would permit, he skirted the pile of honeysuckle and entered the cave. He stopped a few feet inside. Still in the spillage of sunlight, he checked the familiar limestone rocks, the sandy floor, the pale, cold walls for signs of disturbance. His buffalo, deer, and rattlesnakes and Robbie's tepees and totem poles, all done in bright red barn paint, had not faded or flaked. Everything was as he remembered. He removed the flashlight from his pants, snapped it on, and ran its beam through the darkness beyond the arc of sunlight.

The back wall wasn't as high as the mouth, but it was wider. Each side of it opened into a passage. The one on the right veered only a few yards into the hillside and dead-ended, forming a circular room that Robbie called a cul-de-sac. On a large, flat rock inside this room, if no one had removed them, were a cigar box full of stubby candles and a box of kitchen matches. Sam and Robbie had used them to light the secret games they'd played. Through a maze of stalactites and stalagmites, the left passage went on forever, or so it seemed. The boys had gone in once. It twisted, narrowed, widened. In some places, Robbie had to drop to his knees and Sam had to bend over to go through. When they had come to a three-pronged forking of the passage, their courage had flagged. Neither boy had wished to become lost in a pitch-black world of used-up flashlight batteries.

The beam passed over the skull of a dog and a small pile of animal bones that Daddy's tractor had dug up and Sam had saved. There was even a Thanksgiving turkey skeleton that had been scavenged from the garbage. The bones had come in handy for several of the mystery-book and pirate-movie games he and Robbie had reworked for two players. They were fuzzy with dust.

On the ground, he was surprised to find a variety of small animal tracks. Rodents? Chipmunks, maybe? Raccoons? He couldn't remember if he had seen animal spoor in the cave before. He didn't think so, but after a year, he could have forgotten. He shined the light on the ceiling. No bats had come to roost.

Sam thought he heard a faint rustling in the passage that went on forever. He stiffened but heard only the house cat in his chest. No intruder in the cave. He headed toward the cul-de-sac. It seemed like a good thinking room.

Hey, Buddy!

He stiffened again. He could have sworn he'd heard a voice.

Hey! I'm talkin' to ya!

Crisscrossing the darkness with the flashlight beam, Sam searched even though he knew the voice would not have a body. He'd heard it in the nightmare. Sometimes, it told him when to wake up. *You can do it, Ace!* Other times, it would remind him, *Don't worry—just another bad ol' dream.* It sounded just like his own—only tinny like it was coming from a well, from someplace deep and hollow—and this time he was not dreaming. It came from within him. It reached his ears from the *inside*. The voice was more drawled than Sam's—like someone on TV faking a Southern accent—and a little bossy. Crazy people heard weird voices. His knees and elbows locked. He closed his eyes and tried to see inside himself.

Hey, Ace!

"What?" he asked out loud. He didn't want to be crazy, but here he was, answering someone who didn't exist.

Whaddaya mean WHAT? Don't ya even know when you're talkin' to yourself? I'm YOU. You're me. We're us—sort of. But we're still different. Don't YOU think we're not!

His real voice was shaky. "That don't make sense."

It will. We're gonna be just like this.

Sam opened his eyes and stared at the two fingers he'd crossed and held in front of his face. "Oh, foot! This is just me being silly." He uncrossed the fingers and vigorously shook the hand. "Wouldn't Jackie just love to see *this*?"

Whatever ya say, Sam, Ol' Pal, you're the boss, but ya done almost forgot to be scared. I'll take some credit here. Talkin' to yourself'll do that for ya. That is if ya got a smart self like me to talk to.

"Yeah, right." A smart aleck was more like it.

An' ya don't have to say the words for me to hear ya. I can read your mind. Our mind, I mean.

Sam laughed. He liked this game. It was exciting and only a little scary. Just a game. A game he didn't have complete control over. "What do I call you?"

How about SAM? That's my—our name. No, I forgot. Won't do. Too confusin'. Not Ace, either. You're the ace. I'm the wild card. We make a pair! Ha! I'm funny, too. Lessee, now. Ya listenin'? Can't call me Mortimer. Not Bubba or Slim or Doc. Not Abner. Never been fond of Lester. Not Donald— cuz I ain't a duck! Nosirree! Wait! Got it! Ya gonna love this! Pay attention. I'll be Lefty, your left-hand man. We're a southpaw, ya know. Just don't tell your right hand what I'm up to.

Sam giggled. He turned the flashlight off and walked back to the sun-splashed limestone rocks by the opening. "This is too crazy." He sat on the flat rock and tied a loose shoestring.

That's because YOU'RE crazy! Boy howdy, are ya crazy! But we're gonna work on that.

"How do you mean?"

Ya don't get un-crazy if ya don't work on it. I ain't Dr. Collins—that's for sure. Dr. Lefty, thas me.

"I wish you'd make sense."

A penny factory makes cents.

"Be serious."

Bein' crazy is serious. Gettin' over bein' crazy is serious. The dream an' all that is serious. I'M serious.

"I don't know what you mean." Sam was getting tired of playing.

Sure ya do. That's the problem—ya can't admit stuff.

"Aw, come on. Change the record." The fun was over, but he didn't seem to have the power to stop.

Ralph hurt ya real bad, Ace.

The smile fell off Sam's face as easily as it had come. "I don't wanna think about that."

Got to, Hoss. Ya want the nightmare to stop, doncha?

Sam looked at his new white-on-black basketball sneakers. They were laced neatly up over his ankles. The legs of his jeans were cuffed above them, showing an inch or two of blue argyles. The jeans and socks were old and faded. The cat in his chest was a bobcat now, purring husky and uneven. He felt for his atomizer to make sure it was where he thought it was. Every time he breathed in, his chest expanded to the side and sunk in the middle over his breastbone. He coughed. "Yes. Anybody would."

Ya gotta remember ever'thing, so ya can forget it right.

"I didn't forget. How could I forget something like that?"

Disremembered then. Gotta remember ever' single thing, Sam.

"What do you mean—everything?"

Even the—

"Stop it!"

If ya don't just accept it, one night it's gonna choke ya to death in your sleep. Heck, it almost gotcha last night.

"No!"

Ya gotta!

"No, I don't! I most certainly don't!"

Ya gotta remember how it felt!"

"No!"

How it smelled!

"No!"

How it tasted! How ya couldn't get the taste outta your mouth!

"Stop this!" The bobcat became a lion.

How it made ya puke!

"I told you to stop!"

How it almost made ya dead as the Tennessee boy! Almost put ya in a boy-shaped hole in the ground! Made ya WANT to die!

"No! I didn't do it!" The lion roared.

Yes, ya did, but Ace, it's all right!"

"No!" Sam reached into his pocket for the medicine.

You're right. He did it. So ya don't hafta feel so bad! Ya couldn't stop him. Ya wanna believe it never happened, but you're wrong. Your brain tries to hide it from ya, but that trick won't let ya get over it. You ain't a bad kid, Ace.

"Just shut up!" He held the inhaler close to his face.

You're the boss, Hoss. I'm shuttin' up, but for goshsake, use that thing before ya croak!

Sam squeezed the canister and sucked the medicine into his aching lungs. When he could talk, he said, "I'm going home. I'm not afraid of a stupid cave. There's no monster here. No answers, either. I'm not afraid of the woods. It's people that scare me." He stomped out of the cave and slid down the steepest parts of the hill on the seat of his pants. His lungs were beginning to open up and let out the trapped air.

Me, too!

That pesky Lefty stayed with him. How could he get rid of someone who wasn't there?

I'm TERRIFIED of people. They can make ya do things so bad your brain has to lie to ya about 'em—just so ya can live with 'em. Make ya have bad dreams, too. Dreams that take your breath away! Don't we know it!

"I thought you was gonna shut up." He stood up and dusted his butt off with the palms of his hands.

Appalachia had her nose sunk in thick tufts of grass. She didn't even look up.

Okay! OKAY! Shh, I'll be quiet, but I'll be back. Ya need me. Just one more thing—it's important—an' I'm outta here.

"What's that?"

S'posed to pee off the rock. It's a rule.

Sam sighed. He and Robbie had always peed off a big, smooth rock that lay near the mouth of the cave, the rock they used as a lookout into the valley below. They had competed, testing the arc and reach of their aim, marking their territory. A lucky thing. A boy thing. A *normal* thing. Sam needed to do more normal things. He felt obligated to go back. This time he shinnied up the hill without fear of what he might come across.

"I JUST WANTED to be by myself a little while. Sorry."

His eyes were sad and round. He looked pretty sorry to Freida, but the look wasn't enough. "You haven't been riding long enough to go out by yourself. That horse is as big as an elephant. I don't want you doing it again. You hear?"

"Yes, Ma'am."

Freida finished stirring her soup and put the lid back on the pot. "Come over here, son." She sat in a kitchen chair and tapped the palm of her hand on her leg.

He came and leaned against the leg. She combed back his hair with her fingers and kissed his sweaty forehead.

"We need to talk."

"About my horse?"

"No. About the nightmare."

He bumped the toe of his sneaker against a wooden chair rung. "I'm sorry. I don't know I'm gonna wake everybody up until I've already done it. I don't know how to stop."

Freida sighed. "That's not what I mean. We want to be there when you need us. Don't ever feel bad about that. It's what the nightmare's doing to you—that's what worries me. Baby, I think we need to try another doctor. Not Dr. Collins, but someone else who can help us figure out what—"

He leaped away from her as if she'd doused him with hot water and didn't look back at her until he was a safe ten feet away. His hands knotted in fists at his side. Scars a few shades darker than his skin seamed them. "No! I hate psychiatrists and psychologists and people who want to hypnotize me and make me say things that aren't true! Dr. Collins wanted me to say it felt good! It hurt me, Mama! I'll never say it felt good! I won't go! I can't! If I do, I won't talk to *anybody!* I won't say one more word!"

She started toward him, but he quickly backed into the dining room. She halted. "Wait, Sam. Don't be upset. Nobody's going to force you to do something you feel that strongly about. I promise."

"I don't wanna tell anybody else! Ever!"

"Sam, you—"

"You said it wasn't my fault. If it's not, why do I gotta keep talking about it?"

She started toward him again. This time he waited until she could almost touch him before he bolted away. He was crying and wheezing.

The sounds of a hurt animal. His labored respirations chopped his speech, forcing him to spit out a few words at a time. "You said—stay with Robbie.—Stay away from the road,—but I didn't mind you.—You said—somebody could get me,—and they did!—It *is* my fault!—I didn't mind you,—but I didn't do—what you think!—Not all of it, I didn't!—I most positively *didn't!*—What I did—was beg that—horrible man—to kill me!" He had crossed over into hysteria by the time his foot touched the bottom stair. "He's the one—who did it! And if you love me, you'll let me alone about it!"

Freida watched him run up the stairs and across the landing to his room. She heard his door bang shut as A. D. and Jackie came into the house. They stopped just inside the den. A. D. held the door knob as if he might change his mind and go back out. Jackie's eyes had the guilty look of a tattler who wondered if a beating or something much worse had become the end result of her talebearing.

Freida narrowed her eyes at them. "You." She pointed at her daughter. "You have a basket of laundry to hang out. And you, A. D. MacCauley, have a pot of soup to watch. And I don't care if Lyndon or Lady Bird calls. Take a message. I'm going to be busy." Without further explanation, she started upstairs. She had to get a few crucial points across to her son.

TWO DAYS PASSED before Lefty returned. *Lemme get it straight. You're a bad little boy? Bad boys get paid back with bad dreams? That it, Ace? You've had me two whole days. Ain't I learned ya anything?*

"I don't know." Sam didn't want to play with Lefty.

Ya let it go on an' on. Let it be over!

"It won't ever be over. I have to sleep, and when I do, the nightmare brings it all back. If I didn't deserve it, it would all go away. I'd be very glad to let it be over."

Ain't no way one little kid coulda been that bad! What the hell-o did ya DO, anyway?

"I hurt my family. Maybe I did other junk I don't remember—don't start about you know what—and saying I hafta remember. And for the record, Dr. Collins said I forgot a whole bunch of things that would hurt bad if I remembered."

Dr. Collins is a nut! Plus, he's in the past.

"He's supposed to know about people's minds. What if I'm the nut? If I am, then you are, too. So neither of us would know what's what. I could be too crazy to know. Or too bad."

For the gazillionth time, ya ain't bad! Parents punish bad kids. Yours treat ya like—well—like you're important an' special—an' ya are! They act like they're afraid they'll break ya if they ain't careful. Remember the stuff your mama told ya? She tried so hard, Ace, to make ya see. Then your daddy tried. They know ya still hurt. No little boy deserves to get you-knowed an' beat half to death. No little boy can be THAT bad!

"They always want me to feel better. They're like that because they love me, I guess. I'm their kid. They can't help it. They could be as mixed-up crazy as we are."

Not so! They're all ya got to count on. Don't start puttin' 'em down.

"I'm not. I love them."

Sure ya do. Oh, but Ace, the problem is ya don't love yourself. If I can't get through that thick ol' skull of yours, you're gonna spend your whole life pluckin' off all the roses to get to the thorns.

10

Even the deadliest of poisons loses some of its potency with the passage of time, its lethal potential dropping off with pages of the calendar. A body, thrashed and pummeled and broken, retains the faculty to repair and restore itself. Blood and dirt wash clean. Yet, when all possible reconstruction and rehabilitation are complete and the body reset on its forward course, the damaged spirit limps along behind, ever hoping to catch up.

excerpt from *Little Birds* by Brenan Armstrong MacCauley

OVER THE NEXT FEW YEARS, Sam began to grow, all things considered, not unlike other boys—not altogether unlike his former self. After what seemed to his mother an eternity of pain, a grueling, slow-motioned progression began to take place. A weakening of the venomed dreams that had been so relentless. A diluting of the untoward shame. A thinning of the fear that threw its shadow wide between the child and daylight. For all her efforts, Freida was unable to hurry the process. His healing levied high emotional tolls on the family as a unit as well as each separate member. They all paid. Freida could see him with the scars and without and love him either way. But during the lowest times, when pain painted his face with hard, bitter lines, she had to turn her head—take a time-out—just long enough for her own sickness to settle.

He was a beautiful child. Small, compact with hard little muscles and thick, loosely curling wheat-colored hair. Tiny lines formed at the outer corners of his soulful blue eyes when he smiled and between his brows when he frowned. He had a wide, lopsided, straight-toothed grin. Long, curving dimples cut deeply from his cheek bones down past the corners of his mouth. As he slowly approached and passed into adolescence, his outward resemblance to the man who had sired him sharpened. Charles had been handsome and dashing. He had turned heads. To Freida's relief, however, physical characteristics were his only legacy. Charles' stingy, domineering soul had gone with him to the grave. Freida was proud of her shy, generous, and tenderhearted son.

"I DON'T BUY IT. You might fool Mrs. Martin, but I want the truth. What really happened to your fingers?"

"*He* happened to my fingers—like you hadda ask. Bent 'em back till they just started crackin' an' poppin' outta their sockets. He wouldn't tell the doctor at the emergency room nuthin'. It's a sin to lie, you know. So I said I fell off the porch an' tried to break the fall with my hand. It's a sin to lie, awright, but he just stood there an' let me lie my head off to save his lousy neck."

"You could have told the truth while there was someone there to keep him from coming at you again."

"Yeah, sure, Ace. I'd just be puttin' off another beatin' or worse until we got home."

Sam shook his head. Bud's gauze-wrapped hand made him furious. The fingertips sticking out of the bandage were twice the size they should have been and bruised a variety of colors. Bud's daddy often sent Bud to school with new bruises, sprains, and black eyes. The thought of that man bending back Bud's fingers until they broke made Sam sick to his stomach.

"Oh, man. How'd you stand it?"

"I didn't. I bawled like a baby an' begged 'im to stop. An' when he did let go, he wanted me to pray for forgiveness! He's always meaner durin' revivals, but this was the worst. He took me straight from the emergency room to church, an' I got to hear 'im preach about God's love."

"What did you do to get him mad in the first place?"

"I asked if I could stay home from church to study for the midterm.

I've hadda go every night this week. I figured I'd pro'bly squeak by in math an' English, maybe even science, but I'm failin' social studies bad. Now, as soon as we go back in, I gotta take the exam orally because he messed up my hand, an' when I fail it, he's gonna beat the crap outta me all over again."

"You could tell Mrs. Martin the truth. She'd let you make the test up later, and she might know what to do about your dad."

"Drop it, Ace. It wouldn't work."

"Let me tell her. You won't have to say anything."

"No!"

Sam was close to tears over the brutality his friend had to endure. He'd never understand why Bud didn't tell the whole world. Foster homes, places where kids without parents were kept couldn't be as bad as living alone with a madman. Sometimes, Bud talked about running away, but talking was as close as he'd ever gotten to an escape.

"My daddy's okay. Come home with me after school, and we can ask him what you should do."

"I know you wanna help, but you don't understand. Your folks are nuthin' like my old man. Nuthin'. So you don't know how it really is. I can't get away from him. All I can do is try not to make him meaner, so drop it."

"He could kill you during one of his mad spells."

"Please, Sam. Let's talk about somethin' else. It's nearly time for the bell. Quiz me on the cultural oddities of Asian countries. Tell me why the Japanese have paper walls—how they grow rice. Those're things you know more about than me."

WHAT HE LACKED in self-appreciation and confidence, Sam made up for in tenacity, patience, and persistence. Long after A. D. had lathered himself in Ben Gay and retired to the bleachers, Sam stuck to the martial arts lessons, and in doing so gained some assurance of his ability to defend himself. He competed, and more often than not, he won, his style as colorful as his collection of belts and trophies.

Overrun with nervous energy, he bounded back into sports with the enthusiasm of early seasons. Baseball in the spring, football in autumn, whatever struck his fancy in between. He swam, rode his horse, and played basketball in the driveway. And when he exhausted the physical energy, he read everything from Zane Grey to Edgar Rice Burroughs to the *World Book Encyclopedia*.

Freida believed the one place Sam was totally at ease with himself and the world around him was on a baseball diamond. Standing on a slight mound of dirt, a ball in his left hand and an oversized glove on his right, he was in control. The shelves in his room were loaded with trophies and game balls. In Sixty-seven, with no reliable backup pitcher on his team of local thirteen- and fourteen-year-olds, Sam pitched every game. The team took first place in county, second place in state. His coach was quoted in *The Russett Bugle*: "That MacCauley kid's a double whammy against the other team. He leaves them looking at his fast ball and slider, plus he swings a mean left-handed bat. He hit .360 for the season. On top of all that, he rounds the bases like a hungry cheetah." Sam turned eleven years old a month into the season and weighed about sixty-five pounds.

In football, his size made a difference. He stayed with kids his own age and, even among them, was always the runt of the team, but he played like a demon, winning the respect of his teammates. On the football field, he set aside the acclaim of his one-man baseball feats and fell into team play. To be happy, he needed only to know the rules and what was expected of him.

Most afternoons and weekends, the MacCauley woods and fields were crawling with boys. Freida fed and watched over the infestation, and when she was tired of them, she shooed them home. Usually, Sam hung back from the thickest crowds, spending most of his time with Bud Blacknell and Robbie Armstrong. If he neglected his duty as host, the other boys didn't seem to notice. They came right on, taking generous advantage of the freedom and hospitality of the MacCauley farm. As far as she knew, the only things her son refused to share with the masses were his horse and the cloak-and-dagger whereabouts of the limestone cavern.

He and his sister were frequently dedicated enemies—until someone crossed or threatened one of them. Then they became an army united and solid, daring another trespass, courting the occasion for revenge. There were nights, especially during the first year of the nightmares, when Sam took refuge in Jackie's room, her bed. These times could have become perfect opportunities for ridicule, ammunition for public embarrassment, but if Jackie teased him or told another soul, Freida was not aware of it. She realized that Sam, with growing regularity, turned to his sister for advice and support, and that a maturing Jackie could actually differentiate what was fair for sibling rivalry from what was not.

"MOVE OVER."

"Good grief, the least you can do is keep your feet to yourself till they get warm. That's better. That was some fight you were putting up in there."

"I thought maybe I wouldn't have it anymore."

"Well, it's been a while, and that's something. Used to be nearly every night. Reckon why Mama didn't wake up?"

"Door's closed, and I'm glad. I don't want her to know."

"Good thing you got me. Not just any big sister would welcome you in the middle of the night."

"You're an angel. Can I stop praising you and go to sleep?"

"You're wheezing."

"Won't last. I used my medicine."

"I hope it don't take long."

"Don't fuss. I brought my own pillow—see?"

"Guess you want points for it."

"I just want you to be nice."

"At four in the morning? No way. Be still."

"Jackie?"

"Huh?"

"Are you ashamed of me?"

"Of course, I am. You're my brother."

"You know what I mean."

"Um, I don't tell my friends you sleep in my bed when you have a nightmare—if that's what you're getting at. This is private. Family-only stuff. I think I hate that dream as much as you do, but shame don't have anything to do with it. You can't help it. You're shivering. When did you start worrying about how I feel?"

"I just wonder why you don't tell me to get lost."

"Pull that blanket up from the foot of the bed. It's heavier than this one. You know, Sam, it's never been just you. All of us are part of it. Since you got hurt, I've had about every emotion there is. I used to get jealous over you getting so much attention, then I'd get mad at myself for being such a baby. The nightmare always makes me feel sorry for you—and helpless, I guess, because I can't do anything. It doesn't kill me to be nice some of the time—when nobody's looking."

"I just wondered. That's all."

"If I tell you something, will you promise you won't bring it up again? Ever? Not even when you get mad at me?"

"What's it about?"

"Promise first."

"Okay. I promise."

"Sometimes, I get this spooky feeling that one day you're gonna do something really great. Not save the world from the bomb or anything like that. Just that fate gave you some sort of special purpose and that you had to go through all that stuff to help you get ready for it."

"You're way off there."

"Maybe, but if it turns out to be true, remember who predicted it— I told you about those icy feet."

"Sorry. You'd be smart not to expect much from a brother who thinks he's safer in bed with his sister."

"I expect you to shut up and let me sleep. Mama'll be calling us to breakfast in two hours."

"I'll go back to my room if you want."

"Oh, stay. It's no big deal. Just sleep."

AS HER CHILDREN, one close behind the other, began the voyage across the treacherous waters of their teen years, Freida's good-mother radar began to pick up jumbled signals. Undaunted, her maternal weapons honed and gleaming, she swore they'd reach the age of majority with their morals and integrity intact. What was there to worry about? Hadn't the MacCauleys already paid their dues?

II

May 1971

A. D. SIGHED AND FROWNED. Freida ought to take care of some of these conferences herself. Didn't she always pick the topic? Didn't she always decide when the time was right? Didn't she laugh or bully him for something he reported to her afterward? She knew he got all nervous and sweaty.

"I know what you're thinking, but he's so modest around me." She used her sweetest smile, the deceptive one that was supposed to hide her pleasure at getting him to do her bidding. "Besides, you're his father. You're supposed to talk to him. You think your daughter is any easier? She thinks she's in love already."

"Girls do that sooner."

"Are you going to do it or not?"

"Oh, all right, but the problem is you watch 'im too close. There's absolutely nothin' wrong with 'im. He's just turned fifteen. Don't even shave, yet—not regular. Can't expect 'im to get too deep into matin' rituals before his hormones kick in."

"I'm not telling you to take him to a prostitute. I just think he needs to know he can come to us with problems and questions. He's too quiet. We don't know what goes on in his head. Maybe, he's just waiting to be asked."

"He ain't *funny.*"

"He never mentions girls."

"He never mentions hairy-nosed wombats, either."

"*A. D. . . .*"

"I've been through this with 'im before."

"Did you ask specific questions?"

"I didn't ask if he was, you know."

"Of course, you didn't. You can't even say it."

"I can too."

"What if he's afraid or ashamed to tell us? What if he's just too shy to talk about girls? Or ask questions?" She didn't pause for him to attempt answers. "What if he's confused about the sexual feelings he's bound to be having? If you'd read some of the books I have, you'd see just how mixed-up a kid who's been molested can be. I know he dreams exciting stuff fairly often because he doesn't put himself out to cover up the evidence."

"You want 'im to start doin' his own laundry, you tell 'im."

"A. D. . . ."

"Okay, I've already covered this ground with 'im, but I'll talk to 'im again. You can expect a full report in a few days!" He saluted.

A. D. acted a lot more outdone than he felt. Doubts had occurred to him, too, but he couldn't bring his into the open as fast as Freida. He didn't think he could accept a gay son as quickly, either. In theory, he was okay about it, but he hoped he wouldn't have to test the theory against reality. He'd tried to feel the boy out, get some idea of what mysterious forces were silently driving him. Sam had sidestepped every attempt as he would have dung piles in the pasture. What A. D. wanted most for Sam was happiness. Even in an age of diverse life-styles, of hippies, yippies, and flower children, homosexuality was still on the outs with society. He didn't know if happiness and homosexuality could coexist in the same body.

He had watched his son for signs that hormonal insanity had hit, that an incurable obsession with the female counterpart had taken control. A. D. was still waiting. Though Sam didn't say much about girls, he seemed to be doing everything else right. He slept until noon if no one prodded him out of bed. A family of six could feast for days on what he consumed in a meal. His music was an assault of loud, garbled, tuneless lyrics that drove the rest of the family to the brink of mental breakdowns. His hair grew past the curve of his shoulders and hung sheepdog-style over his brow. His clothes looked like rags the Salvation Army had refused. He wouldn't wear them if Freida touched them with an iron. He had developed strong opinions about politics, world hunger, materialism, Vietnam—all popular affairs and topics. Taking a close look at the teenaged children of friends, A. D. regarded Sam as pretty much a part of the current norm—except for the girl thing.

A. D. COULD STILL HEAR the complaining of the school bus engine as it topped a hill a quarter mile down the road. He was waiting on the fieldstone patio. An ambush. In the shade of two giant white oaks, he sat comfortably on a slatted bench of his own carpentry. His workshop had turned out a few nice pieces of lawn furniture. He thought if his brain was as agile as his hands, raising kids would be less a challenge than a hobby.

"Sam?" He raised his voice a little.

Startled out of some deep pondering, Sam halted, then came toward the bench with a question on his face.

A. D. slapped a place on the back of the bench near him. "Park it, son. Haven't seen much of you lately."

Sam took his time, lowering first his butt to the bench then his school books onto the fieldstones between his feet. He stretched his legs straight out over the books and crossed them at the ankle. The length of his legs appeared to be growing a little faster than the rest of him.

"If this is about the dent in the Ranger, as much as I'd like to say she did, Jackie really didn't do it. And on my honor as a MacCauley, I didn't, either. My learner's permit doesn't allow unsupervised driving. So—"

"Your mother confessed. What amazes me is she can see stumps an' fences an' other vehicles when she's in her . . . anyway, that's beside the point, I wanna spend some time with you—find out how your life's goin'." As good an introduction as any, but A. D. caught the stiffening of his son's posture and knew an invisible guard had gone up. "How's the world treatin' you?"

"What specifically did she ask you to grill me about?"

"Huh?"

"She's been giving me the look for days."

"I don't—"

"I gave up cigarettes—I only smoked that one. The woman's got the nose of a bloodhound. Surely, she knows me and Bud were just bullsh— joking about the tattoos." Sam appeared to study the worn toes of his sneakers then suddenly looked up. "You promised not to tell her about the joint."

"I promised to ground you till doomsday if I caught you with another. But I didn't tell her."

"Well, what is it?"

A. D. tried to sound indignant. "I don't know what you mean. This isn't an inquisition."

Sam grinned and spoke with confidence. "It has to be something I'm doing that she doesn't like, something I'm not doing that she wants me to do, or something she thinks I don't already know but probably do. Or the haircut thing again. So?"

"Oh, you're gonna be a real smartass today."

"Sorry. So what is it?"

A. D. thought about giving up and trying a different approach some other time but decided that might not be much better. Honesty and straightforwardness had always come easier to him than tact. "Girls."

"Oh, great." Sam lazily sighed. "What about girls?"

"Oh, just general stuff. They're complicated. Trust me. You can never know enough about 'em."

Sam smiled indulgently. "Want me to explain them to you?"

"Very funny."

"They talk too much. They delude themselves into thinking they know everything. They are critical and cynical and annoying. They can't even get along with each other. Take it from me, I have a sister and a mother."

"Son—"

"They're the ones who have babies. They don't stand up to pee, and most don't have whiskers. What else is there to know?"

"I'm impressed. Since you know so much, why don't you tell me how you *feel* about 'em?" A. D. nudged the boy's ribs and watched for a reaction.

Sam's eyebrows flexed upward and dropped back into place—an unuttered oh, no. A one-sided bashful smile crept slowly across his face. "How I feel?"

A. D. nodded.

"They have their place, I guess."

"Sam!"

"Okay." He brushed some invisible debris from his jeans. His tone was offhand, cool. "They're okay—some are—some more than others. At school, these stupid girls are always giggling and saying silly stuff to me. They get on my nerves."

"What do they say?"

"You know, stuff about the way I look and walk." Sam's cheeks reddened. His voiced dropped to a whisper. "They tell me I've got a cute butt and ask me who I'd like to go out with—or ask me to meet them places after school. Gross stuff like that."

A. D. had all he could do to keep from laughing out loud. "They flirt, huh?"

"Yeah. I guess so. They embarrass me—like you're doing."

"You don't like girls who flirt an' admire your butt?"

"*Dad*—"

"I'm just curious. What kind do you like?"

Sam closed his eyes tightly. When he opened them, he asked, "Do you know who Goldie Hawn is?"

A. D. didn't want to admit it, but he nodded.

"She's my kinda girl."

This was encouraging, healthy. "I reckon you like her best in those bikini things with graffiti all over like on TV, huh?"

"Um, sure, *Laugh-in's* where it all started for me. She's got these wide eyes—this big smile—I don't—" He shrugged.

"I understand perfectly, but skimpy clothes an' a curvy figure don't hurt. Right?"

"Come on, Daddy, I'd like Goldie no matter what she was wearing. I'm sure I'd like her just as well naked."

That's my boy! A. D. nodded to show Sam he understood.

"Can we hurry this up, Dad? I've got stuff to do. If it'll help get me off the hook here, I'll admit to lusting after Linda Evans, too."

"You just sit there a while longer. Your mama an' I have a responsibility to you. Boys your age go through lot of changes—both physically an' emotionally. It's not easy to get through without messing up a few times."

"So let's get it over with. Say what she told you to."

A. D. leaned his head to one side and looked up into the crown of the nearest oak. His lead-ins were not improving. He'd do okay when he got close to the point, but first he had to get there. The boy kept jumping ahead, so A. D. figured if he gave up trying to be subtle, he'd get there sooner. "This is my cart an' my horse. I'd like to say which one goes before the other."

"Okay."

"You know already boys your age have a lot of—um—urges."

"Oh, sh—no! We've done that number before. Come on—"

"Wait a minute. It's important. You were a lot younger an' less mature then. Consider this a refresher course."

"Tell you what—let's make this easier for both of us—if you tell me not to get urges, I swear I won't get them." Sam drew an exaggerated cross over his heart and held his right hand up in an oath.

"Be serious."

Sam lowered his voice again. "Dad, you told me about all that junk—urges, wet dreams, etcetera—everything that comes under the heading 'Puberty.' Once was enough. I'm not stupid. I know what's happening to me, and I'm okay with it."

"You don't have to be embarrassed. This ain't so bad." A. D. knew how his son felt. His own face and neck was hot, and sweat poured down his back. "We oughta be able to talk openly. Besides bein' your father, at one time, I was also a fifteen-year-old boy. I'm familiar with the feelin's. Ever'body has the same want-tos, even girls, an' it's really sad that sometimes young people feel guilty an' ashamed if they—well, if they do somethin' about 'em—like it's dirty rather than natural."

"So we're entering the realm of me doing *it* with somebody or doing *it* by myself—right?"

"Yeah, I guess. In a way. *No!* No, it's not! Cancel that! You've gotta realize—I sure hope you do—that doin' it with another person is totally out of the question for you an' will be for a long, long time!"

Sam sighed, shook his head. He looked vaguely bored. "I'll depend on you to let me know when the time is right."

"Don't get smart with me. I'm tryin' to fulfill my duty to you, an' you're supposed to sit there an' be grateful you got a daddy who loves you. I'm supposed to make sure you don't grow up with a bunch of hangups because you—because of your urges. You know exactly what I'm sayin', so stop making me say it."

Sam nodded slightly. His eyes appeared to lock on the back door. "Did you do it?"

A. D. looked up into the trees again. "Well, of course, I did. I think ever'body does. Ain't nothin' to be ashamed of."

"Do you have hang-ups?"

"No. I don't think so. Not now."

"You were raised by your grandmother. Did she have these discussions with you?"

"No, Sam, but I wish somebody had because I felt lousy a lot as a kid. Sex was the one thing Gramma Addie didn't give me her views on. Once I nearly died of humiliation when she asked me why I was spendin' so much time in the outhouse."

"The outhouse?"

"Go ahead an' laugh. It's funny now, but privacy was scarce in Gramma Addie's house. A closed door drew her like the moon draws water. Until your mother, I never had anyone I could talk to about somethin' that personal. I admit it ain't as easy as talkin' baseball scores, but you an' me ought not to be ill at ease with each other."

"Will you and Ma be satisfied if I say I feel okay about my life? That I'm not particularly guilt-ridden? Not that I'm admitting anything. You're not going into *specifics* with her, are you?"

"I won't say more'n I have to. To answer your other question—as long as we can see you mean it, we'll be as fine as frog's hair. You're important to us. You're important to me. Got any idea how scared I get just thinkin' about all that could go wrong? Growin' up's the hardest work you'll ever do. A whole lot of people go through their entire lives without seein' anything like the pain you've already had to deal with. If I try too hard, don't hold it against me. You know my heart."

A. D. paused and eased his arm around Sam's shoulder, pulling him close. "I want you to know about normal, healthy relationships. When you have questions or need help with decisions, I want to be the person you come to for help."

Sam made no move to resist the embrace. "I trust you. As fathers go, you're not too bad." He looked at his hands. "But you definitely worry too much."

A. D. sniffed, not really caring if a tear came. "Yeah, but you gotta admit your mama's worse. An' when she's worried, we have to do like she says or pay the consequences, don't we?"

"Well, you've done admirably well. So we can wrap this up."

"Sorry, we can't stop now. You ain't raised, yet. I was wonderin'—do you ever have the nightmare now?" A. D. wanted to provide a place for the subject to fit, if needed.

Sam shrugged. "Not often."

"Talkin' about it once in a while couldn't hurt, you know."

"I think I feel what I'm supposed to." A breeze fanned Sam's hair across his face. He brushed it back.

"I don't follow you."

"When I think about what caused the dream, I wonder how any kid who'd been through that could grow up feeling the same things other people do. Looks like just the thought of touching or being touched would be repulsive, but if I listed the top five things I daydream about, at least four would involve some form of touching." He shrugged again.

"But I'd probably be a lot more disturbed by my own filthy mind if I didn't have all your advice and explanations—and hers."

"If I had a tape recordin', I'd play this back for her."

"I'm not kissing up. I know how you two are about each other—always carrying on a bunch of bullsh—sorry. You put up with her acting like she's boss. She's works like crazy to keep you entertained and happy—and, of course, well-fed. That's neat. Now, why don't you ask her something for me, okay?"

"What's that?"

Sam grinned broadly, playfully. "Ask her if she ever gave in to her urges."

"Sam!"

"If she says 'yes', ask her if she has hang-ups."

"Sam!"

"Ask her if she invades Jackie's privacy as much as she does mine. Ask her if she knows how far that evil daughter of hers has gone with Robbie. She's in love, you know."

"Wait a minute! What do you mean about your sister?"

"Oh, never mind. I just wanted to put you on the scent of fresh game. Jackie may not be a problem. Yet. But she's due one of these talks."

A. D. tried to read Sam's face. "If you know somethin' your sister's doin' that might get her in trouble, you better come out with it. She'd tell on you in a heartbeat."

"Yeah, I know. Mama thinks I'm queer, doesn't she?"

"No. Of course not. She only—"

"Tell her to find something else to worry about. Why don't she join a sewing club or something?"

A. D. rolled his eyes.

Sam got up and lifted his books from the patio floor. Halfway to the back door, he turned. "Hey, Dad, speaking of hormones—do you know how to make a whore moan?"

"No, son, how do you make a hormone?"

"Don't pay her!" The screen door slammed behind him.

IN HIS ROOM, Sam's flushed face began to cool. People seemed to go out of their way to humiliate him. The girls at school, his friends, his parents. He supposed his shyness made him more sensitive to some things than most kids, but he couldn't help it. He liked privacy and space. Instead of calling attention to himself, he preferred blending in with the scenery.

He sighed heavily and turned on the radio. *WVOK, the Mighty Six-Ninety.* AM radio at its best. He listened to the mellow broadcaster's voice doing the four o'clock news then put an album on the turntable and switched over from radio to phonograph. Lately, he'd discovered the tragic, haunting work of Kris Kristofferson and dosed himself daily with "Casey's Last Ride," "Just the Other Side of Nowhere," and "Sunday Mornin' Comin' Down." All his pocket-money went to the records-by-mail club that kept him supplied with mood music. Another Kristofferson album was on the way. He stood peering out his window into a thick grove of pink-tufted mimosa trees, listening and humming, thinking.

He understood why his parents thought the bad experiences he'd had as a small child might cause him to be different. He'd read things, heard things. They sometimes had discussions about homosexuality in his presence. These clever dialogues, staged for his benefit, tended to spotlight their liberal-minded views—cloaked ways of saying, "It's okay if you are, son. We'll understand." He wanted to reply, "Save it for some gay person. Hairy-legged men don't do a thing for me. I spend at least eighteen hours a day, *every* day, trying to picture what half the females I know look like naked. I'm fifteen. That's what fifteen-year-old males do. If you hafta worry about me, personally, try worrying about the fact that I'll probably spend the rest of my life doing the same thing I'm doing now. Because I won't ever be able to ask a real girl for a date—much less have a *relationship* with one. But it won't be because I don't have the well-defined urge to!"

He hoped he was wrong about himself, but the way he had it figured, he'd still be taking care of his own urges when he became an old man. Right now, he'd like to tell his parents, "You've done okay. You've loved me in all the right ways."

A noise from outside the window pulled him away from his thoughts.

He looked into the nearest mimosa. A round, dark-eyed face stared back.

Robbie's little sister. Brenan, the Brat, Robbie called her. Sam didn't think she was all that bad, but she tended to be underfoot much of the time. He called her the Sawbriar Princess because once when he and Robbie were supposed to be watching her for her mother to do something in the house, she'd caught them off guard and crawled off into a briar patch. She'd been about two, and Ellen Armstrong had been anything but understanding when the boys brought back her screaming baby covered with bloody stripes. Sam had felt repentant at the time. After three years of hearing the story told and retold by the adult members of his family and hers, he felt amply punished. What would they say about him if she fell out of his mimosa and broke her neck?

Wearing a lemon yellow sunsuit, Brenan straddled a fragile-looking limb close to the top of the tree. Her bare feet swung back and forth in a carefree rhythm that Sam thought could easily upset her balance. Half a Hershey bar poked out of one hand, and her mouth was painted with chocolate. She waved to him with her free hand and grinned a slimy, brown, milk-toothed grin.

Sam pushed up the window. "Get down from there."

She shook her head. "Can't."

"Why can't you?"

She shifted the remains of her candy to the other hand and started licking the chocolate off her fingers. Between licks, she said, "I don't know how."

He crossed his arms. "Go down the same way you came up."

The last of the candy went into her mouth, and she wiped her hands down the front of her sunsuit, making two brown skid marks. She chewed, swallowed, licked her fingers. "There's pissants." She pointed to the branch directly under her. "I'm 'lergic."

He rolled his eyes. "Well, stop moving around like that till I can come out and get you down."

"Okay." She pulled the bib of her sunsuit up over her face and swabbed most of the external chocolate onto it.

A moment later, the five-year-old smiled her most charming smile as she leaned into Sam's outstretched arms. Her sticky hands went around his neck, and she pressed her cheek tightly to his. She smelled of chocolate and grassy, outdoorsy things.

"Thank you berry much," she said when he set her feet on the grass and unwound her arms from his neck.

"Go on home before somebody comes looking for you." He pointed. "And watch where you step. You shouldn't be running around barefoot."

She sighed and looked disappointed over being sent on her way so soon, but she waved silently. He ran a hand over the greasy spot she'd left on the back of his neck and watched her small feet sluggishly drag through the thick grass. At the rate she was going, she'd get across the wide stretch of lawn to her home in fifteen or twenty minutes, instead of three or four. Still, he stood and watched until the kitchen door of the Armstrong house closed behind her.

You're a real mother hen, Ace.

"Shut up, Lefty."

Little kids playing outside alone made him nervous. Someone safe, someone who loved them, should always be watching.

12

. . . deserted ghostway—
not another car in sight.
The motor's but a whisper
in the quietude of flight.
My eyes chase the white lines
through a glistening silver light,
and I curse the devils dancing
in this lonely, silent night.

> excerpt "Lonely, Silent Night" from *Poetic Injustice* by
> Brenan Armstrong MacCauley, 1984

July 1972

EITHER THE SPEED of the Corvette or the whiskey was sending the world reeling by. The blur of telephone poles, mail boxes, and frame houses was making Sam sick. He listened to the spit of loose gravel, the drone of tires and closed his eyes to the kaleidoscope outside his window.

A. D. would have said Robbie was as drunk as a politician's floozy, and even in Sam's own somewhat inebriated condition, he agreed. However, Robbie was lost to reason. It wouldn't do to say anything about slowing down or stopping—unless Sam was certain he was going to puke on the sacred upholstery. Back at the Dance Hall, a fancy name for a clearing in Dark Water Woods, he had made one noble play for the keys that had almost come to blows. Robbie had ended up giving him the choice of riding home with a cocky drunk or walking two miles to the nearest pay phone. Since Sam had held a thread of hope of getting his first sampling of Royal Crown Cola fortified with eighty-proof flame past the detection of his parents—he had crawled into the Corvette.

Thus, he sat rigid and praying on the edge of the passenger seat between Bud's splayed legs. Bud had passed over into La La Land before the Corvette's wheels had started to roll.

Bud was supposed to sleep over with a cousin in Mountain Brook, so the Corvette bypassed Russett Bridge Road and headed straight for I-65 into Birmingham. Sam could picture the pious fit Bud's old man would pitch if he caught his son in this condition. Arlo Blacknell, a minister of the Word, tended to be fiercely opinionated about vices and worldly appetites. In Bud's account, his father had first been ordained a Missionary Baptist minister then converted to one of the Pentecostal groups before giving up established backing to charter a church of his own customized beliefs. *The Faithful Few Assemblage*—hard to say with a straight face—ministered to a congregation of about fifty dedicated worshipers who met in a ramshackle, depression-era two-room school building that had been otherwise deserted for twenty years. The few times Sam had been around the preacher, he had found himself on the receiving end of a divergent host of impromptu sermons and parables. He had swiftly discovered the prudence of avoiding Blacknell and became infinitely more empathic to Bud's peculiarities because of his hapless chromosomal ties to this raving maniac. The injuries Bud wore to school as a result of his father's determination to purge him of sin were severe and many. The teachers had to be blind not to notice or too spineless to intervene.

Exiting the freeway, Robbie began weaving the Corvette down a maze of dark, hilly residential streets. Sam was totally lost. The only thing he was sure of was this area was not the Mountain Brook he knew. Nothing was familiar. No doubt, Robbie was lost, too, but would die before he'd admit an error in judgment, so Sam didn't bother to ask questions. The Vette two-wheeled onto a black strip of pavement that was lined with old castle-like houses with turrets and cupolas. At the end of this street, Robbie swung hard to the left and floored the accelerator.

A dead end street! Sam felt the alcoholic contents of his stomach rolling around inside him. He stabbed the air in a crucial attempt to draw Robbie's attention to the sign.

The Corvette gained speed, and the kaleidoscope outside Sam's window resumed. Ahead, a towering stone building rose up out of the ground. The road ran out in front of the building! Sam yelled, but Robbie was deaf. The Vette had taken wing! Grabbing Bud's belt buckle with his left hand, Sam grabbed the door handle with his right.

He could never say with any confidence in the accuracy what happened after that; he only knew what a network of other people tried to piece together for him.

WHEN HE CAME TO the next day, a bright light was blazing in the dead center of his visual field. It burned through his eyes, into his forebrain. Its glare blocked out the rest of the world. He shut his eyelids, heavy and grainy with fatigue, against the violation.

Voices whispered and hummed in the air. His brain was too tired to sort and clarify them. Other than a tight rumble of air straining in and out of his chest, he had no voice of his own.

His right arm had been wrapped in tight bandages and strung up to a contraption over his head. When he tried to pull it down, pain seared through the arm and into his shoulder and neck. He couldn't find his left arm. If he still had legs, they were numb. Concentrating all the energy he could rally, he tried to move. Nothing. His body was paralyzed. Maybe he was dying. Death could have started working its way up from his feet.

The voices rose, but the asthmatic sounds amplified and pushed them far away. Suddenly, he was terrified. If he opened his eyes again, he would see the gigantic stone church hurtling toward him. Someone close by was crying, sniffing. He was crying, too, his tears sliding toward his ears.

Someone dried his face, and his tears stopped coming. His respirations quieted. Without seeing, he knew the someone. He didn't have to be afraid. The touch of her hand, her strength seeping into the pores of his skin was all he needed. Whatever happened, whatever was to come, she would keep him safe.

Some of the time he was awake. Other times, he slept and dreamed. His dreams were a series of disconnected images. They drifted from funny to sad, from comforting to horrifying. The blinding light gradually softened. He could open his eyes, look around, locate his body parts, and know who was in the room. But no matter how hard he tried, words would not form in his mouth.

Dr. Mark said, *"He's in shock."* His mother and others repeated the words over and over. *"He's in shock."* Three small, simple words, but Sam had no inkling of their meaning. *"He's in shock."* They were probably talking about him.

THE NEXT DAY he kept sorting and arranging the details of the wreck as they were dropped one at a time by his visitors. Soon he would have a complete story. He knew Robbie was alive only because a machine called a ventilator pushed air into his lungs through a hole in his neck. A surgeon had put him back together with only one piece left over—his spleen. Sam heard Dr. Mark whisper to Freida and A. D. that his son wasn't out of the woods, yet. "Not by a country mile." Did Dr. Mark mean Robbie still might die? Was Bud dead? Though he couldn't move or speak, Sam could worry.

A. D. sounded as if he had a cold. "You cry but you don't talk. Why do you keep on cryin'? I wish you'd say somethin'."

He will when he has somethin' to say. He's in shock, ya know. Don't let 'em fool ya—light makes his eyes water. Ain't bawlin'. Ain't scared. Hangin' right in there, ain't ya, Ace?

Yeah. Right. And pigs fly.

Lefty had survived the wreck.

SAM WAS DREAMING about marching down the sidewalk in front of Russett High School. He was wearing a black matador costume —a red cape slung over a shoulder, ruffled shirt, second-skin black sequined pants that glittered in the sun. He seemed to be leading a parade of children costumed to look like tacos, burritos, and rolls of Tums. Bud, in a bull suit with a massive horned headdress, danced beside him. The windows of the school were overflowing with students and teachers leaning out, crying, "Bravo! Olé!" Miss Montoya, the sixtyish Spanish teacher, was moved to tears. Bill Compton, a local celebrity from the Channel Six early morning "Country Boy Eddie Show," brought up the rear, strumming a flat-top guitar and singing "The Greatest Matador."

Abruptly, the dream broke and Sam awoke, embarrassed and hungry, to the sound of A. D.'s voice raised in uncharacteristic, seething anger somewhere outside the room.

"Go on home, Blacknell. You're not goin' in there an' start that bullshit with my son. It looks to me like you'd be thankin' God for your own boy comin' outta this alive instead of blamin' mine for what happened. All three boys were drinkin'. Not one of 'em was a ringleader."

Bud's daddy mumbled something about taking his belt to Bud and about his belief A. D. had spared the rod too long. He then charitably offered to pray for the sins of the MacCauley clan.

A. D. declared that that was just what he needed—some lard can preacher with batshit for brains volunteering to be a messenger between his family and God. "You just stay the hell away from my son, an' you say one more word to my wife, you'll need Sunday's collection for new teeth!"

More things were said, but wanting to avoid hearing the details of Bud's punishment, Sam stopped paying attention. Instead, he devoted his diminished mental energy to retrieving one of his mother's favorite stories. When Jackie was three, A. D. had smacked her leg. The crime that had brought on the punishment hadn't been significant enough to remember, but Freida could narrate, in colorful detail, the dramatic fit Jackie had enacted as soon as she realized she'd been spanked. Deeply traumatized by her screaming, head-banging floor show, A. D. had sworn he'd never again raise his hand to her or any other child. "Whoever thought up this spankin' business musta been one cruel Nazi hatchet man." Over the years, Freida had fiercely loosed many a threat of corporal punishment. *". . . set your butt on fire . . . tan your mangy hide . . . meet me behind the woodshed, Mister!"* Idle threats. Sam and Jackie often joked about their all-bark-no-bite mother. But A. D., permanently civilized by one stirring tantrum, was as good as his word; he didn't even bark.

Reverend Blacknell had better watch out, anyway. A. D. MacCauley's gentle nature with his family wouldn't stop him from decking a crackpot preacher who didn't know when to give up.

ON THE THIRD EVENING of medical captivity, Sam sent his exhausted parents home. He could speak, and with the exception of a broken arm, he could move. A. D. and Freida had begun to feel confident he was going to live, thus the troubled doting had quickly digressed to hostility and profound disfavor. Sam's alcoholic excursion was destined to live in infamy.

"Do you think one of us should stay to babysit?"

"Nah. He's tethered. Don't hafta worry about 'im hittin' the bootleggers an' crawling off through the woods with a bottle of rotgut. Wouldn't get far draggin' that bed behind 'im."

"So let's leave him. I can't fluff another pillow. I'm too tired to be the long-suffering mother."

"Me, too. If Otis here can't hold his own urinal, he can call Barney One-Bullit. Or one of them cute little nurses."

"You wouldn't think a few drinks could cause so many people so much worry and grief, would you?"

"Least we didn't have to bury one of 'em. This time. Came close, but I always heard a miss is good as a mile."

"We'll take turns being relieved and worrying whether our only son will be as lucky the next time he gets thirsty."

"S'pose you'll want me to worry tonight, so you can be relieved."

"That's fair. We'll swap tomorrow."

After staging the sarcastic tribute to his dishonor, his parents had gone, leaving him alone with his shame and remorse.

Nice folks, bad son.

"Shut up."

While Sam was steadily recuperating, things were reportedly looking better for Robbie, too. He'd been successfully weaned from the ventilator and was slowly improving. If Sam's arm hadn't been strung up to a trapeze bar, he would have put up a fuss to see Robbie, so he could make his own assessment. The condition reports may have been altered before he received them.

Bed-bound and sweating, he sat propped behind the dregs of his supper tray. Already shirtless, he kicked and punched the bed covers into a lumpy mound. Propping his bare feet on them, he clicked on the television and sank back onto the raised head of the bed to watch *Emergency!* A few minutes into the drama, the paramedics answered a call to rescue victims from a mangled heap of cars on a busy freeway. Sam snapped the TV off. Not tonight!

Wuss, Lefty sang out.

"Shut up!" Bored, he glanced at a double column of get-well cards and crayon drawings that had been taped to the closet door and in a row under the wall-mounted television set. Brenan, the Sawbriar Princess, had been busy. He figured Robbie also had a growing collection of his kid sister's hearts, stars, daisies, jack-o'-lantern houses, and curly haired stick people masterpieces, all bearing similar messages—"*Get well soon! I love you! Miss Priss had six kittens. I miss you!*", the letters backward, upside-down, some lying on their sides, lots of hearts and flowers. He'd probably put them in a book or something. Poor kid nearly lost both her big brothers.

Doctor Mark had taken Brenan to some place in Atlanta to have her tested. There she'd been assessed to have a genius IQ and moderately severe dyslexia. A classy little kid with impeccable taste in heroes, Brenan had developed a fixation with Sam. She had become a second shadow, spending a great deal of time tailing him around the farm, stretching her short legs to walk in his footsteps, striving to copy every move he made. In return for her adoration, he had became her mentor. He had stolen her training wheels, giving her no choice but to ride without them. He'd shown her how to fold the best paper airplane, how to fly a kite. Through him, she'd memorized most of Marty Robbins' cowboy ballads and sang them loud enough to be heard in Nashville. He'd taken her fishing and made her bait her own hook. He'd taught her to lace her boots, use a slingshot, spit—all the things first grade and her family had neglected.

The cards had come from relatives he barely knew who lived as far away as New York City. However, there was a Hallmark from Tara Mason, the most beautiful, sophisticated girl at Russett High. He'd keep that one. He'd have kept a dead roach if Tara had given it to him.

He fished a book-club-edition novel from the lumpy mound of sheets and blankets. Freida, hands on hips, had sighed heavily and frowned at A. D. when he had dropped it on the bed. If she'd made selections for his reading, she probably would have brought a stack of *Power Boys*, *Trixie Belden*, and *Boys' Life* magazines.

He cracked open the bright yellow-jacketed *Portnoy's Complaint*. Much better than TV, anyway. Sam sure wouldn't want to trade mothers with Alex Portnoy. Freida could be a pain, but that Portnoy woman was definitely too much.

He was on page eighty—well into the chapter "Cunt Crazy" during which Alex beats off on a public bus. The ambiance was getting too strong for Sam's not-so-private spot. Erections had a way of creeping up on him without regard to circumstance. He put the book aside in an attempt to forestall the mood.

As if on cue, Nurse Evans—with her short, snug uniform, dangling stethoscope, long blonde hair, and cold hands—came in to make a routine assessment of his physical condition. He self-consciously yanked the tangle of cover up to his neck to cover his skinny, bruised ribs and the fuzzy promise of chest hair.

DeLane Evans—she had insisted in a deep, throaty voice, he call her *DeLane*—was, without contest, his favorite nurse. Even before the shock that had paralyzed and muted him had vanished, he'd looked into the eyes and cleavage of this ravishing amazon who'd bent over his bed, checked his blood pressure and pulse, listened to his heart, played her cool fingertips over his injured arm. Contrary to his customary shy behavior, he had stared shamelessly. After all, he was in shock. He'd stared until the beam of her penlight blinded him. By then her image had been seared into his brain. With her enormous breasts and pouty lips, she was a mesmerizing, bigger-than-life Goldie Hawn. She came to the left side of the bed. "Shame on you," her sultry voice scolded.

Following her pointing finger to the yellow-jacketed book, he scowled and turned his head toward the window. He felt a blush staining him crimson—starting in his cheeks and spreading in all directions from there. His state of shock had passed, and his timidity had crept back. He believed when she checked his fingertips, she'd find no blood at all circulating to them; it had all gone to his face, neck, and erectile tissues. He brought his knees up to conceal a pulsating tent pole that threatened to raise the sheets. As soon as he stopped fumbling with the covers, she lifted and tucked his left forearm under her elbow and wrapped a blood pressure cuff around his biceps.

Almost touchin' one of them soft, queen-sized mammaries. Ace, you lucky dog! Paradise at your fingertips!

"Oh, don't be embarrassed." She massaged his shoulder then began inflating the cuff with the attached bulb. "I'm a nurse. Absolutely nothing shocks me. I was only teasing. I've read it myself. I've also read *Candy*. You know *Candy?* It's a classic. I've even seen the movie, so you see I'm no prude when it comes to literature or entertainment. Erotica definitely has a place."

We gonna have world-class jerk-off fantasies, huh, Boss?

He glanced briefly at her. Bud had loaned him a ratty copy of *Candy*. Instead of exciting him, it had left him nauseated. He'd returned it to Bud the next day, and when grilled, he'd refused to comment. At least Portnoy was funny.

Hot in here, ain't it?

Lady Chatterley's Lover had been more to Sam's taste. He'd gotten it from Robbie—along with an assortment of clinical sex manuals with drawings, photographs, and written how-tos from the library of an unaware-of-the-lending Dr. Mark. Some of the illustrations had been pretty disgusting, too. He couldn't have admitted to Bud or Robbie that he much preferred heated romance to outright filth, so he usually played along during their perverted conversations, adding as little dirt as was required to remain in good standing as one of the guys. But sneaking glances at DeLane's rounded curves was something he couldn't help.

Hafta be dead not to look.

She winked, wiggled the stethoscope earpieces into her ears, and placed the cold, metal-rimmed disc in the bend of his arm. The air hissed slowly out of the cuff. When it was empty, she stripped it off and reached for his wrist. After a while, she said, "BP's okay, but your heart rate's way up there."

No shit!

Sam was used to female flirtation of a younger variety. DeLane's breathless coquetry was a whole new ball game. She moved around the bed to check his arm, so instead of staring out the window, which was now behind her, he shifted to the open doorway.

Half a woman stared back. One eye. A piece of timid smile.

One slender hand curled around the door facing. The other half of her face was hidden. Then all of her was gone. She hadn't meant to be seen.

Uh, oh!

The room turned cold.

DeLane was still flirting, but all Sam felt was his blood freezing in his veins, his heart pounding like the village drum in an old Tarzan movie. Sweat welled up from his pores.

DeLane didn't seem to notice his distress. She continued to smile and chatter, and finally, assuring him she'd come back to check on him again, she left him alone and defenseless.

An abrupt onset of coughing took his breath and refused to give it back. He lay gasping. The raised head of the bed gave him an easy view of the doorway. It was empty, but Sam, biding long seconds, counted on it filling up again.

His rasping stridor filled the room. Without giving up his vigil, his fingers searched the bedside table for his inhaler. His hand trembled, and his first touch sent the canister clattering to the floor. Held fast by the trapeze bar, he'd have to use the call button to bring someone to the room to pick it up. He looked away from the door to find the call signal that was built into the same control pad as the TV buttons. He found its cord and began following it with the tips of his fingers. It disappeared under the pile of bedding. Just as he located the pad, he heard a noise. The clearing of a throat. He held out his hand for the inhaler before he realized who was handing it to him. His hand stopped in midair.

"It's okay," a soft, shy voice told him. "If you don't want to see me, I'll go."

Slender fingers pressed the inhaler into his hand. His arm slowly settled on the sheets. The asthma began resolving without the medication. The rush of fear from inside him gave out. His pores ran dry. There was nothing to fear. This woman would kill for him. She already had. She owned a piece of him.

Her smile was small, nervous. She expected to be sent away. A thick *Birmingham News* and a less bulky *Russett Bugle* jutted from under her arm. "I read about the wreck in the newspapers. They printed your name. I just thought—"

Sam nodded.

"Are you okay? I mean, is your arm goin' to be all right?"

Sam rubbed his hand across his mouth then offered it to her—an automatic gesture that he didn't try to restrain or analyze. She held it lightly against the front of her blouse and ran her fingers over the thin, white scars. She raised her eyes to his face. He tried to smile, but his lips only trembled. "Not as bad as it looks." He nodded at his injured arm. "How are you?"

An inch-long teardrop-shaped scar dented her right temple. She looked happy. "Not too bad. Not bad at all."

The bullet hole, Lefty surmised.

"Deb?"

Her eyebrows lifted in a return question.

Give her somethin', Sam. Might not get another chance.

She had a beautiful smile—like a little girl's, simple and beaming. Her hair was all brown and straight, cut boyishly short with a thick wedge of bangs. Her white blouse and black slacks were clean and pressed. She'd gained a little weight. No stale odor of cigarette smoke emanated from her.

"Thank you, Sam."

"Why are you thanking me?"

"You made me care. I didn't know I had it in me. I'd never had anybody worth it before you. I've got a good friend now. We have a little house and a whole lot to be thankful for."

"I'm glad."

"The doctor they made me see when I was put up in Tutwiler taught me a lot about not havin' to take other people's meanness. I wished I'd known before. I never woulda hurt you on my own."

He shrugged. The last thing he wanted to hear was descriptions or confessions about things he didn't even remember.

Give her at least a puny 'thanks'. Won't hurt a bit. She'll be gone soon. Give her that much. She gave ya your life.

"What you did for me was pretty terrific. It took a lot of courage. You had to have a lot of good in you even then."

She blushed. "You don't hafta—"

"I think about you sometimes. Not anything bad. I didn't know what happened to you." He tried to swallow a lump that rose in his throat. "I don't hold anything against you, Deb."

See. That wasn't so bad.

Her grasp on his hand tightened. "You're really somethin'."

A bond had held them all along. Spanning time and space and consciousness, it had been forged the day she'd left him standing on a mountain of stone steps. The day she'd killed a man. The day she'd been willing to sacrifice her own life. She had every right to be proud of the courage she had shown.

Though he would appreciate the irony more at a later time, here he lay, once again tied to a bed with Debra Jean standing over him. Trust was a wonderful development. Trust winnowed out fear. The madman was no more. His little boy pain banked on top of her own misery had made her strong enough to save them. Now, they held each other with their eyes, a communion of spirits who were free to be friends, a bridging of unlike worlds.

13

SINCE THE BEGINNING of his senior year, Sam had been barraged with feminine attention. Girls who had shown mild interest last spring had become hungry and dauntless. Making no claims otherwise, they found him fascinating. His shyness only made him more appealing, a more worthwhile challenge. They bumped into him in the halls. They phoned him for help with homework. They you-hooed, wiggled their fingers at him from across the classroom, the gym, the football field. They sniffed out his hiding places. Swallowing back his mortification, he answered them swiftly and courteously. He tolerated the flirting and his friends' teasing. He grinned, flushed, and whenever it wouldn't create a worse scenario, bolted away from them all.

There were dozens of boys at Russett High with the same problem. A few were as bashful as Sam. However exasperating, the female attentiveness also nourished his fragile ego. Almost an even trade-off. Until Vicky.

Vicky was bad news. Vicky wasn't hungry; she was starving.

Sam kicked the lower locker hard enough to put a new dent in the graffiti-etched metal. Vicky was taking lustful lunacy beyond the bounds of decency. Was there no end to how far this girl would go?

No end in sight. Take it from Lefty, she wants ya b-a-d.

"I don't believe this bullshit," Sam muttered.

Ya can stop it. Yessiree. Pull the rug right out from under her, put a brand new crack in that prissy little ass of hers. Or ya can hand 'er the ketchup an' let her eat ya alive.

Sam had kept his mouth shut about the phone calls at all hours of the day and night. He hadn't made a big deal about the notes and underwear—even when they'd fallen out of his locker in front of the crowds who had begun to congregate there between classes. When she threw herself into his arms, fondled his butt, and issued possessive warnings to every other girl in the school, he had simply peeled her off and walked away. He had taken all the measures he could think of to avoid her. He had been pointedly civil during a number of attempts to discourage her. In the mildest of tones, he had informed her that her vigilance was unwelcome—time, after time, after monotonous time. He had been more than fair. Still, she was back for another go.

Gotta play low-down an' dirty, Hoss. Only way girls like her know how to play. She's sampled all the fat-neck jocks. Now she wants a piece of pretty-boy intellectual. Ya can't be bought with dirty pictures. She can peddle her wares elsewhere.

Sam scooped the poker-hand of Polaroids into a neat stack and pushed Bud's leering face away from them. "I'm gonna take care of her once and for all," he declared, as he shouldered his way through the bodies that had gathered, three deep, to try to see what Sam had found in his locker today. He stuffed the photos into the waistband of his jeans. Bud, a.k.a. "the Bear," plus a clamor of catcalls, whistles, lascivious appraisals of this latest segment in the Vicky-loves-Sam drama, followed in his wake. He stopped to select and thumbtack one of the photos over a witch on a Halloween bulletin board. Vicky in nothing but an add-a-charm bracelet, a towel, and a Mona Lisa smile, was now riding a broom across a black crepe paper sky.

A bitch on a witch. I call that art!

Sam's anger dissolved his shyness, stomped flat his easygoing temperament, swallowed up his last morsel of charitable mercy. Vicky continued to throw pieces of herself at him. She deserved whatever he threw back.

Now for the windup an' the delivery.

Down one hall then a left into another, he rounded a sharp corner and found his subject propped against another bank of lockers. She looked up as if she'd been awaiting his arrival.

Vicky's bevy of bitches-in-waiting protectively circled their mistress—a personal team of Secret Service operatives, each one ready to throw herself in front of the ranking bitch, to take the first bullet. But the brainless slut parted them and recklessly met Sam head-on. Her head cocked to one side, trying for a coquettish smile that came off as a smirk. She ran the tip of her tongue seductively over her orange glossed lips.

Thinks you're oozin' hot an' horny after findin' all that T an' A pokin' outta your gym shoes. Good one, huh?

Sam removed another Polaroid from his pants and showed it full-circle to the growing crowd. Vicky in an overfilled halter and skintight hot pants. The hooting and guffawing fell off to a stifled, gasping murmur.

Excellent shock value, Ace.

Vicky's smirk was wiped clean and replaced by a mask of pure, polished horror.

"Stop it, Sam! Those were meant for *you!*" She made a two-handed lunge for the pictures. She was quick.

He was quicker. He pulled a confused but rock-solid Bud between them, making him a Maypole to go around. "No."

"Give them to me!" The command was a shrill shriek. The depraved passion of the past weeks drained rapidly from her face. Her eyes were round with fear and full of sudden hate. "Now!"

"You gave them to me. Remember? That makes them mine to do with as I please, and since you refuse to leave me alone, I *please* to share them."

"You'll wish you were dead before I'm through with you if you don't give them back this red hot minute!" Her reddish hair bounced with the wild momentum of her words. Her stance widened, and her yellow vinyl miniskirt rode high up her thighs.

The crowd leaned in close, straining to catch every word.

Sam had forgotten he'd ever been uneasy around large numbers of people. He barely knew the crowd was there. What concerned him was ridding himself of Vicky. Deep inside, under insulating depths of false bravado, swirled an eddy of foreboding. His hatred for this girl was a person-sucking whirlpool.

"You've had chances to back off—thousands of them, but you wouldn't. Maybe now you'll see what can happen when you throw yourself at someone who's not interested. I've asked you, then begged you, then warned you that you were over the line! You really ought to have more pride than to go on doing stuff like this." Reaching over Bud's shoulder, he shook the pictures in her face but pulled them back before she could get to them.

"Give me those pictures!"

"No," Sam said quietly.

"You're horrible! I would have done *anything* for you!"

"So you've told me. And told me! And told me! You've told every person in this school. The problem is you've already done that for so many guys!" His whole body shook in anger. "I certainly don't want to be confused with someone who cares about your personal or sexual fulfillment, but let me offer you some friendly advice." He stopped to wet his lips. "If the football squad and the wrestling team don't do enough for you, you could try shift change at the mine! You might get lucky at the beginning of the owl shift when it's real dark out! If that's still not enough, try anybody you can find just as long as you stay away from *me!* I don't want anything to do with you! Never have! And I for damned sure never will!"

Vicky jerked as if each word barb stabbed her, but he continued to hurl them. He couldn't stop. "I can't take anymore! Lose my phone number! Stay away from my locker! Keep your underwear under something! These hideous pictures of you nearly naked are giving me nightmares! I passed the first batch out at the pool hall, and even there it was the devil to get somebody to take them off my hands! Even pool hustlers have standards. The one where you're wearing the lacy, see-through thing and a couple of your fingers seemed to *disappear* between your legs really grossed me out! I tore that one up and flushed it down the toilet after all the freshmen in the locker room were through with it! They don't have standards, yet."

That's cuttin' 'er down! T-i-m-b-e-r-r-r-!

The crowd cheered and booed and hissed and gaped. He turned, threw the remaining pictures into air, and saw Vicky was crying before he walked off. He heard the chaos caused by a common grappling for the photographs. A few boys applauded.

A stab of guilt passed through Sam, but it was too late for remorse. He'd already brought the lights down on Vicky Brown.

IT DIDN'T TAKE LONG for the rebound to hit Sam. "Queer." He'd heard the word in the halls with unusual frequency over the past few days. Today, he realized it was directed at him.

Noting the clannish groups of whispering students who'd taken a new interest in him, he had assumed it was due to his sorry outburst on Tuesday. He hated taking it as far as he had. If he'd just stopped before letting go of the Polaroids—but he hadn't. There was nothing he could do about it now. Vicky must have known there was a risk involved in placing racy, revolting, practically nude photographs in his locker. The first batch was still in his nightstand. He'd told her often enough to stop her advances. What he hadn't let himself consider was that some emotional problem might be behind her behavior, pity may have been more appropriate than anger. Nor had he foreseen reprisal.

> The faggot of Russett High School
> Plays Vicky Brown for a fool.
> He asks, "For WHAT?"
> When she offers her twat,
> Cuz only boys put iron in Sam's tool!
> (handwritten limerick Sam found in his locker)

She begged for it, Hoss. Ya warned her plenty, but she wouldn't give it a rest.

Lefty, with his usual supply of opinions, was still on the home side. He'd been known to defect and, more frequently, play both sides against each other.

Sam was now reaping the reward of his deed. Vicky was having her revenge. She was a vulture whose beak was pecking at his eyeballs, her talons groping for his soul. She was bent on ruining him for now and for all time. Judging by the sickening rush of utter despair that was settling inside him, she was going to be a huge success. She was going to swallow him whole.

Of all the routes Vicky could have taken, she had chosen the most direct.

Here in the Heart of Dixie, homosexuality was the deadliest of sins and was viewed with more pious indignation than atheism or the marrying of blood relatives. Alabama, where every town and city could justly be called Bigotsville, ate its young when its young refused or was unable to navigate the maze of accepted society. Homosexuality had never been considered for acceptance. Its mere mention rocked good old boys—even young ones, assholes-in-the-making—to their very cores, forcing them to nervously scratch their balls and their hound dogs and fondle their deer rifles for comfort. They saw it as an abomination sorry enough to justify violence. The doubling of meaty fists followed by a face-bashing was good enough for the fag who tried to share the world of "God-fearin'" Christians. Gays engendered a flaming hatred the faulty brain of the good old boy could never credit as *fear*. Four-lettered fear. Fear of information they were not intelligent or sophisticated enough to process. *"Gimme three points fer that'n, Bubba. Feisty li'l fruit wadn't he?"*

Last night, Jackie had finally broken down and told him what was going on. Sprawled across his bed, she had pleated the front of her flannel nightgown between her fingers and used the folded cloth to daub an incessant flow of angry yet sympathetic tears. "She's saying you're queer, that that's why you didn't want her."

Sam, at first, hadn't been able to digest what she was saying. He'd been horrified. The label alone wouldn't have been so appalling if simple name-calling would be the end of it, but he'd known so much more abuse would follow. "Come on, Jackie. Who's gonna believe that?" He already knew the answer.

"Nearly everyone already believes it."

"Why?"

"Because it's fun to believe something that juicy. Face it—we all love good dirt. We live for it. Sly little Vicky's even made up a lover for you. Says she saw you kissing some guy in the alley out back of Burger King! And those big-boobed, bottled-blondes she cats around with echo every word. Burger King! Vicky says you told her you couldn't get it up for her because girls don't turn you on."

Ohmygod!

"People ought to know me better. They ought to know her. How does she explain her coming on to me so strong?"

"Her story is that she loved you so much, she tried to turn you around with the pictures and lacy underwear and everything. She did it all to make you hot for her. She's got the plot down pat, and she's getting sympathy. Academy award material. Sam, you gotta do something before it goes any further."

Oh, boy!

A low growl had crept into his lungs. Nausea had flooded over him in dizzying waves. He coughed. "What?"

"Start by denying it. Call up one of those dogged little girls who chase after you and ask her out. Have another showdown with Vicky, show everybody she's as big a liar as she is a slut!"

"The showdown is what got me into this." He had no designs on a second. "I wish I could take back the first one. She's only doing this because I hurt her."

No longer crying, Jackie had sat up. "Sam, get a date for the ball game tomorrow. Let people see you out with a female."

Easy for ya to say, Sis.

"I can't."

Lefty had sang out. *Tara! If ya had any gumption at all, ya'd ask Tara Mason. She'd go.*

Sam had visualized Tara shaking her head over the rumor, refusing to believe a single word.

Even if she's already got a date, she'll break it for you.

No, Tara wasn't that shallow. He hoped she wouldn't believe the gossip. He liked her. Her opinion mattered.

"Why, for petesake, can't you?"

Tell her what a wimp ya are.

"Jackie—" He'd seen the logic in Jackie's idea, but if he tried to ask a girl for a date, the words would jam in his mouth. He'd choke, have the granddaddy of all asthma attacks, asphyxiate on his own tongue, go blue in the face and die.

"You do like girls, don't you?"

That had hurt. He'd flashed her a martyred look. She had always been insufferable, but she was also his sister. She was supposed to know him. He'd had to use his inhaler to silence the roaring stridor before he could croak a reply. "Great! Thanks, Jackie! You're making me feel lots better."

"I'm sorry. Being bashful's not a crime." She'd put an arm around him. "But, Ace, this is probably going to get worse before it gets better, and you're going to have to find a way to get through it. I hate to add to it—it's just that—well—it affects me, too. If Robbie was still in high school, he'd be able to do something. He could always make people listen."

He'd seen her sincerity and was grateful for it. So many times in the past, she'd offered her strength to counter his weaknesses. Now, even though he'd become an embarrassment to her, she'd tough it out with him.

"I'm sorry, too, but I can't just call up some girl, especially now that she'd probably think I wanted to use her as cover. And I doubt your back seat lover could do me much good."

Jackie had sighed, giving him her gentlest sad-eyed smile.

"Look, I'll go to the game. I'll confront anybody who tries to start something. Maybe one of the rat pack will call and ask me. If that happens, I promise I'll say yes. Even if it's one of the ninth-graders. I swear."

HE'D LASTED THROUGH THURSDAY at school by constantly reminding himself the assault wouldn't last forever. People would realize Vicky was just trying to get back at him. His friends would come to their senses.

At home, he'd been unable to eat or concentrate on homework. His parents had looked at him for an explanation, but there had been nothing to say. Only a matter of time and they'd know what was happening. The old worries about his sexual bearing would be reborn. They would look at him with eyes full of questions.

Sympathy for Jackie weighed him down. His acceleration through the early high school years had forced her to make room for him in her senior class. The rise had given them too much in common including second period English, the school paper, and the yearbook staff.

None of his generous concerns for others had cut into the pity he'd kept reserved for himself.

On Thursday night, he had tried to sleep but the nightmare had grabbed and held him suspended. A jeering Ralph Sommers had loomed over him while he lay, hands and feet tied to the posters of a bed. Powerless against the shameful violations, his breath had come in ragged spasms. The assault had gone on. And on . . .

He had awakened in a tangle of sheets and a lather of cold perspiration, once again a victim. Just when he needed all his steam to cross the parking lot to the front door of the school, the dream had weakened him. He had cautiously let himself coast back to sleep and was defiled no more by the dream. That night.

14

FRIDAY WAS TEDIOUS at best. Everywhere he looked, someone was pointing, whispering, or pretending not to be watching him for signs of aberrant behavior. A couple of guys asked Sam about his "boyfriend." Holding his temper was tough to manage. Patiently defending himself against their curiosity was next to impossible. Delivering a few tae kwon do kicks to their sneering faces might have made him feel better. Instead of committing violence, he issued glowing denials and shouldered past them.

During third period, Tara Mason grinned sympathetically over her biology textbook. She motioned with her thumb for him to keep his chin up, so some encouragement could still be gleaned.

Tara was his only reprieve.

At lunch break, he passed a smirking Vicky Brown with her entourage in the hall, collected his courage, and yelled, "You really go for blood when you can't get some poor sucker to screw you! Who're you gonna offer it to next? I want to warn him!"

He walked on with a high-pitched chorus of "Cocksucker," "Fairy," and "Faggot" drifting after him.

After lunch, he told his homeroom teacher he was sick—which wasn't a lie—and drove himself home.

AFTER SUPPER, Jackie left to pick up Robbie. Due to a blown engine in his Nova, the antithesis of the Corvette he had once killed, Robbie was once again without wheels, so Jackie was compelled to drive her Maverick on their romantic outings. Sam, sitting behind the wheel of his own car, hoped he wouldn't have much trouble locating them before the game. Misery really did love company, he supposed. He couldn't bear the thought of having to face the mob alone.

Bud had called to say he'd decided to forego football for a movie with some guys from shop class. Sam wondered how much his new and sordid reputation had had to do with Bud's change of plans. All morning at school, Bud had been uncharacteristically cool and quiet. Sam could feel his friend slinking away in the presence of adversity. If he didn't clear himself soon, all his friends would take the same path.

He drove in silence, but his thoughts were busy. Frantic to find some lesson, something usable in this ordeal, he began to see one thing clearly. Prejudice of any kind was wrong. He made a vow; he'd have no part of it. Not now, not ever. People shouldn't be tortured and exiled for being different or following a variant set of rules. The only true sins he could truly believe in was the deliberate deception or harming of another person or the damaging of one's own self. Vicky had hurt him first, then he had retaliated. Now *this*. He had sinned. He had hurt her, and he had hurt himself. The war stopped here. He swore to himself he'd rise above Vicky's revenge, and he'd rise above the all-too-common sport of hating.

He pulled into the parking lot, got out, and trekked toward the football field. A red Baja streaked by him, skidding into a narrow slot near the rival team's bus. "Hey, wait up," a female voice called out the window of the Volkswagen.

He wasn't sure she meant him, but since he didn't see anyone else in the lot, he slowed. He heard a car door slam and the sound of her feet moving toward him across the loose gravel.

"I think I know you. You're the kid from the car wreck a couple of months ago?" A tall blond in jeans, suede moccasins, and a layering of heavy sweaters fell in step beside him. "DeLane Evans. I was your nurse at Northside."

I remember! Tell her Lefty remembers!

"Oh, yeah. The wreck," he stammered.

Smooth! Regular silver-tongued devil.

"You've grown up some. How's the arm? Stan, right?"

"Sam. The arm's as good as new."

"There was another kid in the wreck that you worried about a lot. Did he make it?" Her hair bounced around her shoulders and down her back as she walked. She wasn't Goldie, but she was definitely easy on the eyes.

Relax. She won't bite—but we can pretend.

"Oh, yeah. He's okay. Lotta scars, but he's all right. Wants to marry my sister and become a lawyer. He quit drinking."

"That's nice. I seem to remember you were sort of plastered when you were brought in."

She had to be at least a decade older than Sam, but she didn't seem to notice. Flattered by her memory, he felt an odd easiness with her. "Well, I gave up drinking, too."

"Meeting your date here?"

"Don't have one." He wished she hadn't asked.

"Good. Does that mean I might prevail on you to be my escort?" She smiled and took his arm. "You're so damned cute!"

Jackpot!

His luck seemed to be changing. He took a long, deep, steeling breath. "I don't see why not." He placed his hand over hers and walked toward the football field with her on his arm. He hoped everybody was watching.

"I TRY TO MAKE at least one game a year. It makes me feel like a kid again. I was a cheerleader, you know, and I've always had a thing for football."

I told ya to stay on the team—but, no, ya hadda work on the school newspaper! No time for MANLY sports! Tell her ya still play baseball. Tell her about your fastball.

He could have listened to her talk all night. The self-consciousness that usually killed any fun he might have found in the company of girls had been knocked out by DeLane's bubbly chatter. He couldn't block mental pictures of her and her remarkable bosom, in a white uniform and cap, bending over his hospital bed. Sexy, sultry, sensational DeLane.

Jackie's and Robbie's mouths had dropped open as he walked

DeLane by them. Robbie had choked on his hotdog. Astonished relief had swished over Jackie's face.

When the game ended, he and DeLane hung back until the parking lot was empty. She ran on, asking questions, making his heart thump rapidly. He listened, answered her questions, and, over Lefty's protests, told her about his troubles at school. Neither her age not the fact that he hardly knew her stopped him. For once, he just hadn't cared.

With an expression of concern, she listened, interrupted with more questions, and sympathetically shook her head. When he dispatched the last detail of the story, she asked for a moment to think. In silence, he waited while she chewed a nail and looked up at the stars. Then she flashed a devious grin. "I can help shoot the rumors down, make them bite the dust at Vicky's feet—if you're game for a little theatrical gunplay."

"Sure." No hesitation. He could use all the assistance he could get. "What do you have in mind?"

As they propped against the fender of Sam's dusty Mustang, heads close and conversation low, they began manufacturing a plan.

THE WORD IN THE HALLS of Russett High was Sam MacCauley had a *girlfriend*. An older woman. A real fox. Proof positive he wasn't gay to the ones who wanted to believe Sam. A smoke screen to those who preferred Vicky's story. A small piece of iffy evidence for the fence-straddlers.

Sam waited apprehensively for eleven o'clock study hall and the chance to put the first installment of DeLane's plan to the test. While he waited, he began a slow leak of information to his fair-weather friend, Bud the Bear, who was famous for his inability to keep a confidence.

"I'm gonna cut study hall," he whispered to Bud in his most conspiratorial voice. "If Mrs. Jefferson misses me, tell her I started back with the karate lessons. She'll fall for that. I *think* I'll be back for History."

Bud, bravely standing in the hall with someone who could still prove to be as fruity as a Waldorf salad, jumped at the bait and asked, "What you gonna do?"

"I've got a date." Sam pitched his voice furtively low. "I just need a little *time,* if you know what I mean. If I cut study hall and lunch, I'll have an hour and forty-five minutes."

"In the middle of the day? Who've you got a date with?"

"DeLane Evans. She works evening shift. Three to eleven. So it has to be—"

"That old broad you was with at the game? Some of the guys said she was hot, a real looker. Who the hell you kiddin'? You don't have the balls to ask for a date."

"Don't call her a broad. She's nice. In fact, she's terrific, and she asked *me*. If my folks find out, I'm a goner!"

"Where you takin' her?"

"Well, actually, she's taking me. We're going over to her apartment in East Russett."

"You're lyin'."

"Are you gonna cover for me in study hall or not?"

"Not till I know you're tellin' the truth."

"Okay. She's gonna be waiting for me out by the bus park at eleven. I figure I'll go out the through the gym, circle around back, and meet her there. That's going a little out of the way, but I sure don't wanna get caught! Not before I go, anyway! I don't care if you follow me out to see for yourself—as long as you cover for me. DeLane and I will even wave bye-bye to you."

Less than a minute after the eleven o'clock bell rang, a dozen boys had collected near the bus park, and another eight or ten waited to follow Sam from the gym.

Bud the Bear swallowed the bait—hook, line, an' sinker!

All-in-all, Sam thought things looked promising for the reclamation of his reputation when he slid into the seat next to DeLane. To his delight, she kissed him, ran her fingers through his hair, and then scratched out of the parking lot, leaving their audience choking on a cloud of dust.

His first real kiss!

Oh, yeah, Sam, Ol' Boy! If this ain't the way to go, I don't know what is!

He lay on her bed. A lamb on a sacrificial altar. His fear and guilty misgivings falling to the sensation of her touch.

She worked his penis as if its nerve endings belonged to her, manipulating with a seasoned hand. She did everything he would have done if he'd been doing it alone—and then some—but it felt a thousand times more intense. She seemed to sense when he was close to making a mess all over her and her black nylon sheets and repeatedly backed off just in time.

And she kissed him. His lips, his neck, the tips of his fingers, his nipples. She traced the contour of his ears with her tongue. Having no idea what his role in the activity was supposed to be, he waited. When no instruction came, he simply gave himself to the woman, the moment, the feeling.

At some point, she pulled him on top of her, guiding him into position with her hands. He was almost in when he ejaculated into a gas station rubber. He was devastated, but she consoled him against the resilience of her breasts. After a brief intermission, her fingers came for him again, found his spirit willing and his flesh strong. The second time, he made it all the way inside with perhaps a minute-and-a-half to spare.

When she was through with him, he was surprised he could walk. He was shocked that, after all that had gone on during his initiation into carnal manhood, his legs could support him. There was some feeble trembling down the inside of his thighs and calves, but over all, he had come through unimpaired.

As she drove him back to school, she sang along with The Doors then The Stones while he kept a vigil on the vibrating hump of Volkswagen through the front windshield. Words would have spoiled the aura of afterglow that floated poetically around them—autumn's painted leaves falling, holly bushes rising above snow drifts, butterflies on an April breeze, steam rising off oiled, sun-baked bodies.

DeLane drove past the front of the school to the far side of the parking lot where a group of students habitually goofed away lunch period. A row of buses became a dusty yellow screen between them and the eyes of the school. Bud was perched on the fender of his old black

Falcon. He said something and gestured an announcement to the gang of mostly boys. All of them turned to watch the approach of the Beetle.

DeLane braked a few feet from the assembly. She smiled sweetly at them. With her slender fingers gripping his hair, she pulled Sam to her and kissed him long and hard. A silver screen motion picture kiss. The crowd hooted and cheered. When they finally parted, Sam got out and, with his back to his friends, watched her drive away. She was completely out of sight before he turned. He stepped in their direction, letting a slight grin cross his lips, hang there for a few seconds, and then slide off. He hoped not one of them had the slightest doubt that today he, Sam MacCauley, heterosexual stud, had been bedded by a goddess.

When he'd returned from the other midday excursions—the phony ones when nothing more meaningful than lunch and a friendly game of rummy had occurred—he'd had suggestive comments ready. *". . . that would be kiss and tell, wouldn't it? . . . you men ought to get lives of your own so you can stop worrying about mine . . . it's for me to know and for you to jack-off over! . . ."* A couple of times, he'd said nothing—just walked a little funny. Today was different. Today, he just might tell them a little something. Dangle a select morsel before them.

SAM WENT ON HIS TRYSTS with DeLane two or three times a week. His study hall came before lunch and gave him almost two hours during which no one in authority expressed interest in where he was or what he was doing.

DeLane was more than a fantasy come true, and she proved to be an adroit teacher. She tutored him in the discipline of physical love, of pleasing a woman while pleasing himself. An eager pupil, he made her honor roll as easily as he made A's in school. She praised his swift grasp of technique and style.

Her nights off work were occupied with a man who also had ready access to her body. But, because Sam knew he was on a free ride that couldn't go on forever, he determined to enjoy it without jealousy—right up until the squealing of the brakes.

The only real kink in his affair—he sometimes thought of it as an *affair*—was his conscience. An enormous kink. Lefty would set in, nagging, late in the evenings after a nooner with DeLane and keep going until time for the next. He had little opportunity to enjoy the notoriety that came with such daring. Lefty all but ruined everything. As two-faced as ever, he cheered every kiss, every thrust, every exalted spasm—only to carp about it late into the night and through the early morning.

Your Mama an' Daddy's gonna catch ya. Sure as dirt—as the old man would say. What ya gonna tell 'em? 'I climbed her 'cause, like a mountain, she was there'? 'I feasted on 'er 'cause I didn't like what they was servin' in the cafeteria'? Huh? What ya gonna tell some nice girl ya really like when she asks for a little background information? What about Tara? Ya screw up the best of anybody—ya know that?

Sam knew. The dream didn't let up, either. A nightly event, it was draining him of the energy and ability to keep things straight in his mind. He tried to work on props for the school Christmas play, but his mind wandered. He'd catch himself on a stepladder, holding a paintbrush in midair until someone came along and jarred him back to life. His work on the school paper became a grueling chore. Although there were no major asthma attacks, a smothery heaviness sat on his chest. Old fears made him look over his shoulder and turn corners with caution.

No one called Sam queer, now. He'd become an object of outright envy. Half the boys in the school, from fellow seniors on down, on the sly or right out in the open, coveted the steamy action he was getting with disgraceful regularity.

Still, peace danced beyond the reach of his groping fingers.

What he was doing was beyond stupid. It was crazy. Destructive. Wrong. And it hurt. It was slowly killing him. Soon the pain would spread to his mother and father, his sister.

By mid-November, he began to wonder if he was losing his mind, breaking it off and tossing it away, a piece at a time.

By Thanksgiving, he began wondering what it felt like to die, to go to sleep and not wake up. To sleep and not dream.

15

S AM?—SAM!—-*SAM!"* A. D. stood, hands on hips, patting his foot
on the carpet. He shook his head. His son often required hard-
found patience. *"Sam!"*

"Huh? Sorry, I'll turn it down." The boy pushed a slide on the
phonograph with a toe. The music shrank to a murmur. The foot came
back to its mate which was propped on the side of the bed. The rest of
him sprawled down and over the floor as if he'd taken a tumble off the
bed. His bare feet stuck out of raveled bell-bottomed, hip-huggers gone
thin and white from a year of near constant contact with the elements
and with Sam. A peace medallion on a heavy silver chain lay on his
shirtless chest. Hair covered his shoulders, his ears, and most of his eyes.
Instead of rising, he stared up at his father.

A. D. straightened his grimace into a mischievous smile. This
encounter had the potential for fun. That was, if the problem turned out
to be of the nature he suspected. "Thank you," he said politely. He hoped
his smile was disarming.

Sam smiled back uneasily, a teenager's inherent lack of trust of a
good-humored adult.

A. D. casually looked around the room. To be that of a boy who
looked like a ragpicker, it was surprisingly neat, showing a taste for order
and cleanliness. There were three posters on the ceiling over the bed.
Goldie Hawn, all, and on the closet door a framed charcoal Jackie had
done at her brother's request, also Goldie—evidence the boy still had a
taste for her, too. Two walls of shelves were packed with books, record

albums, academic and sports trophies. A leather encased guitar stood in a corner.

A. D. moved to the double bed and sat next to Sam's feet. He recalled past conversations during which the boy had seemed intelligent enough to handle his hormonal deluges. He hoped Sam was currently doing just that. If he wasn't, A. D. needed to know. Discrediting the recent moodiness and withdrawal as signs of possible danger, he continued to smile as he reached into the zippered bib pocket of his overalls. His hand closed over and retrieved the desired object.

Sam raked his hair off his face and gazed up expectantly. "You want to talk to me, Dad?"

"Yeah, I wanna show you this thing I found in your car." He ceremoniously held up a silver foil package. His smile never flagging, he leaned down and wagged the two-and-a-quarter-inch square at Sam.

The boy came up from the floor with all the grace and speed of a panther at full stride. Once on his feet, he hurriedly tucked his hands in his arm pits and leaned a shoulder against the wall. A comic attempt at casual repose. His expression was meant to denote innocent ignorance but came closer to that of a raccoon trapped by the head lamps of a car.

"I believe you asked me to take a look at the console in the Mustang. Loose or somethin' an' makin' a racket, you said. Well, just as I was crossin' the driver's seat with my trusty screw driver and ratchet in my hands, somethin' shiny caught my eye. I picked it up to see what it was." He waited.

"Um—" Sam scratched the back of his neck.

A. D. could almost see the frantic activity going on in the boy's head in a useless search for an explanation. "Look at this, son." He pointed. "There's some little tiny writin' on the back—so tiny I hadda dig out my readin' glasses. Says right here a man can wear one of these under a black light, an' his dick'll *glow!* It's orange an' has little pleasure bumps on it. Says so right here." He pointed again. "Ever heard of anything like that? Must've fell outta somebody's pocket, huh?"

Sam looked as if he needed to throw up. A. D. thought he probably was carrying a condom around to impress his friends and hoped to the hot place he was right. He'd have to trust Sam to confess if there was more. "Got any idea who'd purchase one of these psychedelic orange pleasure bump things an' drop it in your Mustang right on the spot where you sit when you're drivin'?"

Sam hunched his shoulders, gathered a lot of air in his mouth, stretched his cheeks considerably, then let the air slowly leak out. "Well—"

"I can see you're as stumped as I am. What if your mama'd found this instead of me—the way she jumps to conclusions? As sure as dirt, she'd think you'd tossed your moral upbringin' out on its ear an' fell in with loose an' unclean women. Oh, boy, am I glad you didn't ask *her* to tighten your console."

Sam swallowed. His words came out dry and brittle amid an onset of raspy wheezing. "Dad? I—you see, I—"

"Let's open up an' see what it looks like." Tearing through the packaging, he found the flimsy sheath, shook it loose, and held it up by the reservoir tip. He dangled it in front of Sam's splotchy face. "So that's what pleasure bumps look like—little bubbles that go all the way around. Must be for the girl, or the bumps would be on the *inside*. What do you think, son?"

"I never thought—"

Feeling a mild wash of sympathy for his son's obvious distress, A. D. held up a restraining hand. "Not a word. I know this is a big shock, an' I just keep on askin' silly questions. Don't want you sittin' up nights worryin' about how to deal with this situation. I thought it might upset you—since it was your car an' all—so I worked somethin' out. You just wait here."

He left the room, found a paper bag he'd stashed on the hall table under his hat, and on his way back to his place on the bed, handed the bag to Sam. A prickle of doubt about his handling of the matter ran over him, but he shook it off. The boy was too bashful to be in need of birth control. He didn't even have a girlfriend. And frankly, this was fun. "Go on, son. Open it."

Sam peered into the sack as if he expected a copperhead to rise up and strike. He rolled his eyes. "Aw, Dad."

"Don't thank me." A. D. attempted to keep a straight face, only minimally succeeding. "I know you wouldn't want any of your friends becomin' daddies at a tender age or gettin' the kind of diseases that might make their dicks drop off. Always thought it a good rule of thumb for a guy to hold off on fatherhood until he's old enough to vote an' makin' more money than Saturdays at the car wash or sweepin' out the feed store pays. Now, when you find out who this rubber toy belongs to, you can offer 'im one of these with the suggestion that he read the instructions an' talk to his daddy before using it. That way he'll know how an' when an' if he really wants to. Stuff like that. I'll throw this in the trash where it belongs."

Catching Sam's eyes briefly before losing them again, A. D. stood. "You wanna say somethin, son?"

"Um—I'm sorry."

If A. D. was sure of anything, it was that Sam was sorry. Sorry about getting caught. He held up the orange sheath and torn silver square one last time. "Where'd you get it?"

"Bill's Tire and Lube. Outta the machine."

"Do I need to ask more questions?"

"Um—I—well—"

"No more machines, son. I expect a promise here?"

Sam nodded. He quickly turned his face as if someone had smacked him one.

"Put that box where you mother won't find it."

Sam nodded again.

"And be really careful, son. Your time ain't come yet."

"I will."

"You know you can talk to me?"

One final nod.

He left Sam holding the bag, looking confused, embarrassed, and— a chill ran over him—perhaps a bit guilty.

SAM OPENED THE SMALL sliding door on the right side of his bookcase headboard. Here the box fit with a little extra space around it. Every time he thought about his father's visit, the beast that growled deep in his chest became angrier. If A. D. had known what Sam had been doing, he wouldn't have gotten off with humor. Clearly, A. D. didn't believe his son was actually *using* rubbers.

This thing with DeLane was turning into a horror show. He couldn't remember how he'd let himself get sucked into it. For weeks, he'd let it go on as if she was no more than a piano teacher or a math tutor, and he the pupil. He was caught in a vicious circle of transgression, guilt, nightmares, pain—the circle growing ever tighter, ever smaller. To keep from disappearing altogether, he had to find the guts to say, "Enough!" Each time he came away from her, he felt as if he'd been assaulted. He knew he'd violated himself by being with her. Self-rape. He wasn't ready for the kind of relationship he'd undertaken—not with a girl his age, much less a woman eleven years older. He felt as if his internal organs had been chewed and his heart stuffed with sawdust.

He slid the door back in place and lay down. This was going to be a long night. He could feel it closing in. He dreaded sleep, yet, as if mesmerized by his own fear, he closed his eyes and moved to meet it.

"SHE makes yore prick git big an' hard. Poke 'er two or three times in a row, cancha, Sambo? Must mean ya like her better'n me. Shoulda got big an' hard fer me, boy. Shoulda swallowed my cum. Make yore balls grow big. Make 'em hang low. All that pukin' made me mad, an' when I get mad—well, you know what happens, doncha, boy? Think yore ridda me, but I'm still here. In yore guts, yore liver, yore lights. Makin' a boy-shaped hole in here. A boy-shaped hole to drop ya down. Just like the Tennessee boy. Come here, Sambo. See what I got. All fer YOU! Now, open wide . . ."

Sam woke, coughing and gasping, as the face of Ralph Sommers faded above him. In the dark, he ran his hand over the top of a row of Zane Greys until he found his inhaler. He used it, fought to hold the drug in a few seconds. He no longer screamed for help when the nightmare came, hadn't in years. A boy his age didn't cry and make his parents hold him until the night terror subsided and sleep crawled back. Instead, he stayed alone in his bed, silent and still, cold sweat beading on his chest and stomach, gliding in streams from his armpits. Most of the time, he went back to sleep in spite of the risk of another nightmare; other times, he kept a vigil through the night, standing guard over the child in the dream. The potency of the dream was the determining element. It could be fuzzy and difficult to recall, but now and then, parts of it were clear and as tangible as the bed he lay on, hanging in front of him until the daylight blurred the edges.

Tonight, he'd sleep no more. The luminous hands of his Big Ben windup pointed out 4:25. He wouldn't have long to wait for dawn. When his breathing was quiet, he clicked on his reading lamp and felt under the edge of the bed for a novel he'd been wading through with tedium and a general lack of interest. *From Here to Eternity*. He removed the candy wrapper bookmark but didn't read. Instead, he placed a finger between the pages and closed the book on it.

He sighed.

I'll keep ya company. Lefty magnanimously offered. *Been meanin' to talk to ya s'more 'bout this woman you're takin' down.*

"I'll bet," Sam muttered groggily.

TOWARD THE END of November, he surprised himself by actually saying it. "I need to stop leaving school with you."

"Oh, you think so?"

"It's not you. You're great. It's just—stupid. I can't get away with it much longer. My sister'll tell, or someone'll call up my folks. They'd be really—you know——*hurt*. Kids always say how aggravating their parents are, but mine aren't so bad. I don't wanna mess up any more than I already have."

Why didn't he have the sense to wait until they were dressed before pursuing the subject? She kept doing things that distracted him. Using one of her pink polished fingernails, she began drawing concentric circles on his back. Her breath on the back of his neck made clear thinking impossible.

"Besides, the old man's gonna be watching me super close. You don't just give your son a box of rubbers and then forget about what he might be using them for."

"I'd miss you." She sounded more playful than sad.

"I'd miss you, too, but I'm just a kid. I'd be easy to replace."

"A sophisticated man of the world is what you are now." She kissed a spot behind his left ear. "You learned your way around fast. Plus, you're the best-looking guy I've ever been with."

"I'll bet. Look, it's not that I don't appreciate what you've done for me. I do. I don't know how I'd have gotten through the situation I was in without you. You've been a great friend. You're great at lots of *things.*" He rolled onto his back and took the kiss she willfully pressed on him. Her minty-tasting mouth parted over his. Her tongue ran lightly along the edges of his teeth. When she finally let him breathe, he admitted, "That's one of the things you're very good at."

She straddled his thighs and bent to kiss his nipples. Her hair tickled his chest.

"Please stop for a minute? I can't think when you do that."

She sat back and tipped her head to one side. Her smile was anything but serious.

"DeLane, I've gotta stop coming here—soon."

"Sure, Baby, but you're here now. Let's not waste today talking about the future. We don't have to stop right this minute. We can have a little fun today. Can't we?"

He shivered.

Well, as long as you're awready here, Boss.

"YOU AIN'T REALLY gonna break off with her, are you?"

Sam nodded. He'd been with her today. He imagined he could still smell semen, a scent that always made him queasy.

"Must be outta your mind! How're you ever gonna replace that?"

"Bud, she's too old. It wouldn't last much longer, anyway. Why not quit while I can say I broke off with her? It'll be a better memory that way."

"She looked extremely happy when she let you out today. Strikes me as being one of those nymphomaniacs who can't get enough. You're like a supplement to her man. Bet she'd not get tired of you any time soon."

"I don't know about that, but it will be over sooner or later. I'm just gonna see that it's sooner. I hope that's okay with you!"

Bud's beer can reflected the sun. Robbie and Sam had both left alcohol alone after the wreck, but Bud had taken up drinking as a part of his daily routine. To the 210-pound, baby-faced boy, the best sport in the world was putting something over on his father, the good Brother Blacknell. He was forever bragging about how drunk he'd been at the supper table with his father or in his Sunday School class, always courting a beating, daring and dodging danger. He also lamented the fact that, among his fellows, he was the sole surviving virgin. He swore the lack of female companionship drove him to drink.

Bud had taken up smoking, too, and now blew a series of rings skyward. "Man, I can't buy a piece of tail, and you're gonna turn down freebies. Don't that strike you as abnormal?"

"You make it sound so sordid."

Bud crushed his empty can with one hand, tossed it into a growing pile of scrap metal, and took a deep drag on his Camel. Thanks to him and dozens of other young boozers, the Dance Hall was beginning to look like an alcoholic dump.

Pot-holed, rocky, and garbage-strewn, the Dance Hall was a night-time haven for dating couples to park and do what dating couples do, a twenty-four-hour-a-day watering hole for kids to consume ill-gotten drink in relative privacy, and a den in which dope smokers could pass around homegrown weed. The Dance Hall had been dubbed in some previous, obscure generation, so the boys didn't know how it got its name. The place seemed a little creepy to Sam, and he always complained sorely while he drove Bud there.

"I don't even know what 'sordid' means, but you wouldn't catch me turning down free pussy. Nosirree, not the Bear!"

"I wish you wouldn't talk like that. It doesn't matter what you'd do. I'm going to stop seeing her, and if the whole school wants to call me queer, fine! You, my loudmouthed friend, may quote me on that. I have to live with my conscience, and I'm tired of having to prove myself to the rest of this lousy town."

"Did you get religion or somethin'?"

"Maybe. Would that be so bad?"

"Oh, please, I get enough straight an' narrow at home."

"Are you talking about your dick?"

"For yore information, when I mention that monster, I'm talkin thirteen and a half inches of throbbin' man-meat." Bud slid off the hood of the Mustang, swaggered to the cooler in the trunk, and turned back to look at Sam. "But I've heard ya lose what ya don't use. So I gotta see it gets some exercise real soon. I'd miss it."

"Well, when you get your big chance, I hope it's with a nice girl who makes you lay off the booze first."

"Oh, brother. Ya really gonna stop?"

"Yeah."

"When?"

"Soon."

"Who'm I gonna look up to now?"

"Be serious. I won't attempt to explain my conscience to you, but I really don't want anyone to get hurt—especially my mama and daddy. They think they're raising decent kids."

"Hallelujah, Brother Sam. Yore a saint. My dear daddy would be so proud to have a boy like you. He'd prob'ly forgive you for bein' such a wicked influence if he found out how refined you are. Learn to talk in tongues an' jump over pews with your eyes shut, he'll be tryin' to adopt you! We'd be brothers."

"Your daddy hates me, remember?"

"So? He hates me, too. Just like he did my mother—and *she's* been late for supper since before I started school. He hated her an' my Aunt Millie, an' they both just vanished like peas in a crooked shell game."

"Bud, you don't really think your daddy made them disappear, do you?" This old topic always made Sam's skin crawl.

"Only once or twice a day. When I get away from him, I'm gonna spend the rest of my life tryin' to find out where they ended up. South America, Montana, Transylvania, or some shallow, unmarked grave."

Sam stared uneasily as his friend turned up his beer, lowering it only after it was empty. He couldn't think of anything to say.

"You know me, Ace. I live for sex, murder, intrigue, an' gettin' high in the woods. Do you think I'd be different if my mother had come home that night?"

16

Hope's bridges—all burned down!
Ashes washed up on the ground!
Void and darkness all around!
Lord, can't You see that what once was bittersweet
now is only bitter?

excerpt from *Poetic Injustice*
by Brenan Armstrong MacCauley, 1984

WHAT WERE THOSE things you stuffed into your hip pocket this morning?" Sam froze, but Lefty gasped, *She knows! Run!* The question would have been easy if the items in his pocket had not been Trojans, if the person asking wasn't his mother. Before leaving for school, she'd entered his room just in time to catch him supplying himself for a final encounter with DeLane. Since she hadn't pressed for an explanation at the time, he'd spent the day hoping she hadn't noticed. The pocket in question was now empty, the box hidden. He squirmed into his red and gold high school jacket.

Tell her Bandaids! Packets of Red Hots! Chewing gum!

"My wallet." He gathered up a stack of posters from the counter and tried to make a slick getaway through the back door.

You're dead. May ya rest in peace—not pieces!

"You've had all day to think of something creative."

Had all day to worry himself crazy—not that it kept him outta his lover's arms—or her bed.

A. D., who was busy with coffee and the morning paper that he rarely had time to read before late afternoon, looked regretfully at his son. Sam thought he saw something else in his father's expression. Fear? Betrayal?

He's scared, too, Ace. He gave ya no-nos! Now Mama's gonna ground him, too. To pulp.

Sam smiled one of his practiced mother-pleasers that showed a generous portion of white teeth and good-natured sheepishness. He tucked his hair behind his ears. "Um—let's see—um—I don't remember. Nothing there now. Aw, gosh, look at all these posters. The Christmas play. Bud and I promised Mr. Ellison we'd get 'em put up before it gets dark. Better get going. Bud's waiting."

Nice try.

A. D. pursed his lips and shook his dark head. A signal that said, "Fat chance." Sam wasn't going anywhere until his mother was through with him, and neither was A. D.

"Let go of that doorknob and come back in here." Her irritation was thinly veiled by her efforts to sound calm, her beautiful deep brown eyes flashed a warning.

Sam continued to smile stupidly as he closed the kitchen door. He heard A. D. mumbling something about people getting themselves into a tight, a fix, between a rock an' a hard place. His father's list of analogies ended with a prediction. "Whatever you've done, she's gonna be on you like a frog on a June bug."

"That's enough, A. D. Sit down, son."

Sam reluctantly put the posters back on the counter and selected a chair across the table from A. D. All the poison of his recent fall from honor was coming to a head.

"You don't have to tell me. I know what they were. Yesterday, there was a less-than-half-full super economy-sized box of them in your footlocker. Usually, I don't go near your room except to change your sheets, but when my senses tell me there's mischief afoot, you can forget privacy."

"Shit!" A. D. muttered and gave up all pretense of reading the paper. He shot Sam a look that seemed to warn, *"Be careful what you say about that box."* Then another look that was full of stinging questions. *"How could you let her find it? How could you use over half a box? Why?"*

Sam ducked his head and closed his eyes. He felt his brow knit itself into tight treads of concentration as he tried to think of acceptable answers. The tops of his ears were already burning from the beginning of a stinging blush. An asthmatic wheeze rose in his throat. He sank lower in his chair, staring at the crocheted place mat in front of him. "Maybe, we could talk about this when I get back. It's getting late. What do you say?" The stammered entreaty was drenched in artificial hope.

Look at her, Ace! She's fightin' for control! Fightin' back tears! Look what ya did to her!

"Let me assure you we have time. We have as long as it takes. We have from now on! Now, where did you get that box?"

Oh, no! Not THAT question! Sure as dirt the old man's gonna flip out! Lie! Tell her you're keepin' 'em for a friend! Say you're bein' framed!

Sam knew he really needed A. D. on his side, but considering the situation, there was little hope for that. Oh, well, both his parents preached honesty, the importance of telling the truth. This was the result.

"Daddy gave them to me."

Even though his head was still bowed, he got a peripheral flash of A. D. jerking back in his chair like he'd been fired on by an enemy air rifle or sling shot. Sam raised his head enough to get a good look at his father's face then wished he hadn't. It sagged under the weight of betrayal. The truth had definitely been a poor choice. He heard Freida catch her breath for an assault on her husband.

His own breath stuck. He couldn't push it out of his lungs.

"You bought those things for a sixteen-year-old boy? Your own son! *You!* Abel David MacCauley, how could you!" Her cool had sprouted wings and flown. No one was safe now!

She's usin' full names!

"Freida, let me ex—"

"How stupid can you possibly be?"

"Well, Freida, honey, I—"

"You what? Think about it! You give him money—he spends it. You give him the keys to a car—he drives it. You give him those things and what do you expect he's gonna do? If that box was full when you gave it to him—and for your sake, old boy, it better have been—he must really get a kick out of what he's doing with them!"

Sam's hands came over his face. The fiery flush now covered him down to about the nipple line. He caught broken pictures of his parents through the cracks between his fingers. For the moment, thank heaven, he wasn't required to speak. He couldn't have if he tried. He couldn't breathe.

"If you'd just listen, hon—he was buyin' the novelty kind out of a machine at a gas station. If he's gonna need 'em, he needs to be sure they'll work. Psychedelic colors that glow under a black light might make him easy to keep up with if conditions are just right, but I'm not so sure they're made good enough to keep him from gettin' the clap or makin' babies! Anyway, I didn't really think he was usin' them—just tryin' to make his friends think he was. You know how boys are."

Sam sank lower. His face and neck were on fire. His lungs were in danger of exploding. He'd never last through this.

"Oh, so you wanted make sure he had quality stuff—*just in case*. Is that right?"

"Well, yeah," A. D. said meekly. "You see I thought—"

"You thought? You thought? You *didn't* think!"

Sam searched his jacket pockets for his atomizer. It wasn't there. His hands moved into the front pockets of his jeans. His left hand closed on the canister and brought it up to his mouth. He squeezed, held his breath, squeezed again. Nobody seemed to care that he was smothering. His wrongdoing had killed their concern. After his respirations were a little more even, he tried to brace himself for more humiliation.

"Of course, it was full. I don't have any use for 'em, myself." A. D. nervously continued trying to dig his way out. "What would I be needin' 'em for? After the operation, we don't hafta—you're the only woman—Anyway, I didn't think he was really gonna use 'em—just if he did, he'd have 'em!"

"You're out of your mind! You should have been forbidding him to do anything that requires wearing a rubber! Did you ask him if he was having sex?"

"Not in so many words."

"You're his father, for heavensake. Don't you know he's not old enough to have sex? He gets all the sexual relief he needs in his own bed. I know. I wash his pajamas and sheets. Come to think of it, it's been a while since—"

Sam couldn't sink any lower, so he shifted a little to the side. For some cover, he untucked his hair from behind his ears and let it fall over the sides of his face.

A. D. opened his mouth, but Freida had forgotten him and directed her attention back to Sam.

"Explain to me, your mama, why you need so much protection."

He let his hands slide until he was looking over his fingertips then dropped them from his face. "Why?" he wheezed.

"Yes! And I won't accept any crap like 'it feels good' or 'everybody's doing it' or you 'think you're in love'. It had better be something really noble like some poor young woman is dying and you're her last request! Except it had better not be that because anyone who can do it two-thirds of a box worth can't be too close to dying."

"Mama!"

"I'm waiting." She seemed calmer, but she was still dangerous. A coiled rattler. A cocked pistol.

Anxiously perusing the room for a distraction, Sam spotted a familiar shadowy shape on the dining room floor just on the other side of the doorway leading from the kitchen. Jackie! He was batting a thousand today. He'd never live down this parental confrontation now that Motor-mouth MacCauley had wind of it. He thought about turning her in, but she knew everything and would gladly spill the whole squalid story with embellishments. It was better not to call attention to her eavesdropping.

"Um—um, it's complicated," he rasped.

So lame! Answer her!

"You hear that A. D.? It's *complicated*. Now, you listen to me, Sam Owen MacCauley! I want some answers! And I want them now! How many rubbers did you have in your pocket this morning?"

Great! She's askin' specific questions. No essays. Ya can answer one at a time without havin' to think too much! How lucky can a loser get? Give up, Sam, Lefty pleaded. *Talk about the pain! Tell 'em ya don't know why ya even get up in the mornin'!*

He wet his lips. "Three."

She looked at the ceiling. "He takes three rubbers to *school!*" She told the overhead light fixture then looked sadly at him. She looked scared, too. "Do you have sex at school?"

"No."

"How many did you bring back?"

Give 'em the BIG truth. The trash was symptoms of somethin' bigger'n you. Ya didn't have control. They won't let ya down.

He located a ketchup stain on the front of his jacket. It was the same shape as Florida—panhandle, peninsula, and Keys. He scratched it with his fingernail, but it didn't flake off.

"One."

Freida rolled her eyes. "Oh, I see. You only needed *two.*"

"Do you want it?" He wheezed. Without checking, he knew she'd confiscated the box.

What the hell-o—

As soon as he asked, he knew he'd made a mistake, something his mouth did without consulting his brain. He recoiled as her finger made stabbing motions at his face.

"Is that some kind of joke? If there's something funny here, I don't see it. Now, you get serious, or you're gonna wish you were dead. You hear me?"

Ya wish that awready. She'll hafta pick somethin' else.

"I already do," he said quietly.

She ignored him. "Tell us what you did with the two?"

There were a few tiny lint balls in his jacket pockets. He rounded them up and piled them on the place mat.

"I used them. Then I threw them away."

"Where?"

"Where did I use them, or where did I throw them away?"

"Don't get smart with me!"

"I don't mean to be." He, by trial and error, found out he could roll the lint balls together between his sweaty fingers and make them into one ball. "An apartment in East Russett."

"Who lives in this apartment?"

He put the one big lint ball back into a pocket. If his mother wanted to know what was in *that* pocket, he'd show her. "DeLane Evans lives in the apartment."

Freida's olive complexion changed to the red of bricks. "That nurse who works orthopedics at Northside? The one whose sister dances topless at *Sammy's?*"

"Well, she's a registered nurse. I don't know her sister."

"The nurse with the short uniform who spent hours leaning over your hospital bed after the wreck?"

"Yes, I guess so."

"The one who got arrested during one of those peace marches or sit-ins or whatever they're called and who drives around with 'Make Love Not War!' painted all over a Volkswagen that has its guts hanging out the back?"

"That's her."

"The big-breasted, bleached blond who's thirty years old if she's a day? Is that who we're talking about, son?"

"I said it was! And I believe she's only twenty-seven."

"At last, I know what all the whispering at the grocery store and the beauty shop is all about. Gossip even my best friends won't tell me."

Throughout the remainder of the conversation, during the long stretches when he was not required to speak, A. D. developed a routine of crossing and recrossing his legs, of shaking his head or nodding with each shift in momentum and tone. The whites of his eyes showed all the way around as he volleyed them back and forth between his wife and son. Sam needed his help. Shouldn't a father take up for his son? Couldn't either one of them see that the glue that held him together was melting and dripping on the floor?

Freida, undaunted by the possibility of scarring her son's psyche and crippling him for life, sat down next to him, angled her chair to facilitate looking at him, reached over and touched his shoulder, and whispered, "You may start at the beginning."

Sam heard A. D.'s weary "oh, boy." He checked for Jackie's shadow and found it. He ventured a look at his mother's flushed face. It was wooden and motionless, unmoved by his degradation.

Beg for help! Beg 'em to save us! We're goin' down!

"Ma, I can't. You really don't expect—"

"I'll help. Use your inhaler again. When did it start?"

"A week or two before Halloween."

"How often do you see her?"

"Two, sometimes three times a week."

A. D. whistled softly. Freida silenced him with her eyes. "Do you skip school?"

"Study hall and lunch, sometimes."

"Did your father know all this?"

"No!" A. D. blurted indignantly.

"No. It's not his fault. He said all the right stuff. I promised to come to him *before,* but I already—I wanted to tell him so he'd stop me, but I couldn't. I don't know why."

"How did your relationship with this woman come about?"

"She came to a football game. She remembered me from the hospital. We started talking."

"She could go to jail for statutory rape. You know that?"

"You're not going to have her arrested are you? For Christ's sake, Mama, she didn't use force!" The wheezing came back.

"Don't you swear at me!"

"I'm sorry. Anyway, it's over. I told her today."

"You went through two rubbers and then dumped her?"

"It's not like that. She expected it."

"Did my walking in while you were stuffing your pockets scare you into breaking off with her? Just figured you were caught?"

"No. I'd been thinking about it—even talking about it with her. I never felt okay about it. What you saw just pushed me a little, and I'm glad. I don't want to see her anymore."

"Why did you do it in the first place?"

Sam thought about it. For as far back as he could remember, Freida had made the happiness of her children her top priority. She'd invested huge chunks of herself in putting the broken pieces of his childhood back together. No day had passed without him receiving an excess of her love. She would take the truth of his impending breakdown as a personal failure, but he couldn't stop, couldn't go back and fix his mistakes. She had asked. Now she'd have to listen to his answers. His father would hear. Sam wouldn't leave out anything. He'd tell them first about school, then the nightmare, then the suicidal thoughts. He would tell them how he was barely hanging on. He hated bringing them into the dark and ugly mess he'd created. Still, no one else could help him. They waited for him to further their pain with his own. Looking back and forth between their frightened faces, he suddenly realized he *wanted* to be rescued. He took a shallow, raspy breath. "Everybody thought I was queer."

"What?" Freida's mouth stayed open.

A. D. looked like a man who'd been slapped.

"I'm not, but they kept saying I was."

"Why?"

"I knew some kid would go home and tell his folks, and they'd feel obligated to pass it on to you. It's what you always worried about, isn't it? Or was there more to it? Did you think I'd grow up and start molesting little kids? What else could you expect from a kid who got himself raped nine ways from Sunday?"

"Mygod, Sam! We never—"

"Didn't you, Daddy?" He watched his father's head swing slowly from side to side.

"You're wrong. Freida, tell him."

Sam had never seen her look so spiritless, so miserable.

"Are you saying it's our fault?"

"No. God, no. It's mine, but Mama, if you'll—" To endure her anguish, the look of horror on her face, he hugged himself tightly. "Mama, I'll try to tell you all of it—if you'll get rid of Jackie. She knows, but—"

She grimaced and called her daughter's name, and the shadow disappeared from the dining room floor. Jackie's footsteps beat out the tempo of her retreat on the stairs.

AS SOON AS HE WAS satisfied his sister was out of earshot, Sam had begun the story, and when he was finished, he had told them everything. For once, he'd done the right thing, and in a small way, he was relieved. He concluded by saying, "The thing is I wondered if something really was wrong with me. I don't wonder about it anymore. There's no doubt something's wrong." He paused, ran his tongue over his lips. "I didn't mean to make it worse by doing what I did with DeLane. God, it hurts. And the nightmare's back—nearly every night. It still terrifies me. After all this time, it still makes me sick. I don't know which is worse—staying up and facing the real world or going to sleep and finding Ralph Sommers waiting for me. He lives inside me, and when I sleep, he gets loose."

Sam hadn't cried in a long time. He'd learned to bottle pain, but he'd been weakened by his own words. He felt tremors spring into the ends of his fingers, his lower lip and chin. Tears were bound to follow.

"Why haven't you come to us? We didn't know." Her voice was now soft, maternal. Tears fell from her liquid brown eyes. She still cared.

"It was too hard, Mama."

"Didn't you know we'd want to help?"

"I knew."

A taut hush fell over the conversation. A. D. reached across the table and took Sam's hand. Sam felt the strong, possessive love of his father flow into him.

He supposed he'd known all along that, in one way or another, his DeLane adventure would end up as dinner table conversation. Maybe that was the reason he'd been compelled to go on with it. Giving himself away hadn't been a willful action. It was more like a trick played by his subconscious. With sudden clarity, he realized he'd wanted them to know. He wanted them to reclaim him once more, heal him of this mysterious sickness in his soul. He didn't know if his troubles at school had, by themselves, brought on this surrender. He only saw that once more his life had become unbalanced and unmanageable.

The kitchen, the faces of his parents became hazy. Old terrors boiled around him. He felt incredibly young, dwarfed by the everyone and everything in the room.

"All I want is to be like other people. Not some freak who never knows who he is or what he's supposed to do. I think about being dead a lot. Sometimes, it seems like a good thing." He let himself gaze once more into their frightened eyes. He couldn't have hurt them more if he'd used a club.

Folding under the weight of his guilt, he crossed his arms on the table in front of him, put his head down, and cried.

PART TWO

Hands to Hold

Born naked to this nightmare plantation,
we, spoilers of pious Old South tradition
(hybrids mutated hardier),
plod onward, seek morality, truth—
dodge biblical shrapnel,
help ourselves to small pleasures,
clothe our flesh with light.

We, in preservation of our minds,
skirt fearful conclusions, pain—
catch joy up in our fingers,
contentment in our souls.

We spurn woe-encrusted widows
whose wombs are shriveled, empty vessels,
and sooth-crying cripples who, as we pass,
point with gnarled fingers, withered phalluses
to the smoking maw of their unappeasable god.

And as we pass, uneaten,
we fork our fingers
at the fear-blind evil eyes they flash.
Still, we smile sadly, through our victory,
our pity for their joyless lives
and the bloodless hearts inside them.

"SPOILERS" FROM *Poetic Injustice* BY BRENAN ARMSTRONG
MACCAULEY, 1984

17

February 1973

L EFTY IS GIVING ADVICE AGAIN, as usual. *Call her. Ya know she wants you to. Just pick up the phone and call her. Ya know her number by heart.*

"I wouldn't know what to say."

Start with "Hi, Tara, this is Sam. If you're not busy Friday night, I'd like to take ya out. Nice restaurant. Maybe a movie or skatin' afterward." An' so on. Piece of cake.

"She wouldn't want to go with me."

She'll want to. She likes ya.

"She likes everybody."

I'm losin' patience—fast!

"I want to, really, but she knows about DeLane. Everybody at school does. She doesn't want to go out with a jerk like me."

Pick up the bloomin' phone!

A MONTH LATER, first, a background chorus of giggling. Then an expectant, "Is Sam there?" The youthful tittering continued. A breathless feminine voice tried to shush the laughter.

Annoyed, Freida rolled her eyes. She tapped her foot and frowned at the ceiling. "He's unavailable. May I give him a message?" Freida trapped the receiver between her shoulder and ear and carried the base with her as she resumed dusting the den.

"When do you think he'll be back?" The voice sounded disappointed, pouty. The voices always sounded disappointed, but they never seemed to catch on. They called back for more neglect. If Sam took their calls or called them back, he did so with intricate and thinly camouflaged excuses about why he couldn't talk long, couldn't meet them for hamburgers at Jack's, wouldn't be available for a movie on Friday or Saturday night, couldn't possibly help them study for a history test. He was polite, not wanting to hurt feelings, but he was firm. They were not offended. In spite of his neglect, they could be counted on to call back for more of the same.

"I'm not sure, but I'd be happy to give him a message."

"Well, sure. Tell him Carla called. Have him call me at Yolanda's house. I'll be here *all night*. I'm *sure* he has the number." More background snickering. A rising and falling of young female questions and merriment.

"Carla at Yolanda's. Is that all?"

"I'll tell him everything when he calls. Thanks." A click shut off the gaiety in mid-giggle.

"Don't hold your breath," Freida advised the dead phone line. She looked at the couch and frowned.

Her son lay back, Cleopatra-style, amid an untidy mound of pillows and cushions. The coffee table in front of him was loaded with food, beverage, and the carcasses of previous courses.

"You're supposed to call—"

"I heard. Thanks, Ma. What would I do without you?"

"Take your own calls, I guess. Deal with these little girlfriends of yours all by yourself. Do your own lying." She tried to look and sound outdone with him, but a smile erupted against her attempt to suppress it. He looked so young and sweet and, for a badly needed change, happy. With effort, she shook off the smile before he saw it. "Why don't you go outside, so I won't have to fib every time the phone rings?"

He was eating a thick wedge of lemon pound cake that had been smeared with an inch of peanut butter. Every bite required a concentrated effort and ounces of milk to work into a manageable condition inside his mouth, but the wad didn't stop him from talking. He raised up and looked at her.

"I'm expecting a call from Tara when she gets back from her grandmother's house. Should be soon. Anyway, I wanna watch the rest of this," he directed his words around the unpleasant but impressive mouthful, pointed a finger at the TV set, and laughed. On the screen Wile E. Coyote was lying paper-doll flat at the bottom of a canyon with a boulder on top of him.

She sighed and shook her head. Why females of any age would consider this lug ripe for romance was beyond her. At sixteen, he was a big baby. Gone were the days, however, when she'd worried that he'd never have the courage for girls. He was picky and still had a bit of a problem with shyness, but he was having the time of his life with this courting game. He played instinctively with the pomp and finesse of a master. His awkwardness had evaporated—almost overnight. He made a big show of impatience with his pursuers, but he was clearly eating up every ego-stroking moment.

Three months had been weathered since he'd convinced her he was fully capable of *handling* a woman, and she hadn't come to terms with what he'd done. It had been the first time she'd had to forgive him for anything. An extremely difficult experience, even though she realized how much he'd hurt himself in the doing and the undoing of his affair with DeLane Evans.

For weeks after the initial confrontation, he'd balanced uncertainly on the brink of a complete breakdown. Mark Armstrong had goaded him into accepting a prescription for antidepressant tablets. Adamant in his refusal of further professional intervention, he'd cried his heart out to Freida and A. D. Time and again, he'd pleaded for them to name what was wrong with him, what they saw when they looked at him, why he couldn't feel safe. And, torn apart by his misery, they'd done everything in their power to help him expose the answers he so desperately needed. An impossible task. For nearly eight years, they'd worked in vain to do that very thing. He'd wept until a preponderance of the surface pain had simply washed away, but the old despondency had burrowed deep into him as unmovable and lasting as ever. It could only be shrouded.

The absolution maternal love had tendered was marred by resentment. He'd destroyed her ability to trust. Each time he walked out the door, she wondered where he was going.

"What are you thinking when you look at me like that? Are you ever going to forgive me?" he'd asked one morning after A. D. and Jackie had left the breakfast table.

She'd replied honestly, going on to dump the whole load on him. "I *have* forgiven you because I love you. I've forgiven all I can. But no matter how much I want to, I can't forget what you did. Sometimes, when I look at you, I see you in that woman's bed. That's an image you made, an image I can't erase from my mind. I know you felt trapped in an unbearable situation, but rather than coming to the two people who care the most, you turned to someone who hurt you more. Only after you got caught did it get to be our turn. Nothing we do is going to rebuild your innocence. Still, we're trying. Your daddy and I want nothing more than for you to be well, but you've got to keep in mind that we're healing, too. We work so hard we don't have energy for anything else. We don't even make love anymore."

Silenced, he had lowered his head and left the room.

Later in the day, he'd returned with the familiar heartbreaking apologies and promises.

When she'd reported the incident to A. D., he'd been furious. "Dammit, Freida, he can't take much more. Don't you think he'd have stopped himself if he could have? You think he did it to hurt *you?*" She'd had to make her peace with them both.

Sam's need for solutions had slowly begun growing ever more murky and dense until it was once again hidden away in the recesses of his mind. Then he'd begun to reflect the illusion of wellness. She was not fooled. Inside her son were traumas, raw and painful and enduring. Injuries as unhealed as they had been on that long ago June day when he'd come back to them.

Now that the doomed affair was over, he'd gone out with a few bashful schoolgirls. More and more, he was running with groups of kids, hanging out at fast food restaurants, sporting events, the roller rink. He ignored bold-of-heart girls who called, made the first moves, made no secrets of their flowering admiration. It was his dodging of them that made answering the phone a bothersome chore. But Freida, willing to do anything to help ease him into manhood, covered for him.

At least once a day, every day, she found a private moment to ask questions and give him the opportunity to unburden himself of any emotional trash he'd collected. He shared all he could.

She wasn't blind; she could see why, even in the absence of emotional maturity, he was so attractive to girls. She'd seen the way her own friends looked at him. Though Sam seemed not to have any special concept of his own face and body, the females he encountered found him deliciously enticing. They were drawn to him like fleas to a dog— "like flies to a dead dog" in A. D.'s words. "Can't take 'im to department stores anymore. All them she-mannequins jump off their stands an' try to follow 'im home." Aged by the worry-deepened lines on his face, his field of hopefuls spread wide of high school boundaries. The boy's ingenuity was often stretched to the limit in the manufacturing of excuses to save feelings and thereby safeguard himself. After Vicky Brown, he was terrified of making female enemies. Once in a while, during a creative dry spell, he'd take one of the callers out for a charitable one-timer.

Now, there was hope for a new, healthy relationship with a girl only a year older. Tara Mason was sweet, an honor student, and Sam was showing strong interest. He gone as far as to ask Freida to help pick something appropriate for Tara's birthday.

The worst was over. Sam had come through, a little spiritually hollow-eyed and haggard, but none the less, he had come through. He'd be okay for a while.

He was still a puzzle, a giant question mark. To most people, he seemed so carefree and sunny. He could be the funny guy, the clown, covering up his feelings with a well-defined comedic talent. But sometimes, Freida couldn't see the humor for the guarded, frightened look in his eyes. He was affectionate without reserve toward her and, in a slightly more formal manner, with his father. He'd never been hesitant to say, "I love you." He could touch and be touched, but his circle of intimates was small. His family, the Armstrongs, the Blacknell boy, and a few friends from school. He continued to stand to the rear too much, going to great lengths at times and in various situations to keep eyes drawn away from him. Freida remembered a happy, outgoing, attention-seeking child, and after all these years, she still missed him. She missed that little boy who had shown no fear for anything or anyone. The little boy who had been snatched away from her to be returned incomplete and frail.

He was now beginning to strike out in new, more daring directions. Out of the blue, he'd set his sights on a media career. His plans to become a broadcast journalist were now common dinner table dialogue. Falling into routine attendance of the morning and evening newscasts, he studied Jennings, Rather, Donaldson, Brinkley, and the locals. He read the daily papers and weekly news magazines. If interest and intellectual ability were the only requirements, he'd be an ace, but so much more was demanded of such a job. Sam was not aggressive, and ego wasn't one of his dominant character assets. Freida had her doubts.

The phone rang again and startled her from her thoughts. Ready for another round of song-and-dance deceit, she grabbed it.

"Yes, Tara, he's here. For you, I might even be able to get him off the sofa." Freida turned and cupped her hand near her mouth. "Sam, come get the phone."

He rolled over the back of the sofa and landed catlike on bare feet. Dragging the cord across the floor, he backed into the pantry and closed the door—a privacy custom he'd picked up from his sister who had hundreds of phone hours to her credit. He'd be there a while.

Freida would not be privy to the conversation, so she took her dusting cloth into the dining room where she began working on the china cabinet.

TARA HAD GONE with her mother to visit her married sister in Memphis. Jackie was out with Robert—no one but his mother was allowed to call him Robbie now. They'd probably gone to the drive-in to make out in relative privacy. Neither had a lot of imagination. A. D. was asleep in his recliner, and Freida had gone upstairs to take a shower. Since he didn't have much choice, Sam brushed caution aside and answered the tele-phone.

The caller was an extravagantly intoxicated Bud.

"Sam, baby, I'll pick ya up, an' we'll go over to the Green Top for barbecue."

Sam could almost smell the alcoholic fumes wafting through the phone wires. "No, thanks. You sound pretty drunk, Bud. You need to stay off the road."

"You'd make one helluva preacher, ya ol' butthole. Why don't ya forget tryin' to be my papa, an' les have some fun."

"You know that eating barbecue is *all* you can do at the Green Top. You're only seventeen. They won't serve you alcohol. If you even ask, you'll end up sitting on your butt right in the middle of Seventy-eight Highway."

"If that's the way ya gunna be, I'll just go by myself."

"Where are you, anyway?"

"In a booth outside some dumpy convenience store down the road from Jeff State—I think."

"Which road? Carson? Sun Hill?"

"A paved one with white an' yellow lines."

"And you're gonna just swing by my house twenty-five miles away, *then* drive another twenty for a barbecue? You're not just drunk—you're crazy."

"Correction—a big, messy World Famous Green Top BBQ. It'd be worth drivin' five hundred miles, ten hundred miles. It'd be worth crossin' the friggin' ocean for. Aw, Sam, where's your sense of 'venture? Ya used to be such a fun guy."

"Listen, Bud. Stay where you are. I'll come get you. You can spend the night here, and we'll go back for your car in the morning. There's all kinds of stuff to eat here. No barbecue, but Ma made gallons of chili—"

"I don't need ya takin' care a me, tryin' to make a good lil boy outta me. I go where I wanna go. Neither you nor that ol' fart I call Daddy's gunna tell me what to do. Ya hear?"

"Bud—"

"Go screw yourself!"

"Wait, Bud! I'll drive you to the Green Top. Hold on—"

Bud had already broken the connection. He had just spoken the last words Sam would ever hear him speak.

TOMORROW THE HEADLINE in the Sunday *Bugle* would read: *Local Boy Dies / Two Injured in Crash Near Walker-Jefferson County Line.* The story would identify an elderly couple, residents of nearby Sumiton, and their dead cockerspaniel. The old couple would be listed in guarded condition at University Hospital. There would be mention of empty beer cans, a shattered vodka bottle.

Tomorrow afternoon, Sam would go to the wrecker service in Sumiton to see the car Bud had been driving east in a westbound lane. He wouldn't be able to recognize it as something he'd seen before. He would visit the scene of the wreck on Highway 78, a mile and two-tenths from the Green Top. He would squint at nuggets of safety glass glinting in the sunlight on the grassy median of the four-lane. He would hear on the radio about the old woman dying—then the old man.

Tomorrow evening, he would open his front door to the Reverend Arlo Blacknell. Alone, he would stand, trembling and pale, as this obese man of God raised his high, nasal drawl unnecessarily, dousing Sam with the responsibility of his son's untimely death. Sam would stand accused of owning the blame for every actual and perceived Biblical infraction Raymond Arlo Blacknell, Jr., affectionately known as Bud the Bear, had committed since the age of six. He would stand rooted, shocked, and bewildered until his own father came in from the field and threatened to knock Arlo's righteous dentures down his throat.

Instead of rescuing Bud from himself one more time tonight, Sam would do all these other things tomorrow.

Tonight, he would go to bed wondering what he could possibly do to help a friend who defied reason, a friend whose life was sculpted by undeserved, violent intrusions—beatings, hard words, and a monumental lack of love. He would relive this night a thousand times, but the outcome would never change.

Tomorrow, he would experience one of the emptiest days of his life. The emptiness would linger on after tomorrow had regressed to yesterday.

In a couple of months, he would turn seventeen, graduate high school, and move into a student apartment in Tuscaloosa. He would spend the next four years at the University of Alabama becoming an educated man, a bona fide scholar with a BA and MA. Eventually he'd become a broadcast journalist with WPMS Channel Nine in Birmingham and a fledgling success. He would find his professional niche.

He would never stop missing Bud the Bear. He would forever lament the unfairness of a human child being born to the flip side of humanity. Sam had been brutalized, almost killed. He'd survived because the savagery had ended and strong arms had gone around him. For Bud, there had been no cessation and no arms.

18

Christmas 1980

H E STUDIED THE lighted pathway the moon laid across the rippling waters of Smith Lake—the *moon glade,* Brenan, a young writer fascinated with words and descriptive phrases, called it. Bundled in Sam's down-filled parka, she rattled on about how misunderstood she felt. He should have been fireside with his folks, drinking coffee, sharing memories of holidays past, overnighting in his old bed. Instead, he listened, nodding and shaking his head with apt sympathy, while slowly freezing to death.

Dropping not-so-subtle hints about having a few minutes alone— "We've got a few things to talk over. There's too much going on back at the house. You know how it is."—Robert and Jackie had gone back to the relative warmth of the Nova. Since it had been Jackie's idea to come to the lake in the dead of December, Sam should have suspected an ulterior motive, but he'd let himself believe he was in for a companionable, possibly nostalgic cruise around the lake. If he had known vehicular romance had been on her mind, he'd have given her a hardy "no thanks." He certainly wouldn't have been left on a rocky bank near the dam to entertain a gabby teenager who hadn't had the foresight to dress adequately for a winter's night outdoors.

"Some ride, huh, Ace?" Brenan finally paused.

For Jackie an' Robbie, maybe, Lefty retorted.

"Yeah."

His sister was so pregnant she had to be hauled out of her chair. How, in her current shape, could she accomplish anything meaningful in the back seat of a car? Well, he sighed, at least soon-to-be hotshot lawyer Robert had married her. They could fog up the windows legally, now, but they could have slipped up to Jackie's old room or driven a few miles farther to the lake house where all could have the comfort of a fire.

"Take your jacket, Sam. You're shaking."

"Then you'll freeze. Just keep it."

"I'll go get something out of the car. There's probably lots of clothing lying around by now. They don't need jackets to keep them warm."

Whaddaya call cold-weather lovin'?

"You're not going anywhere near that car."

Wintercourse, of course.

"You don't have to be so careful with me. I know we were duped. I insisted on coming. You were conned into keeping me occupied. They deserve a little interruptus, if you ask me."

He frowned. His sister and brother-in-law were certainly setting a wonderful example for Brenan. "Sit back down."

"Take this, and I will. They won't be long. I heard Jackie tell Mama he's eleven minutes from foreplay to afterglow. Tops."

"I don't want to know. Put that back on."

"You put it on, and I'll sit in front of you. You can lap it around both of us. We'll both be warm then. Move back a little. The jacket and the rock are big enough for us both."

Don't ya dare!

Her idea had made sense until the position had been accomplished, both of them facing the lake. Sam didn't think Mark Armstrong would appreciate finding his daughter sitting between any man's legs, wearing the same jacket. Her nearness was having an unwelcome effect on him, too.

"How's school?"

"Not much going on in the way of excitement. Not fun excitement, anyway. There's this nerd, Davy Harding, who's driving me crazy drawing hearts with my name in them all over the place. He's already been suspended for defacing school property. They made him scrub and paint, but the day we got out for the holidays, I saw a new big old red heart on the back wall by the bus park. Having your name as part of a defacement is traumatic. Plus, there's a freshman jock who—let's just say I hate boys. All boys. This time next year, thank goodness, I'll be out."

In spite of your yammerin', little girl, there's some excitement goin' on right behind ya.

"I know you're smarter than most boys, but surely you run across one every now and then you can tolerate."

"I've seen a few who can read two-syllable words and blow spit bubbles. The same ones who give armpit concerts."

He remembered being fifteen, his maturity and interests lagging behind girls the same age, his nonexistent social skills. He'd been with a group a year older who had looked down on him with the same little-brother distaste as Jackie. He'd spent long school days hiding behind text books, attracting as little attention as possible. Brenan was five semesters ahead. Boys her age must have seemed like morons. He clearly remembered being fifteen, then sixteen, when everything changed. He hoped her sixteenth birthday and the year that followed would be sweet and painless. "It may shock you, but some boys do catch up."

"Don't you start giving me misery about not having dates every Friday and Saturday night. I get enough of that. I hate wasting hours with a dork who lives in a science fiction fantasy or thinks the meaning of life can be found in a B vampire movie or Mad Magazine. Some still read comic books and play with secret decoder rings. Then there are the jocks and the macho men who're used to getting what some girls aren't ready to give. They don't have a clue what 'no' means. The girl's lucky if they can figure out 'leave me alone' or 'get outta my face, jerk.' What's there to like?"

An' ya think Sam understands? Ha!

"You're a little hard on males—wouldn't you say?"

Erections are HARD-ON males. Ask Sam. You've made it HARD-ON him.

"Not the young ones. I guess I go for older guys. Men of the world. Like you said, some boys do grow up."

Don't get his hopes up. Enough of him is awready UP!

"You're just a kid. Stay that way as long as you can. You have no business—none—thinking about men. Haven't I raised you better than to let peer-pressure do a number on you?"

"Never mind the lectures." She laughed and lay back against him. "I'll give you credit for keeping me out of briar patches, literally and figuratively, and for teaching me a few karate moves that may come in handy some day. But, Ace, there are things you couldn't possibly understand."

Of course, he couldn't. His mind's too busy thinkin' nasty thoughts about a sweet, innocent, an' over-stimulatin' little girl who shall remain nameless. Do 'im a favor an' stop squirmin'. If ya don't watch out you're gonna rub 'im the wrong way! An' oh boy, won't we all be embarrassed then?

"Be still. I may be just another stupid male, but I'm glad you're careful. Too many kids mess up at your age."

"I know, and for the record, I don't think you're all that stupid—for a male."

But she thinks ya have the leg bone of a woolly mammoth stuffed down the front of your jeans!

"Thanks."

"Are you still playing doctor with your Puerto Rican medical student?"

Playin'? The fool was serious. Has no taste in women—present company not yet qualifyin' as a woman.

"I see her once in a while."

Once was too often.

Brenan had always shown an interest in the women who passed in and out of his life. Her questions were bold, uncensored, and often well beyond the province of simple curiosity, but she asked them with the same wide-eyed, innocent wonder she'd shown at six or seven. "Why don't the moon fall?" "How come flowers droop when you pick 'em?" "Why are your legs hairier than mine?" "When you eat a cupcake, do you lick the gooey part off first?" He didn't answer all her questions anymore.

"Do you like her a lot?"

"Oh, I don't know."

"Jackie said you took her to Gulf Shores as soon as Thanksgiving dinner was over and stayed until Sunday. That sounds like you like her plenty. Said Freida had a fit."

So did I.

"This conversation just took a wrong turn."

"Okay. I'm curious, so sue me. You used to tell me stuff."

"I used to wipe your nose."

"My point exactly. We used to be close. Guess what."

Closer'n this?

"What?"

"I finished my book."

"Great. Am I going to get to read it?"

"As a matter of fact, I was gonna start hinting around. I'll be finished with the retyping in about a week. If you're sure you want to, I'd like your opinion."

Want MY opinion?

"Let me know when to pick it up."

Sam, Buddy, give her the jacket an' walk it off.

Snubbing Lefty's carping, Sam tightened his arms around Brenan. He wasn't going to let her go until he had to. "In spite of this ridiculous position, Jackie and Robert are going to come back and find us frozen to this rock."

"I'm warm enough, now. Anyway, I realize Channel Nine keeps you busy. I'll understand if you don't have the time."

"I'll make time."

Dispelling the worry of her picking up his physical response to her nearness, she continued to snuggle back against him with the careless ease of complete trust. A numbing gust blew her hair across his face. She smelled of strawberries and musk oil.

"Sam?"

"Mmm?"

"I miss how it used to be when I was little and you were always home."

"Me, too."

"You'll still have to buy a copy when it's published so I can write something really mushy in it."

"I'll buy ten."

" . . . ANOTHER MISSING child report. This morning, seven-year-old Shanna Leigh Gant disappeared from her Cook's Creek residence . . . "

The still photo on the monitor showed a chubby, grinning and gap-toothed little girl with a wild cap of carrot-colored hair. Her wide grin wrinkled her nose and squeezed her eyes to slits. A happy kid, full of mischief.

" . . . parents told police and reporters that Shanna had asked permission to ride her bicycle in the parking lot of nearby Quinlin Elementary School. According to the Gants and their neighbors, the school lot is a popular place for neighborhood children to ride bikes when school is not . . . "

A video pan of a middle-class, suburban neighborhood. Split-level brick and vinyl siding. Mailboxes shaped like barns, covered wagons, birdhouses—some decorated with the red and green of the season. Asphalt driveways occupied by compact hatchbacks, mini vans, mid-sized sedans. Juniper and box hedge. Willows and magnolias. Families standing amid two-dimensional plywood Santa sleighs and reindeer on winter-brown lawns.

" . . . last seen riding her bicycle along the shoulder of Cook's Creek Road in front of the Johnson Heights subdivision at ten-fifteen this morning. Angus McDuff, a local mail carrier and friend of the family . . . "

The close-up of the mailman faded to a shot of a neon pink Huffy with glittery, press-on cartoon stickers. *Rainbow Bright? Strawberry Shortcake? Cabbage Patch?*

" . . . the bicycle, a Christmas gift, was found in a drainage ditch less than a quarter-mile from her home. Officials have admitted clues were found in the vicinity of the deserted bicycle but aren't releasing . . . "

The field reporter's hair blew wild in the breeze.

" . . . was wearing green corduroy overalls over a yellow sweatshirt and white leather high-top sneakers . . . "

Sam's face at the anchor desk. The little girl's picture shrank to a rectangle on the top right of the screen.

After the newscast, Sam grabbed his overcoat and started out, dragging his feet to allow Tommy Crowder time to catch up. He hated covering missing-children stories, especially ones in which there seemed to be no clothes hampers, junk rooms, or tool sheds for them to have hidden in and napped. He hated the stories, but he accepted them without complaint, often volunteering or relieving other reporters of the task. He gave them his best.

"MacCauley?"

He turned. Down the corridor, his partner stood, making no move to get his coat or his camera.

"Yeah, Tommy?"

"Forget it, Ace."

"They found her?"

Tommy nodded.

"Alive?"

This time Tommy only looked at him.

19

January 1981

TO ANYONE WHO might have arbitrarily asked, he would have hotly denied the flagrant desire he was experiencing. He would have argued to the death anyone who braved accusing him of this wholly inappropriate and possibly even perverted lust. This involuntary physical affliction, however abhorrent to him, proved to be a powerful distraction from his more mundane relationships. And he was seldom free of it.

His preoccupation with Brenan was adolescent. She ignited his every nerve ending. He worried that, at some juncture in the misfortunes of his life, some psychological mechanism crucial to his mental health had been mangled beyond repair. These impressions he buried in his heart, and he guarded them as he would have any damning evidence. No confidant shared his dishonor. He lived in fear of discovery.

This was his first love. Until Brenan, love songs had been melodic but empty words. Lyrical poetry had been phantasm and foolishness. The two years he had spent with Tara Mason had been fun, companionable, but void of true passion. When she had moved on to someone else, Sam had nobly rallied an all-out attempt to feel rejection and sadness, but the raw material just hadn't been there. For months, the common interests that had brought them together had lazily waned. The final breakup had been civil and anticlimactic. During the remaining years on the Capstone, the friendship had survived. When their paths had crossed, the greetings had been casual, friendly, and painless. His heart had simply refused to break.

His easy relationship with Tara, now six years in the past, had been a learning experience. He'd come away from her with the courage to talk with other females, ask them out, let them down easy. This allowed an accumulation of experience with a variety of young women. Most he found to be pleasant company, but, unable to visualize one of them in his future, he was content in his single-occupancy. From an efficiency student flat in Tuscaloosa to a three-room, three-story walk-up in Ensley, he took female companionship one brief encounter at a time.

A Roving Action Reporter with the WPMS Eagle-Eye News Team, a broadcast journalist with a regular spot at the anchor desk, Sam was likewise contented with his professional life. His rapid success had been a tremendous ego boost, pushing him into the center of the public eye. His shyness appeared to have given up to confidence—a deliberate pseudo-hauteur—and genuine pride born of a job well-done.

Quite satisfied, until Brenan Armstrong, the Sawbriar Princess, who because of the recent union of Jackie and Robert, was the next thing to a sister-in-law, began to be something more. In the blink of an eye, his heart had breached that cultivated and nurtured contentment. It had deserted him to hang suspended, pathetic and forlorn, over her dark, lovely head.

HE HELD THE LOOSE PAGES of the manuscript at reading level, fixing his eyes again on the title and byline. *Me and Joe, a novel by Brenan Armstrong.* He'd finished the last page, the typed and double-spaced eight hundred eighty-ninth, and tucked it at the bottom of the stack. Closing his eyes and mind against the incredulity of it, he shook doubt aside. A first-rate adult mainstreamer, he had no trouble picturing it in hardcover with a somber dust jacket on display at Waldenbooks, a more colorful paperback on the rack at Kmart.

For the last two years, whenever he'd been around home, he'd watched from a distance—Brenan with her hands full of notebooks and mechanical pencils. Sitting on fence rails, the forks of mimosa limbs, the big rock that jutted out of the hillside between the Armstrongs' half-timber and the MacCauleys' wood-frame farmhouse. Wearing a serious-browed expression of concentration that would have looked silly on most teenaged girls, she'd scratched her pencil in fury over the blank pages, filling them with the words he'd just read. He'd been close enough, on occasion, to hear a new, unladylike vocabulary evolve as she'd impatiently gained typing skills. With a secondhand Royal electric and a card table, she'd homesteaded a make-do office in a corner of the Armstrong dining room. "The Great American Novel" had been her consistent reply to his queries. The reading of her finished manuscript had given him a new mental portrait of Brenan at fifteen. Hers was a well-developed, talented brain that had somehow matured before her body was through growing and changing. Sam wasn't at all sure what to think about the novel or the writing of it, about her adult brain or her youthful body. But he was in love with the entire package.

He put down the manuscript and tried to wade through some of his muddled emotions. Did her intelligence and maturity shave any impropriety off his desire? They made her seem more grown-up without altering the fact that she'd been born six months before he turned ten. Due to complete high school in less than a year, she was propelled by some unknown energy source to achieve, conquer, finish first.

She excited him, made him sweat. Longing, shame, hopelessness, disgust, and a myriad of equally frustrating feelings made his Brenan list. Nothing dampered the flame she kindled; it blazed as bright and uncontrolled as wildfire.

He got up, snapped on the television, and dropped heavily back into his chair. The dark screen lightened and slowly focused on a sharp, brightly colored cartoon France. Sidewalk cafés, Parisians in berets. The renowned Pepé lé Pew was courting a poor little black kitten whose hapless encounter with a brush dripping white paint had left her resembling a pretty she-skunk. After getting a whiff of Pepé, she wrinkled her dainty nose and bolted. She ran as if a hungry hound was on her heels while the love-struck polecat bounced jauntily after her, crooning to her in French-accented English. Every Saturday morning cartoon connoisseur knew the ending, all the foredoomed endings. Pepé was always too nonchalant, and the cat always got away. What would happen if, just once, Pepé dropped the debonair European bullshit and took off after her like a bat out of hell? Would he be stinking up some lonely bachelor pad? Or would he be smugly sharing a bowl of Kitten Chow with that stuck-up little pussy and a den full of half-breed polekitties?

THE *TOONS* HAD ENDED. Some lesser animated celebrity cast was now crammed between the cereal and G.I. Joe commercials. His watch told him he'd slept more than an hour. He stood and stretched, unintentionally catching his reflection in the sliding glass balcony doors. "Boo," he whispered. What he saw was a hairy impostor, an ageless hippy, the Michael Landon werewolf, someone who wasn't altogether Sam.

He was the hairiest TV journalist in Birmingham, in the history of WPMS News. No other employee of Channel Nine would have pushed the boss as far. A week ago, newsroom mogul, Andy Drury, had pulled rank, commanded Sam to get a haircut and a trim and made the appointment for him. What he'd wanted was for Sam to show up for work pruned to a tapered cut with a neat part and a clean-shaven face, the man who had applied for the position over three years ago. What he'd gotten was Sam with an inch off the front and sides, nothing off the back, and a little less bush on the beard. For months, he'd had Drury dangling between old-fashioned reserve and ratings. Between a rock and a hard place, A. D. would have said.

Of course, Sam's hair was always brushed and tamed before the cameras rolled, and considering how much effort went into camouflaging aging anchor Nick Howser's daily razor burn, the beard had advantages. Sam had learned the wizardry of brandishing a snobby air of self-worth, or a convincing sham. His stubbornness about the hair belied any doubt in the quality of his work or his importance to the station. It was his way of saying, "I'm perfectly comfortable running with the big dogs." After all, Roving Action Reporter Sam MacCauley was consistently first on the scene, first on the air, first to get the whole story, and he, if he chose to listen to rumor, didn't look too shabby on the tube—despite the ruff. Other stations wanted him, made openhanded offers. He'd found the interest of women to be as easily aroused as that of adolescent girls and used this ability to bring female viewership to an all-time high. The station's ratings had risen from the basement to the penthouse since he had picked up a microphone and become a pavement pounder. Two years in a row, he'd reeled in Emmy nominations. The beard and long hair hadn't deadened his upward mobility.

With popularity, came clout. Only Dana Rawlings, who had eight years seniority, outranked him. Nick Howser, a thirty-year news hound, was winding down a long career, handing down the reins to Sam with little fanfare. All the others were either slow-climbers who lacked the natural sparkle for serious competing, ambitionless slugs, or struggling come-latelies. He could afford to make some noise. Thus far, he'd insisted on a suitable raise in salary and creative control of his hair. Without a single exception, he played the other eight innings by Drury's rules. Altogether, it was a connection that had made the two of them runaway successes in the news game.

Sam saved the power plays for his job. The illusory arrogance went on with his suit and tie in late morning and hung up to air at the end of the workday.

He continued to look into the glass. His primate-like reflection bore an eerie resemblance to the description of the Brenan's protagonist, a young newspaper journalist, the Joe of *Me and Joe*. His suffering libido tried but fell short of making a correlation. To Brenan, Sam was only another overprotective big brother, an extra, a supplement to Robert, someone who listened and praised, guarded and nagged. She obviously felt a safe kinship with him. Having spent much of her childhood following in his wake, she thought he was someone with whom she could safely share a jacket and body heat.

On Sunday, when Sam had stopped at the Armstrong house to get the manuscript, Brenan had been alone and strangely quiet.

"Is something wrong?" he'd asked.

"Um, just a little post-holiday blues."

"That all?"

"Well, Daddy keeps pushing me to settle on a college. He's hoping I'll let him decide. He really wants me to go into pre-med—since his traitorous man-child studied law. Of course, I'm going to feel like Benedict Arnold number two."

"He'll get over it."

"I guess. He's trying not to be as overbearing as he was with Robert. He's even found this literary agent who's going to take a look at my book, but still—"

Her troubles had afforded him a chance to stay and sympathize. In addition to high school and her writing, she'd already started taking night classes in drafting at the local technical college. She wanted to major in modern architecture, American literature, or geology. Over time, maybe all three. She wanted to keep writing and studying without being locked into any one field. The entire world fascinated her. Once she'd started a project, she couldn't be stopped. Mark would never pack her off to medical school, but he'd wait until the last tick of the clock before backing down.

"Don't worry. You're the spoiled brat who always gets her way. Even that mean old sawbones can't deny you."

"Maybe you're right, but if he doesn't shut up soon, may I come live with you?"

Driving away, he'd felt like a dirty old man. None of the women he'd taken out, spent money on, and slept with had excited him so much.

He sighed and drifted toward the bathroom. This morning, Brenan was supposed to be watching their respective infant niece, Marissa, while Robert studied for his bar exam and Jackie, only nine days after giving birth, ventured back to painting nude males or baskets of fruit in art class. Returning the manuscript was his excuse to see her, if only for a couple of minutes.

The medicine cabinet mirror threw back the startling werewolf likeness. Grabbing a hairbrush, he began to subdue the monster. He couldn't let her see him like this.

ABOVE THE RUMBLE of his now antique Mustang, Sam gave Brenan's novel one last thoughtful poring over. She had written about love—not ecclesiastical fondness nor discreetly closed doors, but a lusty, physical passion between a young dancer and a hard-nosed middle-aged reporter. She'd given them a hardy, graphic sexual awakening after years of simple, mismatched comradeship and shrouded desire. She had narrated the act with a disturbing exactness of thrust and perspiration. He couldn't help wondering where she's done her research. By her account, her dates had been more traumatic than titillating.

Ya wake up in a new world ever' day. She don't tell ya ever'thing. Should know by now some little jailbait females could teach college courses in slap an' tickle.

"Thank you for sharing."

Don't mention it.

The possibility that she'd had firsthand experience made the muscles of his face twitch. He frowned irritably at the manuscript box on the seat beside him. Not only was he bothered by her grasp of sexual pleasures; he was appalled at his green-eyed reaction to it. Sooner or later, she *would* experience life as a woman. Not with Sam. His opinion was beside the point. All she could ever be to him was Robert's baby sister, the Sawbriar Princess. *Finis.* Sign off, flash the scenic logo, and play the National Anthem.

Oh, but you'd fight all the boys on the playground for a turn in the cloakroom with 'er.

"Not tonight, Lefty. I'm not in the mood."

Ya can't bullshit me. Ya been in the MOOD for days. Give your soul away for that little girl!

"I said not tonight, so knock it off!"

Give it ALL to show her some grown-up passion! Be her man! Her first— her only!

"That's enough!"

Yeah, Buddy! Ripened on the vine. Tender an' oh, so sweet!

"You're one sick sonofabitch, Lefty."

Me? I'm sick? Look who's talkin' l-o-v-e! It's YOU who oughta be hangin' your heads—BOTH of 'em—in shame! I'm just sayin' what you're thinkin'—

all I ever do! I AM you! I know what goes on in THIS head. An' it scares the hell-o outta me, Ace! If ya ain't careful, you're gonna take us down, make the DeLane Evans caper look like a carousel ride at Kiddie Land.

"I can keep my mouth shut and my hands in my pockets, but I can't stop loving her."

Love?

"Yes. Love." Definitely love. A wasted, hopeless, choking love. An incredibly deep, glorious, abiding love.

Gonna fork your legs over the wrong fence one of these days.

"Go to hell! Who needs you?"

Yessirree, Boss! Soon as ya get your brain workin' right. Soon as ya can take care of yourself an' find a real woman to take your mind off the kid, I'm outta here. Perhaps. Maybe. It COULD happen. It'll depend on what else you're screwin' up at the time. Till then, just call me tick, cause I'm diggin' in!

"S'MATTER, SON?" A. D. peered over his new bifocals and his seed catalog. "You did the news all last week like somebody was holdin' a gun to your head."

"The matter?"

"I'm askin' what's got you so preoccupied lately? Wouldn't be a woman, would it?" His voice was hopeful.

"I don't know. Maybe."

Sam hadn't stayed long with Brenan yesterday, hadn't even gone inside. He'd stood, in his down jacket, shivering in the wind, and talked to her through a narrow opening in the side doors. *"No, I won't come in. Can't stay."* A few compliments and pleasantries. *"Great story, Bren. The characters and their problems all seemed real. I'm proud of you."* He'd been afraid she'd look through his emotional transparency and see the warped desire that was burning holes inside him.

Freida was out doing her weekly Sunday afternoon grocery shopping. Robert and Jackie had brought the baby by to collect a compulsory round of compliments before continuing on to the other grandparents next door. The house was unusually quiet.

A. D. sat in an old recliner that, after years of communicating with his backside, conformed perfectly to the contour of the man. No one else would have considered sitting in the chair—and wouldn't have been comfortable if they had. Slouching on the sofa, Sam awaited the next question.

"Somethin's on your mind. Wanna talk about it?"

"It's nothing. Just a little tired. That's all."

"So you don't wanna talk?"

"I'm fine. It's you I want to hear about." Sam didn't know if he'd ever be completely at ease around his father again. The heart attack last September would forever be fresh and looming.

A. D. was still thin and weak but indignantly refusing to admit what was visually plain to everyone else. He was forced to take handfuls of pills and participate only in the amount and type of activities prescribed by the cardiologist. An optimist, he swore each day he felt stronger than the day before.

For his own peace of mind, Sam spent more time at the farm than his apartment. He understood A. D.'s aversion to constant scrutiny and his reluctance to accept an unaccustomed and depressing sick role. No one wanted to make him feel like an invalid. Freida and Jackie were better at disguising their worry, but Sam's concern and need to be near his father wouldn't stay covered. If A. D. caught on to how important he was to his son, that was just too bad.

"Need any help around the house?"

A. D. ignored him. "Are you seein' someone?"

"Yes, a very stubborn man."

"You know what I mean."

"Not regularly. Ma said you might want to get out of the house. Why don't we ride up to the lake and take a look at the house? Probably need to some fixing-up before spring. It's our turn. Something will have to be done about the back deck if we want to use it. You'll know more about what it needs."

"Jackie said you called it quits with Carmen."

"And I hear Ma literally danced with joy."

"She wasn't sorry, that's sure. If it's not a woman, what is botherin' you?"

"Why do you think something's bothering me?"

"I've got eyes."

"You can use them to look inside me? Those new glasses have magic power?"

"Son, you're not a bashful schoolboy anymore. You're—what— twenty-four, almost twenty-five? Seems about time you got a little weak-kneed and wobbly."

Sam sighed. He didn't know if clairvoyance was a side effect of heart medicine or if A. D. simply considered the meeting of Sam's romantic needs overdue. "Aw, come on."

"You've got the *look.*"

"Dad, don't."

"The *look.* Sorta dreamy an' puky. Little bit goofy, too."

"Thanks."

"Well—"

"Okay, I'll tell you something if you'll change the record when I'm through." What harm was talking if nothing was said? "Just accept what I give without asking anything more."

A. D. nodded that he would comply.

"Well, I'd say up until a couple of weeks ago, I had no idea what being in love felt like. The way you and Ma are about each other—I knew it was real. It happened to other people but not me." Sam gazed at the interest in his father's eyes. "That's what I believed. Now, all of a sudden, I wish I'd been right."

"You sayin' I'm right? You've been bit?"

"Yeah. Bit—a good word for it."

"I knew it! The *look* never lies."

"Forget it. She's not for me."

"Aw, now."

"I mean it. She won't ever be within my reach."

"You hafta go after her. She ain't gonna jump in your arms if you don't hold 'em out."

"Wouldn't make much difference."

"A married woman?"

"No, she's not married, and you promised you wouldn't ask questions. Let's just say I may be facing a lifetime of wanting a woman I can't have. This love business, the kind that's happened to me, isn't the wonderful thing it's cracked up to be."

"Why are you givin' up?"

"*Because* I love her. Please, don't take this up with Mama."

A. D. sympathetically shook his head. "I don't get it."

"I don't get it, either, Dad. Now, do you want to go to the lake or spend the rest of the afternoon giving me a hard time?"

"DON'T YOU EVER think about havin' a family?"

Why couldn't he ask questions? Did his duty fly out the window when the boy stopped outgrowing his Levis? Wasn't fatherhood a lifetime commitment?

"Aw, Dad. Yeah, of course, I do. Sounds great, in theory, but it's not in the cards. It's just as well; I'm not family-man material. I don't have whatever it is that makes you so good."

A. D. silently noted the compliment as well as Sam's familiar self-deprecation. "How do you know what kinda husband an' father you'd be?"

The warmth inside the car contrasted sharply with the bleak skies and leafless trees outlining the road to the lake.

"I don't even make my own decisions. I ask you or Ma before I buy new socks. You're stuck with a son who'll never grow up."

"You just don't have confidence. You're a good man. It's about time you started givin' yourself some credit."

"There's no point in talking about it."

"Since I can't ask questions, I guess you're gonna leave me not knowing why you don't go after her." He shook his head at the way Sam's hands clinched into fists at the top of the steering wheel. Such a mystery. Why wouldn't he fight man or mountain for the woman he loved?

"Sorry."

"But I'm supposed to be the one person you can tell anything." He deliberately sounded hurt. Sometimes, with Sam, guilt brought results.

Without taking his eyes off the road, Sam removed one hand from the wheel and clamped it onto A. D.'s shoulder. He sighed and attempted a smile. "I could tell you, but that wouldn't put me one millimeter closer to her."

"Well, okay, but for the record, I believe you'd be a terrific family man. You're about as crazy over Marissa as Jackie is. You'd be in hog heaven if you had a kid of your own. Anybody who's seen you with that pesky little Brenan knows you've got the patience of Job."

Sam cringed. "Maybe I don't think of her as a pest." His voice came out as dreary as the January afternoon, but the next statement was sharply ejected. "This conversation is over."

A. D. detected a touch of defensiveness, a wee bit of alarm which hinted at possible chancy plot twists to complicate the mystery.

20

March 1981

S HE'S HAVING PROBLEMS at home. Too long a story for today. Let's just say her dad's a drinker with a bad attitude. Details aren't important." His mother's frown stressed the need for caution and careful wording. Sam dried his sweaty palms on his pants then folded them on the kitchen table. "Her name is Karen Lucas. She's been living with her father in a trailer park in Cullman. She describes him a lot like you do yours, except this piece of work is also a nomad. Since her mother died when Karen was ten, he's dragged her through every town between Mobile and Bangor. She's never spent a whole year at any one school. She just needs to get her life straightened out a little."

"So she's going to straighten out in your one bedroom apartment? How old is she?"

"Twenty-two. She wants to take some classes at Jeff State in the fall. Works evenings, so she can take day classes."

"What sort of work does she do?"

"Dairy Queen, Ma, and she's glad to have it. Jobs are hard to come by."

"Where did she finish high school?"

"She didn't, but she's going to try for a GED."

"Must be pretty."

"Well, yeah. I'd say she's pretty, but what's that got to do with anything?" He tried to sound indignant enough to allay further probing.

"I want to know about the girl you're so much in love with that you move her into your apartment."

"Oh, for petesake! Are you ever gonna start respecting my privacy? The only thing that would make you happy is for me to sign a contract of celibacy like a priest or a monk or something. In a couple of months, I'll be twenty-five years old."

"Big deal."

"Yeah? When you were my age, I was five and Jackie was six! Give me some credit. I don't exactly live under a rock."

"You do have a little money and a good job."

"She doesn't know I have anything more than a paycheck. She's no gold digger, nor is she a news groupie. I doubt she's ever sat through an entire newscast in her life."

"You sure she doesn't have a criminal record or one of those social diseases you read about on health department posters?"

"Aw, Ma, that's not fair. I know where this is going. Nobody knows better what you've had to endure because of me, but could you please forgive me and put the past where it belongs?"

"I'm not trying to make you feel guilty."

"I know, but you are making too much of this."

A FEW MONTHS LATER Sam sat on a stool and watched A. D. carve eyes into the face of a rocking horse he was making for Marissa. "So she's bent outta shape, Dad. What do you want me to do? They just don't like each other. You think I can make two grown women get along?"

"Karen pouts a lot. Maybe, you could help her not be so sensitive. Freida does try to teach her things."

"They both act a little juvenile to me. I'll talk to Karen, but Mom needs to chill a little, too. I expect better from her."

"She believes the two of you aren't suited to each other. You don't exactly seem compatible."

"Maybe not, but sometimes, I'm really glad she's here. She'll leave soon enough."

A. D. folded his knife and dropped it into the bib of his overalls. "What became of the woman you wouldn't talk about? You completely givin' up on her?"

"You promised no questions."

A. D. looked hopeful. "Don't mean you can't volunteer."

Sam sighed. "My feelings haven't changed. I wish that was different. Karen sort of takes my mind off *her*. I'm the user. I never look at her without seeing another woman, never touch her without pretending she's someone else. I hate myself for it."

"You shouldn't do things that make you hate yourself. Your morals are supposed kick in."

"Don't you people ever let up? Nothing's wrong with my morals. Two consenting adults and all that jazz!"

"You said she might leave soon?"

"Yeah, she has grandparents in Tulsa who want her to come out there, start school or something. They've been looking for her since her mom died and that nut-case father of hers started hauling her all over the eastern half of the country. It's going to take a while for her to build up the courage, but she'll go. More than anything, she wants to know what it's like to be part of a family. Can we change the record now? I'm off Sunday and Monday, so Ma can feed me, and I can help with the haying. Karen has to work. That ought to make Ma happy. More than likely, she'll find something else, though. She's only happy when she has a cause to fight for or a wrong to right."

"Sam . . ."

"Okay. That horse's eyes are hers to a tee—wide set and stubborn."

A. D. ran his fingers over the wooden horse face. "I love her eyes, but it worries me how they never miss a thing."

"Oh, take your pills and stop worrying."

"IT'S ME, MA. How are things on the homefront? — Good. Not doing too much with the crew that's clearing the site, is he? — Not yet. Brenan wants me to look at something she drew up in her drafting class first. Since there's no rush and I don't have any idea what I want, I'm gonna see what she's got. After all, I expect to spend the rest of my life in this house."

Anyone passing by his cubical, seeing a large block of text on his computer screen and his phone pressed to his ear, would have assumed Sam was deep into an important story. He was in deep all right—up to his eyeballs in the story of his life.

"I really shouldn't do this on the phone, but Drury's got me working eleven straight evenings. Most are twelve-hour ones. The old guys stranded us when they crossed over to our beloved sister station, and the new ones are jokes. That idiot Roger Garner wouldn't recognize a newsworthy story if it came with a label on it. He's like that Ted guy on *Mary Tyler Moore*. It's good they still have me, huh? — That's the problem. Andy thinks I can do desk and street duty at the same time. You know how things get. Anyway, I've got this thing I want you to know." Sam closed his eyes, steeling himself for a storm. "I hope you're feeling maternal and open-minded today. When I'm through, you can say you told me so all you want, but please, don't freak out. — Yeah, it's about Karen. Now don't start yelling before I even tell you. — Oh, for heavensake! — Yes, that's it! I hate it when you do this. I've never done one thing in my whole life you didn't find out about or just know without even being told. Not one single thing. — Yeah, I'm gonna marry her, because if I don't, I won't have a legal claim to the baby. She could run off and have an abortion. She doesn't want it, but I do. — So it's not your traditional marriage. Karen's agreed to stay only until the baby's born."

He waited but she didn't say anything.

"You crying? — Yes, you are. I'm so sorry. Please, Mama. I hate it when you cry. I know what a letdown I am, but I need you on my side. After Karen's gone, I'll have to go from there by myself. — Yeah, I'm gonna keep it. — So I may be fooling myself, but I'm going to give it my best. A lot of kids have only one parent. It won't be easy, it'll work out. — Oh, Ma, don't make it harder. I messed up. You wouldn't want me to do worse by turning my back on her and my kid. — I'm as sure as any man can be. If it'll make you feel better, I'll get a blood test. It's mine, so drop it. — I know you do, and I love you. Are you going to tell Dad, or make me do it? — I know, but the better you act, the better he'll take it. — All right, have him call when he comes in. Mama? — Um, you know how I hate lying? Well, see, I wanna take back something I said. I really have Thursday off, but I couldn't face you with this, not without preparing you first. — No, I'm not crying. Roger Garner just went by. I may be allergic. — Thanks. I knew you'd be okay. — Thursday lunch will be fine if Karen's welcome to come, too. She'll be my wife by then. — Thanks. — See you then. — Wait! I'm sorry I let you down."

BY NOVEMBER THE PLANES and angles of studs and rafters were beginning to look like a house. A house too big for two people, but Sam already loved it. Brenan had designed it as a project for her drafting class. It was costing more than he could afford, but didn't everybody's? It sat in the center of what used to be the cash farm crop. A lawn would have to be planted and trees brought in, but the ground had been built up into a little rise before the basement and framing began and made the site workable.

Brenan stood near him and watched the workers. "Basement's finished, and those men over there are starting on the walls."

"Still think the lower story will be ready by March?"

"So they say. We'll have Robert and Jackie's hovel in Hoover beat by at least two months. They're going to kick themselves for not letting me draw up something for them."

His heart hammered at her nearness. He stepped back. "The things you're accomplishing at such a tender age is scary. Robert told me about the book deal. I'm hurt. Was I supposed to read about it in the paper?"

"It's a small publishing house."

"I'm still impressed. Does your publisher know you're only fifteen?"

"Sixteen! On the sixth."

"Sorry. Happy birthday! You'll be a celebrity and sell a jillion copies before you finish the one you're working on now. Seriously, Bren, I don't understand. What did your folks do different with you? Robert's smart enough, I guess, but let's face it, when he was your age, he was still reading Power Boys and getting up early on Saturday for *Captain Cave Man.* By the time you were ten, you were teaching me. That's why I'm letting you help build my castle."

"Thanks for the hand up." She smiled broadly as the wind picked up tendrils of her hair and laid them across her face.

"You're welcome. You can, also, give me tips for raising my kid. Suit me fine to have a little Einstein."

"Sam, look at A. D. This is a new lease on life for him. See the way he orders the construction crew around?"

"Yeah. Since he cut back on farming, he's needed a project to keep him away from the checkerboard at Peterson's. Whenever you're around, make him stay off ladders. He thinks he's in better shape than he is."

"How's Karen?" Brenan's smile lost some of its glow.

"Fine. A little on the bitchy side. I sort of take a wide path around her. She won't clean up or cook or wash dishes. I do well to get her to take a shower. She just sits in front of the TV all day and lets things pile up until I get fed up enough to shovel the place out. We'd never make it on a permanent basis. One of us would kill the other. I've started making her walk for the sake of the baby. Some guys walk their dogs. I walk Karen. And she hates it. I do the grocery shopping now, so she doesn't get her Oreos and ice cream. She's having to eat food, and that really sets her off."

"She gives womanhood a bad name." Her smile was gone.

"She's mad about you, too—loves you nearly as much as she loves my mother."

"I'm sorry. I shouldn't even have an opinion."

"I don't like her very much, either, Bren, but I do feel sorry for her. She doesn't know what she wants."

"When she's gone, I'll help with the baby." Smiling again.

"With all you're into, why would you want to baby-sit?"

"Babies are fascinating. I could do something regular."

"I hear they're lots of trouble, but I'll think about it. In the meantime, consider all the implications and talk to Ellen. Then we'll see." He wanted Brenan to love his baby.

SHE ANSWERED ON the eleventh ring. "Wake up, Mama! Hadda call an' tell you 'Happy New Year', did'n I? I'm late. S'awready two o'clock. Two whole hours into the rest of our lives. Happy Nineteen-Eighty-two! — No Ma'am! Ain't drunk. I swear all I had was a few gin-gins an' some beer in silly little bottles. You know I don't drink."

The floor around him tilted, so he held onto the arm of his chair. "I didn't count. — One part gin and one part ginger ale. Or is it the other way around? Jackie made 'em. Anyway, ain't that clever? Gin and ginger ale, gin-gins, I mean. — Not another drop tonight. I swear. Cross my heart. Lean your ear, Mama. I gotta surprise. Is your ear leaned? — Don't fib to me. Can't be done. You can't *lean* your ear. If you try, your head comes with it. — No, please, Mama. Don't hang up. No more jokes. I know I'm sloppy drunk. Knee-walkin', commode-huggin', blind-pukin' drunk. I don't even know how many sheets I got flappin' in the wind. I hadda get drunk cuz I'm heartsick, an' my head's fuzzy, an' I'm really, really scared. That's the surprise! You said I'd find out how scary bein' a parent is. You were six hundred percent right. You're right all the time. An', oh boy, is *that* scary! — Wait! I do too have somethin' to say. Somethin' important. The thing you was rightest about is the baby. It's real! I got an ultrasonic picture of it. It's got arms an' legs an' a heart that beats an' toes. It's awready got toes! It's a human baby. In a coupla months, I'm gonna be somebody's daddy! Don't that scare you?"

Sam dropped the phone while fumbling in his shirt pocket for the picture.

"Mama? Still there? Me, too. I keep lookin' at this little person, an' I'm startin' to like it a lot. Then I think I can't be a daddy! Did'n even grow up all the way, myself. So I start wantin' to back out. — Well, sometimes, things look a lot clearer after a few drinks. The alcohol loosens your brain up. I thought I could do it by myself, but now that I spent the whole evenin' drinkin' an' thinkin', I ain't so sure, I got the questions all cleared up. It's the answers that's missin'. What if it gets sick? Babies get sick a lot, don't they? What if it don't have somethin' it's supposed to? What if it's a girl? Dr. Riley did'n find boy parts. I don't know nothin' 'bout girls. What if it's a sick girl that's got somethin' missin'? Come to think of it, I don't know nothin' 'bout boys when they're babies. — *That's* not what I mean! I mean girl *babies*. You always gotta make stuff sound dirty. — I'm supposed to know about big girls! — Well, it's too late now to go back an' think about these things before I *you know*. I've already *you-knowed*. — Don't lecture me any more, Mama. I stopped doin' it. Ain't that enough? — I most positively did. — A long time. Weeks ago. — Just be-cause! — Okay, but if you promise not to tell. — It's cuz I can't do it with a woman who don't want my kid. Could you? — Y'know what I mean. I did'n do it with her much, anyway. She don't like it. You were right. Daddy was right. Sex ain't nothin' without love. So I quit. — You were right about Karen, too. She's so mean! It's just like I'm pregnant all by myself! — I can't love her no more than she can love me. I tried, but I love somebody else. — Somebody I can't have. Why's my life always so wrong side out? — A nice girl. You'd like her if she was somebody else. — I can't tell you. — Well, of course, I gotta pay the fiddler. We done got off the subject, anyhow. Can we get back to the baby if you're through bein' dirty-minded? — Yes, I still want it. More'n anything, but can I give it to you? — Not forever. Not half that long. Just till I learn. I'm a fast learner. — I knew I could count on you. Les see if I got it right. If I'll give up drinkin' an' callin' you in the wee hours of the mornin' an' lettin' hussies move in with me, you won't leave me alone with it till I know what to do. Is that what you said? — You're the best mother! I always say that! — Naw. She's asleep. It's just me all by myself. Jackie, who, by the way, was pitiful drunk, kept feelin' Robert up. Thought she was gonna have her way with 'im right here on that Navajo rug you got me for my birthday. But for the sake of decency, he took her on home. She's the one you oughta worry about. Your daughter ain't got no manners. — Well, at least, I do my screwin' up in private. Hurts my feelin's the way you an' Daddy always take up for her. No big deal she made a baby before she got married. — Oh, yeah? What about the time they made a wet spot on your bedspread, an' you came after *me*. Tell me you ain't a conclusion-jumper. — Oh, yeah, Brother Arlo called me up to try to save my soul again. Says I need to get the new year started off right. I told him I was gettin' off just fine, thank you. I didn't kill Bud, did I, Mama? —Brother Arlo says I did. — Well, I'm glad, 'cause I miss him. I don't think I'll ever stop. — Am I a bad person? — That's very nice of you to say. You're a good person, too. You mind puttin' Daddy on so I can wish him Happy New Year before my gin-gin level drops?"

"DADDY!" Sam had asked what A. D. was giving Freida for Valentine's Day.

"What?"

"I was just expecting you to say jewelry or flowers or something. I hope you take your pill first! While we're on matters of the heart, what did the doctor say about yours?"

"He said come back in a year. How's that?"

"Great. Brenan says she can't slow you down. If you can keep up with her and the construction crew, you must be in good shape. I just hope you're not overdoing it. Don't look at me like that. You had a heart attack, then bypass surgery. You scared me half to death. As nice as it'll be to get into the house, I don't want you to kill yourself trying to finish it."

"You sit here an' worry. I'm going to the workshop an' make a porch swing for you to do it in."

Sam watched A. D. go. He knew he was stepping on nerves. His own were stretched thin. The baby was due in less than a month. The people at work had started giving him the business. An unusual number of whispered conferences led him to believe some sort of surprise baby party was planned. He was sure Drury would film parts of it for the evening news.

The attorney who was taking care of Sam's and Karen's legal positions had sent Karen to two psychologists. Both had written reports saying that she wanted nothing to do with the baby and would have difficulty if she were to try to take on the responsibility. Karen's problems had been with her a long time. They wouldn't be easy to work through, but she wanted to try. Her grandparents seemed like nurturing people. They would help.

Sam didn't think she would give him any trouble. Freida thought of Karen as cold and conniving, but he saw a wounded young girl who needed someone to finish raising her. She'd never let him get close, but maybe she'd let her grandparents in. After all, they had spent a lot of money and effort finding her.

She never asked for anything anymore, nor did she do anything. Just sat all day in front of the TV set. Wouldn't talk about her feelings. God, he hoped she'd be okay.

Sam and Karen had used each other. The best either one could do now was try to learn something from the experience.

"OH, HUSH your fussing. You're always grumpy in the morning. — I didn't call sooner because I knew you'd insist on coming to the hospital and hanging around all these hours, doing nothing but making me more nervous than I already am. — Sure, I want you here, but you don't need to rush. Take your time. Eat breakfast. You need your coffee. Nobody's going anywhere. — I confess. I'm a basket case. — No, I don't need anything. Don't bring food. You wouldn't expect me to eat now, would you? The nurses keep coffee coming, and that's all I need. — You'll have to call Jackie. I'm out of change. She'll get mad if somebody doesn't let her know in time for her to make sure we're doing it right. — Ohgod, Mama, it's awful. I know I've been told the horrors of childbirth, but nothing I've heard could have prepared me for what Karen's going through. This is my last kid. I'll never put anybody through this kind of torture again, and I plan to be a lot nicer to you, too. — Well, if he's up, then come on, and I'll go back in with Karen. — Yeah. Have somebody at the nurses' desk let me know when you get here. — Be careful. Morning rush-hour traffic will be starting soon. And make sure Dad brings his camera. I've got about ten rolls of film in my jacket pockets. — Oh, yeah, call Brenan, too. It's early, but she made me promise to let her know."

21

March 1982

TINY, DELICATE. A touchable wonder, fragile in her newness. Yet, the first day of her lifetime had already been savored and dismissed. Seconds, then minutes, then hours—soundness quietly supplanting frailty. Straightway she established herself as a reinvented and evolved piece of Sam. The deluge of praise from family, friends, hospital staff served to reinforce the obvious. His daughter was the epitome of perfection. She was beauty and purity and glorious light.

I suppose ya don't notice the curdled stuff she spits all over or the fact that she poops in her pants, Lefty quipped.

"She's gorgeous, son." As she and A. D. were leaving, Freida hugged Sam. "Absolutely gorgeous."

She needs to warn ya about colic, chicken pox, snotty noses.

A. D. nodded. "An angel." He'd never met a baby he didn't immediately love.

Diaper rash, cavities.

Mustering all the humility he owned, Sam replied. "I know."

Distemper shots, fur balls.

When his parents disappeared around a corner, Sam whispered. "She's not a cat."

Wait'll the first time ya hafta stick a thermometer into that cute little butt to tell me how much fun you're havin'.

"THERE'S THIS BONDING thing I have to worry about," Sam told Andy

Drury over the waiting room phone. No mincing of words, no embarrassment. "It's important. Ask Dr. Spock. Ask my mother. Since I'm all she's got, I have to be with her."

"Geez, MacCauley, I hope you don't come down with sore nipples or postpartum depression. My wife got both—all *five* times! She called me every name in the book while I brought her hot tea, Kleenex, and Whitman Samplers. Let me assure you, Ace, I won't be as understanding with you."

"If my nipples get sore, I'll need more time off, so just keep hoping." Unimpeded, Sam, above Andy's unrepressed laughter, reiterated his demand. "I need the rest of this week and the next—maybe even another. I'll know more later what I'll need."

"When I hired you, I didn't figure you for such a liberated woman."

Sam wouldn't let a little bedevilment from the newsroom hinder his attendance at his daughter's feedings, those precious few moments she was awake and in need of his body heat and the sound of his voice. He could be found standing outside the nursery window each time the curtains opened. The rite of passage into fatherhood was a complex phenomenon. It required dedication and time, and Andy Drury could save wear and tear on the blood vessels in his brain by accepting it.

"Bond in a hurry, Ace. Nobody likes dancing with Garner. By the middle of a telecast, his rug's screwed sideways, and his tongue's bleeding from being stepped on. One of these nights, Dana's gonna scratch the smirk off his face with her pretty pink fingernails. But you do what you've gotta do," Drury acquiesced.

SINGLE-MINDEDLY FIXATED on his sleeping child, he watched the uneven rhythm of her quick little breaths. She made his chest and stomach ache in a quirky new way.

A little on the puny side. Lefty observed.

Sam had been ready to settle, happily, for a baby who came with all the right parts in all the right places and those parts in good working order. He hadn't had to settle for anything.

But a little MORE of her wouldn't hurt.

Lefty was right. Five pounds, two ounces of baby wasn't much. His niece, Marissa, born fifteen months earlier, had been a nine-pounder-plus. She'd been big enough to hold on to—but the newborn in the bassinet labeled *"Baby Girl MacCauley"* got lost in his hands. "You only weighed four ounces more," his mother had informed him. "No cause for worry," Mark had reassured. "She'll grow like kudzu. Before long, you'll have to put a rock on her head to slow her down." "Rather have quality than quantity, wouldn't you?" A. D. had rhetorically thrown in.

Freida had tried to prepare him for a red-faced, apelike creature with a lumpy bald head, but her warnings had gone to waste. His baby had come with wispy deep brown curls, and her head was smoothly rounded and flawless. He consistently found something new and wonderful every time he looked at her. A faint etching of straight nut brown brows. A hint of dimples. A pouty little mouth that kept sucking after the rubber nipple was pulled away. Tiny toes that spread and flexed, all in different directions. Freida's tawny skin. Perfect miniature fingers that wrapped, by reflex, snugly around one of his. Her excellence was marred only by an ugly but temporary stump of umbilical cord.

Sam caught his own smile reflected in the glass. Nothing in his experience compared to the emotions coursing through him. The first time she'd been placed in his arms, he'd known she was the embodiment of an extraordinary and unique love, a love that seemed to grow by the minute. Never would he consider her a mistake. Raising her would be no righting of a wrong.

In the middle of a nursery full of infants, *Baby Girl MacCauley*—pretty and peacefully suckling one tiny fist—appeared to have been placed for decoration, a centerpiece. While he stood outside the glass, a sentry keeping watch, she opened her eyes, yawned then closed them again, and was still.

At her request, Karen had been transferred to another floor of the hospital soon after the birth. She had not wanted to see the baby. In the delivery room, she had rigidly turned her head to avoid the sight of the child she had spent fourteen exhausting hours bringing into the world.

Sam considered her insistence on maintaining a cool distance a good sign that he and the baby would have no trouble making a clean break. The papers had been signed and witnessed. The divorce, the relinquishment of parental rights, the severance was nearly complete.

He hoped Karen's realization of a new start would come easier than the other things in her life. She was packed and set to move in with her grandparents in Tulsa. They had offered a family, a home, a job in the cafeteria they owned. Sam had given her a plane ticket, some money, and a promise to help out if she decided to go back to school. A week ago, he'd paid off her car and had it delivered to her grandparents' home. The decision to go to the airport alone tomorrow had been hers. She was growing up, and he considered turning the baby over to him the most solid indication she was going to make it. He'd come to love her in a simple, quiet way—for staying, for giving, for letting go.

In a few minutes, the curtains would close over the viewing window, and shortly after that, the nurses would give him a paper gown and a disposable soap sponge. If he followed directions to their satisfaction, they would give him a rocking chair, a four-ounce nursing bottle, a cloth diaper to use as a bib, and his baby. They would carefully review the instructions he had been given before other feedings, make him answer questions, and then stand aside to critically watch his performance at a distance.

The nurses seemed to regard him with more than a little pity and took the responsibility of getting him off to a favorable start at single parenthood seriously. Attended by at least two at a time, he was impressed by their sincerity and skill. He'd been conditioned to women's hungry reactions and was habitually on the alert around any female he didn't know. With the nursery staff, his caution had proved unnecessary. Only one of the nurses had opened a conversation aside from baby topics, and that had been to argue, with some intelligence, a point of controversy in a political story he'd recently covered. Not one of them had done anything stupid—crammed a phone number into his pocket, offered him comfort in the wake of losing a wife. He was relieved he didn't have to brave carnivores to be near his child.

"Don't you worry, kid. What I can't accomplish with wit and know-how, I'll make up in enthusiasm."

Her eyes opened again, staring dreamily.

"There are lousy parents everywhere having kids for the wrong reasons, having kids when they don't even want them. All things considered, all the good and bad in the world, you could do worse. Don't you think?"

Her puffy lids closed once more. She wasn't worried.

A pint-sized Freida. Be stubborn as a mule.

Tomorrow, he would take her home. Tonight, he would give her a name, the hardest new-baby task he'd faced thus far. As he had so many times in the past, he'd call his mother.

"That one can't be yours. She's too cute."

He tensed, startled by the voice behind him, then turned and gave up one of his most inspired frowns. "Who says? The Sawbriar Princess?"

Beaming, she appeared to concentrate solely on the sleeping baby. Almost by reflex, Sam shifted his attention to Brenan. She made his stomach hurt, too.

Ain't love grand? Now, ya got two little girls to love.

"But I don't think she can hear you talking through the glass, or were you talking to yourself *again?* I understand they have a great psych ward here."

Embarrassed, he shrugged sheepishly. "I'm gonna put a bell around your neck."

"Oh, hush. What're you going to call her?"

"Funny you should ask. I'm having trouble with that very thing. I'm supposed to have my mind made up tonight. They say I'm holding up the paperwork. I'm open for suggestions." Sam felt a familiar, guilty wave of susceptibility to her nearness. He wished she was older. He wished she was the mother of his baby. His wishes were getting more daring.

Sixteen years old! Pack up the wishes, Hoss!

Brenan glared at him with patient indulgence, a look he might have expected from Freida. "Don't you plan for anything? You've had a while to think about names."

"I have, but I can't decide." Whenever he was this close to her, his mouth either locked up or developed verbal diarrhea. During the last seven months, she'd involved herself as much as he'd permitted in the building of his house. Frequent consultation between the two of them had been requisite. He was pleased with the way he'd dealt with this working, if somewhat tongue-tied, business relationship. Around her, he'd kept a lid on his feelings. Now that she'd talked him into letting her help take care of the baby for him to work, he was pelted by doubts. What if seeing her twice a day, four or five days a week proved to be more Brenan than he could handle?

ANY Brenan is more'n ya can handle. Handle her an' you'll need a lawyer or an undertaker.

"You see, the name's important," he said, trying to divert his thoughts. An edgy outpouring followed. "Got to be good, or she'll grow up hating it and have all sorts of complexes. If it's too common, she'll end up in kindergarten with seven other kids who have the same one. If it's weird or hard to pronounce or hard to spell—more problems. Can't be too cutesy or create goofy nicknames. No confusing boy-girl swap-ups—"

Pass the Charmin and the Pepto.

"Whoa. I agree. It has to be just right. But you haven't even narrowed it down to two or three favorites, have you?"

"Not exactly."

She shook her head.

"I first thought about naming her after someone in the family, but that's too much like a junior. She needs her own identity. She can have a middle name that's somebody else's and a first that's just hers. I considered geographical names. I like Britain and Brooklyn, but if she turns out to be chubby, the other kids might call her *Great* Britain or Brooklyn *Bridge*."

An' the Preparation H.

Brenan laughed her tinkling laugh that made Sam think of Christmas carols. She was making fun of him. "That's horrible. Men miss out on a lot of important stuff. Mothers should give their little boys baby dolls to play with. Teach them something useful early on—*before* they have to make decisions like this. Guess it's too late for you. What does Freida say?"

"'Samantha,' but I'm not naming my daughter after myself or a TV witch. She'll have to come up with something else."

Sam studied her as she quietly regarded his kid. If his parenting could produce a young girl with half Brenan's intelligence, vibrant personality, and simple beauty, he'd be one satisfied daddy.

Daddy! There's that word again!

He'd thought the word a thousand times. He'd even practiced saying it out loud to the mirror while brushing his hair. It splashed over him anew. It felt like ice water.

It's the sho-god truth! You, Ace, are that little girl's daddy! Listen to Ol' Lefty—both of ya are adventure bound!

For a moment, alarming visions took him away from Brenan.

"Sam, wake up."

"Sorry."

"How about 'Mariah?' I've sort of had it in mind for my mythical daughter-to-be. Girls do that—name their kids years before they're conceived."

"If I took Mariah, what would you name your kid-to-be?"

"I have plenty time to think of something else."

"Mariah's a nice name."

"Yeah. Remember that little girl who used to live with her grandmother in the house where the Brooks live now? Used to climb the fence to watch you and Robert with the horses. You called her Slick. Mariah's her real name. It's pretty. Not too common, and it goes well with Marissa. As first cousins only a little more than a year apart, they're bound to be close."

Sam smiled. "Mariah." He liked it. He remembered the little redhaired girl as a pest who asked too many questions and got dangerously in the way of the horses, much the way Brenan had, but the name had a nice sound. Comfortable. Feminine and capable of growing from infancy to womanhood. "Mariah. Yeah."

He hadn't planned to hug Brenan, but when he did, that felt right, too. "Works for me."

What the hell-o are you're doin'? Let go of her!

Brenan didn't seem to be as disturbed by his embrace as Lefty, so he let it linger, standing behind her, propping his bearded chin on her shoulder. Both of them visually trying the name on the baby.

Ace!

"You're on your own for a middle name," she said when he released her.

Sam saw something in the flashing of her dark eyes. Something warm but mysterious. Something he'd seen from time to time as she'd told him her troubles, asked his advice, given her opinion. If he could only interpret those eyes the way they had often read the thoughts behind his. This woman in a sixteen-year-old body touched emotions inside him no other woman had been able to reach. When she was close like this, he imagined a parallel reaction in her. An elevation in her body temperature. A trickle of perspiration down her spine. A throbbing of erotic desire that he alone could appease.

She's jailbait, an' if she's gonna keep hangin' 'round, helpin' build houses an' raise babies, ya'd do good ta remember it! Not just a kid—your best friend's little sister an' Big Bad Mark Armstrong's daughter. Dangerous waters, beware the undertow, old man! Besides, you're a daddy, an' it ain't a bit too soon to start actin' like one—responsible an' respectable.

Brenan was unlike any young girl he'd known. She was a geyser of ambition and talent. She had completed high school at the end of the fall semester and was already enrolled in an eclectic list of classes at the University of Alabama in Birmingham. Before next fall, she'd be a published author. By her account, she was nearing a midpoint on her second book. Sam didn't think her own family knew what to make of her, but he had an idea what they'd make of him if he crossed the line.

"Mama drove my car to her Overeaters Anonymous meeting. She's having her old Impala painted fire engine red, and of course, Daddy swears he'll die if anybody he knows sees her driving anything so gauche. I'm in his tank, so I'd better not stay long. He worries more about that

Caddy than he does me. I'm going to the mall tomorrow morning with the list Freida helped me make. Anything you want to add?"

He shook his head. Freida knew what was needed.

"Then I'll be back by noon."

"Great. I should be headed home with *Mariah* by two. That's if some blood test she's supposed to have in the morning comes back okay. Mark said they test all the babies for something in the liver that makes them turn yellow—or something like that."

"You nervous?"

"Petrified's more like it."

"You'll have lots of help."

He sighed. "I'll need it.

"I almost forgot. A. D. finished up the painting and varnishing this afternoon. He'll have the house aired out by the time you get there. My design prof came out. She flipped over everything, especially the fireplaces and the master bath. A. D.'s hired a Mrs. O'Neil, I think, to clean the ground floor tomorrow morning. If you like her, she's available for something regular. After checking her references and asking her a million questions, he's discovered they have common ancestry back in Ireland. So he's convinced she'll be honest and a good cook."

Freida will kill 'er.

Sam nodded. "Sounds like everything's coming together just in time."

"Give A. D. the credit. I swear he walks on water without getting his feet wet. He's got that shiftless indoor crew dancing to the beat—a miracle. Checks every job. If he's not satisfied, he makes them do it over while he watches. You know what a perfectionist he is. I can't wait for you to see the rockers and swings he's made for the porches. I don't know when he's had time to spend in his workshop."

"He is sort of amazing, isn't he?"

"Yeah. Well, I'd better get that car back."

"Thanks for what you're doing, Bren."

"Thank you for the work. I need to keep busy." She smiled, kissed him on the cheek, and ran her palms down the sides of his beard before walking down the corridor toward the elevators. He put his fingers on the spot her lips had touched and followed her with his eyes.

The spot felt warm.

She was beautiful in her retreat.

SAM CONTINUED to stare down the corridor.

Nurses and visitors opened and closed doors, the bustle that ushered in the end of evening visiting hours. A few stragglers stopped by for one last look at the babies. A giant in a felt Stetson, sharp-toed leather boots, form-fitting jeans, and a Crimson Tide sweatshirt painfully poked Sam's ribs and pointed. "My boy there. Nearly leb'm pounds. I'll have 'im passin' an' puntin' 'fore he's a year old. What ya wanna bet?"

Sam gestured with upheld hands that he had no doubts.

As the halls began to quieten, a tired looking young woman in a pink housecoat came out of a room and walked carefully, determinedly to the nursery window. She nodded shyly at Sam.

"That one's mine." She pointed a finger at a bassinet with a card reading *"Baby Boy Freeman."*

"Nice looking kid," Sam offered, charitably. "Big, too."

Not as big as the linebacker over there.

"Big like his father. Is one of these yours?"

"MacCauley. There in the middle."

"Oh, she's beautiful."

Tell us somethin' we don't awready know.

Sam smiled. "Thanks."

"You're that newsman—Channel Nine, right?"

An' a daddy. An' a pervert.

"Yeah."

"I like to see the people you help with *Nine Cares.*"

"Ah, one of the nicest parts of my work. Always a happy ending."

"You look taller on TV."

"Yeah?"

"That wasn't supposed to sound like criticism."

"It wasn't taken that way."

"I wish my baby's daddy was standing here looking proud and happy. He decided early on fatherhood wasn't for him. Took a job in Mobile."

Her sadness touched Sam. "Maybe you and your son will do better without him. I mean if he doesn't—"

"I know what you mean. It's just I wish he'd been, you know, different. It's real scary knowing I've gotta do this by myself, but lots of women do, don't they? This your first?"

He nodded.

"Her mother must be thrilled with such a lovely little girl."

"My wife's on another floor. She hasn't even seen the baby. Wants nothing to do with her. The baby's going home with me, but her mother's not."

Sam was surprised at his candor with this strange woman. Usually, he said as little as possible about his private life around people he didn't know.

The woman was silent for a moment then said, "Funny, isn't it, how some people just walk away from responsibility as if it isn't there."

"It's better to walk away than to stay and cause more harm. My wife isn't ready to be a mother, but she wants her child to have a good life."

"Your job may be harder than mine. For sure, both of us have our work cut out for us."

"Well, if we're able to help those little kids grow up to be decent human beings, the work won't be wasted."

"But can we do it?"

He didn't hesitate. "Sure we can. What other choices do we have? I guess we just have to go on reminding ourselves that, with love and determination, we can give them what they need. I'm scared, too, but I'm also looking forward to having her around. I'm tired of feeling alone."

The young woman laughed. "I'm glad I ran into you. I needed a new way to look at this single parent situation. Oh, look. They're closing the curtains. Feeding time."

WHEN SAM SCRUBBED, gowned, and presented himself for inspection, he was smiling. He could feel some of the frayed pieces of his life smoothing and coming together. He and his child were going to get along just fine.

"Go get your papers," he told the nurse who handed him the paper gown, "and write this down. Her name is Mariah Cathleen MacCauley." He spelled the names then proofread what the nurse had written. "That's it."

Cathleen. Brenan's middle name. She wouldn't care. She'd blame his maleness. After all, he'd never played with baby dolls—except for the couple of times he'd made Jackie's Betsy Wetsy pee her pants. He felt great, and when Mariah was given to him, he held her close to his heart for as long as the nurses would let him have her.

This powerful new passion made him feel as if he had crossed some invisible line from pseudo-adulthood into the real thing. His heart beat with a jolting force. Breathing Mariah's clean baby smell, he whispered her name so she would know. Afraid his beard would scratch her cheeks, he kissed only the top of her head, the tips of her fingers. His fingers trailed lightly over her face, memorizing its contour, its softness. When her hunger had been satisfied, she slept in his arms. She trusted him.

He'd shave the beard off as soon as he got home. He'd ask Freida to cut his hair. Drury would be beside himself with delight, and Sam would get a little closer to his baby.

He reluctantly gave her back to the routine of the nursery, exchanged farewells with Karen, and left to spend his last night in the apartment. Tomorrow night, he and Mariah would sleep in the new house that had grown up out of the fields his father used to plant in soy beans, a piece of Mrs. Meyers's old rattlesnake ranch six hundred yards from the farmhouse. Home.

As he entered the freeway, he thought about Karen. Severing herself from a child she had carried inside her body couldn't be as easy. Surely, many an hour had been spent wondering if she was giving up too much. Over the months, she'd lost much of her shallowness, become aware of her need to grow, to develop the strength to free herself from her past. She was looking to the future, caring what impact her actions made.

In the early hours of her labor, she'd conceded that she loved him.

"You've been better to me than anybody ever has. I'd have to be made of stone if I didn't. You've given me a better picture of myself." She'd told him he had taken care of her, helped break her out of the prison she'd lived in most of her life. Now, her foremost goal was to stand on her own feet. *"I'm ready to take charge of me—just me. I won't interfere with the baby."*

He hoped she'd meant it. He couldn't bear to think she might try to take Mariah back. He'd held her hand when the pains were hard and tearing, then he'd thanked her.

"I love you, too, Karen. Not the kind of love you deserve, but maybe someday, you'll find someone who can give you that."

"Maybe."

"Be good to yourself."

"Sure, Sam. Don't worry about me."

He had kissed her good-bye. If not for Brenan, he might have loved her more.

The freeway traffic was light, and he reached the empty apartment all too soon.

22

THE LONG, DULL WORK DAY before Sam's twenty-sixth birthday was peppered with minor annoyances. Drury had big-heartedly awarded him the next day off—a weekday miracle even for the personal holiday. A day off and a lecture.

Drury's address didn't come as a big surprise. Sam had heard it on other occasions of late. The topic: Pitfalls of Loneliness and Celibacy in Males of Sam's Precarious Stage of Manhood. According to Drury's predictions, without adequate female companionship, Sam could expect to be stricken by any number or combination of afflictions—from bad skin to male-pattern baldness, from impotence and prostate gland problems to jock itch and ingrown toenails.

"Go to hell, Andy."

"See? It's already made you cranky."

If he hadn't known better, Sam might have felt Drury was sincere, but the subject was beginning to be routine and boring, little more than a shabby guise for Drury's everlasting efforts to team Sam up with Marcia Townly. Matchmakers were despicable.

Marcia, a plump, brazen, red-haired vixen whose unstable temperament and alley-cat morals were common gossip fodder in the newsroom, had set her claws for Sam as soon as they'd been introduced. The fact that she was Drury's wife's sister made Sam's refusal to see her socially a sore spot. However, at the risk of further offense, he held his position — not that his firmly restated "I don't think so" checked Drury's efforts.

"Dinner at *Leo's* on me?" Andy tried one last time as Sam sidled past on his way out. "Lobster? Anything on the menu?"

Look, man, he shaved off the beard an' cut his hair. Now, ya expect 'im to take the edge off your sister-in-law's man-craving. Lefty made Sam grin. *Ya don't pay 'im enough for him to buy what he ain't in the market for! Try Under Dog Garner, pride of the newsroom. Divorced times three. Lives with his mama and twenty-nine cats. Bet he'll jump anything that moves an' some things that don't!*

"Naw, Andy. Give it up. I'm going home to my kid. She's the girl for me tonight."

"Maybe if you take her out once and act like a jerk, she'll leave us both alone."

"Forget it. Not in my contract."

"Wait'll you want a favor from me."

"Bye-bye." Sam waved and blew a kiss.

With deplorable regularity, he turned down offers. High school all over again. The phone calls, the flirting, the smell of lust in the air. The fact that his divorce was but days old in its finality or that every spare moment was spent in the company of his infant daughter didn't check the hyenas. They came in salivating packs. But after years of practice, he'd learned a trick or two. He was polite but unyielding. *"Sorry, no. Prior commitments. No, it's not you—it's me. Better luck with someone else."*

Be simpler to tell 'em you're a perverted sonofabitch who's all hot an' horny for your less-than-nubile baby-sitter.

Sam jogged to his car. Marcia was a minor irritation next to his real problem.

In his role as Sam's conscience, Lefty was right on the money. Brenan, the forbidden fruit, had become an obsession. He thought about her when he was awake and dreamed about her in his sleep. Passing thoughts to daydreams to full-blown fantasies.

She stayed with Mariah four afternoons and evenings each week, took classes at the University in the mornings, and worked on her second novel when she found time. Always in possession of more energy than she could spend, the pace hardly challenged her.

Sam had turned the solarium off the family room into a sunny office, so she could work without leaving the baby unattended. On the surface, everything appeared perfectly smooth. Underneath the calm, something spooky was happening. Going home at night was becoming an unsettling affair.

The undertow.

For a while, the arrangement had worked. Mariah and Brenan had made the big house a home. Sam half-expected to walk through the door some night and be greeted by a declaration of abiding love. Half-expected an adamant Brenan to fly into his arms and demand the charade be dropped. *"We both know this is wrong. You come in and I leave. I'm supposed to stay. This is our house, our place. Do you think I ordered that huge custom-made bed for you to sleep in alone or that I'd spend so much time with a child who isn't mine? Haven't I always belonged with you?"* He'd seen her hold his baby girl as tenderly as any mother, her face glowing with love. This fantasy had thrived until only days ago.

Brenan had changed. She'd grown too quiet, too pensive. Her smiling effervescence had gone flat. When they spoke, her eyes looked at anything but him. Something had gone awry. "What happened?" he'd asked himself time and again.

Sam MacCauley happened. She's on to ya.

Only one answer made sense. She knew his infatuation, his preoccupation, his shame. He could see radiant flecks of his disgraceful secret dancing in her eyes. His betrayal of their friendship had aroused in her a wariness. She regarded him suspiciously, mentally preparing to defend herself. What else but discovery and fear could have caused the pregnant silence? She had no way of knowing he'd cut off his own fingers before he'd let them harm her. He would gladly go to his grave in her defense. That was the way love worked.

Hey, Don Quixote, ain't ya takin' the selfless hero delusions a mite far?

"I guess. What can I do?"

Honesty might be a nice change.

"It's possible she's worried about something that has nothing to do with me."

Ask her, but be prepared to bid her a gracious adieu. If by some quirk of fate it's somethin' other than your black-hearted perversion, she might could use some of your nobility an' heroism. Wouldn't that be a hoot?

"I don't want to hurt her." The idea of not coming home to her at night was hateful, but he loathed her sadness even more.

An' what if you awready have?

"Okay, I'll ask. But if it's me, I'm gonna deny everything. I'll tell her she misunderstood and assure her my feelings are no different than they've always been."

Did ya forget, Big Brother?

"What?"

Ya couldn't lie if your life depended on it. Only lies ya ever get away with are the ones ya tell yourself. An' when I'm keepin' score, they don't count.

HUMMING SOFTLY, "Brahm's Lullaby" fading into something elusive and dirge-like she'd heard Sam play on his guitar, Brenan backed away from the crib. After a bath and a bottle, the baby slept soundly on her stomach, her head turned to the side, one cheek flattened against the mattress, her mouth opened and bowed by the position. Her padded butt thrust upward with two incredibly tiny bootied feet sticking out.

For a quarter hour, before finally slipping away to wait for Sam, Brenan had hovered above the sleeping infant. She saw pieces of Sam in every cherubic facial twitch, every small, quick breath. She wondered when Mariah had, for her, stopped being Sam's and Karen's and become only Sam's. When had a creeping love for this tiny person invaded her heart and took its place next to her love for the father? When had Karen ceased to matter? The answers that came to her were no more solid than wisps of smoke, but her two loves were beginning to take their tolls. Her days and nights had evolved into one long and enduring illusion in which this house was her home, the man who lived here her lover, and the baby in the crib her own child.

She couldn't remember a time when she hadn't been in love with Sam. He was a secret she had long kept in her heart, a secret that screamed to be let out. Only Ellen knew. Brenan had first confided her feelings to her mother at the age of eleven and had echoed it during dozens of mother-daughter discussions thereafter. Labeling it "a crush" and "puppy love", Ellen hadn't been overly judgmental, but Brenan had slacked off talking to her. The emotion had become well-defined and potent. Ellen might not understand, now—because now Brenan needed more than daydreams. Her need had become a woman's. It was physically and emotionally unrelenting, and it was driving her crazy.

Get hold of yourself, Bren, she thought, *You're still here. He hasn't told you to get lost, yet. In a couple of hours, he'll walk in and make your heart do somersaults. If you're lucky, he'll have a joke for you, or he'll tell you a little about his day. Then you'll go home and cry on your pillow like the lovesick schoolgirl you are.*

In the family room, she put a ten-year-old Kristofferson album on the stereo — *Border Lord,* one of Sam's favorites — and stretched out on the floor. The music was depressingly fitting for her mood. Too fitting. After a couple of minutes of the weary voice and heavy lyrics, she was more downhearted than ever. Sighing, she lay on her back and stared up at the balustrade of the upstairs landing. She'd always been the oddball, the misfit, the overachiever who was resented and snubbed. Without giving her a chance, people felt threatened and backed away. She'd been thirteen before she'd had the first true female friend. Because of Sam's understanding and attentiveness, the loneliness had been bearable. *Oh, Ace, why is loving you wrong, now? It used to be the safest thing in the world.* The soulful music cast a hypnotic spell that grayed the room to velvety black.

WHEN SHE WOKE UP, the phonograph needle was spinning with a rhythmic thump against the album label, and Sam was kneeling at her side. As his face came into a startling clear focus, she struggled for composure, ran her hand over her mouth. She came up on an elbow and worked her hair back with her fingers.

"Sorry," she whispered, embarrassed.

He smiled, straightened, held out a hand. She let him pull her to her feet. She wished she could draw the hand close to her body, but as soon as she had her balance, she let it go.

He leveled his eyes at her, and his face broke. The crow's feet at the corners of his eyes crinkled. The lines that ran from below his temples nearly to his chin cut smooth gashes, giving him an older, wiser visage. His habitual squint tightened to hide the blue of his irises. Taking a step back, he watched without words while she returned the album to its jacket.

She drew a deep breath and met his gaze. Usually, he viewed her as an actress on a stage. He applauded her, laughed, and teased without making fun or talking down to her. Today, his amusement looked artificial, his smile a sham.

She began her usual recounting of what had taken place during his absence. She'd covered many an awkward moment with a carefully channeled flood of words, and thus, she'd get through this one. "Took Mariah for her appointment at Olan Mills. She wasn't interested in posing, but I think we got a smile. Some woman named Marcia called— message by the kitchen phone. A. D. brought a truckload of food. Your mother had a fight with an encyclopedia salesman, so she's cooking with a vengeance."

"That all?" The fake smile had come undone a little.

She studied him for some sign. A sign of what she didn't exactly know. She was certain her growing anxiety showed. "Yeah, I think so." She walked around aimlessly looking for her things, a headless chicken routine that served to make her more nervous still. "Most of it, anyway. Except, um—" She found her notebook and her jacket, but instead of saying good-bye and heading home, she decided to do some minor prying. "That Marcia person wanted you to call her back tonight. She said something about helping you celebrate your birthday."

"The only Marcia-celebration I'll ever be a part of is the one that goes with her finding someone else to harass. She has a problem understand- ing how I really feel, but she'll catch on eventually. I hope she didn't say anything to offend you."

"She asked a few questions. I think she wanted to make sure I wasn't competition, so I told her I wasn't your wife, mistress, or girlfriend. I may have been a little rude, but I don't usually give my life history to strangers over the phone."

"I'm sorry. Looks like I'm going to have to work a little harder at getting rid of her."

"No big deal. Whatever your plans, have a nice birthday."

"Thanks. A day with my kid and supper with my folks is about all the celebrating I'm up to. Are you in a hurry? I think we should talk."

"All right." *Here it comes,* she thought. *He knows. I must be as see-through as a picture window.* She couldn't do this. She needed time to prepare. No man would want a love-struck kid taking care of his daughter. He wouldn't laugh at her behind her back or make fun of her to his friends. He'd take her feelings seriously, and in the name of decency, he would feel the need to draw a line. A line of separation. Why hadn't she seen it coming? What would her life be like without him?

"Why don't you sit down?" he said softly. After she'd taken a seat, he stuffed his hands into his pockets and moved slowly about the room. "What's up? You seem different."

"Different?"

"Depressed, unhappy. I don't know what, but it bothers me."

"I see." Why didn't he stand still?

"Is the work getting to you?"

"Of course not."

"Am I?"

Her mouth was suddenly dry. "I don't understand."

"I think you do."

Her shrug of ignorance temporarily stopped his pacing. He stood in front of her, looking down into her face. When had he first read her heart? What could she say? "No, really. Nothing's wrong. I'm fine."

"Our families have been close-knit for longer than I can remember— more one family than two. I wouldn't intentionally jeopardize that relationship."

"Nor would I."

"You're a very attractive young woman. I'd have to be blind not to notice, but if I've done anything that made you uneasy around me, I didn't mean to." Sighing, he looked away. "I care about you, but I wouldn't come on to you or anything like that."

She looked at her hands, turned her class ring around her finger. The ring she'd earned two-and-a-half years earlier than the kids who'd been her classmates in kindergarten was an emblem of her singularity and aloneness. Would slumber parties and phone pranks have made a difference? Double dates and rock 'n roll? Had she skipped over too many normal adolescent steps? How could she reply? She couldn't blurt out the truth. She couldn't say she wished he *would* make a pass at her, that she'd jump into his arms quicker than he could blink his eyes. She decided to be defensive. "I never thought you might."

"I just want to make sure I haven't given you a wrong impression."

"I've spent half my life alone with you. In the woods, everywhere. Once I heard Daddy say he'd have to put a stop to my running wild if I didn't have you to watch over me. Besides, I'd let you know in a hurry if you were being a perv."

He sighed. A sound of relief. "You're not a child, anymore. I thought—What is wrong? I'm not just imagining things, am I?" He stopped a few feet away and sat on the edge of the coffee table opposite her.

She tried another innocent shrug.

"I don't mean to pry, Bren. If you're okay, tell me."

Her heart felt heavy and strained. An old windup clock, its pumping was loud and distracting. How could she explain? "Are you worried about how my emotional slump is affecting Mariah? I'm not down around her. She's—"

"I'm not worried about the baby. It would be hard for me to trust someone else with her. It's just . . . suddenly you're not happy."

She ducked her head. If he had already given thought to replacing her, what did she have to lose by confirming his suspicions? "You wouldn't want to hear it."

"Troubles have a way of getting better when they're out in the open. The designated listener doesn't have to be me."

She nodded, a combination nod and shrug. "Yes, it does."

He sat on the coffee table facing her, but her eyes deflected. She couldn't meet his anymore.

"Bren—"

"It's not your fault."

"But, it *is* me?"

"Not anything you've done." She chanced looking at him again—not solidly, but glancing away then letting her eyes flit back. He was staring openly, his bottom lip between his teeth.

"I'm scared of losing something I'm not ready to give up—something that's never been mine—except in my heart."

He released the lip and said, "That sounds serious."

She felt tears welling. She shook her head. She often caught him watching her with a new expression, a new tenderness in his eyes that she pretended was all hers. Pretending helped keep her little girl dreams of happily-ever-after alive. It had been a long time since she'd been a little girl in his presence. He respected her opinions and treated her as an equal. He loved and protected her. Miles from being *in love* with her, maybe, but as long as there was a small chance she was wrong, she'd pretend. The tender look was in his eyes now.

"Don't you know?" She was a crier. Before her question was out, she had to bring her hands to her face to hide tears. Without seeing him move, she felt him kneel in front of her chair. He was wheezing.

"Tell me."

She dropped her hands. Keeping her tears hidden didn't seem important next to his fearful confusion. Taking the wad of tissue he'd pulled from a dispenser on the coffee table, she blew her nose. "You're my best friend—the only person who halfway understands me." She cleared her throat. "Then there's Mariah. I didn't know I'd feel so close to her. I want to be with her, and I want to help finish the house. I don't want things to change. Not *these* things. But they will."

"Brenan—"

Her hands came back over her face.

"All right! Everybody thinks something's wrong with me because I hate being sixteen. The few friends I have give me a hard time. They ask questions I can't answer. Won't let it rest. They expect me to be like them. Daddy tries to make dates for me with the sons of other doctors.

They all tell me to go out, have fun, enjoy my youth. Now, you. Is it unfair to everybody else that I can't be Gidget? If it is, I can't do anything about it. I can't care about the boys who ask me out. I can't because they're not you!"

There, she'd said it. His face froze.

"I can't help what I feel! It's been this way all my life! It's not going to get better! It's not going to go away! I do everything I can think of to find reasons to be near you. I always have. I'm sorry!" Now, she'd finished, and there was nothing but silence in the air around her.

He was still on his knees in front of her. Close enough to touch. His breathing was loud and harsh, but his strong, handsome face was unmoving, his expression bland and unreadable. His eyes, still fixed on her face, seemed at first to have stopped blinking—then they began to blink too rapidly. His mouth opened—then closed.

Too bewildered to cry, she stared back. Her love for him had evolved and grown as she had grown. During all that time, the love had been *her* property. Hers alone. He had to give her something in exchange for her confession. Rejection. Comfort. Pity. *Something.*

He swallowed, his respirations gradually quieting. His eyelids narrowed to thin gashes that concealed any information his eyes might have given. Gradually, a corner of his mouth quivered, twitched into a slight upward curve. A tiny smile. He listlessly shook his head. When his fingers came up to trail lightly down the sides of her face, they were trembling.

Tears ran down her cheeks. His thumbs whisked them away.

When he spoke his voice was low and hoarse. "Don't cry."

When his eyes widened, she found the tenderness she had seen so many times. It *was* hers.

When his shaking fingers began to weave through her hair, she realized something wonderful was happening.

When he opened his arms, she leaned into them. His body trembled with the same force as his hands.

When he kissed her, she knew she wasn't going to lose anything. She was going to have everything she wanted.

23

*A*CE! STARTLED, SAM JERKED AWAY. As if to deny the kiss, one hand clapped over his mouth. Yet, a symbol of his emotional upheaval, the other hand refused to unwind itself from her hair. What had she told him? He'd heard her words. Could he take them at face value? She looked so young and innocent.

Forget ever'thing I ever said, Ace! I wuz wrong! ME—the School of Decency hall monitor! Stop analyzin' an' start listenin' with your heart!

"Bren, I—"

Wide-eyed and unmoving, she waited for him to go on.

"I'm sorry. I promised I wouldn't—" he stammered.

No, you're not! You're not sorry!

"I don't want you to be sorry."

"If you mean what you just said, I—"

"I do!"

Can't ya see she does?

"I've been living with a secret that I'm not very proud of. I shouldn't feel—um—my feelings keep getting harder to hide, and when you started acting so weird, I thought you knew."

"Feelings?"

"I know about fear. I don't want you to be afraid of me."

"Tell me about your feelings!"

"You're too young, I can't—"

"You have to!"

Tell her!

"I'm in love with you, Bren." He finally freed his hand from her hair and tucked it into the other one between his knees. "I've tried to get over you. I've tried!"

"You love me?" Tears poured in continuous streams.

Yes!

"Yes."

"And you're ashamed of it?"

"Yes—no—I was. I've been terrified."

"I'm not afraid. Not now."

Dr. Mark will put the fear into ya! Pro'bly put a great big scalpel through Sam!

"You've never been afraid of anything."

"Oh, yes. That you'd send me away. That you wouldn't—."

He handed her more tissue. "I couldn't send you away."

"So, it's okay—how we feel?"

Love at your own risk!

"Some people won't like it. Your parents. Mine."

"Mama knows."

Uh, oh!

"What does she say?"

"She saw it a long time ago, and she knows she can't do anything about it. It's hard for her to decide how she feels. She thinks you're one of her kids. I haven't mentioned it to her lately, so I hope she's still open-minded."

"What about your daddy?"

"He doesn't know."

"I can't see him approving. He never sees the other guy's point of view. And he always gets his way."

"Not with me. Anyway, I don't care about Daddy's approval. All that matters is how you feel."

"What are we gonna do?"

She shrugged. "You could tell me again."

Yeah! Loud an' clear!

His face blazed as he finally gave voice to his heart's words. "You're the first, the only girl I've ever loved."

"Why didn't I know?"

"Why didn't I?" He took her hands and held them. They were cold. He studied her closely bitten nails. "Are you sure what you're feeling is going to last?"

"It's lasted for as long as I can remember. You've been the center of every dream I've ever had. Good dreams. Until lately, I could handle them because I knew they were only dreams. Then when Karen left, I started hoping that one day you'd look at me. Every time I come here, I let myself pretend I'm home, and I keep right on hoping. After a while, hoping starts to hurt."

She dreams your dreams. The very same ones.

"I want you to live here, too, Bren."

Ya beat all, Ace. She's just waitin' for ya to kiss her again. Seems to me it's all right now.

August 1982

"IT ALWAYS COMES back when I get stressed out. I don't mean to act so weird, but it makes me feel—I dunno—helpless. You need to know what you're getting into."

"You haven't told me much I didn't know. I'm used to your weird stuff. Remember all the lectures? I answered to you for more things than I did to Daddy. You're the strict one, but you were fair and always answered my questions. I've run my fingers over the scars on your hands so often, I could draw them from memory. Don't worry—I'm getting what I want, and I'll do whatever I can to make things easier for you."

"Then you really should stop touching me there. You're making it hard."

"Why do you think I do it?"

"What I mean was you're making it *hard* to be *good.*"

"I don't see why we have to wait. I thought the guy was supposed to be the one who puts the pressure on."

"We can't because your daddy will ask, and our already iffy chances of winning him over will bottom out. I can't lie. He'd know, then we'd have to wait forever; I'd be castrated."

"Then let's tell him."

"Saturday. We'll do it this weekend like we planned. In the meantime, if you don't cut that out, we're going to have another sticky situation."

"GIVE IT A REST, Lefty. I'm tired, and I want to sleep."

Doctor Mark's gonna murder ya! MARK my word—I always enjoy a little pun. Pat it, prick it, an' MARK it with 'B'—dead meat, that's what you'll be. The pun's over, Ace. Ya seen the look on your own daddy's face? Ya heard what HE said?

"I heard."

"Son, pa-leeze tell me ya ain't doin' Mark Armstrong's little girl!" Ouch! Hurts when they have s'much confidence in ya. Don't it?

"I guess after some of the things I've done, he doesn't expect any better, but we talked. He's okay. He's known all along she's the one. I guess he thought it would fizzle."

That pure an' chaste business was a hard sell. Ya ain't got much of a pants-on reputation with females.

"Oh, dry up. A. D.'s thrilled to have outguessed Ma this one time. She didn't seem too disturbed. Besides, we've used up an entire summer trying to think of the least painful way. We've kept everybody in the dark mainly because I'm too chicken to stand up to Mark Armstrong. I've kept Brenan quiet as long as I can. I'm tired of waiting, too. I want to be married to her."

Well, your gonads won't be worth grits when the dissecting's over. An' your mama just don't show it, Hoss. She don't whimper an' break out in a cold sweat like normal people. Headed straight for the kitchen. Cooked till ya can't see over the piles of food. She's prob'ly out now, lookin' for Coxie's Army so she can feed 'em. Oh, boy, she took it real well.

"Nobody needs to worry. I haven't laid one carnal finger on Brenan. I can't say the same for her, but I've been good."

We'll see who believes THAT. Get a notebook to keep score.

"They've trusted me with her all her life. It'll just take some getting used to the fact she's not a child, anymore."

Her birth certificate says she is.

"Oh, get lost."

Ya scare me, Ace.

"What do you mean?"

I hope ya appreciate how hard I work. As sure as dirt, keepin' ya straight is work. Ya forced yourself to do without real love way too long. Told yourself over an' over how undeservin' ya was. Ya ain't changed. If ya had, you'd never've spent three months hidin'. When ya start believin' ya deserve her, you'll have a much better chance showin' the others.

"I'll show them."

Ya just might. Ya showed me.

"Thank you. Now go away!"

Ace!

"If you don't mind, I'd like to sleep and try to build up some energy reserves. Brenan's telling her Daddy her love story tonight, so tomorrow's my turn. You're right about him. I don't think he's gonna be nice at all. So, please, be a good whatever you are, and get lost!"

Sure, Ace, but don't be rude. I got feelin's, too. One a these days, you'll wake up alone an' wonder what happened to Ol' Lefty. Bet on it. Ya gonna miss me when I'm gone.

"You want to test that theory tonight?"

REMIND HIM IT AIN'T polite to murder a man in his own home.

"You should calm down enough to realize what you're saying." As practiced, he kept his voice low and even. He'd tried to be prepared, but he was standing in quicksand with nothing to grab onto if he started to sink. He wasn't sure a mere mortal could hold his ground in a confrontation with this iron man. For protection, Sam had recovered his infant daughter from her crib. She slept, softly snoring, while he held her at chest level.

She ain't big enough to save all your vital organs.

"I'll have you know I'm perfectly calm and well aware of what I'm saying. You're the one who needs to rethink his position." Mark's eyes twitched. He was as far from calm as Sam had ever seen him. "My daughter is not of a marriageable age. She won't be for quite some time, and that, my dear boy, is *that*. Now if you want to talk about another subject, I'll listen."

"Oh, Mark. I hope you don't expect me to give up or go away." Sam sat down in an ornate oak rocker Freida had bought for a song at an estate auction. Mariah had developed an avid, and often loudly proclaimed, passion for motion, so Sam and Brenan had logged an impressive number of hours in the rocker. He hugged her tightly.

Deep breath. That's it. Let it out slow. Ya start wheezin', ya won't get a word in sideways. Be dead in the water. A floater. A belly-up guppy. Keep that baby in front of ya. Even Dr. Mark wouldn't hit a little girl.

"Please, let me explain."

"Explain what? You *think* you're in love with her. She *thinks* she's in love with you. You're both stark raving insane!"

Even though he wasn't a big man, Mark made a room look smaller. Sam's family room was spacious. Most of the furniture was grouped in an intimate semicircle around a large fireplace and a fieldstone hearth that rose eighteen inches above the floor. Except for a strewing of blue, ivory, and rose area rugs, a few tables laden with houseplants, a coat rack, and an enormous old upright piano, a considerable expanse of hardwood floor space was free from clutter.

Sam glanced around the room to avoid looking at mark. The room was two stories high with a view of the balustrade that fenced the upper landing and hallways and brightened by a quartet of skylights. The second story was accessed by a wide, straight staircase. The family room opened to the morning room, the dining room and foyer, the alcove outside the master bedroom where Mariah's nursery had been set up, and the solarium that aspired to be Brenan's office. Sam loved this room, the rustic wooden heart of the house, as he loved every feature and facet. Brenan, only a few years past Lincoln Logs and Tinker Toys, had helped build it. He wanted her to live in it with him.

He gazed up at a man he regarded as a backup father, a man who had been privy to Sam's most personal and painful secrets as well as his triumphs. He wanted to believe if he was patient and persistent, Mark would come around. Brenan's happiness was at stake. Sam, though only a rookie parent, was beginning to realize how much a daughter could change a man's point of view.

Laterally and vertically, as Mark paced erratic pathways around chairs, tables, and the C-shaped sectional sofa, he filled the whole place.

"Mark, please listen—"

"I don't have time for this right now. Even on the weekend, I have patients I can't trust to that flighty resident, Simpson, so I have to go to the hospital. I'll tell you what," he said condescendingly, "if your father will arbitrate, we'll schedule a meeting at my house for, say, three o'clock. I'm only agreeing to this because you are the son of a friend. I'll give A. D. a call from the hospital. We'll put our cards on the table and all that malarkey. I'll say 'keep your paws off my child.' *Then* the subject will be closed."

Sam nodded. He was in no position to refuse Mark's crumbs.

"She said you haven't done anything to her."

"I haven't."

Mark gave a smug, dry grin and saw himself to one of the two sets of double glass doors that opened onto the back porch.

Good. We'll have nearly three hours to prepare our case. We'll subpoena Dr. Joyce Brothers an' Abigail Van Buren to testify on behalf of true love. Dr. Ruth an' A. D. can explain human nature and urges. An' we'll need character witnesses . . .

"I'll see you then." Mark opened one of the doors then angled back around. "And, Sam, lose the baby. She's not winning points for you. And be forewarned, if I find out you've been anything more than a friend to Brenan, that baby won't save you. The United States Marine Corps won't save you. Understand that?"

Sam nodded again.

24

MARK'S STUDY OFFERED no hiding place, so Sam parked in the open on the armrest of the leather-upholstered chair his father had taken.

A. D. nodded politely, a gesture of artificial formality, as always his sense of humor keen and untiring. If Mark decided to be mean, Sam hoped A. D.'s presence would serve as a buffer. He had no idea why his father had been chosen to referee, but since he was here, Sam hoped he was going to be an ally. A son pitted against a treasured friend—who had the home field advantage?

There could be no backing down, no weakness showing. He had to be forthright, force Mark to see. Before leaving home, he had fortified himself with a stiff dose of theophylline. The drug had made him even more jittery, but if necessary, he'd sit on his hands to keep them still. He had to gain Mark's sanction, assure him that *No* with a capital *N*——one of Mark's personalized negatives—or no spelled any other way was the wrong answer.

Brenan, with Mariah in her arms, appeared in the doorway. The baby was kicking happily and drooling down Brenan's arm. Both seemed to beam pleading expressions that conveyed a powerful message: *"Don't goof up after we've made it this far!"* His life minus either one of them would be no life. Brenan wiggled her fingers, then she and the baby vanished down the hall.

Tucking his shaky hands into his armpits, Sam waited. A. D. discharged a loud, drawn-out sigh. Lefty was quiet, too cowed by the formality of the ordeal to spread his usual ceremonious hell.

Mark came into the office then leaned back through the doorway into the hall. He looked both ways as if checking for spies, then he shut the door. When he boosted himself backward to perch on the edge of his desk, his feet swayed ten or twelve inches above the floor. A little shorter than A. D.'s five feet, ten inches, Mark was stoutly put together. He could give the illusion of great size and strength when he chose to do so. Sam, who had once been the smallest kid in his class, had rallied until he topped off a quarter of an inch short of six feet, but in this room, size wasn't measured in feet and inches.

A family practice physician, Mark had the ability to command, empathize, teach, and gracefully accept the adoration of his patients. He'd developed an impressive following, but the good doctor had a dark side. Most of his life Sam had heard wild and comic accounts of Mark's dictatorial tirades on the staff of Northside Community Medical Center. Dr. *Adolph* Armstrong. His adeptness at getting his desires met by the quickest, most efficient, most ruthless of means had earned him a variety of behind-the-back nicknames. If he knew or was concerned about his notoriety, he kept it to himself. He'd commanded one and all under his dominion for twenty-two years, and thus far, he'd given no indication of relenting. He effectively kept his patients happy and the hospital staff muttering under its breath.

Until now, Sam had been one of the chosen few on Mark's good humor list. He hoped he wasn't about to be permanently ousted.

Mark sat breathing heavily and dangling his feet. A. D. mumbled something that sounded like "*oh, boy.*" No one seemed anxious to get the interrogation underway. Finally, Sam caught the gaze of Mark's blue-black eyes and declared, "I'm ready!"

Mark scowled, "This isn't an amicable gathering of friends. You are the enemy! You're supposed to be on the defense, and I'd appreciate you remembering that. Now, you may begin by telling me what in blazes you think you're doing with my daughter."

"I told you. I'm going to marry her," ventured Sam. Still pleasant, with a mere ghost of a crack in his voice. He heard a distinct intake of air from the chair.

"And I've already told *you*—you'd need my signature, and since I have no intention of signing anything, you are wasting your time and mine." Mark's eyes flashed, Satan-like.

Sam remained outwardly unruffled. "I think you will."

"You're a long way from changing my mind."

"If I don't, Brenan will. Her happiness is important."

"And just how is she going to do it? By asking her mother to take her to a doctor for help in deciding what kind of birth control suits her? That's precisely what she's done."

Sam felt an involuntary warmth spreading up his neck. Disconcertion still had a way of turning him a glaring neon red, making a fight for composure more troublesome. He couldn't afford to squirm and talk in circles today. He had to radiate confidence and unwavering conviction. He swallowed back cowardice and said, "In light of everything, that's appropriate."

Mark jumped down and stood in front of the chair. Hands balled into fists, arms locked at his sides, he looked ferocious. "You said you weren't having sex with her! You *swore!*"

"I'm not." Sam despised being called a liar, and by his count, Mark had questioned this truth twice today. "But I didn't say that was a permanent arrangement. She's going to be my wife. Wouldn't you agree she should see a gynecologist beforehand? I believe Ellen made the suggestion, and I think it's a good one."

Mark had begun pacing a short trek in front of Sam and A. D. He halted only long enough to frown and eject. "Oh, you and Brenan think Ellen's already gathering up wedding cake recipes, but she's not rooted in your garden, yet! All she wants is to keep in Brenan's good graces. Teenagers are difficult. She knows we're *only* parents. We're not in the best of positions here, and I certainly don't appreciate you creating this situation!"

"I understand your concern, but you won't try to see things the way Brenan and I do. I'd say we're the ones facing pretty awesome odds, but our love's real. No matter how stubborn and unbending you are, it's not going to blow over."

"She's only sixteen! Let me remind you there are statutory rape laws in Alabama."

Sam chose to ignore that. People liked to threaten statutory rape, even when they had no true concept of the law. "Let's get back to Brenan. Why can't we talk about her in terms of her intellect, her maturity, her accomplishments—not her age? She wrote a book! She designed my house! Does that sound like the resumé of a child?"

Mark halted again, his lips set in a dangerous-looking line. "For crying out loud, what difference does any of that make? She's still in her first year of college. Never even dated the same boy more than twice. What does she know about commitment?"

"Not one of us could keep her from going on with her education. She's academia personified, so drop that excuse. You could talk to her about why, when she got old enough to date, she wasn't too thrilled about it? Let her tell the whole story this time. Teenaged boys aren't even close to her mentally. She's told you how disgusting it is to have to fight off those obnoxious little score-card keepers? For her sake, listen!"

Mark sneered and waved his arms wildly. "Oh, she hit me with all that garbage. She's been madly in love with you since she was three months old."

"I don't think it's been that long, but it's been long enough for you to take her seriously."

"Oh, now you want to tell me about parenting! You have *weeks*—*months* of experience being a father!"

A. D. watched the words volley back and forth between his son and his friend. He looked like he'd rather be stranded in the Mojave. Sam still wondered why Mark had invited him to be on the sidelines. The support of an old friend? A witness to anticipated violence? Whatever the reason, he nearly startled Sam off the arm of the chair when he suddenly spoke up.

"Sam?"

"What?"

"Why not explain why you an' Bren are in a hurry to marry."

Sam pitched back a why-don't-you-stay-out-of-this look.

"Well, son, you gotta admit it's a tad on the abrupt side."

"An understatement, if I ever heard one," Mark added. He returned to his desk perch. "Start at the beginning and tell me everything. It won't change my mind, but I'll listen."

"Aw, Mark. We went through all of it this morning."

Mark took a small, wicked-looking knife out of his pocket and began cleaning his nails. "I think I missed something."

"Be realistic. You know we want to be together. There's nothing difficult to understand, but if you need help with it, A. D. is great at explaining human urges. If you have confidence in him, you'll see it's okay for us—-*any of us*—to have them. And, let me assure you, Brenan and I have them, and it's getting harder by the hour to do the honorable thing."

"I couldn't care less about your urges. We're talking about my daughter."

"Okay, I didn't want to do this, but Ellen was seventeen when you married her. Don't give me a song-and-dance about how women were expected to marry earlier, how they were more mature back then. I doubt if she was more mature. And I feel justified in asking—*after all you've asked me*—did you wait until the wedding? Deny yourselves? Did you wait because you didn't want to lose the respect and support of your families? Or did you sneak around until you got caught?"

Both Mark and A. D. visibly stiffened.

"Wait a minute here—"

Sam cut Mark off. "I don't expect you to answer. I just want you to think. Brenan and I need our families. We want you to be on our side, and we've talked this to death, trying to figure out the best way to gain your blessings—not cause pain or destroy friendships and family harmony. We knew her age was going to a big factor. All we could come up with was to be honest, and that's what we've done!"

Mark's chest sunk in, his bloated superiority deflated. His voice was low and icy. "Since you know how old Ellen was when we were married, then you must know she was pregnant. She became a mother when she should have been a high school senior. She couldn't go to school that year because pregnant students were not allowed. She finished high school the following year while her mother took care of Robert. I was just out of medical school and went straight into my residency earning nearly nothing. We lived in a two-room garage apartment on Southside until Robert was four—just to keep from having to live with her parents.

"I know you have a nice house, and financially you're probably in fair shape. But you have a baby and a divorce the ink hasn't dried on. And I'm not convinced your ex-wife isn't going to decide she wants that baby back. She didn't seem very stable to me. Both you and Brenan are starting careers that require devotion to succeed. You look at my point of view now!"

"My kid's not an issue in this."

"The hell she's not! Brenan sees herself as her mother!"

"It's a good thing, too, because she had to bypass a lot of resentment to get over Mariah coming from Karen. When she offered to help, she was doing it for me. The emotional ties came later. She loved me *first,* so I think it's great she and Mariah like each other."

Mark's face settled into a tired mask. He was used to having his way, no opposition, no struggle, no questions. "Sam."

"Wait one more minute, Mark." Sam shot A. D. an apologetic expression. "A couple more things, then I'll be through. I hate to use the fact that *your* son has been having sex with my sister since *she* was sixteen, maybe even earlier, or that she, too, was a pregnant bride, but I will— because you seem much more concerned about *your* daughter who hasn't been seduced by your best friend's son—the shoe's on the other foot kind of thing.

"Still, Robert and Jackie are happy. They were meant for each other. You and Ellen seem happy. I don't know how to prove I can be trusted, that I love her as much as I say I do. All I can do is remind you that you know me. You know the mistakes I've made and how I've dealt with them. Nothing's been covered up. You know Brenan loves me. I hope you also realize if you don't stand by her, you'll lose her. That's a loss I don't think you can handle. I swear to you I don't want that to happen. She needs you. Don't make her choose between us."

A. D. and Mark looked apprehensively at each other, but Sam continued. "Things weren't perfect when you married Ellen. A. D. married my mother even though she was newly widowed with one infant in her arms and one inside her. Both marriages have worked. They're still working. We don't have a perfect world, but love goes a long way toward making this one seem like a good place. Talk to your daughter. Listen and decide what you have to. Now, if you're out of questions, I have some work to do."

Mark, humbled and shrunken, simply nodded for him to go.

A. D.'s brow wrinkled into a network of frank amazement. He looked up at Sam, lifted one hand, and waved him on.

ELLEN AND FREIDA were complaining about the inferiority of Y chromosomes while they tended steaks Mark had thrown on the grill and left to burn. A. D., stinking of insect repellent, was asleep in a hammock he'd strung between two water oaks behind the lake house. Jackie, Robert, and Brenan had taken a grocery list to Road's End, a small town two miles away. Mark was nowhere in sight, and Mariah was missing from her crib. Sam, with Marissa's chubby little arms tight around his neck, had completed a room-to-room search and now headed outside.

Mark must have taken the baby. But why? And where? He hadn't spoken to Sam once during the hour they had been together. He hadn't said much to anyone.

"Told us to watch these then went back in." Ellen dabbed her face with a towel and pointed at the back door with a meat fork. "Ought to be back out by now. He's the idiot who wanted to cook out in this inferno. When you find him, tell him—"

Leaving his mother and Ellen on the patio, Sam began another circuit of the grounds.

"Bird." Marissa patted his face to get his attention and pointed.

He stopped and followed her finger. "Yeah, that's a cardinal, a red bird."

"Bread bird." She was solemn in her attempt to show off her verbal skills. Tangles of sunny curls framed her round face. She was as light as

Mariah was dark. She waited for the praise she knew would come.

"That's *very* good. You talk like a big girl." He hugged his niece. Since becoming a father, he hadn't had much time to spend with her.

"Big girl."

"Yes. Let's see if we can find Grampa Mark and Mariah."

"Ry-ya? Baby?" She frowned.

"Yes, honey. Looks like you have to share everybody with that baby, huh? Just moved right in on you, didn't she?"

He took the short straw-cushioned path to the pier and immediately spotted Mark sitting on the far end with his back to the shore. From this angle, Sam couldn't see if his daughter was there. Marissa began bouncing excitedly in his arms. "Paw!"

"You're the only person I've ever known who could get excited over seeing that old man!" He stepped onto the pier. He could see the top of Mariah's head, now, and even though Mark didn't turn around, Sam knew he had heard them.

"I hope you're not planning to drown her."

Mark glanced over his shoulder. "Why the blue blazes are you following me around?"

"My kid was missing, and I don't trust you. You haven't been in a good mood."

"You're a mother hen. This child is going to be as neurotic as an old woman by the time she starts school. Well, as long as you're here, sit down. You make me nervous standing behind me."

Tightening his grip on Marissa, Sam sat and dangled his legs off the end of the pier. The lake was down. The water was seven or eight feet below the soles of his shoes.

"Baby." Marissa frowned.

As soon as she saw Sam, Mariah put out her arms.

"No, baby!" Marissa was ready to show some of her mother's temper.

"For the sake of peace, maybe we'd better swap." Sam held out the indignant toddler.

After the exchange, Marissa sat pouting in Mark's lap while Mariah lay back contentedly against Sam's shoulder. Sam noticed Mark had had the foresight to bring a nursing bottle and a spare diaper. "Why did you come down here?"

Mark gave up one of his famous hard-eyed glares.

"The women are hot, in more ways than one, about being left to do the cooking."

Mark sighed. "If you must know, I was taking some time to—to get better acquainted with my new grandchild." He turned to look out over the water. "I can't have her thinking I'm just someone who gives her booster shots and looks in her ears."

"I see." Sam found it difficult to keep from jumping up and doing a victory dance. His grin couldn't be suppressed. The old man had relented!

Mark looked back at him. "Wipe off that smirk. You won, but you don't have to gloat."

"I'm not gloating." Sam pointed to his mouth. *"This* is gratitude and relief!"

"Well, go on then. Take this one, and leave that one. This one needs her seat covers changed—besides, I've got some time to make up with that one."

They swapped babies again. Marissa's lips puckered up as if she was trying to decide if a protest might be in order.

Sam tipped his head toward Mariah. "She'll be more than payment enough for your signature on a piece of paper."

"You'd better get one thing straight. Ellen and I are her grandparents. We are not *step*-anything. Go back and tell your folks to move over. We have to share both of these babies."

Sam stood. "I'll do that."

"One more thing—I want a promise."

"Let me hear it."

"Brenan's not nearly as tough as she'd have you believe. As much as she loves you, you could break her heart like that." He snapped his fingers. "Give me your word you'll do right by her."

"You have it."

"Well, go on, and leave us alone. Mariah's safe with me."

25

SEPTEMBER 5, 1982, 9:40 P.M., a Sunday. Her fingers turned the dimmer switch a twist too far. The room was suddenly full of deep shadows. An abrupt spell of modesty?

Ya know better, Ace! She's been comin' on too strong for that! You've hadda fight her off for AGES! She's all revved up!

Brenan had made no secret of her impatience with waiting for things to be squared up with her parents, with Sam's need to be certain no war would ensue. In spite of her readiness, first-time anxiety was likely. "I'm not scared," she whispered as if she'd read his thoughts. He used one finger to lift her chin, leaned forward, and kissed her. During the lingering kiss, he reached around her back and felt for the circular control. Just a little light, still soft and unobtrusive. He'd waited for this moment too long to have it take place in total darkness.

When the kiss broke, they stood, eyes locked, each trembling inside the other's embrace. Sam's fingers found buttons, fumbled them open, parted her thin, gauzy blouse back over her shoulders. The blouse dropped to the floor. Staring at his reflection in her fluid brown eyes, he began to walk her backward toward the bed. On the way, her white lace bra fell.

Brenan had tears for all meaningful events. Tonight, she smiled at him through overflowing pools of them. The salty taste lingered on his lips and tongue. He kissed her again, this time easing her with him onto the bed.

His body sloped across hers, rested lightly against her, his weight on his knees and the palms of his hands. Slowly, he moved his mouth over her face and neck, sampling one tiny spot of firm, blushing skin before moving to another. He felt her fingers meet at the back of his neck and lace together in his hair. An involuntary tightening of his arm and thigh muscles dropped more of his weight onto her, causing her small, perfect breasts to flatten against his bare chest. His own nipples stiffened. Every nerve ending in his body began to flex and quicken.

The wedding was set for September tenth, but the honeymoon started tonight.

Lefty felt compelled to keep the cautions and critique coming. *Pace yourself. Slow an' easy. Don't wanna go puttin' short of the cup! No hurry; she's not goin' anywhere! No! Wait! Letdown alert! When ya finally get stuff you've hadda wait for, it ain't good as it's cracked up to be!*

Wrong. The feelings that surged through Sam at this moment were that good. The nearness, the heat of the woman in his arms was creating sensations greater than orgasms he'd had with other women. There would be no disappointment. None. Nada.

He sat back, peeled down his frayed cutoffs, and kicked them over the edge of the mattress. His heart rate launched a swift upswing as Brenan lifted her hips and stripped away her tennis shorts and panties with one smooth gliding motion.

All veneer and window-dressing cast aside, he shook his head. It rattled. He'd only glimpsed her body in pieces and sections—lovely and flawless pieces, certainly—but he gasped over the stunning perfection of all the pieces, seamlessly put together. Lean, firm, sturdy. Tan and shiny with the flowing polish of youth. He would not have believed the existence of this exquisite beauty had she not made gift of it. Could being in love have slanted his perspective? Maybe every man saw the woman he loved in some unearthly light—or any man who fell victim to a bolus of testosterone, a wickedly selfish libido. Were the extremes of her elegance visible only in light of the moment and his enormous need for her? He would have to touch every piece to judge for himself.

Before falling silent, the overprotective Lefty dropped all caution and screamed, *Disregard the priors! Forget all that other stuff! Ya ain't blind!*

Ain't crazy! What ya ARE is the luckiest man in the universe! Look at her! All yours!

He bit his lip and shook his head again. It sounded full of loose coins.

"What is it?" asked a voice that came to him as tinkling music. Tinny music boxes. Christmas carols sung by angels. One-finger piano ser-enades. Chimes of ancient timepieces.

"You, Brenan," he answered. His fingers began to touch, to explore, to pioneer—blazing pathways he hoped to follow forever. "You're all of it. You're everything that matters."

Her hand trailed after his, tracing the places he had caressed. She chased him with her fingers, let him lead for a while—then caught up. With the palms of her hands splayed through his chest hair, she pushed him off her and onto his back. Making her body a lid to hold him down, she exhaled his name, her breath drawn like a satin scarf across his neck and shoulders.

While she played him, Sam gave no self-conscious thought to the image of his own body. He knew what he looked like to other people and was neither arrogant nor proud. More often than not, he was annoyed with the response his physical appearance evoked. From the time he was fourteen years old, he'd been ogled, fondled, and harassed by starry-eyed females and lechers of both, and sometimes uncertain, genders. Hyenas, carnivores all. As a child, the mothers of playmates had embarrassed him with their crooned exclamations and the incessant smoothing of his hair. Later on, the unsolicited advances of perfumed and sultry women had kept him out of bars, grocery stores, elevators. He had gone from a pretty boy-child to a coveted piece of meat. His looks had demanded guarded, unpublished phone numbers, obscure parking places, added security measures at the TV station. In his mind, his features were much less a bonus than a handicap. Only Brenan's opinion meant something. He loved the sweet, simple adoration in her eyes, because he knew she saw more than the lines of his face and the musculature of his body. She saw something many never bothered to look for. She saw *him*.

Outside the bedroom, in her little alcove, the baby slept in peaceful oblivion. Except for a crescendo of laboring respirations, the bedroom was still and hushed. The rattling inside Sam's head quieted at last. Nothing intruded the electric force field that had erected itself of their passion around the oversized, platformed bed.

Inside that shielded orb, a new inner dimension waited to be opened, a completion of their union. He moved her again to her back, opened her—first with his knees then with his fingers, oiled himself against her folds.

She moaned his name.

He pushed, met resistance, recoiled.

"Push!" Her command was eager, breathless, staccato.

As he tried again, he envisioned stretching, bruising, tearing. He saw a pained blurring of her eyes. Still he pushed.

Tara had been a virgin.

Who cares?

Karen. A virgin.

So you're Triple Crown Virgin Champ!

Had he hurt them? No memory of imposing pain surfaced.

They weren't Brenan!

She wouldn't let him draw back. "Don't stop!"

Instead of accepting utter defeat, she thrust against him, forced an opening, pulled him into her.

A possessive internal fist fastened around him. It squeezed him, strangled him. Startled, he drew back and hovered above her. Watching the last of the pain harden in her eyes, he saw steaming flecks of determination, glowing red coals inside those beautiful eyes. She arced once more, met him in the air above the mattress, and he fell like an anchor into her.

Her warmth and wetness eddied over him. He fought for purchase, found none. He surfaced, floundered, sank—a float tied to a lead sinker, bobbing in the chasms of a wild, stormy surf. He no longer needed breath—the small liquid sounds of her pleasure sustained him. Her orgasmic buoyancy carried him with her up and over the rising swells, through the combers, across an eternal glassy ocean. This was a scene she was directing by instinct and need. This was what she'd promised all

along, what she'd begged to do for him. He'd never deny her again. Her
name echoed, reverberated inside his brain. *Brenan!*

His struggle ended. Her wet heat became a whirlpool that sucked him
deep into her center, into the blood and marrow of her. There, shivering
with sensory exhaustion, he drowned.

3:15 A.M. HE RELEASED a deep sigh. They'd made love a slower but no
less heated second time, the main course after the appetizer. Then they'd
slept, awaking later for a third, the dessert, a conclusion, drowsy and
sweet.

Though exhausted, he couldn't seem to shut his eyes. He sat against
the carved oak headboard, hugged a pillow to his chest, and watched her
sleep. Just to be touching her, feeling her, he gently slid one leg against
the straight plane of her back. Strands of soft brown hair had tumbled
over her forehead, and all the lines of her face had slackened and flowed
back into that of the child Brenan. He'd waited an eternity for her to
grow up and take her place next to him. She filled up an emptiness he had
never been able to name. His love for her was not a dangerous undertak-
ing that could ruin him. The danger had passed.

Next to him, she lay on her side. Lulled to sleep by the universal
rhythms of human loving. Her motion had been sweet and tender. It had
also been famished—as unbridled and glorious in reality as it had been in
anticipation. All the sexual experiences of his past, lumped together, had
been reduced to a single candle flame in the glowing torridness of his
world set fire. "I hope I'm what you need. I hope I'm enough."

He eased under the sheet that covered her, pressed his body into her
back and buttocks, into the warmth of flesh on flesh. In her sleep, she
turned and permitted herself to be enveloped in his arms. He pressed his
face into her hair. Flinging away the undercurrent of trepidation that
had, all his life, seemed to cloud every hint of fortune that had come to
him, he closed his eyes. Then he was able, at last, to fall asleep amid
lingering pulses of desire and happiness.

ON FRIDAY, AS HE finished up an appeal to animal lovers across the area to adopt a pet from the humane society, he visualized Brenan balancing the baby and a bowl of pureéd pears in front of the TV screen. He'd asked her to take an hour out of the chaos of her wedding day to watch.

Before daylight, he'd gotten a call to come in early to co-host "The Morning After Show" with one of the regulars, Paige Stewart. The other host, Mark Evert, had gone on a spur-of-the-moment assignment that would involve spending most of the day at City Hall. Sam, according to the station manager, was being offered the better deal. Andy Drury, rarely awake before eleven, yawned. "After nine-thirty or so, you can honeymoon the next two weeks. That's two weeks without me, Ace. Besides, if you don't do it, I'm gonna give Garner your job—permanently."

Sam had thought about it. "I'm already scheduled two weeks off. I'll do the show and take another week. That's three. If you don't believe me, ask Garner to count them for you. Rumor has it he can go all the way up to six or seven."

"In your dreams, MacCauley." Drury sounded big and bad.

"Up your ass, Andy."

"You do know I hate you?"

"Don't hurt my feelings. See you in three weeks." And Sam had hurried off to the station. He'd use the misdirected opportunity to surprise Brenan to herald their union on the air.

Throughout the first three quarters of the show, Paige made a variety of references to build up the audience for Sam's sharing some tiny morsel of his private life. *"Have your hankies ready. Call your friends and neighbors. Call your sister and your mother. They won't want to miss this!"* She created such mystery that, by the time the cue came, he wanted to back out.

He also, in keeping with his nature, began to worry that Brenan's age might come up and spark something controversial. In the photo he'd brought, she looked older than sixteen, but a lot of people knew her. Some self-righteous loudmouth could easily create a nasty situation. Then there was Karen. His marriage and subsequent divorce had never been given public airing, but Mariah's birth had been heralded.

His doubts came along too late. Paige finished the lead-in and grinned expectantly at him.

He took a deep breath and confessed to his fickle public. He was getting married. Unexpectedly, he was saved from having to go into details, cut off by the loud clamor of horrible crashes, glass shattering, female screams, objects falling from great heights, funeral dirges. Sirens and wailing. Chaos and doom. An elaborate arpeggio of studio sound effects. Some clown's idea of cuteness.

When the racket died down, Paige jumped in with a dramatic interpretation. "That, my dear friends, I'm sorry to say, is the sound of hearts breaking all over the Channel Nine viewing area."

Sam's face stung under the inevitable blush. Not caring that a camera was fixed on him, he rolled his eyes and shook his head. Sometimes, people went to great pains to embarrass him.

Part Three
Wolves and Lambs

Beware of false prophets, which come to you in sheep's clothing, but inwardly they are ravening wolves.

THE GOSPEL ACCORDING TO ST. MATTHEW 7:15

(Underlined in red ink in Reverend Arlo
Blacknell's cloth-bound King James Version)

26

July 1984

I DON'T KNOW what to believe," Sam said, singling his friend and camera man Tommy Crowder out of the sweaty crowd. "One big outdoor nuthouse."

"See that lady." Tommy's grizzled head tipped toward a white-haired, sixtyish woman who was standing alone in a patch of shade on the sidewalk. Her arms were crossed tightly over the front of her sleeveless blouse as if, in this late afternoon ninety-eight-degree oven, she felt an arctic breeze. "Says she's been here from the beginning, but I don't know about putting her on. She's in control and makes sense, and she knows the sonofabitch. Wouldn't you know she's got a doozy of a speech impediment, like my mama after the stroke? The devil to understand. Everybody else I talked with—morons." He raised his eyes skyward.

Tommy's message was strong but his voice was as mild as if he was inviting Sam to Sunday School. "That cop—that gorilla on steroids—told me to get out of his face or we'd be history. I assure you, I was nowhere near his ugly mug."

Sam, who had also been trying to get a straight story for ten minutes, shrugged sympathetically. "I can't report that according to one neighbor this is all a big joke, that according to another the guy's a dangerous pervert, and to still another he's a confused and lonely man-child who just needs a mother's touch."

Chaos ruled the sidewalks of Hyacinth Court and Red Valley Road in Southside. By the time Sam and Tommy had reached the scene, the police had pushed most of the crowd to the opposite side of the road from a dilapidated green clapboard house that had become the central hive of the commotion.

The crowd was not especially daunted by police barricades. It pressed itself as close as it was allowed. Not at all embarrassed over its macabre curiosity, it watched with the greedy leer of buzzards. A dark, ghoulish party atmosphere reigned. Up and down both sides of the street, small window unit air conditioners whined and wasted electricity while the occupants of the houses sweat-watered tiny lawns and cracked pavement. The windows and doors of the houses without air conditioners gaped open behind frayed and curling screens.

Outside, housewives held babies, yelled at toddlers and each other. Fanning themselves with folded newspaper, elderly people huddled in clannish groups of twos and threes. A few men of indeterminate ages and able-bodiedness milled around. They wore billed caps and stained tee-shirts that didn't completely cover their beer guts. With serious faces, they shared their man's-eye-views with the people standing closest to them. Altogether, this was a racially mixed, indolent neighborhood of soap opera addicts, porch-rocker royalty, and government-funded hypo-chondriacs who were starved for excitement and recognition. Today, they were getting huge doses of both. Sam regarded them with growing distaste and categorically avoided each and every person who deliberately tried to lure his attention.

"I just got fourteen different accounts. If you think your girl's reliable, tell me what she said, and I'll do it as hearsay." Sam touched the remote receiver that was plugged into his right ear. "We gotta do something soon. Back at the ranch, Drury's pitching a screamer for some coverage to come in before the competition gets here. I'm afraid he'll rupture something."

Crowder hunched up his shoulders and began. "Well, Ace, it goes like this . . . " He gave Sam a quick rundown of Essie Lockhart's version of the hostage-taking, smoothly shouldered the camera, and began counting down from five.

Sam stood with the sagging front porch of the green house as his backdrop and spoke into a hand-held microphone. Through him, the local public heard the first tentative account of the sickening excitement taking place. He slickly relayed a story of Troy Lovell, a young unemployed nurse with a grudge, a man who had been fired from his job at a local hospital only days ago. A man whose volatile temper had recently cost him his live-in girlfriend. A man with a vendetta.

Lovell had allegedly gone to the apartment of his ex-girlfriend where her two preadolescent daughters were latch-keyed and defenseless. The ex-girlfriend, a laboratory technician at University Hospital, had been at work, and there had been no one available to stop Lovell from showing the girls a stiletto and marching them seven blocks east to his home. When he had led them past Mrs. Lockhart, who had been sitting on her front porch, they'd called out for help. Lovell had angrily responded by pulling the blade of the knife across the neck of the older girl, drawing a thin stripe of blood. The act had been sufficient to convince Mrs. Lockhart and other stunned neighbors, also watching from porches, to let him pass unhampered. More than enough to silence the cries of the terrified children.

According to Mrs. Lockhart, Lovell had been known to verbally and physically assault the girlfriend and had shown signs of being deeply depressed and angered by her leaving. On one occasion during the previous week, he had told a group of neighbors his girlfriend would regret refusing a reconciliation. Though he hadn't gone into specifics, his threat had sounded plenty serious. A hunter and arms fancier, Lovell was known to possess several handguns, two antique twelve-gauge shotguns, and at least one high-powered deer rifle. The stiletto, Mrs. Lockhart believed, was one of a matched set of four antique silver daggers that Lovell enjoyed showing off to the neighbors.

The children were thought to be about eight and ten. It was rumored that a cruiser had been dispatched to bring the mother to the scene to try to reason with Lovell. In the meantime, Channel Nine's Eagle-Eye News Team would remain on the scene and update the viewing audience as developments occurred.

Roving Action Reporter, Sam MacCauley, offered a melancholy smile, lowered the microphone, and nodded curtly at the camera. His traditional silent signing off. His trademark closing.

AN HOUR PASSED. Traffic sounds and human voices came from every direction, but the green house was as hushed as a tomb. The police, the media, the variegated audience played a waiting game.

Oily sweat dribbled down Sam's spine. His short-sleeved dress shirt was heavy and clinging. His tie had been discarded. The circumstances, more than the heat, made him feel sick.

He thought about his two-year-old daughter. Mariah was a bright, curious little tomboy, full of questions, tricks, and an assortment of talents. She added an extra dimension to his life. The very notion of someone holding her away from him, putting a knife to her throat made him shiver. That kind of picture often popped into his brain in much less grisly circumstances. He was a what-if worrier who had to be ever on guard for his family. Bad things happened to those caught looking the wrong way.

During the first stages of a rare headache, the crystal sharp portrait of a small boy burst uninvited into his mind . . .

. . . terrified, dirty, sweating. Shivering against a sun-heated handrail, watching a woman wave and drive away. Too weak and scared to go in . . . "Jesuscrist, buddy, what happened to your hands? Somebody sure messedja over." . . . They say, "It's not your fault" again and again until he almost believes . . .

Vivid, lifelike, the boy's image stayed with Sam when he interrupted the scheduled newscast to relay the latest events. And it endured after the update was over.

Here ya go again, Lefty sighed. *Callin' up the old bad stuff. Ain't ya got enough to think about here?*

THE GHOULS REALLY get off on this, huh, Boss? Bet these're the same ones who pull over to get a closer look at car wrecks.

At 5:20 p.m., the mother arrived on the scene. The camera captured her standing on the scraggly lawn. The audio equipment picked up her pleading cries. An added bonus for the titillation of the viewing public, the camera was rolling when Lovell showed himself in a window holding up a Springfield 30.06 semiautomatic rifle for inspection and effect. When the scared mother saw this nut cowering behind one of her children, holding the rifle with one hand and the gleaming stiletto under the girl's chin with the other, she panicked and had to be wrestled to the ground to keep her from charging the house.

The message Lovell tendered was simple; the woman would suffer as he had suffered through her rebuff. He was going to kill the girls. *Nothing, nobody* was going to stop him. But not until their mother paid her dues in miserable atonement. If the cops came for him, the girls would die all the sooner. *"Just be sure, bitch, you know what happens when you fuck with me! See what happens when you pull Ol' Troy's chain!"* He taunted the police. *"The longer you leave me be, the longer these little brats draw breath—the longer you got to figure out how to get them away from me!"* Every word was caught and transmitted. A delay of a few seconds probably permitted *bitch* and *fuck* to be dubbed over with silence before airing.

The little girl in the window wore her hair in a ponytail tied in a purple ribbon bow.

AT 7:23 P.M., he did a live stand-up report: "Since roughly 3:20 this afternoon, Troy Lovell has acted out a gruesome drama in which the fates of two small children are uncertain. . . . Thirty-one-year-old Janice Stiles, the mother, has been taken to the emergency room at University after collapsing on the lawn . . . Police, including Lieutenant Edward Englewood, who heads up the S.W.A.T. team, are refusing to give out any strategies they have formulated. When questioned about the possible use of tear gas, Englewood told reporters . . . still a waiting game . . . a full report at ten. Until then this is . . . "

The sad smile. The lowered microphone. The abrupt nod.

AT 10:01 P.M., he was back on the air: "Stillness and silence are all that can be witnessed by the vigilant congregation around the house at 4211 Red Valley Road where seven-year-old Rebecca and ten-year-old Danielle Stiles are being held captive by a man who has threatened to take their lives at some unspecified . . . since no lights can be seen in the house . . . has been no word on the condition of Mrs. Styles who was taken by ambulance . . . this is Sam MacCauley reporting for . . . "

A LITTLE BEFORE TEN-THIRTY, he called home: "Hey, Bren, looks like I'm gonna be here through the night or until this nut does something. — I know, Baby. Nobody understands. If I were you, I'd turn the TV off and leave it off. Find something more pleasant to do. How about writing a short story with a happy-ever-after ending? — A place called the Allnighter Convenience Store a few blocks down Hyacinth. It's a classy joint with an awning that's hanging by a prayer and a sign hand-lettered in red crayon announcing shirt and shoes are not required. Owner has a sense of humor. Tommy swears there's a decent deli. — He's gone in for coffee and sandwiches. He'll want to call Jo when he comes out, so I'll say goodnight now. — No, I'll be fine. Listen, if you don't want to be alone, call Ma or Ellen. They wouldn't mind. — Just an idea. I'm not too thrilled having you alone. — If she wakes up, give her a kiss for me. — Always. I'm always careful. Got too much waiting at home not to be. — I love you, too, Bren."

12:19 A.M. THE EVE of Independence Day. By the inadequate light of ill-spaced and tree-shielded mercury vapor street lamps, Sam stared at the scars on his hands, road maps permanently drawn, but now faded to fine, hair's-breadth etchings. Time had almost scoured them away, but inside his palms, the damage was still distinct. The white suture lines stood raised and knotted. While the specific events that had come with the making of the scars were hazy and insubstantial, the fear and helplessness were always fresh and eager to be experienced all over again. He didn't want to think about scars any more than he wanted to think about two children inside a dark, brooding house with a madman. But he rarely had control of his thoughts. Were the girls bound?

Gagged? Had they been given water or food? How long would they be alive? What scars would they wear if they were allowed to live?

The police were getting nowhere with the situation. They stood like sentries at the corners and angles, consuming copious amounts of coffee delivered by self-appointed caterers in the crowd, and waiting. No one wanted to give the order to storm the house and startle Lovell into carrying out his threats. Each time one of the officers tried to talk to him, he yelled back a standard, "Shut up! I'll blow their fuckin' heads off!"

No question, the man was unstable and his actions impossible to predict. The newsroom's hasty research into his background had turned up little except high school and nursing school records showing him to have an IQ of 138 and a somewhat abrupt bedside manner. His academic performance had been superior. Only the clinical, hands-on internship was dotted with minor attitude flaws. Dana Rawlings had contacted the last nursing supervisor he had worked under, a few people from his childhood neighborhood, and his father. They had all given testament to small idiosyncrasies, eccentricities they had noticed but hadn't felt serious enough to cause concern.

Only Janice Stiles, Essie Lockhart, and a couple of other neighborhood personalities gave believable voice to his severe mood swings and increasing brutality toward Janice and her children. His father, a resident in a nursing home in Dothan, admitted to having been a strict disciplinarian when Troy was growing up. A believer in lashing bad behavior away with a belt, George Lovell had conceded to the Dothan reporter that the boy had been a *"double handful"* when he hadn't gotten his way. *"Couldn't do a durn thing with 'im when he set in ta wantin' somethin'. Not one thing, 'cept take the hide offa his back. Hadda fix the little asshole's wagon somehow, didn't I?"*

The loss of Lovell's job had come as a result of an extreme number of absences—nothing sinister. Who, what was he? A smart, white-uniformed Jack the Ripper? A pissed-off Florence Nightingale? A spurned, angry lover? An unhealed victim of abuse? At this late stage of the game, did it really matter?

DAYLIGHT HAD DONE LITTLE to relieve the grimness of the ordeal. The media, including Sam and Tommy, had been pushed farther back from the house. A series of attempts at speaking with Lovell had been executed with what appeared, from Sam's vantage point, to be scant or no progress. A woman in a pickup truck had delivered dozens of boxes of Krispy Kreme doughnuts. These were now being passed through the crowd. The sidewalks and lawns were strewn with cans and bottles, Styrofoam, plastic, paper. After a sleepless night, the festive pantomime resumed.

Sam shook his head at a pass of the doughnuts and shuddered when Crowder took three from the box. As far as field partners went, Tommy Crowder was the absolute best. He could anticipate most of Sam's needs. He was soft-spoken and caring, but he never got caught up in the emotional heat of assignments. Or if he did, all Sam saw was calm, clear eyes set in a placid, fifty-year-old face. Tragedy didn't seem to affect Crowder's appetite, either, but Sam didn't know how anybody so close to this house could eat. "No thanks," he said when Tommy held out the box one last time before sending it down the line.

AT 6:45 A.M., at the prompting of Crowder's finger, Sam began a five-minute rundown for *The Morning After Show* to be aired at seven. The mother had returned and was sitting in a drugged stupor in a folding chair on the sidewalk. A few relatives and friends, some in hospital whites and gunmetal grays, flocked around her in anxious attendance. Overall, the content of the report was dull. Nothing encouraging or new. But as a veteran herald of the news game, Sam was adept at extracting something from nothing with a flair coveted by many of his contemporaries. He was out of patience with the S.W.A.T. team for not rescuing those children and having this atrocity aborted. With slick cunning, he said as much in his report. Only the most savvy law enforcement officers listening would know whether or not they'd been insulted.

Ya call a spade a spade, huh? Call a baffled bunch of public servants who can't pull miracles out of their pockets imbeciles an' assholes on TV. Wonder why they don't remember your birthday or tell ya their secrets! Will the real a-hole please stand up?

THE EARLY-AFTERNOON sun was near its zenith when the screaming started.

"No!" Sam heard himself demanding. After nearly twenty-two hours in the thick of this dark suspense, he had counted on a better ending. *Anything* would be better. At that instant, the psychopath was putting a screeching conclusion to hope. High, clear screams, the beginning of the end. The deep, lowing wail of the mother rose amid the frenzied shrieks slicing through the thin walls of the old house to fill the expectant neighborhood.

The S.W.A.T. team launched into action. The weary crowd became a still photograph, flyblown and dripping sweat, stupefied by the act of straining forward.

Only one child was screaming now.

Janice Stiles, restrained by the hands of two uniformed cops, continued pulling and twisting, battling to be freed.

Tommy's camera minded the swarming of the house. Policemen poured through windows and doors. Sam tried to narrate into the microphone but kept losing his place in what he was witnessing. He noticed an unsteadiness in the hands that held the camera and realized that the horror had finally gotten to Tommy.

The last shriek from inside the house was snapped off as if by the click of a radio knob, the flick of a light switch. The mother understood what the crowd did not yet grasp. Her last wail died, and she sank to the pavement between the two officers.

The S.W.A.T. storm was too late. The onlookers could go back inside their houses with the taste of morbid excitement still on their tongues. Troy Lovell had claimed his bounty.

Soon Sam would put down his microphone, go home to his wife and child, but the young mother would never again hold her children. He would gratefully take his family into his arms. A desperately mental search for a meaning, for something he could understand proved fruitless. No moral, no reason, no rhyme.

He wiped perspiration from his scarred palms, one at a time, onto the fabric of his pants. He hoped Brenan had taken his advice and stayed away from the television. He didn't want her to hear the next segment of his coverage, the grand finale.

He would wait for official confirmation to make his announcement. It wouldn't be long in coming. A squirt from his atomizer relaxed his lungs enough for his voice to be clear.

Being Channel Nine's Roving Action Man-on-the-Street was suddenly shaping-up to be one of the dirtiest jobs in Birmingham.

27

New Year's Eve, 1985

HER SCREAMS WERE ripping him open, shredding his insides. And he wasn't, by any means, discounting what the cause of the piercing screams was doing to her. An hour ago, he'd been reduced to pleading on her behalf. "The epidural's not working. Bring out the hard stuff! Put her down for the count! Listen to me! Knock her out! Now!"

Dr. Tristan Riley, who had, over four hours time, become sadistic and deaf to reason, calmly shook his head and, in his clipped, down-under accent, made excuses for letting her suffer. "I've given all the analgesic I can for the pain . . . She's fighting the medication . . . For heavensake, Sam, you of all people, know how she *is* . . . carries on nearly this profanely during a routine exam . . . frightened more than hurting . . . If *you'd* calm down, she probably would, too . . . I'd be more than happy to give *you* a pill . . . Chill . . . " *And so on . . .*

How could he calm down when he and everybody else in North Birmingham had to listen to the bloodcurdling sounds that came out of his wife's throat? When everyone, except Dr. Riley and the mercy-poor maternity staff at Northside, was going to require professional help if it wasn't over soon?

Between contractions, she would settle and, with a tongue thick and dry from the narcotic, vehemently deny the pain was all that bad. "You know what a big baby I am." Occasionally, she would drop into an exhausted, short-lived sleep. It was an on-again-off-again horror show, and the pains kept coming back, each one sooner and more ferocious than the one before. They made great jagged mountains and cratered valleys on the monitor screen and its paper tape printout. And in spite of her efforts to bravely bite them off, the screams came.

Several times, she pointed to the exit side of the curtain, sending Sam to the waiting room. "Go see how the others are doing. Take a walk. Get some coffee." He heard the unspoken, "You're driving me crazy," and obediently went out each time, long enough to give her a break from his restless presence. Long enough to reassure his parents, his in-laws, Robert and Jackie—and any passerby who showed one iota of concern—that there would be no more babies of his bloodline. His wife would never go through this again. If she survived this excruciating impasse and wanted more babies, they would have to be gotten by some other means. He vaguely recalled making a similar manifesto in these halls once before. No matter. He meant it this time.

On one waiting room trip, he used the courtesy phone to call his daughter. A cold and fever had forced him to leave her at home with the housekeeper, Mrs. O'Neil. Mariah, who was three months short of her fourth birthday, had been supremely indignant over being left out. She'd been tediously prepared for the birth experience and had expected to be a part of it.

"Why does it take so long for babies to get out?" she asked. "We been waiting and waiting. I'm tired of waiting, Daddy."

"I'm sorry, Rye. I can't make it happen any quicker. We just have to keep waiting. Why don't you draw Mama some pictures? That will help you pass some time. I'll bring them to the hospital tomorrow."

If Sam could believe his parents and in-laws, his daughter was smarter than either he or Brenan had been at the same age. Actually, he had little trouble believing. She was already reading Dr. Seuss and simple storybooks. Brenan had spent a tremendous amount of time playing what she called learning games with her. The games, short exercises Brenan made up as she went along, were fun and educational, and they were having a profound effect on Mariah's ability to concentrate and accomplish new skills.

"'Kay. Whatcha think she'd like?"

Even though Mrs. O'Neil had assured him Mariah's temperature was down, he didn't like the sound of her croupy cough. He made a mental note to ask Mark to check her over on his way home.

"Let's see. You do tremendously nice rainbows and butterflies. How about some of those? And your hands? Hands are my favorite."

"Well awright, but I'd rather be with you."

"I know."

"All Mrs. O'Neil wants to do is watch TV and take naps. That's no fun." Sam heard her long-suffering sigh. "She read me a story about a bear who wears a red cap and drives a boat and catches fish. You ever heard something so stupid, Daddy?"

Sam remembered the storybook from his own childhood.

"Oh, it isn't stupid at all. Was his name Bobby?"

"Yep."

"Well, there you go. Bobby used to live in a cave in the woods behind the lake house. Used to borrow your Gramma Freida's deep-fryer to cook his fish. I always thought he was pretty smart—for a bear."

"You're silly." Her croupy laughter ended in a fit of coughing. When the cough subsided, she said, "Mrs. O'Neil wants me to take cough syrup. Do I have to?"

"Yes. Be good, and I'll call you back later. Okay?"

"'Kay. I love you. Tell Mama."

"I will. Love you, too, Rye."

"Bye, Daddy."

Sam hoped a new baby in the house wouldn't be too big an imposition for Mariah. She was accustomed to being center of the MacCauley universe. Only Marissa had ever invaded her space. But Marissa's intrusions were short, and lately they had been welcomed. The two girls were learning that interacting was more fun than playing alongside each other, glaring and jealously guarding treasured toys. A friendship was forming. But a baby couldn't be sent away after a couple of hours. The time and attention a newborn demanded could be translated as a takeover.

WHILE BRENAN THREATENED him with castration and attempted to wring one of his hands off at the wrist, Sam tried to focus on the coming of the baby. The last day of 1985, a birthday too soon after Christmas. Sorry kid. Maybe we'll give your birthday parties in July.

He'll have to stop causin' all this commotion an' come out before ya can call this his birthday. If he don't get a move on, he may not make Easter! Bet he's hearin' all these naughty words his mama's sayin'. Where'd she learn to talk like that?

By the day after the drugstore test had shown a positive result, Brenan was convinced the baby was a boy. *He* had never been an *it.* Sam halfheartedly wondered if Brenan would be disappointed if her prediction turned out wrong. At this point, he'd be satisfied with a puppy if she could be free of pain. Two epidurals and a paracervical block had failed to numb her. Dr. Riley was setting up for an old-fashioned saddle block.

The latest contraction ended, and she came out of it sloshing over with tearful apologies. He flexed his cramped, aching hand and looked at his watch. The ordeal was now in its eighth hour. He was exhausted, and Brenan was about used-up. Both were overcome with relief when Riley snapped off a rubber glove and said, "I think we can go to the delivery room now. The little sucker's finally gotten curious about all this unladylike racket you're making. He's coming out to see for himself."

ADAM BENJAMIN MACCAULEY. Ben. Four-pounds-ten. Eighteen-and-a-quarter inches long. Wisps of wavy brown hair, and a set of lungs to complement his mother's.

Sam shyly carried his squalling, flannel-wrapped son into the corridor where the family waited to be introduced. Ellen and Freida reached at the same time. Freida was quicker.

"The nurse said to keep him warm." He frowned, cleared his throat, and patted his foot while his mother unwound the blanket, exposed and inspected the tiny body in front of a small crowd.

"Look, Ellen. Isn't that cute?"

"You know, Mama, there are some things you could simply take my word for."

When both grandmothers were satisfied everything was in order, Freida rewound Ben's covers and handed him back. Sam blushed and graciously accepted a round of compliments and congratulations.

No surprise to anyone, the grandmothers cried. Robert was forced to swipe a roll of toilet paper from the men's room to staunch the flood. Mark repeatedly cleared his throat and continued to pout over not being invited into the delivery room.

Jackie and Robert, who while waiting had idly discussed the pros and cons of having another baby themselves, insisted on turns at holding the screaming infant.

A. D., blinking hard, sniffed and muttered, "Good lookin' boy, and loud, but don't you all think he's kinda small? If he was a catfish, we'd hafta throw him back."

28

July 1987

BRENAN WATCHED SAM WALK to the door and look both ways down the hall. His respirations sounded harsh and forced. Almost everyone in the waiting room followed him with their eyes.

"Did you remember your medicine this morning?"

"Of course, I did. I've been taking it more'n six years."

"Doesn't hurt to ask."

Sam turned, came back, and stood in front of his father. "What do you think's taking so long?"

"It'll take as long as it takes, son."

"It just seems like they've had long enough to operate on everybody on sixth floor." Sam's hands dug deeply into his pants pockets as he started moving again.

Brenan got up. To halt his pacing, she hemmed him in a corner. "Look, Ace, I know you're apprehensive. Waiting's hard on everybody, especially A. D." She kept her voice low. "Don't you think your fidgeting might make him even more nervous?"

Sam nodded unhappily and sat down next to his sister. Brenan took the chair on the other side of him. His hand closed around hers and squeezed. She knew it took all his willpower to sit there. His frequent tight, weary sighs were about as bothersome as his pacing. She wished she had some means of calming him, but nothing short of an "all clear" from the surgeons could accomplish that. She dug into her purse with her free hand for his bottle of Theo-dur, opened it, and held it out to him. "Take one." Obediently, he dry swallowed the caplet she shook into his palm then chased it with cold coffee from a cup he'd abandoned under the chair an hour ago.

A. D. sat across the room with Robert and Ellen. Now that Sam had stopped asking questions, his father sat in silence, his eyes fixed on his hands, no part of him moving. His worry took a form much different from his son's.

Mark had left them to put his staff privileges to work toward getting some advance word from surgery.

The other people in the waiting room were strangers. They were divided into small groups, talking softly and worrying among themselves about other surgery patients. One woman, in spite of *No Smoking* signs on all four walls, repeatedly replaced one glowing Virginia Slim with another. She casually flicked her ashes and butts into a soda can, ignoring the frequent coughing of her otherwise silent male companion, Sam's wheezing, and the disapproving glances of the people around her. The tension in the room was as thick as Freida's Cajun black bean soup.

Sam's asthma reacted as much to the tension as to the smoke. The stridor had slowly grown audible and resistant to bursts from his atomizer. An elderly lady with her purse tucked snugly into her armpit had already offered him a list of home remedies. He had given the appearance of courteous listening, but Brenan had known his breath sounds disturbed the sweet old lady much more than Sam. She hoped the theophylline would calm his breathing without adding to his agitation.

The evening before, she had eavesdropped on his attempts to explain cancer to Mariah. He had tried to keep his voice light, but even the five-year-old had seen through him. He was talking more about her grand-mother than a disease. "She might get sick. If they can't get all of it out, she *will* get very sick."

"How does it make people all that sick?"

"It grows inside them until it sort of fills them up. It makes parts of a person's body not work anymore. If it's only inside the one place, her uterus—you remember what that is—the doctors will take that out, and she'll be okay. She doesn't need that part anymore."

"The doctors will get it all out, won't they? Even if it's somewhere else, too?"

"I hope so, honey. I can't promise."

"They *better!*"

"They'll do their best."

"Grampa Mark would get it all. Why can't he cut it out?"

"Grampa Mark's not a surgeon. He doesn't operate on his patients. He sends them to other doctors for that. Gramma Freida's doctors will try very hard to make her get well. One of them is the same doctor who helped when you and Ben were born."

"She won't feel them cutting, will she?"

"No. She won't feel anything because she'll be asleep."

"How did she get it—cancer?"

"Nobody knows. But a lot of women get the same kind, and many of them get well."

"She's not gonna die is she, Daddy?"

"No, honey. I don't think so."

"Then why are you crying?"

Brenan didn't think Sam was far from tears, now. His face was pasty except for bright streaks of red across his cheek bones. He loved his family with a fierceness that threatened his emotional equilibrium every time there was sickness or injury. Ever ready to tend, defend, and watch over his people, he worried too soon and too long—and more often than not, unnecessarily. Brenan could get only part of the way toward understanding his intensity. She ached to know the reason behind his fears, his insecurities, to alleviate some of the weight he carried. On numerous occasions, he had attempted to help her, but he had always ended up scrambling her even more. If he started making sense, some unconscious switch would trip. Although she hadn't given up hope of getting past his defenses, staying faithfully beside him was all she could manage today. This time, his uneasiness was founded in plain, hard reality. The abnormal cells growing inside his mother were real.

Brenan's father returned to the waiting room without much of an update. "I guess Tristan expected me. That Aussie's posted guards. Wouldn't let me past holding. *His* orders. Now, I have nurses telling me what to do. If it wasn't for the situation, I'd—never mind. They did say she's weathering the surgery well—strong vitals, that sort of thing. Sorry."

They were forced to keep waiting.

Brenan leaned close to hear Sam's whispering.

"It's ironic."

"What do you mean?

"She's always jumping me about swearing—like words are so power-ful. *This,* cancer is what's profane, Brenan: people sitting around waiting to be told if it's going to destroy somebody they love and need. The fucking F-word doesn't mean shit."

A half-hour later, Dr. Lonnie O'Casey, the oncologist, and Tristan Riley finally brought word. They believed they got it all. Everything looked good. Of, course, they'd be watching.

When the doctors had gone and A. D. was allowed to go to his wife, Sam turned to Brenan. His face told her the relief provided by the doctors had done only a marginal amount of good.

"When was your last checkup? Your last Pap smear? How often do you get them?"

When he had her answers, he turned, with the same questions, to Jackie. He would have moved on to Ellen if he hadn't known she and Freida had gone to the gynecologist together.

February 1990

"BREN, CALM DOWN and tell me what the woman said. — Well, it looks like if she really believes God wants you dead, she'd let Him take care of the arrangements. Has Mrs. O'Neil left, yet? — Good. Ask her to wait until A. D. gets there. I'll call him. If I can't find him, I'll come home. — Just make sure the house is locked and the alarm's on. — The key's on the bedroom mantel, but I don't think you need to get that out. You don't even know how to load it. If you're that scared, if you think there's any chance you're going to hafta defend yourself, you ought to go ahead and call the police. — She gave her name and said she was a member of Arlo's congregation, didn't she? Shouldn't be too hard for them to find her. — Listen to what you're saying, honey. Death threats are against the law. It's their job to find her! — Okay, I'm sorry, but I don't know what else to do. I've never had to deal with crazies coming after my family. The fence is nearly built. The electronic doors are on back-order. The motion sensor lights and cameras are already up. The dogs are trained to rip apart anybody who tries to get to you or the kids. You won't let me hire a body guard. What else is left? — No, it's *not!* You didn't do anything wrong! It's the fault of the sick society we're forced to live in. There's nothing evil about your book. *Pulpits* is a novel. These loonies can't tell fact from fiction. You can't help that. — I know. To them, everything that brings comfort or pleasure is a sin. Money, sex, your book. Baby, I hate to say it, but if they're right, we're going to hell. — Oh, I was only trying to lighten the mood with a little humor. — One thing's certain, you shouldn't have to go into hiding because a bunch of religious nuts don't like the story-line. They don't give God much credit, do they? — What's the use of being on your way to fame and riches if you can't feel safe in your own home? — I love you, Bren. The thought of somebody hurting you is too much. Their scaring you is bad enough. Don't deny it. You're tough act doesn't work on me. Fear can make your life miserable. These nuts are afraid, too. That's why they have to act out against things they're not able to understand. They've been brainwashed into seeing evil everywhere they look. They have to stamp it out to keep it from blocking their road to heaven. Take them seriously! Let me get someone to stay with you and the kids when I'm not there. — Yes, we *will* talk about this again. Now, I'm going to call A. D., and you're going to let Mrs. O'Neil take over answering the phone like she's paid to do. And leave that gun alone until you've had some lessons. If you tuned in this evening, you heard me report a four-year-old shooting himself with a .22 he found in the glove box of his mother's car. The kid died, Bren."

WHEN HE KNEW A. D. was on his way to Brenan, Sam pushed back from his desk and stared at the phone. All phones were beginning to be sources of dread. A storm of hatred had been ticked off by Brenan's newest novel, *Pulpits,* which had been on the stands and in the bookstores since late fall. She had written a story of religious fanaticism in Alabama and the South. A story so realistic, people whose minds were already so Bible-muddled common reason was wasted on them mistook her for the Antichrist.

These people pored over their Testaments, dredging bits of scriptural meat to back up their cries of blasphemy. The story was about one minister, a composite of many, who had allowed the straight and narrow to wrap around him in a vicious stranglehold. His dogma had jumped the bounds of established Pentecostal doctrine and developed a cult following of a few likewise crazed individuals who worshiped with him, first in tents then a hastily constructed shanty church. Brenan had taken the families of this preacher and his followers and explored the harsh conditions of their lives in the light of religious obsession. Her research had been in-depth and thorough, her portrayals accurate and representative of the real victims she'd interviewed. Victims who had retreated from society into mental institutions, chemical stupors, and other dismal hermitages.

Fiction with the clear ring of truth, the book grabbed both attention and acclaim. It disappeared from shelves as soon as the boxes were unpacked, yanking Brenan into the spotlight alongside it. Success proved fickle and fragile. Unknowingly, Brenan Armstrong MacCauley had dared the hand of fate, and she'd had to take cover when it came slapping after her.

The South took its religious beliefs and denominational variations gravely. Its radical sects spurned believing that Brenan found no fault whatsoever with any individual's freedom to worship. They couldn't see that her grievance came in when pietistic fervor was imposed on children and otherwise innocuous victims, when blameless people were hurt. Rather than simply documenting facts, she had produced a powerful piece of fiction that bespoke her convictions to the fullest, thus bringing a rush of bigoted indignation down on her head. Her contenders saw her as a sinner, a demon-possessed charlatan straying from the wide path to hell long enough to pick a bouquet of backsliders and weak-hearted Christians to be used as trinkets in her wooing of Satan. They believed the mouth of hell would gape wide for her. Some of these good Christians were so frightened of her word power, they were eager to help her get there—all in the name of a vengeful God.

Arlo Blacknell had reappeared on the scene as leader of the most adamant hate group. After a few telephone rows and sidewalk face-offs, Sam could see the man's psychosis had deepened. His threats smacked of violence, madness. Of all the hecklers, Sam feared Arlo and his *Faithful Few Assemblage* the most.

On top of all the Brenan-inspired anger, Arlo still blamed Sam for Bud's demise. Sam finally saw something positive about Bud's death. It had freed him from the sadism of his own father.

After a few of his importune calls, Arlo's hate-filled essence lingered to invade Sam's sleep. Slithering into the vague format of old nightmares, he assumed the form of a cloven-hooved devil standing over a bed where Brenan lay bound. *"Hell's gates swing wide for the likes of you, Miz MacCauley!"* A madman pulling a stiletto across a little girl's throat. *"God's will must be done, little lady."* A stinking, grease-spattered mechanic hovering over a bleeding boy. *"Yore ol' man ever do this to ya, Sambo?"* Bogeymen, past and present. Throughout the nightmares, the high, ringing screams of children filled Sam's ears—where they echoed long after he awoke.

The threats his family had sustained over the previous weeks had left him feeling too small and inadequate to keep them safe.

To protect Brenan and the children, his parents and in-laws, he was in the process of building a fort around the properties, sequestering the three homes from the rest of the neighborhood. A. D. escorted Ben and Mariah to their classrooms in the mornings and returned for them in the afternoon. Precautions were considered before shopping trips or visiting friends. Privacy was elevated to seclusion. Still, Sam worried that not enough was being done. Until the hot bloods began to cool, he would have to be alert.

By EARLY JUNE, the calls and letters had nearly stopped. *Ease up a little, Ace. Take some of the restrictions off. Let 'em feel normal an' alive for a change. Take it from Lefty, a vacation's what you need. If anybody's got one comin'. . ."*

"Well, maybe, we could slip off some place where no one knows us. The beach, maybe. Everybody loves the Gulf."

Sounds good—long as you don't smother 'em the whole time.

"I'm not all that bad."

Hoss, you're the wettest blanket in these here parts.

"I do whatever it takes to get by. I can't just dangle my family in front of a bunch of raving lunatics who hate them. They're dangerous. They want Brenan and everyone associated with her taken *out!"*

They're all talk. Gotta spout off at all you bad boys an' girls to win their brownie points with the Big Guy. With all the THOU-SHALL-NOTS they gotta go by, they can't get permission to attack with anything stronger than words.

"These aren't reasonable people. The couple who followed us around the mall—do you think they were rational?

No, but I doubt they were dangerous.

"I took my family home, anyway."

Ya gotta start venturin' back out some time.

"I can't take my wife and kids to a restaurant or a movie without risking them being harassed or hurt. The vacation sounds like a great idea, but when we get home, the guard goes back up."

When ya get home, start takin' it down a piece at a time. Take your life back bit-by-bit. Won't seem so radical that way.

"Maybe."

29

April 1991

M R. MacCAULEY?" The voice of a child. Timidly uneven and low. Probably male. Polite, undecided. Talking to an adult— sometimes the hardest thing in the world for a child to do.

"Yes. May I help you?"

"Uh, sir—I'm—ah, my name is Justin. You don't know me, but I— uh—"

"What can I do for you, Justin?"

"Well—see—I heard you talk about—about grown-ups messin' with kids. On TV, I mean. That was you, right?"

A black child, no more than ten or twelve years old.

"That's right. Do you want to ask me something about the story?"

"Yessir, if you got time. It's awright if you're busy."

An abused child, maybe?

Why else would he call, Ace?

"I've got time. It's okay."

"I was wonderin'—could you tell me—uh—why they do it? The hittin' an' all? When nobody ain't done nuthin' sometimes? Or don't know they've done it?"

Uh, oh.

Sam shivered. "I'm not sure anyone knows what makes some people mistreat other people. It's probably a little different with each one, but the important thing is, nobody should get away with it. Do you know someone who's hurting a child?"

"Uh, I just wanna ask about it. I cain't really say nuthin'. Do you think some folks just *like* to be doin' mean stuff to kids?"

Asks good questions, don't he?

Sam felt a trickle of cold sweat run down his neck under the collar of his shirt. "Yes. I think some people like scaring and hurting people who are smaller or weaker. It makes them feel strong and powerful. It makes them feel big. Are you alone?"

"Yessir."

"Did you call because you know someone who's being hurt?"

"You said kids should tell. Sounds good, but sometimes it don't do to tell. Tellin' could make it real bad."

"You mean the person who's doing the bad things might find out and do worse things?"

"Yeah, like that, an' they just say you're lyin' an' stuff. They tell other people, 'he's lyin',' an' they believe it 'cause they take the grown-up's word over a kid's."

"There are people you can tell who'll believe a kid first. They'll also protect him. There *is* a way out."

"My brother, Jason, says ain't nobody gonna help boys like me an' him."

Told ya!

"Jason's wrong. I put a lot of work into that story. I met many of the people who take care of abused children every day and guard them against the people who have hurt them."

"You talked about sex abuse—not just hittin'."

Oh, boy.

"Sometimes both happen together."

"Did you ever know about it bein' a boy that got messed with? You know, a man doin' sex stuff to a boy—*not a girl?*"

Sam's heart became a closed fist inside his chest. "Yeah, Justin. I'm afraid I have. It's not just girls."

"It's queer things they do to boys, ain't it?"

"No. The things they do are brutal and terrifying. Sexual abuse isn't real sex; it's cruelty, rape."

"Does it make the boy queer?"

The fear an' pain's universal. Yours. His. Same ol' ones.

"No, it makes the boy very frightened and unhappy. It makes him feel ashamed to admit what's happened to him—even though he has *nothing* to be ashamed of. Sometimes, he feels no one will love him or that everyone will think he's bad, so he doesn't talk about it. The truth is, any person who hurts a kid should be kept away from all children, some place where he can't do it again. And the kid needs someone who knows how to help him feel good again. There's only one way for the right things to get done, and that's for the kid to tell."

"Some things are so bad nobody would understand about 'em."

"One time, I thought the very same thing, but I was wrong. There are people who realize that a child is helpless to keep an adult off him."

"Just say the man's big like Bo Jackson, only mean, an' would kill the boy if he told. Just say that boy lay still an' let that man do it so it won't hurt so bad an' he won't get hit so much. An' just say that boy's mama knowed an' didn't make 'im quit. Just say that."

As if to hold back the rising swells of nausea, Sam ran his hand across his mouth. Suddenly, he was drenched in icy sweat.

Be careful!

"That boy would need a grown-up who wanted to protect him while the police went after the man—and while they tried to find out why the mother lets the bad stuff go on. If I knew about something like that happening, I'd want to help. I'd want to make sure the man couldn't get to the boy anymore."

"You're a white man. What about if the boy was black? Jason says nobody, not even grown black people, don't care what happens to black kids."

"Some people don't care, but a lot of people, black and white, do. They care a whole bunch for all children. For instance, color wouldn't make one bit of difference to me."

"Why?"

"Because I know if I start hating someone because he's a little different, I'll end up hating a lot of people. Everybody is different from me in some way. I'd be cheating myself out of friends. I need friends. I need all kinds of good people to choose my friends from. That way, I'm sure to get the best. Do you mind that I'm white?"

"I don't think so. Can I call again sometimes?"

Don't hang up, kid! Don't leave us not knowin' what's happenin' to ya nor where you're callin' from! Stop him, Sam!

"Sure, Justin, you can call me. Do you have something to write a number down on?"

"Yeah, but I already looked it up. *I called you.*"

"Oh, I know, but I want you to be able to call me at my house. Sometimes, it's hard to get through here at the TV station. I'm in and out a lot, but you try any time you want, okay? If you can't get me here and I'm not home, talk to my wife. She'll give me your message. Her name is Brenan." Sam gave Justin his home number. "What if I want to talk to you? Could you give me your number?"

"Oh, I better not. I ain't home much. I'll just call you."

"Justin, do you need help today?"

"Aw, no. I'm goin' over to my Granny Kay's. Anyway, it ain't me I was talkin' about."

"Will you watch the news again tonight?"

"Sure."

"There's another part of the story tonight and one more tomorrow night. I want you to pay close attention."

"Well, all right. I gotta go."

"Wait. Will you call me if you need help?"

"Maybe."

"I'd want to help."

"Why?"

"I've got kids. A girl and a boy that I love very much. If someone was mistreating them, I'd want them to tell."

"But I ain't your kid. You don't know me."

"Listen, Justin, I got hurt when I was little—by a man—just like you asked about. If I hadn't, I don't know how much I'd care. I hope it would still be a lot. But the fact is, I know how much it hurts and how hard it is to talk about."

Silence.

"You still there, Justin?"

"Yeah."

"If you needed to, would you call me?"

"Yeah. I guess."

"I'm glad you called. You sound like a nice kid. Maybe we'll get to be friends."

"I really gotta go."

A click. A dial tone.

Oh, boy.

Sam set the phone back into its cradle and got up. He walked to the newsroom's front desk.

"Rita," he told the secretary, "the last call you put through to me was from a little boy named Justin. If he calls back, even if I'm busy, even if I'm on the air, I want him kept on the line until I can talk to him. If I'm not here, ask him to call me at home. I gave him my number, but kids lose things. He's the one person you can give it to. And make sure you tell Betty and Drury and anybody else who might answer the phone. Post a note where it'll be seen."

"You're not trying to set up a hotline here, are you?" Rita's brown face and her toasted almond eyes appeared comically disapproving. She crossed her arms tightly. He had been her bad child for years. "If you are, I am not on the line."

"Just this one kid."

"Sam, honey . . . "

"I know I can count on you." Sam thought that, next to his father, Rita Williams had the most beautiful and gentle brown eyes in the world. He knew he was her pet. She baked pastries and left them on his desk. She called Brenan to tell on him when he was working too hard, getting too involved, wasn't eating the way she thought he should. She nagged when he needed nagging, and she took up for him when something happened behind his back.

"Sure you do. Oughta be ashamed—taking my favors for granted. I've spent twelve years screening your calls for sex-starved bimbos and brimstone-spouting preachers, and now—"

Sam leaned down and kissed the overweight, fifty-eight-year-old secretary with exaggerated passion—first on the lips, then the neck. "Remember his name is Justin," he whispered into her ear.

When Rita caught her breath, she gave him a glare of charitable lenience and shooed him back. "One of these days, Ace. One of these days, I'm gonna turn your skinny little butt over my knee and give you the spanking you've been begging for!"

He laughed. "One of those steamy fantasies of yours, no doubt!" He shuffled back toward his desk. Halfway there, he spun to look back at Rita. "Thanks a lot."

"Get me your mama's oven-fried chicken recipe, and we'll call it even."

"Why don't you ask for Elvis? I'd have a better chance of getting him for you."

BRENAN WAS ATTENDING a two-day writer's workshop in Nashville. Both Ellen and Freida had gone along as sidekicks.

Sidekicks, my foot. Bodyguards, Ace. She wrote a book. She made some kooks mad. The mama hens've gone along to keep the hawks away from their chick. They take the place of high fences, trained dogs, an' electronic surveillance when she goes to towns like Nashville. Towns below the Mason-Dixon Line. Towns where hot-blooded maniacs an' tract-passin' Christians are sometimes the SAME folks. A year an' a half, an' they ain't forgot.

A. D. and Mark had stayed at Sam's house to watch Ben and Mariah until Sam finished the ten o'clock broadcast. When he got home at eleven-thirty, he found the two older men in the family room playing Nintendo and arguing like schoolboys. Soon after his appearance, they gave up the game, refused to stay the night, and headed out on foot for their respective homes—still raising their voices in overdone, colorful accusations.

Sam called from the porch, "Can't you two play nice?" He locked up and made a round upstairs to make sure the kids were okay, then leaving a trail of clothing across the bedroom floor, he flopped onto the bed.

The child abuse story and the phone call from Justin had his stomach knotted, his lungs screeching.

He had titled his story "Innocence Unclaimed" in reference to the misplaced guilt children always took on themselves. For his research, he'd gone to federal, state, and county agencies, to halfway houses and foster homes. He'd talked with police officers, attorneys, and child molesters who were doing time in jail or out on probation. He had been thrown out of a Parents Anonymous meeting. He'd interviewed medical doctors, nurses, and psychologists. He'd sought the advice of school teachers, ministers, and day-care workers.

He'd written and processed volumes of material into eight three-minute segments for airing in order, each one twice a day at six and ten, for eight consecutive days. He also had two fifteen-minute segments scheduled for "The Morning After Show" next Monday and Tuesday and an ultimate hour-long airing of all the material plus live studio interviews with experts on Saturday, the twentieth, with a repeat airing on the twenty-third.

The publicity was shocking and compelling. He'd used a home video of a gorgeous toddler in a tee-shirt and droopy training pants. The child appeared happy and carefree as he sprinted across a toy-littered lawn. He played peek-a-boo with the camera by repeatedly pulling his shirt over his face. Laughing, he tried to get a drink from a garden hose. Then Sam's voice came in as a freeze-frame stilled the little boy, his lips pursed near an arc of water at the end of the hose. "This is Elijah Roberts. His father filmed this movie last summer at their upper-middle-class Forestdale home shortly before Elijah's third birthday. On February first of this year, after fourteen days of inconceivable suffering in a Birmingham hospital burn unit, Elijah died. He died because he didn't get to the bathroom in time on a day when his mother had taken a few extra pain pills for her headache. He died because his mother, on the agitated down side of her narcotic high, doused him with charcoal starter fluid and set him on fire . . . "

News director Andy Drury had handed down the assignment with specific instructions to get the public's attention, to make known the grisly statistics of Alabama and the nation, to present the disgusting details with such a stark and graphic picture no one with eyes or ears could fail to see and hear. Sure, the story would grab ratings—Drury would never discount ratings—but it also would educate and perhaps even spur some positive action. After all, Drury was a Big Brother, a Boy Scout leader, the father of five, and a charter member of the Christian Faith Church in Avondale. He was as concerned as anybody that Alabama ranked near the top of the nation's child abuse statistic list.

Nearly a decade after the beard had been shaved off and the hair cut almost short enough for Drury's taste, his relationship with Sam was craggy and pockmarked with the battle scars. Whenever the two locked horns, kicked sand, and shouted insults, a creative process clicked on. An idea, a solution, a *story,* perfect and whole, was born. Their contentions ended in double victories, the journalistic equivalent of simultaneous orgasms. Their brand of tough love was magic.

Drury had not known about Sam's childhood traumas, but he'd had no doubts that Sam MacCauley would get the story. People would pour their souls out to him. They would grandstand, cry on his shoulder, and he would treat them with dignity. So appointed, Sam had begun the research with a queasy stomach, a fresh supply of asthma medication, and a rigid squaring of his shoulders. He had taken "Innocence Unclaimed" all the way.

He had edited and fine-tuned. The finished product was one of a few in his career that had truly satisfied him. He was likely to receive a respectable amount of recognition for the story. The network had picked it up for one of the news magazines. But the story had levied an emotional toll, pried loose crusty old memories and resurrected vintage nightmares.

At times, during the years since he had first called himself a man, Sam had known a mystic beading-up of tiny memories among the raveled fibers of his dreams, along hazy edges of awareness. Only misty leftovers of the screamer nightmares that had soaked his childhood and adolescent sleep, these dewdrop recollections evaporated in the clean, dazzling light of day. At rare moments, though, he could revive the horror, intact and undiluted, and relive it with a depth and clarity that left him shivering. These times came when there was another crisis, another crippling molestation of his heart and spirit, or when he crossed paths with another limping victim. Most of the time, he could block the memories as if they didn't exist. Oh, he knew they were everlastingly *there,* embedded inside him, silently, stealthily screening, sorting, and shaping his directions and values before allowing them to rise up into his brain. They preordained his behavior, his interpretations, the trigger and speed of his reflexes, his thought processes. They magnified his capacity for loving while narrowing the channel through which the love of others was shunted back to him.

Sam knew the dark magic of the memories but denied their power over him as a criminal denies his deed. Seldom did he give those spirits-of-horrors-past credit for a part in the making of the man he had become. He preferred to believe he had passed into adulthood whole, unscarred, and without encumbrance. He was willing to let the demons have his subconscious and unconscious minds, let them have the bleeding soul of the little blue-eyed boy of his youth. As long as they left him alone to wallow in forgetfulness, they could have what they wanted. The effect of his self-induced ignorance was gratifying and soporific, and for twenty-five years, it had been his forte.

The child abuse assignment, the sporadic threats to Brenan, the accumulation of day-to-day pressures and strains began to wear thin the fabric of his protective shell. Marbled by a quarter century of darning and patching, the threads had become brittle and delicate, rendering vain attempts at further mending. All he could do was wait for the truth on the other side to seep through and demand to be acknowledged. He told himself he needed this truth, needed to deal with it in the open, yet he dreaded the day he would wake up and remember. Would it destroy him?

The research for "Innocence Unclaimed" had unearthed nightmares that touched him from the outside. Now, there was Justin.

Flattening his body on the mattress, Sam let out a long, deep breath. As soon as he closed his eyes, a nightmare would come. It would be vivid and menacing. When it ended, he would remember only shards of it, and the jagged edges would cut him. But he was too weary to stay awake and outlast it.

30

April 1991

THE PHONE RINGING after midnight at the MacCauley house usually meant someone from WPMS was calling with something that wouldn't wait for morning. A big story, a human tragedy the viewing audience would hover around their sets to be a part of. It usually meant Sam would have to get dressed and go out into the night, but true to his nature, Sam invariably thought first of other things: family illness or misfortune, Arlo Blacknell or one of his followers up late worrying about MacCauley sins, disease, danger, death.

He lifted the cordless phone off its charger in the same motion he used to bring himself off the bed.

The phone had not awakened him. Instead of sleeping, he'd been rehashing his conversation with Karen and the reactions of his wife and daughter when he'd told them about it.

After a nine-year silence, Karen was asking to see Mariah. Reluctantly, Sam had promised to call her back with a decision. Ultimately, he and Brenan had left it up to the child.

Mariah had agreed to a once-only meeting. A natural inquisitiveness had won out over fear of the unknown. Since the age of six, she had known the circumstances of her birth, and Sam thought, overall, she had seemed unimpressed. The twinkle of curiosity he'd seen in her eyes at the prospect of meeting Karen had needled him a little. He was certain Karen could make no legal claim, that his daughter was in no danger of being taken away. Still, he wasn't thrilled to have this near stranger barging into the lives of his family. If he gave his permission, Karen had told him, she would like to have her visit take place in June, two months away. Sam intended to put in a call to his attorney before giving her Mariah's answer. Just in case.

The ringing of the phone knocked Karen temporarily out of mind. Wriggling into a hooded terry robe as he walked, he carried the handset to the window seat. Brenan was likely in her office with her phone switched off. In his mind, he saw her sunk deep in her latest novel, lost to external stimuli.

"Hello."

At first all Sam heard was panting and a soft rustling.

"Hello," he repeated.

"Mr. MacCauley?" A nervous whisper.

"Justin?"

"Yeah. Can you hear me?"

Sam flipped the volume control switch on the phone to the maximum position. "I can hear you. Are you okay?"

"I guess. Mr. MacCauley?"

"Sam. No Mister anything. Okay?"

"Sam. Uh, you said you got hurt. How old were you? Do you mind talkin' about it?"

He minds.

"No, I don't mind. I was nine."

"How did you get help?"

"There were two people. One of them didn't like being a part of it and let me go. When I got back home, my parents helped me."

"The people who did it didn't live with you?"

"No. A man I didn't know forced me into a car with him."

"Oh—"

"Each case of child abuse is different, Justin. Some are very similar, but no two are alike. All of them hurt a lot."

"But if you gotta live with the guy who's doin' it, you cain't stop it."

"Yes, you can. You don't have to live with him."

"Those places where they put kids that get took away are just as bad—

foster homes and them other places where there's lotsa kids. I heard all about 'em! My friend, Reggie, got took to one when his mama got put in the hospital. That's where he got it *done* to 'im. Beat 'im nearly to death, some woman did! He ain't right now! Got no feelin' in one of his arms, an' his mouth hangs down on the side! He cain't even talk plain."

Oh, no!

"Whoa. I know things like that happen, but the services provided for children are getting better all the time. The bad places are being shut down. Now, they're watched very closely to make sure the kids aren't mistreated." Sam hesitated.

Not the whole truth.

"If you need to get away from someone, I'll come get you—and Jason, if he'll come with me. I don't know if the people who make the decisions will let you stay with me while the problem is being taken care of, but I'll do my best. I think they might, at least long enough for things to be safe for you to move in with your grandmother. No one at my house would hurt you."

"Why do you wanna help so much? I ain't even told nuthin'."

"I think you've told me a lot."

Careful!

Sam had discussed Justin's first two calls with Brenan. She'd been interested and sympathetic. While he was putting together "Innocence Unclaimed," she'd been close by, funneling suggestions and bits of her own research. She wouldn't object to providing a temporary safe house to the boys. Maybe he wasn't being wholly realistic, but he'd made contacts that might assist him in gaining sanction for such an unwonted placement. A. D. and Freida would know how to talk to them, what to do.

"I never even said it was me."

"Is it you?"

Justin cleared his throat. "Sometimes. When it ain't me, it's Jason. He's thirteen. He says I better not tell nobody."

Sam looked out the window into the hazy blackness beyond the sprawl of the outdoor lights and wondered what he was getting himself into. Justin's calls brought a fluttery feeling to the pit of his stomach. Maybe that was a warning to turn him over to some person with the authority, resources, and experience for helping a child in trouble. But he couldn't. The boy was more afraid of that than of the person who was hurting him.

"I'd like for you to tell me what's happening to you and your brother. Will you do that?"

"I dunno. Jason saw you on TV. Said ain't no white man gonna help us. You might feel sorry for us, but that's all."

"He doesn't know you've called me?"

"No. He said I better not. He's out with his homies. Mama an' Jerome—they're sleepin'."

"Jerome's your mother's boyfriend? He lives with you?"

"*We* live with him. Sometimes, he goes on trips for a few days, but he always comes back. Sometimes, me an' Jason get to stay a few days with Granny Kay, then he comes an' gets us."

"Does he beat you?"

"If we don't do what he says or don't do it quick enough."

"When you called the first time, you asked me about sexual abuse. Does Jerome hurt you that way, too?"

Sam heard Justin's hard intake of breath. After a long pause, the boy started talking. *"S'awful* what we gotta do for him. Mostly me, cause he lets Jason go out an' makes me stay home. It hurts—ugh!" The sound of Justin's words were cleanly cut off. All that Sam heard before the phone went dead in his hand was a groggy, adult male voice growling, "What the hell . . . "

Images of a boy being beaten, possibly raped by the man with the groggy voice, made a return to bed out of the question. He didn't know Justin's last name or how to go about finding him. With all the options available for the phone, he was certain one of them could pull up a caller's number, but that particular technology was of no use tonight. The only one of the new services that had appealed to Brenan enough for her to sign up for was Call Waiting.

There was absolutely nothing he could do to help Justin tonight.

IN THE KITCHEN, he poured a glass of milk, crawled into the breakfast booth, and stared at the glass. He thought about how the nightmare lurked in his bed, waiting for sleep to paralyze him. Each time he awoke, he remembered a little more. Hidden somewhere was a message that never quite stuck in his waking memory. Justin's latest call had interrupted tonight's dream.

Both Justin and Jason were safe in their beds. Jerome was out of town. To keep from waking his sleeping brother, Justin's voice had been held to a whisper, but it had been lighter, more animated than usual. He still held the information Sam wanted, his trust growing. Only a matter of time.

He drank the milk, ran water in the glass, and went up the stairs. In the dim landing light, he picked his way across a myriad of model train tracks and stepped into the room where Ben slept on a top bunk. His guardian angel, Howie Mandel, watched from the ceiling. The five-year-old had sunk himself in the synthetic down of a Darkwing Duck sleeping bag. His burnished gold hair and lashes were shining, his face sweet and babyish in the faint glow of the nightlight in the base of his Chip 'N' Dale Rescue Rangers wall lamp. His heroes guarded him well. Sam kissed his son on the forehead and again on one soft cheek.

The boy's bowed mouth puckered slightly as if returning Sam's kiss and then settled back, his lips slack and parted. He turned over and was still.

Averting a second crossing of the tracks, Sam cut through the children's bathroom to Mariah's room. He noticed a stack of hardcover novels beside her bed just in time to dodge them. She had gone to bed with questions about the mysterious woman who was coming to see her in a couple of months. After work, he'd found her awake and stayed with her a while. He hoped her sleep was dreamless and untroubled. However rare for him these nights, he knew the blessing of peaceful oblivion.

Small for nine years, she lived in a big world. In September, she would be making a place for herself in a group of towering sixth graders. The decision hadn't been easy. After testing and retesting her, the public school system couldn't seem to find a place for her. Third grade was a disaster that would soon be over. Even with a part-time gifted program, she endured her school days with kids who had only a birth year in common with her. They resented her for her aptitude and the attention it captured, for Sam's and Brenan's public accomplishments, but most of all for her dissimilarity. She carried on with admirable tenacity, pushing her coping skills to their limits.

The Paragon Fine Arts Academy, an unconventional private school established only three years back and already gaining a reputation as a progressive and innovative success, had gladly accepted her application. During the mandatory interview, she had told the panel she wanted to follow the footsteps of Stephen King, Steven Spielberg, and Connie Chung, and they'd welcomed her enthusiastically. *"Just the kind of passion we're looking for in our students."* She'd been given the grand tour and introduced to Paul Jackson, who would be her teacher. The course of study would begin with a handful of gifted and talented sixth graders and take them collectively through middle and high school. A basic education would take second place to challenging language arts assignments and media-oriented courses. The group would publish a weekly newspaper and a monthly literary magazine and would be taken on regular field trips. Most of her classmates would be residential students from other states. Mariah would be one of only four day students in the entire school.

The whole concept had grabbed Mariah's fancy, so Sam and Brenan had enrolled her, and a week later, her best friend, Deejay Windham, followed. Deejay had shown interest and promise in most of the same things and would be one familiar face in a room full of strangers. Eleven and ready for sixth grade, he was Mariah's self-appointed body guard. He gave them one more reason to be optimistic about the school.

Mariah lay on her side, and Sam had to skirt the double bed to see her face. So gentle and innocent. Her dark hair had been woven into a thick braid and thrown behind her head. The baseball shirt she wore as a gown was bunched around her hips, her quilt kicked over the foot of the bed. Instead of books, stacks of video tapes made navigation difficult on this side of the bed. Most of them Michael Keaton movies. She was as avid for

Michael as Ben was for Howie. The purple gorilla who shared her bed was called Michael for her silver screen idol.

Sam covered her, kissed her, and slipped out to the stairs.

He'd kill anybody who put a hand on one of his kids.

Brenan's office door was ajar. Eerie electronic light spilled through the crack. Resisting the urge to clear his throat, he stood in the crack and waited to be acknowledged.

"Hi." Brenan looked up.

"I'll come in if you insist," he answered hopefully.

"I insist." She kicked a castered desk chair toward him. Her smile was welcoming.

"Thanks." He sat and rolled close to her.

"Let's have it, Ace."

He shrugged.

"Oh, come on."

With a little more coaxing, he began. He told her about Justin's call. While he had her ear, he dumped everything on her. The nightmare, his dread of Karen's visit, Brother Arlo's fixation with the MacCauleys, all the *what ifs* that were currently bugging him. By the time he was finished, Brenan had printed up her hardcopy and the computer's screen saver had kicked on. She was empathetic, he was yawning, and the mantel clock was striking two.

"I'd better get you back to bed. You've got to sub for Paige on 'The Morning After Show' in a few hours, and you'll be all fuzzy if you don't get a little sleep." Brenan pushed him toward the bedroom. When they reached the bed, she pulled the robe from his body and dropped it on the floor, peeled back the covers and held them for him. She made a wonderful surrogate mother.

"Stay until I go to sleep?" He deliberately sounded pitiful and lost. He fixed his eyes into his saddest, most childlike expression. He knew he wasn't playing fair, but he was cold. He needed her heat. Besides, he didn't often intrude on her work.

She looked down with a small, resigned grin. Her dark hair fell around her face, shading parts of it. Her simple, natural beauty took his breath. His love for her raised a familiar tightness in his chest.

"I can do better than that," she whispered and began dropping her clothes on the floor. She rummaged through the drawer in the bedside table until she found something that she brought to bed with her.

"Move over, Ace."

He didn't have to be told twice.

BRENAN WOKE AFTER Sam had already gone to the station. She had intended to get up after the lovemaking for an hour or two of editing, but his warm, muscular body had pulled her down into the depths of sleep with him. She had gone willingly and had no morning regrets.

Still drowsy, she stretched and pulled his pillow tightly to her chest, curving herself around it as he had curved his body around hers. Lately, he'd been depressed and restless. Over the years, he'd gone through brief similar bouts. She hoped his good spirits would return as quickly as they always had. She hated seeing him unhappy.

Her second thought of the morning was of Karen. Karen was coming to see Mariah. Brenan wanted to be all right about it. She wanted to feel secure in her own relationship with Mariah. She wanted to be benevolent in her attitude toward Karen. In reality, she felt petty and uneasy. Old feelings of jealousy and resentment had wasted no time in slinking back.

Her thoughts drifted to Sam's getting caught up with a small boy in trouble. He was so easy to read. His emotions showed on his face, as cleanly cut and molded as a drama mask. Justin had touched something inside him, something intensely personal. She hoped he was up to dealing with this child.

From outside the bedroom came the noises of morning. Ben and Mariah were moving about the family room and kitchen. Calliope music, punctuated by beeps and ringing bells, told her at least one of them was playing a video game. They were probably already dressed for school and waiting for breakfast.

She rose slowly to a sitting position and stretched again. Her toes curled. She halted in mid-yawn.

"Uh, oh," she breathed. She clicked her tongue at the sight of an unopened contraceptive sponge lying on the sheet between her feet. She'd only taken one from the drawer, so this had to mean she'd exposed herself to millions of frisky sperm. Oh, well, she didn't track her periods very closely, but she thought she was probably safe. Besides, this wasn't the first time she'd gambled. If she lost, a baby wouldn't be a disaster. She and Sam both loved babies. Babies didn't last long enough. They grew big and independent and left an emptiness.

Brenan threw the sponge back in the drawer, dressed, brushed her hair, and made herself ready to face her children and the day.

31

YOU FIND IT HARD to trust people, but to get away from Jerome, you'll have to have faith in somebody." Sam was running out of things to say to Justin. Over a three-week period, the boy had phoned Sam several times at work and home. During his first home call, he'd been caught. Believing Justin was talking about his problems to his grandmother, Jerome had jerked him away from the phone, slapped him around and promised worse if the boy didn't keep his mouth shut. Both Justin and Sam had been grateful harsher consequences hadn't ensued.

Justin was more furtively cautious now, waiting until he was alone in the house. Slowly, he began to describe, in sickening detail, episodes of beatings, sodomy, and emotional battery that left Sam shaking with impotent rage.

Justin wanted help but was terrified of repercussions. Sam repeatedly offered to go to him and each time was refused an address, a last name. He'd considered having the calls traced but worried that a surprise visit, either by Human Resources or by Sam, could prove disastrous. He didn't want to risk losing the nominal progress he'd made in gaining Justin's confidence. Frustration and depression, as dark and threatening as storm clouds, hovered.

When he was nine and suffering, Sam had had two parents, unshakable in their devotion, to come home to, to engineer his recovery. What would he have done if only strangers had been available to care for him? Would he have been able to accept comfort from them? Would he have gotten well without Freida and A. D.? He asked himself questions he'd never before thought to ask. No answers came. He simply didn't know how to proceed with this child about whose well-being he cared deeply.

He kept trying. "You can trust me."

"Aw, Sam. He ain't done it so much lately."

"If he's done it at all, it's too much."

"Anyway, we figured somethin' out. Me an' my Granny Kay. She's gonna tell my mama she needs me an' Jason to come stay with her at night cause she's scared an' not feelin' good. She knows Jerome's mean as the devil to us. She's gonna call Mama tonight when she gets home from her job at Sears. She don't want us around anyhow, so she'll let us stay if Jerome don't say no."

Ask what Sears store. Ask where his grandmother lives.

"Are you going to tell me anything more about you? You know I could find you if I really tried, don't you?"

"I cain't, Sam. You cain't fix everything, but you can be my friend an' not look too hard for me."

"All right—for now. I hope your plan works out."

"It might." Justin didn't sound all that sure.

"Look, I've told you about my two kids. I can't stand the thought of somebody doing to them what's being done to you and Jason. It makes me feel sick to know you're still having to go through it. You and I— we're friends—even you've said so. I like you a lot, and well, it's getting so I have a hard time when you hang up. I *really* want to get you away from that man."

"I know, but you cain't. You don't understand. I ain't no slum kid, Sam. Jerome—he works for—I cain't say, but he's got a big wood desk with glass on top of it an' great big windows in his office. Gotta whole room full of secretaries. People *know* him. He's got two Caddies, a new one an' a old, old one that looks new. An' he bought a bran' new Park Avenue just for Mama—just wrote a check for it. Nobody even asked to see his driver's license. He can pay all the lawyers he needs to say I'm just a lyin' little kid. Nuthin' poor 'bout Jerome. But I'd rather be out on Windover Street with Granny Kay than up on this hill with him. Mama's gonna marry him so she won't hafta work no more. Won't turn a hand to help me an' Jason. She can be in one room hearin' us hollerin' in the next an' not even come see what he's doin' to us."

AFTER WORK, Sam found Windover Street and drove its length several times. It ran through a six-block section of a time-frozen, mostly black neighborhood that was defined by old, sagging front-porch dwellings that had been built in the twenties and probably hadn't seen adequate upkeep in thirty years.

He was vaguely familiar with the area because last winter he had covered a series of arson fires in a row of warehouses a couple of streets over. Also, this was one of Rita Williams's childhood haunts. The secretary had a thousand humorous, heartwarming, as well as heart-breaking tales of growing up black and impoverished in Birmingham. Some had taken place on Windover.

He looked carefully. There were a few ragged fences, two rusty gym sets, and fewer than three cars per block. A peaceful, old-fashioned tract, a little outside of the rougher, too common crime-infested despair holes. A six-block representation of a way of life Sam knew only secondhand. He could come back in the daylight, knock on doors. Someone would know a Granny Kay and, if that person recognized Sam's face from the TV, might even point out her home to him. He decided he would do just that as soon as he figured out if it would help to deliver Justin and his brother into safe and loving hands.

"COME ON, Sam, wake up. It's Justin. He sounds like something's wrong."

Sam gradually broke the surface of a sound, dreamless sleep. Morning sunlight streamed through the bedroom blinds. He sat up, put one hand over his eyes, and took the phone.

"Yeah, Justin?"

"He come got me." The boy's voice was husky from crying.

No! Lefty's alarm went off.

Instantly, Sam was alert. He swung his feet off the bed and leaned forward with the handset pressed to his ear. Brenan, who had only retreated a few steps, stood still, waiting.

"He took you away from your grandmother?"

"Yeah. He says he missed me, but he let Jason stay. He says Jason ain't good like I am. He just wants me."

Think of somethin' quick, Sam! Ya gotta!

"You can't stay there. You've got to let me come for you this time. I swear I'll protect you."

"I cain't talk about that now, ain't got time. He's comin' back 'fore lunchtime. Says he's gonna bring this friend of his. Says his friend'll give me somethin' if I treat 'im nice."

Friend! Ohmygod!

"Tell me how to get there. You'll be gone when he comes back."

"You said this ain't my fault. Jerome *made* me do it. God won't blame me. Right?"

"Of course, God won't blame you. Nobody will blame you. Are you going to tell me—"

"So when I die, I won't burn up in hell?"

"No, Justin. You're a good kid. You won't be punished for something you couldn't stop from happening. Now, let's quit talking about dying, and tell me how to find you."

"Stop it, Sam. I wanna tell you somethin' an' I ain't got much time. You're a good friend. I believe you wanna take care of me. It ain't your fault you cain't. You told me I don't hafta take blame for things that ain't my fault, so I hope you know how not to do that, too. *This* ain't your fault. Just be happy it won't happen no more."

I don't like this!

"What're you talking about?"

"I got his gun."

What!

"What!"

"I wish I'd got you for a daddy. You've been real straight with me, an' I'm glad I got to know you." Justin's voice was still hoarse but calm. "Your kids're lucky."

"Justin, no! Please! Leave that gun alone!"

"You don't understand. I want to go to heaven. Granny Kay says God don't let nobody get hurt in heaven. She reads me stuff outta the Bible that makes it seem like a great place to go to. I ain't scared a bit."

DO somethin'!

"No! You don't have to do that! I can help *you!*"

"You think you can, but you cain't. He'd come after you. You got a family that needs you. You've been my friend. That's all you can do. I love you, Sam. I look at you on TV an' make like I'm your kid an' it's me you'll be comin' home to when you get done there."

"I love you, too. You feel like my kid. I need to do something, Justin! *Please, let me come get you!*"

"Don't you get it? Jerome will kill you. He'll pay somebody to kill you or your kids. He'll get you. I cain't let 'im do that, an' I cain't let 'im do it to me no more."

"Wait!"

"No, there is somethin'."

"Anything! Just don't—"

"Tell about Jerome on TV when they git 'im. He won't know about you 'cause it'll be me that gets 'im caught. He won't know you're my friend—just a newsman on TV. I sent a letter to my Granny Kay an' Jason. I mailed it. The law'll have to put 'im up when they get that letter. I said everything in it."

"Justin!"

"You just go on an' tell his name an' what he did so he cain't get to nobody else. His name's Jerome Watley. Will you — No! Oh, Sam, he ain't supposed to get home, yet! They're comin' in! They're laughin' an' . . . "

Sam heard a thud. The sound of the phone falling out of Justin's hands, hitting a table or the floor.

"Justin! For godsake, Justin, pick the phone back up!"

Sam looked at Brenan. She stood a few feet away in the same spot she'd occupied since she'd turned the handset over to him. Her eyes were fixed fearfully on his face. A whisper. He turned. Mariah and Ben stood as still as statues in the bedroom doorway. Their faces were also painted with fear. They'd heard him pleading with Justin. They knew something terrible was wrong, but he couldn't comfort them. He was powerless to do more than struggle for breath and listen to a concert of noises on the other end of the line.

Shuffling. Scraping. A mechanical click.

Justin mumbling to himself—probably no longer aware of Sam's presence on the phone line.

Then a voice, rising above the gruff, garbled, shocked reactions of Jerome and his so-called *friend,* came all too clearly through the phone lines.

"Get back, Jerome! You cain't do it no more! I won't let you! Not no more! NOT NO MORE! NOTNOMORE!"

And an explosion.

Sam held the phone in front of his face and stared at it. He couldn't think of anything else to do with it, so he held it out to Brenan. She put it to her ear, listened, then pushed in the antenna and flicked the switch off.

"The line's dead," she whispered.

"The line's dead," Sam echoed.

32

June 1991

S HE HELD HER HAND over her eyes and watched Sam and the Explorer disappear around the bend in the driveway. In a couple of hours, he'd return with his first wife. He looked as if he'd rather drink poison than make this trip to the airport, but instead of taking comfort in his dread, Brenan felt her anxiety grow. Sam hadn't been happy in a long time.

Standing on the front steps, Brenan tried to telepathically send her support down the empty driveway to him. A deep gloom had settled on him, devitalizing him, gnawing away at his spirit. She brooded over the changes she had seen him go through. He didn't even confide in her.

Dragging blame behind him, Sam had pulled through Justin's suicide. Hands in his pockets, face averted from the ice blue casket, Sam had stood dry-eyed in the chapel and at the graveside. Then moving a distance from the small gathering of mourners, he had posed in front of Tommy Crowder's camera and tried to formally report the incident. But he hadn't quite pulled it off. His cool professional style had gone tepid, flat. He'd made too much of an emotional investment in this elusive telephone child. In trying to publicly explain his relationship with Justin, he'd given voice to the guilt he'd otherwise denied. Then he passed some of it around. "*When are we going to stop letting beasts who masquerade as human beings brutalize and terrorize children? Justin Kelsey took the only way out, the only way he could see. He told me about his mother in the next room refusing to answer his cries. His last calls for help were directed at me, and I waited too long. I failed him. No amount of hindsight is going to give him another chance. I shouldn't have waited for the right time because the right time is only a myth. I shouldn't have waited for him to be ready because his judgment was contaminated by the abuse. At the end, he worried more about me than himself. He saw death as freedom . . . "*

Throughout the ordeal, there had been no tears—only blue and gray shadows that had darkened Sam's face to a stony mask. The nightmare had kept him from the solace of sleep. Tears might have helped.

Justin's letter to his grandmother and the report Sam had given the police had set in motion a series of reactions. A domino effect that had eventually slammed into Jerome Watley and knocked him down. When the time came, Sam would be required to testify. Brenan dreaded that day and what it might contribute to his depression, but he seemed to look forward to it as the means for a reckoning. He was clear in his intent to make Watley pay.

An up-and-coming politician and a top-level executive for one of Birmingham's oldest mortgage and investment companies, Ludlow Financial Services, Inc., Jerome Watley had denied everything. Judging from what Sam could find out through his journalistic sources, the combined medical evidence of both boys, half of it postmortem, would stand as powerful testament in court. Jason, in his shock over his brother's death, had forgotten his resolve to never tell and given police an explicit account of abuse beginning the day their mother had moved them into Watley's home over two years ago. The children's mother had disappeared, and the warrant for her arrest had gone unserved.

Jason had been remanded to the custody of Vera Kelsey, his Granny Kay, who lived on Windover Street. This time the arrangement was permanent. Mrs. Kelsey had gratefully allowed Sam to pay funeral expenses but politely refused a cash gift for Jason. "If he ever needs something I can't pay for, I won't be too proud to ask. In the meantime, I thank you."

At home, Sam had become mechanical in carrying out the routines of his daily life. Except for the hours when he was working, he made himself an odd shadow following the movements of his family. Brenan didn't know if this new stick-tight, protective posture was for her and the children or for himself. From work, he called to check on them too often. She began to notice a lot of small changes—and bigger ones.

As days and weeks passed, their lovemaking became touched with a new and stormy urgency. A torrid undercurrent began to flow with his movements, with the sounds that came involuntarily from him. Afterward, he fell into fretful sleep riddled by bad dreams he would later claim he couldn't recall. "Screaming. That's all. Children screaming." Twice, he'd awakened her in the middle of the night, wanting to make love. Actually, Brenan thought what he wanted and took from her during those times was a little more earthy and elemental than loving.

As if untoward grief was not enough, he presently had to deal with Karen. He'd made a dedicated stab at lightheartedness when he left the house. He hadn't wanted to add his worry to her's or Mariah's. He had tried too hard. Brenan was uneasy.

She was concerned about Mariah, too. The child was behaving as if this day was just like any other—not the day she was, for the first time, to meet the woman who had given her life. At last check, she was in her room apparently absorbed in a Michael Keaton movie. Playing it cool— an act, a way of holding onto a feeling of normalcy.

When Brenan and Sam had tried to prepare her for meeting Karen, Mariah had made the statement, "I'll be okay just as long as nobody refers to her as *my mother.* " She had pointed and said, *"You* are my mother. I'm relieved this woman didn't want a kid. Just make sure this Karen person knows I'm not going anywhere. Grampa Mark said Daddy robbed a cradle to get you for me, but since you're happy, he guessed the end justified the means—or something like that. Anyway, Mama, I'm glad I have you."

Even Sam, who hadn't seen much humor in anything for a while, had smiled at her quoting Mark.

In an effort to be honest with herself, Brenan conceded her own worries. Karen had been married to Sam. She had lived with him, slept with him, given him a daughter. All before Brenan had made any claim, but she still felt the sting of leftover jealousy pangs from the days when she'd loved him in lonely silence. Sam was anything but excited about seeing Karen. He'd never looked at her with tender longing. But the little pangs kept hitting.

Brenan hadn't been feeling well physically. All morning, she'd been queasy. Her usually insatiable appetite had been off for several days. She hoped this disruption of their lives would soon be safely behind them— for all the combined reasons. With tension so thick in the air, she hadn't written a word in a month that she didn't immediately delete.

The only person in the house who wasn't nervous about Karen's impending arrival was Ben. He had his attention focused on adding another hundred feet of track to his railroad line. The new track would pass by Mariah's bedroom door, rising to run along the baluster that overlooked the foyer, dropping to make a U-turn loop in the seldom-used play room and returning along the opposite side of the hall. A. D. had cut two arched openings in the bottom of the playroom door to facilitate the entry and exit of the train. The railway presently covered considerable floor space. If someone didn't put brakes on the railroad-building soon, the second story would be unfit for pedestrian traffic.

So far, no one begrudged Ben the space. The tracks could be stepped over, ducked under, or skirted. His trains made him happy. He was also happy in his ignorance of other people's problems and was fortunate enough to have no especially pressing ones of his own. Brenan stopped for a minute to watch his track-laying before going on to Mariah's room.

Batman had ended. Another movie was beginning. *Touch and Go*, a favorite. Brenan wondered how many times Mariah had sat dreamily through this one.

"Move over, kiddo." She settled onto a heap of pillows beside Mariah. They smiled at each other, snuggled close, but didn't speak. After all, the idolized Michael Keaton was playing hockey on the TV screen.

MARIAH HEARD THE Explorer coming up the drive. Forgetting her resolve to be cool, she climbed over her mother to look out the window.

At this distance, she couldn't even recognize her daddy through the darkly tinted windshield of the wagon.

"They're here," she announced. "You'll stay with me, won't you? In the same room?" She hoped she didn't sound too much like a baby. She searched Brenan's face for some indication of her true feelings about this stupid meeting.

"Yes, honey, I'll be right there. I wouldn't leave my kid."

Mariah's stomach felt all fluttery. She hated doing this. Although she was curious about this woman, wanted to know what she looked like, how she talked, Mariah would rather be behind some two-way mirror, looking through. She wanted to be the observer, not the observed. She'd known about Karen for a long time. Until lately, she hadn't thought much about her, and when she had, it was to wish she didn't exist. Mariah had the best mother in the world, and her name was Brenan—not Karen. Brenan had taken care of her since she was born. Brenan had loved and wanted her. That made her Mariah's true mother. That woman had better not think she could come here and squeeze herself into Mariah's life. She'd better not try.

A few times, Mariah had asked Gramma Freida about Karen. Her grandmother hadn't had much to say other than to answer specific questions, but Mariah could tell her relationship with Karen had not been a joyful one. In fact, once Mariah had overheard Gramma Freida tell Gramma Ellen there had been no love lost in Russett, Alabama, when *that woman* decided to move on. Gramma Freida always had opinions, but her criticism was usually more in fun. She didn't say the kind of things that would hurt someone's feelings on purpose. She *seriously* didn't like Karen.

Mariah had another reason for hoping that things would go smoothly and be over quickly. Something was wrong with Daddy. He had been really sad when a little boy he'd made friends with killed himself with a gun. Daddy had heard the gunshot over the phone. He'd been sick or something ever since. Lately, when she looked at him, she thought she could see something even more wrong that made his eyes look blind even when he was trying to pay attention to her or Ben. He was too softhearted, anyway. He always wanted to do things for people. She felt sorry for him and wished she knew how to cheer him up.

A car door slammed, then another. Mariah flinched.

"Come on," she said and put out her hand for Brenan to hold. "Let's go get this over with."

THE DRIVE BACK home took a little longer than usual, because they stopped at a Food Plus Mart for chips, candy, and fountain sodas to be consumed on the sly in the wagon. Brenan was nearly as bad as Freida about fat, sugar, and empty calories—with a rare exception for choco-late. She wouldn't accept that now and then people, especially kids, needed junk food. Sam and Mariah felt no shame in satisfying that need today. A bag of peanut M&Ms, a Chocolate Soldier, and a jumbo pack of Pixie Stix were stowed in the console, waiting to be smuggled upstairs to Ben. Everything else disappeared into Sam and Mariah during the ride home.

Straining upward to see through the windshield, Mariah sat in the passenger seat with the shoulder harness bisecting her diagonally. When Sam glanced at her, he found her profile stunning. He loved her in a way Karen, on her smartest day, could never understand.

He credited his ability to love Mariah and Ben so completely to the selfless, untiring way his parents had loved and nurtured him. But recently, he'd become afraid for them and for Brenan. This fear, different from his usual caution, was based not on rationale but a deep, obsessing dread submerged somewhere inside him. All of a sudden, he would be seized by the need to be watchful, on guard. After a while, the uneasiness would let up—only to return, more frightening after a brief respite. For days, the feeling had been strong and unrelenting. Today, it showed no sign of abating.

"What's going on in that brainy head of yours?" He tried to sound light and playful.

She turned her face to him. The corners of her mouth dipped downward. She shrugged. "Just thinking. About her—Karen. I don't know what I thought she'd be like."

"What *was* she like?"

"Well, she wasn't extremely stupid or ugly or anything like that. Not what you'd call the mother type, but not too bad. Nervous, I guess."

"Do you think you'd ever want to get to know her better? Spend time with her?" He glimpsed a flicker of uncertainty crossing her face.

"You didn't make any arrangements without telling me, did you?"

"Of course not. It was only a question."

"Then no, but I told her she could write. I didn't promise to answer, but I might. Anyway, I'm okay with the family I've got—most of the time. I'm one of these people who gets stubborn and set in their ways early on. I like things to stay the same, and I like to be able to depend on the people around me. I need to know what to expect. Know what I mean?"

"I think so." He knew exactly what she meant.

They both sighed. It was over.

Karen had come and gone. Sam's world was unmoved and sound. But was it really? Why couldn't he feel the soundness?

He and Mariah had taken Karen to the Cranford, a nice motel near the airport. Tomorrow, she'd fly back to Tulsa. A couple of hours was all she'd wanted. He thought maybe she'd planned on staying longer but had been more ill at ease than she'd expected.

She'd been smiling and quiet, asking only uncomplicated questions. "Do you like school? What do you like to do? Do you have lots of friends?" Short, simple, impersonal.

Mentally, Sam had applauded some of the changes he'd observed in her. She'd seemed to have lost much of her self-centeredness and grown. She had finished a cosmetology course at a vocational college in Tulsa and was currently working at a salon in a shopping mall. She still lived with her retired grandparents. For a short time, she'd been married to a truck driver who had been less than decent to her. After the truck driver had gone out of her life, she'd joined a Baptist church and appeared to have found some peace for herself there.

She hadn't asked for anything—money, sympathy, or another visit. Sam had offered to help her finance a salon of her own, but she'd shaken her head. "Thanks, Sam, but I'm doing things for myself now, and it feels good. I already owe that to you."

Things had gone better than he'd expected, but he was all too relieved to see her go. Mariah was his child, and Brenan's, and he'd hated putting her on display for a woman who was just passing in and out of their lives on a whim.

He and Mariah had helped Karen settle into her room at the Cranford. They'd had dinner with her in the motel restaurant, adding another hour to the visit. As they were saying good-bye outside her room, Mariah had, to Sam's amazement, allowed Karen one brief, stiff hug. Later, in the parking lot, she had wrapped her arms around him and, without saying why, hugged him tightly.

He reached over, ran a finger down her cheek. "You managed things just fine today."

She smiled. "So did you."

"Thanks. I have something I want you to know."

"What's that, Daddy?"

"I really wanted you—even when I thought I'd be raising you by myself. Karen didn't know how to care about another person back then. Her life had been pretty horrible. She didn't even care about me until it was too late. At first, I was temporary shelter or something like that. I hope you don't feel that she rejected you."

"Why did you live with her? I mean, if you didn't love each other, why would you want to?"

"I hate to answer that because I don't want you to know how selfish and dumb I can be."

"Whatever it was—I was born because of it."

"That's true, and you have the right to know."

They reached the driveway, but Sam decided to pass on by it. If Mariah noticed, she didn't comment.

"Brenan was sixteen, and even though she seemed older, I thought my love for her was wrong. At that time, I never would have believed she had the same kind of feelings for me. I was ashamed and fearful, and just to keep from going crazy, I tried to forget her. Karen just happened along. She needed to get away from a father who emotionally abused her, and I needed someone to take my mind off Brenan. Maybe I should be ashamed of that, too, but I'm not. Karen ended up with a better life—not perfect, but better. And I got you. No regrets here."

"It didn't work, did it?"

"What?"

"Forgetting Mama."

"No. You can't replace people you love. Bren loves you and me without holding Karen against us. Terrific, huh?"

"Yeah, but today was hard for her. She wasn't feeling good, anyway. We need to be extra nice to her when we get home."

"I think you're right. Let's run up to Billie's Flowers and buy her a cactus or something before we turn back toward home. You can give it to her while I bootleg the goods to Benjamin."

33

THE INDEPENDENCE DAY SKY above and below Red Mountain was glittering and garish. The main show was over, but the mingled fireworks displays of the various points of the city were nearing a peak dazzle. Sam was free of the newsroom and one of the most exhausting and least productive evenings of his life. He wasn't impressed by the blazing heavens.

Nothing specific had soured the work day, only a running total of small inconveniences that had added up. All he wanted to do was put the day and the drive home behind him and enter the relative calm of his own home. After the ten o'clock newscast, he practically flew off the mountain.

Holiday traffic made his flight a bumpy one. A mile from home, he fished a black plastic remote control from the seat beside him, and held it restlessly as he steered. When he finally wheeled into his own driveway, the dashboard clock showed 11:22—not exactly record timing, but close. His thumb stabbed the center of the remote control pad with more force than was needed, and the gates of the security fence that guarded his family in his absence swung open. He glanced up the hill to the northeast of the house and shuddered at his wasted effort. Even home would fall short of a peaceful sanctum tonight—at least until the home boys were through playing.

At this hour, Mark, Robert, and A. D. would still be armed with enough bottle rockets, Roman candles, and variety packs of fireworks to last until sunup. They'd probably return in a couple of hours with their pockets bulging with fire cracker and sparkler overkill. The three men, usually four counting Sam, had kept a major chunk of Russett's citizenry up late every Fourth of July as far back as he could remember. Before rounding the house, he caught a peripheral blur of three women seated on the Armstrongs' patio. Another look told him Brenan wasn't one of them.

Independence Day required serious celebrating. After all, the freedom of a nation or an individual was a precious commodity with distinctions not to go unsung. Every year, as soon as the world was dark enough for a spark to show, the Armstrong-MacCauley Brigade lugged boxes of carefully selected and culled fireworks to the rocky overlook on the hill near the cavern mouth, possibly the loftiest perch of the near foothills, and proceeded to give the locals a free show. Marissa, Mariah, and Deejay, as well as any kid who might be visiting, followed. This year, Sam had reluctantly agreed that Ben could go.

Before leaving for the station, he had dumped a handful of plastic-wrapped disposable ear plugs into the bib pocket of his father's overalls and using the tip of a finger firmly against the older man's chest, insisted, "Make sure they wear them. You'll be held accountable for any hearing impairments. Also, I'll be counting fingers when I get home."

It seemed to Sam his dad got a little younger in his behavior with each passing year. His father-in-law wasn't much better. The two had never lost the knack for playing. Throw in Robert, a perpetual adolescent despite a boring but lucrative corporate law practice, and a dangerous combination existed.

The free shows were legend, as much tradition as backyard barbecues and the faded old flag that hung heavy and unwaving, but nonetheless proud, on its pole at the union hall. Families who couldn't see the fireworks well enough from their own yards and people from neighborhoods outside Russett gathered at a popular fishing hole to the south of Russett Bridge. Sitting on tiers of beer-cooler and lawn-chair bleachers and the rough elbows of low-forking limbs, they watched from the creek bank.

On the occasions Sam didn't have to work, he dutifully tagged along. He hated to put a damper on their fun almost as badly as he hated to leave them without someone to supervise and nag them into keeping their body parts intact. This afternoon, he'd rounded up the children and lectured them on the behavior and precautions he expected from them, then he appointed Marissa fire marshal. She was an enthusiastic tattletale who had a natural bossy, belligerent peal in her voice—traits handed down by her mother. She'd suffice as pinch nagger this once.

Sam drove under a sky twinkling with artificial stars and parked in the garage. He jogged lightly through the house.

Instead of homey peace and warm arms, he found an irate Brenan sitting in the dead center of their bed with the cordless phone and a box of tissue in her lap. She jerked her head up to look at him, her brow crinkled into a zigzagged line. Her face was shiny with tears. A tissue ball sailed through the air in front of him, almost making the cold fireplace before it ran out of momentum and dropped inches from the hearth.

His mind already grappling for a safe greeting, he pulled up short of the bed. She was touchy these days. So was he. The emotional climate of the household seemed to be blowing both of them considerably off kilter. "What's wrong, Pooky?" He settled on showing concern for her obvious distress.

"This phone!" Her chin was trembling; tears spurting anew. "First, Arlo called to tell me if I don't publicly retract every word of *Pulpits,* God's going to demand a ransom of my blood. How can fiction be retracted? Then your ex-wife called. She wants to give Mariah a diamond and emerald ring her grandmother gave her. I told her she'd have to talk to you. That was about ten. She's already called back, trying to sweet talk me into being gracious and using my influence. Arlo's called back twice!" The tears that streamed from her lovely dark eyes were whisked aside by angry swipes of her close-bitten fingertips. She crawled on her knees to the end of the bed and thrust the handset at him. "Here. If it rings, you deal with it," she said as she brushed past him. No attempts to put on her tough-gal show tonight.

"Wait, Bren." He threw the phone back on the bed and started after her. She stopped in the doorway with her back to him. She rigidly allowed his arms to circle her, his chin to rest on her shoulder. Her cheek next to his was hot and wet. "Come on back. I'll turn the phone off. The kids won't be back for a while."

She hesitated, unmoving for a few seconds, then nodded and followed him to the bed.

"DO YOU THINK SHE'S going to be trouble?" She lay beside him, holding his hand flat against her bare stomach.

"Karen? I don't think so, but we'll deal with her if she decides to be. Mariah's ours—yours and mine."

Brenan became silent and dropped into a weary sleep without asking any more questions.

Sam watched her breasts dip and rise with her breathing. They looked larger, the nipples darker. She'd put on a few pounds, adding a softness to her features, a difference so slight he doubted anyone else would notice.

There was a difference inside her, too—a much more intrusive incongruity. She was keeping something from him, and he was wary of what it might be. He couldn't ask, could only brace himself, give her opportunities to explain. He felt as if the warmth had been bled out of her by some dark, alien force. Unless he called her name, she didn't look up when he entered a room. He couldn't hold her attention in conversation. She kept her feelings to herself. And now, their lovemaking had gone stale.

Lately, every time they had been intimate, the union had been stiff and perfunctory, stirring none of the accustomed excitement. Their bed had grown cold. He couldn't recall the last time she'd said, "I love you."

As he watched her sleep, he resented the intrusion of his own thoughts but knew he had to face the reality behind them. Tonight, she had put on an act designed to convince him he'd given her something he hadn't. All too plainly, he saw that he'd come nowhere near touching her. The center of his chest burned over her attempted deception. She should have told him what she wanted, what she needed, if she simply preferred to be left alone. How many times had she put on this act? How many times had he been taken in by it? He hadn't called her on it. The pain of her sham was too strong, too fresh for that tonight.

Thinking back over what had just taken place, he shuddered. Sex should never be taken or given—only shared. It should never become an obligation. And it should not leave a man feeling as if he had wounded his lover's soul. He'd have to watch closer for signals. He wouldn't let himself believe a permanent alteration was taking place in the life they'd made together. While he'd dealt with Justin, she'd administered to him. She must have found his despondency taxing and hard to comprehend. He would give her space, wait for her to come to him. He could be patient. He could do anything for a while.

When he heard the sound of his children and the others coming in, he covered Brenan, left her sleeping, dressed quickly, and went out to greet them. It did little to improve his mood.

ABOUT ELEVEN IN THE MORNING, when Brenan took to her office to begin her day's work, Sam trekked up the hill with A. D. and the kids to clean up the fireworks shrapnel. The place was a rubbish heap of shredded paper, blackened matches, and sticks from rockets and sparklers.

At noon, he checked his wristwatch and shook his head. Time to get dressed for work. Before he left the makeshift grounds crew, he fussed until A. D. finally promised to sit out the rest of the cleanup. Sam looked into his father's tired eyes and told him plainly that the kids would do the job. "They'll also tell on you if you get off that rock before they're through. It's too hot for me, so I know you must be feeling the heat."

"Nag, nag, nag. That all you can do?"

"You taught me to take care of the things I care about so I'd have them a long time. You're not easy to take care of, you know." Sam pointed at his chest then turned his finger in the direction of Ben, Mariah, Marissa, and Deejay. "I need you. They need you. And living down in the valley are a whole lot more people who need you. So behave."

A. D. made his compliance look grudging. A show of uncontested acceptance would have embarrassed him. A man needed his pride. "You act like I'm an old man."

"I do not."

"Yes, you do."

"I act like you're important."

Sam yelled at the kids to stop dawdling and get the job done.

THE PHONE WAS ringing when he entered the house.

He scooped it off the kitchen wall. Karen.

"Did Brenan tell you I called?"

"Yes."

"She tell you why?"

"Yeah. Look, I don't think it's a good idea for you to start giving Mariah gifts. She's satisfied with the way things are, and I don't want to mess that up."

"I promise not to make a habit of it. It's just so she'll have something of mine, something of *me*. I'm no more her mama than any other strange woman, but I have feelings. It'll just be this once. I didn't give you any trouble after she was born, and I won't now. Just let her have this."

"Fine, Karen," he sighed, "but after the ring, I want you to confine your communication with her to letters—words on paper. Leave it to her whether or not to answer. If there's ever anything more, it will have to be because she asks."

"I understand."

"Just don't expect anything from her or us. Brenan, Ben, and I are her family. She's glad she met you, but she's also a little unnerved about it. Please, understand." He hated having to say these things. Rejection always hurt.

"Sure, Sam, I swear. I can see she's happy, but God, I wish I had someone like her."

TWO DAYS LATER, Sam removed his sunglasses and waited for his eyes to adjust to the glare ricocheting off the marble headstones and the ivory baked-clay mounds of earth. In only minutes under the July sun, perspiration had soaked his clothes and hair.

In an era of flat green expanses broken only by uniform markers with

small built-in vases and *rules,* the old swept cemetery was one of the last
of its kind. Here, the rule was no rules. Old people took care of inherited
family plots in the manner that best suited their tastes or economic
means. No grass grew. Any weeds that shot up in the spring were pulled
before the rain of flowers on Decoration Day, an annual gathering that
fell on a select Sunday in June. Sam couldn't recall which one.

Around him were whole family plots of eight or ten graves outlined
in brick, cinder block, white picket and single graves overlaid by solid
cement slabs or mounds of marble chips. A few anonymous final resting
places were measured only by two rocks. Leaning, crumbling stone
markers dated back to pre-Civil War days, evolving forward up to the
newer, straighter, squat designs of the near present.

In the center of the graveyard were a scattering of unmarked cairns.
A century old, these mysterious rock piles had been a childhood source
of speculation and intrigue for Sam and Robert during the many trips
they'd made to the cemetery with A. D.

Few interments had occurred in Bent Pine since the late sixties when
Russett Memory Garden first opened its ornate wrought-iron gates.
Bud's tiny marker was one of the newest.

Raymond Arlo Blacknell, Jr. / Jan. 22, 1956 — Mar 31, 1973. No
Beloved Son of . . . , no *Rest in Peace.* Only the barest of mortal statistics
etched into a stone the size of a Cheerios box.

The hillside was decked out in artificial flower groupings from last
month's Decoration. There were no flowers on Bud's grave. Someone
had cleaned around it. The dirt had recently been mounded back up.
The tine marks of a leaf rake were still impressed into the earth. The
keeper of a nearby plot whose graves would have been cheapened by a
mess so near? Someone who'd known the grave would go untended?
Someone who had felt badly about a forgotten soul? A. D.? As soon as he
got home, Sam would order flowers for Bud. Bud wouldn't know, but
Sam would. He couldn't leave the grave looking like nobody cared. "You
were important to me, Bud the Bear," he whispered. "I haven't forgotten." He would ask A. D. to remind him in time for other Decoration
Days and special times in between.

A. D.'s parents, his baby brother, and his grandmother were buried near the dark back of the graveyard where irregularly spaced cedars grew and became nuisances. Sam skirted the perimeter until he reached their graves. Shaded by two fat, conical cedars, this plot was well-tended and the trees carefully pruned. The wilted remains of the flowers A. D. had placed there in June had been replaced by recessed pots of crisp yellow chrysanthemums and pink tea roses. No plastic or silk in summer. Not for A. D. MacCauley's people.

A. D.'s maternal grandmother's name had been Adelaide Haisten, but her grandchildren had called her Gramma Addie. A. D. had brought the tradition down to his grandchildren. *Gramma* Freida, *Gramma* Ellen, *Grampas* A. D. and Mark.

She had taken A. D. and his brother, Henry, after their parents died in an early morning house fire. At the time of the fire, A. D. had been four years old, and Henry less than a year. A neighbor had pulled the boys out of the burning house but hadn't been able to rouse John and Omie MacCauley from their beds ahead of the smoke and flame. Gramma Addie had already lost a husband to tuberculosis and two sons to the first World War. Then two months after the fire had taken her daughter and son-in-law, her Baby Henry had succumbed to diphtheria. Gramma Addie and A. D. had become a family of two. Yet, lovingly and without bitterness, she'd raised her surviving chick to the age of seventeen. He'd been a senior in high school when a sudden stroke snatched her away, too, leaving him to finish up by himself. She had called him Abel David long after school yard mates had dubbed him Shady A. D. The two had loved each other with a fierceness born of common tragedy and loss. She had given him her strict values, respect for himself and others, and a taste for simple living.

Sam had heard so many Gramma Addie stories, he believed he knew her. A large woman with a sense of humor and the strength to carry on while her kin were picked off in ones and twos—A. D. often referred to her as a fine piece of work. Sam gave her credit for the strong, generous man that was his father. In his eyes and heart, no other man had ever come close to A. D.'s stature. Sam, as well as his mother and sister, were fortunate to have this man instead of the one whose place he had filled. He nodded a silent thanks to Gramma Addie's headstone.

A fifth grave shared the plot—this one smaller than Henry's short mound. *Abel David MacCauley / September 8, 1959 – October 1, 1959 / son of A. D. and Freida who will be forever thankful for those twenty-three days.* After fruitless surgery and struggle, Sam's brother had died of a heart deformity. Afterward, Freida had gone through two first trimester miscarriages and suffered bouts of anemia and depression. *"Of course, we both grieved. He was our baby. Your mama, though, was torn up for a long time. Wouldn't admit it, but deep down she thought she needed to give me a child,"* A. D. had told Sam several times when he was growing up. *"Her first husband didn't leave her enough self-confidence to fill a thimble. No offense, son, but I sure am glad you didn't turn out like him. Coldhearted skin flint. Your mama had a tough time believin' I loved her for a lot better reasons than just what she could do for me. Took a lotta talkin' to convince her all I needed was her an' the babies she'd already given me."*

Sam had intended to visit Justin's grave which was in one of the big, monotonously flat cemeteries in Birmingham. Walking away from this old one, away from the Bent Pine Primitive Baptist Church, a deserted one-room block building where services were no longer held except on Decoration Day, he changed his mind. He had conjured up enough ghosts for one day.

"Tell me about this ransom of blood you keep bringing up to my wife. Somebody just might take that as a threat on her life."

"Take it as ya will. God's not mocked. He ain't one to let people who blaspheme agin the Holy Ghost go unpunished, neither. He'll take His revenge in His own good time, Mr. MacCauley. B'leve that! Ya didn't repent for the way ya took my boy off an' taught him the things ya did. Didn't even have the decency to own up to givin' him the likker an' dope, puttin' him up to sin with women. You an' the Armstrong hellion ain't got me fooled, but I blame you a sight more cuz Bud thought ya wuz his friend. He wuz easy led. Now, tell me how ya live with knowin' ya innerduced him to the very thing that killed him?"

Old fart don't even know Bud was a virgin, Lefty cracked.

Sam didn't answer. He didn't hang up, either. He wanted to hear all this old coot had to say so he would have some idea how seriously to take the threats against Brenan.

"Can't answer, can ya? Well, ya done worse in beddin' down that little piece a devil's garbage ya married—them *two* pieces ya married. That last un—she goes whorin' fer Ol' Scratch ever time she puts a word on paper. She's evil. She don't repent an' be saved, she'll be put down by the Almighty. Mark my words, MacCauley, ya just may go down with her."

Tell 'im you'd rather go down ON her.

Brother Arlo was still preaching when Sam put the receiver back in its cradle. He was no closer to figuring out what to do about this madman but was glad he'd intercepted the call. Brenan was nervous enough without having to listen to this trash.

He quickly thumbed through the front of the phone directory, found the listing he was looking for, and lifted the handset again. The least he could do was change the number one more time. It always took Arlo a few days to get hold of a new one.

This week of unwelcome phone calls and graveyard reunions, of growing uncertainty, of loneliness and rejection, had Sam hoping desperately for a change soon in the coming.

AIN'T DOIN' NUTHIN' but starin' at the keyboard. Looks like writer's block. Might welcome a break. Tap on the glass, smile, crook your finger, an' see if she'll come out an' play.

Early August, standing on the porch, watching Brenan through the window, Sam felt like a voyeur. Mark and Ellen had taken Mariah, Ben, Marissa, and Deejay to Point Mallard for the day. Freida had abducted A. D. and departed with him for a shop-till-you-drop excursion in the clusters of factory outlets in Boaz. And Brenan was *working.* Except for Lefty and the dogs, Sam was alone.

Now's a good time to talk. Nobody 'round to bug ya.

Still covertly observing his wife, Sam frowned.

She's confused, too. Both of ya can ask questions, answer 'em, an', ya know, TALK. Remember how? You'll ask, "What did I do wrong?" An' she'll tell ya, an' you'll say "I'm sorry. I won't ever do it again—cross my heart." Then you'll kiss an' make up, an' stuff'll get better. We'll all be friends again.

Sam sighed. Brenan sat with her elbows on her desk, her chin propped in the palm of her hand. Her beauty held up to profile, to any angle. If she turned her head to the left, she'd see him. She probably wouldn't like him watching her on the sly. She no longer wanted him to glance at her from across a room.

What're ya standin' here for? Ya don't wanna always be on the outside lookin' in. Go on. Do it.

Sam really needed her to explain what was amiss.

It's gonna get worse. An' worse!

"Ohgod, Bren, I miss you!" The whisper felt like a sob.

PLEASE, Sam. Go fix things for us. I miss her, too. Don't be nervous— I'll tell ya what to say. Might be just waitin' for us to make the first move. Bet she is. Won't know till ya try. If anybody knows how stubborn those Armstrongs can be, it's us.

Sam was terrified of talking to her. She might tell him *things*. I-don't-love-you *things*. Get-out-of-my-life *things*. *Things* he couldn't face.

Ya ever knew me to say please before? Never! I never did! Only for Brenan. PLEASE!

"I can't," Sam hissed. He slid quietly around the corner and down the back steps.

Without a hand to hold, he roamed the yard and fields. A couple of canine shadows, the German shepherds, Mandel and Keaton, somberly trailed after him. He led them to the stable where he had once kept Appalachia. A. D. had hung onto one of the mare's offspring, a gelding named Rufus. Though the biggest, most fierce-looking of the four remaining horses, Rufus was the best saddle. Smart and even-tempered, he was the only horse Sam allowed Mariah to ride without his close supervision—as long as Deejay or Marissa went along. He was a firm believer in the buddy system for children. The more buddies, the better.

He wasn't comfortable enough with any horse to let Ben ride alone.

The boy was too small and light, so Sam rode always double with him, using his own arm as a safety belt. Ben loved riding, so Sam tried to take him out a couple of mornings a week.

Lately, he'd missed a few outings with his children. Their eyes asked questions he couldn't answer. He couldn't say, *"Justin Kelsey will never ride a horse or play basketball or swim in the lake, and I'm the reason he can't."* He couldn't say, *"If I couldn't save him, how can I protect you?"* He couldn't even make excuses, so instead, he didn't say anything.

The horses didn't hold much interest for him today. Nor did anything else on the farm—except the woman in the glass office.

Sluggishly, he made his way back to the house. Once inside, he took the most direct route to the bedroom, kicked off his shoes, and dropped onto the bed. For a long time, he lay on his back, looking at the ceiling, concentrating heavily on feeling sorry for himself. Somewhere, he had taken a wrong turn onto a strange new road and couldn't seem to find his way back to the old one.

He had nothing to do. Nowhere to go. No friends to talk to.

Even Lefty had gone tight-lipped and pouty.

34

LOW-DOWN, SIMPERING, excuse-making coward! If you had any balls at all you'd have tracked down that jowly faced sonofabitch years ago and blown a big, gaping hole between his beady little eyes! Then I wouldn't have to be afraid to answer the phone! For all I know, you probably gave him the number!"

Duck an' cover!

On the first Sunday in September, Sam huddled in a corner of the breakfast booth next to his father-in law. Brenan, forehead wrinkled and fists clinched, sat on the other side. For days, she'd been eerily quiet, avoiding physical, verbal, and visual contact with Sam whenever possible. But, oh boy, she was full of spit, venom, and cat claws today.

So she's bitchy! She's also so scared an' upset, she's shakin'! Do somethin', Soldier!

Pulling in an exasperated breath, she turned and transferred her attack to her father. "And you! Looks like you'd do something even if *he* won't! Attila Armstrong! You, who would crush under your soft Gucci-leathered feet the career of any slightly impudent nurse or resident! But let some psychopathic redneck preacher harass your own daughter, your own flesh and blood, your own gene pool, and you just sit around sipping iced tea with the likes of *him* and do nothing! Never mind! Maybe I can sue that crazy old fart for Biblical malpractice or something—without any assistance from either one of you!"

Sam knew Mark was making a special effort to be careful what he said around females these days. Ellen was having a rough go of menopause and stubbornly refused to take the medication Tristan

Riley had prescribed. In this new and volatile Ellen, Mark had met his match. Her fuse was always glowing. She had cowed him, put him on guard around all women. If Sam had been in a better mood, he might have laughed at the tentative voice his father-in-law used when he spoke to Brenan.

"But, honey, when Blacknell first started this business of calling, you told Sam and me that—"

"Since when does anyone listen to me? Oh, everyone listens and does the exact opposite of what I want, but when it counts, when I need you to step in and do something—oh, never mind."

Not good. Definitely, not good.

"What happened to 'Let him alone, he'll eventually get tired and go on another crusade'?" Some of the sweetness had leached from Mark's voice. "What happened to—"

She spoke through clenched teeth. "I don't know why I'd expect a man, *any* man, to understand—or even care!"

"Brenan, that's not fair!" Sam couldn't keep his mouth shut any longer. Her assault had escalated for a quarter hour—since Blacknell had gotten through with another of his heckling calls. Sam had never seen her behave this badly. "You stopped me from taking care of his threats two years ago. You stopped me two *months* ago! I believed he was crazy and dangerous then, and I haven't changed my mind. He must go to a lot of trouble to get our new numbers. He shows up wherever we happen to be. If you want to press charges, I'm with you. If you want me to shoot him, I'll do it, too! Just don't order me to back off then blame me for not doing something! Now, if you want to talk—not scream—about what's really bothering you, I want to listen."

Mark energetically nodded his agreement. "Me, too."

Me, too.

Brenan's bottom lip pressed out a little farther than the top. Her frown deepened. She stared at each of them then crossed her arms and looked sideways at the ceiling. The pouting lip trembled, then the small-clefted chin. Young and pitiful. Sam's heart contracted in shame. She was hurting. He couldn't figure her out. Had he not been afraid of a rebuff, he would have put his arms around her and pulled her close.

Do it anyway!

Mark asked if she was going to cry. "Tears—a woman's most powerful weapon, and you, my dear, use them splendidly. Otherwise, I wouldn't have let you marry this cad. You're *good.*" He winked at Sam while continuing to rag Brenan. "Get that from your mother. If the dam's about to break, give me some warning so I can run for high ground. Get plenty bawling at home."

Why don't he knock it off? Ain't things bad enough awready?

She gave them another one of her exasperated looks.

Then, caught up in the moment and hoping to lighten it somewhat, Sam made a mistake. "Bren, do you have your period?"

The flattened palms of her hands made a loud splat when she slapped them on the table and used them to push herself up. She didn't look back on her way out of the room, but even with her back to him, he knew she was crying.

Jerk! Asshole!

He ran after her.

She slammed and locked the bedroom doors in his face. A muffled "Go to hell!" came through the thick wood panels.

"I'm sorry." He doubted she heard over her sobbing.

See what ya caused? Can't do anything right!

Dejected, he returned to Mark. He was emotionally paralyzed while his marriage rocked like a sailboat in a storm.

If you'd be nice to her, she might talk.

Mark's eyebrows went up. "Maybe she's sympathizing with her mother—a hysterical menopause."

Maybe Dr. Bigmouth oughta go home.

"Maybe," Sam muttered.

"Could be PMS. What do you think?"

Could be the wimp she's married to.

Sam sighed. "I wish I knew."

"Maybe she's not getting enough."

"Enough what?—Oh. If she's getting any, she's got me beat." Sam studied his fingernails while Lefty did an imitation of a bugle sounding "Taps."

IF ONLY SAM KNEW that months would pass before her next period, some of his careless digs would certainly dry up. Brenan couldn't remember her last period. She'd tried. She'd never kept up with them. No inconspicuous red markings on the calendar, no mental notations. She let them go by with little fanfare or inconvenience.

Some things she remembered vividly—like the last time they had attempted to have sex. Oh, yes, she remembered that. The memory, not a fond one, was at least six weeks old. Somewhere in the middle of the venture, he had issued one word—an acerbic "Shit!"—then stopped and moved away. No explanation of why he couldn't, wouldn't, or didn't want to continue.

The whole spring and summer had been long, dreary, tiresome, full of emotional peaks and valleys for Sam and everyone who cared about him. She'd tried to show compassion, but, protecting his misery, he had turned away. She saw his failure to share his feelings as rejection, a sign she was not important enough to be let in. Other arcane forces were at work, opening up a gulf between them. Initially, during the prolonged silences Brenan had felt Sam's confusion and unhappiness almost as acutely as she'd felt her own, but then hers had begun to grow.

She knew she'd been a bitch in the morning room, but against the buildup of tension, anger, and ignorance, her pressure valve had blown. She loved Sam and wanted to understand, but right now, he was driving her up that overly clichéd wall. His failure to rescue her from her inner turmoil was disappointing enough without him leaving her to the manipulation of that fat caricature of a minister. Blacknell's obsession had always put her on guard, but his threats had taken on a malicious tone that surpassed any of his previous soothsaying. He wanted to hurt her and was spending an enormous amount of time trying to create a tenable design for doing it. A heart-to-heart with Sam should have been her first consideration, yet she ensconced her emotional dilemmas as selfishly as he. Tit for tat.

Hormones. Could hormones be responsible for bouncing her from rage to despondency? Or was Sam's behavior a more likely cause? Her first pregnancy had been an adventure full of exotic food, nervous energy, glittering compliments, and indulgence. He'd pampered her. This time, before she knew another baby was growing inside her, he'd shoved her aside as if she was no more vital than an old newspaper.

What about the nightmare? The worry lines cutting into his face? The long silences? Was she the problem? Some of it? All? If he'd let her in, make her privy to the mystery, she'd ask questions so rapid-fire he'd barely have time to catch his breath. Only he could open that door.

On the evening Sam and Mariah had driven Karen to her motel, he had come home in a good mood. He'd seemed surrounded by an aura of lighthearted relief. That night he'd wanted her. He seemed to have put Justin and Karen behind him. He'd been eager, attentive, and sweet, paying close mind to her responses, tailoring his touch to them. The sex had been athletic, steamy. He'd given her everything he had. After that night, he'd rendered little or nothing of himself. His emotional swan song.

The few times they'd tried to be intimate had been more chore than pleasure. He'd been only half there, taking an inordinate amount of time to climax. Only the presence of semen denied he was faking his orgasm. During these passionless encounters, she'd begun feigning hers. She had uncertainly acted out a few before giving up all pretenses at feeling anything. She guessed "Shit!" had meant he'd given up, too.

She hardly knew this strange quiet man, but she desperately missed *her* Sam—the man who lovingly looked after her, who made the scary world a tolerable, safer place. She wanted Justin Kelsey, or whatever had him, to give him back.

She hadn't been to Dr. Riley or bought any drugstore tests, but she knew the swollen breasts, the cranky stomach, the small bulge just above her pelvis wasn't going to go away. She'd denied anything was happening to her body too long. She couldn't remember when she'd started making a game of lying to herself, but the game had ended. A new one was underway. She knew she should tell Sam and see her doctor, and yet she couldn't speak up. Nothing held her back from blowing up at him over some imagined slight, but she was unable to tell him about his own child. He would think she'd tricked him, that she'd gotten pregnant because she was scared of what was happening. He might become angry and back even farther away. She'd wait a while longer. Things could get better.

THE PHONE STOPPED ringing before Sam got to it. Justin?

No, Ace. Not Justin.

Brenan must have answered in her office. The in-use light on the cordless charger glowed red.

Sam coaxed his sleep-blurred eyes to focus on the mantel clock. 4:15 a.m. Calls at this time of the morning were seldom pleasant. As usual, his first waking thoughts were of Freida and A. D. Calls after midnight would always pull up the memory of his father's heart attack. And Justin. Probably, this one was the newsroom. He lifted the handset and listened.

"—Genesis to Revelations. All ya ever need in this life is there. Miz. MacCauley, you nor nobody else don't need no other book to explain things to 'em. God keeps puttin' it on my heart to warn ya about that. His wrath is a mighty fearsome thing to go a-messin' with. Yore book is a slap in the face a God. Why, the ol' devil hisself wouldn't have no better."

Sam listened to a couple of minutes of scripture-quoting and rough-grammared commentary. The old man was short of breath, panting as if turned on by his bedevilment of Brenan. Well, she was a gorgeous, sexy woman. Sam supposed even psychopathic clergymen lusted. They probably just denied it to themselves, swallowed it, and let it come back up as scriptural vomit. He heard Brenan's tired sighs and wondered why she didn't just slam down the phone.

"Why don't you an' yore husband bring them little younguns a yourn an' come up to the parsonage after it gets daylight. I'd shore like to share some litature an' Bible verses with ya. The Lord's laid this burden on me for yawl, an' I can't let it just be water off a duck's back. I can't let it slide down in that ol' cesspool of iniquity. He wants you to stand up an' say you done made some big ol' mistakes. Then He can forgive you an' make you clean an' whole an' innocent like a newborn baby."

Sam heard Brenan's sudden intake of air. He would have bet she was fueling herself for a verbal homicide. The voice that came over the phone was calm and low-key, but the words were solid. "You are stupid and insane, Reverend Blacknell, and you may, at any time, drop that old burden in a cesspool or any receptacle of your choosing. You'd accomplish more by throwing rocks at the broad side of a barn than spitting Bible verses at me. At least, you'd stand a *chance* of making contact. When I read the Bible, I get something you haven't found."

"Miz MacCauley, this blasphemy hasta stop. Now, lissen—"

"You heard my wife!" Sam jumped in, hoping an intervention would at least would win some points with her. "You've bullied her enough. Badgering a woman—-*that's* really Christian of you."

Amen! Lefty seconded.

"I expect a man of your black-hearted character to be a challenge. I expect to be cussed an' spit at. I expect to wrassle the devil for your soul. What I don't expect to do is give up. I had to give up on my own son in the prime a his life. You might recall the road he was led down by his drunken, fornicatin' friends. You call me tryin' to bring that little woman a yourn into the fold badgerin' if that's a word ya like, but God tells me to witness. When God says 'go,' a man's gotta go. When God says 'spread the Word to the lost, evil, an' downtrodden,' a man's gotta do that, too. Another thing, Mr. MacCauley, God ain't gonna wait much longer for his sheep to come in. His patience is a-wearin' mighty thin."

Throughout this latest oration, Sam prepared himself to wage a full attack, put an end to the harassment once and for all, but as he opened his mouth, Brenan charged through the bedroom door.

The look on her face snapped his lips together with eye-blink swiftness. Her right hand came palm up at him. No time for questions, he lowered his eyes and placed the phone in the outstretched hand. As soon as she moved the switch to the off position and dropped the handset onto the charger, she spun at him. Her right forefinger stopped an inch from his nose.

Run, Ace—tuck your tail an' run!

"Bullied? Badgered? True enough! But don't be jumping to my

rescue. I'm not frightened anymore—annoyed is more like it—with Blacknell as well as certain members of my own family. I will apologize for that little outburst yesterday. I can see where that would make you feel obligated to defend me. You and my father may blame my emotional instability on any phenomena or female malady you wish. I'll just consider the source and let it slide into that ol' cesspool of iniquity. The truth is I'm living in the Twilight Zone—the fucking Outer Limits—but I'm in control, now. I think I can honestly assure you it won't happen again. Your services as my protector are not required."

She said the F-word! Look out! She NEVER says the F-word!

Staring at her finger so close to his eyes, Sam's vision blurred again.

Said she don't need ya!

He moved his gaze on up her arm to her face. She looked mean and unforgiving, and so stunningly beautiful his stomach hurt just the way it always had.

Face it, Boss. Ya can't win. All ya can do is play the game by an ever-changin' set of rules.

"Have I made myself clear?"

As clear as a whistle. As clear as rain.

So damned beautiful. He closed his eyes, nodded that he under-stood—even though he didn't—and whispered, "I'm sorry." He didn't understand at all. He wanted to say, "I need you."

Say it!

He wanted to say, "No matter what it is, I'm sorry!"

Say it!

He wanted to say, "This is making me sick."

He wanted to say, "Come back to me."

He wanted to say, "I love you."

Say it!

He wanted to plead for forgiveness, another chance. He wanted to say so much!

Say it! Say it! SAY IT!

Instead, he said, "I understand. I promise I won't bother you again. If you want me to do something, you can let me know."

35

O N A TUESDAY in mid-September, Sam reached into a box and took out some well-creased papers. The letters and crayon drawings were a little yellow around the edges. To Sam, they were priceless.

July 31, 1972
Monday afternoon

Dear S.,

I guess I'm one of those people who lets boredom drive them loco. Bored is definitely one of the things I am. The hospital finally sprung me, but with my arm in a cast, I'm not exactly free to have fun. It still hurts, so I swallowed a Percodan—pardon me, I swallowed a mistake. That stuff does a number on the brain. Here I sit at my desk, writing myself a letter. Next time, it's aspirin for me.

Now that they're pretty sure I'm not dying, the old people have turned to ice. They're really giving me the biz about the Wild Turkey or Jack Daniels or Evan Williams—whatever the firewater was that Robbie sloshed into our RC Colas that night at the Dance Hall. Mom keeps telling me how she can't believe a man child of hers would be so idiotic, and A. D. gives me that HURT look. Begging for forgiveness hasn't done much good. Man, I don't think they remember being sixteen or making stupid mistakes, but they did make them. Oh, yeah. When A. D. runs into an old friend he grew up with, the first thing they say to each other is, "Remember when we blah, blah, blah . . . " It's always some prank they pulled or some scrape they got into and almost got killed or sent to jail. It's just different when it's me or Jackie doing those kind of things.

It's too hot to go outside. When you sweat inside a cast, the itching and stinging can drive you crazy. The smell don't do much for your popularity, either. I don't remember TV being this boring, and when I try to read, my mind starts playing hopscotch through a lot of old memories. Most of them should have been shot and put out of their misery years ago, but some are kind of neat. I remember one time when A. D. had the stores and used to take me up to the one in Russett on Saturdays when it was only open half a day. He'd put me to work sorting nails and washers or something small and let me think I was being a big help. It was after I started school. I guess I was six or seven, and I was sitting on a high stool at the counter sorting stuff into little boxes. A. D. was at the register, and some guy came up to pay for something. The guy said, "MacCauley, that boy looks more like his daddy every time I see him. Down right spooky, ain't it?" A. D. just took the guy's money without answering, but when we were alone at the counter again, he picked me up off the stool. I wrapped my arms and legs around him and let him hug me all he wanted. Back then I didn't care if people saw us. I hugged him back, and he whispered, "Don't ever let anybody make you believe you're not mine." He's mad at me now, but he'll get over it.

A. D. was always bringing materials home and making stuff for me and Jackie. We had more toys made of wood from his store than we had bought for us already made. Good toys that didn't fall apart or stop doing what they were supposed to do. He's always been good "with his hands"—that's the way Ma puts it when she's bragging. My twisted mind could make something else out of that, but she means he does good work in his shop. He can take one stick of stove wood and whittle it into nearly anything. Jackie's artistic, too. She's starting to paint some neat stuff.

Ma's in the kitchen, and even in this awful heat, she's baking bread and frying dried apple pies. It doesn't bother her when she's doing "mother" stuff. She just kicks up the A/C and oven to high and lets them fight it out. She's all for Women's Lib. She says one woman is worth two men. She just doesn't want to be a truck driver or a coal miner. Cooking and bossing her family around is her thing. I wouldn't mind her finishing up those pies. She's always saying what a picky eater I was when I was little to be such a pig now.

I didn't tell anybody about Deb coming to the hospital, but I wasn't embarrassed. She apologized for hurting me. I don't remember what she did. I wonder if she has bad dreams. I don't as often as I used to. Mostly I dream about naked women like Miss Allen, the girls' gym teacher, or Haley Mills. I can't believe I'm writing this stuff down.

Bud's not allowed to be friends with me or Robbie anymore. (Like that will stop him!) His daddy's wigged out over the drinking and the wreck. According to him, it's all mine and Robbie's fault. Looks like he'd be glad Bud didn't die or end up like Robbie who is going to be in the hospital a long time. Bud's okay. A lot of people don't understand him because he's a trash-mouth who does disgusting things to get noticed, but he gets treated bad at home. I hate what happens to him. Bud needs someone to defend him from his own father.

Mrs. Armstrong brought the Sawbriar Princess over this morning. She had more pictures to give me. Her flowers and trees are the same size, but I made like they were fine art. She kissed my arm so it will get well. She's a cute kid (for an Armstrong), and she's pretty smart (for an Armstrong). She talks a lot, though, and that can get on your nerves. She tells everybody I'm her boyfriend. I wish Tara would look at me the way Brenan does. I'm going to put her drawings in a folder so I can tease her about them when she gets bigger. Maybe I'll put this crazy letter in the folder, too, so I can look back and see what dumb things I thought about when I was sixteen and bored. It'll be my own private time capsule.

Jackie's having fits about Robbie. They used to fight all the time. Now they'd rather kiss and whisper things they don't want me to hear. She'd better watch out because A. D.'s gonna blow if he finds out daddy's little girl is being taken down by his best friend's son. I don't want to think what Ma might do to Robbie. It wouldn't be pretty. People are more that way about girls than boys. The boy gets blamed as if the girl doesn't meet him halfway. With Jackie, it was probably two-thirds of the way.

Last night I heard the old people doing IT, and it nearly drove me crazy. While I was in the hospital, Ma moved my bed and their's against the same wall. I couldn't very well bang on the wall and yell, "stop it!", so I put my headphones and Carly Simon on to drown them out. I hope if I ever need any pointers, I have the guts to ask him, because she sure sounded like she liked whatever it was he was doing! (I'm even grossing myself out here.) Anyway, A. D. came up a while ago, and I got up the nerve to tell him I didn't think our beds should be against the same wall. He got all splotchy in the face and said he'd take care of it. Later I heard him moving stuff around in their room.

Bud talks about IT all the time. He embarrasses me, but I feel sorry for him. His daddy caught him whacking off and beat him with a belt and then with his fists. Bud came to school with his eyes swollen almost shut. He told the teachers he'd had a fight with his cousin, and they acted like they believed him.

Once this girl named Lisa came up behind me in the gym at school and pinched me. She said out loud in front of a bunch of people, "You've got the cutest bum!!!" I nearly died. Sometimes girls whistle and yell dirty stuff they'd like to do with me. I try to act like I don't hear them. If looking good to other people is supposed to be so great, why does it make me want to crawl into some hole and pull the hole in behind me? When I look at myself in the mirror all I see is a skinny kid who looks too young and soft to be sixteen. (Soft like a kid, not a sissy.) My nose and ears are too big. I don't see what those girls think they see. No matter what I look like, people shouldn't say things to embarrass me, and they shouldn't touch me. Nobody has the right to put their hands on you when you don't want them to. I would never do that to another person. But if it was Goldie and she WANTED me to. . .

If this is the kind of thing I'm going to start doing when I get bored, I'd better find a hobby. It's too bad I can't play my guitar with one hand. I think I could write a really sad song today. Next time I hear somebody say, "I'm such a poor correspondent," I'm going to tell them to try writing a letter to themselves. You can really let your hair down doing that.

Well, I've enjoyed as much of me as I can stand. TTFN.

Mine truly,

S.

Dear S.,

When you leave private letters lying around, what should you expect? I found this one to be particularly interesting. I never knew you had such girl trouble.

I think you should talk to us old people about your visit from Deb, but I won't make an issue of it. Your letter contained a number of topics that could stand some discussion. You're a good kid. After learning you chose Carly Simon over eavesdropping, I'm sure of it. Our giving you "the business" and "hurt looks" has nothing to do with forgiveness. It has to do with coming face-to-face with the death of someone whose place we could never fill. It has to do with love.

Sincerely,

One of the old people

(guess which one)

P. S. Your sister is going to be miffed about the personal info, but she ought to be over it by the time she gets out of her room—1975?

SAM DIDN'T DIG THE LETTERS and drawings out of the file box often, but when he did, they took him on a journey back in time. A few pages of notebook paper, written under narcotic influence and thereby free of inhibition, said so much about the young man who had liberally poured his heart out over them. His mother's embarrassing reply multiplied the value. The drawings were the tip of the relationship he would have with the artist as she grew from child to woman. There were other things in the file folder. Letters A. D. and Freida had written to him while he was at the University. Bud's eighth grade report card, proof of the one time the boy had made honor roll. A snapshot, stolen from a family album to keep Freida from showing it to company—Jackie and Sam, ages three and two, naked in a backyard wading pool. Notes Brenan had left on the refrigerator that contained small personal messages with which he couldn't part. Hand-drawn birthday and Fathers' Day cards from Ben and Mariah. Things that had to be kept in a fire proof file box because, just like the people who spoke through them, they could never be replaced. He added Justin's obituary and a few newspaper clippings about his death and then put the folder away.

Roaming through the sleeping house, he stopped to study a family portrait Jackie had painted. For her own home, she had done an enormous mural of everyone on both sides of the family, including herself. It was a perfect depiction of a family picnic at the lake. Sam had been after her to do a duplicate for him. Hanging on the wall opposite the breakfast booth, the painting before him was no more formally posed. Sam, Brenan, and the kids wearing pajamas and robes and eating breakfast. Jackie, having inherited some of their mother's need to feed people, usually incorporated food into her work. As a gift for A. D.'s last birthday, she had painted Freida at work in her beloved kitchen. Her talent was amazing, her oils almost as sharp and true as photos.

He stared at the faces in the painting. Each one was happy, content to be having something as ordinary as a meal with the others. Talking, listening, sharing. Being a family.

He desperately wished he could go back in time—to live again a few short months, to live them right and fix all that had become broken during them.

36

I T'S NOT JUST YOU, Daddy." She sat across the booth from him. "It's Mama, too. The kids know you. Everybody in the city knows you. They also know you're married to the notorious Brenan Armstrong MacCauley. For Pete's sake, Deej did a book report on *The Lasting Kind.* Mr. Jackson made *Poetic Injustice* part of the language arts curriculum. Can't you see how it's going to be when they find out I'm your kid? I'm very proud of both of you, *but. . . "*She made her mouth a wide, flat line. Her wry face.

"You don't want to be publicly associated with either of us? I guess that's understandable." Sam took the milk back to the refrigerator.

"That's not what I mean. If you'll get still and listen, I'll tell you. That's better. You know kids can be so totally lame. Last year at Smith-Briley, they couldn't let it rest. They all thought since you're on TV and Mama writes books, then I must be a snobby brat with an attitude. Nobody took time to get to know me. It's weird enough being nine in a room full of sixth grade giants, but over all, it's not too bad. It's a lot better than being with a bunch of brats fighting over who gets first turn on the playground swings. I don't want to goof things up."

"I thought you'd found your niche at PFAA. All your classmates have similar abilities, so the competition is more equal. You've led me to believe they pretty well accept you."

"They do," she sighed, "and Mr. Jackson *likes* me. That's a first for me. My old teachers acted like I was put in their classrooms just to make their lives miserable. They took every point of my IQ over 120 as a personal insult. Intelligence isn't a disease at Paragon, but who knows about family fame and fortune? Some kids have to have scholarships, and their parents have to get loans."

Sam sighed, too. He vividly remembered the last two school years. The kids and even some of the school personnel had given her a difficult time. He deemed her IQ more responsible than Brenan's books or his face on TV. The poverty-stricken county and city school systems had no choice but to place advanced students in part-time gifted and talented programs and otherwise mainstream them in regular classrooms. Advanced students frustrated teachers who were not able to challenge them or had no time to move outside normal classroom structure. Worse still, they were perceived as threats by students who couldn't compete with them. The decision to let her skip grades four and five no longer seemed radical. She was at long last showing her mettle. She'd made friends and was now heavily into slumber parties and phone marathons. Some evenings, she actually had to study.

Having Deejay in the same class had worked well, too. If possible, the two had grown closer. Mariah needed a solid friend, especially now. The tension at home was running high, and Sam knew, whether he saw it in them or not, the children were feeling it.

"Okay, Rye, if Deejay and Mr. Jackson haven't blown your cover, I won't, either. I'll see if Dana can do the newsroom workshop and tour. If she can't, I'm sure Roger Garner would *love* to—not that *he* has anything to teach you. I'm sure all of you have already mastered yawning and scratching. By the way, how did you keep Deej and Jackson from giving you away?"

"I talked about it with Mr. Jackson at my interview, and he thought it would be okay for me to be incognito for a while. I told Deej it was your idea to give me some time. He'd do anything to keep on your good side—and that of your wallet. Face it, Daddy, the boy's a freeloader."

"He's worth a few tuition dollars. And I do not have a bad side. I'll call Mr. Jackson and tell him I'll get a replacement because I can't make it. You may run into me at the station, but we'll be just two strangers crossing paths."

"That's not what I want. Why don't you listen? I didn't plan to hide you forever. I'm going to tell them. I was already planning to. You or Mama will have to come to the school, anyway. Open House comes before the field trip—next Thursday, I think. I'll have to let it leak out between now and then. I just want to set some ground rules."

Sam looked into Mariah's stubborn blue eyes. "Well, let's hear them."

"I wrote them down," she said as she reached into the back pocket of her jeans and produced a folded sheet of paper. She pulled the paper across the edge of the table to straighten the creases, then cleared her throat. "First, under no circumstances are you to refer to me by any of the following ways: your little girl, Rye, sweetheart, or any other term of endearment. I am your daughter or Mariah—nothing else."

She was serious. He smiled. "Got it."

"Next, Deej is not my *little* friend. You can't say anything about being proud of me. You will not talk about cute things I did when I was a baby or mention Ben and me in the same sentence. No feminist, football, or bodily function jokes—nor any jokes about Mama's books. You're really not funny, except when you stick to the simple stuff. And last," she stopped to point her finger sternly, "Michael Keaton's name had better not come up!"

Sam drew an *X* across his chest with his left hand and held up his right. "I agree to all your specifications—*carte blanche.* On my honor." He thought he saw something in her eyes that had nothing to do with her school. Accusations? Confusion?

She pushed the paper around her cereal bowl and across the table. "Keep this. You'll need it for reference. Mama's list is totally different. Um, I almost forgot. There is one other thing. Don't wear the tie with the sad-eyed basset hound on it."

"Aw, Rye. It's my favorite, a birthday present from Deej."

She rolled her eyes. "I know. You've worn it three times a week ever since. I'll get a pencil and add it to the list."

WHEN MARIAH SPOTTED Deejay through the window and went outside to him, Sam stayed in the booth with his morning *Bugle.*

Over the paper, he watched as his daughter and a boy twice her size and two years older mounted bicycles and peddled out of sight. If he or Brenan happened to stumble upon them, as likely as not, they'd be sprawled, each with a book, on some grassy hillside or propped on separate limbs in one of the mimosa trees. During the warmer months, they stayed close to the pool, but the rest of the time, they roamed around with a pair of German shepherds tailing after them. Sam trusted the big, fair, soft-spoken boy. He also trusted Mandel and Keaton. The dogs had been trained to be expert kid-watchers. If not for the dogs—in light of Blacknell's threats and others of the kind—the kids could not have gone out without an adult.

Deej came almost every weekend. His mother, a registered nurse at Northside, tried to schedule double shifts on weekends. The overtime kept the mortgage payment current and her big-footed son in sneakers. A single mother, she'd once worried about the boy's lack of male influence. Deej's fortuitous discovery of Mariah and the MacCauley commune had delighted Margaret Windham. Now, the boy had Sam, A. D., and Mark—a package deal. The fact that a little girl was the main draw didn't worry Margaret. Her son had the opportunity to view a farmer, a doctor, and a TV journalist in their natural habitats—and when Robert was around, a lawyer. She didn't have to forego much-needed extra income to go in search of a father-figure for her son.

Deejay's connection with the MacCauleys had come about acciden-tally on his ninth birthday. He had shown up at the front gate one Saturday morning. His face, behind constellations of freckles, had been paler than his platinum hair. He'd come dangling an arm that had been broken in three places and sputtering a tearful request to use the telephone. Sam had gone looking and found the boy's bicycle wrapped around the gnarled roots of a water oak at the end of the driveway and, close by, a pair of wire spectacles, minus the lens.

Brenan had called Dr. Mark who'd brought a temporary splint. The boy's crying had stopped immediately, and while waiting for his mother to arrive, a friendship had bloomed. He and Mariah exclaimed over the same books, music, and movies. One thing had progressed to another until they were joking, laughing, gesturing. Although he looked more like a Swede, Deejay was to become a naturalized appendage to the Scots-Irish MacCauleys.

After the arm had been set, the bicycle and eyeglasses replaced, Sam had insisted, "That old tree probably jumped right in front of him. Always been a bit on the shady side. If it'd been one of the sweet gums—that would be a whole other story."

After that, rarely a day had gone by without Deejay. On weekends, he usually hung around from early morning until his mother or grandmother came to collect him for supper. He breezed through books alongside Rye and was curious about everything that moved, made a noise, or lay totally inanimate. While she was a cynic and realist, he was a dreamer, a defender of underdogs, a believer in lost causes. She was fire. He was water.

After some wheedling, Margaret had given in to Sam's persistence and allowed him to take responsibility for PFAA tuition. The Academy was a forty-five minute drive one-way, with a stop halfway at Ben's new school. An extra ten minutes had to be figured in for a stop at the Windham house. Ellen, Freida, and A. D. took turns driving them in the morning and Brenan collected them in the afternoon. Everyone thought of Deejay as family and considered him whenever plans were made.

Deejay had missed a few weekends of late. Sam wondered if he had picked up on the dark undercurrents flowing through the household. Immediately, he wished he hadn't thought at all.

Perhaps, though, things were not as bad as he feared. Brenan had actually spoken this morning. On her way into her office, she'd come by the kitchen for a mug of coffee. On the table in front of him, she'd put down a Zip-Loc bag containing several pre-filled, disposable syringes. Epinephrine, his just-in-case-nothing-else-works asthma medication.

"Daddy left these last night," she had explained in an almost conversational tone. "He said for you to chuck the old ones. Don't forget the ones in the wagon and at your mother's. Let him know how you're fixed for Theo-Dur and your aerosol."

It wasn't *"I love you dearly. I want things to be the way they used to be.*

You're the best thing that ever happened to me," but it was *something.* Several sentences in a row, more than he'd been getting. After mulling it over, he supposed asthma medicine could be considered personal subject matter.

Upstairs a train whistle cut through the Saturday morning lull. Sam heard a distinct "All aboard!" followed by running sneakers on the stairs. Ben, wearing a blue-and-white-striped engineer's cap and overalls, burst into the kitchen.

"Daddy, bring your guitar up an' sing me the song about the railroad bum who got kicked off the train an' had to sleep in the rain. *Please.* I'm running the freight train with open boxcars. The hobo camp is all set up." Ben finished and stood waiting.

The excitement in his eyes was reason enough for Sam to nod and head toward the bedroom for his guitar. "Sure, Ace. I'll meet you at the hobo camp pronto," he called over his shoulder.

The hobo camp was under the trestle that spanned Big River Canyon near Big River Village which were technically located in the hall outside the door to Ben's room. A. D.'s deftness with a pocketknife and a paintbrush was shown off here. Hoboes eating out of tin cans, playing harmonicas, and relaxing on the ground were spread around a campfire and under two tin-covered lean-tos braced against a green candle-wax hillside. All this detail was arranged near a clear acrylic river with moss-covered banks and a red-rock levee. The miniature scale was almost perfect.

Sam sat on the floor beside Ben. He leaned back against the open door frame and tuned his old Fender acoustic. When he was satisfied, he began strumming. Ben smiled and swayed side-to-side, keeping time. They both loved the old Jimmie Rodgers's hobo ballad passed down by A. D. Both A. D.'s father and grandfather had ridden the rails during the early part of the century.

Ben got up and pulled a small, stringless flat-top guitar from under his bottom bunk. He sat back down and began to strum along. Everyone, including Ben, was more enthusiastic about his guitar when he played without strings. His imagination took him through the notes and chords. Sam had promised to give him lessons as soon as his hands were big enough, but for now, Ben seemed happy to be a part of the hobo camp sing-along.

The old song, bluesy and sad, made Sam feel lonelier. He heard movement on the stairs and looked up just as Brenan reached the top riser and sat down. Fifteen feet away. Her presence made the company special. It also created a strangeness that didn't belong among family members.

Brenan smiled at Ben, and he grinned back. She forgot to smile at Sam.

"Sing 'Railroad Lady', Daddy," Ben said when the first song ended. "Mama likes that one. Grampa A. D. says when I get bigger he'll get me a horse if you'll let me have one, an' I'm gonna name her Railroad Lady."

Sam glanced at Brenan. She shrugged slightly. Neither a *yes, do* or a *no, don't*. It was more of a *do whatever you like* shrug. She used to have an opinion. She used to sing with him. And when she sang, her voice was rich and full of emotion.

"That's a passenger train song," he told Ben.

"The hoboes don't care. They're just glad they got music."

Brenan shrugged again. Closer to a *yes, do* this time.

While Sam strummed an intro, Ben left his guitar on the floor and the train running. He picked his way through the tracks and crossed the landing to sit next to his mother. He rested with his back against her.

Sam sang.

Brenan's arms circled her son, a child with her doll, she rocked him, almost imperceptibly. Ben sang the parts he knew.

The train made a complete round trip every two minutes. Tiny circles of smoke puffed out of the smoke stack. The whistle was programmed to sound as the train approached crossings. The whistle and the chugging of the wheels added a forlorn quality to the music. Sam's loneliness heightened and filled him.

The train was midway into a third trip through the rooms and hall of the second story when Sam started on a third request. "The Streets of Laredo, The Cowboy's Lament," a folk song that had traveled in various

forms, personas, and settings through Ireland, Scotland, England, perhaps other lands, before the American cowboy adopted it as bunkhouse
lore. It was the saddest song in the world.

> *As I walked out in the streets of Laredo,*
> *as I walked out in Laredo one day,*
> *I spied a young cowboy wrapped all in white linen,*
> *wrapped in white linen as cold as the clay . . .*

PART FOUR
If You Loved Me

Deep into that darkness peering,
long I stood there wondering, fearing,
Doubting, dreaming dreams no mortal
ever dared to dream before;
But the silence was unbroken,
and the stillness gave no token . . .

—EXCERPT FROM "THE RAVEN" BY EDGAR ALLAN POE

37

THE STORM HIT PRECISELY at six-thirty, November first, the first clap of thunder simultaneous with the fade from the station's logo at the end of the newscast. Instant gratification, giving Dan Stircy, the weekend meteorologist, a direct hit to his credit.

Sam liked Dan. He was young, twenty-six, but seemed older, and was one of the newer members of the weekend night team. A gentle giant, six-and-a-half feet of hard, rippling muscle, Dan had six inches and seventy-five pounds on Sam. Standing next to Dan was like standing next to an oak tree, feeling its deep-rooted, unbending strength emanating up and outward. A Michael Jordan look-alike—same face, same enormous smile, he'd been with the team on a regular basis for about a year.

Lately, Dan had been frequently asked to sub at the weekday weather map for veteran Frank Davis, who had been infinitesimally easing into retirement for months. Sam enjoyed working with Dan. Everyone at the station had taken to him—everyone except Garner who, on general principal, hated everybody. The team treated him much the way they had Sam when he had joined them twelve years ago. Dan had gotten a few breaks and used them productively to win respect necessary for successful navigation in the business. Even-tempered, submissive, and resourceful, he counterbalanced the brassiness of the other anchors and, thereby, made Andy Drury's professional life a little nicer.

Shortly after the six o'clock broadcast, Dan stopped by Sam's desk with two Styrofoam cups of coffee, black for himself, light for Sam. "I don't know if coffee's what you need, Ace, but you do need something."

"Gotta quit reading my mail, Danny, but thanks, anyway."

"Where'd the 'Ace' come from—ace reporter?"

"No, it means I'm not a wild card."

"What?"

"It has something to do with me being my own imaginary playmate. Too crazy to explain. Nice call on the storm."

Dan eased his mammoth frame into a folding chair and crossed his feet over a corner of the desk. "I'll take that as a compliment, but it's still a storm. John Q. Public, who has a Friday night date, wishes I'd been wrong. Looks like we're in for a bout of crappy weather, and you look like you're all dressed up for it."

"You're full of praise tonight."

"Can't help being curious, and subtlety's not my style."

"If you've got specific questions, let me have them."

"What's thrown you into this tailspin? The Kelsey boy?"

"Oh, I dunno."

"Dana told me he really got to you. She thinks his death was the start of something you're not bouncing back from. By the way, she wasn't gabbing; I probed. In fact, after the first couple of questions, she told me she didn't want to play anymore. Tightest-lipped black woman I ever met."

Sam took a sip of the coffee and grimaced. "The boy figures in somewhere—sure he does. I should have seen it coming—someone else might have, but I didn't. If I had, I could've stopped him. Anyway, that was six months ago. He's dead. That's not going to change. At least his brother's in a decent home, and that human scum, Watley, is in jail. You know several boys came forward with stories of Watley molesting them?"

"But only one left you holding the phone—"

"He's only a part. My whole life's a whirling carnival ride. I'm sorry if my moping is spoiling the atmosphere of the hallowed work place."

"I'm not complaining, but if you need a therapist, Dr. Danny's on call. Pro bono, for you, of course."

Sam considered the offer and then surprised himself by divulging, "It's a domestic thing, Doctor. A pregnant wife who's beginning to get royalty checks for more money than I make in three months. A pregnant wife who has become very independent—no, she was never dependent—*detached*. She's detached herself from me. I don't get to have an opinion or make decisions or even be consulted about anything. She has this certifiable nut preacher who calls at least once a week to browbeat her with God's wrath. Plus, there's a group of his backup fanatics all pissed-off over her religiously controversial material. They want to assassinate her. They probably don't know she's pregnant, but as crazed as they are, I suppose they'd like getting two for one—Devil's spawn, you know. They don't like me, either. I see them as grave threats to her, but she only takes them seriously when she's really mad at me. I'm an old-fashioned guy. I love my wife, and I want to defend her. I want to slay dragons and windmills for her, but she won't let me. Did I mention she's with child?"

Dan gnawed his top lip and was silent long enough to make Sam wish he'd kept his mouth shut. When the weather man began to question and hypothesize, his words put a whole new slant on Sam's troubles, causing him to feel immensely more depressed.

"Is money at the top of the heap? Doesn't everybody like money? Or is it the detachment? Or the psycho preacher and his entourage? Because it seems like it's the pregnancy you've fixated on."

"The detachment, I think. Or not. Maybe it's the baby. She shouldn't be pregnant. I don't think she should. See how confused I am? I feel left out, abandoned, insignificant. Kid stuff, huh? On top of everything else, I've managed to accumulate a tremendous amount of self-pity. Does it show?"

"Stop me if I say too much, especially since you said the love word. Mind you, I'm just throwing out possibilities, but I think, somewhere in there, I heard some weighty doubt of the did-she-or-didn't-she brand of parenthood concerns. Could it be this detachment thing came before the pregnancy? That's a conclusion I could draw from the way you're talking. She is away from home sometimes, isn't she? Writer's conferences, workshops, publicity things? And you miss prime time loving by working the dreadful *evening* shift—think you might have something to worry about there?"

The muscles in Sam's neck stiffened. Though he'd provided the opening, he didn't appreciate this insinuation. The signal thumps of a headache pulsed in his temples. "I don't think—"

Dan blurted in as if Sam's answer wasn't needed. "I'll remind you that a woman who's not protected from conception isn't protected from sexually transmitted death sentences, either."

Sam leaned forward and held up his hand. "No she's not—"

"Whoa, Sam. Don't tell me. I'm not asking, I'm not suggesting, and I'm not trying to be your mother. I just thought you might be wondering about it and needing to sort it out, gain some perspective. You're so down. You don't hide it very well. A man could get super messed up over a woman like you've got. Smart, sexy, successful. A wet dream for most guys—I say that only as a compliment. I've only met Brenda once. You remember, at Houser's retirement get-together? I didn't know you then, but the two of you seemed so right. Everybody was *looking*. I mean, she was there on your arm, and you looked proud. And I distinctly recall you making some lighthearted jokes about the money that was rolling in since the last book. Didn't seem like you were jealous, just that you were glad she was doing so well. Money can't be what you've gone into the despair pit over."

"It's Brenan—B-r-e-n-a-n, not Brenda." Sam knew he sounded petty. "And of, course, I was—am proud of her, and, you're right, the money's really not the problem—not the big one, anyway. I don't even know if Brenan's the problem."

"Man, you had it all together when I came here, then you changed. One day, you were the sharpest guy around. You played this game like a pro, and the next day, the fun was gone. You dragged in and got through, but the spark had died. If your wife's not messing around, then—"

"There's something wrong between us—but not that."

She wouldn't do the cheatin' thing, would she Ace? Answer me!

Pain hammered Sam's temples.

Maybe ya oughta look into it, huh, Sam? Couldn't hurt.—Yes! Yes, it could! It could rip ya into little pieces! But it's the kinda thing a guy's gotta know.

"So if the kid's yours, why're you so worked up over it?" Dan asked. "You're always crowing about your kids. Being a daddy's not a new deal."

Because he don't OFFICIALLY know she's pregnant.

Sam rubbed his temples with the tips of his fingers. "Bad timing. Unplanned. That's all."

"You're not Catholic, are you?"

"No."

If she let another man touch her—other men can make babies, too.

"Are you allergic to latex?"

"No!"

Oh, Ace, she didn't! No way! She's mad at ya, sure, an' full of spiteful female hormones, but she'd never ever—

"Then you had control of the timing."

Sam caught himself reluctantly smiling with only a shade of bitterness. A man as big as Dan didn't have to be shy about speaking his mind. "I can't believe I'm sitting here letting you lecture me. You're no marriage counselor. You don't work for Planned Parenthood. You're a bachelor. What do you know?"

Dan picked up a double gilt-lace frame from Sam's desk. One of the photographs was of Brenan at seventeen sitting behind a stack of books, crisp first-edition copies of her novel, *Me and Joe*—her first autograph party at The Book Mark. Her pen was poised over the inside cover of a book. She was laughing and beautiful. The other was a candid shot of Ben and Mariah sitting on the back steps playing with a stray cat. No stiff, formal poses. Sam had taken both pictures, tangible samples of the family portraits he carried in his heart.

Dan put the frame back down. "You're listening because you know how smart I am. I know how babies are made. You've already got two kids—make that two-and-some-fraction. How many do you think you'll make before you figure out how you're doing it?"

Sam gave Dan an aggravated frown he didn't altogether feel and shooed him out. "Draw me a diagram when you've got a minute. You've got a storm to watch, and I've gotta get back to my work."

THE RAIN HAD STOPPED, but every time he met another vehicle, Sam had to use his wipers and washer fluid to scour off a spray of muddy slime. His week-old Explorer, next year's model, kept a hold on the slick pavement as he pushed the speedometer past sixty. Its purchase hadn't cheered him as much as he'd hoped. A forty-minute drive took him out of the city, over twenty miles of interstate, down the rural two-lane blacktop that was his passage home. It gave him plenty time to ponder his parley with Dan.

Although the pregnancy troubled him, he hadn't taken up the possibility that Brenan could have been unfaithful. Now, he permitted a *what if* to be born. A lion growled in his chest. What if she'd met some man on one of the trips? A one-timer? An on-going affair? A man who excited and satisfied her, eliminating her need for Sam? A man who had taken his place? That would explain her reluctance to tell him about the baby. It would explain why she didn't want him to touch her. The picture of her in another man's arms left him in a cold sweat.

He dug into his coat pocket for his aerosol inhaler and silenced the lion. The pain in his head was close to unbearable. He was disgusted with this feeling of being small and helpless, disgusted with himself for waiting in the dark for her to come to him, fed up with playing ignorant. Tonight, he would demand answers. If Brenan was asleep, or pretending to be, he didn't care. She'd had five long weeks to get her story all worked out.

You're gonna start somethin'! Better watch out! She'd better watch out! She don't deserve the attitude you're takin' home to her. Besides, what're ya gonna do if she tells ya that baby she's carryin' ain't yours?

"Shut up!" His vehemence dampered Lefty's commentary.

IN NEAR DARKNESS, Sam ambled through the utility room and kitchen. He stopped at the sink, snapped on a light, found a bottle of aspirin in a nearby cabinet. He chased four tablets with a glass of water and snapped the light back off.

In the family room, he found Brenan clearly wide awake and watching Arsenio Hall's monologue. He couldn't remember the last time she had been visible when he came in from work. Usually, she was in bed or closed up in her office.

When he approached, she looked up—another rarity of late.

"You're up." A stupendously dumb thing to say. Obviously, she knew she was up. "I'm glad."

"Oh?" Brenan muted the TV and tossed the remote control aside. Arsenio's monologue settled into pantomime inside the big-screen that she'd had inset into the stone wall to the right of the fireplace apron. Her voice was dry and formal. No tinkling music. No Christmas carols.

He sat down beside her, leaving a cushion between them. "I need to talk to you. Is there some reason you stayed up?"

"Same thing—to talk, but you may go first."

Sam recovered his wallet from his hip pocket, opened it, removed a folded insurance statement and a laboratory slip. He held them out to her. "Why don't we discuss these?"

Brenan handed them back. A flicker of anxiety crossed her face. "Another coincidence, we picked the same topic."

"Why don't you cut to the part where you tell me what's up?"

Give her a chance!

"Well, as I'm sure you've gleaned, I'm pregnant."

"Those papers are five weeks old. I've had them nearly that long, and I've been waiting, counting off one day at a time. I can't say I'm pleased with being left out. Tell me."

She didn't deflect her eyes from his face. "Sam, you know how things have been with us. I didn't want to believe this could be happening *now*. I went to Tristan hoping he'd tell me stress had thrown my periods off, that some persistent bug was making me feel lousy. Every time I started to tell you, I'd feel—I don't know—uneasy. No—sick's a better word. I'd feel sick because I don't know you anymore. You're so remote. I kept putting it off, hoping for a better time. You don't talk to me unless it's something you can't get out of, and then you're just some polite stranger sharing necessary information. I've been waiting for an opening, a right time, but whenever we're in the same room, the tension is so strong I can't think. Like now! I know you feel it. Anyway, finally, I got it—

there's not going to be a right time, so I picked tonight. I've been sitting here thinking it could become a starting place for us to communicate."

"Seems to me you're a little turned around in some of your descriptions. I don't guess that matters anymore."

"I can't justify holding back. I won't try. I was wrong, and that's that."

"How did this pregnancy happen?"

Go slow. Lefty warned.

"I guess we were careless."

"We?"

"Okay. *I* was careless. Is that how you want me to put it? The keeper of the sponges? The designated sperm killer?"

"That's not what I mean. When did the carelessness take place? When have we met the requirements for making a baby?"

Jerk!

That hurt. Her stoic face sagged. Her chin began to tremble. He knew then, with all the certainty he'd ever need, she hadn't been unfaithful.

"Is it mine?" He went ahead with the question hoping to make her defend her secrecy.

No fair!

Tears sprang from the corners of her eyes. "What do you mean? I haven't—I wouldn't—How can you do this to me? I didn't do any—" She covered her face with her hands.

Why don't ya just hit her? That wouldn't hurt any more'n what you're doin' now!

He wasn't ready to end the attack. "When did it happen?"

She dropped her hands. Tears caught and shimmered in her dark lashes. She shook her head. "All this time I've wondered about you. I've wondered if another woman is why you act like you do. But then I'd think about the child abuse story and Justin's death. Then there was Karen coming to see Mariah. And the two years of living behind fences that I caused. I thought maybe those things were reasons. I've tried to convince myself that you're going through a bad time, something you feel you can't share with your family. I keep telling myself it's something you'll get over. But still, I've wondered."

Anger shook him. She wanted to turn the guilty tide away from her. He kicked the coffee table across the floor. It banged against the rise of the hearth. He stood and leaned over her, aiming his finger at her face. *She'd* wondered about *him!* Who was suffering here? He was a man who would give every material thing he owned to have her look at him again with love, with desire. Never could another woman give him what she had given. She knew he loved her! What kind of game was she playing? He clinched his teeth and shook his finger. He opened his mouth to tell her what *he* thought.

She shrank back.

See what you've done!

Her sudden fear startled him, made him retract the accusing finger, straighten, and turn around. He ran his fingers through his hair. When he turned back around, all he felt for her was pity—and love.

"I'm sorry." He swallowed. "It's just you've known all this time. I needed to know, too. I had a right to know. What am I supposed to think? How am I supposed to feel?"

"I don't know what you should think and feel, but I do know one thing: there's a great deal wrong in a relationship where people can't talk to each other."

"Then tell me what it is, Bren. I don't have a clue."

She silently stared at the fireplace.

"Fine. Don't answer, but listen when I tell you another woman is the last thing I want."

Sam sat back down and gazed at the muted TV screen. After a while he asked, "How far along are you? I can't tell by just looking at you."

"I'm not sure. I'm having an ultrasound in a few days. That ought to be fairly accurate. Close to four months, I guess. I don't remember my last period, and the last time we were together isn't something I want to remember. I don't mean that to be hateful, but it's the truth. You know how awful it was."

She's right, Boss. Can't fault her for tellin' the truth.

He nodded sadly.

She shifted, rearranged her position, looked at him with sad, weary eyes. "Sam?"

"What?"

"I'm sorry, very sorry I hurt you. The pregnancy came as a shock. If you think it was something engineered, you're wrong."

"Why would I think that?"

"Well, sometimes women try to fix ailing marriages with babies. I'm not one of those. That's what I meant."

Ailin' marriage! She hit that on the head, too. That's exactly what ya got here.

Sam dismally shook his pounding head. "I wish you had. It's a sorry shame to bring a child nobody wants into the world."

"You bastard!" She became loud and indignant, almost hysterical. "You didn't hear me say I don't want it! All I said was I didn't intentionally—oh, never mind. I can't make you care about this baby, or me. The truth is, I do want it, and if your feelings don't change, if you hold what I've done against our innocent little baby—that'll be the *real* shame."

She called ya a bastard! Gonna just take that? Sure, ya are. The truth hurts, but it's yours to keep all the same.

"When have I had the chance to care? How did you think I could care for a baby I didn't even know about?"

"You're right, Sam. I tried to sneak this one right past you. I wanted it all for myself, and I wanted you to turn into a stranger who doesn't look at me or talk to me. A stranger who acts like I'm not here!"

Uh, oh!

"That's not fair!"

"I've apologized, Sam. That's all I know to do."

"Well, as long as you're sorry . . ."

Stop provin' this bastard thing, Sam. Put your arms around her! Tell her it's okay. If ya try, ya can work somethin'.

"We've accomplished so much with all this communicating. Don't you think?" She stood and began walking toward the bedroom. "But I'm tired, now. I'm going to stop communicating and go to bed."

Go after her! There's still time!

Exasperated, Sam threw his hands up. He heard the soft clap of a door closing upstairs and wondered ruefully which one of the children had been listening.

Man, you're gonna lose her. We're gonna lose her! I love her, too, ya stupid sonofabitch.

The pains banging in Sam's head felt like a series of implosions.

38

MARIAH TRIED TO LISTEN to what Daddy was saying, but her mind kept stepping off the track. Except for the light from the T.V., the room was hazy and full of November shadows. She'd been in the habit of watching the five o'clock news for longer than she could remember. At first, she'd watched just because of Daddy. Now, she watched even when he wasn't working. She liked learning about the things that were reported. Everyone should know as much as they could about the world they lived in. The older she got, the more important Daddy's job seemed. Lately, he'd worked so much, TV was just about the only place she saw him. Now and then, he hurriedly passed by her at home. Sometimes, he stopped for a brief chat. Other times, he didn't bother to speak.

Her grandfathers called her a news junkie. She was seriously considering becoming a broadcast journalist and had made the mistake of telling them. They teased her about following in her father's footsteps. *"Like father, like daughter."* They'd think *following* when she landed a top spot like Katie Couric or Connie Chung with a major network or CNN! She also wanted to write blockbuster movie scripts and bestselling novels. She hadn't tried to talk about her ambitions with either of her parents since the beginning of the school term. They'd become so preoccupied, they probably wouldn't be interested, anyway.

Tonight Daddy's image, complete with his stupid basset hound tie, filled the screen. His face was a little green, but she didn't feel like adjusting the color. She was angry at him. Green was good enough. It suited him.

As usual, Daddy was anchoring with his partner, Dana Rawlings. Dana was as much Mama's friend as she was Daddy's. Her family and Mariah's did things together—trips to the zoo and Rickwood Cavern, Oak Mountain and Smith Lake camp-outs, backyard barbecues. Mariah's admiration for Dana was one of the reasons she'd made her career choice.

Instead of paying attention to either Dana's or Daddy's news reporting, Mariah let the stories sail past her, plucking a few shreds and crumbs as they went by. Five unattended children, all under seven, had died in a house fire in Tarrant. A Bessemer man had shot his mother nine times. Some nut had tried to climb the Vulcan statue on Red Mountain, gotten tangled in his ropes, and had to be rescued by the fire department. There was more about the shortage of money for Alabama schools. Mariah was concerned more with the messenger than the message.

Daddy kept going on about the tragedies and events of other people's lives. It was time he started showing concern for the problems he had at home. She felt neglected by nearly everyone, but most of all by him. He had changed the most.

She inspected his green face. He looked different. Gloomy, unsmiling. Always before, she'd been proud of his looks. He was the best looking man on the news team—and just about everywhere else, too. In fact, only Michael Keaton had ever ranked higher with her. But Michael was more cute and weird-looking than handsome. Her friends thought Daddy looked sexy. Some of them got crushes on him and asked her all kinds of crazy questions. What was his favorite food? His favorite color? What was his sign? What did he wear to bed? Now, his face reminded her of someone who had been sick a long time, and when he was home, he acted that way. He looked a little like some pictures she had seen of people dying with AIDS. He used to jog, ride horses, work out on the machines in the rec room over the garage, and play ball with her and Ben. He didn't do any of those things now. He just watched them like he thought they might run away or hurt themselves. He watched but didn't talk. And when they tried to get close, he stopped paying attention.

Mama was nearly as bad. She and Daddy used to be fun. Every day they'd get something going. Phony arguments or made-up games. They used to play. They used to embarrass everybody by hugging and kissing and whispering. Mariah missed the silliness and laughter. She missed the interest they used to show.

This morning, before school, Mama and Daddy had come into the kitchen while she and Ben were eating breakfast. Mama had sat down with them while Daddy, in his bathrobe, stood beside her. He had cleared his throat like he was going to speak, but Mama had been the one who'd told them they were going to have a baby sister or brother in a few months.

Mariah wasn't blind. Anybody with eyes—except maybe Ben—could have seen something that obvious. Daddy had cleared his throat again and gone back to bed. Mama had stayed a few more minutes to answer questions. No one had asked any. Ben hadn't even looked up from his cereal. One of them should have cared enough to ask him what was wrong.

Mariah hadn't mentioned lying on the landing one night last week, listening to them argue in the family room. They'd shouted so loud she couldn't help hearing. They should have known.

"It's like we don't matter as much as we used to," she thought. *"They do stuff for us like they have to—not like they want to. Daddy can be in the same room and not even see us or Mama. And Mama tries to stay in rooms and places where Daddy don't usually go. They are always hiding and dodging each other. Even Deejay and Marissa don't like to be around them anymore, and Ben's getting quieter and weirder every day."*

The phone rang and shook Mariah from her thoughts. "I'll get it!" she shouted just in case anyone cared. She looked up at the television. The five-thirty network news had replaced the local broadcast. The rumble of Ben's train floated down the stairs. Mama put her head through her office door and asked for a message to be taken if the call was for her. "Put the answering machine on after this one, Rye. I thought it was on."

Mama wanted the answering machine on in case that stupid preacher, Blacknell, called. She had told Mariah and Ben to hang up on him.

"Hello."

"Rye, it's Daddy. You watch the news?" Daddy used to sound happy when he called home. Now all Mariah heard was sadness.

"Sort of. Not really. I wasn't paying much attention."

"This new baby thing takes some getting used to, huh?"

Mariah thought having a baby now made about as much sense as going barefoot in snow. "I guess."

"Is your mama busy?"

"Yeah. She said take a message."

"I see."

Mariah heard his disappointment, but she didn't feel sorry for him. Not much. "She might not've meant you. I can ask."

"No. That's okay. I'll talk to her later. I've gotta go, anyway. I'll try to call back before bedtime. I love you."

Mariah waited. She didn't feel like saying it, but after a while, she admitted, "I love you, too, Daddy."

"Bye."

"Bye, Daddy."

Mariah put the phone down. She felt cold as she walked toward her mother's office. At the door, she raised her fist, knocked twice, and waited for Mama's voice to invite her in. The sounds of sniffling and nose-blowing came before the invitation.

The brass handle turned in her hand, and Mariah pushed through the heavy, carved-oak door into a room that held books, files, computer equipment, and Mama's polished oak desk. It was a corner room, and two of the walls were mostly glass looking out onto the south and east sides of the wraparound porch and the lawn and woods beyond. A tinted skylight shaped like a lemon wedge added more light. A sunny room that usually felt cheerful, but today it had the feel of rainy days and forgotten promises.

Mama sat at her desk in front of a blank computer screen. She didn't even have it turned on. She looked at Mariah with eyes pink-rimmed from crying.

Mariah walked slowly to the desk and put her hand on Mama's shoulder. "That was Daddy. He'll talk to you later. He said he'd try to call back at bedtime."

Mama nodded. "Did he say why he called?"

"I think he just wanted to talk to you. I guess he's lonely."

"Oh."

"Mama, why do you cry so much?"

Mama tried to hug her, but Mariah stepped back. She didn't want her mother's arms around her.

"Being pregnant can cause your emotions to sort of get away with you. I've heard lots of women cry all the whole time."

"You didn't with Ben. At least, I don't remember."

"Well, every baby is different."

Mariah had given Mama chances upon chances to tell her what kind of trouble their family was having, but all she'd gotten for her efforts were stupid answers. She'd asked both grandmothers, both grandfathers, and Aunt Jackie if they knew what was wrong. They had seemed just as confused and worried, but they had said things that were meant to help her feel better. They had cared. Nothing could make her feel better as long as she was shut out. Being shut out made her mad.

"You know something is happening, and you won't tell me. It's something big. You and Daddy try to act like everything is okay, but I'm not blind or dumb. Ben's not either. You're both doing wrong."

Mama's mouth opened to say something, but Mariah was no longer in the mood for excuses that might even be lies. She turned and went back through the door, then she started running. She wouldn't let Mama call her back. She ran up the stairs and into her room. She hoped Mama heard the anger in every step.

BEN'S SISTER RAN past him in the hall. She didn't even look at him before she slammed the door to her room. Mad.

He shut down his trains and crept across the crisscross of tracks that made twisted routes around the floor of his room, the upstairs hall, and the tops of the rails that looked down into the foyer on one side and the family room on the other. He had laid new track in the playroom, and now most of the second story looked like the web of a giant spider who couldn't spin straight.

He was tired of traveling, so he lay back on his bed and thought about the good times he'd had with his trains. He thought about the times Daddy or one of his grandfathers had crawled around on the floor and taken make-believe trips with him, the times Daddy had sat by the tracks, strumming his guitar and singing hobo and cowboy songs. Sometimes the whole family sat by the tracks or on the stairs and sang or just watched the running of the trains. Those were the best times, but even by themselves the trains were special. Usually no company was required for them to be fun, but he was lonesome. He wanted Daddy to be here with him, to talk to him.

Someday, he'd have a brother or sister who might want to play with his trains. If Mama or Daddy made him, he would have to share, but he would never volunteer. Rye didn't bother them. She knew the railroad was his special thing, the thing he made decisions about without having to ask anyone else.

His coal train was just like the ones that used to run all over Alabama. Even though not many real ones were still running, Daddy had taken him to see one and to a museum that just had coal mining stuff and old brown and gray pictures of coal trains.

His passenger train was like the Amtrak Grampa Mark had taken him on to New Orleans and back again—just for the ride. The front of the engine was shaped like a bullet.

Ben's favorite was his freight train, his hobo train. It had boxcars with sliding doors, miniature livestock, an engineer, and a red caboose. It even had tiny hoboes with bandana bundles and arms and legs that he could bend and fix like he wanted beside flickering camp fires made of glass or inside the boxcars. He had piggyback trailers and cattle cars, railroad crossing signs and gates, trestles and handcars, houses, trees, and picket fences. Round puffs of real smoke came out of the smoke-stack.

Grampa Mark and Grampa A. D. had bought every single thing they could find to add to the M & A Railroad—MacCauley & Armstrong. What couldn't be bought, Grampa A. D. had carved out of wood or made out of tin, wax, plastic, or glass. All set up, it was what Daddy called a majestic rural rail. It passed through farm country. No city. No burbs. Just peaceful countryside.

Every day, Ben sank hours into pretending he was riding those narrow rails. He knew the hoboes and brakemen. He knew the farmers and their families. He knew them as friends with names and faces. He was the engineer who sat at the window under a plume of black smoke and tipped his striped cap when he passed a friend. The trains made him feel happy.

A long time had passed since Daddy had played with Ben. Mama had tried once to play with the trains, but she didn't know how. All Rye wanted to do was read books. She would probably play with him for a little while if he asked, but it wouldn't be much fun. Everybody in the whole family seemed to always want to go off by themselves and be left alone.

Ben hoped all that was going to change soon. He hoped everybody would go back to being like they were supposed to be. Once in a while, he liked somebody to pay attention to him. He missed his family.

39

THE WATERY GLOW of the outdoor security lighting flowed between glass-enclosed louvered blinds, painting the bedroom with eerie, luminous bars. Asleep in this prison of yellow light, Brenan lay facing Sam's side of the bed. In keeping with her recent habit, she took only a narrow ledge, leaving him a vast expanse of custom-made bedding.

Thanks to Roger Garner's hernia operation, this was the first night Sam had been off work after eighteen straight. His family had barely noticed he was home. He didn't know what he'd expected from Brenan. He tried so hard not to expect things. But, still, he'd been hurt when she had gone to bed at nine-thirty without even saying good night.

As he shed his clothes, he recalled a time when she would have waited for him or cajoled him into coming with her, a time when she would have met him halfway across the bed. He lamented the experience of curving himself around her while she slept. He could almost feel his face against the coolness of her neck and shoulders. Holding her was a privilege for which he was hungry. How distant had the loving and holding and oneness fled?

Too far, Hoss! She's had 'er fill! Lefty shrieked then immediately countered with a retraction full of bitter denial. *Wait! Ain't so! Hang on! She'll come back!*

How long could he go on without real answers? Her answers. Why couldn't he talk to her? Why couldn't he ask? Every time he tried, his heart rose to stopper his throat like a cork in a bottle, or a caustic rage took over, transforming him into a vengeful, crazed man, flowing over with accusations and grudges.

You're a chicken, a Holly Farms reject who won't even TRY!

Wednesday had been Brenan's twenty-sixth birthday. Her aversion to overblown celebrations had held the party down to lunch in her parents' dining room. The MacCauleys. The Armstrongs. The Rawlings. Smorgasbord and mulligan stew. Her presents had been small and personal—except the one from Sam.

He'd bought a heavy gold-and-diamond ankle chain months ago during a trek with Brenan through The Galleria. The anklet had been part of a three-piece set with a bracelet and a double-strand necklace. She'd stopped for a browse at a jeweler's display window and made some comment that had led Sam to believe she'd liked the ensemble. So while she'd harassed a Radio Shack salesman about computer software she had no designs on buying, Sam had backtracked and bought the ensemble. Forty-five hundred Master Card dollars, and yesterday, he'd been uneasy when he handed the second piece of the set to her. He'd given her the bracelet in September for their wedding anniversary. He supposed by now, she'd guessed he was saving the necklace for Christmas. What had seemed romantic and intimate a few months back, now felt gaudy, tasteless. She'd accepted the second gift with the same quizzical expression as with the first. Earlier, he'd noticed she was wearing both pieces—but she hadn't said goodnight.

So young, so beautiful, she appeared to be commuting into an illusion, a lovely but transparent hologram. He ached to feel close to her, important to her. Standing there, looking down on her, thoughts, thick and poison, came from nowhere to burst through, to explode into shrapnel in his brain. The floor, the firmness beneath his feet shifted. Afraid of losing his balance, he crawled onto his side of the bed where nothing moved.

He lay enveloped in silence. A few feet away in the hush, the woman he loved slept and dreamed and held herself away from him. A few feet away. Miles away. Light years away.

Lying on his back, he watched the ceiling tiles above his head run together to form an unbroken, blackened expanse. Onto the black, he projected his thoughts, lighting it with color and motion. A movie screen.

The mind movies, classics, reruns many times over, flashed across the ceiling in a crazy, jumbled succession, creating a mess that his brain immediately began to sort and put in sequence. Finally, sound came—voices released from subliminal storage compartments. The movies were pieces of his life, tangible, touchable pieces of his spirit, of him. The pieces fit together—sometimes smoothly, sometimes leaving wide, abysmal gaps. Some pieces were homey, nostalgic. On better nights, they would have made him smile. Others were portraits of hell.

He felt movement in the bed. The ceiling screen flashed off. He went on staring into the dark as an old, familiar warmth spread itself across his side. A hand, soft and light, trailed down his body, paralyzing him. He caught and held his breath. Was she moving in her sleep? Acting out some erotic dream?

Brenan!

But the hand moved with a purpose, a rhythm, creating a living, pulsating vertex gorged with blood and yearning. An execution with an objective, a goal. A groping, an extraction of sensations he hadn't known for an incredibly long time.

She's doin' it on purpose!

"Sam?"

His name came in a cool breath that drifted above his ear. Had he imagined it? The sound of her voice could be a trick of his own desire. He tried to swallow the alarm that rose like acid in his throat. If he turned to her, the fire of her touch would cool to ancient ashes. The passion would be his alone and wasted. If he went into her, she would lie corpse-still, waiting for him to be done. She had taught him a confusing ritual of pleasure regressing to panic and pain, and he had memorized it. He could take no more false starts, no more rejection.

But he wanted her! He needed her! Not just the memory of her. Not just a sample of her. He needed her touch to be genuine, but its new fickle nature had denied him too often.

He was trapped. He would look, only look, try to see what she wanted, but he wouldn't answer. Not yet.

In the gloom, he found her features clouded and ghostlike, eyes lost in black holes. If he could unmask them, expose their intent unaltered, he'd know how much of himself to lay open. He told himself the decision to play was his to make, but all the while, her hand milked the ante from him.

"Sam?"

With the tips of his fingers, he touched the groping hand. It became still but kept its possessive hold on him.

"Sam? Do you want to try?"

If he had meant to speak, the effort would have been squandered. Her kneading fingers had strangled his answers.

"Shouldn't we at least *try*?" Her lips were slightly parted and glistening in the thin light, her breath measured and balmy on his skin. Her breasts, heavy from the pregnancy, brushed against him with each breath she drew. Her nipples were firm and pointed beneath the thin fabric of her gown. She knew he wanted her. She held the proof of his need in her hand.

Four enduring months of declining hope at once melded with his urgency and her offering. Every part of his body trembled with terrible expectation. He possessed no power to resist. He had to know if anything was left. Before the groping hand could release him and the warmth remove itself from his skin, he reached for her.

In his quivering arms, she was solid and accessible. When he kissed her, she did not recoil. She graciously accepted his hands, his fingers, and returned to him touch for touch. When she opened to him, he entered slowly, greedily tasting the sensations. She lifted to meet him, and he took their joining for a celebration, a reunion.

He was balanced on an invisible honed edge when she tensed, the cage of her arms and legs tightening around him. An arching of her back flattened her pregnancy-thickened abdomen against him. Her breath came in raspy gulps. He should be able let go, now, to collapse inside her, to finally rest his fear and pain.

But some phantom sensation halted him. A sound, a movement, a feeling wrenched him back. His hands moved to her shoulders then her face. Realization washed over him in freezing waves.

She was sobbing! Her shoulders jerked in ragged spasms. Her cheeks were slick with tears.

Roughly breaking out of the tangle of legs and arms, he shoved himself to the foot of the bed.

"What's wrong?" She pulled herself up, covered her body as frantically as he had fled her embrace, and sat glowering at him. His lungs closed against the air in the room. His breathing became a grating, fragmented, futile exercise. He was phenomenally stupid! He'd never learn!

"Sam? Tell me!"

He wanted to slap her. What right did she have to demean him? Did he deserve this crippling humiliation?

He found his jeans on the floor by the bed and pulled them on. At the door, he spun around. She sat with the sheet pulled up to her neck. Her sobs were loud and wet. Her streaming eyes shamed him. Anger relented to pity.

And love. No matter how hurt, how angry, the love came fatefully through to confuse and complicate. Whatever had made her treat him this way, whatever had made her change was something she couldn't help. She had wanted to love him, but it had been too hard. The thing he could clearly see was her pain and recognized it as plain and cutting as the misery inside him.

"I'm sorry," he said as calmly and distinctly as he could. He looked around the room until he spotted a canister of Beclovent on the floor by the rest of his clothes. He bent and picked it up, but instead of using it, he slid it into a pocket. He'd use it when he got out of the room. "Please, stop crying, Bren. It's over. I'm through touching you."

He heard her call his name, but he was on his way outside to think. He couldn't let her call him back. He had to know what to do. Where to go.

HE STOOD ON THE STEPS of the old-fashioned wraparound porch. A cool, light autumn wind lifted strands of his hair. He hardly felt the breeze on his shirtless body. The asthma was subsiding. He looked around and stared at things that belonged to him but now seemed part of an alien world.

During the construction of the house, the porch had been Brenan's pet project. It had received first consideration. Its wide plank floor and siding and brown-shingled cover surrounded the entire house except for the junction with the garage. The cream-stuccoed second story seemed to grow out of it. It housed a gymnasium of swings, hammocks, rocking chairs, scrolled iron tables, antiquated gliders, and a large doghouse for the German shepherds. She had screened a section of the cool eastern side for bug-free summer evenings. During suitable weather, foliage plants in hanging pots trailed tangled green vines and runners over the broad sitting rails. Flowering shrubbery grew in jungle profusion all around. Rose, camellia, azalea. A fair-weather heaven for watching the sun go down or entertaining guests.

Dressed to the nines in chasing lights and evergreen boughs, this porch had been the big attraction in last year's *Channel Nine News Family* Christmas spots. Filmed on a cool Saturday in late October, they had featured the news staff, spouses, and children. No script. They had simply come for an evening party that had been recorded in indolent spurts on video tape then later cut and spliced into festive but homey scenes. Ben and Mariah had been in two that had aired several times daily throughout the season and were being slated to rerun this year. In one, they had been eating oranges with Garvey's little girl and Dana's two boys on the stone steps. Mariah had sworn she'd die of embarrassment if she had to watch it again. In the other, Dana had been helping a circle of kids make origami birds. The next morning Sam, Brenan, and the children had played in the fake snow before vacuuming it back into thirty-gallon plastic bags. This memory of happiness past served as no insulation from his misery. It merely illustrated how far he had fallen.

On this November night, the porch was only wood and nails, mortar and stone.

The dogs came to investigate his appearance then, yawning, returned to the dog house around the corner near the garage.

Sam was alone. Pain coursed through him. Liquid fire. Nothing escaped the searing flow. Not his body. Not his soul. A cruel fantasy sprouted. In it, he returned to the bedroom, pushed Brenan onto her back, and ignoring her pleas for him to stop, forced himself on her. Time after time, until all his grief was spent. He shook off the sadistic illusion.

"Oh, Bren, I'm so sorry. I couldn't hurt you like that—or is that what I just did?" He leaned against a post and cried in miserable, wracking sobs as he hadn't done since he was a boy. The sobs came as blows battering his body from the inside.

He loved her, and even after all the rejection, he needed her. He needed her to be the way she was before, to care enough to give him answers, to come all the way back.

He had jerked away from her one thrust away from orgasm, and physically, he hadn't moved far from that. His erection was a sickening reminder of his shortcomings as a man. It was proof of his incompetence in dealing with his own emotions and responses. His body had no respect for his pride. He touched himself through the denim of his jeans. He felt strained and sore. Pathetic and weak. Without thinking, he opened his zipper.

And when the joyless act was finished, he cried harder for his losses. The loss of the life he loved. The loss of his family unbroken. And Brenan. He'd have no life without her.

40

E DIDN'T SLEEP but endured the remainder of the night on the sofa in the family room. He couldn't make himself go back into the bedroom for a shirt or a blanket, so he built a fire. In the flickering blue and yellow flames, he sought answers. There were no answers, no magic in the fire. The only answer lay deep inside his bruised and aching heart. During the first cold, dark hours of morning, he made a decision he hoped, for Brenan's sake, he could carry out.

Before seven, Ben drifted groggily down the stairs. Sleep had skewed the waistband of his *Ninja Turtles* pajamas sideways and rakishly curled his hair. Yawning, he gravitated to Sam's lap. Sam hugged him.

"I know you didn't get up to see *Bobby's World,* Daddy." Ben referred to Howie Mandel's early Saturday morning cartoon show. Howie appeared briefly in non-animated form at the beginning and end of each half-hour episode, and Ben, who regularly declared himself Howie's biggest fan, set his alarm so he wouldn't miss it. A sly deal with a local video store supplied Ben with a steady flow of Howie posters which were rapidly papering over the ceiling of his room.

"No. Not exactly." Sam checked the mantel clock. "You've got over half an hour to wait."

Ben got down and headed for the kitchen. "Gotta eat first. Want some Kix?"

"I'll pass."

Sam detoured to the bathroom in the foyer then joined Ben in the kitchen. While the boy got out cereal, milk, and apple juice, Sam made coffee.

"You don't get up early. Did you have a bad dream or somethin'?" Ben asked.

Sam sat down in the booth across from his son. He tried to rub the chill from his bare arms. "Sort of."

"You'd make me put on a shirt or a robe if I was cold. What kinda dream?"

"I don't think I can explain."

"The kind you can't remember real good?"

"I guess so."

"You're wheezin'."

"Not much."

Ben crunched his cereal and talked between bites. "I'm at the end of my last tape. Just got room for today if I use EP. Can I get some before next Saturday?"

"*May* you."

"May I?"

"Sure. Remind me, okay?"

"I will. Deej says he's got a tape of a show where Howie's in Hawaii. He says I can't watch it 'cause Howie cusses an' pees in the ocean. You think he's lyin'?"

"That sounds like some of the things I've seen Mr. Mandel do." Had the selection been up to him, Sam would have picked a different hero for his son—not that he had anything against Howie. He just didn't like to think of a man who stretched rubber gloves over his head and inflated them with his nose as the Roy Rogers of today.

"One time, I saw him go to hell on 'St. Elsewhere' before Rye told on me for gettin' up at midnight to watch it. He got shot in the hospital, an' the bullet went through his heart. The other doctors got him alive again, but while he was still dead, he went to heaven an' hell an' the desert. Hell was a big lake, an' heaven was a big giant yard with flowers an' stuff. If you'd buy me enough tapes, I could tape 'St. Elsewhere' while I sleep. I might want to be a doctor."

Sam managed a smile over the rim of his coffee mug. "I'll think about it."

"Daddy, do you think somebody could get shot through the heart an' not die?"

"I don't know. Sounds unlikely."

Ben put down his spoon and ran to look at the clock. At five years, his sister had been able to read anything that came into her hands. Ben's reading was fairly impressive, but he was better with numbers. He had mastered clocks months ago. The result of Brenan's patient tutelage. He came back to his cereal and announced. "Ten more minutes."

Sam wondered how long it would be before he would next sit through breakfast with his son. How could he tell his children he was leaving? How could he make them understand what he couldn't? His stomach cramped, a balloon expanded inside his chest, and his coffee grew cold. He'd wait a little while longer. He didn't want to spoil *Bobby's World* for Ben.

WHEN BEN, in his twisted pajamas, ran back up the stairs, Sam poured fresh coffee and carried the steaming mug to the bedroom. He found Brenan sitting on the denimed window seat. Her face was turned to gaze out over the back lawn and orchard.

After what had happened in this room last night, after what had happened on the porch, he hated to look at her, hated for her to look at him. Shame burned on his face. He stood in silence until she turned to look at him.

"Coffee?"

Her eyes were swollen, and her cheeks were blotched red. She hadn't slept, either, he supposed.

"No, thanks."

He heard a slight edge on her polite refusal, put the mug down on the night stand, and sat on the unmade bed.

Get it done, Ace. An' no bawlin'. Ya know I hate that—almost as bad as I hate you an' the way ya mess ever'thing up!

A fit of harsh coughing came back to him magnified by the stillness of the room. Brenan's eyes lingered expectantly on him. When he tried to speak, a sudden onset of stridor ate his words. He crammed his inhaler into his mouth and squeezed. The canister was empty.

Can't buy a break, huh, Boss? Not one. Loser.

Impatient, he threw the inhaler against the hearth and got another from the drawer in his bedside table. This one worked.

"Brenan—"

Throughout his coughing and fumbling, she waited, her swollen eyes rapidly blinking.

"I can't do right by you anymore. I can't go on hurting you the way I did last night." He stopped to use the inhaler again. "It's time for me to give up."

Can't get more up front than that.

She stopped blinking. "What do you mean—*give up?*"

"I'll leave."

"Leave?"

He nodded. "I wish you'd talk to me before I go."

She pulled her feet onto the cushion and drew her knees against her chest. Her loose bathrobe gaped open with the movement. She quickly lapped the edges tautly around her legs and tucked them under her. "Where are you going?"

"A motel, I guess. At least for a while."

"Great!" She shook her head. Her Alabama drawl flowed with syrupy slowness. "You just do that! Get yourself a nice room!"

His emotions were blistering coals. Love. Pity. Hate. Anger. All snapping and glowing. All rising hotly to the top. Anger seemed to be surfacing as the momentary winner.

He crossed the floor to stand over her. Her wounded expression pushed him back a step, but it registered too late to take the fire out of his voice. "What's your fucking problem? You act like I'm sticking knives in you!"

"You! You're my problem! My only problem!"

"Well, if I'm all you've got, when I'm out of here, you'll be problem-free. Pretty stupid of me to think you might be willing to give something of yourself to help me figure out what's going on. You can just keep on playing your mind games without me. Keep everything for yourself! Your secrets! That goddamned haunted bed! *Everything!* Don't you break down and tell me one fucking thing! There's nothing I need to know. Not how you feel or what you want! Not one word about last night."

She cowered on the window seat, shrinking from his ranting.

Stop it!

As abruptly as it had come, his anger fizzled, giving up to pity. Anger didn't have a chance. Her wide-eyed gaze wrung his heart, but he refused to cry. He had done a lifetime's worth of that during the slow creeping of the night. He ran his fingers through his hair. "Look, this is too hard. I don't mean—I didn't mean to—I'm really sorry. I've gotta go out there and tell my kids that I won't be staying here anymore. How am I going to do *that?*"

"You're the one who's doing the leaving."

"Yeah, I'm the one who's going to have all the fun. Listen to me, Brenan! Our kids are gonna need a reason I don't have to give them! What happened to us?"

"I wish I knew," she said quietly. She turned to look out the window. "Maybe we should calm down and think about this. Maybe, if we try hard enough, we can work something out. You don't have to go today." She turned slowly back to him, but he couldn't look at her.

Stay. There's a chance. Ya heard 'er say it.

"Yes, I do. I'm not strong enough to keep this up."

"Fine, Sam, but what about me?"

"What about you, Brenan? You haven't told me about you. I don't know what you want."

Just that it ain't you.

He made himself glance at her. She looked so young and scared. If she would open up, give him a way to make amends, he'd do whatever it took.

"When you leave, are you going to someone?"

"Oh, come on—"

"Are you?"

"You know, if you want to start the cheating bit all over, I'll give you the opportunity to explain the fine points of this pregnancy. If it happened without me . . . " The anger was back.

I can't believe you're doin' this!

By the time he shut up, she was crying too hard to answer.

Still, cruelty surged through his veins. "Why don't I just tell you? It's been months since we made it all the way to the finish line! I guess, at least in theory, it's possible for a few stray sperm to get loose if I get *in* but not *off.* Isn't that something we were told in sex ed class? Sure, we had a few failed starts, but I wonder what the odds of getting pregnant from a dry run really are?"

She hadn't been with another man. She'd convinced him when he had confronted her last week, but if he could make her mad enough, she might defend herself. If it increased his odds of producing one tiny scrap of information, he was willing to hurt her in the process. Her pain would never equal his.

Push the screw in, an' turn it. Teach her to fuck with you, Pal. Uh, oh, sorry. Poor choice of words!

Instead of replying to his vulgarities, she went into the dressing room and came back with a photograph and a small sheet of paper. She handed both to him, sat back down, then drew her arms up to hug herself.

An ultrasound image of a fetus labeled at the bottom: MacCauley, Brenan *A./11-7-91/Gestation 23 weeks.* Nearly six months! The paper was a typed report form confirming the information on the picture, a projected delivery date of March 5, 1992, and the fact that no abnormalities were noted.

Uh, oh!

"Last night I put those with your wallet so you'd see them. I guess you didn't look," Brenan murmured. "From now on, we'll just call him *my* baby."

Sam stared at the picture. He'd been so self-absorbed, he had pushed the baby's existence out of his mind. This was the first time he allowed himself to feel something for this child. Guilt was something. It was a start. Confusion was something. This baby was real, and it was supposed to be as much a part of his life as Mariah and Ben. He was supposed to know and love it.

You're s'posed to stick around to raise it!

"Brenan, I—I didn't mean—"

"I don't care."

"I know it's mine. I just—"

"No matter what you know or don't know, what you mean or don't mean, you're leaving. Why don't you start packing? You can tell the kids on your way out. They'll have a right to feel deserted, because that's exactly what you're doing. Justify it any way you have to, but keep in mind nobody asked you to go."

SAM PUT HIS SUITCASE, a hanging garment bag, and his guitar in the Explorer. Then he walked back through the garage and into the house to finish detaching himself from his family.

In the family room, Brenan had set the stage.

The kids sat side-by-side on the sofa. Ben was already squirming over his separation from his TV set. He had taken time from the cartoons, probably during commercials, to dress in a sweat shirt, jeans, and Nikes. Mariah, roused from her accustomed Saturday morning sleep-in, looked bored and drowsy. Sam watched as Brenan moved to the foot of the staircase.

His show, now.

He sat on the rise of the stone hearth with only the low coffee table keeping him apart from his children. Mariah had two shallow lines frowned into the space between her brows. The lines indicated she knew something out of the ordinary was taking place, and she was anxious to get done with it. Ben sat forward, restlessly swinging his legs off the edge of his cushion.

"What?" Mariah asked.

If his daughter had hopes of going back to sleep, he was about to kill them.

Don't know why I stick around. Ya never learn. This time you're doin' it big. Gonna break some little hearts, Ace. Some little ones an' some big ones. How ya gonna live with it?

Sam swallowed, rubbed his hand across his mouth, and began. He'd barely stumbled through three or four sentences when the changes started.

Mariah tilted her head to the side, her eyelids blinking too often. Poking one cheek out with his tongue, Ben grimaced. They were catching on quickly.

"You two kids are the most wonderful parts of my life—and your mama's. We'd never hurt you on purpose. But I'm afraid what I have to do is going to hurt."

Mariah tucked her arms together and bowed her head. Sam saw a tear fall. It darkened a small circle on the sleeve of her gown. The first tear. There would be others. Ben moved his tongue to the other cheek. His legs swung harder, faster. Brenan had disappeared into the bedroom.

"At first, it might seem scary because you're used to all of us being together. You may think if one of us didn't live in this house—sometimes one parent has to—I'm not really leaving you. I'll be with you a lot, and if you need me for anything, I promise—"

"No!" The word came twice in close succession. Mariah's was an incredulous whisper; Ben's was closer to a shriek. Their faces blanched with shock and disbelief. Ben kicked and slid across a narrow span of cushion and abutted tightly against his sister. She grabbed him, dragged him close. Here they sat, huddled protectively, cringing as if they expected a beating.

"Please, listen before—"

"No!"

"Ben, please—"

"What did we *do?*"

"Nothing. You and Mariah didn't—"

"Then who did?"

"It's not that simple, but I'll take all the blame—"

"That's right, you will! If you don't want us, just get on outta here.

We don't want you, either!" The boy got up and ran to the double doors. He pointed. *"Go!"*

"Ben!" Mariah yelled. She ran after him, but he circled her and came at Sam. His *I hate you!s* became a chant that resounded off the walls.

Sam dropped off the hearth to his knees. He reached to catch his son, but the boy's sneakered foot connected with a spot an inch above Sam's belt buckle, forcing him back on his heels. Twice more he took the impact of his son's foot before he was able to grab the small shoulders and physically end the attack. He spun Ben around, and pulled the small back against his chest. Still, Ben kicked the air and Sam's legs.

Brenan came from the bedroom and started toward them, but Sam waved her back. No matter what part she had played in his impending flight from home, this was his fight.

Mariah stood in the middle of the room with her back to all of them, arms crossed tightly, head tilted to one side.

Sam endured. Slowly, Ben ran down and became limp in his arms. The *I hate yous!* dwindled to tired sobbing. Sam turned the stilled body around and hugged it to him. He motioned Brenan to the sofa and carried Ben to her. "I love you," he told the now docile child then placed him next to his mother.

He passed in front of them and stopped near his daughter. He lightly encircled her in his arms. She wrenched away, narrowed her eyes to slits, and hissed, "I hate you, too!"

"Mariah! *Wait!*"

Her reply was the slapping sound of bare feet on the stairs, punctuated by the resonant slamming of a door.

41

THE PERKY BLONDE young woman behind the desk of the Northgate Grayson Inn exuded a pungent, sex-scented curiosity. Her breasts, roughly the size of A. D.'s fishing creels, appeared to put significant strain on the seams and buttons of her man-cut uniform jacket. "Hey, I know you. You're that guy—MacCardy or something? You do that 'Nine Cares' thingy, don't you?"

Sam nodded wearily and slid his Visa card toward her.

"MacCauley. Sorry. Your house being sprayed or something?"

Her coy smile was laced with the heavy bouquet of Wrigley's Juicy Fruit. Her cologne smelled cheap, flowery, strong. Fruit and flowers. Overripe bananas and wilted honeysuckle.

Fly bait.

"Or something."

"I'll just bet everywhere you go in Birmingham, people recognize you. Don't that get annoying?"

He shrugged.

Her inquisitiveness was as readable as an electronic marquee. She'd not object to giving aid and comfort of the bimbo brand. Snap your fingers, blink your eyes, toss your head—She'd come running. Hips, lips, finger tips! Another carnivore.

No thanks! Not if you was the last one left—an' ba-lieve me, there's plenty man-eatin' hyenas left! Pull in your claws! Ya won't be havin' MacCardy-MacCauley meat for dinner tonight!

"How long will you be needing the room?" She asked amid a series of elaborate gum-poppings. While she ran her eyes over him and waited for his answer, she twisted a clump of her pale hair around a finger.

Good question.

"A week, I guess."

Her black-penciled eyebrows rose with animated interest. "That long?"

He rolled his eyes and hoped she noticed.

"I've read *all* your wife's books. She's *marvelous.*" The spoken. *"Why aren't you at home with her? A split, maybe? Dare I hope?"* The unspoken.

He contemplated telling this woman to stop squandering her charm, that he would never fall prey to her purple-shaded turquoise eyes and wet, pink-frosted lips, that he thought Brenan's books were probably miles over her bleached-out head, that a billion units of penicillin and a recommendation from the Surgeon General wouldn't make her one speck more attractive. Instead, with a psychic warning of Vicky Brown flashing in his head, he uttered a grudging, "Thanks."

"Will she be joining you?" A laughable attempt at shrewdness.

The joinin' business is all over. She's un-joined 'im. That's why he's gotta put up with the likes of you.

Sam's polite coolness was going. "Well, this week she's photo whaling off the coast of Nova Scotia. Research for a new book, you know. Next week, I think, she's backpacking in the Italian Alps, but I can't say she won't drop by. Listen, can we hurry this up a little? I'd like to get settled in before I have to go to work."

"Sure." She handed his credit card back, the tips of her brightly painted nails grazing the pads of his fingers. Her pink lips pouted with undisguised disappointment and bewilderment. "Room 201. That's Building Two. It's directly behind the office. If you get back before one, there's a great band playing at The Greeting Place—that's the lounge." She pointed across the lobby to a set of black metal doors. "The Blood Letters—that's the name of the band. A little hard—punk, you know, but they're cool. You've probably heard of them. I get off at ten-thirty and go by there almost every night."

Thanks for the warnin'.

He took the key and was almost through the glass, chime-rigged door before calling out one last perfunctory and acerbic, "Thanks."

ROOM 201 WAS STARK and sterile. Clinical neatness in shades of aqua and gold with dark wood-stained paneling and furniture. A big bed and a small television set. Sam dropped his luggage and guitar and perched on the edge of the bed. He slumped forward, his elbows digging into the tops of his thighs.

Everything felt empty. The world, this room, the chambers of his heart, his soul. He had no concept of what his life was supposed to consist of from now on. He was a family man who had set himself apart from his family. Not by choice, but by what?

You're in deep poopoo now, Pal. Lefty, spokesman for wisdom and doom, chided. *Ain't never been worth a tinker's dam on your own. Plus, ya gotta tote those pitiful little faces around the rest of your stupid, pathetic life. Add 'em to your collection at The Sam MacCauley Museum of Horror—way down in here! This internal trash dump is fillin' up fast. Not much room left, but on the outside, Ace, if ya didn't have me an' hard times, ya wouldn't have nuthin' at all!*

"Can't you ever be nice to me."

No, I hate you. Ya tear down your children's world, an' then ya run! Sayin' "I love you" don't amount to beans if ya ain't there when they're the hurtest they've ever been. Everybody's gonna hate ya.

"I hate me, too."

Hey, Ace, how come ya gotta hard-on? Explain it to me. You're disgustin' . . .

"Leave me alone."

What's it called when ya get all hot for a dead relationship? Necrophilia? Necromania? Somethin' like that . . .

"Shut up!" Sam hissed through his teeth.

Yessirree. Anything ya say, Boss, Lefty replied, and the world fell abysmally silent.

The room blurred. Sam sat in the same position until it was too late to get to work on time. He dialed the station and told Drury he was having car trouble. "I'll be in after a while."

"You mean the new one's already on the outs?"

"I said it was, didn't I?"

"The brand new Explorer you took half a Tuesday off only a couple of weeks ago to go pick up?" Drury asked suspiciously.

"You wanna fuck me, Andy, you'll hafta wait till I get there."

"Drop the shitty attitude on the way."

"Whatever," Sam answered quietly.

BEFORE THE FIRST broadcast of the evening, he took a call from A. D. He wasn't prepared for a social call much less the raking over his father put him through. His first reactions were hostile and defensive, but before he finally put down the phone, he made an all-out but failed appeal for sympathy. "Dad, please give me a chance. I can't explain now. Just believe I had to or I wouldn't have done it."

"You've moped around here for months, refusin' to tell us what was eatin' you. What is wrong with you? Didn't you see what kind of condition your kids were in when you run out?" A. D. wasn't buying anything but Sam's stupidity and selfishness. He hung up while Sam was still pleading.

Sam tried to call back. He wanted to ask A. D. to buy some video tapes for Ben. He wanted another chance to explain. When no one answered after a dozen rings, he gave up and stared at his blank computer screen for a long time.

"Hangover?" Dana, who had traded a shift with weekend anchor Gail Abernathy, leaned into his cubicle and asked.

"No."

"Well, partner, you need to get the red out before the cameras roll. You look like a Walker County back road. Drury's pee-ohed at you, anyway." Dana's tone was friendly enough but tightly laced with reality.

Sam pulled open a drawer and rummaged through it until he found a bottle of Visine. He held it up for her to see. "Anything you say, Mom."

"Now, be a good boy, comb your hair, and do up your tie. We're on in fifteen minutes. Afterward, you can buy me a cup and tell me all about it." She smiled, blew a kiss, and disappeared.

When she was out of sight, Sam held up two middle fingers in her direction.

"Take one to Andy—your pick!"

SAM GOT THROUGH Friday evening's newscasts in spite of Dana's maternal prying and Andy Drury's ruffled feathers. He made it past the nightmared sleep of Saturday night, but Sunday morning was yet to be conquered. The alternating sunlight and cloud-cover had brought anything but cheer into the room, so he'd pulled the chintzy drapes. The phone had started ringing about eight.

So far, Freida, Jackie, and Ellen had called to give him hell. Robert pointedly hadn't talked to him when Jackie called with her, "What the Sam Holy Hill do you think you're doing?"

Determined not to play favorites, he was curt and rude to one and all. If they wanted to draw and quarter him, let them. He didn't have the long-suffering grit to ward them off. There was no patience in his reserves for courteous banter or self-defense, so he gave them a pat "Come and get me, or go to hell."

The only people Sam wanted to talk to were Mariah and Ben, but when he tried, Brenan was unable to get either one to come to the phone. They were adamant in their denying him an opportunity to open the door his leaving had banged shut between them.

Brenan neither asked for nor offered information. She responded with only a minimum of civility, but before he hung up, she had warmed a bit. She admitted that she, too, was worried over the children's refusal to see him. "I don't suppose it's any consolation that they won't talk much to me, either." She promised to encourage them to open up about their feelings and to call him if they showed any sign of willingness to talk. She promised to reassure them, tell them how much he cared. That was all he could ask of her. That was fair.

But it wasn't enough to quiet his worry. He needed them as much as they needed him. Nobody's needs were being met.

After he put down the phone, he showered and called out for lunch. He wasn't hungry, but he couldn't remember the last time he had eaten.

He thought maybe Friday evening. When the food came, the smell made him feel queasy. After a few bites, he took the bulk of it out to a sidewalk garbage can.

As he drove to the station, he felt weary and lightheaded. With his mind full of other distractions, he had to try twice as hard as he should have just to get through traffic and make the correct exits and turns. Putting the window down didn't help his ragged breathing. He'd have to get rid of the asthmatic stridor before air time or Drury would have only one anchor, and the newsroom crew would have to put up with an ugly tantrum.

Ya ought to feel big an' powerful—bein' able to screw up ever'body's life without even tryin'.

42

O
N MONDAY, though he'd been scheduled an off-night to compensate some of the extra shifts he'd pulled, by noon he'd been summoned back to work. He'd anchored the five and six o'clock broadcasts with Dana. Then, drowsy with physical and emotional fatigue, he had weaved his way back to his office cubicle, propped his feet on his desk, and tried to coax his brain awake.

Here he sat, silent and sulking. The routine of the newsroom had become so scrambled Drury was actually sending Sam out to do inane fillers. Three weeks ago, two morning anchors and several members of the behind-the-scenes crew had abruptly and smugly walked out of WPMS into more lucrative positions at the CBS affiliate, one of three stations which sat in a row on Red Mountain next to Channel Nine—the second mass traitor exodus in a decade. The stretching of the staff to cover the loss and the breaking-in of newly hired replacements heaped strain on everyone. In his constant state of grief and self-pity, Sam scarcely had time for riveting headlines, much less fluff.

The rival Birmingham stations—among others, including the networks—regularly offered Sam generous contracts, but he wasn't a man who embraced change. Neither fame nor fortune tempted him. His loyalty wasn't for sale. At WPMS, he was prosperous and comfortable, a big fish in a small pond. And home was just down the road. It used to be.

Drury's whip-cracking and Sam's smart-assed defiance wasn't doing anything toward the good of either one or the newsroom. Nor was the foolish assignment Andy had handed down making Sam laugh. A rookie job requiring only the minimum of preparation, the story should practically write itself, but Sam's ability to concentrate wouldn't budge past his personal sorrows.

The story was more ridiculous than newsworthy. Lyle Tyler, a local street corner and park green evangelist, was claiming Jesus Christ had returned to Earth in the form of a goat. A nanny, at that! Tyler had been dragging a scruffy, stinking goat around the city for a couple of days, holding spot services wherever he could shag a bit of attention. Another hapless nut that fate played jokes on.

Sam tried to recall his last decent, serious assignment. Garner could have had this one with Sam's blessing, but the irritating oaf, having worked two evenings after returning from sick leave, had called in sick again. Word around the newsroom was Garner had developed some sort of postoperative infection and needed extra days to recuperate. Sam, the Faithful and Stupid, had been tracked down to fill the slot.

Stop bellyachin'. Andy woulda give ya the story, anyway. Betcha Tyler's one of Garner's relatives an' the goat one of his old girlfriends. Conflict of interests or somethin' like that, huh?

"I guess."

Sam stared at the papers in front of him, but his lethargic brain refused to deal with the words printed on them. He flipped the computer on then off again. In a few minutes, he'd go to his scheduled interview with Tyler, turn on the bluff and bluster, and wing his way to a story. Having thus excused himself of the business at hand, he began bending jumbo paper clips into letters of the alphabet.

He tipped farther back in his chair, and with the paper clip letters, he spelled *IDIOT* across his chest. He was working on *IMBECILE* when a sudden clamor startled him. He jerked his feet to the floor, knocking his address file off the desk. Rolodex cards and paper clips took flight around the cubicle.

Only the phone. Jumpy, ain't ya? Need a pill for that?

"MacCauley," he answered gruffly.

"Sam, it's Mark."

What the hell-o does he want? Ya think he's finally caught on to the fact that it's open season for nincompoop son-in-laws?

"Yeah, Mark?" Sam tried to backpeddle to a milder tone.

"Son, you need to come over to Northside. Brenan's here. She started spotting, and Freida brought her in. Um—she's hemorrhaging steadily now."

Dread prickled Sam's skin. "Spotting? Hemorrhaging? Does that mean she's losing the baby?"

"Actually, she already has."

"Aw, hell."

"Nearly a fullterm boy. By rights, he ought to be alive now. Sorry to be so blunt, but the packing won't slow the bleeding for long. Tristan needs to clean the uterus of any placental fragments and control the blood loss." Mark, contrary to his normal matter-of-factness, sounded unsettled. He was worried.

"But she'll be okay?"

"Physically, I suppose. Emotionally, I just don't know. She's wild and hard to deal with. Won't let any of us stay in the room. Won't talk." Mark paused. Sam heard him take in a long breath. "You need to come on, now. There'll be plenty time for questions after she's been taken care of. She's not capable of making decisions, and the hospital looks down on incompetent patients signing their own op permits. You need to sign for the procedure."

"I'm on my way."

Sam passed Dana's cubicle on his way out. He stopped in the aisle and called back to her. "Take a message for me, will you? I have a family emergency. Somebody else will have to do the loony with the goat. You're by yourself for the ten o'clock. And tell Drury if he wants my butt, it'll be at Northside Medical Center. He'd better work out something for tomorrow, too."

"One of the kids?" she asked.

"Brenan." He started walking away.

"Nothing too serious, I hope."

Dana worried about everybody. The last day or two, she had devoted herself to him in particular. She, Rita Williams, and Dan Stircy were the only ones he'd told about leaving home. Brenan had gotten the news to

Dana first. He'd been waiting for her to take sides. He looked back into eyes large and round with concern. The eyes of a friend.

"Me, too. Thanks."

"The baby?"

He wondered which one of them had known about the pregnancy longer. "Yeah."

"Call me."

"Sure, Dana. I'll call."

FREIDA AND ELLEN were in the fifth floor waiting room. Sam walked by them as if he didn't notice. Mark had met him at the elevator and filled him in on the details.

Brenan was in a room on a medical-surgical floor next to obstetrics but far enough away that she wouldn't hear crying babies. Riley had admitted her for the night. Due to her distraught state, a psychiatric consult might be necessary in the morning. Sam had to go to the nurses' desk and sign the permit before going to the room. The kids were home with A. D.

"Be careful what you say, Sam, but don't let her run you off. She needs you." Mark's last words before Sam left him standing in the corridor.

At the door to Brenan's room, Sam stepped aside for an obese nurse with a pink angelic face. The nurse motioned to him, and he followed her a few steps away from the door. "You're Mrs. MacCauley's husband?"

"Yes."

"She's being prepped for surgery. When the other nurse comes out, you may go in. Dr. Riley wants to speak with you before he takes her downstairs to do the operation. I'll let him know you're here. And Mr. MacCauley, she's very fragile right now. She says she doesn't want anyone with her, but Dr. Riley wants you to stay, anyway. He thinks she doesn't really know what she needs. The sudden loss of a baby can be an extremely difficult experience for both parents, but sometimes a mother needs a bit more understanding and patience."

He nodded and thanked her.

She smiled sadly and walked on.

Sam stared at the closed door.

The baby was dead. Was it his fault?

If all the babies in Birmingham died, it'd be your fault!

He supposed his parents and hers, everybody, thought so, too. Brenan would blame him. He waited, and when the second nurse came out of the room, he took a long, fortifying breath and went in.

Her face was wan and still. Her drowsy, dark-circled eyes seemed fixed on the bag of intravenous fluid that hung on a metal pole near the foot of the bed. She blinked but did not otherwise react to his presence in the room.

He walked to the bed. "Brenan?"

Someone had pulled up the metal rails as if they thought she might try to run away. The IV tubing ran through a computerized pump that was attached to the pole below the bag. The pump, housed in a blue rectangular case, produced a rhythmic hum. A red digital display kept track of the rate of infusion in milliliters per hour. The clear tubing then made a path across the bed and disappeared under a wide strip of tape on the back of Brenan's left hand.

A hospital identification bracelet had been affixed around her right wrist. She didn't stir when Sam picked up her hand to read it. *MacCauley, Brenan A. / Tristan Riley / 524.* A series of numbers followed, but they meant nothing to him. Yellow hospital gown, tied at the neck. Clean white sheets. Built into the rails, finger controls for adjusting the bed, operating the TV, calling for help. All very clinical and cold.

He put her hand back down.

"You'll be going to surgery soon. You know that, don't you? Dr. Riley explained, didn't he?"

An almost imperceptible nod.

"You understand what he's going to do?"

Another nod.

"You want to talk about it?"

Nothing.

"It must have been painful."

Nothing.

"What about now? Do you hurt? Did they give you something for pain?"

Nothing.

"What can I do to help?" His chest tightened, and a warning wheeze arose.

She wet her lips with her tongue. They were dry and chapped, her voice softly husky. "You can leave."

"I don't think so."

"I don't need you here."

"Maybe, but I lost a kid, too. It wasn't just yours."

"*It* was a boy."

"Did you see him?"

A slight nod.

"Did it happen here or at home?"

"The emergency room. They wouldn't let me hold him."

"Why didn't you call me?"

"Freida was close."

"I could have met you here."

"I didn't want you."

"I see." He tried to take her hand again, but she wouldn't let him. She tucked it under the sheet.

As he looked down at her, a spot of blood no bigger than a nickel appeared on top the sheet between her thighs. He was sure it hadn't been there when he came in. He stood still and watched. Slowly, the spot grew.

As big as a quarter. A half-dollar.

"He looked like nothing at all was wrong." At last, she looked at him, her eyes bright in the center of dark, hollow circles. "Only little. And he was dead. I begged them to let me hold him, but they took him out of the room. They kept saying 'not now—we have to stop the bleeding'. I could have held him while they worked, but they wouldn't let me."

Sam didn't know what to say, so he kept quiet and monitored the blood on the sheet. The spot was maybe three inches in diameter now. He fought to keep his own breathing under control. Somehow, he'd stave off a full-blown asthma attack for her sake.

"There's no reason for you to stay."

"There is. You shouldn't be alone. Blood's coming through the sheets. I think I should call a nurse."

"No."

"But—"

"I said *no!*"

"Why don't you want me here?" He blinked rapidly, took a shallow breath and held it, hoping to restrain the tears that stung his eyes and made the room look shimmery and blurred. Brenan didn't need that. He didn't need it, either. He'd cried too much in the last few days. A lifetime's worth of tears.

"I want to be alone."

"I won't bother you. I'll just be close if you need something."

"I won't need you."

Tears fell in spite of the deep breath, the blinking, the struggle to make them stay put. He palmed them away. "What if I need you? I feel things, too."

"You didn't want him."

"Bren, I—"

"You said you didn't want him!"

Sam swallowed and tried once more to hold her hand. This time she let him. "I do now!"

The hand was warm and limp. He felt her face with his other hand. It was warm, too. Maybe, too warm. Feverish. He pushed her damp hair back from her face. Her forehead was burning, and her cheeks were beginning to flush red against the pallor.

"I didn't make it easy for you to want him," she admitted.

He shook his head slightly, hoping she'd see it wasn't important now and whispered, "It's okay, Bren."

When she closed her eyes, one fat tear squeezed out of each. The blood stain was as big as his hand.

Sam was reaching to push the call button when Tristan Riley came through the door.

43

E SAT STARING at a pile of blood-soaked sheets. A heart had been opened and drained over them. While he'd been selfishly enveloped in his own pain, giving up little concern for the baby growing inside her, Brenan had cared. She had loved. She didn't believe he had never truly denied the child—not deep down inside him where truth sometimes hid when his mind was impaired. If only he could put the baby, alive and healthy, back inside her. He ached for her to know how wretched he felt, ached for forgiveness she couldn't deliver because, in a moment of cruel, self-indulgent anger, he'd said he didn't want it. Now, she intended to maintain her pain and loss separate from his guilt and belated remorse.

He left the accusing, bloody bed and ambled slowly toward the waiting room to present himself for the judgment of the others. Mark wasn't there. Robert and Jackie had taken places next to their mothers. All sat in plastic chairs that connected one to another at the armrests. Jackie, Freida, Ellen, Robert. Mental fingers pointing. Judge and jury, all in a row.

Afraid to go all the way in, Sam supported himself, shoulder against the door frame. He looked at his watch. Five past nine. Visiting hours technically over, the MacCauleys and Armstrongs had the room to themselves. He cleared his throat. "Tristan said it might be two hours before Brenan comes back to the room."

All but Robert peered up at him.

"She wanted me to ask you to go home and wait there. She doesn't feel she's up to seeing anyone tonight."

"I'm not leaving!" Ellen practically screamed at him. "Surely you don't expect us to go home while she's in surgery!"

"No, Ellen. I simply gave you her message. I don't think she'll see you when she wakes up, but you might be able to talk to Tristan or something. He said the surgery waiting area on third is full of people—a wreck, I think—so he suggests everybody stay here. He'll come up when he's through."

Ellen set her face in a hostile glower. "Does she want you to stay? Does she want *you* in the room with her?"

Sam regarded them all. Robert leaned forward, elbows on knees, head down. He saw sympathy in the faces of his mother and sister. He was the son and brother who had done the wrong only because he hadn't known what was right. A well-intentioned screw-up. They pitied him the same way they would have a child who had fallen from a tree or rode his bicycle into a ditch.

"Yes, I think she does."

Ellen's scowl deepened, an exhibit of supreme disbelief.

Jackie came at him. "Come on, Sam. Go with me downstairs. I need food." She swung back around to the others. "Would anyone like us to bring something back?" She hardly waited for the replies before she pushed him out into the corridor.

"Ellen's ready to come after your eyes with her knitting needles." She hissed when they were out of earshot then began a speech that lasted to the door of the second floor canteen. "She's got Brenan pissed off. I can't get her to tell me the whole story—I'm certain my having blood ties to you is the reason—but from what she has told Robert and me, they had a fight. She said some nasties about your leaving, and Brenan retaliated by ordering Ellen out. I wish I knew what she said. This isn't like Ellen. She's usually the peace keeper. Then Mark got onto her for being so bitchy and refusing to take medication for the hormone roller coaster she's on. Now, she's pissed at him. Menopause must be one wild pony ride. Anyway, Daddy's leaning toward Bren's corner, so Ellen's also on the outs with him. Mama's trying to keep her head, but who can say how long that'll last. Ellen keeps making off-color remarks about your character in front of her, so she's already breathing hard. If she blows, won't be enough left to bury. Robert hasn't made up his mind, yet, but he's worried. As you know, he won't say much until he decides, but he's worried.

"And, oh yeah, the big, *big* thing is Brenan called Mama when the pains and bleeding started. Insult to injury for Ellen. Salt in the wounds. Somehow or another, that's your fault, too. So, brother, you'd better lay you butt low around her!"

They can kill ya, but they can't eat ya, Lefty said sunnily.

Sam didn't have a rejoinder to her rapid-fire commentary, so he shrugged and asked how much caffeine she'd had today.

They can kill . . .

"I'm serious, the waves are getting high. You and Brenan better get back together soon—before the MacCauleys and Armstrongs find themselves in a civil war. The Hatfields and McCoys never had an Ellen nor a Freida." She led the way through a maze of tables, only a couple of them occupied, to a small one in a back corner.

Sam sat, crossed his arms on the tabletop, put his head down, and whimpered. He glanced up as Jackie's mouth opened to continue. "Please, don't. Brenan's in surgery. Blood was gushing out of her when they took her. Isn't that and a stillborn son enough for me to deal with?"

"Two good reasons for you to go on back home. I can list other reasons—with your living children topping the list."

He raised his head. "She doesn't want to live with me."

"I don't believe that. She loves you."

"She used to love me."

"That's garbage! You're killing her, slowly, a degree at a time. She doesn't know how to survive without you. And ditto for you. You can't not go back. You've gotta open up, tell her how scared and mixed-up you are. Don't you realize whatever's brought on this split is totally unrelated to her and the way you feel about each other—just the way you feel about yourself."

"That doesn't make sense."

"It will. I just hope it doesn't take too long." She touched his sleeve.

"Listen, I don't want to dig up anything, but I've seen you do this kind of overreacting before."

"What do you mean?"

"The nightmare. You're having that again?"

"Yeah. So?"

"The things in the nightmare are what it all goes back to. That man left you feeling defenseless. Your guard is never down. These feelings of inadequacy are part of you. Most of the time, you work around them, but sometimes you let them take over. Then through them, you try to destroy yourself in the daftest ways—like with DeLane Evans. Even your mother-hen syndrome goes with it. You protect all of us to death then trash yourself. You may not understand it any better than we do, but you do know exactly what I'm talking about."

Lissen up, Ace. She's got your number.

"This is different."

"No. The child abuse story you spent all those weeks on got to you. You worried yourself sick over that little boy, Justin, and when he pulled that trigger, something in you blew. We see it every time we look at you. Sam, that kid didn't want to put guilt on you. He saw death as his only way out, and he called you because he wanted you, as his friend, to share his relief."

"Jackie, please," he whined. He wouldn't hear anymore.

Lefty blurted. *The nightmare—again an' again. An' again! You an' Ralph an' Debra Jean. An' Justin! But Ben's there, too! The trailer's rockin'. Ever'body partyin' together! You dream about Ben, an' Ol' Ralph won't let you get to your son!*

She sighed. "Okay, no more. Not tonight, anyway. I'm going to make an order. What do you want?"

"Nothing."

"I'll get you a cream cheese danish. Let Mama have a food fit. It'll release some tension. While I'm gone I want you to rehearse telling me that you're not still crazy about your wife. Practice, and be able to tell me you don't love her. Then I'll shut up for good."

He watched her navigate the rope maze to the counter and return with a bag full of chips and nauseating, sugary pastries wrapped in clear plastic. She put the sack on a spare chair.

"Well, can you say it?"

"You know I can't."

"Then go home with her tomorrow. She needs you to take care of her. Don't take your grieving off in separate directions."

"She doesn't want me. It hurts, so let me stop saying it."

"She wants you. Just a couple of days before you left, she said she wished she could figure out what to do to make things right. She said you'd turned your back on her."

He sighed. "She probably meant she didn't want to talk to me after I had it out with her about not telling me she was pregnant. You know the story. I wanted her to tell me, but she never did. By the time I asked, she was very pregnant by—even she didn't know just how very. Then, I asked if it was mine."

"Oh, Sam, you didn't!"

Yes, he did. I heard 'im. Treated her just like any ol' whore, like her feelin's didn't count!

He nodded. "We hadn't been intimate in a long time."

"You couldn't have believed she was fooling around!"

"I don't know what I believed. Why she'd go so long without telling me? It would've crossed any man's mind. Anyway, I said a lot of stuff, and so did she. She wasn't talking much before the fight, but afterward, she hardly spoke at all. I can't undo the damage, but she didn't do right, either." Sam didn't think he couldn't accept all the blame tonight.

"You didn't have sex in all those months? Why?"

"That's no concern of yours. Now, I'm going back to Brenan's room and wait for her." He thrust back from the table and stood, knocking his chair on its side. Leaning, bringing his face close to hers, he ejected searing words through his teeth like missiles. "I can't keep people from believing whatever they want, but the truth is I'm working with the only choices I have. When you see Ellen, give her a message for me. Tell her Brenan needs her more than she ever has, and she's going to have to dump some of her childish rage to help! Tell her I don't fucking care what she thinks about me! I don't need her goodwill, but her daughter certainly does! *Got that?"*

Jackie gave a resigned sigh and nodded.

He sauntered out, leaving the chair where it had fallen.

"OH, GRAMPA, it's all right. He can sleep with me. It's scary for him—all the bad things happening. He's little."

A. D. nodded assent. He noticed that Ben didn't waste time crawling under the covers next to his sister. They'd been too quiet since he told them about the baby dying and their mother having to stay in the hospital. Ben had asked several times if A. D. was sure his mama would get better and come home. He still didn't seem convinced. A. D. could give them mountains of love, but Freida would have done a better job at soothing their fears.

What bothered A. D. more was the fact that neither of the kids had mentioned Sam. Not once. He'd been away from them two days, and on the outside, it was as if they had erased him from their lives. He knew they needed to talk, ask questions, express their feelings. They just didn't know how to go about it. He tried to get them started. "Your daddy's gonna stay at the hospital with your mama tonight. He's there now."

"Why?" Mariah obligingly asked.

"Because they need each other. He's that little baby's daddy—just like he's yours. You know he cares about you all, honey. You feel hurt an' confused right now, but don't cheat yourself into believin' he don't love you. You're adjustin' to a terrible shock, but you didn't lose your daddy. He's just unable to be what you want 'im to be right now."

"Gramma Ellen told Mama she thinks he has a girlfriend, then they started fussing. Mama told her to get out of his house if she couldn't talk any better about him."

"Ellen's not thinkin' too good, either. She's got some problems of her own. I don't know how to explain, but it's not her fault. She even thinks Mark has a girlfriend, an' tell me, who'd want an old grump like him for a sweetheart?" A. D. paused and waited for a smile. Nada. Zero. Zip. No humor here. "Tell you what, when Gramma Freida comes over, ask her about what happens with women who are goin' through menopause. If you can't remember the word, ask her about a woman's 'change of life.' Okay? Think you can remember to do that?"

Mariah shrugged. "You don't think he's got a girlfriend?"

"No, honey."

"He could get AIDS."

"Rye, you don't really think he's betrayed your mama. That's not why he moved out. Right this minute, he's with the woman he wants. Sometimes, I think he loves her too much, but his thinkin's all jumbled-up. He's hurtin', an' he's awful upset about not bein' on good terms with you guys. He keeps callin', an' you won't come to the phone. It's breaking his heart. You gotta let 'im show you how he feels, an' you gotta tell 'im how you feel."

Mariah stared up at him with large, empty eyes. She knew just enough about common vices to create imaginary motives and mischief for a father whose trustworthiness was already in doubt.

Throughout the conversation, Ben pretended to be asleep, his eyelids fluttering with his effort to keep them closed.

A. D. wished Mariah a good night and kissed them both, just as he had kissed Sam and Jackie through many years of bedtimes. He left the door ajar and a light on in the hall.

Feeling the tension of the evening tightening the muscles of his back and legs, he descended the stairs and walked to the laundry room to try to do something about the bloody things Freida had stashed in the washer to keep the kids from seeing them. He picked up a telephone on the way. He'd have to call the waiting room to ask her how to wash them. She would know.

Before he reached the laundry, the phone in his hand rang "Hello. — Oh, for cryin' out loud. Not tonight, Blacknell. — Well, sure, Arlo. I'll look those verses up right now, if you'll just tell me how many jerk-offs you get over a call to my daughter-in-law."

IN ROOM 524, the bed had been remade with crisp white linens. All traces of Brenan's blood was gone. The top sheet and blanket had been fan-folded to one side and the height of the bed raised to facilitate the movement of a patient from a stretcher. A mat of disposable linen savers covered the center of the mattress. In anticipation of more bleeding?

Sam called the newsroom and gave Rita a synopsis of what was happening at the hospital. "Tell Dana I'll call tomorrow."

"You don't sound so good, Ace," Rita told him.

"No shit!" He responded sharply and was instantly sorry.

Ya really know how to treat an old an' treasured friend!

"Look, Rita, don't pay attention to me. I'm too tired to think. I'm sorry. Okay?"

When he hung up, he loosened his tie and flung his suit coat over the arm of a high-backed arm chair. With a paper towel and blue liquid soap from the dispenser over the sink, he washed a thin residue of studio makeup off his face.

Hands in pockets, he walked to the window. There was nothing to see except a view of the parking deck, the chrome and glass of the front lobby entrance, haloed street lights. He watched the traffic light on the corner change from red to green and back to red before he returned and slumped into the chair. All he'd eaten today was an English muffin with coffee from the motel's continental breakfast bar hours before he'd gone to work, and although he had no appetite, he was hungry. His stomach had been upset the last couple of days, and now it was really grumbling. He should have taken Jackie's offer of food.

Spend your whole miserable life wishin' ya'd done somethin' ya didn't or regrettin' somethin' ya did. Lemme tell ya, Ace, it's makin' ya old fast. Old an' lonely. Only you can stop it. Find the brake an' step on it.

Tristan Riley came in, followed by Mark, both in slate-colored surgical scrubs. Riley's were stained with small spatters of blood. Circles of sweat ringed his armpits. Sam stood up.

"She's okay. Ought to be back here in less than a half hour," Riley told him. "I removed the remains of the placenta . . . "

Sam listened closely to the doctor's account. He needed to understand.

" . . . running fever, quite high. Urinary tract infections are fairly common. I wouldn't say it had anything to do with the abruptioplacenta—the precipitous birth. I've started her on intravenous antibiotics. If she's doing well tomorrow afternoon, she can go home on oral medication."

"What happened?"

"The placenta, the afterbirth, separated from the wall of the uterus. That usually happens after the baby's born and doesn't need it any longer. Yours was alive and apparently healthy prior to the separation. The tearing cut off his oxygen and blood supply and caused the hemorrhaging. Now just what caused . . ."

The doctor's explanations went on while Sam sought to grasp the reality of this horrible thing that had taken place inside Brenan.

" . . . usually close to term, and that gives us a chance to save the infant. Brenan was delivering when she got to the emergency room. It's my belief the baby died shortly after the bleeding became heavy, maybe an hour before the birth. It's a shame, Sam. He was mature enough to have had a good chance outside the womb. Both the ultrasound and my calculations were way off. I don't see how Brenan could have gone so long . . ."

Sam tried to clear the confusion by shaking his head. "You're saying he might have lived if she'd come to the hospital sooner?"

"Maybe, but no one could have seen this coming."

"Could stress have brought it on?"

"This isn't a my fault/your fault situation. Don't make it one. There was a spontaneous interruption of blood flow, an accident, the same kind of accident as a stroke or the blowing of an aneurysm. Hormonal fluctuation may . . ."

Theories didn't help Sam understand what he was hearing.

"The only way we could have saved your baby would have been to predict the placental tearing—the exact time of it. I'm sorry as I can be about this, Sam, but I'm no prophet."

Mark cleared his throat and touched Sam's shoulder. "I think I'll go fill the others in. I'll come back."

When he was gone, Sam asked. "What can I do for her? I've never dealt with anything like this."

"I'm having Dr. Pinkard drop by in the morning. He's a psychiatrist who's really good with the unique and sensitive problems caused by loss. You don't object, do you? Good. She may need some convincing and encouragement. If you're here, that might help. We'll see what he thinks. Someone will talk to you about your wishes for the baby. The hospital will take care of the body if you like, but you can also have it released for burial. I don't want you to have to face that tonight, so we'll take it up tomorrow. To answer your question—pet her, absorb her anger and pain for a little while. You don't look so great yourself, but she's devastated. She's normally dramatic, but this time she's not acting. Don't lose the patience you've always had with her."

"I won't."

"Do you want to see him?"

"The baby?"

"Yes."

He wasn't certain he did, but he nodded.

"Then come with me."

At Sam's request, they stopped at the waiting room. He thought Freida and Ellen might like to go. Ellen refused to acknowledge him when he called her name, but Freida joined them.

MARK WAS WAITING in Brenan's room when Sam got back. His father-in-law looked older, more haggard than Sam remembered.

"Tristan said he had to give her blood. Your blood. The nurses had better take cover."

"Very funny. We were a perfect match. They did a type and cross-match as soon as I got here—on Ellen and Robert, too. With the HIV virus, transfusions are risky procedures. I guess I don't trust the new screening methods, yet. Ellen couldn't give because she's a bit anemic. She was loudly disappointed." He lifted his brows as if to convey his helplessness in appeasing Ellen's frame of mind. "Robert gave, too. So there's some on standby, but her hematocrit's okay for now."

"No one told Riley that Brenan and I aren't living together. At least, he doesn't act like he knows."

"We're hoping that's a condition that won't last. Don't look like that, I'm not going to start tonight."

"I saw him, Mark. The baby. He looks like—well, okay."

"You expected something else?"

"I don't know what I expected. I've been indifferent, dosing myself with self-pity, and suddenly it's too late to pay attention. Everything I care about seems to be going to hell, and I can't stop any of it. I don't understand what's happened to Brenan—what I've done to make her this unhappy. I've alienated my kids. And I've lost a son. How did I do all that?" Mark's sympathetic, fatherly hand on his shoulder was a load too heavy. Sam reverted to the chair and dropped wearily into it.

"Son, if you think you've done it all without any help, you're giving yourself way too much credit. Brenan hasn't said much, but what she has shared doesn't make her sound innocent. She admits she was secretive about the pregnancy. Wouldn't say why, just that she regrets it. I see in her the same fear I see when I look at you. Breaks my heart—and mine's a tough one to break."

"You know I didn't want to leave home?"

"Yeah. I also know you didn't have to. I know I said I wouldn't start. Look, Sam, Ellen can't make up her mind which one of us is the devil incarnate. I'd watch her if I were you. If you tangle with her, you don't stand a chance."

"She's not really—"

"Don't get me wrong. I love her dearly, but if she don't start taking some hormones and an antidepressant soon, I'm going to have the same address as you."

Sam tried a smile. He hoped what he managed to produce looked like a smile. "Warning noted. Thanks. And thanks for not turning on me yourself."

Mark shrugged and rearranged things on the bedside table. "A while back you made a promise. I'm still holding you to that promise, and I'm going on the assumption that you've kept it. I don't think you've meant to cause my daughter to shed the first tear. In fact, I think you want more than anything to be with her. If I'm wrong, you'd better hope I never find out."

"You're not wrong."

"Tristan wouldn't let me go in with her."

"Good. That would have given her something else to be pissed about."

"Well, she made it pretty clear before they took her into the operating suite that she wants to see no more of me tonight. She told me to take everybody else, including you, home with me."

"I'm not going." Sam was prepared to argue.

"I'd be incredibly disappointed if you did."

WHEN THE EMPTY stretcher was rolled into the hall, Sam was allowed back in the room. The nurse he had met earlier brought coffee and a newspaper before she reported off to the eleven-to-seven shift. He had gratefully accepted.

Holding the Styrofoam cup in both hands, he slouched in the chair while Brenan eyed him hatefully through the bed rails. He stared back. If there was conversation, she would initiate it. She was unmistakably stoned on some narcotic. Her eyes held the same glossy wildness as when she'd taken Tylox capsules for a broken ankle a few years back. For three solid days, she'd been a trial to live with. The drug would have to wear off before she would sleep. In the meantime, he would tread lightly.

He picked up the somewhat rumpled, nearly day-old paper, but when Lyle Tyler and the Jesus goat peered at him from the front page, he'd dropped it beside his chair.

"You're only here because you feel guilty. You could do that in your little impersonal motel room, and I wouldn't have to put up with you." Her voice was a stout attempt to sound hard.

He tried to give the impression he could overlook her rancor. Fighting for composure—and losing—was getting to be routine. Her heavily drawled words were quite successful *inside*.

"You don't have any right or reason to be here."

"Brenan, I don't want to argue. You've been through a lot today. You've been hurt the most. Nobody's going to dispute that, but it hasn't been easy for me, either. You could be a little more agreeable. You really shouldn't be alone."

"I can push one little button and have all the help I need. I wouldn't be alone."

"I would."

"You chose to be alone."

"That's not exactly true, and whether you accept it or not, or even care how I feel, I'm affected by this. Before you went to surgery, I thought you'd decided not to shut me out. We have a child to put away. Shouldn't we do it together?"

"Oh, all right, stay!"

He bent forward in his chair. "I saw him."

Her forehead wrinkled. She raised the head of the bed with the electronic control and leaned over the top rail. "The baby?"

He nodded.

"Where is he?"

"He's not in the morgue—just an ice-cold, closet-sized room. No sign on the door. They've wrapped him in a blanket and put him in one of those little beds like they use in the nursery."

"They haven't done anything to him?" Her voice was eager.

"I think we get to decide what's done—"

"They're not going to cut him up—an autopsy." In her growing excitement about the physical sanctity of her baby's body, the hostility dried up.

"Only if we ask. There doesn't seem to be a reason. Riley thinks he was healthy, that something happened to the placenta."

"He looks normal?"

"Yeah. He favors Benjamin—the shape of his face, around his mouth a little."

"Yes. Yes, he does. And you. I saw that much. He looks like you, Sam."

Sam's shoulders tightened. Her meaning got through. "Yeah, because he's mine. I don't need confirmation of that."

She stared up at him with an unreadable expression. It looked almost like pity.

He wished he could hold her. Since he couldn't, he closed one hand around the bedrail and whispered, "He was almost ready —Tristan said he was."

"Yeah, he told me, but I honestly didn't know. I could feel him moving in September, maybe late August, but still I didn't think—I guess I wouldn't let myself think. It didn't show that much, did it?" Her eyes widened in a startled expression. "Oh, Sam, I wouldn't have deliberately waited that long. I swear!"

"Brenan, don't. I don't care about that now. The most important thing tonight is dealing with the feelings we have about losing him. If we keep bringing up the things we did and said when we were angry and— when we were more than angry. I said stuff I didn't mean. I don't know why."

"You know he's yours?"

"Yeah."

"He must have been conceived around April."

"Well, that's good. Things weren't so bad then. I hated thinking it happened after—" He got up and stood by the bed, grasping the rail with both hands to keep them from trembling. "I hope you know I love our kids—all of them. I never believed you were unfaithful. I only wanted to make you mad enough to talk to me."

Looking directly at her was more than he could do so he found the blue pump on the IV rack. "Not long ago, we were close. Now, I don't know what we are, but I'm truly sorry for the way I've treated you. I won't ask for forgiveness. I don't deserve it, but, Bren, don't make me an outsider. I'm not used to being out of your life. I'm having to face too much too soon."

She nodded and lay back. Her hostile expression had been replaced by one of sympathy or tolerance. He was thankful for either one.

Trying to feel a little of her heat, he pressed close to the bed. He couldn't hold her, and that felt enormously unfair. "Would it make you feel better if we had some sort of service?"

"Yeah, maybe, if it's just you and me. I can't take anymore of everybody standing around, feeling sorry for me." She was losing some of the drugged glow. "He should have a name."

"A name. Sure."

"In the emergency room, everyone kept calling him the fetus. I hated that. He's our baby, and he should be named."

"Do you have something picked out?"

"Maybe." A grimace of pain crossed her face—only to be immediately erased by her hardheaded determination to keep it covered. She squirmed until she seemed more comfortable. The effort left her short of breath. He pretended not to notice.

"You remember how you didn't want Ben named after you? You said you didn't want him to have to share a name with anybody."

"I remember."

"I think—I mean—wouldn't it make this baby seem more like a part of our lives if he could share something with you? He's very real to me but you—I'd like him to have your name." She hesitated and looked into his eyes. "I don't mean a junior. Just Sam Owen MacCauley like your parents gave your brother A. D.'s name. When we talk about him, we can call him Owen. I know we'll talk about him once in a while."

Sam swallowed and nodded. He was dangerously close to crying again. His voice cracked. "I'd like that."

44

U NDER A SHEET and a heavy woven blanket, Brenan at last was sleeping. An infrequent muscle twitch rippled the covers. In near darkness, Sam squinted at his watch. Half past one, Tuesday. A nurse on her rounds adjusted the ticking IV pump, hung fresh antibiotic solution, checked Brenan's blood pressure, pulse, respiration, flirted a little with Sam. Brenan was still feverish. The nurse made her sit up to swallow Tylenol. Throughout all this attending, she scarcely roused.

As soon as the nurse left the room, Sam dug the old medication bag out of the trash and matched it with the newly hung dose. This nurse didn't inspire the confidence he'd felt in her chubby evening shift predecessor.

The room and the halls outside were ghostly quiet, the silence of sick people sleeping. Stiff from sitting so long, he stood, yawned and stretched, then left the room in search of more coffee and reading material.

At the nurses station, the nurse who had checked on Brenan and another cut from the same cloth—twin Barbie dolls in white uniforms—looked up from a green plastic flip chart they were studying. They smiled, openly ogling him as he passed. He was far from flattered by their earthy whispers, but their behavior triggered a memory that was not altogether unwelcome.

Fall of '72, Lefty chimed. *DeLane.*

DeLane wasn't someone he thought of often or without regret. She was a shame-filled era gone by. Years passed without his sparing her a whole thought. Tonight, he allowed himself to wonder what had

393

happened to her, if she still work here at Northside, if she ever thought about him, if she'd taken other boys into her bed. Then he tucked her back into his memory. He didn't want to invite a renewal of that guilt and humiliation. He was currently overladen with both.

He bought a large coffee and a sandwich at the canteen, took the stairs back to the fifth floor, and stopped by the waiting room for something to read.

A solitary figure occupied the room. She sat just inside the door. He didn't see her until after he'd picked up a stack of magazines and started out. Ellen. He stopped and stared.

She appeared considerably calmer than she had earlier. She had a finger tucked into the pages of a splayed paperback copy of Brenan's first novel, *Me and Joe*. She stared back, her eyes glittering with what Sam perceived to be utter exhaustion and, possibly, the first dawning of regret for the way she'd lashed out at everyone. He remembered the message he'd angrily dictated to Jackie and cringed. He hoped it hadn't been delivered.

"I thought you'd gone."

"I couldn't." Nothing in her tone gave an intimation of her emotional state.

"You can't accomplish much here."

"I haven't gone near her. I've done no more than ask the nurses about her. Now, if you don't mind, I'm reading."

"You act like she's done something to you. Can't you see what losing the baby has done to her?" He tried to explain how Brenan's loss was too personal to share so soon. "If you want to help, get some rest so you can be there when she needs you."

Giving advice to her was courting another attack, but he took the risk. Her problems and his were casualties of separate wars that had somehow collided to become the fabric of a common, more complex one. He didn't want to fight her. She was someone he loved and respected. The loss of her trust was another trauma to absorb. She'd been his staunchest ally when he and Brenan had announced their intention to marry. Throughout his childhood, she had been his best friend's mother—his own *other mother*. His mother's best friend.

She ran her fingers over her mouth but didn't speak.

"She was sleeping when I left the room. If you want to look in to see for yourself she's okay—"

She swallowed and looked away. When she carried her eyes back to him, she gave a small nod.

He arranged the coffee, food, and magazines so he was able to extend his left hand to her. She pointedly refused the hand but followed. At room 524, Sam grasped the metal door handle.

"Just wait!" she hissed.

He let his hand fall from the handle and turned around.

Ellen had crossed her arms and propped her shoulder against the far wall. She released one hand to motion him to come then quickly tucked it back. She shivered as if she was cold.

He moved as close as he dared.

"I can't go in. She told me in no uncertain terms to leave her alone. When she wakes up, tell her I'm sorry—that I shouldn't have said what I did. Will you do that?"

"She's not thinking clearly. Why not let old arguments—"

"Will you just tell her I'm sorry?" She turned to go.

He blocked her. "I won't apologize for you. Brenan has nothing to give tonight, but you can give her something. You can stop blaming her for my failures."

"She let you stay."

He wasn't going to admit how hard Brenan had tried to get rid of him. "And you have a problem with that?"

"Why you? You ran out on her." Still soft, still under control, but her words were full of the slight of her daughter's rejection and of her new disdain for him.

He pitied her, but he was tired of defending his right to a place at Brenan's bedside. "She's my wife. That baby's my son. Whether you approve or not, I'm supposed to be here with them."

"But I'm her mother." Grudging envy raised her voice slightly. She covered her eyes with a trembling hand.

"Then act like it." He placed his free hand on her shoulder, but she jolted away, turning her face to the wall.

"What kind of husband were you before she lost the baby? How were you taking care of her then?"

"Do you want to go in and see her?"

"Who did you dump her for?"

"Stay here." Sam started toward Brenan's room. Ellen's goading had succeeded, found its mark, but even though he was shaking with anger, he wouldn't let her see the wound.

Her voice rose a little and followed him. "I don't know what awful thing you've done, but it made her turn on all of us."

"If you don't keep your voice down, she'll hear you. Just stay there quietly for a minute, will you?" Without waiting for an answer, he disappeared into the room.

When he opened the door again, he found Ellen where he'd left her. He held the door for her. "Come on." She came slowly, comically slinking, scraping the door frame to avoid touching him, her sullen eyes flashing as she sidled toward Brenan. On a television sit-com, her act would have been funny.

He took a possessive stance at the foot of the bed.

The covers rose and dipped over his wife's chest. Her dry lips were slightly parted. The blue-gray circles under her eyes were deepening against the pallor of her face. A few hours of grief and pain had left marks.

Ellen clamped a hand over her mouth. Her shoulders shook.

Brenan's eyelids eased open, giving the impression she had sensed her mother's presence, but Sam had found her awake and warned her.

Ellen dropped her hand, tried to smile. Brenan seemed to put great effort into crimping her forehead into a frown.

"Sam said I could come in."

The remark reminded him of a child playing one parent against the other. *"But Daddy, Mommy said I could!"*

Brenan found him at the foot of the bed and gave him a sour little smile.

"I'm sorry, honey." Ellen made no move to touch her daughter. "I know this breaks your heart."

"I'm okay."

"I had no right to talk to you like I did. I know it upset you, but I wouldn't have had this happen for anything."

"I'm all right, Mother, but I'm tired. Please, go on home."

"Please, don't hold it against me. I never—"

"Please, Mama." Her eyes seemed to beg him to do something. Bringing Ellen in was another miscued decision to his credit. She selfishly refused to let go of her own guilt long enough to tender one paltry measure of comfort. He'd expected her to offer maternal concern—instead of demand Brenan perform something as difficult as forgiveness. Freida would never have been so self-centered. Her absolution could wait. Brenan was too tired and too wounded to support someone else's wretchedness.

Yet, she tried. "Nobody did this, Mama. Not me. Not Sam moving out. Not you with all your anger. It would have happened if everything else had been perfect. Now, I want you to go home. Sam will take care of me. He's the one I need right now."

BRENAN SAW SOMETHING wonderfully steadfast in Sam's face that overrode the terrible way she'd treated him. The old tenderness lurked in his eyes, in the deepening crow's feet and facial hash marks. In her sore, sorrowing heart, she welcomed his presence. Though she didn't tell him, she was thankful for his refusal to leave, for asserting his right to stay.

He wanted to do the right thing. His tears had touched her, made her feel his sincerity and his need to be here. His leaving, and the incidents leading up to it, had hurt more than she had known was possible. She couldn't hold him blameless, yet, she realized something had gone wrong inside him, something that had torn him from her against his will. Deliberate injury wasn't in Sam. He'd told her numerous times he didn't understand the problem. Now, she believed he might be telling the truth, and she knew, from this experience, ignorance could be malignant.

Before the bleeding and contractions took her child, the urgency to know had been consuming, overwhelming. It had controlled every thought, provoked her into throwing up fences between herself and the people who were working themselves to distraction trying to console her. She had wanted neither their help nor their attention; she had wanted Sam's.

That fundamental need to know would return, but for tonight, he was here. He was helping. He cared, and that was all that mattered. When she was stronger, she would try harder.

She watched him through eyes narrowed to slits. Physically, he was the embodiment of perfection. Strong face, drawn handsome by deep lines of humor and character. Eyes that laughed and cried with equal passion, their deep midnight blue irises faithfully guarded by possessive, squinting lids and straight, heavy brows. Every piece of him blended, nestled with all the other pieces, engendering a splendid male body. Wherever he went, heads turned, eyes widened to follow his movement. Females from puberty to dotage vied for his attention—a nod, a wave, an obliging smile. Jealousy would have eaten Brenan alive if Sam had once shown anything less than contempt for the gawkers.

In his work, his looks, coupled with his natural gift for persuasion and the ability to grab trust, had made him stand out from many of his colleagues. Talent alone wouldn't have made him shine. When other reporters were turned away, he got exclusive interviews. He transcended the expectations of everyone from his producers to the organizers of charity fund-raisers. Everyone wanted him on their teams. WPMS executives fetched and toted to keep him happy. He was their Golden Boy. Their quickness to jump and bow filled him with power. When necessary on his job, he used this power, but in his private life he seldom pushed. He waited his turn, stood aside for others to go first, left the power to rule where he felt it belonged.

She had anxiously followed his recent decline. The Golden Boy was losing his gloss and taking on a prosaic, lusterless patina, the filmy telltale of immense unhappiness. He looked a decade older. Rocked by some private, internal storm, Sam was going down. She willed herself to believe his inner soundness would be restored, and that that of their marriage would follow.

Too tired to think beyond that particle of hope, she needed his arms around her, his breath on her neck, his hands in her hair. She had read stories about people making love with frantic abandon during times of tragedy and loss. The kicking in of some obscure psychological defense? A temporary detour from reality? Her desire was simpler. All she wanted was to hold her child and her husband. But she couldn't touch either one. Her child was dead, and she couldn't ask her husband for his arms.

Frequently adjusting the angle of the magazine to catch a ray of light from the recessed entry fixture, Sam feigned interest in a *Reader's Digest*. The overhead lights hadn't bothered her, but he'd snapped them off anyway. "Try to rest," he had urged in his tumbling waterfall voice. Did she want something to drink? Did she hurt? What could he do? His words had splashed her—water words dropping from a great height into a rocky pool. His rich, nearly accentless broadcaster's voice had always thrilled and exhilarated her. Tonight, it made her heart feel as empty and battered as her womb. "Sam?"

He looked up. "I thought you were sleeping."

"No. Bring your chair over here, and turn that light on. The one on top. I want it on. That's better. Now put this rail down. It makes me feel caged up."

Sam minded her directions until the last one.

"I won't get up. Just pull the chair closer and stack those magazines here beside me."

He gave her a curious glance. "Are you going to read?"

"Maybe." She continued to conduct him until she was satisfied with the location of his chair, the magazines, and him. When he was sitting close enough to touch, close enough to hear his soft wheezing, she fingered the front cover of a magazine then dropped it back into the stack. She looked into his face. In spite of the circumstances, she adored him. He might have a room at the Northgate Grayson Inn, but tonight, he was beside her, loyally standing guard, a shepherd with an injured lamb.

A tender smile cracked the corners of his eyes and mouth. It warmed her. His nearness was almost as soothing as being held, almost as warmly comforting. She felt sleep closing over her. "I'm glad you let her in." Her own words would be her last conscious memory of the night. Something she hadn't meant to say but was pleased she had.

SAM CLOSED THE *Reader's Digest* but held it, infrequently tapping it against his knee. His thoughts hovered around his lifeless son. *Owen.* The name helped solidify the image of the tiny infant he'd found when he had peeled away the folds of flannel receiving blanket. A familiar little face had floated up. Though sketched in soft, immature strokes, Sam had known those features all his life. They were his own. He had touched the diminutive, perfectly forged fingers and toes. Until a few hours ago, they had flexed, fanned, curled inside Brenan. Death had stilled them. Translucent pink skin with an undercoating of mottled blue-gray stretched over an exquisite miniature skeleton. An ounce shy of two pounds. *"Mature enough to have had a good chance outside the womb."*

Sam had rewrapped the baby and held him firmly to his chest. Ignoring the questioning faces of his mother and the doctor, he'd attempted to tune himself into the baby's fading life force, to pick up any lingering vibrations left over from the process of dying. He had wanted to know what suffering his child had undergone before all sensation had fled. Unborn babies dreamed, sucked their fingers, slept and played in their liquid nurseries. In his, Owen had smothered and died.

Holding his son had told him nothing about the pain of death, so he had asked Freida. Dr. Riley, with his education and experience, had been there, but Sam had wanted to hear what his mother believed. Her heart heard things other people missed.

Freida had answered that there must have been a brief period when the baby had felt *"something—not very long, not very strong."* He hoped she was right, that Owen hadn't suffered.

Walking away from the cold room and the lifeless body, Sam had felt Freida's hand flat against the center of his back, adding her strength to his. At the waiting room doorway, Riley had slipped away, and Sam had given himself up to a full, steeling embrace from his mother. As countless times before, he'd helped himself to the solace and strength of her body heat.

His thoughts drifted, trailed through time. Remembering what Jackie had said in the canteen, he held his hands up, opened his palms and studied the network of stringy white scars. Perhaps, she was right, the malevolence of the dark days of his childhood had returned to haunt him. Or had it been there all along, insidiously reshaping him into a man Brenan couldn't love?

He leaned forward and put hands on the bed. After all this time, old scars shouldn't matter. But they did. As long as the nightmare had its hold, they would matter.

Brenan's breathing was slow and deep. Sleep, a short time-out from her heartache. "I'm sorry," he whispered. "You shouldn't be punished for my weaknesses."

He was no stranger to suffering and sorrow. They had come to him in many different packages. They had always left scars.

AS THE NIGHT WORE ON, the nurse who had annoyed Sam earlier made hourly rounds. She was about Brenan's age with long, luxuriant spiral curls. Her makeup was dark, her cologne heavy. The lines of her underwear showed though her clinging uniform. Several times, she tried to initiate conversation, but he affected interest in reading, doling out short replies, verging on rudeness. By the time she came in for six a.m. vital signs, she had apparently given up on sparking his interest and assumed a sulky, quasi-professional attitude.

Sam moved the chair to give her room to work and watched as she hung a new bag of antibiotic. No longer bothering with well-mannered discretion, he again compared the drug name and dosage labels on the new bag with one he lifted from the trash. Brenan's eyes hardly opened while her temperature, blood pressure, heart and breathing rates were measured.

When the nurse suggested he wait outside while she checked for bleeding and took care of her patient's more personal needs, Sam walked to the window and looked out, sending the impression that either he hadn't heard or was unwilling to comply. It didn't matter which. He had no intention of leaving Brenan alone and at the mercy of this twit. Behind him, he heard an irritated and exaggerated sigh. He stayed at the window and listened.

"How are the cramps, Miz MacCauley?"

"Not too bad." Brenan's voice was thick with sleep.

"Let's get you up to the bathroom and into a clean pad. The bleeding may pick up some after you get up."

"I can do this myself."

"I need to walk with you."

"No, thank you."

Good for her! Nurse Goodbody better watch out.

Sam grinned out the window. Brenan was waking up testy.

"You may get dizzy the first time up, Miz MacCauley. And you've got this big old machine that has to go, too."

"It has wheels."

Dr. Mark would be so proud. Nurse bashin's in the Armstrong blood, ya know. Now, she's got a double dose.

"I don't think you realize how weak you are."

"I'm fine."

"Also, your urine has to be measured."

"Why don't you go on to your next patient and check back a little later. I'll give you a full report then."

"I shouldn't—"

"Yes, you should!"

Sam continued to grin to himself at Brenan's and the nurse's growing annoyance with each other.

Doncha just love these little verbal cat fights?

"Mr. MacCauley?"

Sam couldn't get rid of the grin before he turned to answer. He didn't really care. "Yeah?"

A flush showed through the artificial pink on the girl's cheeks. "Your wife seems to have a stubborn streak. Will you please keep an eye on her until she's back in bed?"

"Certainly."

"I'll have to chart that she refused my help."

"You do that." He winked.

Brenan sat on the side of the bed and frowned as the nurse finally gave up and sashayed out. "Chart this!" She put her tongue out at the door then turned to Sam. "Thank you. Now, why don't you get some coffee or have breakfast or something?"

His smile became stubbornly fixed. "Not right now."

Her defiant expression slowly waxed to annoyed resignation. He was witnessing a first. Even though her principles and independence were the issues, she was giving in without a fuss.

She came out of the bathroom, dragging her IV pole behind her. Sam had waited by the door to walk with her to the bed. He felt her trembling through the thin cotton gown and knew a lot of determination was required for her to walk upright. Under his stabilizing hands, her body felt as fragile and light as papier-mache. He hated to let go when she was safely back in bed, but he was grateful she'd let him do that much.

As she instructed, he wrote 320 ml on a small pink sheet of paper the nurse had left on the over-bed table then glanced up, hoping she'd give him something else to do. Any fatigue he might have experienced earlier had been replaced by a restless energy, a jittery second wind.

She sat in the center of the bed with her feet pulled under her staring down at the hospital gown. When she raised her gaze to him, her eyes were glistening, wide and childlike. "Sam?" She pulled her top lip between her teeth in response to some physical or spiritual pain he couldn't read. Her tremors were visible from where he stood. She put a hand on a spot of white sheet near her. "Sit by me."

He sat on the spot she'd touched and watched her face for some sign that would show what she wanted. He gave her the hand she reached for, allowed her to carry it to her body. She gently touched the tips of his fingers to one breast. The nipple was hard, the breast distended, full. The cloth of her gown was wet and sticky with the initial yellow flow of milk, the antibody-rich colostrum. Instantly, his muscles tightened to an aching hardness. She should have been given an injection of medication to dry her milk before it began to flow. Karen had been given one when Mariah was born. Routine procedure for non-nursing mothers. His jaw muscles cramped, his teeth ground in fury. He silently damned Riley and all the twit nurses who should have aborted this! Because of this inexcusable omission, Brenan's breasts were full, ready to nourish a hungry infant.

The first of her sobs, grievously silent and wracking, overcame the tremors and pressed her breast more tautly against his hand. When they became audible, he put both arms around her, pulled her to his chest. Her arms crept around his back. "It's not fair. They should have let me hold him. I should have had that much." Then her convulsive weeping suffocated her words.

At that moment, he would have given anything he owned, would have performed any act to be able to put a living infant to her breast. As his respirations steadily progressed past the purring kitten, the rusty hinge stages, she cried for both of them.

"I know," he exhaled the words with considerable strain.

After a while she became limp in his arms. Lowering her onto her pillows, he stood, caressed her face with his fingertips, then cautiously backed away. Her swollen eyes followed his movement. Taking a moment to quiet the stridor with his inhaler, he gathered air into his lungs. "I'll be right back. Nobody's going to stop me from bringing him to you. This time, I swear, nobody's going to stop you from holding him."

He turned and walked out of the room. Down a series of corridors, through a set of double doors, past the curtained windows of a nursery filled with warm, living infants. And finally into an unheated room by the nursery, a closet-sized room the hospital used as a holding place for stillborn babies.

45

"S O HE SENDS in a fidgety, mustache-chewing shrink to ask stupid questions, and while that nonsense is going on, he gives *you* my instructions and discharges me! That's just great!"

Brenan was immediately sorry she'd yelled. She couldn't hold back her fluctuating swells of rage. Throughout the long night, Sam had been wonderful. He'd brought the baby and put him in her arms, giving her one small moment and a memory of the sweet, stilled face to keep. He didn't deserve her outbursts, but for so long, he'd made her feel helplessly forlorn and cheated. She wanted answers to questions she couldn't bring herself to ask, questions she shouldn't have to ask.

"Why didn't he wait to talk to me?"

"I guess he thought since you're so upset you shouldn't be responsible for remembering everything. He'd already examined you and tried to get you to stay for another day. You were the one who insisted on going home. Remember?"

"So?"

"He was only trying to give what you wanted. Besides, he's going to see you in his office in two days. If you have specific questions before then, we'll call him."

He looked as brittle as a walking corpse. Brenan's self-pity didn't keep her from feeling sorry for him, too. Pity was abundant. "Oh, I'm sorry. I know you didn't do anything, but sit down. You're making me nervous." She waited until he was seated before asking, "Well, what did he say?"

"He said take these." He held up a trio of prescription slips and repeated the doctor's instructions. Antibiotics, pain medication, pad count, activity and rest. "He thinks you should talk to someone about your feelings instead of using them as weapons against other people. He said that—not me."

"I hope he doesn't expect me to see that—that—that Doctor Pinkard again."

"After the way you reacted? Um—your *reactions* are why they held the baby—Owen—away from you yesterday. Riley would have let you see him this morning, anyway. I told him I thought you'd have been better if they'd let you have him right away."

"What are the rules of etiquette for the mother of a stillborn baby?"

"He just didn't want to make it harder for you."

"Go on."

"A nurse is supposed to come in with suggestions about what you can do to be comfortable until the milk dries up. He's really sorry about that."

"Is that all he said?"

"No."

"Well?"

Sam leaned forward and looked between his knees at the floor. Brenan thought she caught a glimpse of a bitter smile. "He said it would be better if you didn't get pregnant again for a year or so—at least six months. Some women do, trying to replace what they've lost, but it takes a long time for your body to heal completely. He said, even while you're bleeding, it's possible to become pregnant. Since there were no tears or episiotomy, you should heal fast externally. But—um—no intercourse for ten days or until you're comfortable with it. I guess he doesn't know about our current living arrangements."

Even his discomfort chafed her. She folded her arms. Her mind flashed back to the last time they had tried to make love, and she felt her eyes spontaneously narrow and her heart shrink in her chest. She'd like to block the memory forever, put a retaining wall between her and the hatred it evoked. She knew there was a reason, an argument for his humiliating rejection, but since none had been offered, she wanted to shove aside all images of it. The best she could hope for was that he'd get over this phantom malady and come home.

He *would* come home. She had stopped believing his leaving might be permanent. His behavior here at the hospital had gone beyond obligation and had told her a lot about his true feelings. He cared. He didn't just care—he still loved her. The baby's death had hurt him, but long before that, he had lost control of something deep inside him. He'd been reduced to a terrified little boy in a man's body. And he was profoundly unhappy.

HE DROVE SLOWLY, watching the blacktop for rough patches and potholes. Once home, instead of helping her to bed, he was forced to turn her over to a conglomerate of both families, each individual waiting in line for a turn at being her caretaker.

After driving to the pharmacy in Russett and returning with her prescriptions, he tried to find an opening for a moment alone with her. Failing that, he finally told her in front of her mother and brother what time he'd pick her up tomorrow morning, gave her the bottles of pills, and reminded her to use his beeper number if she couldn't reach him at the motel.

He then tried to see Ben and Mariah, but they ran from him. He saw them watching the comings and goings in the family room through the upstairs balustrade, but they saw him, too. As soon as his foot hit the first stair, his children disappeared. At the top, he called out. No answer came back. A room-to-room search, including closets, bathrooms, and around the corners of large pieces of furniture, failed to reveal their whereabouts. Their hiding was no children's game.

Just the sound of their voices would have meant something. Even if they had been angry and accusing. Even if they'd only been talking to each other. The second story was silent except for the whisper of slow, uncertain footsteps and raspy breathing, both of which belonged to Sam.

On his way out, he found A. D. and Mark standing by the glass doors. "Why don't you to try to get some sleep?" Mark asked. "Why not stretch out in one of the guest rooms? As tired as you are, you shouldn't drive."

Before Sam could respond, A. D. struck out at Mark. "Leave 'im alone so he can go back to his impersonal motel room where he don't have to deal with the responsibilities of his family."

Mark attempted kindness. A. D. stabbed Sam through the heart. The kindness fell short, but the knife blade came through. Sam didn't acknowledge either.

He was behind the wheel of the Explorer when he saw his children again. They were crouched on the porch floor at the end of an antique wooden glider. They were watching him with eyes alert to every move he made. They didn't have to worry. They didn't have to be prepared to run. He had no desire for another rebuff. He'd had his fill of rejection. He only looked at them long enough to let them know he saw them. His hand automatically lifted in a small greeting.

He cranked up and drove away without touching his son or his daughter, without hearing the sound of their voices.

He left with a little more pain than he'd brought with him.

46

WEDNESDAY, AND A sixty-degree, gray, moldy-smelling gloom had fallen. Although there had been no significant rainfall since Sunday evening's parade of thunderstorms, there had been little sun to relieve the dreariness or dry the standing puddles that camouflaged potholes and turned the waterlogged, baked-clay shoulders to deadly slicks. The humidity made each breath feel like an intake of oily swill. Ugly, cheerless, the environmental mood seemed to leach through the pores of Sam's skin to further pollute his more delicate spiritual climate. He sighed and glanced at Brenan. Her lovely eyes were glazed and fixed on something far beyond the windshield. If the day had been perfect, she would not have seen the sun.

He pulled into the garage, opened the door for her, took her arm and held her fast until they were inside the house. She moved with the slow, water-treading pace of someone compensating pain and weakness. Under his touch, she felt feverish. He was afraid if he let go she would give in to the pull of gravity and the weight of the box she refused to relinquish and sink to the floor.

The box was not much bigger than a child's lunch kit, but instead of pink or blue cartooned plastic, it was made of solid cherry, unstained but lacquered to a high gloss. The glue-sealed, domed lid was hand-carved with roses, intricate sprays of baby's breath, a date and a name. A. D.'s loving, fancy work, it looked like a treasure chest with gold hinges and diminutive padlocked hasp.

Sam didn't think all of the elaborate carving could have been completed in a day, maybe the name and date but not the delicate florals.

There was too much painstaking detail. Still, he hadn't asked if there had been another intended purpose. He had gratefully accepted its offer, and when Brenan was satisfied with it, he'd made a pointed effort to thank his father.

"It's perfect."

A. D. had simply nodded.

This morning, Sam's father had said little. He hadn't mentioned the baby except to throw two short sentences into a family circle conversation about a receptacle for the ashes. "I got somethin' you might wanna use. Look it over an' see." Sam couldn't remember the last time A. D. had touched him. A hand on his shoulder would have supported him a great distance.

Family milled through the lower story of the house. As soon as the kitchen door closed behind them, Sam sensed an intuitive herald calling the others to him and to Brenan.

Brenan must have felt it, too. She dragged him along with a new strength in her stride, ducking the most-traveled path for the dining room and foyer. She wanted to make the relative privacy of the bedroom before the well-meaning crowd closed around her. She gave it her best, straining toward the bedroom with Sam in tow. Instead of speaking, she barely took time to nod as they passed Freida in the dining room. Mark and Robert were left waiting at the bottom of the stairs. Sam pulled the double doors together almost in Jackie's face—only to turn and find Ellen sitting on the bed, holding a pose of ownership. Brenan sighed heavily. She had given a magnificent effort and had almost made it. She frowned with unconcealed displeasure at her mother then, apparently deciding to disregard her presence, turned to Sam.

"The mantel?" She gave the carved box to him. This was the first time it had been out of her hands since the funeral director who had supervised the cremation, had placed it there.

He took it to the bedroom fireplace, stepped onto the hearth and placed it on the mantel shelf. He paused and ran his fingers over a carved rose. The box felt empty, not enough ash to make a discernible weight—after all there had been a scant two pounds before the burning. Positioning the name to the front, he gazed back at Brenan. She approved with a gentle nod.

Ignoring Ellen, he asked, "What should I do now, Bren?"

"You really ought to see about the kids."

He'd been hoping for something easier first, something small that would permit his courage to gradually start flowing, but he nodded. The children had been put off too long.

"Take something for that fever and try to rest. Okay?"

"Yeah. Unless the kids need me, I want to try to sleep."

Sam detected a message for Ellen in Brenan's words.

She angled close to him and whispered, "You don't have to stay after you see Ben and Mariah—we'll be okay—but you don't have to leave, either. It's up to you."

He nodded. She had softened up over the last two days.

"Thanks, Sam."

"For what?"

"For not letting me run you off."

He shrugged.

"I didn't make it easy." She offered a thin smile.

He wanted to take her in his arms the way he had at the mortuary, the way he had in the hospital. He believed she would allow him to hold her for a while in *this* room, on *this* horrible day, but Ellen's glowering stopped him cold. Would there ever be another opportunity for his arms to go around her?

Pointedly eyeing Ellen, he tried to convey a plea for her not to start something after he was gone that would further add to Brenan's exhaustion. She stared back defiantly.

"You've never made anything easy, Bren." He tried to smile. "I'm used to it."

IN THE FAMILY ROOM, A. D. and Freida sat holding hands, shoulder-to-shoulder in the center of the sectional in front of a low fire. Mark, Robert, and Jackie were at the booth in the morning room. They sat speaking softly around mugs of steaming coffee. Sam made eye contact with all without verbally addressing any of them. There was nothing to say.

Through the glass walls of Brenan's office, he saw Marissa and Deejay, just in from school, sitting in a porch swing, clearly arguing about something between the covers of an *Omni* magazine. Neither Ben nor Mariah was with them.

Sam made a hurried circuit through the morning room, kitchen, dining room, and foyer, and when he didn't see either of his children, he took the stairs by twos. At the top, he stepped over the model train tracks and through Ben's open door. The rails were silent and the room deserted. "Ben?"

No answer.

He called again at the door to the bathroom that separated the boy's room from his sister's. No reply came. Sam retraced his path to the landing and headed for Mariah's room.

He knocked on the closed door.

A sharp "I'm busy!" came through this wooden barrier.

"Mariah, I'd like to come in." He tried to sound confident, tried to make uncertainty come across as authority.

It didn't work.

"It's your house." Spite, sarcasm.

He pushed the door inward. She was sitting in her low, thickly cushioned cane rocker. Instead of looking at him, she tipped her head back and defiantly studied the ceiling. Had he expected her to cower? Her feet curved under her, and her arms were folded around an open Stephen King novel that was roughly the size of library edition dictionary. *Needful Things*. The title and author brought a chill to the back of Sam's neck. *Needful Things* sounded like morbid reading for a child who was already angry and frightened and depressed.

He sat down on the bed. "Can you spare a little time?"

"I'm not stopping you from talking." She shrugged and leveled her eyes on the door behind him.

"You know where your mother and I have been today?"

She shrugged again.

"It was a hard thing to have to do."

Another glib shrug. Her vexed sigh irritated him. He tried to keep focused on the fact that, in spite of her nervy reactions, she was only nine. He'd always been reasonably comfortable with her blown-up IQ and abilities because he'd been able to see the child within. Today, all he saw was a dangerous weapon pointed at him. A whetted sword aimed at his heart. The coldness on her face upset his concentration, and when she casually announced, "I don't care how hard things are for you," he exploded.

"What *do* you care about? Do you care what your mother's going through? Do you care that on top of everything else, she's physically sick? Do you care that she could use more compassion and less grief from you? It's plain you don't care at all what you're doing to me."

Mariah threw her book over the arm of her chair. It hit the floor with a thud. Without wavering, she caught and held his eye. "I didn't make this situation, but I'm doing the best I can to get through it. I don't know how to help my mother or my brother or my own self. You can stand there acting like it's my responsibility to make things better, but that don't mean I can do it. You caused this! You take care of it! And if you don't want to hear exactly what I think, you'd better stay away!"

"Oh, it's pretty obvious what you think of me." He tried to snuff the childishness from his voice. "You could give me a chance. You want things to get better between us, don't you?"

"I want you to get out of my room."

"Mariah, please—"

"My brother's hiding from you! How does that feel?" Suddenly, she was flushed and spewing large tears. Leaning forward in the rocker, furious, her floating eyes dared him, challenged him to make her stop. "Men are supposed to have these really special relationships with their sons. Boy, I'll bet you're proud of yours!"

Sam's head jerked to one side as if she'd slapped him. "Why are you doing this?" He couldn't stop tears from raining. He had no parental power, no protection, no defense of any kind.

Instead of giving him an answer, she sniffed and scowled.

"You know where Ben is! Tell me!"

"He doesn't want you to know!"

"Tell me where he is!"

"No! He trusts *me!* Don't you think it's good he has someone he can trust?"

The blue of her eyes became the steely gray of dirty sidewalks. Her tears gave off the hard glint of frost crystals on window-glass.

"Whether he knows it or not, he needs me!"

"He needs you to go back to your damned old motel room! He needs you to leave him alone!"

He sought to avert the tide of sickness and panic that was rising, wave after nauseating wave, inside him. "Where is he?"

An unrelenting stare.

He blotted his face on the sleeve of his jacket. There was so much he wanted to say, but the more he readied his mouth to speak, the farther away the entreaties leaped from him. "Mariah, please! Doesn't it mean anything to you that I've just lost a kid?" An appeal for sympathy was all he could manage.

There was no pity in the room. No pity in the child.

"Count again! Not one kid! Three! She held up and wagged three fingers. "You've lost three! You are *nothing* to me! *Nothing* to my brother! *Nothing at all!* Now I want you to get outta my room!"

He gave into her demand. The instant her door slammed behind him, he started running. Over the miniature railroad, through the library, across the outside deck, down the rec room stairs into the garage. He couldn't face another person.

The new Explorer cranked and swiftly rolled through the gate he'd left open for a retreat he'd never imagined would be so fleet and urgent. And gutting.

IF DADDY HAD slowed down only a little on the steps or in the driveway, he might have heard the sounds made by the two pairs of feet that had formed a posse, a wild chase like in the old cowboy movies his grandparents were always watching. Ben's sister really wanted to catch Daddy. She cried out for other chances to be good, yelling "I didn't mean it!" over and over.

The chase wasn't exciting. It was frightening. Ben ran just to keep up with his sister. He couldn't lose her. If she caught up to Daddy, she might leave, too. Mama couldn't be counted on any more than Daddy. She was so sad because her *other* son had died she didn't feel like being a mother to him. Mariah was all Ben had left. So he ran after her and risked catching up to the person who had caused him to need hiding places.

When Daddy's red and gold truck was out of sight, when there was no chance of catching up, his sister stopped and took his hand, giving him no choice but to run back into the house with her. He was glad to hold on and ran as hard as he could to keep from breaking her grip. He wished somebody who knew how to explain things in a way he could understand would tell him what to think, what to feel, who could be depended on to care.

THE RUNNING FEET never caught up. Sam heard nothing above his own breathing. He didn't know that he could have looked over his shoulder and seen his children framed in his back windshield. He didn't know he could have jumped out and caught them up in his arms. He didn't know until it was days too late.

And because of his ignorance, when he was far enough along the twisting, tree-lined driveway for the house to have fallen behind the skeletal oaks and the evergreens, he pulled over and wept himself empty and dry.

RUNNING AS HARD as she could manage without pulling Ben's arm off, Mariah sailed through the garage, kitchen, and family room, past a half-dozen curious faces. She shook off her brother's hand and threw one of the bedroom doors back so hard it hit the wall, bounced, and slammed behind her, almost smacking Ben, who was still close on her heels, in the face. She hurriedly jerked it open again and pulled him into the bed-room.

Her breathing made short and raspy noises and stifled her words before she could push them out. It sounded almost as bad as one of Daddy's asthma attacks. She was supposed to knock on closed doors and wait for permission to enter, but she had broken so many rules that one more wouldn't matter. She headed straight across the room and stopped when she was close enough to touch her mother's knee. She stopped so fast Ben bumped into her.

Sitting on the bed with her back against the headboard, Mama looked up from the treasure chest Grampa A. D. had made to hold Mariah's special things. He'd been working on it when Mama had to go to the hospital. Now it was a casket. She'd been promised another, but she didn't want one anymore. She read the engraved name that was upside down to her. *Sam Owen MacCauley.* Daddy's name. The *Owen* part was slightly bigger than the rest.

Mama didn't look mad, just surprised.

"That's him?" She was still short of breath and spat her words out fast. Mama nodded.

Mariah felt sadder and more wicked than she ever had before. Her heart beat so hard she felt it pulsing in her neck and ears. Inside that little chest was the *one* Daddy had meant he'd lost. He'd needed the other *ones* he believed were still his, but he didn't get them. Oh, no. Mariah, who had turned evil and poison, had seen to that. She had to make Mama bring him back. She had to tell him how feeling alone and unprotected could make a person turn bad.

She'd treated him like all the bad stuff was his fault. Maybe it wasn't. She'd seen the sorrow on his face, in his eyes. And his love. She'd seen his love even before she'd screamed those awful things that had made him start crying and run away. She hadn't been able to stop herself. She had to find him and tell him what she was feeling *now*. No matter how hurt they both were, she loved him. She knew how badly he needed to hear her say it and how much he wanted her to see *his* love.

"What's the problem?" Mama scooted off the bed, carried the chest to the mantel, and came back. She seemed to have a hard time making a smile. Her slender arms slipped around Mariah and drew her close. Ben kept a few paces away from them. Mama curled her finger for him to come, but he shook his head.

Mariah tried to slow her raging need to fix things. She knew her mother was weak and grieving. "I'm sorry about the baby and everything and for acting so mean."

"It's not your fault, honey. No one's been their best. We didn't set out to neglect you. Once we all get started working together, it'll get better. Did you talk with your daddy?"

Even though they felt warm and doting, Mariah pushed through Mama's arms and turned her back. She didn't deserve to be hugged. She decided to tell the truth and take whatever punishment came. "Yes, I talked to him. That's what's wrong."

"I don't understand."

"I ran him off. I can't even describe how bad I acted."

Mama sat down on the bed. Her smile faded. "He's gone?"

"Yes, Mama. I'm sorry."

"Ben?" When Ben looked up, Mama motioned again for him to come. "Did you see him?"

Ben took small, slow steps, crawled onto the bed beside her, and drew his feet tightly underneath him. He propped his elbows on his knees then rested his chin in his hands. His unhappiness made him look like a storybook waif.

"Did you see him?" Mama asked again.

Ben didn't look at her, but this time he answered. "He didn't see me."

"What does that mean?" Brenan raised his chin with her fingers. Mariah could tell she was afraid to hear his answer.

"Um—I was hidin'."

"I see. Why did you hide?"

"I'm scared of him."

"Why, Ben?""

"I kicked him."

"Did he kick you back?"

"No."

"Then why are you afraid?"

"It's not that kinda scared. I can't talk to him, Mama. I don't know why." Ben's voice was soft and sadly sincere. His accent as slow and richly Southern as Brenan's. "You know, sometimes you just can't do somethin'?"

"Oh, Ben, he's your daddy. Don't shut him out."

"He don't like me, or he would've stayed here."

"You won't accept his love—he didn't stop giving it. You can blame him for not being what you want him to be, but you won't give him a chance."

"Maybe so, but just the *thought* of talkin' to him makes my stomach hurt. I'm goin' upstairs now. I'm tired of talkin'."

Mama let him go and stared at closed door after he had gone.

"It's not Ben's fault," Mariah explained. "It's mine. I need Daddy to come back so I can tell him."

Mama sighed. "As tired as he is, he can't even find peace in his own home. Mariah, your Daddy needs you as much or more than you need him."

The tears her alarm had momentarily driven back came flooding into Mariah's eyes. The plain and simple truths she was hearing shamed her. The room and her mother became a shining blur. "Call him on his car phone. Maybe, he'll turn around."

Mama shook her head. "I thought if he stayed until everybody else left he might—but now—Mariah, I won't call him. You'll have to do that yourself."

"What if he hears it's me and hangs up before I can say what I need to? He hates me! I gotta have time to make him see—"

"He doesn't hate you. The problem is he's like me; he's had about all he can take right now. I'm not calling, Rye. Mend your own fences, then maybe next time you won't be so quick to tear them down."

"But you told us you're still friends. It's worse than you think. You'd hate me, too, if I told you. Please, Mama!" She hated begging. She hated herself for putting another weight on her mother's shoulders.

Mama looked pale and tired. Her voice was thin but firm. "Tell Gramma Freida. Maybe, she'll help."

"No, Mama, you don't understand." As she began to repeat the words she'd used in her attack on Daddy, Mariah watched panic come into Mama's eyes. "And then I told him he didn't mean anything to me! I'm scared, Mama! What if I killed all his love? What if he can't get over it?"

Mama's voice was so low Mariah had to strain to hear. "Why did you do it?"

"I guess I wanted to make him hurt as bad as me, but now I think he already does. I'm bad!"

"Oh, Rye. How far have we let you down? How much damage have we done?"

"I don't know, Mama. I don't know what's happening to any of us, but I do know it makes us act like different people—not nice people, either."

"Baby, I'm so sorry. I want to help, but I can't right now. I'm so tired I can't think, so worn out and confused nothing makes sense. So is your daddy. You can't know how it feels. You're getting close, but as long as you can carry all that anger, you're not there, yet. I'm failing you. I want to be here for you. Maybe, soon—please hang on a little longer."

"It's okay, Mama. I understand, and I'm really sorry for making it worse." She let Mama hug her. "I love you. I don't think he'll listen to me, but I'll try." She turned and ran back to her room. Under her breath, she whispered, "I don't deserve anybody's help, anyway."

47

S AM WAS TEMPTED to yank the phone out of the wall and throw it across the room. If it didn't stop ringing soon, he'd go completely out of his mind. It had been jangling when he unlocked the door and hadn't stopped for more than two minutes at a time since—over an hour. A big part of that time he'd spent kneeling on the cold tile in front of the toilet, trying to purge some of his misery, the only thing in his stomach.

The persistent caller was probably Freida or A. D. hoping to give him grief over upsetting Mariah and running out. He supposed he could have the motel operator do something to hold his calls. He could leave. There were ways to handle these things, but Sam couldn't think. Could not think.

Answer the phone!

"No!"

Might be Brenan. Or not. Might be one of the others. They all want your balls stuffed, mounted, and hung over the fireplace with a little gold plaque. But what the hell-o do ya need balls for? Ain't no good to ya if ya can't even answer the phone.

"I can't!"

It might be important!

He reached for the burring phone.

"Yeah?"

A sticky silence, then, "Daddy?" Soft and hoarse and tentative, but unmistakably his daughter. He sank to the bed. His chest seemed to collapse inward. There was nothing of substance left inside him, but still he nudged the plastic-lined waste basket closer with his foot. He listened to the malignancy of the telephone.

"Daddy?" There was no storm of hatred rampaging through her faint, cracking voice. No sharp, serrated insults.

He struggled to clear his throat. Failing, he jammed a Beclovent atomizer into his mouth.

"I'm so sorry!"

He felt the vibrations of her pleading apology through the miles of wire, hardware, and plastic. He tasted the cold burn the medicine left on his tongue. The smothery gasping settled to a feeble wheeze. He coughed.

"Daddy!"

"You don't have to do this. I understand." He didn't, but he wanted to. He wanted to say what a better parent would say.

"Then you'll come back?"

"Not tonight. Soon."

"Why not now?"

"I can't. I don't know why." He knew why. He simply couldn't take any more. None! Zilch! Not a single iota more!

"How soon?"

"When I can. It's too hard now." He didn't know if he could ever go back.

"I swear I didn't mean what I said!"

"You're not the reason. It's just—" Yes, she was. It wasn't Brenan. It wasn't his parents or his in-laws. It was his bitter little girl and his invisible little boy.

"*Any* of it! I don't even know why I was all that mad. Please, Daddy, forgive me! Come back! I'll do better!"

"There's nothing to forgive. You're having to face a lot of ugly things. Your anger isn't too unusual." Oh, but it had cut his insides to stringy, useless pieces.

"Do you love me? Why don't you even say my name?"

"Yes, Mariah, I love you." But there was a darkness to his love. He was afraid—no, terrified—of it. She held too much power over him. Her tongue could eviscerate. Her eyes could burn holes. But love her? He certainly did!

"I won't ever do anything that bad again. Believe me!"

"I believe you." But he thought she might do it all again. He'd created a great instability in her.

"Then come back. I need you. We all need you."

"I'll come when I can—as soon as I can." She had told him to leave her alone, and he'd done just that. Now she could, please, do the same for him. A barter. An even swap.

"Am I too late?"

"No. I want to be there, but I'm sick, honey. Not just the asthma. I'm really sick." He figured he was going to be sick a long time, a dreadfully long time.

"But if you're sick, you need to be where your family can look after you. Maybe, somebody here could come get you."

"Please, try to understand. I can't come." That house wasn't his home. As much as he loved them, he wasn't even sure the people who lived there were still his family.

Her voice sank from its throaty hoarseness to a low, broken whisper. "You'd come home if you wanted to. I wish I could take it all back, but I can't. Now it's hopeless. I made it hopeless. That's what you're telling me. Isn't it, Daddy?"

"No, really, I—" What could he say? She was catching on. Smart girl. She knew hopeless when she met it.

"I meant it when I said I was sorry. I meant it when I said I love you. I hope you know that."

"I do. And I meant it when I said I love you." God, yes, he loved her. He had loved her the whole time she was screaming, cursing, and hiding his son from him. The whole time.

"I'm sorry about the baby."

"I know." The wheezing began to pick up.

"Ben was in my closet."

"Oh?" The wheezing grew into loud stridor. The heaviness in his lungs began to grip and squeeze with a vengeance.

"Use your inhaler!"

He squeezed off another puff and held it in his constricted lungs as long as he could. Only a little improvement.

"Stop worrying. We'll just forget it, okay?" Sam almost laughed at the joke. He'd never forget what she had done to him. This might be the most memorable day of his life. He wouldn't forget any part of it. He took another hit from the inhaler. He should go to her, hold her. Maybe in a little while.

"You won't forget, and I won't forget."

"Mariah—"

"I'm only nine. You could try to see."

"It's just—"

"It's *just* that I was right to start with. You can just forget you ever had a daughter."

"Mariah, don't—"

Stop her, Sam!

"I hope you never come home."

No!

"Wait, baby, I—"

A click.

Too late! Always too late!

A dial tone.

Always!

A nauseating silence. A silence like death.

DEPLETED BY HIS CONFRONTATIONS with Mariah and further weakened by the asthma and vomiting, Sam kicked back and fell into a dog-tired sleep. The nightmares came and went, but when he awoke, he was unable to recall any part of them. He was none the less sure they'd been wild. All the symptoms were present—sweat-drenched clothes, knotted bedding, pounding heart, screeching lungs. He ran his fingers over his lips. His mouth was sore. He must have bitten his lips and tongue.

He got up and drank a glass of water from the vanity sink. His eyes felt scratched and dry. The man in the mirror looked like a scarecrow, a stick man in baggy clothes.

Peering around at the open suitcase, the tumbled bed, he thought about Brenan, in her debilitated condition, having to deal with the hostilities of Mariah and Ben. She needed to be able to count on him. He splashed a handful of water on his face, and reached for the phone.

On the third ring, Brenan answered.

"I'm sorry for running out so quick. You okay?"

"Yeah, I'm all right. What about you?"

He dismissed her query without an answer. "Have the kids given you any problem?"

"I know what they did to you, if that's what you mean. Must have been pretty bad. That's my fault. I haven't done much to help them understand."

"No, I won't let you take the blame. I just want to make sure they've settled down. I don't want them worrying you tonight. You need to rest. I should have stayed. Brenan?"

"Yeah, Sam?"

"Mariah begged me to come back, but I couldn't face her."

Her judgment was silent.

"I'll drive you to Riley's office tomorrow. You're supposed to be there at one. I'll talk with the kids after that."

"Uh, I promised Mama she could drive me. I had to give her something to do. You don't need an official reason to come here. Don't you think seeing your kids is reason enough?"

"I guess." He was disappointed. Taking her to the doctor should be his job, his right. He needed that time with her.

Before he hung up, he tried to explain the sickness in his heart. Nothing he said made sense—even to him—but Brenan listened patiently to his pathetic rambling.

He almost got hold of the courage he needed to ask her why he was no longer good enough, to ask if there was any chance he might redeem himself. But at the last moment courage dodged him, soared past, and disappeared. Without it, he couldn't ask.

He realized he was selfishly giving her one more damaged soul to worry about, but that knowledge didn't slow him. If he'd been the kind of man she needed, he'd have been next to her, soaking up the warmth of her body and sharing her sorrow. Tonight, he was keenly aware that all he had left of his relationship with her was a sterile voice on the phone and the plain reality that never had he been more alone.

Brenan promised to call if she needed something, but Sam didn't think she would.

48

EARLY THURSDAY AFTERNOON, Sam called to ask Brenan about her doctor visit. For hours, he'd been scraping up the bravado for another encounter with Ben and Mariah. Bracing his spine against the straight plane of the headboard, he took a deep breath, punched the numbers, and listened with the trepidation and resolution of a man with a deadly mission.

However, no backbone was needed. None at all.

Ellen answered the phone and hesitated not a second in informing him that Brenan was *"just fine, thank you—still running a high temperature, weak as a dishrag, scared to death about her kids, spending hours in bed holding a box of ashes, and drowning in her own tears—but doing as well as could be expected under the circumstances."* His mother-in-law went on to remind him no one in the house was interested in taking his calls, that Mariah was shut up in her room and Ben had spoken fewer than five words all day. If Sam wanted to come over and see what he could do to make matters worse, she supposed no one could keep a man out of his own house.

Shuddering, he quietly put down the receiver without waiting for her to finish her colorful attack.

Thursday night, he slept long enough to dream.

AROUND LUNCH ON FRIDAY, after narrowing his choices to either going to work or back to bed, he picked up the telephone and dialed the newsroom. Drury was in a meeting, so Sam left a message with Rita. "Tell him to expect me when he sees me. Take down my new number.

You or Dana may use it, but don't give it to the old man. If he wants to fuck me, he can call my beeper."

"You need anything, Ace?" Rita countered his harshness with soft-spoken concern.

"Yeah, I need you to keep a check on my wife. If you think she needs something, let me know. Remind Dana to do the same."

"Sure, baby, we'll be regular little bird dogs. I hope you're eating right."

"Don't worry about me, Rita. I'll be okay as long as you keep Andy off my tail."

AFTER EVENING ROUNDS at the hospital, Mark, full of charitable concern for his muddled son-in-law and apologies for Ellen's meno-pausal transgressions, stopped by with deli subs that Sam couldn't eat. "Let me give you a shot to settle your stomach. You've got to start eating." This mild man, with a worried face and his hands in his pockets, was not the Dr. Armstrong seen by the world at large. He was merely a father whose only concern was the well-being of his children.

Mark's kindness was wasted.

"You're like my own son. It's rough watching you and Brenan break apart. Plus, you're ripping my grandchildren to pieces. I won't leave you alone until one of you starts doing what it takes to make things right."

Sam hadn't been able to think of anything to say, so after a while, Mark had stamped down the sidewalk. "You promised you'd take care of her!"

AFTER SPENDING SATURDAY listening to distant traffic sounds and the internal derogations of Lefty, darkness came and Sam went out for bottles of vodka and Coke. Then back in room 201, he proceeded to get himself and Lefty drunk. About the time the alcohol, in an otherwise empty stomach, began to warm him, replenish his dried-up tear ducts, and succeed in putting Lefty down, sleep made a grab for him. But he wasn't wasted enough to face the nightmare ogres—those humanoid fiends who waited resolutely in his head for his eyes to close so they could ambush him from the inside. In a rising panic, he rallied for combat. Afraid sitting would make him more vulnerable to nodding off, he stood in front of the mirror and stared at his reflection until his legs wobbled beneath him. "What's the use?" he muttered, refilled his plastic tumbler, and dropped into a chair. When it seemed his gritty eyelids would shut in spite of his struggle, Mark returned and saved him.

"Oh, now you're a sot."

"No, I'm a stupid, snivelin', self-centered jackass!" Sam was surprised that, in his inebriation, the description came out right on the first try. Well, he was a news anchor. His mouth was his living. "My father told me so. My mother-in-law an' brother-in-law said practically the same thing. There you go."

"Stop whining, and eat."

Mark had brought Chinese food in a box—wormy-looking sprouts and shrimp the size of Spaghetti-Os. Sam obediently ate from the box with a plastic fork. Soy sauce on saw dust washed down with tepid alcoholic swill.

"Why's ever'body always wantin' to feed me?"

"Because everybody hates to look at a stupid, sniveling, selfish whatever-you-are who won't take care of himself."

"If they did'n keep comin' here, they wouldn' hafta look—now would they?" The booze made the room and Mark misty. It certainly wasn't tears because Sam had stopped crying. He hadn't cried all day. He found tissue and blew his nose anyway. Then his mouth started asking questions. "Do my kids talk to you?"

Mark sighed and shrugged. "Mariah tells me to get lost or, sometimes, to go to hell. No one's been successful in enforcing the 'no swearing' rule. If I can catch his head pointed in the right direction, Ben looks at me like he almost remembers me. The trains have stopped running. The whole house is a tomb."

"Why ain't somebody helpin' 'em?"

"We've all tried. It's going to take you, Ace."

"I can't."

"Maybe not while you're drunk, but I expect you'll do something soon. It could be as simple as admitting you're afraid and asking them for help—help them by letting them help *you.*"

Mark didn't understand. Sam pointed to his head as an illustration. "The problem is that things inside here are all cut up in tiny little pieces. I can't put 'em back together the right way, so I hafta keep startin' over. I shoulda known I couldn' have normal things—like a family. It's my fault or it's not. I can't make up my mind. I hurt the people who care about me—the people I care about. That's unnormal. After a while, some of 'em—like Brenan—only feel sorry for me for bein' so stupid. Oh, man, I shouldna made babies."

"Don't you think you're being a bit dramatic?"

"Another defect, I guess."

"One thing you're not running short of is self-pity. You seem to be living in some Gothic cathedral built of whimpering and self-loathing."

Sam thought about that. "Stones," he answered. "Sticks an' rocks an' spitballs."

"What?"

"My cathedral's made outta sticks an' stones. Life's always throwin' rocks at me. I just picked 'em up an' used 'em to build my cathedral. Big sonofabitch, too, wouldn't you say?"

"So you see yourself as a martyr?"

"Hell, no. I thought we got that straight. I'm a stupid, abnormal, self-centered, whimperin' jackass."

Mark rolled his eyes. "You're hopeless."

"My daddy told you that. Did'n he?"

"Everybody's patience is wearing thin."

"You remember when you did'n want her to marry me?"

Mark nodded. "You got her, anyway."

"Yeah, but goin' without her now is ten times as hard. See, I had her heart in my hand—right here—an' it just died. Now, she's heartless. She can't love me or forgive me. It's like there's this big glass mountain between us that's too steep and slippery for me to climb over and too wide to go 'round. I see her sittin' on the other side all sad an' disappointed an' thinkin' that sweet little baby woulda lived if his daddy'd been the right kinda person. An' here I stand holdin' a dead heart. I'm nothin' without her. The only time I ever felt like a man was when I was holdin' her."

"You should have gone into theater."

"I shoulda gone into a fuckin' monastery."

"Sam, sober up and go home."

"I told you—I can't."

Mark found the vodka bottle and poured the last of it into the sink. Sam couldn't rouse a protest. *"Now,* you're going to sleep. Go pee, first. I can't abide bed-pissing drunks."

Sam staggered toward the bathroom. "I'm only doin' this 'cause I was gonna go anyway." When he came back, Mark was still being bossy.

"To bed. Take your shoes off first—and your belt. That's good. No, not on top of the spread. Pull it back. You'd probably be more comfortable if you took your pants off, too."

"Why do I hafta mind you?"

"Because I'm in charge."

"Who made you king?"

"It's my turn. Now, go to sleep."

"I don't wanna sleep."

"I'm going to sit right here beside you to make sure you don't get up."

The darkened room and the coolness of the sheets were soothing. Maybe, the nightmare wouldn't be too bad.

"Tell 'em I love 'em when you see 'em. Tell 'em I'm sorry. Tell my little girl if she ever wants me again, I'll come. I swear. If she calls, I'll come anytime." He tried unsuccessfully to snap his fingers. "Just like *that!* You tell her I said that. Then tell her to go ahead an' call, cause I want her to. An' tell Ben he don't have to hide. I won't hurt him."

"Go to sleep, son."

During the night, Sam broke through several times, never coming completely out of the drugged sleep-hold, but waking enough to realize Mark was nearby.

LIFE BECAME A SUCCESSION of flawed efforts to mend and maintain relationships. Strained, unsolicited visits from A. D. with his dark, accusing eyes and Mark with his misguided sympathies. The mandatory calls from Freida who would never give up, never admit failure, never accept the fact that her mothering could only cover so much ground. Sam's automatic and pitiful leave-me-alones were wasted breath. His ill-fated attempts to persuade his children to pick up a phone and speak to him were squandered time. In spite of the pains, the relationships suffered all the more.

At some fateful moment, during his hours of staring at first one wall then another, of lying in one position until parts of his body became numb and useless, a shadowy conviction tapped him on the shoulder. The seed of an idea, old and familiar, a discarded design from another heartbreaking era of bad dreams, struck the fertile soil of his suffering and began to grow. Overnight, its kudzu-eager runners crept around his heart and mind. Its vines winnowed out healthier thoughts and desires. He heard whispered promises in the rustling of its foliage. *No more night-mares! No more chaos! No more pain!* The notion of not being, not *feeling*, was fascinating, obsessing.

He had reported suicides, accidental deaths, a spectrum of life-endings. Slowly, he allowed his brain to turn them over, study them, envision them, adapting them to fit his purpose. A suicide dressed up as natural death. He made mental cut-and-paste lists. Only a few graphic pictures in his mind—the faces of his family, innocent but shouldering the blame—gave him the bare strength to fight the rampant growth. Ceaselessly hacking and pulling, he managed to keep himself just ahead of it.

On top of everything else, his body played pranks. He was physically sick. Asthma, gastrointestinal ailments, headaches. Lastly, throbbing erections, a running sequence of hardy, aching, long-lived erections that amalgamated into one enduring physical condition fraught with pro-longed exacerbations and brief remissions. His grief, his suicidal imagery, his concentrated despair had no observable influence on his intractable penis. His hand could not break the hold. The back porch stint had been his farewell to ejaculatory relief.

Through this ludicrous phenomenon, his feelings of weakness and failure deepened. The erection remissions could only be counted on during arctic showers, bouts of gastric upheaval, in the presence of company, and during those tense periods of time when he held his breath and waited for someone to come back and break the news that neither Ben nor Mariah would be accepting his call.

49

S TOP IT!" A. D. visually followed his son's trek to the window. Here Sam stopped, parted the drapes with one hand, and stood looking through the glass—a caged animal wanting out.

"It's a reasonable question, son."

"You know how I feel about her!" When Sam turned around, his face was a red flame. He looked at the bed instead of A. D. "And you know how hard this is for me."

Anybody with eyes could see Sam was being eaten alive by grief, but A. D. hadn't come to support or give comfort. He'd come to apply more pressure, to turn the screws one more twist, in hopes making the pain worse would ultimately make it better. Thanks to his own big mouth, their relationship had already fallen on rocky ground. "I thought when the baby died you were tryin', but you didn't keep it up. Doesn't matter how bad your family's sufferin' long as you can sit here like an old dog, lickin' your own wounds."

Though the temperature outside in the fluctuating rain and drizzle was near seventy, the motel room was cool. The dampness found its way in and hovered, dank and oppressive, almost too heavy to breathe. The harsh sound the thick air made as it passed in and out of Sam's lungs put A. D.'s nerves on edge. "You need help, son. A counselor of some kind, maybe. Brenan's not much better, but she is tryin' to get through to the kids, showing 'em some love an' tryin' to convince 'em to talk to you. An' here you are, ready to let everything you ever wanted an' worked for go to hell! No fight! Nothin'!"

A. D. wanted Sam to look him in the eye, let him see if there was something there he could recognize and use. But Sam, hands stuffed into his pockets, stepped slowly about the room, stopping at intervals to examine the wallpaper, the alignment of the hangers on the rod, the motel's disclaimer on the door. If his glance crossed A. D.'s face, it showed no pause.

"I'll leave, but I'm comin' back with your children. You're gonna face 'em with an explanation."

"You think I haven't tried?"

"You gave up mighty easy."

Sam stopped his tour of the room and, for an instant, looked directly at A. D. "You think you know so much! Well, you don't have the slightest notion what I'm going through!" Sam turned and resumed his aimless pacing. "And you don't know what I've tried—nor how hard."

"Might know more'n you think. I know at least part of the reason you ran off after comin' back from the funeral home."

"What? That I didn't even see my son? That he hid from me? That Mariah didn't want me in her room? That she said I was nothing to her or Ben? They'd spent a couple of days with you, so I guess you all have an exclusive club or something."

"You didn't give 'em time. They ran after you, but you didn't even look back!" A. D. frowned. His patience wore thinner with each footfall Sam allowed to touch the carpeted floor. "You ought to see 'em, Sam—really see 'em. It's not anything they got from me. I don't run you down in front of 'em. I try to help 'em feel better about you an' themselves. They're so pitiful. Can't be sent to school in that condition. They don't play. Hell, they don't do anything normal. It's scary just to look at Ben. Walks around like a little ghost. Won't talk to anybody but Rye—an' don't say much to her. He looks through Brenan like she's not even there. She asks questions, tries to get through, but he just sinks deeper down inside himself. An' Rye, she's a whole different ball game. She's got this standard go-to-hell for ever'body, includin' her mother. If anybody gets too close, she pulls out the big time sarcasm an' profanity. You're not the only one she ordered outta her room. Told Ellen to get the f-word out! Imagine how impressed Ellen was. Talks tough, but she's only actin' out what she feels."

"They tried to stop me? Shit!" Sam spoke softly to his reflection in the mirror over the sink.

"Yes. Now you expect them to shrug and go on?"

"Expect? I didn't expect Brenan's whatever or a stillborn son or the kids' anger. I couldn't stop any of it, but blame me! I should be blamed! But I can't take anymore right now!" Sam came at A. D., taking slow-footed, deliberate steps. His voice seemed to rise decibels with each syllable. A. D. shrank back against the door as the scorching words slammed into him. He watched tears well up and slide down his son's face. "You're accusing me of not giving a damn what kind of pain I'm causing! I don't understand! Is anybody hurting more than me? When have you tried to listen to my side of it? You say you want to help at the same time you're calling me a coldhearted bastard? What you're saying is I've lost you, too—right?"

"Sam, listen—"

"No, Daddy, I've listened all I'm going to."

"Let me try to—"

"Get out!"

"Okay, but I'm comin' back with the kids."

"I'll deal with my kids!"

"An' you'll do it today." A. D. started to the door then turned back. "It's a big responsibility you're neglectin'. I don't hear anybody else talkin' straight to you?"

"Well, listen again. There's Ellen. She been very frank with me! And don't forget Mama and Robert and Jackie. And I'm expecting to hear from Marissa and Deejay just anytime."

"You're over-reactin'. Let's see," A. D. brought his wrist watch close to his nose. "Ten-twenty. Oughta be back by half past eleven. I think I'll bring Ben first. Both at the same time might be a dab too much."

Sam took a strong breath and let it hiss out through clenched teeth. "They don't want to come here."

"Oh, don't I know it? Don't wanna see you at all—so they say. Ben put a snapshot of you on the railroad tracks. Run his coal train right over you. Here. I got it outta the trash. Call it a souvenir." He took a mangled photograph out of his shirt pocket and handed it to Sam. "Your little girl swears I don't have a chance of dragging her to see the lousy s.o.b. who wouldn't even come home when she begged him to. Same child who ran for all she was worth tryin' to tell you she was sorry. It's time to force your way back into their lives. Not when you think you're ready—now!"

The lines of Sam's face tightened as he turned the battered photo over in his hands.

"DON'T BRING THEM against their will!" Sam yelled hotly, as if he believed A. D., at this advanced stage of the argument, could be swayed. What he wanted was to be left alone. Left to his solitary occupancy of the king-sized motel bed. To his new home where he had everything he needed to sustain his dejection. Ice bucket with plastic cup. Remote-controlled cable TV. A view of another two-story block of motel rooms. Vending machines and ice just around the corner. Four hangers attached permanently to a rack so he couldn't loose them. He didn't have Brenan or Mariah or Benjamin—or Baby Owen, who had died because Sam hadn't loved him soon enough. He had a phone he was afraid to answer. He much preferred the phone to be silent and the door locked against intrusion, questions, opinions, pity, contempt. Staying in this room kept interference to a minimum.

He splinted his sore abdomen with his hands, sat back against the wood veneer headboard, and pulled his knees against his chest. He was tired of pacing the floor, waiting for A. D. to give up and go home. He wondered what fiery convictions his father would have if he knew all of Sam's woes. What would he say about a body that, in the midst of personal holocaust, refused to give up its doomed craving for a lost mate? An absurd erection that pulsed like a metronome hours each day? Could he explain why Mariah and Ben hadn't given him an opportunity to speak before they'd turned on him? What about the absolution of guilt? Could A. D. show him how to forgive himself for the shattering of his children's security and happiness? Or his inability to breathe life into a dead baby? Or stop a bewildered friend from crawling into the mortal obscurity of a bottle? Or keep a young boy from squeezing a trigger? What about his lurid fascination with suicide? The new and improved Ralph nightmares, complete with Ben's face, the ear-splitting screams of little girls, and bone-jarring explosions? No, A. D. couldn't fix any of those things. Sam shook off his thoughts. "I'll see them tomorrow before you take them on whatever adventure you've planned."

A. D.'s brow creased, and his mouth pulled into a tight circle. "They'll be gone until Sunday. They need more than a few minutes. Take 'em to the mall. Get 'em somethin' new for the trip—some games to play indoors if this rain don't let up. Buy 'em pizza an' ice cream. An' please, sit 'em down an' tell 'em how important they are." He leaned in the shadows against the door with his arms crossed and his feet spread apart. Only one lamp glowed feebly in the curtained gloom. A. D.'s face darkened to murky shades of gray. The silver streaks at his temples stood out stark against the black.

"Okay, I'll go tonight. You can go back and tell them—"

The opening of the door cut the words off cleanly. Dreary, dusky light poured around A. D.'s dark silhouette as he stepped onto the sidewalk and looked back into the room. The rain hitting the pavement sounded like a chorus of cicadas. "Talkin' to you's like talkin' to a tree! You don't run off, but you don't listen, either! I'll be back in an hour with my grandson, an' you best be prepared. I'll hold Rye till after lunch. The rest of your day is for them."

Sam forced himself to stand. "Wait—"

Issuing a long sigh, A. D. eased back into the room and let the door close softly. He came close enough for Sam to feel his breath. "Aw, son." The wistful sadness in the beloved voice he'd found comfort in all his life made Sam shiver. The daddy voice. He searched for a trace of the old parental devotion. He closed his eyes and called up a childhood scene.

"Open mine first." A. D. holds out a box. Inside is a jacket. Soft black leather with silver zippers. The one Sam had pointed out from the sidewalk in front of Loveman's window. The one he'd dropped hints about since October. $129.95 plus tax. This Christmas, Sam is twelve. "Your mama

thinks it's on the pricy side for a kid, but I told her I was buyin' it, anyway. So don't you go gettin' me in trouble by rippin' off the pockets or snaggin' big holes in the sleeves. I bought it big so you can get more'n one winter out of it. Now, you go make a fuss over whatever that thing is she got you." A. D. turns to give Jackie a gold locket with her initials formed of small diamonds. Freida only pretends to be mad. "If you kids wanted a pet dinosaur, your daddy'd drive himself crazy trying to figure out how to turn back time."

The daddy voice pulled Sam back. "Never thought I'd take another side against you, but you've turned dangerous—not just to yourself." He moved closer again and raised his arms, palms up. Sam thought those work-roughened hands were going to turn and drop to his shoulders, but they simply swept back down, a conclusion to a shrug. A. D. exhaled loudly and shook his head. The door clapped shut a second time, and Sam, at least for a short time, was left alone with his motel things.

50

HIS HAIR STILL WET from the shower and his belt cinched to a new hole he'd notched with his pocketknife, Sam opened the door. Ben, holding tightly to his grandfather's hand, kicked at the door jam with the toe of his sneaker and didn't raise his head to look up. Their jackets were water-spotted and their hair damp from the rain. Sam moved aside to let them in.

The boy, at five, was Sam in miniature. That's what other people said, but Sam didn't see it. Translucent blue eyes beneath thick umber lashes and brows. Milk chocolate hair that curled wildly in humid weather. Cleanly-cut dimples, strong, defiant chin. He wasn't like Sam; he was beautiful and perfect.

A. D. gently pushed Ben into the room and started out again. Ben stayed with him, step for step.

"Don't leave me!"

His grandfather stopped.

When Sam heard the boy's plaintive whisper, his heart contracted. "Ben?"

"I want to go home!" The small voice was louder, more urgent. Tears sprang from the corners of his eyes as he wrapped his short arms around one of A. D.'s legs.

The stomach cramps that were the residual of days of diarrhea, vomiting, and anxiety grew and nearly folded Sam in half. His breath stuck in his throat. He could only watch in crippling anguish while his son tried to climb into A. D.'s arms.

"Remember, we talked about this on the way over." A. D. patiently but firmly put the child back on his feet. "Now turn around. See? Your daddy's not mad at you."

"No!"

Sam stood rooted while A. D. dropped to his knees in front of Ben. "He's scared, too, Ben, because he thinks you don't like him anymore. You two hafta get started bein' friends again. I'm goin' now, but I'll be back in a little while with your sister."

Ben permitted A. D. to push him a few steps closer to Sam. Still, he didn't look up, and when his grandfather had gone, he stood shivering no more than three feet from the door. He didn't answer when his name was spoken, but he let Sam remove his jacket and lead him to one of the room's two molded plastic chairs. As Sam lifted him into the chair and knelt in front of him, Ben's face turned willfully to the drawn curtains.

Sam didn't have any idea what might break through the boy's armor. He searched the hostile profile for a clue.

This wasn't the boy who wore Ninja Turtle pajamas and got up early on Saturday for *Bobby's World*. Not the kid who road the rails with gentlemen and hoboes, ladies an' livestock. Not the boy who laughed all the time and never ran out of things to say. This was some angry old man who had snatched Ben's body.

Sam reached to brush back a snarl of curls that dangled over Ben's forehead but changed his mind. "I messed up, son. If—"

"I hate you!" Ben looked at him for an instant, his face full of rage.

Sam tried not to react, tried to keep his voice gentle. "I didn't mean to, but I really messed up. I don't expect you to understand something I don't understand myself, but—"

"I hate you!"

"See, I need you to help me get things right between us."

"I hate you!" His anger was losing momentum. Now, he stared stubbornly into Sam's eyes.

"No, you just think you hate me. You want to hate me because I hurt you, but down deep, you still love me."

"Stop saying stuff like that!" Ben jumped around Sam, putting the chair between them. "I kicked you! I kicked you, an' you left an' didn't come back! Don't you care if I kick people? Don't you care I kicked you? Or that I didn't even know if I wanted a baby brother?"

Sam knelt, pried the child's hands off the back of the chair, and drew the rigid little body to him. Ben twisted and pulled, but Sam refused to let go. He'd not give up this time.

Gradually, the boy began to relax. His small hands came up to cup Sam's face. His stormy blue eyes fastened, questioning, searching, on Sam's. "Don't you care I hid from you?" His hands slid back down. He became limp, flattening himself against Sam's body. "Don't you even care how scared I get?" he whispered.

Warm urine spread unnoticed across Sam's abdomen. He hugged his son tightly, pressing his face into the narrow hollow of the boy's neck. When he was able, he whispered, "I care."

A. D.'S LEGS FELT HEAVY and old as he climbed, in the rain for the third time that day, the back steps of his son's home. The desolation that hung over this house was beginning to eat through his skin. Mandel and Keaton danced unrecognized at his feet. He seemed to be walking under water, treading against the current, and he was tired. No, tired didn't quite cover it. He remembered the breakdown or whatever it was that Sam had gone through as a teenager. The confusion and despair of late was the same sickness grown hardier. Holding his hand and letting him weep until he was hoarse and dry wouldn't be enough this time. A. D. hoped forcing him to take responsibility for his children would help him focus somewhere outside himself and allow him to develop some perspective. Then maybe he'd realize his greatest enemy, the only being from whom he needed sanctuary, lived inside him. Sam was a good man with big heart, a good son, steadfast in his love and loyalty. Until recently, he had been a dedicated husband and father, but once again his internal enemy had gained the potency to reduce its host to child victim. His use of the term Daddy, not A. D. or Dad, was a reliable indicator. Jackie had always called A. D. Daddy. Most Southern fathers were Daddies until they died. Only in the context of feeling diminished and overwhelmed did Sam regress. A. D. winced. If he kept mulling, doubts would get in his way.

Through the glass doors he saw Brenan sitting in a curve of the sectional with her head bent over a folder that rested open on her lap. Probably the same manuscript she'd held all morning. A prop, a guise of normalcy to hide behind. At least, he thought with some relief, she wasn't holding the box.

He pushed the bell, and when she looked up, he pressed his palm against the sensor plate, releasing the computerized locks.

"Come take some of the chill off," she beckoned.

He was the privileged one. Brenan was no longer speaking in civil terms to her own parents. She was primarily ignoring Mark, but Ellen was once again the dreaded opponent—not that there had been more than a flimsy truce since Sam had moved out. Ellen had been on her way out when Brenan had let A. D. in at eight this morning. She'd passed him on the back steps without bothering to speak, but her ire had flashed brightly. He didn't know what had transpired but wasn't surprised that something had. Ellen, paranoid and deaf to reason, had come up with scenarios that doled out extramarital lovers to almost everyone. She had gone as far as to ask Sam, during one of his many attempts to reach the children by phone, if he'd considered the stillborn baby might have been fathered by another man, thereby implicating Brenan with all the other cheating hearts. Mark and Robert were threatening hospitalization and psychiatric therapy. Mariah was threatening grandmatricide. Ben refused to show himself when she was in the house. Freida and Jackie whispered in the background, Brenan was issuing ultimatums right and left to one and all—except A. D., who would have been flattered if manufacturing an emotional cure for the whole bunch hadn't fallen to him.

Both Mark and Ellen had started off eager to rescue their daughter. They might have been beneficial if they'd followed the same game plan, but just as he and Freida had done, they had taken opposite corners. Each mother had chosen her child while the fathers had crossed over—not quite so precise in analogy, but close. The heavy issue with Mark and

Ellen was the fighting that kept rising between them. Ellen's miserable battles with menopause made her a formidable enemy for any soul who dared to cross her. Her tangents had repeatedly driven mighty Mark to his knees and cast Brenan farther away from the aid she needed.

How long could he and Freida remain cordial enough to keep tipping their hats when they crossed paths? He couldn't deny that she had a way with emotional matters. In fact, the plan for making Sam deal with the kids alone had been hers. She'd casually masked it in small talk and fed it to him with supper. Via some psychic scanner in her brain, she could feel people out, diagnose their maladies, and prescribe treatment. If the dose was taken, the sickness got better. Perhaps her history of successful cures was the reason A. D. tended to routinely play devil's advocate. A little good-humored friction was refreshing, and the few times she'd been wrong had been sweet. But this time the sport wasn't there. Both sides must win. All or nothing.

Brenan tapped a cushion near her, but A. D. chose to stand in front of the hearth, soaking up the warmth of the wood fire.

"How'd he do?" She closed the folder and tossed it aside.

"Not too happy, but he stayed. Hafta wait till I take Rye to see. I couldn't tell how Sam's goin' to handle the job. He's so scared himself. Both may be still starin' at the floor. How big a problem's Rye gonna be?"

"Can't say. She wants to go, I think, but she's frightened. She's too stubborn to admit to either. She has some kind of on-going psychological war with Sam. She's afraid she's pushed him too far. Fear's new to Mariah." Her voice was flat, her expression a void. Her customary animation had died slowly over the past few months. No longer the eternal teenager, she looked all of her twenty-six years. Actually, A. D. believed she looked a little older. He didn't expect they'd ask for her I. D. at the taverns today. The breakup had aged her. The loss of her baby had added a generous measure of bitterness to her face.

"Let me fix you somethin' to eat."

"Look, A. D., I appreciate all you're doing, but ease up. Believe it or not, I have lunch waiting for you and Mariah, so let that be proof I can actually move. Sometimes, I simply choose not to."

He gave her one of his famous childlike grins. "Well, where is the little tyrant?"

"In her room reading *Scarlett*." Brenan managed a smile.

"For petesake, she's nine years old! What happened to Nancy Drew an' little prairies with houses on 'em? Don't she read anything normal?" His mild static was meant to be funny, but Brenan's rough smile vanished.

"Being smart isn't a disease."

"I didn't mean—"

"Oh, I know. Why don't you go up and get her? Use whatever weapon is necessary, and if she puts her middle finger up for a little nonverbal communication, break it."

A. D. was on the stairs when the phone rang. He paused, waiting for the answering machine to collect a message.

"Brenan, it's me. Pick up." Sam. Trouble already?

He started back down but heard Brenan lift the receiver. "Hello—I was hoping he would—Sure." She hung up.

"Sam wants you to bring clothes for Ben." She passed him on the stairs. "I'll get them."

MARIAH GAZED FIRST at Sam then at her sleeping brother. She frowned. Behind her, A. D. also frowned a question. Ben's soft snoring and Sam's wheezing were minor challenges to the stillness of the room. "A siesta—too much Tex-Mex for lunch." Sam heard the false glibness in his words and tried to wring it out before going on. "Chicken fajitas brought over from the Border Cantina next door. Um—he wasn't dressed for going out. Knocked out right after he ate."

"I guess that's because he's tired. He has these bad dreams that wake him up at night," Mariah said in a tone that made Sam wince. She was ready to spar. "Doesn't eat much, either."

"He ate lunch." He caught his defensiveness and again changed his tone mid-response. "I think he's feeling a little better." He closely watched her for a reaction.

Her features were blank.

A. D. cleared his throat and held out Ben's clothes. "I'll come back about eight."

"I'll take them home."

"Sure. It's better you take 'em."

Then A. D. was gone, leaving Sam to face another injured child. He didn't think this one would be any easier than the first. Mariah, the child he had fought doubt, circumstance, and tradition to keep, fixed her bright, soulful, night-sky eyes on his face and held him silently captive.

You first, Ace. You're the big one.

Fate could have given him a daughter with any combination of dispositions, abilities, or visual attributes. Considering her birth mother, she could have been beautiful, chaotic, vain, selfish, and incapable of making the first decision for herself. Instead, she was a remarkably precocious, stalwart little girl with a gentle heart—gentle until notably provoked—and an IQ thirty points higher than her father's. Dark hair and skin the color of good bread, her resemblance to Freida was extraordinary, and her artful brandishing of her grandmother's expressions and outspoken opinions had brought applause at many a family gathering. Her looks pleased him. Karen was dark-haired but with showy green eyes and a milky complexion—pretty and delicate and soft. As Sam had been as a child, Mariah was small, sinewy, and athletic. Due to her atypical acceleration through the levels of childhood and the pain he'd thrust upon her, she was old for only nine years. Old and judgmental. Feeling the parent-child roles in reverse, Sam yearned for her to hug him, to make the first move toward reconciliation. He almost held out his hands for her but checked himself. He needed her to come to him, to forgive him without being asked.

Actually, she made the first move DAYS ago—remember? Lefty reminded.

"Sit down." He took one of the chairs and with his foot pulled the other close to him.

She obediently sat. Not a grain of forgiveness was evident.

"Has your mama talked to you about my moving out?"

"No."

"She hasn't told you why?"

She hesitated, still judging him with her eyes. Then she spoke, harsh and accusing. "How could she? She doesn't know. Why does Ben need more clothes?"

"He wet his pants. I find it hard to believe she hasn't said anything at all."

"She said ask you. Ben doesn't wet himself. What did you do to him?"

He frowned. "Not going to give me a chance, are you? Up until a few days ago, you trusted me. Couldn't you give me the benefit of a doubt?"

"You better not've spanked him."

"No. You know I wouldn't hit either one of you. He's okay, honey. No, not okay. He's still confused and unhappy, but he knows I want to be part of his life. He knows I love him."

"Then why the hell did he pee his pants?" As it had done in her bedroom, the blue of her eyes turned a cold, dirty gray. He should have made himself go to her that night. No. He should never have left her room. He should have taken her into his arms and held her until all the ugliness bled from inside her. But, putting his pain first, he'd run. He'd refused to return when she was desperate for him. How could he explain the sickness that had taken over his judgment, his ability to deal with people he loved with all his heart?

"When he first got here, he was upset and crying, and he wet his pants. Ask him when he wakes up if you need to verify my story, but don't embarrass him. And leave off the swearing."

"Grampa says maybe you and Mama will talk if we're not there, so he's keeping us out of school and taking us up to the lake house for the rest of the week. Some vacation that'll be. Will you talk to her after we're gone?"

"I don't think your grampa meant you had to be gone for us to talk. You haven't stopped us. We just haven't been ready, yet. Other things have had to be dealt with. But, yes, I'll try. I hope you don't feel like you've been in the way."

"Yeah, yeah. Did you stop wanting to be married to her?"

"No."

"I'll bet."

"Mariah, neither your mother nor I planned a breakup. I don't think she did. It just happened, and I'm trying to figure out what caused it. I left because I believed it was best for her. I must have done something, maybe a lot of somethings, that made her feelings for me change. I can't explain until I know."

Mariah sighed. The same exasperated sigh she used when Ben wanted to watch "The Simpsons" instead of "Cosby." The look she gave Bobby Cox on the TBS Superstation when the Dodgers or the Cubs laid into her beloved Braves.

"You're so stupid."

That ya are, Lefty piped. *Are we unanimous on that?*

He nodded.

"I don't like her being by herself five whole days. She doesn't look right. Losing the baby made her sick. She tries not to cry around us, but we know."

"So do I."

"Then why don't you do something?"

"What?"

"You're her husband. You're the one who's supposed to know." She rolled her eyes over his pathetic ineptitude. "Anyway, she gets scared, especially when she gets those crazy letters. That Blacknell guy called again the other day. He said the baby's dying was God's way of punishing her for writing that book. I heard her tell Dana."

"I realize she's having a rough time."

"Will you be nice to her and check to see if she's okay?"

"Yes."

"Will going to see about her be any different than coming back that night? Will you be too sick?"

"I'd come for you, now."

"Nobody's asking you to do one damned thing for me, and nobody's going to. But you will check on Mama while we're gone?"

"Yes."

"Daddy, you just made a promise."

Daddy. She'd acknowledged a familial tie. A start, maybe. "I know."

"You'd better keep it. You're supposed to keep promises."

"I will."

"Do you have a girlfriend?"

"Of course not!"

"Did Mama make that baby with somebody else?"

"No. Why would you ask that?"

"You asked. I heard you."

Sam remembered a door closing upstairs the night he'd argued with Brenan. "I said things I shouldn't have—things I didn't mean. I hurt her a lot even though I knew she wouldn't do something like that. I thought if I made her mad, she'd tell me why she was unhappy. It was a terrible thing to do. We talked later, and she knows I didn't believe it."

"Are you still sick? You haven't been on TV."

"I took some time off."

"You don't have AIDS?"

"No."

"Grampa A. D. said you might lose your job."

"Your grampa talks too much."

"You're skinnier." She looked around the room. "What the hell do you do in a dump like this?"

"Sit right there and feel sorry for myself." He pointed to the bed. "I wonder what's going to happen to us as a family." He stopped when his bottom lip began a warning twitch.

Mariah got up and walked to the bed. Her brother lay on his stomach, his head turned away from her. Sam's tee-shirt came below his knees. He had kicked the thin motel blanket down around his feet. In his sleep, he turned toward her. His cheek was pinker than the rest of his face, a wrinkle from the bedding had pressed into it.

"He was pissed when Grampa left with him. Don't look it now, does he?" She walked slowly to Sam.

"Don't say pissed. No more swearing or bathroom jargon. Period."

Her brow crinkled. Concentrating. She slanted her head first to one side then the other. Her gaze met his without faltering. A step closer, then another—until she stood between his knees. "Okay."

"I'm sorry I hurt you, Baby."

"I wish I'd never starting saying bad things to you."

"I know. You didn't say anything a hug wouldn't cure."

She rocked a little on her heels. "I don't know how to feel."

"It's all right for you to keep loving and trusting all the people you loved and trusted before—even the ones who do things you don't understand."

"I guess." She stopped moving and peered into Sam's eyes.

"We need each other."

"I'll never understand." Her wry face came back. "Okay, Daddy, if you're stupid enough to want to, you can hug me."

WHILE TRYING TO HELP Ben find the final flat-sided piece of the puzzle's border, Sam paid close attention to the only end of the conversation available to him.

"I kinda feel sorry for him, Mama. He bought us all this stuff, and he's got this big puzzle to finish. — Yeah, Ben's fine. He took a nap and ate half a pizza! — If you don't want to be alone, I'll come home. — You sure? — Oh, all right. I admit it. You were right. I'm just not used to apologizing."

She caught him looking and turned her back. Her brassiness tuned down to a stout whisper he could still pick up. "He doesn't look good. I think he's sick. — Because after he ate some pizza, I could hear him throwing up in the bathroom. — I think he wants to come home but don't believe you'll let him or something — Well, maybe I don't understand everything, but he loves us. I know that. All of us. — Mama, it wouldn't hurt you to listen. He's not even mad at me. — If you believe that, why don't you ask him to come back? — Well, someday somebody in this family's going to have learn to explain. — Hold on. I'll get him." She called over her shoulder. "Ben!"

Ben reluctantly left the table and took the phone from his sister. "Yep? — Well, yes, I'm talkin'. — I can, now.— I dunno, I just can. I'm talkin' to you, ain't I? — Um, it's got a barn an' cows an' stuff on it. We couldn't find one with a train or cowboys. — A thousand pieces. Grass an' sky're always the hardest parts. — Okay. — Eight o'clock. Got it. — Yeah, I can remember. — I will. Promise. — 'night, Mama. — Aw yeah, me, too."

Ben put down the phone and ran back to the table. "She says she'll have breakfast ready at eight o'clock, and Grampa A. D. will pick us up at home, so you gotta take us. I forgot what time we're supposed to leave, but that ain't important 'cause we'll already be there. You can eat, too, Daddy. She said so."

WHEN THE KIDS WERE ASLEEP, Ben, again in the oversized tee-shirt, in the middle of the bed, with Mariah next to him on the side next to the bathroom, Sam tuned in the News.

Garner was doing Nine Cares. An elderly Tarrant man had received a four-hundred-dollar water bill after a main had geysered in front of his home. Garner had gotten a quick cancellation of the errant bill and now stood shoving a microphone toward the grinning, toothless mouth of the old man. A one-phone-call job, and Garner was beaming his self-importance over the airwaves. Birmingham had a hero!

Good deal, Garner! Lefty addressed the TV set. *Bet ya kiss Drury's ass nitey-nite every time Sam don't show! May get his job, yet. But he'll get by. Bet on that!*

Sam gave Lefty a thumb up.

Yeah, boy, he'll survive the whole shebang—long as he's got these two great little kids. May not have another thing in this whole screwed-up world, but he'll have these kids. Enough for any man—an' then some?

Lefty turned his attention from the TV to Sam. *Ya got plenty to live for right here. Plus, ya got me, Ace. We're doin' fine tonight, huh? Next ya can work on gettin' Brenan back for us. I got some ideas on that.*

"You always do."

Sam clicked off the set and slid under the covers next to his children. He searched for a small hand, found one, and held it until he, too, fell asleep.

51

THE NIGHTMARE SHOULD have been but a half-remembered wisp of shadow, growing dimmer and less ominous with time. The boy-Sam had wrestled and perspired through it hundreds of nights. Then somewhere around the bleary edges of his coming of age, the man-Sam had managed to lock it inside where, for a time, it had remained jailed and dormant—infrequently testing or slipping the latch and easily recaptured. Now, with the helter-skelter collapse of Sam's world, it had escaped, and its power was growing. No less deliberate and uncompromising in its night-hold, time had not softened the isolation and powerless rage it evoked. Yet, it *had* changed. In the past, its clarity had muddied in the light of day. Steadily, the muddy waters were beginning to clear and the details show through. Pictures of a defenseless child, not always a nine-year-old Sam. Justin, Mariah, Deejay. More and more the protracted scenarios were of Ben. All children from his life. The station wagon stopped, not by a country road but beside a labyrinth of toy trains. *Only a dream,* he would remind himself. At some point along its relentless course, he always forgot, his forgetfulness giving passage to a guise of grotesque reality that took command of his heart rate and claimed an unfair share of his breath.

. . . He fell tumbling as if from a lofty elevation, his descent slowing as he neared the bed where his son was lashed. A few yards above the bed, his fall ended, and he hung suspended and helpless to rescue Ben from the stinking, grease-stained hands of the mechanic called Ralph. Sam would

just as well have been a pair of disembodied eyes and ears. He could do no better than watch his beloved child struggle against the knotted baling twine, watch the flesh of the small hands split, bleed, gape open under the cordage, listen to the hulking figure in the doorway laughing through tobacco-blackened teeth, listen to the soul-piercing cries. "Daddy! DADDY! DAAADDDDDEEEEE!" and to the pleading, "No! PLEASE, NO!" Sam remembered the taste of those words because he had screamed them, too. He had screamed and begged, knowing Daddy couldn't hear and begging wouldn't help. A choking panic rose in Sam's chest as the Ralph-monster crept toward the bed. "Leave him alone! Not Ben! Please, not Ben!" "Why, if it ain't my old friend, Sambo! Hey, Benji, did Sambo ever do this . . ." The monster turned, looked up, bowed slightly before turning back to the child. Sam had to save Ben! "You can't have him!" Frantically, he searched for a crack in the mortar of the dream, found the tiniest rift, and began to wildly claw his way to wakefulness . . .

When he climbed, gasping and sweat-soaked, out of the nightmare, Sam found himself staring up into the anxious face of his son.

"Bad one, huh, Daddy?" On his knees, Ben leaned protectively over Sam.

Sam shook off the stupor of the dream. He tried to smile. "Yeah, a bad one."

"You said my name. You said 'Not Ben'."

"I must have been dreaming about you."

"Don't you remember?"

He remembers.

"Not much. Just that it was scary."

Ya do, too.

"You always say dreams ain't real. They can't hurt you. But I wonder. I dreamed Deej socked me in the mouth with his fist an' look." He wiggled a front tooth with his tongue. "Whatcha think of that?"

They can hurt.

Sam felt his smile broaden and become honest. He wished he knew how to tell his little boy how good it felt to be with him, how much love was reserved just for him. "I reckon it's about time for those teeth to start falling out, anyway. You'll be six next month—right after Christmas.

"New Year's Eve."

"That's right. Looks like you'll have a visit from the tooth fairy long before Santa gases up his reindeer."

Ben hadn't given an ounce of credibility to the Easter bunny, but he had challenged his cousin Marissa to fist fight over Santa Claus. *"Take it back, or I'll punch your lights out!"* This tooth fairy business could go either way.

"Must've been loose a while, Ace. Looks ready to fall out."

Ben turned his head toward the lighted bathroom doorway. "I didn't tell nobody. Grampa Mark noticed, but I didn't tell him."

"Did you want to surprise everybody when it fell out?"

"No. I wanted you an' Mama to know first."

Sam swallowed back a lump that sprang up in his throat. "And you didn't feel like talking to us? Right?"

Ben's head bobbed up and down. He continued to look away.

Going on six. First loose tooth. No one to care. A little kid alone in a dismal grown-up world. "I'm glad you're giving me another chance. I never meant for anything bad to happen."

"Grampa Mark says I'm gonna be singin' a song—somethin' about wantin' my front teeth to grow back for Christmas. I don't think so. Daddy?" The boy turned back to face Sam.

"Yeah?"

"How come you ain't mad?"

"Mad?"

"About me an' Rye? About what we did?"

"I am, son, but at myself—not you or your sister. You didn't know how to react. How could I get mad at you about something I caused? I hope you know how much it means to me to have you here tonight. I've really missed you."

He drew the boy down and cradled him. Ben gave no resistance.

Instead, he seemed to welcome the embrace, and he permitted Sam to hold him until he fell asleep.

Sam also slept, this time, without intrusion.

A. D. ASKED MARIAH AND BEN to give him a minute alone with their daddy. Reluctantly, they meandered back to the kitchen where Brenan, Freida, and Mark were having coffee and discussing trivial subjects—all covertly marveling over the change in the kids after one night with Sam. A. D. was no less impressed.

"I'll take a little credit," he mumbled to himself. *"Now, I just hafta smooth over the row I plowed to get here."*

He watched Sam drift, hands in pockets, toward one of the two glass walls of Brenan's office and stand placidly looking out on the shadowy, cloud-covered day. He'd always been lean and well-muscled, but now he looked reed-thin and brittle. With offhand politeness, he had turned down breakfast except for coffee and a slice of toast Mariah had willfully pressed on him. Although he'd stayed at the table until the children had eaten, he'd spoken only to them or when keeping silent would have been more awkward. For sly, brief moments, he'd gazed at Brenan with such longing that A. D. had shivered, knowing that Sam was totally blind to how furtively Brenan had peered back.

"Son?"

Sam reeled around, his face a question he didn't bother to put into words.

"It was a risk, but it worked."

Sam ran his tongue around the inside of one cheek and looked at Brenan's computer monitor.

"It's been so hard seein' you apart from your children. I can't help but think what it mighta been like if somethin' like this had happened between us—you, Jackie, an' me—when you were little an' needin' all the lookin' after you could get. Ain't it bad enough that we're not doin' so good now? I wanna keep the closeness we've always had. You gotta forgive me."

Sam stretched his fisted hands as far as they would go into the depths of his pockets. He filled his mouth with air, let it hiss slowly through closed lips. He regarded tiers of clippings, book reviews, odds-and-ends on Brenan's bulletin board.

"Anyway, you can't hold against me what was mostly your mother's idea. I hafta mind her. She'd put me outta the house."

Frown lines cut deeply into Sam's brow and temples. His eyes, mere slits, returned his father's gaze. He wet his lips.

"Sam?"

Sam opened his mouth, lightly grazed the edges of his teeth with his tongue. He removed one hand from its pocket, fingered a mug of pencils, and nodded. A slight, barely perceptible movement, a faint lifting of one corner of his mouth, a gesture so small someone else might have missed it.

A. D. felt relief burst in the pit of his stomach.

Sam turned back to the window wall. Sighing, A. D. crossed the room to stand beside him, brought a hand to his back. They stood looking at the stone path that led to the pool. After a while, Sam asked, "What's wrong with me?"

"A theory's all I've got."

"Well—"

"You keep pain bottled up for long periods of time, years, then you let it have you again."

"Why?"

"Because it still makes you feel small an' helpless. An' guilty. You let it live inside you, an' that gives it power. Part of you has been nine years old way too long. I wish I could do it for you, but only you can do the soul-cleanin' you need."

"I'm not strong like you."

"That's one of the self-defeatin' lies you keep comin' up with. You create an' believe 'em. You live by 'em. You're stronger'n me by a country mile. I'd have buckled an' give up long ago if I'd had to live under the standards an' judgments you've set for yourself. Your children reacted to your leavin' with the same fierceness you've taught 'em. No, don't you get mad again. You asked. You've put on the longest one-act drama of all times—months of it, an' we're all glued to front row seats. It was touched off by that little boy you couldn't help—no, byjoe, you did help 'im. You cared. Let 'im know he didn't deserve the pain. You couldn't do more'n that! But when that child shot 'imself, he jarred somethin' loose inside *you!*"

"Little kids shouldn't have to suffer. The adults who bring them into the world should take care of them. I went to all these places and talked to *all these* people. Child abuse isn't rare. It's as common as runny noses. All the people and organizations who claim to be working to stop it aren't making a dent. The people who could do something don't care. You couldn't help what happened to me, but you put everything you had into getting me over it. Justin's mother knew and did absolutely nothing to save him. She let that pervert kill him."

"So you hafta take the blame because his mother won't? You hafta take your own family apart because of all the no-accounts in the world?"

"Is that what I'm doing?"

"I'm just a simple farmer. I don't know much psychology, but I know you. If I sound like a busted record, so what? Lookin' at you today, I see the same expression I saw on your face when you told us what that sicko Sommers did to you. Your mama an' me could say it's our fault you can't be happy, that we didn't do the right things or try hard enough. But we did the best we knew how. Nothin' was more important than gettin' you through. Not many places to turn for help back then, but one thing we learned was if you pack somethin' down inside you, it grows, gets meaner an' stronger. Get it out! Let it go! Accept that what happened belongs in the past an' that the only power it has to keep jerkin' you around is what you give it!"

Sam continued to peer through the window. His forehead almost touched the glass.

"You deserve better. You were wrong about the children. They came back just as soon as you had 'em hemmed up long enough to make 'em hear you. You're dead wrong about your wife, too."

Sam turned. "That's one thing you don't understand."

"We'll see. Rye said you promised to spend time with Bren. You do that. I think she might be ready to talk." A. D. didn't know what else to say, so he waited.

"I'd go back to her if I could. My craziness, or whatever you want to call it, changed her. I'd have done anything to please her, but she wouldn't talk. She could've stopped me."

"So you say, but no matter how much you love her, you've gotta find some answers before you can be what she needs. When you finally accept that no one or nothin' else in your life—not your job, not your inability to stop the injustices of the world, not your relationship with Brenan, not the way you feel about yourself as a man—should have a thing to do with a freak who's been dead twenty-six years."

SAM TRAILED THE KIDS upstairs to help with their packing. His silence broken, Ben dispensed a stream of questions and opinions. Mariah, having dropped the profanity, competed with her brother to be noticed and heard. The need for reassurance had all three of them searching out small opportunities for hugs and kisses. *"I love you this much, Daddy!"* *"So? I love you THIS much—plus an ocean!"* These demonstrations of affection fed his hunger. His words fell short. He hoped the touch of his hands told them more. They had traveled a full-circle. Their voices were again sweet and enthusiastic. They called him *Daddy*. They were weary, but they were going to be okay.

Mariah made Sam promise to eat. With her anger subsiding, she switched to mothering. Freida had taught her well. She reported his nausea to Mark and was rewarded with a bottle of Phenergan tablets. Sam swore on his honor he'd take them. He crossed his heart. He'd make a trip to Food World.

"Well, just make sure you get healthy stuff."

Being important to her felt good.

When they were leaving, he stood beside Brenan and Freida and waved. He watched until A. D.'s mirror-black Bronco II rounded the bend in the driveway. Some of the grief and dread of the preceding days began to recede, leaving a sticky residue of soreness, fatigue, and regret— and the belief that the days ahead, if not full of happiness, would be bearable.

As soon as the wagon was out of sight, Freida said her good-byes and started walking toward the farmhouse. Mark had already sped off to morning rounds at the hospital. Shuffling here and there, catching crumbs of conversations, Sam deduced that Ellen was spending the day with her sister in Fairfield and that she and Mark planned to meet A. D. and the kids at the lake house early in the evening. Freida, reciting a list of pressing chores that must be done first, had half-promised to join them by Friday. Sam thought his mother may have lingered, not for chores, but to keep a mindful eye on Brenan and him.

When Brenan turned to go back in, he hung back. At the door, she turned. Her eyes were unreadable in the shade of the porch. "Are you coming in?"

He couldn't.

Ya gotta!

"I think I'll take a look at the horses. If you don't mind, though, when I get back, I'd like to pick up some clothes. I haven't figured out a laundry routine, yet—but I'm working on it." He tried to make his smile light and informal.

She shrugged and left him alone on the steps.

Coward! Perfect opportunity to get with this woman, an' ya go slinkin' off. Stupid, craven, spineless wimp. Get my drift, Ace? Did I leave out anything?

He had every intention of talking to Brenan after a courage-building walk, but he'd found the old farm courage-poor. He wished he could stroll right in and tell her how much he cared, how sorry he was, how desperately he wanted to come home. But wishing was as far as he could go.

Hey, Hoss? Remember what your daddy says 'bout wishin' in one hand an' spittin' in the other? Which one fills up first?

Instead of going back in, he drove to the station. He wanted to ask Dan Stircy, who had just hooked the full-time evening weather slot, what was being said about his absence and to see Andy Drury about arranging more off-time. Moreover, he wanted to check in with Dana. As Brenan's sounding-board, she knew things. He considered Dana research for the temporarily postponed but inevitable confrontation with his wife.

HE FOUND ANDY DRURY and Dan in a conspiratorial pose behind the desk in Drury's office. Standing behind the desk chair, Dan leaned deeply over Drury's shoulder staring at a place on a chart marked by Drury's finger. As Sam approached, they looked up.

The chart was a printout of the newsroom staff's time schedule. Even upside down, Sam found his name and followed it to a line of red X's. He put his forefinger down next to the last X. "I'll need a few more of these," he said coolly.

Andy stiffened, his face freezing in a hard glare. Behind his back, Dan shook his head as if to say, "Whoa, boy!"

"How many?" Drury's voice was under provisional control.

"I'm not sure. A few. A week—maybe more."

"Though I sympathize with your trouble and loss, you must realize I have a newsroom to run. Holidays and all. I need you. I'll have to hire a temp if you're not back by Monday."

Sam smiled. He wouldn't cower with false humility. No begging or bargaining. This was the one place where he could exert power. It felt good to hold the right cards once in a while. "I can't help what you have to do until I get back. Now, put a week's worth of those little red X's by my name."

"MacCauley—"

"I've brought you good luck, Andy. Ratings, awards. You wanted an Emmy—I got you *two.* When you tell me to crack a story, I crack the effing story! You worked me eighteen straight days last month then gave me one lousy day off. I don't recall one word of appreciation. I bust ass through holidays, vacations and every weather condition that exists. You won't fire me and lose your cushy little job in the doing. Birmingham doesn't know who you are, but she *loves* me! Now, you put me down for the off-time, and be glad I'm not demanding a raise!"

Something sulfurous hit the fan. Dan straightened to his full, impressive height and took a step back to watch the clash from a safe distance.

Drury stood, squared his shoulders, and wasted the next five minutes giving Sam hell. Sam retaliated by yawning, cleaning his fingernails with his pocketknife, and reading the bulletin board. It was a purgative exercise for both men. When the boss finally wound down, Sam smiled pleasantly and said, "I'll call with an update in a few days. Thanks for understanding. I do hope you were this sympathetic with Garner when his hernia strangulated."

"You think you're indispensable." Drury's ire was rushing back. "May pull a stunt like this one day and find your balls are smaller than you thought."

"But they'll always be bigger than yours." With that, Sam saluted, congratulated Dan on his new slot, and walked out, leaving Drury red-faced and shaking with impotent fury.

He blew kisses to Dana and Rita who huddled together in the hallway near the office trying to show no interest in Sam's arrogance or the raised voice of Andy Drury.

HE HAD TOTALLY forgotten his most important reason for going to the station. As he was angling into a parking space outside his motel room, he remembered. Dana and Brenan were bosom buddies. There was a modest chance he could have gleaned another take of his situation, a clearer one than the family's myopic point of view. He knew Brenan and Dana had *talked*.

52

S AM'S EYES SANK deep behind wilted, blue-veined lids. Hair fell over his brow in tangled straw-brown clumps. His cheeks were beginning to hollow, and his body sagged inside his clothes. If not for his perverse hard-on, the new hole he'd carved in his belt would not have kept his pants up.

Every breath was scented with Brenan's essence. Hunger for her superseded the need for food. He had tried to keep his promise to Mariah, tried to eat but barely kept down an ounce or two of liquid or a few saltines at a time. He slept too much, preferring the classic nightmare to more palpable day terrors. His kids were gone. Brenan was as dead to him as Owen. Bleary-eyed, he stared at a now familiar scarecrow in the motel mirror.

Used to be so cute, Lefty told the scarecrow.

The scarecrow stared back without comment.

Take a shower, ya bum! I ain't lettin' ya go nowhere—'specially not your mama's house—like that!

"I'm not going!"

Oh, yes ya are. Ya promised, an' I aim to get ya there.

Sam sighed. Lefty was beginning to grate on his nerves.

Can't go without a bath. Just ain't done. Ain't a matter of pride—which you ain't got, noway. Pee-uuu! Ya stink! Raised ya better, she did.

"I know."

Poor thing thought she was raisin' ya to be a man, but a man wouldn't let himself go like this. A man'd be home with his family steada layin' sorry

461

here in this dump! Even a little bitty PIECE of a man'd know what the hell-o went wrong.

"I've already agreed with you."

He stripped off his tee-shirt, unfastened his belt, let the jeans that no longer fit pile around his ankles. The scarecrow evaporated, further diminishing the reflection into a skeleton with a zany, dogged erection, a stick man in a bawdy comic strip. A tear glazed one cheek, sliding slowly down a whisker-shadowed crease. Seconds later, another snaked down the other side.

You're round the bend, Ace.

Sam turned from the stick man in the mirror, kicked the jeans across the bathroom floor. Moving slowly to the tub, he turned on the tap, and when steam began to waft, he pulled up the lever and stepped around the curtain into the spray. The tears on his face and any that may have followed were soon washed away.

"I COOKED." Freida used her hug to frisk his arms and chest as if to judge the extent of the emaciation that had taken place. The baggy sweats he'd worn would have covered some of his weight loss if she had only looked. He held as much of his body as he could out of reach. Although the erectile joke his body played was blocked by her nearness, he wasn't safe. Her uncanny radar could zero in on his most humbling secrets, extract confessions before he could clamp a hand over his mouth. Through her, his privacy suffered.

"Eat. We'll talk after you've had a good meal. I made dumplings—chicken and apple—low fat, of course, and I have fresh bread ready to come out of the oven." She scooted him in front of her into her sunny, old-fashioned kitchen much the way she had to his milk and cookies after a day at school.

Thirty-seven years in the South had scarcely filed the spiny edges off her New York accent. No slow drawl for Freida, her speech was clipped, shaped, and executed to show she meant every word. To neighbors, she'd forever be A. D.'s Yankee wife.

The rich aroma of spices and baking bread evoked more memory than appetite. He sat in the chair she pointed out and waited for her to lift the bread board from the oven. Two perfectly round, mahogany-crusted loaves were held out for him to admire. Though the corners of his mouth felt stiff, he forced a smile and watched her take a heavy china dinner plate to a trio of steaming pots on the stove. "I'm really not hungry."

She turned, holding the plate steady. A hearty mound of dumplings had already been dipped onto it. "Oh, yeah? What have you eaten today? Remember, it's me you're talking to."

"Nothing," he admitted. He should have taken a Phenergan before he came to his mother's house where food was not to be refused. "But my stomach's not quite right. A bug or something. You know how these things are."

She set a heaping plate of hot food in front of him, and carved a chunk of bread to go with it. "I know how grief is, son. If you don't have strength to fight it, it'll eat you!"

Her mouth was set. He'd have to eat. Thirty-five years old didn't seem any different from ten when he was with her.

"While you eat, I'll give you *my* version of *what's what.*" She put a tall glass of milk beside his plate and took a chair across from him. She'd told him *what* was *what* at this table on more occasions than he cared to recall.

Ignoring small quells of nausea, he lifted the fork.

Her fixin' won't work. Too many pieces lost or broken.

"How do you like these tricks your father and Mark are playing?" Her voice was light but loaded.

"Tricks?"

"Oh yes. The real reason your father and Mark kept the kids out of school and took them to the lake house—a hoodwink. It started as an attempt to get them away for a while, take their minds off things and give Brenan a break. But when the dropping-the-kids-at-the-motel trick worked so nicely, the lake excursion took on a whole new objective."

"Yeah?"

"It's supposed to get you and Brenan together without any distractions. Doesn't seem to be working—yet."

He put down his fork, coughed.

"Having Dana Rawlings and Rita Williams call Brenan and report back to you isn't the deal you cut with Mariah."

"I'm going over there. Probably tonight."

"Mark and your daddy don't mean to cross you. When A. D. does things for Brenan and takes up for her, he hopes it'll aggravate you so much you'll take back the job. You could treat him nicer. And both of you and Brenan ought to be ashamed for giving Mark the cold shoulder. All in the world he wants is to help. The cool cucumber number is a first for him."

"Is this where you tell me Ellen calls me dirty names, hangs up on me, and tells my children I have a mistress because she thinks it's for my own good?"

"Don't start on Ellen. No one can get along with her. See, not all messes are your fault."

Her explanations were unneeded. A. D.'s heart was in the right place, but it still hurt to be pushed in and out of his good graces. Both fathers were decent men whose hard feelings would soften in time. Sam was grateful for their wishes, if not their methods, to help his children.

"Brenan's not writing. Called off the workshops in Atlanta and Charleston. Of course, she's not up to going. Her face stays all puffy and red. Just sits for hours in her bathrobe and sloppy old pajamas staring at the fireplace, only getting up to stoke the fire or go to the bathroom or the refrigerator. I think she's put on a few pounds—maybe just fluid retention, maybe not. Grief does different things to different people."

Sam swallowed a difficult clot of chicken he had been holding in his mouth. Visualizing his wife fat and disheveled didn't hinder a small stirring in his pants. "At least she's not having to go through the motions of a bad marriage."

"Which one of you was doing that?"

He didn't bother with an answer.

"She says you got up in the middle of the night and walked out. Just like *that.*" She snapped her fingers.

He felt her eyes searching his face, waiting for the missing account or a denial. He had neither. He'd never known Brenan to lie, but if a little playing with facts made her day-to-day life easier, he wouldn't hold it against her. Whatever it took to make her feel better was fine. Alone and physically compromised by illness and the birth process, she was mourning Owen while bearing the burden of the kids and the rest of an emotionally overwrought family. At the hospital, over the phone, during the brief moments they'd been alone, he picked up feelings of guilt, pity. Guilt over not being able to love him anymore. She didn't deserve this. The wreckage of a once-perfect love lay at his feet. She held answers to the *what?* questions. The *what did I do? what could I have done? what can I do now?* questions.

"You should go to her."

"I will."

"Today?"

"If I can." He knew that wouldn't satisfy her, but he didn't know what he'd be able to do. What if he couldn't play fair? What if he bawled and begged her to take him back?

Freida sighed and frowned. "What happened, son?"

He shrugged.

She sighed again. She was tall, big-boned. Her brown eyes were full of intelligence and compassion. Her body language was easy to read. Her solid, darkly handsome features were testaments to her inner strength and determination. Sitting next to her, he felt insubstantial.

"She said it was as if something inside you got unplugged. She told me things she'd never have mentioned if she'd been able to stop. She usually guards her privacy and yours so well. But she was out of control, and all this stuff kept pouring out. Son, you two aren't telling the same story."

The few bites he had eaten shifted uneasily in his stomach, and he pushed the plate back. "Give me an example."

"Well, okay." Her voice dropped. "But let's go in the den. Cover your plate with a napkin. Good, boy. You may want to come back to it later."

They sat, face-to-face, feet tucked under them, silent and staring at one another from opposite ends of the sofa. Thoughts of Brenan threatened to bring the early stirring in his genitalia to disgraceful maturity.

"Just like two Indians having a pow-wow." Indian-style was a natural posture which she attributed to Native American blood of centuries past still flowing strong in her veins. Somewhere back down the line an Iroquois and an Italian had been in the same woodpile. Owning only half her Native American ancestry, he sat thus, using the position to create many folds in his baggy sweats to augment the minimal restraint of his Jockeys.

Serve ya right if she notices that boner an' gives ya the granddaddy of all lectures. Who but a sicko would loll around his mama's house with a dick hard enough to crack walnuts?

"I hate to say it, but you look like something the cat didn't quite get covered up. And old—too old for me to be your mother." The silence was broken.

Sam ignored the comments of both Freida and Lefty. "You were going to tell me something about Brenan spilling her guts." His wife's name felt thick and cold in his mouth.

"Here goes. I stopped by the night before last to leave her some soup I'd made. With the kids at the motel with you, I knew she wouldn't cook. It was still early, but she was already in her jammies. Her hair was all messy like she'd been in bed, and she'd definitely been crying. I could have cried, myself. I don't know what's depressed her more—you or the baby. You, I think. She realizes she couldn't have prevented the baby's death, but she blames herself for you. Anyway, she wanted me to stay a while, so I took her into the kitchen and brewed her some hot tea. Mostly, I just sat and listened. I noticed she's chewed her nails down to the quick and keeps gnawing at them. When her fingers aren't in her mouth, she's twisting a lock of hair or spinning her wedding band around and around her finger." She halted and waited for him to say something.

He couldn't think of anything.

"You may not know, but a couple of days before that she started running fever again. She'd quit taking the antibiotic Riley gave her for the urinary tract infection. Mark raised Cain and got her on something stronger. He calls her every time a dose is due to remind her to take it. Can't remember to take the medicine she really needs, but I could swear she's taking too many of the pills for pain and rest. You know how depressed people do things they shouldn't because their judgment is off. She needs someone to watch over her."

"So, at least for now, she's better?"

"Physically. She asked about you. She doesn't need lies, so I admitted I'm worried. She wants me to make A. D. leave you alone. She's concerned that he's leaning too hard. If it means anything, he tries to get her to come to you." Pausing only to draw a hasty breath now and then, Freida ran on, "I see you haven't taken off your ring, either. Those bands are symbols of love and commitment between two people—not a paper marriage. They usually come off when the love is gone!"

He nodded. He'd never give up his wedding band.

"Anyway, she'd been misting up off and on, but then the real boohooing started—to say the very least! She asked what I thought. All I could say was that she ought to know more than me. She said she was more in the dark than anybody realized, that she'd never been more confused. Then she just fell apart. I don't know how else to describe it. She started saying that for months you'd been a polite stranger, showing no interest in her, not really talking except when you had to. She can't remember when it started, but for the most part, she blames Justin Kelsey's suicide—and, by the way, I agree. Then, whenever she could talk, she began describing in Technicolor the downward spiraling of your sexual performances."

Oh, shit!

The nausea raged back. A faint wheeze growled low—or was it fear clotting in his throat? His teeth clamped painfully shut. *"You're over the line now!"* he mentally shouted.

Her dark eyes were squinting and puzzled. "The things she told me doesn't fit—not if I'm to believe what you've said."

"I haven't said anything about—"

"No, I don't mean that. Both of you—oh, never mind. You can just squirm around. I wasn't exactly comfortable hearing a blow-by-blow account. Your wife had a lot pressing to get out, and you really ought to hear it from her. Then tell her what you're feeling, and figure out for yourself *what's what!*"

"Tell me what she said!"

Don't, Ace! Are ya losin' it? She'll really tell!

Her head dropped. She flexed her fingers and regarded them absently before touching the tip of one finger to her own wedding band. When she spoke, her words were directed at it. "You'll resent hearing it from me."

"I'm sorry I yelled, but I need to know."

She continued talking to her hands. "Very well, but don't get mad later on."

He nodded.

Here it comes!

"She said, a few months ago, you began to have difficulty making love. First you seemed to lose interest for weeks, then when you were with her, you took an unusually long time to—um, finish. She thinks you were only fulfilling a duty to her."

Told ya! Right off the bat!

He felt flushed. His stomach knotted. He didn't want to listen, but he had to. He had to know anything she could tell him about Brenan. "Go on."

Freida fumbled under the sofa for her box of sad-movie tissue. Her eyes were bright with tears, her pupils large. "After a few times like that, you weren't able to do it at all, so you stopped trying."

Sam looked at his hands now. "She told you I was impotent?"

"She specifically said you were impotent with *her.*"

"She thinks there's someone I'm not impotent with?"

"No, I think she knows that's not what's wrong, but in the beginning the possibility of another woman crossed her mind."

"There's no one else, and I don't believe she ever truly thought there might be. Either she's lying, or you've misunderstood."

"Sam, listen to me. I'm not doing this to save *my* marriage. To tell the truth, I'd rather be cleaning the toilet, but you said you wanted to hear it. Tell me what to do."

"Finish what you started."

"All right, but remember I'm just the messenger. She said—um, let me think a second—oh, yeah, she said you couldn't keep it up for her, but that you had no trouble whatsoever jacking-off into the rose bushes. That's pretty close to verbatim. Now, you decide if I've misunderstood, if she's lying, or just *who* doesn't understand."

53

A LIE! *NOT A LIE!* Not the truth, but not entirely a lie. How could he dispute the technicalities with his mother? He had no defense for his flimsy manhood, so she'd go on believing partial truths. His erection melted, and the throbbing moved upward to settle in his chest. The air in the room grew dense and rank. The liquid in his eyes made his mother's strong face go soft and blurry. "I don't know why she'd say—" He untangled his legs and got up. "Excuse me."

"Sam?"

In the bathroom, he vomited. He was surprised she didn't barge in. As a child, he'd never been permitted to be sick in private. She'd always been there, swabbing his face with a wet cloth, crooning reassuring mother-words. The stick-man scarecrow was in this bathroom mirror, too.

Sam sat on the edge of the tub and waited for a wave of dizziness to pass. So many things in his life were unfair. His weaknesses, his stupidity jinxed him. Never had he been free of confusion or doubt. He couldn't think of one plausible reason why his own mother hadn't deserted him decades ago. Still, she loyally kept trying to save him from himself.

When he'd regained a degree of composure, he washed his face, Listerined the bitter acid from his mouth, then trudged back to the den. Facing her took every scrap of courage he could marshal.

Freida looked empty and scared, too. She reached to take his hand, but he couldn't let her have it. Not now. He had to sit on his hands to settle the tremors. Worse, still, he had to hear the rest of Brenan's story. "Sorry. Your good food doesn't seem to be doing much for my stomach."

Time to go, Boss.

"Mama, I'd like you to start at the beginning and tell me everything Brenan said."

Fool! Ain't gonna like it, Ace. I don't like it!

Freida shrugged. "Stop me when you've heard enough." She slowly began recalling the intimate specifics of Brenan's tale.

Sam flinched, chewed his bottom lip, and tried to avert his eyes from her face but was unable to hold back regular injured and astonished glances. He fan-folded the excess material of his sweat shirt, inspected the weave of the upholstery. Each segment of the story was *partly* true. He wanted desperately to point out the inaccuracies, absolve himself in some small way. But she was miles ahead of him in the use of sexually unambiguous terms. Obviously fortified by parenthood, she looked him in the eye, when he'd let her, and spat out a litany. He could only shake his head in mute denial.

When she finally wound down, he was exhausted. He felt betrayed by the woman he loved and the mother who should never have become privy to his bedroom failures. Betrayal and shame. What he wanted to feel was hope. *If* Brenan had indeed said all those things and *believed* them, a chance for reconciliation existed, a chance they had been wrong about each other. *If*, an uncertain word. No real promise to it. Hadn't he been there?

"Sam?"

He flashed his gritty, stinging eyes at her to show he was listening and quickly returned them to the study of his left thumb.

"Sam?"

She wanted some kind of response. He didn't have one. How could she expect a man with an ounce of self-respect to endure this humiliating address and, afterward, discuss its strengths and frailties? What ugly mental portraits Brenan had painted in his mother's head! Her pathetic son caught dumping his misery into the shrubbery like a schoolboy, while his poor, rejected wife watched in humiliation and horror. A coward, choosing flight over fight.

A man don't get more pitiful than that.

"Sam?"

"What do you want me to say, Mama?" The anger in his voice startled him.

"Don't turn on me. Please. My interfering may seem like it's at an all time high, but for once, it was an accident on my part. Let me assure you I didn't get even the tiniest thrill out of Brenan's story nor from my passing it on to you. My interest here is *you!* When you're unhappy, how can I just sit back and do nothing? I've watched you hurt just about all I can for one lifetime. You deserve better! Why can't you let go of the pain and give yourself permission to be happy?"

He wasn't expected to answer, but he felt he owed her eye contact. He fought the need to look away, more so after the tears came back. The ache in his chest swelled down into his stomach, up into his throat. Over growing wheezes, he listened.

"From the beginning, the love between you and Brenan showed as plain as day. It still shows. You've come so undone you can't see it. Watching you fight your inner battles has clouded her vision, too. But to the rest of us, the love shows!"

"I don't deny my feelings for her."

"But you deny hers."

"Would I let myself hurt like this if she wanted me?"

She began another story angle. "This is what happened. You came across a child who was suffering the way you suffered. To you, his pain and yours were one and the same."

"We were talking about Brenan."

"That little boy killed himself as much in your presence as if he'd been in the bedroom with you. It was too much. You withdrew, and anyone who came near got shoved away. Even Brenan wasn't allowed to share your pain. Since she was five years old, she's brought every problem she's had to you. Suddenly, you're the issue, and she feels there's nowhere for her to turn."

"Justin was my problem. She was never beaten or molested—why should she be burdened with that kind of nastiness?"

"Justin was a part of you, and through you, a part of her. And while the hurt was still fresh, Karen breezed through. Your *first* wife. No threat, but did Brenan know? Here Karen is looking and acting like a different person and you offering her money to start a business. Brenan's raising a child that Karen gave birth to. Naturally, she felt a little threatened."

Sam's shoulders jerked. She was not going to use Karen against him. She was one subject he could respond to without reserve. He could hang defensive sentences together like pearls on a string. "Brenan is Mariah's legal mother. Karen has no claim to her! It was a one-time meeting! A few hours! Everybody's curiosity was satisfied, and Karen disappeared! Maybe Brenan was a little nervous, but she knew Rye only wanted one look. What child wouldn't?" He paused to think.

Seein' Karen after all these years mighta brought back some ugly memories! She's told ya how hard it used to be seein' ya with Karen. It WAS disgustin'. Makes ME sick to think about it. Ya know ya only let her move in to keep the other hyenas off ya, an' to take your mind off Brenan. An' then, 'cuz ya felt so bad usin' her like that, ya let her treat ya like dirt in front of ever'body. Most men who let women cleat 'em are madly in love. You were just plain pitiful. If seein' Karen sparked memories like that—coulda been repulsive enough to make your wife take a good close look at ya! Maybe, she didn't like what looked back!

Freida pulled a wad of tissue from the box and blew her nose. She sounded tired. "She says she loves you in words a child could understand. What more do you need?"

"You don't know everything!"

She *didn't.* She had Brenan telling her he was impotent and cruel. She didn't know the reason he couldn't make love to his wife. She could judge him all she wanted while that truth rotted inside him. All the truths were Brenan's, and for all her bedroom confessions, she wasn't giving up the ones he needed.

He closed his eyelids and found Brenan behind them. She stood as stiffly unyielding as she had been in his arms. Cold, wooden, transparently beautiful—but not really there at all.

"She needs you, son."

He opened his eyes and tried to laugh. His laughter sounded like weeping. He felt himself losing direction, losing control of some elusive, integral part of his character—the part that should have reminded him, "*This is your mother! You don't say these things to your mother!*" The strange laughter that leaked from his tightened lungs rapidly died, giving way to a ragged flux of words and sobbing that spewed from him with projectile force. He was powerless to do more than attend his own ravings.

"Whether it was Justin or Karen or me all by myself—I've lost her! It started months ago, and it ended the morning I gave up trying to get her back. All that's left is for us to work out some friendly terms for our kids. You think you have the whole story, but listen, anyway. She dropped me out of everything. She talked about the kids. She talked about her book. She talked about the weather! But she didn't talk to *me!* I hoped it was some temporary thing—hormones, the pregnancy—-*something!* I waited for her to get over it and come back to me!

"And the pregnancy. Can you imagine how much that hurt? I found papers from the doctor, and I waited for her to tell me! I waited weeks before I asked her why. Said she was waiting for the right time. Said I was too remote—whatever that means. I was thinking she was only a couple of months along and wondering who the hell had impregnated her. Couldn't have been me! Turned out she was pretty damned close to full term. If she truly didn't realize just how long she'd been pregnant, she could have told me when she *did* know—What was she afraid I'd do? She couldn't talk to me, but think about what she's managed to tell you. Some of it lies, too! Yes, Mama, Brenan really loves me!"

"Sam—"

"Give me some credit. I had to stop hurting her. I didn't know what I was doing wrong, but whatever it was hurt her! It hurt her a lot. I couldn't wait anymore for her to change back. It was too hard to sleep in the same bed and not touch her. I'd wait as long as I could, then I'd try, and every time, she just lay there waiting for me to be done with her! So I'd stop. I guess that where the misconstrued impotence comes in. Her feelings matter. She was willing, but she hated it. She'd go to bed as soon as the kids were down and pretend to be asleep when I'd come in, or she'd stay up all night in her office trying to make sure I didn't have many chances to come on to her! Must've been horrible for her. How do you think you'd feel about having sex with a man you didn't want?"

"I wouldn't do it. Not now. Not voluntarily." Her voice was a dry whisper. He didn't want her to look, and mercifully, she didn't.

"What if that man was your husband?"

"I went through that very thing before A. D. came along and showed me I didn't have to belong to anybody. I've never referred to Charles Smith as your father because I hated him and the way he treated me. He believed he owned me, and as his possession, I was to be available for his every whim. He never gave me a choice. Son, you're not like him. Brenan knows her wishes mean a great deal to you. I had to learn that no one owes sex to any other person. Brenan wasn't raised in the Dark Ages or in my father's house. She doesn't have to be taught self-respect. She wasn't playing the 'good little wife.' With you consistently pulling back, she didn't know you wanted her. During all that time, neither one of you spoke up and said what you really felt. Listen to yourself. What you're telling is not so very different from what Brenan said. One story from different points of view."

"All that sounds good, but it hurts too much to believe things are better than they are. The night before I left, I thought she felt better about us." He sighed bitterly. He'd come too far to stop. She only had one version of that night.

"She looked like she was asleep when I got to bed that night. Sleeping was hard for me. Had been for months. Always too much quiet. No distractions. Nothing to take the edge off the loneliness. All the bad thoughts and fears pushing and shoving at each other, each one trying to be thought first, each hoping to be the scariest. I can't describe how I hurt. I lay on my side of the bed in the dark. Then I felt her move close to me. It had been so long since she'd touched me. I thought she might still be asleep, that she might not know what she was doing, so for a while, I didn't even move. Then she asked if I wanted her." He held out empty hands. "At first, it felt like she was there with me. Then she started crying! Her whole body was shaking, her face all wet with tears! I was trying so hard, needing to please her, and she was sobbing like a baby! Letting me use her! Trying this time to play her part all the way! Doing what she was supposed to do—living up to what's in the fucking contract! But it was just too awful for her to keep up."

Sam brought his hands to his face. He wanted to cry into them, hide behind them, but he had to finish. He had to hear himself say it. "I went outside to try to figure out what I was going to do. Bawling like a little kid. Still, I wanted her! I wanted to understand! Every part of me ached! There was only one pain I could do something about. I didn't know— she shouldn't have been watching, and she shouldn't have told you!"

He dug his Beclovent out of his back pocket and used it.

"The next morning, before I left, I asked her what was wrong. All she'd say was that it was me. All me. I lost her. I lost a son. I almost lost Ben and Mariah. I don't have much left I can live without."

A stack of soggy tissue had collected on the sofa between them. He had fresh ones knotted in his hand.

"Did you ask why she was crying?"

"I didn't need to."

"You might have saved a lot of hard feelings if you had. I'm scared for you and the family you made. It's like I'm watching it die a slow, screaming death. If you don't do the right thing soon, you and I both will be occupying a penthouse suite at Bryce." She found a tissue and gave her nose one final blow. "I take that back. You and Bren will be the ones in lockup. I'm the sane one. I'll be here raising your kids. I just hope they lock you in the same room. Perhaps, then you'll talk."

The phone rang. "I'm a mother who knows what's what," she added as she reached for it. "Hello. —Yes, honey. — Of course, you may."

He felt Brenan before he heard her, even before his fingers found the phone. His testicles tightened. "Hello."

"It's me." The articulation was thin and timid, Brenan's voice diluted. "Your mama came by the other night. She mentioned you might want to talk. I thought you were going to stay a while yesterday, but—"

He looked for Freida, but she had left the room. He could hear her moving around the kitchen.

"Um, yeah, she told me she spent some time with you. I wanted to come back in the house, but I couldn't."

The earpiece was mute for a few seconds then the small voice came through. "You said if I needed you, I could call, so—"

After all he'd just gone through, his impossibly hopeful penis pulsed inside the folds of his clothes, giving full attention to the cherished voice on the other end of the line. "You should have known she'd tell. Why, Brenan? Why did you say all that stuff?"

Silence again. Then a whisper. "I didn't—it's just—I'm sorry—it's so hard. I've never been this alone before."

He'd never thought of her as being alone—not like he was alone.

"Sam?"

"What?"

"Hasn't this gone on long enough?"

He swallowed and ran his tongue over his lips. A seed of hope cracked open in his chest, germinating in spite of his willing it to die. "I'll come over."

He placed the humming receiver on the cushion next to him and used the last tissue in the box to swab his face. His hand slipped inside his pants to rearrange a clumsy bulge. It would show when he stood up, but he had scarier things to worry about.

"I GUESS I'LL GO." He stood behind Freida while she busied herself with things on the stove. He wanted to hug her, but since he couldn't, he tried an apology. "I'd like to be a better person, especially for you. The truth is I don't know how. I love you, Mama, and I'm sorry you got pulled into all this."

When she turned around, she was smiling, but her eyes were still brimful of tears. She finger-combed his hair back from his forehead and kissed his cheek. "I wish you knew the wonderful person you are. You'd kick the clutter out of your mind and allow yourself to accept the love that's given to you. I know you love me, even when you don't say it for a long time. I love you, too. So does your wife. And you deserve that love." She waited, but when he didn't reply, she asked, "You going now?"

"Yes. Does that make you feel better?" He'd started hoping. The seed had swollen and burst, its roots reaching through him, filling him with treacherous veins of hope.

She touched her fingers lightly to the spot she had kissed. "You need to eat. Don't you want to try again before you go?"

He shook his head.

"Then take these. For later." She loaded a stack of Tupperware containers and a foil-wrapped loaf of bread into his hands, then she held the door for him.

He knew better than to protest.

"There's more than enough for two," she said and touched his face again.

The strong, decisive lines of her face had returned.

54

S AM MULLED OVER LEAVING the Explorer in his mother's driveway and walking, but after a quick assessment of the brooding, indigo clouds, he decided to drive. Walking back in the rain was one misery he could forego.

After stashing the food containers on the back seat, he opened the driver's door and got in. He sat behind the wheel for a short time holding his keys, rattling them first in one hand, then the other, stalling. The hope that had soared only a moment ago was flagging, the fears skulking back. His foot slipped off the clutch and killed the engine twice before he got it running.

Weaving along the sloping curve of his parents' asphalt drive, he tried to disregard the hot streaks of pain that struck repeatedly through his abdomen and the harsh sound of his breathing. He strove to think only of the coming encounter, rehearsing in pantomime what he might say, lip-synced make-believe dialogue as he inched up to the steel gates of the eight-foot chain link fence—a major part of an elaborate security system he'd installed two years back, after the first of the threats to Brenan's well-being. Here, he braked and got out. The onerous fence with its close, thick-linked mesh camouflaged the details of the house and outbuildings. Only from the top of the far hill could the enclosed house and grounds be clearly seen from the outside. Standing on the rocks outside the mouth of the cave, one could look down as if peering into a box. Even that half-mile vantage point gave Sam movie-enhanced visions of scripture-drunk snipers sitting on those rocks, watching his family through the cross hairs of high powered, long-ranged weapons. Why hadn't he fenced in the whole hill? Who knew how far a fanatic would go?

Tell me, Lefty, who's the most likely to hurt her tonight?

Giving his lungs a chance to settle down, Sam slowly walked along the fence. The wind gusted, causing his sweat shirt to balloon and whip against his body.

The religious maniacs were out, armed with King James Versions, pocket-sized New Testaments, and, perhaps, more assailable weaponry. *Pulpits*, with its controversy and its success, had brought an onslaught of requests for appearances on talk shows and at workshops. Brenan had been obliged to hire a part-time secretary to coordinate and manage the business side of her writing. The devout nuts hadn't given up. The calls, though waning in frequency and fervor, kept coming.

Pulpits was in its sixth, maybe even seventh printing—Sam couldn't remember—and had been out in paperback close to a year. By Spring, Brenan, with the guidance of an experienced screenwriter, was slated to begin adapting the story for a TV miniseries.

The sudden notoriety had made things spooky for a while, thus the added measures to insure the safety of the household. Eight-foot fences, topped with coils of razor wire, had also gone up around his parents' and inlaws' homes, but they no longer felt the need to keep the gates closed and locked during the day. Brenan, who had been profoundly affected by the rush of menacing letters and street-corner confrontations with irate Christian soldiers, embraced the strength of high fences, locked gates, motion sensor lights and alarms. He was glad she kept using them.

He walked back, and before he had time to lose his nerve again, he thumbed the remote and leaped into the wagon. The gate swung smoothly open and closed automatically behind him.

On the back steps, Sam felt a stab of resentment. So many times this set of wide stone risers had been the gateway to home, where the living took place.

Not anymore, Ace. Just any ol' visitor, now.

He shook the sneering voice from his head, readjusted the stack of food containers to be held by one arm, and walked to the glass doors. Keaton and Mandel nuzzled close for a hasty pat and then trotted off as if that was all they expected. For an instant, he wondered if he ought to ring the doorbell, but since Brenan was expecting him, he let himself in.

He surveyed the family room, the stairs and foyer beyond, the closed door of Brenan's office, the open archway to the morning room. Empty. He made a circle around the staircase. The kitchen, dining room, foyer, the little alcove that served as an entrance to the master bedroom and as a nursery when the children were babies, before they were independent enough for rooms of their own.

Back in the family room, a fire burned low. Something A. D. had reported inched up into Sam's mind: *"Poor thing keeps a fire goin' for companionship. Stares into the flames as if she was starin' into the eyes of a lover. Wouldn't surprise me if I come up on her whisperin' sweet nothin's to it."* Freida had mentioned Brenan's comfort fire, too. Without analyzing the move, he laid on more wood.

Look! Lefty exclaimed.

Brenan came out of the bedroom wearing an ivory eyelet cotton peasant blouse with a loosely gathered cornflower blue skirt. The blue of the skirt was sprinkled with tiny pink and ivory flowers. She was barefoot and beautiful. Her appearance sent his state of arousal rocketing to new levels.

"I'll be right out." She padded back into the bedroom.

Oh, Ace! She dressed for ya!

The old-fashioned ensemble was the first clothing he'd bought for her without consulting Freida or Ellen first. On impulse, he'd bought it in Muscle Shoals during a Tennessee River fishing weekend with A. D. and Mark. As he awaited her return, images of that fated but memorable weekend, now three years in the past, climbed up into his head.

No time to mosey down memory lane. Ya gotta be ready when she gets back. Ready to charm her back into your arms.

Torrential rains had kept the three men off the river banks. Full of vim and restless energy, they'd spent the entire Saturday shopping. An indeed bizarre exercise for any one of them, the spree had burgeoned into an adventure. In the rain, they had gone from shop to shop, from market to mall, filling the camper shell on the back of A. D.'s old Ranger with an eccentric array of merchandise. The collection had run heavily to novelty items and big boy toys but was not neglectful of those family members waiting at home. They had eaten horrible, artery-clogging food and laughed at everything because everything had been funny. They had maxed out their Visa and Discover cards.

Stop woolgatherin'. She'll be back in a minute.

A. D. and Mark had decided three-year-old Benjamin needed a train set. No brightly colored toy on a pull string—a railroad line complete with depot, farms, fully-operational locomotive, dozens of cars, and miles of track. In the toy store, they had insisted on assembling the entire set for a trial run. A. D.'s imitation of a train whistle had raised the hair on Sam's arms. Embarrassed by the show of enthusiasm, he had wandered about the store, inspecting Barbies, bicycles, whole shelves of Fisher-Price toys, pretending he didn't know either one of them. At some point, the manager had reached his limit of their playful banter and sound effects and asked them to purchase the set or pack it back into the boxes. They had split the six hundred dollars worth of miniature railroad and accessories and whistled—*"Here, boy!"*—for Sam to help carry it out.

Any second now!

Sam regretted that he had not taken part in the acquisition of that first magical train set. The tremendous and lasting pleasure it had delivered to Ben would never be equaled.

Whatcha gonna say to her? Ya plannin' to talk toy trains?

Pleased with their purchases, the trio had gone home from the fishing trip on Saturday night without baiting the first hook. On the long, rainy drive, Sam had taken the wheel while the older men snored, A. D. with his mouth open and his head tilted over the back of the seat and Mark with his head slumped on A. D.'s shoulder. To drown them out, he'd tuned in the Grand Ole Opry on WSM out of Nashville—more static than music but rich in Old South ambiance. The day had been one of those great times that couldn't be explained to or appreciated by someone who hadn't been a part of the experience, the rare kind of day that came only when everyone had forgotten they existed.

Touchin' story, but we got a woman to woo! When she comes in call her somethin' cute an' sweet like "Precious" or "Pooky" like ya used to when ya was tryin' to make up to her for doin' somethin' stupid—or "Ohbaby" like ya used to in the sack during those last slow pulses when the afterglow wuz settin' in.

Sam wondered if Brenan had turned over memories of that night when she'd made the choice to wear the skirt and blouse. Could she have chosen them deliberately to spark his memory? Had she rehashed his waking her at two in the morning to give them to her? And what had happened afterward?

Ohbaby!

He'd been worn out from the fishing trip and the drive back. But if he'd craved sleep, waking her up was the last thing he should have done. She'd come at him like a starving animal, and an hour later, she'd tossed him aside like a gnawed bone. He pictured himself lying on his stomach, used-up and forgotten, fighting to stay awake while she festively tried on the clothes, tore through the other bags of unrelated merchandise, and admired her reflection in the mirrored walls of the bedroom. Ivory, blue, and a deep rose pink, her colors.

She reappeared, stopping a few steps into the room. The skirt's wide waistband was a little snug, but the overall picture of her thus dressed and in a pair of blue canvas slippers was stunning. From beneath the ragged bangs of her it's-supposed-to-look-like-*this* haircut, she peered timidly at him, eyes wide and her delicately curved lips set in docile blandness.

Ohbaby!

Freida had been right about the fluid retention. It created a slight blurring of Brenan's softly rounded facial features. She wore no makeup, never wore any at home. He preferred her natural sunny complexion, anyway, but he supposed the opinion of a husband, once removed, was no longer a factor.

"I let myself in. Hope that's all right."

She shrugged and walked to the couch.

"Ma sent food. It's in the kitchen."

Flashbacks of the sweat-suited scarecrow produced a self-consciousness that made him hurry to sit down. He needed to look good for her, but he was having a bad-body day.

She headed straight to her customary spot on the sectional while he scrambled for the last cushion on the other side.

The churning in his stomach heightened with the realization that he was perfectly set up for a final refusal by this woman who, not so long ago, had made his life wonderful and full of meaning. She could finish breaking him with a word. He hated her for this potentially volatile control, hated her for making him feel like a stranger in his home, and in spite of all that, he loved her beyond reason. All the love and hate in the world seemed to have come together to feed off him.

Gorgeous, ain't she, Hoss?

The calm was palpable. She would have to break it.

Remember how she feels in your arms? How she smells?

He remembered the feeling of her moving, fluid and feline beneath him, moaning softly to the beat of his thrusts.

History, Hoss. Ancient fuckin' history. The pun's over.

The clock in the foyer stuck twice. Two in the afternoon. Sam bit his bottom lip.

"What did Freida tell you?" Brenan finally asked.

Go easy.

"I doubt she left out anything. You didn't leave out much. I'm surprised you didn't call Jackie over to do illustrations." He couldn't reel in the needling statement, nor did he especially care. His taking the offense was justified. This was his last chance to recover a portion of his spent manhood. She had broken the code that protected the dignity of lovers—or lovers passé.

"I didn't think she'd—"

"You gave her a responsibility to fulfill, and no matter how good she's always been at interfering, it was hard for her to tell me what a sorry excuse for a man I am."

"What? I don't believe—"

Aw, Sam . . .

He slipped from offense into a pity-seeking mode. "She's my mother! *My mother!*"

"I'm sorry!" Her mouth twitched.

"You know her. She always means well, always intends to do what's best for her family. But do you realize what she's going to do about this? She's going to discuss it with A. D.—to see what he thinks. Then she'll get depressed and have to talk to Jackie or, worse yet, *your* mother! And so on! Couldn't you have ripped me apart some other way?"

"I said I'm sorry! What else can—"

"Well, as long as you're sorry, everything's fine!" He got up and stood facing the fire. The sweat pants didn't have front pockets, so he tucked his shaky hands into his armpits.

"I can't take it back." Her voice was soft and anxious. "I'll call and ask her not to talk about it anymore. There's not much else I—"

He spun around. "You could've told the truth!" He hadn't meant to do this.

Ya came here to TRY to get her back, Ace! That's all that got ya here! Put down your guns!

Tears pooled in her glassy eyes. "I know I shouldn't have talked, but I didn't lie. I was—oh, the only lies I've heard came from you! Not that you've told me anything! You've tried to make everybody think I ran you off! I asked you to stay. You might be surprised to find out how few of them believe you. Daddy, maybe, but tell me one other person who does!"

She's right. Her table's full, an' you're playin' solitaire. Your mama wanted to believe but couldn't pull it off.

Brenan's lips trembled. Tears flowed in steady streams.

He had never been able to abide her hurt crying. He walked to her and sat on the coffee table in front of her.

Do somethin', ya jerk!

"Aw, Bren." He tried to tame his voice. "I don't want to do this. I've never wanted you hurt. It just keeps happening. What went wrong between us? What did I do? What started it?"

"You left me. You left me a long time before you actually walked out the door." She swiftly whisked the droplets from her cheeks. Sam saw the chewed, angry-looking tips of her fingers. She'd bitten her nails before during stressful times, deadlines, the *Pulpits* threats, but never like this.

She dried them in the folds of the skirt as if the salty tears stung the raw nail beds.

"I don't understand. You told Ma I was the one who stopped caring. That's what she *said*. I can't begin to explain what it feels like to be me— to live apart from you because I'm not what you want anymore. It would've been so much better to have never had you at all." He blotted his eyes on his sleeve.

Brenan's brow crinkled with deep, bewildered lines. "I didn't want you to go. I asked you to stay so we'd have a chance to figure things out. You didn't even tell me what I did. I don't know if it would have made losing you easier, but it's my right to know. I keep wondering what you'd have said if I'd asked in the beginning—before it got so bad—but I couldn't! You were too strange even then."

Sam didn't trust himself to interpret. Could she be giving him a crack to crawl back through? How screwed-up could his mind have become?

"I made a big mistake about the baby. That's just one more thing I can't take back. I lost him! Don't you think that's punishment enough? Oh, I hate you for running out!"

As if to draw farther away, Brenan pressed herself into the cushions. Her voice dropped low, became less strained. "At the hospital, you cared! Surely, I didn't imagine it. I felt it so strong! You still have something for me. I don't know exactly what. It's love on some level—I hope. Sam, I need you here. I want to go back and be like we were before this horrible mess. If I thought it would work, I'd beg you to come back!"

Yes!

Instantly, he was beside her, holding her as she sobbed. Never mind the silences. The polite little games. The pregnancy she'd kept from him. The failed attempts at making love. The way she had cried that last night.

Your fault! Not hers! Hurry! Make promises! Tell her you didn't understand!

No. Too big a risk. Too soon. He had to preserve whatever emotional strength he had left. But as he held her tightly against him, lightly stroking her back, he couldn't stamp down a steady billowing of hope. His body shook with her weeping.

"I don't understand," he said. "You pushed me away."

"If I did, I didn't know."

He further gentled his voice. "Don't you get it? You don't have to say things you don't mean."

She pulled back to look at him. "All I did was try to stay out of your way. Tell me how I pushed."

His efforts to explain made no sense, even to him. "Just the way you acted," he concluded, "and the way you looked at me."

"What?"

He told her how unwanted he had felt.

"You can't put all that on me. Tell me when you sat down by me, talked to me. Have I forgotten?"

"I don't—"

"No you don't! Because it didn't happen. You ought to know by now if I hadn't wanted you to touch me, you wouldn't have!"

Ever thought of that?

"But you—"

She pulled back her arms, crossing them tightly over her breasts and lowering her face over them. "That last night, I came to you. I wanted you—but you couldn't."

"You were crying."

"You jerked yourself away from me like I was burning you!"

"Dammit, Bren, you were crying."

"What does that mean?"

"You were *crying!*"

"So? I cry. You used to make jokes about it."

"Not when we're making love!"

"Are you saying now you can't live with me because I cry?"

"Of course not!"

"Then what?"

"If it made you cry—"

"Those were tears of relief, Sam. I was happy, but then—" She hid her face in her hands and sobbed. "As soon as I started coming, you jerked out of me! You'd fulfilled your obligation, so you could quit! That hurt!"

"Ohgod!" he gasped.

"Why didn't you just tell me you didn't want me?"

"Bren, I—"

"I followed you. I saw what you did!" Her wintry voice gushed, ice water pouring over him. "You just kept on humiliating me!"

"OhgodBren!" Reality broke through. She was telling him he'd thrown her off as if his job had been finished—an unpleasant job. She had experienced the same elating hope followed by the same crushing rejection he had felt. Then he'd committed a final act that she had perceived as the utmost degradation.

"Can you imagine how I felt?" She was screaming now.

"I swear I didn't know!"

"Know what?"

"That you came."

"How could you not know?"

He held out empty hands. "At first I thought—"

"Don't say I rejected you!"

"Brenan—"

"You left *me!"*

"I didn't understand. Let me try to explain—"

Her voice dropped, and when his arms encircled her, she collapsed against him. "What about the other times, Sam? When I wasn't crying?"

"I wish I knew."

Tell her! Beg for mercy. Do somethin' right for once!

"You used to want me."

Tell her!

"There's something wrong with me that makes me incredibly dumb." Pulling her into his lap, holding her head to his shoulder, letting his fingers glide through her hair, he began to unravel his misconceptions. He explained his emotional march from doubt to dread to destruction. "I felt so useless. I suppose, without realizing it, I gave you all the responsibility for fixing me, and when you didn't, I decided you didn't care. And if you stopped caring, then I must not be worth caring about. That's as close to an explanation as I can get."

"You should have talked to me."

"But I couldn't. You were all I could think about. I was losing you and couldn't for the life of me figure out why. On top of all the emotional grief, my physical need for you has been burning holes in me. I thought if we could make love, we'd be okay. All those times, I tried so hard to make you *feel* me. You could have said no, and I wouldn't have bothered you."

"You believed I didn't want you?"

He nodded.

"If you'd known, you wouldn't have backed off?"

He shook his head.

"What about now? After all that's happened?"

"I'm dying without you."

"Then prove it."

"How?"

"Show me."

His breath became nearly impossible to draw, but asthma wasn't causing his distress. "Are you saying you want to make love?"

"Yes!"

Ya hear that, Ace?

Trembling, he put her down on the sofa, then dropping to his knees in front of her, he stared up into her face. "Is it all right? I forgot what Tristan said."

"He said ten days. It's been eleven."

He reached up and caught her chin in his hand. He needed her to say one more thing.

"Brenan?"

"What?"

"Do you love me? You said you hated me."

She slowly nodded. "You really can't tell? Look, Sam, love and hate are sometimes part of the same thing. Even when I hate you, I love you."

Ohbaby!

He stood and gathered her into his arms.

"Can you do it—no pushing me away, no stopping—even if I cry?"

"Oh, yes," he whispered as he carried her into the bedroom. *Ohbabybaby!*

He certainly could.

AND HE DID.

And she loved him—as she never had and as she always had, reaching into him, stroking his very essence. Cracking open and stripping away his armor, she returned to him, and he let go of all else but her. He loved her because, at last, he could, and without a breach or parting, he loved her again. Then he lay with her, their whispered words reaffirming a commitment that had suffered. The words flowed in smooth, painless currents, full of hope and promise. They got all the way in.

When words were no longer needed, they slept.

And awakened.

And he took her once more.

When the gentle rhythms of their loving slowed, he knew the rejoining was complete. The tenderness and warmth passing between them were the only truths that mattered.

The healing had begun.

THE CLOCK IN THE FOYER struck four. Rain splashed the roof in cold, repeating waves. Thunder grumbled above the valley. An occasional flash of lightning threw a flicker of brightness into the bedroom. Otherwise, the room was darkened by the gloom of the afternoon storm.

Motionless, he floated in relief and happiness. He knew she was aware of neither the darkness nor the rain. She slept, he imagined, seeking the strength her love for him demanded. In her sleep, she snuggled into the arc his body formed around her. A perfect fit. Two fragments curved and curled into a whole, one indistinguishable from the other.

PART FIVE

Sam's Heart

Well I declare! Sharon thought with pure disgust. *Just lookit that red face an' them wild eyes! I've seen that very same look on Charley lotsa times—always right 'fore he blows his jism. Why, that fat ol' preacher's a-gittin' off on all this hooey—all this hoppin' up an' down on one foot then t'other, a-slappin' that Bible agin his leg! Mama needn't think she'll be a-gittin' me back here fer another one a-these beatin'-off sermon preachin's. That Brother Travis's got his Bible jist like Charley's got his Penthouse. What's the difference? Don't neither one a-them do nuthin' fer me.*

EXCERPT FROM *Pulpits* BY
BRENAN ARMSTRONG MACCAULEY, 1989

55

February 1992

TRAILING LONG SMEARS of silver and violet, the sun succumbed to the shaggy arms of the pines, the bony fingers of leafless oak and gum. Sam, stalling, hands in his pockets, monitored the deepening shadows through the panes of his parents' seldom-used front door. Behind him, A. D., Freida, and Brenan skillfully produced small talk designed to stave off his discomfiture. Quality small talk, no awkward casting about of meaningless drivel—a truly amazing talent from Sam's point of view. Living with him had given them ample practice. Though grateful for their efforts, he felt like a cross between a kid on his way to the principal's office and a specimen under a microscope.

This evening's get-together was to be a surgical probing into the mystery and taboo of his mind. Or his heart? His soul? First to Brenan and then to Dr. Maurice "Call me Maury" LaFayette, he'd excruciatingly put his feelings of helplessness into words. He had mentioned the unmentionable and waited for judgment. Gradually, speaking and questioning had become less intimidating, and Maury, aside from his psychological dictum and slang, was turning out to be okay.

Maury called the task at hand "Exploring and Confronting." "E and C" were either the third and fourth or fourth and fifth rungs of the *Recovery Ladder*. Sam didn't care for the analogy; therefore, he often lost his place on the *Ladder*.

"Fact and fallacy must be separated so that you only have to deal with the

bare truth. Fear, regret, and guilt tend to recreate reality, especially as you grow into adulthood. This process keeps the wound open and festering indefinitely. If you can go back all the way and take a good look, you'll likely be able to let go of the health-impeding emotions."

The speech, orchestrated to gain Sam's approval for therapy utilizing hypnosis and regression, had received an enthusiastic nod from Brenan that succinctly overrode any personal misgivings. Now, six weeks into it, the going was slow and monotonous, and though Brenan's confidence continued to run high, the progress was impossible for Sam to judge.

Taking a deep, steeling breath, he faced his family.

The conversation glided to a graceful end. The resulting silence was an implied starting place for him. The eagerness in his parents' eyes belied the offhand casualty they'd tried to propagate. Long ago, they had pledged themselves to his protection and salvation, and even with all the setbacks, they'd never relented. They wouldn't quit as long as success was still out there somewhere. Appreciative that he could still bring his troubles home, he walked toward them.

Brenan sat on the floor a little to the side of the sofa. Her knees pulled tightly to her chest, she leaned back on A. D.'s threadbare recliner. In the beginning of their relationship, he'd told her what he'd remembered. He hadn't deliberately held anything back, but he hadn't known how to share the feelings. Instead, over the years, he'd unconsciously shown them through his overprotection, his possessiveness, his intensity. He knew now she'd been a part of his pain all along, and his attempts to keep her separate had only potentiated the hurt.

For a moment, he stared into her eyes. Her determination and love were as real and solid as any object in the room. She fought with him and for him—and when necessary, she fought *him*.

The nightmare had ignored the reconciliation. Brenan had consequently witnessed its full potency, heard him cry out, felt the bed move with his thrashing. Numerous nights, she had thrown herself over his body, shielding him until normal sleep came. In her pursuit of relief for him and for the fear he had established in her, she'd found Maury. "People do it all the time, Sam. They go back and find the truth that somehow got covered up. It may hurt more in the beginning, but facing it and forgiving yourself could make life a lot more comfortable." After a couple of weeks of long walks, he'd assented.

She smiled sweetly and raised a confident thumb. He lifted his chin, an unspoken acknowledgment, swallowed hard, and turned to his parents. Waiting for him to open the conversation, A. D. flipped over an empty palm, and Freida raised a curious brow.

Sam cleared his throat. "Well, Ma, I remember when you were the resident psychologist."

She frowned. "And that's changed?"

"Guess not. You're still getting business." While many people embraced the anonymity and distance offered by a cool, paid-to-care outsider, Sam valued the familiar.

"For now, I'm only your mama. What is it you need?"

"A mother's memories dating back to the summer of '65." He didn't see anyone flinch.

His parents hadn't asked the kind of questions Dr. Collins had asked. *"Did anything Ralph did to you feel nice? If you knew you wouldn't be beaten, is there any part you'd like to do again? Do you touch yourself, Sam? Do you know what orgasm is? You don't have to be ashamed. Sexual pleasure and curiosity are normal—even in children. We all have those feelings. Now, isn't there something you'd like to tell me?"*

"He hurt me!" Sam had screamed. Dr. Collins hadn't wanted the truth, but his parents had believed Sam. Now, here they sat, side by side, touching at the shoulder, serious and waiting, emanating a tremendous love. Braced to endure once more. Primed to invest whatever emotional energy was required. As concerned for the adult son as they had been for the little boy.

Sam coughed, bent forward in his chair, mentally promising this to be the last time. No more rehashing. "I remember coming out of Peterson's Store . . . "

He didn't remind them that not so long ago he had almost lost his family. He didn't bring up names—Justin, Karen, Bud, DeLane, Owen. His life was a series of passages in an open book. They knew him better than he knew himself. They would start with Russett Bridge Road and help him connect the dots until the crimes against him were yoked. A picture would form.

" . . . and starting home." Quickly, he gave them the memory scraps he'd held onto, then he held out empty hands. "So . . . "

He watched Freida's hand feel its way into A. D.'s. To give or receive strength? "I'm the one who let you go."

Sam squeezed his eyes shut and prayed she wouldn't cry.

"No." The word was spoken with finality, a command to be obeyed. "Nosirree," A. D. repeated. "We're gonna tell this like a story—beginnin' to end. Don't be slappin' guilt around like mayonnaise on a sandwich. We've all gotta do a better job livin' with what we can't change. Ain't that what this is all about?"

She cleared her throat and nodded, thus appointing A. D. spokesman. He waved a finger at her and then Sam. "You didn't do nothin' wrong. It's time you started believin' it."

Sam nodded. He was trying. He had always tried.

"We never liked you kids walkin' on that road. Mostly we worried you'd get run over by some hot-roddin' . . . "

The outline of a canister of Beclovent stood out through the fabric of Sam's shirt pocket. He ran his fingers lightly over the bulge and leaned closer, his elbows resting over the spread of his knees. He felt a vague spark of alarm during one fleeting instant of eye contact with Brenan. Then for the better part of an hour, he was okay.

" . . . marks on your body told a lot of the story. Looked like he tried to rip you apart with his hands, but for a while all that had to take a back seat. You were *alive*. We were selfish. What mattered most was . . . "

Sam used the inhaler once and aborted an asthma attack before it could gain momentum.

" . . . tellin' each other all these years you needed to face up to the whole truth, but we had that quack Collins sayin' . . . "

Freida blew her nose too often but sat stolid beside him. A. D. glanced at her for a reaction. She shrugged her shoulders and told him to go on. "You're doing fine."

Brenan got up and moved to Sam. She sat back down on the floor between his knees, leaning her head against his crotch.

" . . . wouldn't answer nothin' Collins asked, an' what we learned had to be dragged out of you. You thought we'd blame you or stop lovin' you, I guess, an' I don't see that we ever completely convinced you different."

"I knew you didn't blame me." It was the first time Sam had interrupted. "And if I blamed myself, I didn't realize. The scars and the nightmare—I blamed the man who caused them."

"You blamed all of us plenty. We were supposed to keep bad things from happenin' to you. Parents are protectors. They're supposed to work miracles, do the impossible."

"No."

"Can't you see it's all right?"

"No. Justin's mother could have saved him, but you couldn't get to me."

A. D.'s eyes were round and glistening. "Even as a child, you hated lies. You'd tell the truth even if it got you in trouble. Most of the time, that was a good thing. When the truth was too painful, instead of lying, you blocked it out. That's where the trouble comes in."

"I accept that." The wheezing returned. "I can't even face up to it in my sleep. I wake up knowing I've just been through it again, but I can't remember what *it* is. When Justin told me what he was going through, I couldn't even visualize a man doing such disgusting things."

A. D. shrugged sadly.

"I keep thinking about the child abuse story that prompted Justin to call. Every interview, every case I researched made me feel sick, but I didn't relate any of it directly to me. During the interviews and articles and when I was listening to Justin, I must have heard descriptions of the very things I've repressed." His words were croaks between wheezes.

"It caused your asthma." The conviction in A. D.'s voice was strong. Freida nodded to show she agreed. Brenan tipped her head back to look up at him.

"You were wheezing when I picked you up at the Sheriff's office. The first major attacks came with nightmares in which you was relivin'—I don't even know what to call it—oral and anal rape, sodomy, I guess."

Sam felt the lines his face tighten. He stared down at the top of Brenan's head. He touched her hair. The stridor grew stronger, louder. "I told you that?"

"In the beginnin' you described it real plain. Bein' kicked an' beaten. Him threatenin' to cut off your tongue or your penis if you didn't do what he wanted. But soon you'd only say he did *things* to you, made you do them, made the woman do them. *Things.* We didn't know psychology, didn't push. We didn't know the importance of talkin' or rememberin', so we let you forget. We wanted to forget. As much as I suspected it was wrong, *I* let you forget. Bein' sorry don't do a lot of good—"

"Stop." Sam compressed the atomizer and held his breath to contain the medicine. After he let it go, he said, "You made the no-guilt rule."

A fine beading of perspiration dotted A. D.'s face. "Listen, son. One act of rape ain't no different from another in its badness. You endured 'em all. Most of 'em left marks on your body. The worst thing I think I ever saw in my whole life was a pattern of small bruises on the back of your head an' neck—ten of them, Sam. *Ten* bruises caused by fingers clamped around your head. The bastard's thumb prints were pressed into your temples! He used his hands like a *vice!*"

Sam slumped. Every expiration sounded like the creak of un-oiled hinges. He shook his head. How could he have forgotten?

"You always woke up from a nightmare with an asthma attack. You only have them when you feel threatened or have to deal with stress. Listen to you now. You must unconsciously link every bad thing in your life to that sonofabitch. Sommers an' the asthma go together. He almost choked you to death back then, an' sometimes, in the nightmare, he still tries."

Sam pulled himself straight in the chair and watched Freida go into the kitchen then return with one of the pre-filled disposable syringes Mark kept prepared for severe attacks. She put the syringe and a sterile-wrapped alcohol pad on the table beside him and raised her eyebrows. He made a face to show he didn't want the epinephrine, but he knew if his lungs became much tighter, he'd give in.

Freida left again, disappearing into the utility room. This time she brought out a small stack of neatly folded clothing. "These have been in my trunk of keepsakes close to twenty-seven years. This morning I decided you should see them, so I washed out the mothballs. There are other things in there you're not ready for yet, but—" She sat, took an item from the bundle, shook out the folds. "See how small? If you look at the inseams, you'll find bloodstains that didn't wash out."

Sam glanced then turned his head. "Why did you keep them?"

"For you. Do you believe anyone small enough to wear these could defend himself against a two-hundred-pound man?"

Sam shrugged. "Of course not, but—"

"But what, Sam?" she asked.

"If I'd minded you, it wouldn't have happened at all. That part was my fault."

A. D. opened his mouth to protest more blame-taking, but Sam quickly switched directions. "This fear used to lurk in the back of my mind. It wasn't even possible, but it scared me just the same. I guess, it still does."

"What's that?" asked Freida.

Sam placed his hands lightly on Brenan's shoulders. "That he could come back. I'm older than he was when he died, and yet, I'm afraid one morning I'll open my eyes to find him sitting on the edge of the bed—smelling like grease and spoiled meat. I'm a grown man who's afraid to turn corners because a monster from childhood might be waiting."

Mental pictures began to form piecemeal as he listened to his own unexpected admission. Ralph Sommers's small, deep-set eyes, open and staring out of doughy sockets, challenging and full of dark humor. Cruel lips, twisted and bloody, silently sneering. Debra Jean's hair matted with blood. Blood on white sheets and gloved hands. Everywhere, blood and gore. Mark angry and shouting. A. D. frantic, reaching, pleading. Sam looked at his hands and saw them swaddled in bloody gauze. The air in his lungs became solid and immovable.

The forms of his wife and parents moved around him in a blurring mist. A needle bit the flesh of his arm. Though the air was softening, converting back to gaseous form, too much stayed in his lungs. He couldn't force enough out before his lungs strove to take in more. He hadn't had an attack like this since—when? The date on the syringes usually lapsed, and they had to be replaced with new ones. He willed himself to push air in and out, willed his vision to clear. Slowly, he pulled back the materiality of his family and the room.

Brenan perched protectively on the arm of his chair. His mother and father sat forward on the sofa.

"Something happened at the hospital." Neither a question nor a statement.

For a moment, no one reacted. Bloody visions floated in and out of Sam's head, but they no longer hampered his breathing. Ralph Sommers *had* come back—at least once.

Brenan excitedly jumped to her feet and faced him. "You mean there was more?" Before he could respond, she turned to his parents. "How much can a kid live through?"

A. D. cut his eyes toward Freida. "Hon, why don't you an' Brenan—" He tipped his head toward the door. "It might be better."

While Brenan, angry and breathing hard, waited for someone to acknowledge her consternation, Freida rose, pushed the bundle of clothes into Sam's hands, and took her daughter-in-law's arm. "Yeah, honey, let's go see if Ellen needs some help with that string quilt she's trying to get the hang of."

At the door, they both looked back. Sam could see Brenan didn't want to go, but he waved her on. "It's okay."

He dropped the clothes on the floor by his chair. His hands felt dirty.

56

THE LITTLE PILE of clothes on the floor tugged at his eyes. A pair of kid's scuffed-toed sneakers poked out from under a time-yellowed tee-shirt. Ralph's. That shirt had been worn by an animal before it had temporarily concealed wounds inflicted by the animal. Sam's shirt had had orange and blue stripes. It had been ripped off him and used to wipe up a puddle he'd vomited on the floorboard of an old car. Funny, little details kept sprouting while the big ones stayed buried.

He kicked the shirt off the pile and cringed at the sight of dingy, once-white underpants and shoes no more than eight inches long. The jeans, faded white at the knees, lay sprawled to the side. They were smaller than Mariah's, nearly small enough for Ben. *His* things. *Things* he'd worn. On the day the old station wagon had rolled into his life, he'd been only slightly bigger than his six-year-old son. He tried to appear detached, indifferent, as he picked up one of the shoes, turned it over in his hands, ran his fingers over the brittle, grayed laces. "Keds," he whispered.

"From that little shoe store at Five Points. Keds for you. Red Goose for Jackie. An' those oxblood penny loafers you both wore to school."

"Those were Buster Browns, I think. Mama would pout because you wouldn't try on shoes." He smiled. He was relieved that he no longer had to fight for breath.

"When I needed shoes, I did. Never had more'n two feet, did I? Work boots an' black lace-ups was all I needed. I wore those stupid red plaid slip-ons in the house just for her."

"But you'd run put your boots on when there was a knock at the door." Dropping the shoe, he gave his full attention to his father. "Took to Nikes well enough after we nagged you into your first pair, huh?"

Those sage, creamed-coffee eyes. When working the haying or the harvest or just taking a walk in the sun, Sam had seen those eyes masquerade as gold and green, but indoors they were always a warm, creamy brown. After the heart attack, A. D. had lain on his back in an intensive care cubicle, his chest and head raised a prescribed thirty degrees. Above the tangle of oxygen prongs, subclavian lines, and monitor leads, his eyes had remained closed for long intervals. Sam had stood between his mother and sister, staring down in terror on the closed lids and bloodless face. Then came the surgery that had split open the chest, cracked the breastbone in half, transferred blood vessels from thigh to heart. All the while, Sam had lived, with the oppressive fear of death in constant attendance, for those eyes to open. And at last, they had. He loved those eyes, the thick black brows that sheltered them, the strength and goodness of the man behind them.

The smothering further relented. He felt no fear of another episode as his mind continued to heed old questions as if hearing them for the first time. The answers, seeming as foreign as slices of someone else's life, continued to come, single-filing in, dragging others along behind them. The gaps were filling.

A. D. held up the empty syringe. "Been a quarter century since I gave you the first one of these. Still amazes me I can do it. Don't look at me like that. I'm gonna tell you what you wanna know, but first I'm gonna get us some hot coffee."

Sam didn't argue. Lefty bubbled up to fill the silence of A. D.'s absence. *It's all down here, Ace. Heaps an' heaps of ugly. Mounds of stink. Yessirree. It's ALL here!*

He would look. If he couldn't see it all today, then soon. He felt young, inexperienced, and breakable, unfit to process what he might find. The earthy, rudely outspoken Lefty could always see, recognize, and deal with more. But Lefty, only a component of Sam's shattered ego, a separateness incapable of mainstreaming with the other elements, kept secrets.

Boy howdy, it's deep! Lotsa buried trash! I see it. Always could—if I looked. I'm lookin' now. Yuck! Your turn! Do it right. See it for what it is. Water under the bridge. Yesterday's news. Then shovel it out like blowfly stable muck.

Sam nodded then shifted around to make sure A. D. hadn't caught him responding to thin air.

You was like any old thing to Ralph. He didn't care that ya couldn't breathe. Debra Jean kept on beggin' "He's had enough!" but all he cared about was pain. Pain turned him on.

Closing his eyes, Sam assembled a composite, one feature at a time, of the man who had hurt him. A black and white two-dimensional face on a wanted poster. Front and then profile.

Got off big time on torture. Pain an' cryin' an' fear excited 'im. He's dust, but he still makes ya sick an' crazy. Can't go on lettin' a corpse rape ya ever' time ya go to sleep. Are ya hearing? His dick is dirt! Keep on at the real problem.

"What is the problem? An old memory? A lost memory?"

No! Guilt! You're eat up with it! Been totin' 'round blame that ain't even yours! Ain't that somethin'? Ain't got nuthin to do with beatin' or rape or ropes. It's for bein' alone on the side of the road! Blamed yourself for the hurtin' your family went through an' all the while thinkin' maybe ya deserved what ya got. A little kid, scrawny, immature youngun who thought an' acted like a nine-year-old! Real kicker is ya ain't learned much since or you'da shed that guilt! Your body grew, an' your mind grew—all but one little piece—a strong, stubborn little piece that bullies all the other pieces.

A. D. put a mug of perfectly lightened coffee on an end table next to Sam and carried another to the sofa.

Here comes the scariest part of the nightmare. Just tell yourself you're ready an' glad it's finally comin'.

Sam picked up the steaming mug. Coffee usually helped ease the asthma. The caffeine and the steam. Over the rim of the mug, he examined his father's face. Through the steam, it looked younger, the lines air-brushed to smoothness. "I give," he said softly as he caught the flash of A. D.'s small, easy smile.

"You're already lookin' a mite on the relieved side."

Sam shrugged. Maybe it was relief he felt. The dread had definitely gone thin.

Here comes old news. A stain that came out in the wash. A dried up mud hole. Ain't real no more!

"Evidently, you've recalled some of it."

"Just flashes. Ralph and Deb swaddled in bloody sheets."

"Ambulance brought 'em to Northside. Both near-dead but hangin' on. You were in the corner of one of those long wards made to hold a half-dozen emergency patients. Somebody rolled Ralph right in next to you. I turned around an' saw more blood than I thought a human could hold, an' it was still gushin' out of 'im. The bastard was wide-eyed an' lookin' around."

An' grinnin' all black an' slimy—just like by the road.

"When you saw 'im, it took me, Mark, an' two orderlies to hold you. Seemed like you were tryin' to bust a hole through the wall behind you to get away from 'im."

Sounded like a kid blowin' through a straw into his milk glass—blood gurglin' out a hole in his neck, but his eyes were on you, Ace.

"You got loose an' ran out in the hall smack dab into the woman's stretcher. There was blood all over her, too. She was unconscious, an' a nurse was holding a towel to her head to stop the bleedin'."

Ya thought Ralph got her for tryin' to help ya! Now, he'd finish ya both!

"You just sorta froze up for a few seconds, then you started climbin' on the stretcher with her, tryin' to get her to wake up an' run with you."

"Wake up, Deb! He's here! Gotta get away! Please, Deb! He's HERE!"

"Somebody finally got you pulled off an' gave you to me so they could go back to workin' on her. Mark got Sommers's body out before I carried you back. Still you fought like a tiger, pointin' at the spot where the stretcher had been. He was stone dead by then, but you couldn't be convinced."

"I'd seen blood on him before. My blood. Maybe not like that but—"

A. D. bobbed his head. He closed his eyes, squeezing out an unexpected spate of tears. "Death was too good for 'im."

"I didn't believe he *could* die. For a long time, I thought all of you were lying so I wouldn't be afraid. I expected him to come for me." He felt beat after beat of emotion slam into him. Ralph hadn't died in the garage. He'd lived long enough to get in one more assault. Sam's memory came alive with depth and color. The exact tint and shade of the sunken eyes that had raided a thousand nights' sleep. The cruel mouth contorting tortuously to form a final violation.

"Ralph said something to me, didn't he?"

A. D. sighed. "An' to me."

"What?"

"I can still hear every word like it was yesterday. He said, 'I broke 'im in for you, MacCauley, but he won't forget who fucked 'im first.' Then I think he tried to wink an' said, 'Ain't that right, Sambo?'"

"WHY ARE YOU CRYING?" Outside, the world was dark and the air had turned cold, but the need to escape walls and doors had sent the two men into the night. In nearly identical down jackets, they sat, backs to the wind, on a fieldstone garden wall they had erected together. The coolness eased the last traces of constriction in Sam's bronchial tubes.

"I wanted to make you feel safe. A father ought to be able to do that much."

"Whenever I was with you, I *was* safe." Sam touched a tear that slid down his father's face. "Cut this out. You were terrific then, and you still are. I wouldn't dredge it all back up, but I've got to get over it somehow."

"I hope you're convinced we never blamed you. We spent days believin'—knowin'—you were dead. No way I can describe it. Gettin' you back was a miracle. Can't describe that feelin', either. We played by ear an' made mistakes. Lately, all the many kinds of child abuse have made the priority list. Adults are goin' for counselin', joinin' support groups, readin' books, goin' on talk shows, workin' to get their lives back. You need more'n me, Freida, an' Brenan can give. You're finally doin' right. Just don't expect that LaFayette guy to care like we do."

Sam smiled now. "I haven't been able to hold up my end, but you and

Mama never fail—even though you keep having to do more. Without you, I'd have lost everything. Brenan loves me, but I need her to tell me ten times a day, and after what I did to them, Ben and Mariah need the same thing from me."

"You need to see yourself worthy of Brenan's love."

"As long as I can't grow up and be the man she needs, I'm not worthy of her."

A. D. found his handkerchief and loudly blew his nose. "I don't want to debate, son, but I'd like us to make a deal. You're pretty good at keepin' promises. Until you get what you're searchin' for, keep tellin' Brenan what you feel, and come to us when you need to. Your wife an' kids are too precious to be careless with. You already know what life without 'em is like. Love 'em, take care of 'em, let 'em love you, an' please, promise me you'll put some effort into loving yourself."

Sam tried to look confident when he nodded. He almost lost his balance when A. D. clapped him firmly on the back.

"Do all that, an' someday, I'll take you fishin'."

BRENAN AND FREIDA found Sam asleep on the rug in front of the hearth and A. D. snoring in his recliner. Exchanging a questioning frown with her mother-in-law, Brenan shook her head. Peaceful slumber was not what she'd expected. Near the door, a paper grocery bag had been filled, its top folded neatly closed. She didn't have to look inside to know its contents.

"Up, Ace." She nudged him with the toe of her running shoe. "That's it. Stand up. Daddy will be home with the kids soon. It's time for the rink to close." An atmosphere of serenity had given the room a just-like-any-old-evening feel.

When he was on his feet, rubbing his eyes and yawning, she held his jacket open. "Put your arm in here. No, that one first. Good." She turned to wave a good-bye to Freida and pushed Sam gently in front of her.

He allowed her to guide him around the furniture to the door, stopping only to pick up the bag and tuck it under his arm.

57

THERE'S TWO OF 'EM," the gas station attendant who'd given the final directions had shared. "Sisters, I reckon. You that newsman, aintja? Gonna put them little ladies on the boob tube or somethin'?" "No" was as detailed an answer as the attendant would get—and a perfunctory "thanks" for the directions.

Sisters? Had he driven a hundred-and-fifty-mile goose chase on a March Sunday? What hard evidence did he have? Initials, a last name she might not use anymore, a piece of address in a phone directory. A surreptitious call to a colleague who ran a weekly community newspaper within the same phone exchange. A handful of hastily researched maybes. He might have taken more time to verify his findings, but he wanted to see her *now*.

Crossing his fingers over the steering wheel, Sam parked the Explorer behind a clean white T-bird in a jonquil-lined driveway. In five or six strides, his blue-jeaned legs covered the distance to the bottom doorstep. The house was a neat, shrub-trimmed brick square with a poured-concrete stoop. He paused to zip his blue and white nylon jacket. The breeze that puffed out of the west was light but chilling. He wavered a little, wondering if he was doing the right thing. Of late, the conviction that finding peace meant finding her had become strong. Pushing uncertainty aside, he ascended the steps and knocked.

The door eased open. The right place after all. He watched the weight of recognition settle on her face. He attempted an uncomplicated smile to put her at ease and show his intentions to be benign.

No shock or dismay clouded her expression—only mild curiosity.

Silver highlights frosted her short, loosely curled brown hair. Time had sanded the scar on her temple to near smoothness. In neatly creased slacks, a pullover appliqued with a glittery sunburst, suede oxfords, wire-rimmed eyeglasses, she could have passed for one of the ladies Freida and Ellen invited for brunch in order to catch up on gossip and extort recipes. The breeze carried a faint aura of sweet musk oil.

He waited, wanting her to go first.

After a moment, the corners of her mouth twitched up, and her bright eyes widened. A handsome woman with an air of simple dignity. "Well, I do declare." She held the old-fashioned scrolled screen door open with her right hand. The left one floated up to her mouth.

"I would have called ahead," he explained, gesturing with empty hands, "but I wasn't sure I'd found you. You might've told me not to come."

The hand that covered her mouth drifted to the sleeve of his jacket. It came down so gently onto the fabric, he scarcely felt the feathery touch on his arm before she carried it back to her mouth. A little surprise but no genuine alarm. Her words, spoken in a light, flowing drawl, chimed with sincerity. "I haven't been any place in the last twenty-six years that didn't have a little space left over for you. In some little way or another, you were always there and welcome."

He understood and nodded. While the wintry breeze riffled his hair, his eyes and his heart filled up with her. Though he hadn't known until this instant, she'd been with him, too.

She took her hand from her mouth again and held it out. "You don't have to stand there shivering. Come in where it's warm." Taking his arm, she led through a tiny mirrored foyer with brass sconces and into a sitting room.

The room was a quilted paradise. Curtains, cushions, upholstery covers, throw rugs on the gleaming hardwood floor, all quilted patchwork in shades of rose, aqua, and beige. A room Brenan would have loved. A Dutch Girl quilt graced the wall above a winged loveseat. Sam knew the pattern well. Over the years, Freida and Ellen had made Dutch Girl and Boy quilts for everyone inside their circle of family and friends.

He'd slept under one most of his life. He also recognized a Nine-Diamond custom fitted to twin ottomans, an Eastern Star upholstering an easy chair, and a Double Wedding Ring on another wall. He couldn't resist leaning close to the nearest chair to verify the quilting had been done by hand. Through the various forms of artistry in his own family, he'd come to treasure hand-crafted work. The stitches were tiny and uniform but clearly hand sewn.

"My friend, Marion, and me—we enjoy needle work. Passes the time and gives us something pretty to look at when we're through. I guess, we overdo it a little."

Dark, polished paneling and a mirror-topped upright piano show-cased the bright quilted fabrics. Clear glass figurines of forest animals ruled over dinner-plate-sized tabletops and quarter-round corner shelves. A room in a storybook cottage.

"It's beautiful," he gestured with his eyes. "All of it."

She let go of his arm and pointed to the easy chair. "Please have a seat. I've got coffee hot."

The soft chair tried to swallow him. He almost turned down the coffee, but remembering he had once been afraid to accept food and drink from her, he said, "Coffee would be great."

"Cream and sugar?"

"Cream, thanks."

While he awaited her return, he perused the room. There were no photographs. Every room in his mother's house had family faces smiling through rectangles and ovals of glass. Freida had chronicled his life, Jackie's, those of her grandchildren from birth to the present on her walls. She'd found space for Brenan, Robert, and a mix of relatives and friends along with a dozen of Jackie's painted homescapes. His own home was a Mariah and Ben gallery. Without pictures, this room, though lovely and warm, gave off an air of loneliness, a hollowness only a child's clutter and fingerprint smudges—and pictures—could dispel.

He knew so little about this woman. How could he ask questions? How could he expect her to answer?

She put a cup and saucer on a near table and sat down on the sofa.

Steam, like streams of wood smoke, rose from the cup.

"Why'd you come, Sam?" Her eyes were wide and curious.

"I don't know." He took a sip of the hot coffee and put the cup down on the saucer. He'd never been any good at saying things about himself or his feelings. "Well, yes, I do, but—"

"You want to ask me something?" She waited, smiling.

"I needed to know how you've done."

Her brow furrowed in interest.

He went on. "I've spent most of my life trying to put a few horrible days behind me. I don't think those days were any easier for you, so if you don't want to talk about—"

"No. No, Sam, I don't mind."

He could see in her smile that she didn't, so he began. "Let's see, where do I start? Not long ago, I asked my parents to help me piece together what happened. I'd repressed so much. My mother showed me the clothes and shoes I'd worn. My father started giving all these horrible descriptions, and the more he said, the more amazed I felt. Then all at once, I remembered. Now, I can see why my life's been so hard. I want to change that. You were with Ralph a lot longer than me. I need to know what you did to—" he held out empty palms. *Get by? Survive?*

"I know what you want, and I know you can sure drive yourself up the wall trying to do the impossible. We're not gonna get over Ralph. He left his mark. You came from a family and a home where you were important and tended to. It was easier for me because I was born to it. Even I hurt you, too."

He put up a hand to stop her. "Wait. I didn't come to—"

She waved him off. "At times, guilt nearly did me in. Took many a year to come to terms with myself. I'd get to thinking I wasn't even scratching the surface, but now I know that every dab of progress I made added up to me becoming a person I didn't have to be ashamed of."

"Deb—"

"Used to eat away at me—what I did to you. Had to forgive myself and keep telling myself that you understood."

Refusing to look away, he shut his mind against the acts she had performed on him. "You were in no position to say no."

"And you were?"

He shook his head.

"See? No reason for faulting ourselves." She grinned shyly. "I've kept up with you on TV."

Kept up?

"It's got so I think I know you right well."

"How do you mean?"

"Last summer and fall you were sick. Anybody who'd watched you as close as me could see that. Heartsick, not just bodysick. Wasn't just the little boy shooting himself, was it?"

"No."

"Marion taped the child abuse story while I worked evenings. That got attention around here. People talking about it at the grocery store and the hairdressers'. I hear a lot of cases got reported because of it."

"Record numbers, but has anything been done to help? Judging from what's come back to me, not much."

"A rain barrel fills up a drop at a time."

"Only if it's raining."

Her face tipped intently to the side as she scrutinized him. "Something must be going right. You're better now, but for a while there, it looked touch-and-go."

He didn't take the time to contemplate her accuracy in reading him. He'd known Freida to home in on secrets of the mind and heart too many times to wonder over another woman's ability to do the same. Everyone who had followed the story knew Justin had ended his life while Sam held the phone. Dana Rawlings's sensitivity in taking up the slack caused by Sam's stunned grief had brought soft hearts all over Alabama together to mourn the meaningless tragedy. The caring had come too late for Justin.

He nodded. "I went a little crazy. Almost lost my family. No, that's not right. I went a lot crazy and walked out on my wife and kids. There's this thing inside me that takes over the way I think. It makes me doubt everyone and everything."

"You're separated?"

"They took me back, but they can't let go of the fear that I might mess up again. There's so much damage to repair." He sighed, unsure if he was making sense. "I've always held them too tightly. Protected them when they didn't need it. I know how awful it is to live in fear. Now, they're scared and holding tight, too. I've got these two little kids, Deb. They—we all need some peace." In wonder, he sat lamenting his life in a strange house, bending the ear of a woman he hardly knew, unfairly imposing on the one historical tie between them. As a terrified little boy, he had begged her to save him. And she had. Was he doing it all over again? *Can you save me from myself, Debra Jean? Can you finish what I've only started?*

"Peace comes from inside. It's not something another can give, but I can tell you about me. Might help, because even though we came from different places, we ended up in the same boat. First, would you mind me looking at your hands?"

He slid to the edge of the chair and held them out. Consciously bracing himself against a flinching recoil, he permitted her inspection, her turning them over, tracing the lines of scaring with the tips of her fingers. He seldom touched anyone other than his people. Even the cordial handshaking ritual disconcerted him, often prodding him to override it when possible with his own customized, coldly polite gestures—a practiced nod, a comic salute. But her touch was relaxed and familiar, her caress a communication of tenderness.

"These hands are what saved us both. They told me I had to get us out. I'd been around dirt all my life, so I didn't know much different. But I'd never seen nothing more cruel than Ralph's putting a rope across your raw flesh and pulling it so tight it cut deeper and bloodier than the time before."

Slowly, he withdrew his hands, slid back in his chair, and sheltered them in his arm pits. Debra Jean also sat back. With no further bidding, she told her story. As her words drew a picture of a little girl conditioned from birth to abuse and hopelessness—so different yet akin to a carefree little boy yanked from his haven of innocence and ripped apart by a hungry beast—he wondered which child's plight had been worse and decided it didn't matter. No competition existed.

"My daddy was all the family I had before Ralph, and he wasn't right in his mind, either. Made me do a woman's work from the first time I can call up a memory. Cooking, washing, making a garden. I probably wasn't more than ten when he started bringing men home—sometimes one at a time, sometimes two or three. He'd say 'Debra Jean, you be nice to my friend Ed'—or Hank or Louie. That meant I was supposed to go to the back room with one of them and do what they told me to do. Before they left, they'd give Daddy some money or a bottle of whiskey. To him, one was as good as the other. I don't remember Daddy hitting me, but if one of his *friends* slapped me across the room, he wouldn't bat an eye.

"Started bringing Ralph around not too long before the law got him and took him to Bryce. Daddy done something or other to make a public disturbance. I never even knew what it was, but it showed the law he was crazy enough to need locking up. I was about thirteen and Ralph was near twenty. Ralph was already working on cars and making a little money. Not much, but enough to buy an extra bottle every few days. When Daddy got picked up, Ralph told everybody that Daddy'd signed and we'd got married. That's how come I was with him all that time. Didn't have any other place to go. Didn't even know things could be better some place else. Since I was 'married,' I didn't go to school, so there I was keeping house for Ralph instead of Daddy. Looking back, I thank God I didn't get pregnant. Either Ralph or me didn't have what it took, I guess. Anyway, it would've been an awful shame to bring a baby into the house with Ralph.

"I got out of Tutwiler in April of sixty-seven, less than two years after I went in. After the truth about Ralph got out, murdering him didn't seem so bad to anybody. You were eleven then, or close to it. I moved in with Marion. Been with her ever since. She got out a week to the day before I did and found us a little house to rent cheap. Got us jobs at a chicken hatchery and egg farm. There was a bunch of those around these parts back then. We washed eggs and made enough to eat good and buy an old junker to get us around. We went to the movies or the auction barn on Saturdays. Marion's good to me. If we don't agree on something, we just talk it out. I used to have these old dreams about Daddy and Ralph, you and that other little boy. Marion'd put her arms around me and talk to me till I felt better. I don't know the nights I went back to sleep with Marion holding me like I was some young'un she'd took to raise.

"Then she got education-minded. Made me study and go to adult education classes at the high school. With the little grade school I got as a kid, I could read and spell pretty good, so it wasn't too hard. I was twenty-eight years old when I got my GED. Then me and Marion both went to junior college to be LPN's. Now, we both work at Hollow Ridge Nursing Home just this side of the river. When we put in our applications, we just left blank the part about 'have you ever been arrested . . .' We must not look like criminals because we got hired. We figured we'd be good with old people. Don't mean to brag, but we do get on with our patients. They're sort of mine and Marion's babies. Been here nineteen years. If we'd been close to Chesterville or most anywhere in the counties around Birmingham, somebody might've known me and got me fired. Must've looked different when I got out because not long after I did, I walked right by some people me and Ralph went to church with, and they didn't know me. My hair was all brown by then and cut short. I wasn't so skinny anymore, either." She grinned. "Could be they didn't look too close—you knew me right off years later."

Her matter-of-factness was amazing. He couldn't relate to her ease or frankness. "I'm glad you were able to separate yourself from the past. You seem content."

"I am. Not just content—happy. Marion gets some of the thanks. She went to jail because she burned her trailer and tried to collect the insurance. Her husband made her do it then lied his way out of it. They got divorced while she was in. Neither one of us ever wanted another man. No offense to you, but we'd been burned. So we stay together, and if we do anything somebody else might not approve of, we keep it to ourselves. Love don't have to look the same for everybody."

She paused, but the only response he had was a nod of agreement. He didn't care who made her happy, or how. He was, however, tremendously relieved that she *was*.

"I kept the name Sommers, and Marion took it, too. She didn't want to keep on using her ex-husband's, but Ralph was dead and Sommers is common enough. Nobody ever put two and two together. Everybody that knows us thinks we're sisters. One widowed, one divorced, both using our maiden name. She's not but three years older'n me, and we've got the same color hair—except now she's got more gray in hers. I tease her about it. Everybody, even Marion, calls me Dee. I'm too afraid Deb or Debra Jean will set off a memory.

"You sure look good, Sam. I'm glad you had a nice family to go home to, and I'm glad you grew up to be the kind of man who values his wife and children. They must be wonderful people.

"Well, listen to me, I'm just all over the place. Running on like a river. What I meant to tell you is that after I got out, I started seeing pictures and write-ups about you in the *Russett Bugle*—always a couple of days late, because we got it in the mail. The first time was when you won a prize for having the best science fair project, and a few days later you won something else in a school contest. Then every week almost, there'd be something. Sometimes, it'd be on the sports page. Little League, Karate tournaments, football. I got a whole scrapbook full of *you*. Marion and me even went to some of your ball games, mostly tournaments, when we figured there'd be a crowd to get lost in. If you remember two crazy-looking women in sunglasses and big floppy sun hats—that was us. Marion's the only person I ever told about you. I hope you don't mind—about Marion or the scrapbook."

Sam shook his head. He didn't know why she had wanted to keep it, but he didn't mind.

"I always was afraid if you saw me, you'd get upset. I thought you probably hated me. Then when the need to get one good look at you got too strong, you were real nice about it. Most teenagers, I hear, are sorta hard to get on with under the best of circumstances, but you were an angel."

"I owe you, Deb—Dee."

"Aw, no." Tears fell freely as if she wasn't aware of them. "I had to give up a lotta regrets just to keep on going. The only one I couldn't let go of was that I didn't kill Ralph before he ever laid eyes on you or the Tennessee boy."

Sam's turn to give something in return for her chronicle and for saving his life had come. He spoke slowly, trying to feel out the words. "You're one of the bravest, most giving people I know. In the beginning, I didn't understand why you waited. Then I learned about the holds some people have over others and how hard those holds are to break. It took monumental courage to break loose. By the time I saw you again, I knew."

"It meant a lot to me. Healing medicine. You didn't hate me, so I must be okay. That was how I took it. Sam, coming here was the best gift you could give me."

"I came here for you to make me feel better, and you have. I haven't given anything back."

"You gave me the grandest thing in the world—the ability to love another human being. You helped get me started on a learning path. All along that path, I learned so many things. Things I can hold. Things that make me feel good. You helped me learn that I'm not bad, that I can help people and they can care about me. I never knew what love felt like before you. It started when we, you and me, got outta that trailer and ran, but when you got in that wreck and I saw you—that finished the job for me. I've been a different person. Even Marion says so. I can look at my own face in the mirror and like what I see. I still feel sick over that other boy. He deserved to live, too. But the truth is I didn't kill him, and I didn't know I could've saved him. Ignorance isn't a sin in my book. I just tell myself at least Sam didn't die. Just think how helpless we were—you more than me—then you'll see we don't have to take the blame."

She got up, moved about the room, found a box of tissue and brought it back with her. After drying her face, she sat back down on the edge of the sofa and raised her face to look at him. "You're right. I did have to be brave. A person can be told something so much they believe it. I'd been told I was dumb and weak all my life. Both Daddy and Ralph dared me in their own ways to try to run away. Always, they said how bad it would be when they caught me. Well, I fixed Ol' Ralph where he couldn't catch me, and here we are today—you and me—as free as birds!"

Sam smiled. "Most people who are abused for long periods of time become cruel and abusive to other people, but you—you're very special, and I'm glad I came."

"Aren't you sweet? Would you happen to have a picture of your wife and kids on you?"

Sam brought out his wallet, opened it, and withdrew three plastic laminated photographs. "My wife gets them waterproofed because I have a habit of getting caught in the rain." He handed one of the pictures to her. In the photo, he was standing behind Brenan with his arms around her.

"She's beautiful. I've seen pictures of her on her books. She looks too young and sweet to be such a powerful writer. I hear she causes a stir sometimes."

"That she does." He grinned, shook his head over the truth in her comment, and gave her the other two pictures.

"My daughter, Mariah, just turned ten, and my son, Benjamin, is six. He's temporarily short a few teeth."

"The girl has your eyes, but the boy is you all over."

"So I hear."

She studied the pictures a long time, constantly changing the one on the top of the stack. "You ought to be the happiest man alive. Just look what you've got—a wonderful family, a job where whole cities and towns adore you, and your looks—you've still got your good looks."

A revived blush warmed his face. "Why don't you just keep those? I'm sure Brenan has dozens more. She's big on pictures."

Deb looked pleased. "You know that tape recording you made is partly what got me off with a light sentence, don't you?"

Tape? He had no memory of a tape. "I don't know what you mean."

"The tape where you told what happened. My lawyer got the judge to let him play it. Of course, they never used your name. Nobody knew it was you."

"I don't remem—" But he did. He remembered Mark holding a microphone, asking questions. An old reel-to-reel recorder spinning its spools. A. D. sitting with him on the couch in Mark's office. A woman writing in a notebook and a man in a suit standing in a corner. "What did I say?"

"You said Ralph hurt you—not me—and that I took you to get help. You didn't have to say what Ralph did. They had those pictures with your face blacked out."

Pictures? Where were they, now? Who had them? When Freida had handed him the bundle of clothing, she had made some remark about having other things she didn't think he was prepared to see. Photographs.

The taking of photos was suddenly a sharp image in his mind. Mark had taken those, too—at his office in the clinic, with no one else but A. D. in the room. Explaining that, with pictures, no one else would need to look at him, they had stripped him and stood him against a wall. A. D. had wept quietly while Sam, naked and shivering, had carried out Mark's directions. His daddy, a man who had never cried, a man who could now compete with the most accomplished of criers.

Deb's voice broke his thoughts. "They said because I took the gun, loaded it, and drove to the garage, it was premeditated. The tapes and the pictures and the corpse of that other boy proved I had reason to fear for your life and mine. They figured I had to do something drastic."

"You shouldn't have had to serve time at all. They should have given you a reward and held a banquet in your honor."

"Your mama and daddy sent me a letter. It was sort of like an award. I still have it. Wouldn't take nothing for it. Want to see it?"

A warning wheeze sounded in his chest. He didn't know if he wanted anything to do with such a letter, but he caught himself nodding too late to stop. While Deb was out of the room, he sat rigid. Why had his parents kept these things to themselves? Even though A. D. had presented the gristly parts of the story, Sam was finding parts his father had left out. Big parts. A letter. Pictures. A tape recording. What else could there be?

Deb brought back a brown-edged piece of old-fashioned tablet paper. Lined, five-by-seven inches, folded once to fit inside a small tailored envelope. He opened the page and read:

September 20, 1965

Dear Mrs. Sommers,

Thank you for our son. We hope you will soon have your freedom. If you should need anything, please do not hesitate to ask. We may be contacted at the address on the envelope. Again, you have returned to us a precious part of out lives, and we will be forever grateful.

Sincerely,

Freida and A. D. MacCauley

HE'D INSTANTLY recognized the fluid handwriting.

The memories Deb had pried loose grew crystal clear. Mark had taken pictures and made the recording. He had patiently explained every word, every move, allowing the final decisions to be made by Sam. No one had forced him to do anything. No one had kept anything from him. If he had asked, one of his parents would have answered. Knowing his people were honest and open to his needs had gotten him through all the trying times. They hadn't changed. The wheezing subsided.

"You never asked them for anything, did you?"

"No, Sam. I didn't need to. They paid my lawyer and hospital bills without being asked. All I needed after that was to know you were all right. The little snippets I collected for my scrapbook told me a lot. A boy don't do well in school if his parents don't care what he learns. They don't go to ball games and yell like crazy when he does good and say 'good try' when things don't go his way if they don't treasure him. I watched them. And I saw you standing in the middle of those ball fields, cutting your eyes to make sure they were paying attention.

"You were the first person I loved. I lived a long time just on *that*. Now, I've got Marion, of course, and friends and a whole bunch of little old people who make my life full of good things. I count my blessings every day that comes. You need to do that, too, Sam, then you won't have much time to worry what happened too far back in the past to matter now."

Listening to her was therapeutic, every word worthy of keeping and appreciating. The awkwardness he had feared had not found a way into the little quilted room. After more than an hour, he called Brenan to let her know where he was, what he was doing, and that he would be a little longer than he'd expected.

He turned down a supper invitation, but he drank a second cup of coffee and stayed long enough to meet Marion. Even though he doubted they would, he asked them to visit his home and meet his family. They encouraged him to come back, and he knew he would. They had made a spiritual exchange, acknowledged kinship. Each had declared, "You are important to me, and you deserve to live free of shame and guilt."

As he was leaving, he allowed Deb to press into his arms two handmade quilts—one for each of his children. When he placed the folded patchwork on the seat beside him, he realized he was going home to tell Ben and Mariah who had made them and how he had come to know this woman. He was going to do his best to help them understand that sometimes he still hurts, that he was truly sorry for letting that hurt flow over onto them. He hoped in sharing what he'd learned about himself, he'd impress upon them the need to think, be wary, and be safe.

58

April 1992

S INGING SOFTLY, Sam neatly stowed a suitcase, a garment bag,
Brenan's brief case and IBM laptop in the trunk of her Cougar.
He took his time backing the car out of the garage then thumbing
the door closed with the remote control before he circled the house and
parked by the back steps. After pausing to evaluate the soundness of the
engine's droning and take a gas tank reading, he shut off the motor then
hurried back into the house. At three a.m., the world was still dark and
silent and chilled.

Brenan was scheduled to appear with him on an early taping of
today's "The Morning After Show." Wanting to capitalize on the
backlash of her recent stint on "Geraldo," the station was holding out its
arms. Seeing it as an easy plug for the coming release of her new novel,
Little Birds, Brenan was willing. During her encounter with "Geraldo"
and a panel of irate clergy, she had obligingly raked up old grievances on
the matter of religious fanaticism in Alabama and the South. She had
soap-boxed on spiritual quacks and fools, and immediately after the
show's airing, a tide of incensed piety began to roll. To make matters
worse, *Pulpits* was being made into a six-hour NBC mini-series—a
supreme insult to those who had fought tooth and nail to have the book
banned, succeeding only in keeping it on the bestseller list for a stagger-
ing number of weeks. WPMS wanted some of the sensationalism, a piece
of the Brenan MacCauley public-feud-pie. Sam was going on with her in
hopes of serving as a catalyst in yet another chancy engagement.

Once again, the MacCauleys and members of the extended family were looking over their shoulders and approaching blind corners with caution. They'd probably have to seclude themselves permanently after the new book hit the stands. Brenan hadn't been able to restrain her sentiments in that one, either. The point of *Pulpits* had sailed right by the very zealots who wanted to crucify the author. *That* had been the issue all along. Officials of a half-dozen different denominations, including two of the major Pentecostal groups, had gone public in Brenan's defense, at least to say they had interpreted no denial of God nor an infringement on an individual's right to worship. A few of them agreed with her outright, that some persuasions fostered abuse and the closeting of defenseless participants, such as children. But the hardcore sects were deaf and blind to reason—Brenan's precise argument to their competency.

"Geraldo" had ushered in a new batch of threats, some of them smacking loudly of violent intent. Sam had hired a security service to provide a perimeter guard for each of three eight-hour shifts daily. The MacCauley compound had become a fortress, his parents' home and that of his in-laws enclosed therein. The fence had been expanded to surround the hillside and cavern. He'd been compelled to make security improvements at Robert and Jackie's house in Hoover and at the Smith Lake property. Brenan's new wealth and another mortgage barely paid for these extravagant measures.

As soon as this morning's show wrapped up, Sam and Brenan would drive to the Birmingham Municipal Airport to board a 7:01 flight to Jacksonville, Florida. Brenan was slated to head a workshop dealing with the writing of Southern fiction at the Florida First Coast Writers' Festival. They wouldn't be back until Sunday. An annual event on Brenan's calendar, due in part to a number of her friends living in Jacksonville, the Festival was one of the few workshop weekends she enjoyed being a part of—the only one she'd agreed to do this spring. With the revival of the threats, Sam was more than a little skittish about the openness her participation in a writers' forum created. There had been only sparse publicity about the Festival in the Birmingham area and most of that had come through Brenan's circle of literary friends, but worry-prone Sam was not consoled.

Brenan's secretary screened the contents of the mailbox for threats. Letters also came in the mail to both sets of parents. All were shunted away from Brenan. The three households had developed an angst about answering the phone. Even with all the efforts to hold them back, a significant number of the heckling messages found their way to Brenan. Notes were tied to rocks and bottles and lobbed over the fence. Crude, hand-painted signs appeared on trees near the driveway. Some of the intimidations had originated in Florida and South Georgia—Jacksonville's domain. All had been stored, but there hadn't been time to determine how many, if any, had come from Jacksonville or its close proximities. Sam knew Brenan's scheduled participation in the Festival had been well-publicized in that area.

When he'd failed to talk Brenan into canceling, his decision to go along had been automatic—if for nothing else, to make sure she was careful. He'd probably spend most of the weekend as her shadow, a tagalong trying to blend into the background, but that would be better than not knowing what was happening to her. Despite her roaring objections, he was giving serious study to applying for a permit to carry a handgun. Robert and the females were dubious, but Mark and A. D. agreed with Sam. A man had an obligation to defend his family.

He went back through the house and found her, barefoot and in her underwear, shouting into the bedroom phone. Considering the time and the angry flush on Brenan's face, he knew someone had betrayed them again.

"Where did you get this number?"

Her cheeks were scarlet with fury. As she paced around the room with the cordless handset pressed against her ear, the antenna erratically stabbing the air, her eyebrows came together to form a wavy brown line across her forehead.

No doubt, Brother Arlo. Otherwise, she would have let the answering machine log a message. The unpublished number had been changed again only weeks ago. The family, the kids' schools, Brenan's agent, and a handful of WPMS employees were the only ones who had been given the number. All had also been given strict instructions to keep it confidential. Either this guy had friends at the phone company or someone they trusted was blabbing. Every time the number had been changed, Arlo had come up with the new one. Sam just couldn't endorse the theory that God was giving them away.

He couldn't fathom what about this ominous preacher fascinated Brenan. Even though she was left in a state of undiluted rage afterward— answering machine be damned—she nearly always intercepted when she heard his voice.

"Well, let me tell *you* something *Reverend* Blacknell. First of all, my husband didn't write *Pulpits*—I did! He didn't read a single page until it was finished, and therefore, he had no influence on its writing. Second, he had nothing—*nothing*—to do with Bud's drinking or his death— except that he probably saved Bud's life a few times beforehand by keeping him from behind the wheel of a car when he was too drunk to know his own name. Sam cared about your son. That was more than you can say. He was Bud's friend. What happened was a tragedy you can keep on your own doorstep. *You* were the one who gave him a set of rules so strict no human could follow. Your fanaticism and your belt cost you your son. Do you really think God was behind any of the beatings?" She noticed Sam watching her and rolled her eyes. He reached for the phone, but she kept it at her ear and shook her head. She chewed a fingernail and tapped her foot on the carpet as she listened to the voice on the other end of the line.

"That's where your stupidity flashes like a neon sign. I've heard the story from sources other than Sam. Bud came to you for help, and you, drunk on self-righteous jargon, quoted scriptures and told him he was going to hell. You stood up at his funeral and ceremoniously committed him to your so-called hell, and when you did, you sold out your son *and* God. You can thump your fancy, gold-monogrammed Bible until you wear a hole through the cover and still be ignorant as a fence post. — Oh, yeah? Well, the next time you waddle your fat, holy hinny up to a pulpit to send out the message that *God is Love!,* I hope you use some example other than the dooming of a confused and abused young boy like Bud to the eternal fires of your hell! With that one, God comes off looking rather sadistic! And furthermore, I never once criticized the Church of God, the Assembly of God, or any other Pentecostal denomination. I profiled religious fanatics and snake handlers and soothsayers—lunatics like you who sit in judgment of anyone who refuses to contort themselves into pretzels in the aisles of your alleged sanctuaries. — Save your prayers, or better yet, pray over this: if you use this number again, the police can have you! We have your threats on tape, in letters signed by you, and God knows how many witnesses who are *praying* for a chance to swear on the Bible the details of what I've put up with from you. I'm ready to press charges now, and when I do, my husband is going to report everything on the evening news. On top of that, *Unsolved Mysteries* will be looking into the disappearances of your wife and sister-in-law. Could it be God wanted them wiped out, too? Some folks are still wondering. Good-bye, Reverend Blacknell! God bless you!"

Purged of her anger, Brenan hung up and turned pleasantly back to Sam. "Next time he calls, I'm going to turn him in."

He hoped she meant it. She was too quick to tell off her adversaries, this one in particular. She was good at it, but he was edgy, fearful, nearing the realm of paranoia about possible retaliations. Blacknell was beyond recovery. Sam had watched this man's psychosis develop and define itself over the years. He believed the man was an explosion waiting to be set off. He recalled the thrashings Bud had taken at this monster's hand. The rod had not been spared. The child had never once been good enough. The love of father and Father had been only meaningless, hollow words to a boy who would have given up anything, walked any mile, or performed any act to have pleased *either* just once.

Brenan was afraid, too. Only her closest family and friends would spot her substituting sarcasm and bravado for overt fear and trembling. Acerbity, denial—along with an overindulgence in chocolate, sex, and Super Nintendo—had likely kept her out of a padded penthouse suite at Northside.

"You should have put him on with me."

She gave him an impatient tilt of her head. "Oh? I think I handled him just fine. Besides, he's caused enough rows. I'm still embarrassed about one in particular. I've gone back to being tough and independent, but I still let you tail me around, guarding me. That's why I'm letting you go to Jax with me."

"I'm sure he's more pissed now than when he picked up the phone. And this business about letting me go with you is bunk."

"The old hypocrite won't think twice before he calls again. He's convinced the devil's working through us. You turned Bud into an alcoholic, and that makes you liable for his driving himself into the grave and pulling two people in with him. He says the old couple were Lutheran; therefore, they went to hell with Bud. Missing the chance to convert through an untimely death won't keep Old Scratch from getting them, I guess. In his delusions of grandeur, I used him as a model for Reverend Travis in *Pulpits*. Not really a delusion, I did use him and a dozen other pew-jumping, spit-slinging zealots and would-be-Jim-Jones maniacs who nest all over the South. They'd be laughable if they weren't responsible for screwing up so many lives."

"You expect me to disagree?"

"Remember all those churches we visited while I was doing research? That tin-sided barn where they brought out boxes of copperheads and rattlesnakes? That cult in Louisiana that didn't even have a building, just a cemetery full of ancient, crumbling cairns the congregation sat on during the services—waiting for the Resurrection, the vaults to open, the dead to float up out of their shrouds? If people are so bent on carrying on such morbid traditions, why are they so sensitive about them?"

"You're asking me?"

"I'll tell you why? They're so worried about the hereafter, they can't live in the present."

"Amen!"

"Don't you go sassing me, you pagan varmint. Help me find my Nikes. I'm dressing for comfort. What did you tell me happened to Bud's mother?"

Sam thought it was convenient and utilitarian that Brenan was forced to stop for air once in a while. "You should have your story down pat before you use it as a weapon."

"Yeah, yeah. So?"

"She and her sister vanished into thin air one summer when Bud was about four or five."

"And they were never found?"

"Neither hide nor hair. The sister had a husband and two sons she lived with in Mountain Brook. Her family may still live there. I haven't heard from them since Bud died. He used to hide out at their house when he was afraid of a beating. The sister's husband tried to get the police to look into Arlo's doings because he believed they might find something to connect him to the disappearances of the two women."

"Did they investigate?"

"Probably not like they should have. Arlo insisted the women had run off with other men."

"But there were two of them. A double elopement?"

He shrugged. "Police didn't want to tangle with clergy. If it had happened recently, Arlo wouldn't have been passed over so easily. A minister commanded a lot of respect back then."

"Good ones still do. A sincere pastor does an awesome job for his congregation. Support, comfort, hope. They deserve respect and admiration even if their beliefs aren't yours. Arlo wouldn't know God from Jay Leno."

"Still, you shouldn't make idle threats about things you don't even know about. I'm sure he's touchy on the subject of his wife. Did he say anything new?"

"Of course. After reminding me he'd bought a .22, he said God sometimes exacts vengeance on people who've had the chance but refused to repent and undo their sins, people who continue to lie down with swine. Suppose that makes you a pig. He said—and I quote—'I'll have to do what the Master bids.' Sounds like *Dracula's* Renfield. 'The blood is the life' sort of thing. Probably eats flies and spiders, too. Anyway, he said he'd have to do whatever was necessary to get by anyone who stands in the way of the Truth and the Light. He's playing Christian soldier. I hope you don't take that babble seriously."

"I take seriously this man's desire to hurt you, and so do you. Every time you talk *Pulpits,* he thinks you're talking about him. He thinks you've insulted him on national TV as well as on paper. Plus, you insult him for real every chance you get—on the phone, to his face. Now, you've practically accused him of murder. He's a Christian soldier, all right, and you're the infidel foe. Add to that his feelings about me and the fact that I'm the swine you lie down with, and you'll find he's got plenty incentive to rid the world of your evil impact."

"Stop sermonizing. We're going to be late if you don't shut up and finish getting dressed."

He could see agreement in her eyes. Now might be the time to push a little harder. "Bren, baby, if we don't do something soon, I think he will try to hurt you. If he did off his own wife and her sister, he'd just as easily—"

"Okay, next time, I'll turn him in—like I said I would."

He gave her his exasperated look. "The *next* time?"

"The very next." She formed a flirty pout. "I promise."

"Why not now?"

Her fingers stole under his undershirt and teased a nipple. "Too much paperwork. We'd be late."

She slid her body against his, slipped an arm around his neck, and bit his earlobe. She didn't play fair. Her fingers snaked between them, tugged at his belt. Sam found her fumbling with his clothes distracting, and for the time being, his worries about Arlo were relegated to the back of his mind. A push from her sat him on the bed. "You know, we *are* going to be late."

She shoved him onto his back and climbed astride his thighs.

"Bren—" His protest was weak.

"You're much too tense. We've got to release some of that pent-up stress."

"What about the show? Mark and Paige? The free publicity? The 'I'm sorry if I've offended anybody' thing you've been rehearsing?" Her bra fell across his face.

"They'll wait."

"DID YOU HAVE to tell the entire population of North Alabama you're on your way to the airport?"

"I didn't think much about it."

"With dozens of crazies out there who want your butt?"

"Unless you're tired of it, my butt's taken."

He gave her the look he kept reserved for such comments. He was irritated with her lack of due caution. When he had declared he was going with her to Jacksonville, her reaction had been pure delight, but not for the designated reason. *"Great! We can go down to the beach at St. Augustine late at night, walk in the surf, make love by the dunes. Sand's nice and pearly there. Maybe we'll go to the old fort, and Ripley's Believe It or Not Museum on Sunday before we start home. You know how much I love that place. You can pretend to fall for that tongue-rolling thing and crack everybody up behind the two-way mirror like last time."* Not, *"Great, Sam! I'll feel safer having you around!"*

Sam wasn't ready to stop fussing. "You might as well take out an ad that reads 'Come Get Me!' or 'Catch Me If You Can!'"

"Sam, I can't screw you to shut you up on a busy freeway. Can't you fizzle out on your own this once?" As she threaded the Cougar through traffic, Brenan casually popped a Garth Brooks tape into the player and raised her voice enough to be heard above the singer's playful backwoodsy twang. "Personally, I think, under the pluck of their symbolic swords and staffs, those maniacs are all cowards."

"You should be more careful—that's all."

"Okay. Starting now. You're sweet to be so concerned."

"I'm concerned because I love you, and I'll probably keep nagging because I'm crazy about your method of shutting me up."

"I love you, too, but you gotta admit sometimes you worry about bogies who aren't there." She smiled then started singing along the tape—some song about wearing boots, getting drunk, and having friends in low places.

He shot her a hurt look.

She stopped singing. "I didn't mean it like *that*. I'm the luckiest woman ever. It's great to have you sticking up for me. Just chill. Let's enjoy being together. You're the best, Ace, and with you as my armor, nobody's going to get to me."

He envied her confidence.

59

E ARLY—FOR ONCE. All the preliminaries taken care of with unusual dispatch, leaving a half-hour to wile away, Brenan wanted food, her customary second breakfast. Weekdays at home, she ate breakfast with the kids before school and a couple of hours later again when Sam emerged in search of coffee and nourishment. She had the metabolism of a house fire.

At an airport restaurant, while she ordered and ate, Sam drank strong creamed coffee and kept an eye on her and the bustle around them. He'd selected a side table and sat with his back against a glass wall—a trick learned from old cowboy movies.

Just 'cause you're paranoid don't mean there ain't somebody out there really tryin' to get ya. Lefty vied for cuteness.

Mentally, Sam appraised the people who came and went, those at other tables, those who stood at the windows watching the traffic of planes and airport vehicles. A lot of people were going places today and stopping long enough to give a spot of business to the restaurant. Though nothing appeared out of the ordinary, he momentarily permitted himself to imagine he and Brenan were being observed as warily as he studied the crowd.

Paranoids have a new support group—Paranoids Anonymous—but they won't tell ya where they hold the meetin's.

He almost laughed aloud. He'd never learn moderation. His life had been devoted to stewing over everything that came under the realm of possibility.

The ol' "What If" game.

If Brenan paid any mind to his persistent disquiet, she withheld comment. Just as well—it was slacking off, permitting him to pay closer attention as she ran through a spectacular diversity of upbeat topics: the workshop, her interview with "Geraldo," her expected appearance on "Today" prior to the airing of the mini-series, her quest to snag a invitation from "Oprah." "Oprah has experienced the South up close," she said with surety, "and she would plead my case with sincerity and tears."

A toddler girl at a nearby table initiated a game of peek-a-boo with Sam. A chubby moppet with a wild tangle of platinum curls and blue jeans with ruffled pockets, once she caught his eye, began a ritual of covering and uncovering her face with a colorful copy of *Green Eggs and Ham.* Each time she lowered the book, she put her tongue out and giggled, and he countered with one of the silly faces that had evolved over years of playing with Rye and Ben. She pointed to the cartoon being on the cover of the book, leaned closer, and whispered, "Sam-I-am."

Though categorically opposed to any child flirting with a stranger, he shook his head and put a finger to his chest. "No, Sam-I-am."

The little girl thought his contradiction was exceptionally funny. Her laughter rang above the clamor of the restaurant.

Brenan rattled on, subject to subject, slowing only long enough to give the little girl a stingy smile. A philosophical conversation she'd had with Jackie about assisted suicide. Some new ferns she'd ordered. The crew that was getting ready to plow up the sagging old driveway and scrape it for repaving. How cute A. D. had looked asleep in Ben's spare bunk when they'd left him to babysit.

"Hush! and sit there!" A woman Sam assumed to be the mother lifted the child into a chair and turned to resume a conversation with a companion at the table.

Brenan teased Sam about the approach of his thirty-sixth birthday and a tiny lock of white hair above his left eyebrow.

The child's feet had scarcely touched the floor when the woman yanked her by one arm back into the chair. "I told you to stay put!" A resonant smack landed on the child's hand.

Whoa, Zorro!

"That was my fault," Sam started, shaking with anger, "I—"

"She knew better!"

The woman's curt reply and instant dismissal stung. If she hits the little girl in a public place, what does she do to her in private? Brenan shushed him. "Starting something will only make her angrier, and *who* will she take her anger out on?"

She was right, but it didn't make him feel any better.

Brenan got on with her monologue, drawing a portion of his attention back to her, leaving the leftovers to the child who sat pouting in her chair. He tipped his head back until it touched the glass and listened as she skipped from topic to topic. She was well back into her enchantment with St. Augustine when she suddenly stiffened and halted mid-sentence. "Sam!"

He jerked, expecting to witness another assault on the little girl.

"It's—" She strangled on her cry of alarm. *Then* she was completely hushed and frozen, her eyes fixed wide on something or someone near the center of the tables.

Sam pivoted, saw and felt and heard everything almost all at once. An arm's length away, he beheld the two-fisted grip of cigar-like fingers on an oiled gray pistol, the look of perfect contempt on a flabby, one-eyed face. He saw the blur and heard the sounds of panic—the rumble of people scattering, chairs falling, tables being knocked over, the little girl's startled cry as she was hustled away—then a calm voice ejecting ironically from a winking, hate-filled face, *"Our Father Who art in Heaven hallowed be Thy Name . . . "*

He saw his own hands fly across the table and push his wife with a force that sent her and her chair crashing to the floor.

She can't die!

"Thy kingdom come . . . Thy . . . "

He heard a detonation, felt the painless jolt of a bullet tearing into his left shoulder, slamming him backward into the wall. He saw a spray of his blood splatter-paint the face and arms of the man who had pulled the trigger.

"will be done . . . on Earth . . . "

He saw one eye in the fat face disappear once more to allow its mate to take aim through the upright sight of the gun.

"as it is in Heaven . . . Give us this day . . . "

He heard Brenan's scream, saw the man sidle closer and point the gun straight down into her face. He heard, *"No!"* burst from inside his own throat.

"our daily bread . . . "

He felt his body turn into a coiled spring, propel forward. He heard the second blast and the crunching sound of the bullet splintering his breastbone. He felt a jolt shoot through him as his foot made solid contact with preacher's skull, a hoarded particle of the martial arts training from long, long ago.

Like ridin' a bike!

He saw Reverend Arlo Blacknell go down into oblivion a second before he felt himself falling, sliding slowly down a bloody glass wall into a seated position on the floor.

Help would come for Brenan before the preacher regained the senses he would need to pull himself up. Help would come . . .

Sam sat upright as if the bullet had nailed him to the wall. He searched for Brenan, located her directly in front of him. Peering down at the place where her hands pressed against him, he watched thick cords of blood slide between her fingers and over her hands. When his eyes found hers, he smiled. There was nothing he could do but wait for the blackness he knew would come. In the seconds before it arrived, he saw with crystal clarity all the layers of himself reflected in Brenan's eyes. For the first time in his life, Sam saw what she had always seen, what his mother and father had always known was there—the ordinary virtues that justified the love they continued to invest in him. Thick overlays of guilt parted to show uncontaminated pools of decency, innocence, goodness. At his core, underneath insulating folds of fear, doubt, and pain he'd never been strong enough to overturn, he found the child's innocence that had gone unclaimed. In Brenan's panic-wide eyes, he found truth.

See? I told ya! We all told ya!

He tried to sort his thoughts, so he could think them one at a time. The bullets had been for her. He was glad he'd stolen them. She always saw the goodness inside him. When he wasn't able to love himself, her love made up the deficit. The bullets had weakened him. He'd have to finish thinking later.

In the mist over Brenan's head, he saw willowy spirits floating toward him, reaching, hands glowing with soothing warmth. A. D. in his overalls. An aproned Freida. Mariah and Ben. And others. Familiar, nurturing apparitions who came to serve as spacers between him and death. He heard them call his name, heard them cry for him, felt their tears rain down on him.

Brenan was alive. She would not die today. The others would protect her. No longer needed, his fear soaked into the floor and away from him. Then the darkness came. And for a brief and enchanted time, Sam didn't feel or hear or see anything that he recognized as a part of the world as it was known to him.

60

I T IS WITH GREAT SADNESS that I interrupt this portion of 'The Morning After Show' with news of an event of a very disturbing and personal nature to the WPMS News Team as well as to many of you. Less than an hour ago, news anchor, Sam MacCauley, was shot by an unknown assailant at the Birmingham Municipal Airport. According to witnesses in an airport restaurant, a man approached a table occupied by MacCauley and his wife, drew a small-caliber handgun from beneath his shirt, and fired two shots at close range—both of which struck MacCauley in the upper part of his body. Mrs. MacCauley was apparently unharmed. MacCauley's co-anchor, Dana Rawlings, is presently on the scene. We'll be joining her shortly for a more in-depth account of the shooting.

"MacCauley has been a respected personality at Channel Nine since he was hired as a Roving-Action Reporter in '77 at the age of twenty-one. Mrs. MacCauley is the author of bestselling novels, *Me and Joe, The Lasting Kind,* and *Pulpits,* as well as a new, yet-to-be released novel entitled, *Little Birds.*

"This morning the MacCauleys taped the promotional interview segment of *The Morning After Show* that aired just prior to the beginning of this report. Evidently, they had gone directly to the airport and were waiting to board a flight to Jacksonville, Florida, where Mrs. MacCauley was scheduled to take part in a weekend workshop. According to sources in the studio, Sam made comments suggesting he was going with his wife as a protective measure after a bout of threatening phone calls from representatives of local religious groups who were offended by the nature of the novel, *Pulpits.*"

Mark Evert looked up for confirmation that the live report was ready. Paige Stewart had fled the set in tears, and Andy Drury was presently storming between the cameras five hours before he usually graced the station with his presence. Mark had seen Brokaw and Donaldson stumble along the breaking of emotionally disturbing stories. The Birmingham audience would forgive his hesitation and confusion. Sam was Mark's colleague and friend, someone who evoked both respect and, at times, mild pangs of jealousy. Sam would have a tough go of reporting one of his own associates downed by bullets.

Andy Drury, casting his stormy eyes on Mark, gestured wildly at Dana's sorrow-stricken face centered on the monitor screen.

Mark bobbed his head slightly. "We go now to Dana Rawlings on the scene at the airport. Dana, can you tell us . . . "

THE MICROPHONE would not be still in her hand. She'd never lost her composure during an assignment. She supposed there really was truth in the first-time-for-everything adage. She hadn't gotten past the initial shock and disbelief, but reporting news was her job. "Mark, as you see, around me is a lot of activity and, uh, confusion. Sam has just been taken . . . "

Andy Drury had called her at home. She'd almost gotten out the door with her car keys in her hand and her boys in tow when she heard the phone. Reluctantly, she'd picked it up and listened in stunned incredulity. "Hello," and, a moment later, a perfunctory "Okay" had been her entire contribution before gently replacing the receiver and turning to her two sons. "You'll have to take the bus after all. I have to do a story." They had made frustrated faces and fussed a bit, but she hadn't told them the man they fondly called Uncle Sam, a man they esteemed second only to their father, could at that moment be dying or dead. Nor had she permitted herself to believe.

The solidity of the crowd had parted to let her through. Tommy Crowder, his camera balanced on a shoulder, caught her attention and signaled her to hurry. In front of him, a team consisting of a doctor, a nurse, and two paramedics had been working around an unmoving figure on the floor. The glass wall behind them had been turned into a mural of bloody designs. A blood bath. The colorized version of an old slasher flick. The floor had told its own story with littered paper, plastic wrappers from medical supplies, and still more blood. One of the paramedics had held an IV bag connected by a clear flexible tube to the man on the floor.

Dana had strained to see her partner's face, but it had been angled away from her. From his thighs up, his clothing had been saturated in brilliant shades of maroon and crimson. Nothing about the recumbent body had seemed alive. Nothing had moved.

"I called his father-in-law. He'll notify the MacCauleys. They sure don't need to hear it on the tube," Crowder had told her. He'd looked no more ruffled than the times he'd worked with her on political or human interest features, but there had been something extra in his voice that Dana had taken as distress. He'd logged as many hours with Sam as he had with Dana, and their bonds were tauter than professional camarade-rie. Sam owned pieces of them both. If he died, those pieces would be lost.

"Has anyone said how bad it is?"

"They don't have to. Just *look*. Dana, honey, he's not gonna come through this."

"Don't give up, yet. As long as they're working on him, there's a chance." She'd clung to feeble hope. "Where's Bren?"

Tommy had nodded toward a table.

Dana's eyes had searched the crowd in the direction he'd indicated until she'd found her friend.

Brenan had been a statue, sitting silently with Sam's blood drying on her hands and clothes, her face fixed on the grotesque scene in front of her. Dana had gone straight to her, lightly touched the steel set of her shoulder. "Brenan?"

Brenan did not lift her hypnotic gaze from Sam and his circle of attendants. Dana stayed beside her a few minutes until she saw Robert and Jackie Armstrong roughly part the crowd and stumble through. Dana could not do anything for any of them, so she went back to Tommy to do her report.

When the report was over, Sam, his family, and attendants were gone. The bloody wall and floor, the medical litter, the thinning crowd of gawkers were left to bear the truth. Someone had fired a gun. It happened all the time in Birmingham. Dana and Sam had reported thousands of shootings. They had stood at the scene of hundreds. They had felt some sickening unnamed human emotion for each victim. Shootings. Stabbings. Beatings. Neglect. Gross representations of man's inhumanity to man, and they had reported them all. But Dana would never do *this* again—not a friend, not someone she loved. Andy Drury might have thought she'd want to be the one, but she would give him an enlightening earful as soon as she got the chance.

"Tommy," she handed him the microphone, "I can't do this again. There's Channel 6. They can interview all the eyewitnesses they want. They can have the story. Would you please tell Andy I'm going to the hospital?"

Tommy nodded. "I'll call in. As soon as I get packed up and squared away, I'll swing by for Rita. We'll meet you there."

61

A BADLY DAMAGED ENGINE, his heart shivers and stalls, shivers and stalls. A signal of death? No, Sam doesn't think so. Soon a spark will catch. The eruption of pain that for a long moment mushroomed inside him has vaporized. The swishing breath sounds have quieted. The din of the crowd has left his ears. But dying? Dead? No. He still feels. He still knows. And the blackness no longer shrouds him.

Pulling away from the wall, he leans forward, stares down at black-rimmed holes no bigger than dimes. Except for a few telltale grayish-purple stains on the blue of his shirt, the blood has disappeared. Perhaps, it has soaked back into him, loading itself again into his veins and arteries during the stoppages of his heart. Brenan's hands have also vanished.

A man's gotta do what a man's gotta do, Ace.

Struck by a sudden urge to rise and plunge through the oxygen-sucking crush of bodies, he stands, takes a few wobbly steps, looks back. Another Sam remains on the floor to play the protagonist in this lurid drama. Brenan attends the wounded facsimile, sees only the bleeding replica. He has to leave her with the gory mess and this hollow twin. There's no other way. "I'll come back. I promise."

Not hollow, Boss. I'm here.

"Come on." He commands, impatiently curling a finger.

I can't go, Ace. Lefty's voice hisses out of the clone. *I have to guard it. Make it breathe. Make it thrive.*

"What if I need you?"

Ya need me here! I'm the spare tire, Ace. Only need me when you've got a flat. An' you're flat out HERE, Hoss!

"But what if—"

What if pigs had propellers? What if hogs had wings? You're on your own. Go!

The choice isn't his to make. He must go alone.

Happy trails, Pard!

"I love you, Brenan." She looks so frightened. He hopes she will be safe until the force spurring him away returns him to her. He hopes someone will take care of her, take away the gun. "I'll come back." The promise comes from his heart. It wells up and out of him like the crimson stream that still bubbles out of the twin and sluices through her fingers. Then for a second, her eyes flash toward his face, a face he knows she cannot see. "I'll be back," he vows once more. Many times in the past, she has heard his soul's whispering. When Brenan sets her mind to do something, she usually does just that. Intent on holding back the bloody tide, her stubborn hands compress the bullet holes. Her love glows like a fire burning around her.

Alive, breathing, he walks, tentatively at first, then with mounting determination. No one turns to watch. When the hard, cold glass and steel of the airport magically melt into the grass and dirt of his home hillside, his footsteps fall cushioned and easy. He slows to take in cool morning air, then speeds up to gain an unclear destination. His leg muscles feel corded, taut.

The long walk has extracted a high cost from his reserves of strength and endurance, but what matters is that he has reached the top of the hill. All the noisy ado is below him. Below. Behind. *Beyond.* Here is tranquility and light.

Choosing the biggest rock by the mouth of the cave, the lookout rock of his boyhood, he sits down to rest. The cool breeze brings echoes of the left-behind noises. Excited voices, the rustle of paper, *lub-dub, lub-dub,* then perfect stillness.

The early morning sun is warm and bright—bright enough to dispel gloom and fear, warm and soothing on his face. Dazzling specks of magic dance in the air above the dewy green. No such thing as carpet rides, genie lamps, leprechauns—oh, but the world is full of glimmering magic. The valley is a greening panorama. Spring rainfall has the creeks and branches flowing and the water tables high. A few atypical cold snaps initially slowed the budding of trees and wildflowers, but they are coming along, lush and emerald, in cascades of new foliage. Having survived the angel-hair frosts, the flower-starred sugarsnap vines A. D. has set out in a corner of the south field have crept five feet up their wooden stakes, and the nearby rows of scallions look like a deep sea of waving grasses. Heavy gates block the view of the fish pond and the foot bridge across the creek. A uniformed guard trudges alongside the fence. Soon the gates will gape open and the guard will be discharged. Visitors will again be welcome, fear banished.

Although his parents' house is hidden in the evergreens, Sam can see a bit of the freshly tilled and seeded kitchen garden. His father walks between the rows of lettuce, carrots, and spindly tomato plants. Soon Freida's kitchen will be redolent of summer. Soon friends who drop by will not leave empty-handed.

The A-frame roof of the Armstrong house rises out of a hill to the northwest. The one window showing in the white-and-brown half-timber peak is that of Brenan's old bedroom. Now, only out-of-town company and overnighting grandchildren sleep there. Brenan sleeps in Sam's arms.

Sam's house, outbuildings, the pool and pool house, and immense spans of lawn are all visible from the rock. He glimpses his children throwing tennis balls for the dogs to fetch. They are waiting for Freida to come out and drive them to school. They don't know about the preacher. Or the bullets. *Yet.*

His valley, the place he was born to inhabit. Peaceful, bucolic, welcoming. Up close, a Norman Rockwell print; at a distance, the picture on a jigsaw puzzle. Home.

Sunshine highlights the few meandering cumulus clouds in silvery tinsel. In front of Sam, the world is bright and sharply drawn. He stands on his shadow. Behind, in the cave, sunlight falls short. He respects the contrasts of light and shadow and darkness because they illustrate the extremes and depths of an hour, a day, a lifetime. The temperature is sixty-five degrees, fifty-five inside the cave. Peace and hope abide all around. He releases a long, cleansing breath, and the pain that tries to reclaim his center is expelled. He inhales the delicate scents of spring. Honeysuckle and pine, clean air and freedom. Nothing is driving him toward any kind of action. To rest and think, to take advantage of the tranquility, he leans back against the cool limestone. His mind drifts along, charting a mental inventory and evaluation of the people in his life.

Brenan has wrapped up a deal for her latest novel. Since Thanksgiving, after the love came back, she has written like a machine. *"Eight hundred forty-one pages of pure magic,"* she describes it. Sam thinks it's her best work. Although he doesn't ask and she hasn't said, he knows this one is his story, fact-based fiction, more so than *Me and Joe*. And — surprise! — it has a happy ending! In it, she likens wounded children to fallen sparrows. She calls it *Little Birds*. He touches the bloodless hole over his sternum, dead center between two buttons. Behind it lies a heart that has been bruised by countless symbolic sticks and stones—now a bullet. He hopes Brenan won't let the bullet change the ending, a last minute edit before publication. He wants to live happily ever after in this one.

She says she isn't afraid he'll stray back off into the Twilight Zone, but he knows better. They are both afraid. Fear sometimes shows in her eyes, her voice, the touch of her hands. When he notices, he holds her, makes the promises all over again. And when they make love, they say what they feel, what they need. The fire between them again burns bright and hot, kindled by old passions, old needs, and new ones.

Sam has come a long way since autumn. He has learned to reach for hands that will pull him back from the edge. He is learning to speak of Fear and Confusion as the falling rulers of his soul, and he has begun to await the end of their reign.

Arlo Blacknell will bother Sam's family no longer. There are laws, mental institutions. A keeper of keys will claim his body. His god has already eaten his mind and soul. His disciples will be pariahs in search of a new chief to foster their fugitive spiritual dogmas. Sam hopes they will find a true leader and stop confusing Blacknell's god with God.

Life in the valley will go on. Some things will change. Some will never change.

As always, Freida is obsessed with feeding people. She still bakes bread and cooks for her children—and anyone else who looks hungry. She avidly reads labels and refuses to allow a grain of bleached flour or visible animal fat to cross the threshold of her house. On the outs with processed sugar, she probably already has her fruit jars washed and jugs of clover honey ready for the first ripe plum or strawberry. The silent breath-holding when she goes for checkups continues, but there's been no sign of the cancer returning. How could the part of her that gave life to him and to his sister become the part responsible for taking her from them? They need her. Their children need her. Outspoken, warm, and funny, Freida never changes. Truly, a great lady. Sam smiles, knowing a mother who doesn't change her strengths and beliefs for popularity points can be depended on.

The kitchen garden, the scallions, and the sugarsnaps are about the extent of A. D.'s farming, but that's enough to keep him happy and his fingernails dirty. His woodworking shop is productive and gaining respect outside the family. Now and then, he takes an order for a rocking chair or a picnic table, but most of his pieces are snatched up by members of the family as soon as they are turned out. He's down to one blood pressure pill a day, and Mark says his heart is as strong as a young boy's. Since the trouble, Sam doesn't always know what to say, but with A. D. explanations are unnecessary. The father-son respect is intact, and the bond is sturdy. Sam will never see A. D. through adult eyes. He'll always see the daddy who wouldn't give up on the son. A. D. is a rare and astonishing man no matter what kind of eyes see him. A rescuer. A fountain of wisdom and strength, courage and tenderness.

Ben has gone back to happily riding the rails. The boy laughs and sings. He runs and yells. He watches "Bobby's World" in cartooned pajamas. He does little boy things, plays noisy, reckless games. He climbs and hides and makes annoying sounds to enhance his play. And he tries so hard to trust. Some of his questions cut Sam to the quick. "You won't leave us again, will you, Daddy?" Every few days, that comes up. *"I didn't want to leave in the first place. I don't think I'd ever do it again."* "Why can't you just say 'no', Daddy?" *"Maybe someday, I can, son."* He hugs the boy every chance he gets. Touching is good for them. Sam has put strings on Ben's guitar, and stiff little fingers are stretching to make the first chords. This time next year, the boy will be strumming "Railroad Lady" and "Waitin' for a Train" all by himself.

Mariah's doing fine. Her rancor has cooled. She watches Sam too closely, but seldom criticizes anything more personal than his tie or his approach to a news story. She is reading *Nicholas and Alexandra* and driving everyone to distraction with questions and opinions about Russian history. Snubbing Fitzgerald and Hemingway, she's ordered the complete works of Steinbeck and Faulkner. She's waiting on Dean Koontz, Robert McCammon, and the Kings—Tabitha *and* Stephen— to write something new and heart-rending or horrific. She can't decide if she wants to be a writer, a movie director, or a broadcast journalist. Sam thinks she reads too much adult material, but Brenan says leave her alone, that censorship is unconstitutional and the epitome of small-mindedness. Sam says, *"okay, okay"*; he's outnumbered anyway. She may ask him to explain the sensual passages of D. H. Lawrence, but she's still a little girl searching the *TV Guide* for Michael Keaton movies and roaming the woods with Deejay and the dogs. She lets Ben sleep with her when he feels the need.

Both children feel the guilt Sam created. He hurt them. They fought back. Now, they have to forgive themselves for their intrinsic reactions. He can't teach them a process he hasn't mastered. "I'm sorry. It was *my* fault." What else can he say?

Robert and Jackie have decided to live an adventure. Courtesy of an old friend from law school, Robert has been offered a position in a firm in California, an L.A. law practice to begin in early summer. Their house in Hoover is for sale. Jackie's already packing up her easels and brushes. She has always dreamed of doing sea and snow-topped mountain scapes. In California, she should be able to do both. She's thinking about opening her own gallery. Los Angeles is too far from home.

At eleven, Marissa's already showing some of her mother's aptitude for drawing and painting, but she'd rather be painted. Around Christmas, she informed the family she was going to become a model, then in the weeks that followed, proceeded to starve herself pencil-thin. A few days of therapy at Doctor Freida's kitchen table straightened her out. She's eating, now, and looking for a new career. She hasn't been completely sold on the move to California, but she's playing her mother's old Beach Boys tapes and trying to get used to the idea. All are ambivalent.

Each time the wind shifts, Mark talks about retiring, but he's been doing that for years. Sam figures Mark will be wearing a stethoscope around his neck another decade. He still needs the hospital to serve as a pressure valve. People around home ignore his bluster. For the first time in his career, he's taken a young partner. Watching this alliance develop has strong entertainment potential. If the younger has the tenacity to endure the pomp of the elder, he'll have the finest of mentors.

Ellen seems to be about through changing. The medicine—after she finally gave in and began swallowing it—has done amazing things. She is drifting closer and closer to her premenopausal relationships. Her smile and sense of humor have returned though she still finds joking with Sam awkward. Wanting to put things right, she's making an effort. A few nights ago, she conjured up a batch of sticky black walnut divinity and coolly delivered it to Sam. A peace offering if he'd ever eaten one. All that fat and sugar. Brenan gave them *looks* that dubbed them partners in crime. Ellen made him promise not to tell Freida about the candy. The silences between them have been long and wearing, but since the two of them can share a secret, a flat-out reconciliation can't be long in coming.

News is still being made, and Sam has been reporting it with finesse and flair. During the past year there have been wars and rumors of wars, coups, and to Mariah's optimum joy, rumors of another Batman movie. Cannibalism, Satanism, earthquakes, storms, UFOs, skinheads, Michael Jackson, Liz, Madonna, and both armies fighting the abortion wars have all made headlines. The world watched a man beaten savagely by officers of the peace—Los Angeles, California, United States of America, Land of the Free, Home of the Brave—then a few men tried to tell the world not to believe what it saw. The nation's President puked in Tokyo and on international television, but his upset stomach didn't appear related to the beating in L. A. AIDS awareness increased, but so did the number of victims. *The Silence of the Lambs* made horror movie history. Country Music celebrated a miraculous revival. According to popular opinion, the best jokes are running for President—so not all the news is *new*. On the homefront, Birmingham broke her own record for the number of murders in a year. Proclaiming a matter of principle, the mayor of Birmingham spent a night in jail. *And so on, and so on . . .*

While Brenan has devoted herself to word-processing, Sam has been throwing his energies into his spiritual reclamation. He now accepts himself as the one vehicle essential for his healing. Daily, he is growing, learning, and becoming stronger. He doesn't know how to judge his progress, but it *is* happening.

Today, an assassin's bullet has opened him, readying him to receive something—but what? answers? a nightmare antidote? He turns to face the dark maw of the cave. He feels no need for Lefty's voice to calm fears nor a canister of Beclovent to maintain the patency of his lungs. All by himself, he is ready.

His vision blurs. The brilliant colors around him soften to pastel smears. Close by he hears a rhythmic *blip, blip, blip* echoed by a weak *lub-dub, lub-dub, lub-dub*. The sound of voices, sirens run together. A mixture of smells floats on the renewed breeze—coffee, blood, bacon. Sensory fragments of the ado around the Sam-twin on the floor in the airport restaurant. A telepathic message assuring him people are taking measures to save a shell for him to inhabit when he returns. Sunlight swirls, mixes with the darkness of the cave, creates a mist of constantly changing forms. When his vision clears, cave and valley are gone. He shakes his head, but he can't bring them back. A process has begun. The rock beneath him dissolves.

62

IS SHOES COME lightly down on a beaten, tree-lined foot path, a dark pathway he instantly knows with a sharp and focused clarity begins and ends in his childhood. A *time* path. Someone at the other end—which is indeed the *beginning* of the path— is waiting. Someone who is hurting. Someone who has a secret to share. Someone impatient and needy. "I'm coming," Sam whispers, using his voice to abort a shiver of fear. Walking first, then running, he treks down this narrow avenue that curves in and out of time folds, sending him through and past the crimes and failures of his life without disturbing the interstitial spells of peace.

At each bend, he finds a forepart of himself, each one younger than the one before, each thirsting for recognition and for forgiveness. To each, he nods a pardon. "Not your fault. You were only human." One milestone at a time, he jogs forward, thus, taking himself back, farther and deeper into his history. The exonerated self-images cheer, beg him not to slow his pace. At crossroads, they point the way, assure him a panacea for all awaits. So he runs, his shoes slapping the hard-packed earth in smooth undulations. Now with eyes only for what lies ahead, he no longer turns to the Sam likenesses. He glides with the momentum of their pushes and is grateful for their shepherding.

A dim apparition in the distance startles him. Small and indistinct, a forlorn little ghost. Fear replaces the urgency. No longer sure he wants to go on, he balks. His feet become heavy and laggard but refuse to stop. The distance closes.

In front of what seems to be a flight of iron-railed, concrete steps oddly set in the middle of his path, he stumbles and at last draws to a halt near the mournful figure. Not a mere image, wavering or ghostlike, but a child of flesh and bone. A pathetic boy whose wounds are as fresh as the remote pulsing hole under Brenan's hands. Except for blood-stiffened underpants, the spare, battered body struggling to support itself against the handrail is naked. His eyes, full of suffering and isolation, are the color of a cloudless night sky.

"Ohgod, it's *me!*"

The boy nods.

Horrified, Sam kneels. His arms go around the small, fragile body. The boy curves against him with a baby's trust, a confidence born of instinct, belonging. His bleeding hands ease around Sam's neck.

"I waited and waited. I knew you'd come."

"You knew?"

"I didn't know when, but I knew you'd come back. It's been such a long time." The child-voice of the boy is softly urgent.

Sam feels the blood from the boys hands seeping into the chambray collar and yoke of his shirt, staining the back to match the front. His heart opens again and begins pumping. Fresh blood floods over the clinging boy. Sultry little-boy heat soaks into Sam's pores. It circulates inside him, a substitute for the spilled blood, warming internal crevices and corners that have known only coldness and neglect.

"You have to love me," the boy says. A command, not a plea.

The desperation of the embrace tightens, each one of them intent on keeping his grip on the other. Cheek-to-cheek, their tears mix. Beneath Sam's hands, the boy feels tiny and delicate, yet solidly tenacious. Holding him stanches the spillage of blood.

"I've always loved you."

"No! You blame me! I left the store, and you blame me!"

"No!"

"I've waited ever so long for you to forgive me. I can't keep waiting. If you forgive me, you can love me. If you love me, we will heal."

"I don't blame you. Now, I know better."

The boy abruptly breaks away, shaking off Sam's attempts to pull him back. He crosses his arms and stamps his feet. His lower lip protrudes in a pout. He puts his bleeding hands over his ears and screams, *"That Sam-I-am! That Sam-I-am! I do not like that Sam-I-am!"*

"Green Eggs and Ham! You're quoting Dr. Seuss! Dr. Seuss is dead! He's dead, but we're not. Please, come back!" Sam holds his arms out. He has a flaming need to hold the boy.

But the boy shakes his head. Under darkening smears of Sam's blood, his face and chest are mottled in blue, black, purple, and yellow bruises, deep red scratches and raised welts. His lips are split and swollen. His thin ankles are deeply ringed with oozing red ditches. His poor *hands!*

"Please!"

"I didn't let him have us! You were there! You couldn't stop him, either! We were only nine!"

"I know!"

"I wanted to get home first! I didn't believe about bad people until I saw the man!"

"It's okay!"

"No, it's not okay! She said it could happen, but I didn't mind her! We didn't mind her, Sam! It was never okay! But she forgave us! Daddy forgave us!"

"Of course, they did!"

"We were just a little boy!"

"I know!"

"Then forgive me!"

"I do!"

The boy looks into Sam's eyes. *"How do I know?"* His face is skeptical.

"I forgive you, and I'm sorry I waited so long. I didn't know how!"

"You have to feel forgiveness! If you just say it, it doesn't count!"

"I feel it! We couldn't stop any of it! I can't give back a single minute, but I can start now. Please let me hold you."

The boy edges back into Sam's outstretched arms. *"You mean it? You swear?"*

"I mean it! I swear!" Sam gently strokes the slender back, caresses the sharp protrusions of ribs and shoulder blades. The boy stiffens with excitement.

"Then you can love me!"

"I do! Very, very much!"

His words are true. Sam's feels a rush of pure love coursing through his arteries and veins. The little-boy-Sam has been suspended in time, alone in his suffering, needing this reserved love, so long withheld, to make him well—the boy's suffering, so much like the man's.

"Look!" The little hands are held up for Sam to see. They have stopped bleeding. Scabs are forming over the wounds. The bruises and welts are fading. The edematous lips are shrinking back to the angles of their natural bow. Sam smiles through his tears and hugs himself tighter.

"Say it! I want to hear it! Say 'I love you, Sam!'."

"I love you, Sam, and I'm so glad I found you." Sam's excitement is no less than the boy's. They rock back and forth.

"Look, Sam. My hands!"

Front and back, the wounds are gone. Only a crisscrossing of fine white lines remains. Sam compares his hands to the boy's. The patterns of scarring are the same.

He tilts back to look at the rest of the child. He can find no bruises. The skin is clear, smooth, and lightly tanned. Pale lines ring the sun-browned ankles. The underpants are clean and white. The tears have dried, and the boy's smile is stunning, the big-toothed grin of a happy kid. Tiny lines crinkle at the corners of his squinting, night-sky eyes. Thick curls, the color of bread crusts, pitch over his smooth forehead. He is as handsome as the boy in Freida's picture albums. As innocent as the sweet face framed on nearly every wall in his parents' home.

"I love you, Sam!" The youthful voice rings. It might as well be singing *"Ready or not, here I come!"* or *"Red Rover, Red Rover, let Sam ride over!"* or any of a thousand chants of children. It is full of the vibrant sounds of playful happiness.

"I'm so glad I found you!" Sam repeats, and the boy throws back his head and laughs—a fountain of laughter that splashes cleanly over them.

Sam draws his child-self close again. Slowly, an absorption begins to take place. The molecules of the child shift, change, enter and become enmeshed with the structure of the man—sucked through the small hole in his chest, reuniting the two into one being. Halves becoming a whole, no piece missing, no piece leftover. Sam hugs the boy until there is nothing left to hold.

Inside, he feels a stirring. The process of man and boy permanently fusing. From his heart, the tell-all marks of years of pelting stones are evaporating like dewdrops in the sun. Sam searches with his eyes and fingers for the bullet holes.

He smiles, lifts his face to a clean, cerulean sky. He is a man who will not forget his past. There will always be memories and scars, pale railroad tracks on the backs of his hands, raised cords in his palms, hairless circles around his ankles—the written history of his twenty-seven-year ordeal. The healing will never be perfect, but it will be sufficient. He will battle his fears in the open.

"I love you, Sam," he whispers one last time, and stands to begin the walk home.

Home, where the best days of his life are waiting to begin.

With every step, he feels a little stronger, a little lighter, his heart a little sturdier.

63

PARTICLES OF PURE white light fall dappled onto the footpath. Somewhere ahead, it is all of a piece, alive and beckoning. Effortlessly, he runs toward it, back the way he came. The Sam images rush to greet him. With cries of triumph, they slam into him, become one with him, each in his turn, each a little older than the one before.

The light glows brighter, closer, streaming between trees, washing over him. The strong, rhythmic *lub-dub, lub-dub* of his heart and a mechanical *blip, blip, blip* resound in his brain amid sweet, sweet lilting voices. Brenan's, the children's. Lefty's.

Hurry, Boss. Ya done your job, an' I done mine. Time to put us back together.

At last, he reaches the light and allows it to embrace him. Slowly, as it softens, people and things begin to show through.

Eyes closed, his clone lies on a hospital bed. Bandages cover his shoulders and chest. Plastic tubes sprout from him.

Crawl in here, Ace. You ALL come in here with me.

He creeps onto the bed and lies back into the body that has lived in spite of the bullets. He opens his eyes.

We're all together now. All for one, an' one for all.

Two frowning, questioning faces loom above him.

"Mama, come here. His eyes are open!" one of them says.

Ben in his engineer's costume. He and Mariah look tired and hollow-eyed. Both sit on the bed watching him.

His mouth refuses to make words, but his eyes take in the beautiful people, his ears savor their voices.

"Sam?" So fearful, so lovely. Brenan!

"Go easy, Bren. May not come all the way to, yet."

"He knows me. I can tell. Don't you, Daddy? I'm Ben. I been sittin' here a long time—just waitin'. I prayed God wouldn't let you die."

"Hush, Ben."

"Rye's still scared, but not me. You're gonna get well fast!"

Freida leans to touch his hair then takes her hand to her heart.

"You're gonna be a-okay, son." A. D. seconds Ben's position.

Brenan frowns but appears unharmed. He tries to smile.

"You saved Mama's life, Daddy. Then she saved yours. Gramma Ellen's gonna make you some fudge."

"Over my dead body."

"Freida, stop with the dead-body talk. Makes me nervous."

He willed his cheeks to draw out the corners of his mouth.

"Look, he's smiling. See, Rye. Told you."

He is tired. Pain radiates from the center of his chest, steadily building, but he can withstand pain and fatigue. In time, they will go away. The light has gone soft. Brenan's eyes swim in tears. She hasn't spoken since she said his name, but those eyes talk to him. The others are near, anxious but happy.

"Say something, Daddy."

Wet your lips and give it a try, Ace.

"Ben! Mama, make him stop."

Sam licks his lips.

Watching between the crush of bodies around the bed, Debra Jean—Dee—leans against the door frame. She lifts a finger in a tiny wave.

"Go on, say something. I know you can." Ben's patience is going.

Ace!

Sam takes an exhausting breath and whispers, "Sam I am."

His ears ring with sweet laughter and *blip, blip* and gentle applause. Amid these joyous sounds, his eyes willfully close, and sleep draws him down past all the pain.

64

THREE MONTHS HAVE PASSED since the shooting. Ben lets the corner divide him in half. Standing this way, he can tip his head to one side, his wrist watch side, and see Daddy talking to a tall black man who stands behind a little counter selling hats, belts, and wallets with pictures of horses and stuff made into the leather. He can tip the other way and see a man with a bristly white mustache, white hair, and black eyebrows. The man is wearing a black *Batman Returns* tee-shirt and keeps curling his finger at Ben. Ben, Rye, and Deej have shirts just like that, only smaller. Aunt Jackie sent them from California. Ben only wears his shirt when Rye and Deej have theirs on and only because it makes them mad. He'll take Ninja Turtles and Rescue Rangers over Batman any old day.

The man in the tee-shirt is rattling some keys that probably go to his car. He looks like he wants to hurry and leave but has to wait on something. There are two glass doors behind him, and Ben can see part of the parking lot and a bunch of cars through them. The man stops curling his finger then looks at his watch, the parking lot, and back at Ben.

When Ben looks around Daddy's side of the corner, he gets a little bored. Daddy wants to buy Grampa A. D. a new straw hat to wear when he goes out in the sun. Looking at hats is not a lot of fun unless you want one yourself, and Ben doesn't. Still it feels good to be going places with Daddy. It has been a long time since Daddy could drive or even walk in the yard without getting too tired.

A preacher who was crazy shot Daddy two times with a real gun.

Grampa Mark says one of the bullets went all the way through Daddy's heart and that *that* would have killed most people. He said it's a good thing the bullet had eyes and Daddy was made out of kudzu vines and pine knots. Grampa Mark is a doctor, but he doesn't always talk like one.

The white mustache man is still rattling those keys. The rattling makes Ben nervous.

Daddy says, "Look at this, Ace." Ben looks up. Daddy puts on a Chicago Cubs ball cap and shows Ben. Ben tells him to take it off. All the MacCauleys are Braves fans. Daddy takes off the cap and rubs his hand over the bullet scar on his shoulder. When he moves his arm a lot, his shoulder hurts and he has to rub it. He has a lot of other scars. He has a long one with prints of the stitches still showing that goes across his chest under his nipples. The scars are not important as long as Daddy is getting better and stronger all the time. Most of the time the big ones are covered up, and the little ones are hard to see. Anyway, who cares what he looks like under his shirt?

When Ben turns back to the white mustache man, he isn't bored. He feels creepy—sort of like when he wakes up in the middle of the night and doesn't know why. The man wants Ben to come to him. Well, Ben has news for the man. He would never go to a person he didn't know.

A strange man hurt Daddy when he was a little boy. He told Ben and Rye about it. He brought them quilts made by a woman who sneaked him away from the man. He said she saved his life. He said the man tied him up and made the scars on his hands and the white circles around his ankles where the hair won't grow. He said the man used the same kind of string Grampa A. D. uses to tie up bales of hay. The man did things to Daddy. Ben knows they were bad things that hurt for a long time, but he doesn't understand much of what Daddy said about them. Daddy made Ben and Rye promise to always mind the rules he and Mama give them. The rules cover talking to strange people, taking things from them, and wandering off in stores and malls, so that man can just rest his finger. Ben isn't coming.

Daddy wants a certain kind of straw hat with one of those green things in the front brim that Grampa A. D. can look through without the sun hurting his eyes. Grampa A. D.'s old sun hat is really old and curled up the sides from fanning with it. The salesman doesn't have one, but he will order it. He can have it by Monday or Tuesday—Wednesday at the latest. The salesman writes down Daddy's phone number at work, and Daddy says for him to give a message to Rita when the hat comes in.

No one in the family tells the phone number at home except to special people. The TV station has to call Daddy on his beeper. The preacher who shot Daddy is in a jail for people who are sick in their heads, but a person can't be too careful when there are so many nuts out there. Ben heard Gramma Ellen and Gramma Freida tell that to Mama. They said nobody wanted Mama to quit writing books, but we'd all have to get false noses to wear to Food World. They were trying to sound funny because Ben and Rye and Deej were listening, and they don't like kids to worry. Ben knows that preacher wanted to shoot Mama, too.

Daddy only *tells* the news on TV now. Somebody else has to go out and get it. He says he won't be a desk jockey long. He says his feet are itching to pound the pavement again. He says soon nobody's secrets will be safe. Ben is used to the way Daddy talks, and he understands most of it.

Everybody says Daddy nearly died saving Mama's life. Saving a life makes a person a hero. Just a few days ago Ben asked if it was true. Mama said yes, so Daddy really is a hero. Mama was sitting next to Daddy, and he was hugging and tickling her. He said if he hadn't, she'd have haunted him the rest of his life. Then he kissed her on the mouth. They act silly, just like they used to before the bad stuff started happening. Ben is glad to have both of them. He likes everybody to stay together and love each other.

The strange man shows Ben a wad of dollars he has in his pocket and makes motions with his hands that look like he's playing a sign language game. He's saying Ben can have some of the money. The man's eyes are the color of the sky on stormy days and his skin is suntanned. Even with white hair, he doesn't look old like a grandfather.

The salesman tells Daddy it's too hot for old people to be outside, anyway, because it's ninety something in the shade. "Dog days a-comin', ya know," he says, sounding like one of those people who want you to think they know better than you. Daddy tells him Grampa A. D.'s only fifty-nine and knows not to stay out long in the heat.

Ben thinks Grampa A. D. can take the heat better than Daddy. Daddy isn't all the way well, yet. He got all sweaty just walking from the parking lot to the mall and through Sears. It's a good thing he doesn't get asthma attacks like he used to. Those can be scary all by themselves.

The salesman knows Daddy got shot and that he's a news man. He says, "Folks sure missed you." Some women at Sears said the same thing. Because Daddy works on TV, people act like they know him when they really don't. Women always act stupid around him. Daddy wears sunglasses when he goes out. He doesn't like people to bother him. The sunglasses don't always work very well—like today.

The white mustache man tries one more time. He holds his hands up in front of his chest, flops them over into doggy paws, and makes a pitiful face like he's begging. He sure looks goofy. Why doesn't he just give up? Ben doesn't shake his head or motion the man to go away. That would be the same as talking to him.

Daddy buys some cowboy belts for himself and the grampas and one for Deejay. He buys some of those stringy ties that cowboys wear for dress-up. He asks Ben if he wants a hat or a belt. Ben likes his engineer's cap, and he has a brown cowboy hat and a vest with fringe on it that he wears when he rides his filly, Railroad Lady. He doesn't want another hat, but he likes cowboy belts. If there's one small enough, Ben would like that. He holds his arms up while Daddy tries one on him. It's a little big, but Ben is growing.

The white mustache man looks mad now. He just stares at Ben and makes his mouth look mean. His black eyebrows run together to make one big eyebrow. Ben's skin wants to crawl off his bones. He grabs Daddy's hand and holds it tight.

Daddy pulls his hand back to get some money out of his pocket to pay the salesman.

The white mustache man notices and starts walking toward Ben. He must not see how close Daddy still is.

Ben slides around Daddy's side of the corner then squeezes between Daddy and the tall counter. His ear presses against Daddy's stomach and hears the growling inside. When he stretches to look back around, he doesn't see where the man went.

Daddy puts his sack of belts under his sore arm and reaches his other hand back to Ben. He smiles down and squeezes Ben's fingers a little. Ben likes the way it feels to be Sam MacCauley's little boy. Because he is so small, he likes the way it feels having someone big beside him, someone who will take care of him no matter what, someone who is his daddy and who loves him a lot.

Ben squeezes back.

"You're holding on pretty tight," Daddy says. "I didn't know you had a grip like *that!*"

"Yeah," Ben answers. "I don't wanna lose you in this crowd. Mama wouldn't like me having to drive myself home. She fusses when I lose my socks. Can you 'magine what she'd say if I lost something big as you?"

Daddy laughs. He always knows when Ben is trying to be funny. He always laughs at the right time.

They walk nearly right up to the white mustache man who pretends he doesn't care what Ben is doing. He still looks sort of mad, but he is staring at something or someone *behind* Ben and Daddy. He points at his watch, then shakes a fist like he's pretending to clobber somebody.

"You couldn't lose me if you tried," Daddy says.

The white mustache man is smiling. He is smiling like grown-ups do when they sneak up on a kid who has made a giant mess and got his clothes so dirty they won't ever come clean. Sort of like they expect the kid to do that kind of dumb stuff but really wish he wouldn't. Not really mad, just sort of like *oh, well.*

Ben slows down to look.

Now that the man isn't paying attention to him, he's curious. Maybe the man has found another boy. If he has, Ben is going to tell Daddy. Daddy slows down, too, because he's still holding Ben's hand.

A woman with a lot of store bags hurries around Ben. She smells like flowers. She walks right up to the man.

"Okay, okay, okay. We can go now," the woman says. "You can just stop making all those faces. You haven't missed a single minute of your old ball game. Just wait'll you see what I got *just for you.* "She sounds silly and flirty like Mama does sometimes.

"I thought you'd never come out. You trying to buy out the mall?" The man jokes with her and gives her that funny look again. He takes some of the bags from her. They start walking together toward the glass doors.

"Come on, son," Daddy says and gives a tug for Ben to come with him down the aisle, but Ben doesn't come, yet. He looks back and sees a store that sells women's underwear and the weird stuff they sleep in. The store is right across the aisle from the hat and belt store, right behind the place where Ben had been standing. The white mustache man probably hadn't even looked at him.

Ben feels pretty stupid. Oh, well, better safe than sorry, Gramma Ellen always says.

When you put both his grammas and both his grampas together, you get a lot of sayings. He isn't allowed to repeat some of them. His favorite is one of Grampa A. D.'s. *"You hafta treat your woman twice as good as you do your dog if you want her to lick your hand."* Ben doesn't understand what it means, but it sounds funny, and it always makes Gramma Freida say, *"Shut up, Old Man!"*

Daddy hits Ben on the head with the sack of belts. It doesn't hurt. It wasn't meant to.

"Come on, Ace, stop daydreaming," Daddy says and pulls Ben along by the hand.

Daddy is wearing what Gramma Freida calls his up-to-no-good-grin. She says Ben has one just like it. Mama has another name for that grin, but it's one of the things Ben isn't supposed to say.

Ben walks fast enough to keep up. "We came in that way, Daddy." He points.

"I know, but the food court's this way." Daddy leans down and says in a sneaky whisper, "Let's go eat something we're not supposed to before we go home."